The Year of Thamar's Book

Lucy Beckett

GRACEWING

First published in England in 2018
by
Gracewing
2 Southern Avenue
Leominster
Herefordshire HR6 0QF
United Kingdom

www.gracewing.co.uk

ISBN 978 085244 935 6

.

Typeset by Word and Page, Chester, UK

Cover design by Bernardita Peña Hurtado

ita errores et falsae opiniones vitam contaminant, si
rationalis mens ipsa vitiosa est, qualis in me tunc erat
nesciente alio lumine illam inlustrandam esse, ut sit
particeps veritatis, quia non est ipsa natura veritatis.

And so mistakes and false opinions contaminate life,
if the rational mind is spoiled, as then it was in me. I
had no idea that, if the mind is to share in the truth,
it has to be lit from a light outside itself, because the
mind itself is not where truth is.

Saint Augustine
Confessions 4.15.25

Il faut un grand courage aujourd'hui pour se déclare
fidèle aux choses de l'esprit. Mais du moins ce courage
n'est pas inutile.

It needs great courage these days to declare oneself
faithful to things of the spirit. But at least this courage is not in vain.

Albert Camus
La nouvelle culture méditerranéenne VI

Chapter 1

Jamila

April 2015

It was raining hard, so she paid the driver before she got out of the taxi.

"There you are, madame", he said. "Café de la Paix. With rooms. You see? There's no hotel in the village. Should be OK for a night or two."

"Thank you, monsieur."

She watched through the rain as the taxi swung round, splashing in the puddles of the empty square. The headlights dazzled and then passed her, and the rear lights disappeared as the car turned at the top of the square, back towards the town. Silence. She shivered. Surely, so much further south, it should have been warmer than Paris. It seemed colder.

There was a lamp each side of the door, lighting dimly a terrace with little wooden tables, wooden chairs tipped forwards against the tables, all sopping wet. She looked up. There was an awning rolled up above the door, for sunny days. She heard male laughter from inside, then a deep voice speaking.

The bell of a clock across the square struck eleven. Was it in the church? The Mairie? It was impossible to tell in the dark. She took a handkerchief out of her coat pocket and wiped the rain from her spectacles. She hoisted her travel bag and her everyday bag on its strap more firmly on to her shoulder— she had brought only a few night things and her laptop—and opened the door.

Silence. She shut the door behind her. The warmth misted her spectacles. She wiped them with thumb and forefinger and saw five men, two of them old and stiff as they turned, looking at her, not hostile but curious, or so she hoped. These two and two others were sitting at a square table. A game of belote had been suspended by her appearance. One man, pencil in hand, was about to write numbers on a pad. There were glasses of wine on the table. The fifth man, sitting astride a chair to watch the game, stood up and with one hand turned the chair round to face the table. He wore a long, faded blue apron. The *patron*.

"Good evening, madame."

"Good evening, messieurs."

"What would you like?"

"I am . . . I was hoping you might have a room for the night."

"But of course."

A shout over his shoulder. "Hortense!"

The door beside the bar opened. A woman appeared, wiping her hands on a tea towel. She smiled.

"Madame would like a room for the night."

"Of course. Good evening, madame. Have you eaten?"

"Yes, yes, thank you. A sandwich on the train."

"Madame has come by train? Here?"

"Yes. And a taxi."

"Well! Congratulations, madame, for finding us. And on such a wicked night. The rain! Allow me, madame, your coat—it's so wet. It will dry in the kitchen."

She took her coat.

"Come with me, madame. And you—", she said to the still staring men, as if to a bunch of naughty boys, "you get on and finish your game. Time to go home to bed. You'll be in trouble, Marcel, if you don't get home soon."

A sheepish laugh round the table.

"Come in, madame". Hortense held the door by the bar open for her. She saw the brightly lit kitchen on one side. Good cooking smells. On the other side was a narrow staircase. Hortense switched on a light for the stairs, bare wood, no carpet, but the light above in a many-coloured glass shade.

"Please. Follow me, madame."

A wooden door with an old-fashioned latch.

"This is our best room. My apologies for the cold, madame. We had no idea that tonight, in this horrible weather—" She

2

closed the shutters and drew the curtains.

"Of course. Please don't worry. I shall be fine."

"No. It is like the refrigerator in here. Wait—I'll fetch you a little stove, only electric, you understand. A moment—"

The room was bare, clean, friendly, the floor dark boards with a rag rug by the bed. One light, on a night table beside the bed. Crisp curtains at the window, white cotton with a pattern of small flowers, and another long curtain, the same cotton, drawn across a basin—she looked—with shiny taps, soap, and a clean towel.

Hortense came back with an electric heater which she plugged in and turned on.

"This will help a bit. Now, I will bring you a hot-water bottle, and perhaps a tisane? To sleep well?"

"Please don't go to so much trouble. It's so late and I'll be fine."

"No, madame. It's a cold night and you have had a long journey. Where have you come from today?"

"From Paris."

"From Paris? So far? You must be very tired. Wait, please, for a little moment."

She sat on the bed, tired indeed, and found she was almost in tears. She had had no idea what to expect, in this village in a part of central France where she had never been before. She realised that she was a stranger, a Parisian and a foreigner in more ways than one, in the deep country. When she and her husband, once a year in August, left Paris for a holiday, they always went to Rouen, where his family lived. When the children were little, they had spent days at the seaside, at Honfleur or Trouville, and sometimes took a picnic to the woods or the small fields of Normandy. She had never in her life travelled so far alone. She hadn't known how it would be, or how she would be when she arrived, and everything she had come for was still to do. But she had certainly not expected such kindness.

The good Hortense knocked and came in, a hot-water bottle in a knitted cover under one arm, the other hand spread to carry a small tray with a steaming cup and saucer, and some biscuits on a plate.

3

"You are too kind, madame."

"Not at all, not at all. Now, you have a good night's sleep. It's very quiet here, you will find. Until the traffic starts in the morning, and there's not much of that. The toilet is next door, on the right. And when you get up, come down for breakfast, in the bar, whenever you are ready. We're always up early."

"Thank you."

"Good night, madame."

Hortense shut the door gently. She heard her go back down the stairs, and shortly afterwards heard the men in the bar leave. "Good night Hortense, Pierre. Goodnight, Marcel. Goodnight." She imagined them shaking hands as they parted in the rain. Their footsteps faded into the night.

She had thanked Hortense, not only for the hot-water bottle, the biscuits and the tisane, warming her hands as she held the cup, but also for not asking her why she had come.

When she had finished the tea she got out her laptop, opened it beside her on the bed, and sent her husband an email.

All well so far. The journey was fine. Kind people here. Love to you both, J

She woke to the sound of shutters banging open downstairs and the smell of coffee. Once she remembered where she was, and why, she lay in bed for a few minutes, wishing she hadn't come, wishing she was at home with Jean-Claude and Joséphine—Bernard was away at his university in Nantes—deciding what to do in the half-term holiday which had just begun. Then, warm and comfortable, she was surprised to find that being alone so far from home was also actually enjoyable. Enjoyable and even exciting: what would she discover today? Perhaps nothing. But she would have done her best.

She got up and opened the curtains and the shutters. The sun was shining. The square, not as big as she had thought, was empty, puddled and glistening from last night's rain: pretty houses and cottages, some washed white or creamy yellow, some built of rough, large stones, all with reddish-brown tiled roofs; a church, not big, with a modest bell-tower; the Mairie, also small, with five windows on the first floor, a steep roof and the flag of the Republic. No one about except, on the far side of the square, a young woman in jeans with a baby in a pushchair and a little boy beside her on a scooter. Out of a small van two men, probably the driver and the shopkeeper, were taking trays of what looked like fruit and vegetables and carrying them through the open door of a dark shop. A boy on a bicycle, two baguettes under his arm, one hand on the handlebars, whizzed across the square and disappeared down a path.

She looked at her watch. Nearly eight o'clock. How long and heavily she had slept. And of course it was Sunday morning. She opened the window. The sunshine was already warm, much warmer than at this time of year in Paris. Small birds were singing, and throaty pigeons. On the chestnut trees outside the café there were bright new leaves. A spring day, almost like summer though it was still April. She stood a little longer, as if taking a photograph of the square, to keep, to look at when she was back in Paris, before she had to spoil the morning with conversations and complications.

Downstairs the belote table was laid for her breakfast with a clean checked cloth and white china. She sat down.

"Good morning, madame. You have slept well, I hope." The *patron*'s wife, in a fresh apron, appeared from the kitchen and put a jug of yellow tulips on the table.

"Good morning, madame. Very well, thank you."

"Very good. Very good. A *café complet*?"

"Please. They're so pretty, the flowers."

"From the garden this morning."

Her breakfast was delicious.

"More coffee, madame?"

"Please, so good, your coffee."

"Thank you, madame. And would you mind signing our register, just your name and address. Here is the book. Is it just for one night, your visit?"

"I should like to stay tonight as well, if my room—"

"No problem at all. We have very few visitors at this time of year."

"And possibly another night. I'm afraid I don't know yet."

"The room will be for you as long as you need it, madame."

5

She wrote her name, her address in Paris and yesterday's date in the columns of the book with the pen that was attached to it with a string. She felt that the woman was studying her more closely than she yet had.

"Excuse me, madame. Your first name, such a pretty name—is it North African?"

"Yes. I'm glad you like the name. I was born in Algeria, but I don't remember it at all. I have lived in France since I was a baby. I have an identity card which—"

"No, no, madame. There is no problem. Not at all. Excuse me. I should not have said anything. We don't see many North Africans here, so far from the Mediterranean, and so far from Paris."

This was the moment she had been putting off as long as she could. The *patron*'s wife had not asked her why she, an Algerian who lived in Paris, had come, by train and taxi, to this village in the heart of France, but she could feel the question in the air as she drank the last mouthful of her second cup of coffee, and now she must deal with it.

"You see, madame," she said. "I am here to see if I can find someone, or perhaps find out about someone. For an old friend, you understand. You may be able to help me yourself."

This was clearly a lucky idea. The *patron*'s wife put the coffee pot and milk jug on the bar, wiped her hands on her apron and sat down opposite her at the table.

"Willingly, madame. Anything I can do to help."

"Well—It's a bit complicated."

"Of course." The *patron*'s wife leant forward. "You can tell Hortense. I am very discreet."

She smiled. This was evidently not the case, but it didn't matter. She might need half the village to help. With a surge of confidence that surprised her, she began:

"Not long ago, actually a few weeks ago, this old friend died. She had been very ill for some months so her death, a peaceful death, was not too sad."

"Thanks be to God."

"I was helping to look after her. Before she died she asked me to do one thing for her, one little thing, she said, though I

6

thought it might be quite a big thing, quite difficult. She had hidden away among her things a small carved box, a wooden box carved with flowers and leaves, an Arab box, you understand—my friend was an Algerian. She told me where to find this box. Then she asked me to wrap it very carefully in paper and to tape it up in her presence so that she could see it was sealed. I did all this, and then she asked me to find someone, someone she knew a long time ago. She wanted me to find him so that I could give him the box. 'He is old now', she said. 'If he is still alive, he is old. He may be dead, but you will find out.' She gave me the name of this village. She said he was born here but she didn't know if he had lived here later in his life. She hoped he would have come back here at some time. 'I know French people', she said. 'They always go back to their village.' Isn't that so?"

"Well, they do, of course." Hortense smiled as she said this. "Very often they do, if they can. But it is not always possible. What is the name your friend told you? I know everyone in the village, I think. Perhaps not everyone who comes here just for holidays. We have too many of them. Their houses are empty most of the year, which is not good for the café, for the shops, you know. They're not country people. They come from Lyons, even from Paris. Like you. But they are rich of course."

She looked down at her black suit, one of her two suits for work, respectable, neat, but evidently not expensive, evidently not new.

She smiled back at the *patron*'s wife. "No, we are not rich, madame; you are right."

"O, I beg your pardon, madame. I didn't mean—"

"Of course you didn't. Don't worry. It's of no importance. Do sit down again, madame."

To her relief, the thread was broken. But she must pick it up. How?

The *patron*'s wife sat down and folded her hands on the check tablecloth, looking at her kindly.

"Your husband, madame. You have left him in Paris?" She had said "we are not rich"; she wore a wedding ring.

"Yes. He was happy for me to come by myself. He is at

home, with our daughter. My husband is a schoolteacher, in a *lycée*, but the schools in Paris are on holiday for a week from tomorrow. Our son is away. He is a student in Nantes."

"A student? That's excellent. He is a clever boy?"

"Yes. He works hard. He says he wants to be a writer, and he's studying political science. Perhaps he will be a political journalist. One day."

"That's a very interesting career, I'm sure. You must be proud of him."

"Yes. He's a good boy, sensible, but also idealistic. He wants to go away in the summer, to work in another country, perhaps for MSF. We have never taken the children abroad."

"MSF: what is that?"

"*Médecins sans frontières.* Doctors who go to foreign countries where there has been a disaster or people are very poor or there is a war, to help. They are very brave."

"Very brave, but their poor mothers, like the mothers of soldiers—"

"I know. I don't want him to go away, to some dangerous country. There are so many wars. But he says he needs to do something useful. Of course he isn't a doctor. He wants just to help, as a driver, or a record-keeper. He's good at computers." She paused, looked across the table at the friendly face of the patron's wife, and said, "His name is Thomas."

"Your son is called Thomas?"

She tried to keep hold of her voice. "No. My son is called Bernard. The man—the man I'm here to find is called Thomas. Monsieur Thomas. Jacques Thomas. Have you heard of him? Do you perhaps know him? An old man, if he is still alive."

"Thomas. Monsieur Thomas. Jacques Thomas. I don't think I have heard that name in the village. Jacques Thomas." The *patron*'s wife narrowed her eyes and looked out of the window at the other side of the room as if a man called Jacques Thomas might be walking across the square towards the café. Instead, an ancient Deux Chevaux pickup truck rattled to a halt outside the window and two young men in dirty overalls and baseball caps jumped out and came into the café.

"Morning, Hortense." Rapid handshakes. "Two coffees with

shots. We've done a couple of hours in the vines already. Any chance of a croissant?"

"You are lucky boys. I fetched some earlier for madame."

"Terrific."

Quick stares, a nod from one of the young men. They weren't as surprised by, or as interested in, her presence as the older men of the night before. Of course. She was old enough to be their mother.

The *patron*'s wife had gone into the kitchen. Almost at once she returned with a different pot of coffee, cups, sugar, croissants, napkins on a tray. She served the young men from behind the bar, taking a bottle of *marc* from the crowded shelf to lace their coffee. They stayed standing at the bar, ate two croissants each, very fast, dipping them in their coffee and biting off great chunks.

"Thanks, Hortense, you're a star", one said, turning to go. "These vines won't prune themselves."

"Hey", said the boy who had nodded at the stranger, "it's your turn, Gérard."

"No it's not. Is it? O well, OK". He turned back, pulled some coins from his pocket, chose a few, and pushed them across the bar.

"That's exactly right. Now, off you go. Work to be done."

"'Bye, Hortense. Madame", said the second boy.

"Good bye", she said, as if she knew him.

The *patron*'s wife gathered up the breakfast things from the table and the bar and stacked them on a tray.

"Wait, madame", she said. "I'll find my husband and ask him about Monsieur Jacques Thomas. My husband was born in this village. He's lived here all his life. I come from further away, you see, Saint-Christophe, you wouldn't know it, naturally, coming from Paris. Wait a moment." She took the tray into the kitchen, balancing it on her knee with one practised hand as she opened the door with the other.

Waiting, obediently and gratefully, she took her laptop out of its case. A message from her husband: *Glad it's going well and you have met kind people. Joséphine and I are going to the Picasso Museum—free tickets today and I thought we'd have a look at the renovations. Joséphine not keen but I persuaded her. Good luck with the day. Love J-C*

Good. She needn't send another email until the evening.

After a few minutes the *patron* appeared, backwards, having pushed open the door with his backside. He was carrying a huge basket full of logs. Now she saw that there was, in the wall with no windows and beyond two more tables, a wide, old-fashioned fireplace. No wonder it had been so warm last night.

"Good morning, madame. You had a good breakfast, I hope?"

"Very good, thank you."

"Hortense says you are looking for a Monsieur Jacques Thomas?"

"That's right."

"How old would this gentleman be?"

"I'm not sure. Quite old. In his seventies anyway."

"I think I may know him—well, not know him exactly, but I think I may know who he is, or who he is now."

Was this good or bad? She tried to keep as still and calm as she could.

"How do you mean, who he is now?"

"It's a bit complicated."

He was standing in front of the log basket that he had put down beside the fireplace. She looked down at the tablecloth, knowing he was studying her face.

"Are you all right, madame? Can I get you anything?"

She met his look, kind, a little anxious.

"A glass of water perhaps. Thank you."

He went behind the bar, poured Perrier into a tumbler for her and for himself a glass of white wine, brought them to the table and sat down opposite her where his wife had sat earlier.

"Now look, this may not even be the man you're trying to find. I don't remember that he was called Jacques, though he may have been. The story goes something like this.

"When I was a small boy, that would be in the nineteen-sixties, there was an old lady called Madame Thomas in the village—

10

well, not quite in the village. Her house, a nice old house, not large, you understand, but nice, just beyond the village on the road out to Saint-Roch, was next door to the primary school—that's to say it was the school then. I went to it myself as a kid. They knocked it down when they started taking all the little kids from the small villages in a bus, to the school in St-Christophe. A fellow built a house and a garage there, sold petrol, serviced cars, but he couldn't make it pay—you have to travel to St-Christophe for petrol these days—and now another fellow lives in the house and repairs farm machinery in the yard, tractors, vine-weeders, harrows, grape-pickers, all that sort of thing.

"Anyway, Madame Thomas. She was a formidable old lady, very devout, but she was kind to us children, and she had a lovely big dog, a German shepherd dog, but gentle and quiet. We used to take him for walks—to tell the truth, I think he took us for walks—and she would give us a few centimes for our time.

"The château—it's a short way out of the village, in a pretty park—was a convent in those days. Nuns, you know. We never saw them, but Madame Thomas used to walk to their chapel every day for Mass, not a long walk but long enough for an old lady, and she would do it every single day, even in the winter, even in bad weather. Came the time when she was too old, too frail to leave the house, and her dog died. I can't remember exactly when she died herself, probably when I was fourteen or fifteen. A long time ago, you understand. She left her house to the commune and different people lived there for years, old people who had given their house to a son, young families who couldn't afford a house yet, that sort of thing."

She was finding the story unaccountably soothing; listening to him she felt far away from ordinary life, happily attentive, not impatient for him to reach Jacques Thomas.

"I beg your pardon, madame", he said. "I am talking too much. Hortense always says I talk too much. If you run a café you get used to talking."

"Not at all. It's most interesting, the story. I know so little about life in the country."

She did not say that her only memories of life in the country were dim, far away and frightening: a camp, huts for dormitories, lines of washing, barbed wire, mud to play in or cracked ground baked in the sun, she, a very small child, and her mother, picking bits of gristle and bone out of the stew they were given to eat, and saving some of the day's portion of bread so that the three- or four-year-old she then was would have something to nibble before she fell asleep each night.

"And I have been to Paris only once in my life. My father took us to the circus and we climbed to the top of the Eiffel Tower. It rained all the time."

She laughed "What bad luck. Paris is so beautiful."

"So they say. But not as beautiful as Burgundy."

He looked out of the window as if the village square and the chestnut trees in the sunshine belonged to him.

"You haven't seen Burgundy yet, have you? Our woods and hills and vineyards. I could show you—never mind now. Where was I? Yes. Madame Thomas. Very good."

He paused and she looked across the table at him.

"Well", he went on. "There was a young man who came back from the war, the war in Algeria, you understand, wounded, I suppose, or perhaps not wounded but damaged in some way. For a while she looked after him, until he was more or less better. I was too young to know anything about this at the time but later, long after he had gone away again, I have no idea where to, old people in the village said he was her grandson and she had brought him up because her daughter, the young man's mother, had disappeared during the war, the real war, the Occupation and all that terrible time. No one saw him when he came back from Algeria, because of the state he was in. I don't know anything about that, except that people said he didn't want to see anybody. Maybe he was a little . . . wrong in the head, you know. Soldiers have these problems sometimes. Then he went away, several years before the old lady died, and no one heard anything of him again until, well, it must be many years ago now. How many years? Perhaps fifteen, perhaps more, when I come to think of it. The years go by so fast. In any case, whenever it was, he came back. He was definitely the same man, and he still didn't want to meet anyone, but this time he had been properly injured, wherever he had been. He has a very bad scar which he does his best to hide. So he's shy, as well as perhaps a bit strange. He comes into the village first thing in the morning, just to get bread and the newspaper and a bit of shopping. Apparently he comes to the church when there's a Mass; he sits at the back and goes out at the end before the rest of the people. He doesn't like talking. He never comes in here, for example. He calls himself Thamar, just the one word, like a film-star or a rock-singer. You know, like Fernandel, or Bono. Only people with long memories know he's called Jacques Thomas."

"Where does he live?"

"In her house. In Madame Thomas's house. One way or another the house was empty at the time he came back, and the commune let him have it. Perhaps he was just lucky, or perhaps there was something in her will about him having the house if he needed it. I really don't know."

"How does he . . . does he work?"

"He's old of course. I suppose he has some kind of pension. And he does work, yes, he works. He looks after the garden of the château. No nuns any more. They got fewer and fewer and older and frailer and were taken away to another convent somewhere. Years ago. The château is a nursing home now, for old people. A good place to die if you can afford it. I could tell you—"

He broke off, looking out of one of the windows that faced the square.

"Ah! Customers. Excuse me, madame. They'll be back from Mass in Saint-Roch." He stood up, pushed his chair in neatly and smoothed down his thick, greying hair. As he went to the door he said over his shoulder. "There's Mass here only once a month these days. It's bad for business." And, on the terrace, to a middle-aged couple and three teen-aged children, "Good morning, mesdames, messieurs, what can I get you?"

While he shouted to Hortense for coffee and fussed about at the bar pouring fizzy drinks, she picked up her laptop and went upstairs to her room. There was a lot to think about.

She stayed upstairs for an hour, during which she decided several times to go back to Paris that afternoon and not to bother this old man who disliked meeting people and did the gardening for the nursing-home in the château. She decided as many times to stay, to try to see him: wouldn't it be merely cowardly to go home now? She heard the café fill with people for aperitifs, then for lunch. When the noise died down, she went downstairs. One family was finishing lunch inside and several other customers were talking and laughing over their coffee on the terrace. She asked the *patron* if there were still some lunch.

"It smells delicious."

"But of course, madame. Sit down, over here." He quickly cleared on to a tray the plates and glasses from a table in the corner, took the tray into the kitchen, came back with a clean paper tablecloth to replace the one he whisked away, and laid a place for her.

"Three minutes, madame. Would you like wine with your lunch? We have excellent . . ."

"No thank you. I would like some water. That's all."

She had brought with her a detective story, an old Simenon novel which Jean-Claude had told her she would enjoy. She had started it yesterday on the train. She couldn't remember the beginning and now only pretended to read it as she ate some lunch.

The café was empty, though one couple and a man drinking by himself were still outside on the terrace, when the *patron* came to take away her coffee-cup and her glass.

"Monsieur", she said. "You were very kind this morning to tell me the story of Monsieur Thomas. I—" She didn't know how to go on.

"You would like me to take you to the house?"

He smiled at her. She saw he was pleased he had guessed correctly.

"Thank you. If that's possible? When it isn't a difficult time for you."

"Sunday afternoons get quite busy, and Hortense likes an hour or two off on a Sunday after all that cooking and washing-up. Monday mornings are always quiet after the early rush, and Hortense, when she's done the shopping, will be here washing and ironing—she can serve anyone who does come in. We get the odd lorry-driver and the dustbin men on a Monday morning but not many others. You can stay till tomorrow?"

"Yes, of course."

"I'll take you to Madame Thomas's house in the middle of the morning. Mind you, he's a funny customer, this Thamar, as I told you, very timid. He may not open the door, even if he's there in the house. And he may be out working at the château, though I'm told he usually takes the school holidays to work at home. In any case, we can give it a try. And at least you can see where he lives."

"Thank you. Thank you so much."

All going well. I have discovered a really interesting story, but am a little afraid of where it may take me. I have some help. I miss you and Joséphine. I will stay tonight and come home tomorrow evening if I can. Love J

The next morning she woke up much more than a little afraid. Today she didn't have to think out where she was; her room, the smell of coffee made by someone else, good Hortense, the sense of the sun shining beyond curtains and shutters, the sound of the *patron* thudding up the wooden stairs in his boots and shortly afterwards thudding down again, then the creaks and rattles of the awning over the terrace being unrolled and fixed for the day: all were as familiar, and as unthreatening, as if she had known them all her life. But a dream had haunted her night, a dream she had woken from two or three times and tried with her conscious mind to banish, but which haunted her still now that she was properly awake. She had lost a child, not one of her own, a strange child, a little boy for whom she and she alone was responsible. She left him in a dark street but in front of a lit shop. She told him to wait for her. She would be back very soon. She had to find something, fetch something. She couldn't do it. She didn't know what it was. She went back to the shop. The child was gone. There was no one in the street.

15

The shop was shut, its lights out. She searched and searched. She wanted to call out but she didn't know his name. Once she woke up crying. Now she was awake, wide awake, and all was calm in her room, with the smell of coffee and the wooden stairs. But the clutch of the dream wouldn't let her go.

She got up and opened her laptop.

Well done. Of course stay another night. Look after yourself. We are fine. Joséphine must do some homework today so I'll do some work too. Love from us both. J-C

Now she was crying because Jean-Claude was kind and full of support, as he always had been. But also because he had no idea, however much he always said and always would say he understood, of what this journey meant to her. How could he possibly understand, with his steady, prosperous, respectable parents in Rouen, who had made such a visible effort not to look as if they minded when he married an Arab girl from nowhere, with his brother, a lawyer like his father, and his sister with her dull husband and her three dull children? It wasn't his fault, he tried his best, but it was simply not in him to understand. He knew the bits of the story she had been able to tell him, he knew the surrounding history, because history was his career and he was always good at facts, but of the soul, her soul, perhaps even his own soul, he knew almost nothing. The soul was not a subject which could be managed, have notes taken on it, ordered and summarized and taught, so it did not even interest him. Not that she could deal with the restlessness in her own soul, the restlessness that she often thought was all she knew of her own soul. She had been given so much that was evidently good, a good husband, children who were well and seemed reasonably happy, though she worried about Joséphine, who wouldn't talk to her, a safe and comfortable flat in Paris with evening sunshine through the windows and plane trees in the street, a good job which she could do competently with a mixture of efficiency and common sense, even her mother's peaceful death, after a life which she knew had been sad and often hard: all this, being French, being educated, being lucky in all sorts of ways, should amount to a contented life. It did. It did not. There was always something she missed, perhaps had missed when she might have discovered it, perhaps would always miss. What?

Thinking, she had stopped crying. She washed her face, got dressed, looked at herself in the small mirror on the wall by the basin—she could see she had been crying; she hoped the *patron* or Hortense wouldn't notice—and combed her hair. Thinking about Jean-Claude, about herself, had helped because it reminded her that she was used to being alone. This she did know how to deal with.

With what was to come, she would just have to do her best.

As she ate her breakfast at her corner table the café filled and emptied with workmen, all in a hurry, the *patron* at the bar, Hortense in and out of the kitchen with coffee, bread, croissants, for one old man two hard-boiled eggs which he put in his pocket. One or two of the customers gave her a friendly "Good morning, madame", and smiled. Some stared at her in brief curiosity. Most ignored her.

The square today was noisy, cars, motorbikes, farmers' pickup trucks, a tractor with an empty trailer, a big lorry full of cows or calves or bullocks on two levels inside, pulling up near the café, setting off again with an unnecessary roar of the engine.

She wished she knew more about life in the country.

Yesterday afternoon, with all that the *patron* had told her turning over and over in her mind, she had gone for a walk, across the square, past the church, a duck-pond and an old, silent mill on the edge of a stream, which someone with a good deal of money had made into a picturesque house, a few cottages, a farm with hens, and then the sign with the name of the village crossed out, on its other side the name of the village clear, and along a quiet road between peaceful fields. This was the road she had travelled in her taxi, but in the dark and the rain. Beyond the fields, on both sides of the road were wooded hills, with what she thought must be vines planted in rows on the slopes below the woods. There were flowers, yellow and white, in the grass beside the road, more flowers in the fields, and under groups of trees, their young leaves fresh in the sun, small gatherings of cows, beautiful creamy-white cows, five or six together, one or two with calves beside them or suckling, the rest clearly not far from giving birth.

It was soothing just to stand at the wall beside the road, in the flowery grass, and watch the gentle cows. There was almost no traffic. An occasional car. A tractor drawing a mysterious machine behind it. A young man on a bicycle with a small, noisy engine—she had never seen such a thing in Paris—stopped beside her, alarming her for a moment. She looked up and down the road. No one in sight. But the young man said, "Hello, madame. Are you lost?" "No, no, thank you. Everything's fine." "Very good", he said, and puttered off on his bike.

She realized how odd she must look, here, in her city black suit, her spectacles—they should not be surprising in the country, but she felt they were—and her darker-than-French colouring, perfectly ordinary in Paris, not here.

This was the country of his childhood, to which he had returned, a number of years ago, according to the *patron*. No wonder he had come back. So beautiful, as the *patron* had proudly said, so cared-for and somehow kind.

What else, far from here, had happened to him? The story was still full of gaps, long years the *patron* knew nothing about. What might she discover? Bad things? Good things? But of course he might refuse to see her, refuse to talk to her. Then she would have to go home to Paris, taking with her in her bag the carved box, wrapped and sealed, to Jean-Claude and to her ordinary work at the school, her ordinary days in which usually she was quite content, with nothing more to carry back with her than the bits of story the patron had told her. She felt the crush of disappointment as if it had already overcome her.

She had walked on for another twenty minutes. The sun was low in the sky, the hills and woods on one side of the road were becoming indistinct; on the other side the line of shadow was creeping upwards as the sun went down, the trees at the top lit gold with the last of its light, something, accustomed all her life since she was a small child to city streets, that she had never seen before. When the road narrowed and began to wind uphill through woods, she could no longer see the sky, the evening was dark, suddenly much darker than it had been out in the open, the silence had changed so that she could hear sounds among the trees that she didn't understand, and she was afraid.

She turned and walked quickly back to the village—it wasn't far after all—and met no one as she walked.

Now, sitting waiting for the *patron* to have time to take her to Madame Thomas's house, she realized that, whatever happened today, she wouldn't forget her walk, the mild beauty of the fields, the flowers, the white cows in the green green grass, the darkening wood like the forest in a fairy story. The walk had unlocked something in her. She had no idea what it was.

Sitting at her table in the café with the book she wasn't reading open in front of her, she searched her memory for something, somewhere, that her walk reminded her of.

She managed to remember. About fifteen years ago—it must have been that long ago because Bernard and Josephine were about seven and three years old—Jean-Claude had taken them all out for the day from Rouen. It was August, very hot, and Bernard had got sunburned on the beach the day before. Her mother-in-law had said: "That child shouldn't play on the sand today. The sea is bad for sunburn. Put him in a loose shirt and take him into the country. You could have a picnic. Trees and shade are what he needs." Her mother-in-law had gone to the shops to buy the picnic, bread and cheese and tomatoes and sausage and peaches, a bottle of wine, orange juice for the children, and packed it all in a basket for them. Jean-Claude, who always obeyed his mother, and thought his wife ridiculous for saying "she does this kind of thing to show what an incompetent mother I am", borrowed his father's car and drove them, not far, for perhaps half an hour.

The Seine, now a huge river, much wider than in Paris and flowing in great loops towards the sea, appeared from time to time, gleaming in the sun. Bernard was thrilled every time he saw it. "Look, look, the Seine again! Can we have our picnic by the Seine?"

"Of course we can. That's where I'm taking you. A place we used to go to when I was your age."

"With grandmama and grandpapa?"

"That's right."

"Is it a nice place? Can we play in the river?"

"I'm afraid not. The river's too big for playing in here. But it's a lovely place."

She couldn't remember the name of the tall, bare, wonderful, ruined church in the green fields and trees of what was almost an island in a bend of the Seine, surrounded on three sides by the river. Grand churches usually scared and oppressed her, she wasn't sure why. Perhaps because when she was growing up her mother had often told her that except for the White Fathers—she had no idea who they were—the Church had been most cruel to her people, especially, she had heard, in the cities, and had despised them and their religion. Not that her mother was religious. "You are lucky to be here, to live in France, to go to school in France, where no one bothers about religion. Religion does so much harm. I think it has always done more harm than good." But somewhere in her mother, who was never able to put it into words, there was a memory, or perhaps a remembered legend, of holy Muslim people, long ago, in the mountains where she was born. And distant recollections of that world made her mother fearful of Catholics. She had caught this fear from her mother, so that Notre-Dame in Paris, where at about ten years old she had been taken with her class at school, had only frightened her, enormous and dark and heavily carved and decorated with almost black pictures. Here and there were little banks of lit candles: she had thought that only one candle needed to fall and the whole church might catch fire. And the west front of the cathedral in Rouen which Jean-Claude had often stopped her to admire, as they walked in the city, his home city—" Don't you see how beautiful it is? Different in every light, as in the Monet paintings."—also struck her as threatening, an elaborate wall of carved stone that might, almost that was intended to, fall on her, crush her. She had never been inside the cathedral.

But this ruined church, its towers tall and pale, with simple arches, its columns and roofless windowed walls like an avenue of stone trees against nothing but sky and grass, seemed quite different, without menace. And the slender white tower with its layers of arches, other fallen walls, a smaller church, the great square, labelled "cloister", that must have been a garden once, with an ancient tree in the middle, surrounded by more ruined buildings—what did it all mean? Bernard loved it and forgot about wanting to play in the river. He and Joséphine ran about in the grass, climbed on the broken walls, hid from each other, soon calling out if they thought they might not be found, and when they had got tired of playing were pleased to sit against a low wall in the shade of some trees for their picnic. Joséphine, hot and sticky after eating a peach, fell asleep with her head on the napkin that had wrapped the bread in the picnic basket.

"Papa", Bernard said. "Were all these walls houses for people?"

Jean-Claude taught history in the *lycée* where she worked as the director's secretary, and Bernard always asked his father for information, knowing his father would always be able to produce it. "Not exactly. But a lot of men lived here once, close to the church, in all these buildings, and not just one lot of men but old ones who had been young and young ones who would grow old here, for hundreds and hundreds of years. They were called monks. They spent hours every day in the church, saying their prayers."

"What's prayers?"

"Well, it depends. In a monastery, which is what a house of monks was called, they all said prayers together in the church. People who believed in God, and most people did in those days, thought that if you said, or sang, a fixed set of words at fixed times every day, God would listen and perhaps make the world a better place."

"Did he?"

"Did he what?"

"Did he listen? Did he make the world a better place?"

"I'm afraid not. You see, God isn't really there. It's just that people used to think he was. And the world doesn't get better, because people keep making a mess of it, having wars and treating each other badly."

"So all this prayers stuff was really a waste of time?"

"Yes. I suppose it was. But at least it didn't do any harm. Or not much. The monks could have led more useful lives."

Lying on her back after her mother-in-law's inevitably perfect picnic, watching the pigeons circling the high towers of the abbey in the hot afternoon, and listening to Jean-Claude, she knew he was wrong. She said nothing, and couldn't have explained to him or to anyone else her reasons for knowing this. She was simply sure that whatever the life of those who built this church and lived here had been like, and it was hard to imagine, it had not been a waste of time, not useless. She closed her eyes; Jean-Claude would think she was asleep.

"Why did the church get the roof taken off and the walls get knocked down?"

"Well. There used to be lots of places like this in France. All of them were closed during the Revolution. The monks were sent away and most of the monasteries had their buildings knocked down, like this. You know about the Revolution?"

"Yes, we've done it in school. 1789. The Fourteenth of July. Liberty, Equality, Fraternity. What do they mean, papa? Miss told us we should always remember Liberty, Equality, Fraternity, but she didn't tell us what they mean."

"It's complicated, Bernard."

"Grown-up? You always say it's complicated when it's grown-up."

"Grown-up, yes. But you're a clever boy so I'll try to explain. The Revolution happened because lots of people thought things had been very unfair for a very long time."

"Did the monks who lived here think things had been unfair?"

It was typical of Bernard to enjoy using the word 'monks' which he had just learnt.

"No. Or maybe yes. I don't know. Perhaps some of them did. In any case what the poor people wanted, and most people were poor then, was a fair share of everything. In those days the king and a very few grand families owned nearly all of France, and the Church—the monks were part of the Church—as well as owning a lot of valuable things itself, supported the grand families and the grand families supported the Church. It was all part of how things had been for hundreds of years—we call it the old order. You see?"

"Sort of."

"Anyway, the poor people, because there were so many of them, and some clever men in Paris helped them, managed to get rid of the king and the grand families and . . ."

"Did they kill them?"

"Quite a lot of them, yes, they did."

"Did they kill the monks?"

"No. Not usually. But they told them they weren't monks any more and they smashed up the abbeys and took the lands and the valuable things and the money the monks had."

Silence. She opened her eyes and saw Bernard sitting beside his father, his arms round his knees, looking up at the ruined church. Eventually he said:

"Wasn't that a bit sad?"

"No. It wasn't sad. It was good. Things have to change, Bernard, and the Revolution was a great change for the better. People who had been kept poor by the rich and powerful were freed to do what they wanted, live where they wanted—that's what liberty means. Equality means everyone being counted as the same, like in your class at school. And fraternity means people being kind to each other."

More silence. Bernard was a thoughtful child.

"They weren't very kind to the monks. And anyway it doesn't work, does it?"

"How do you mean, it doesn't work?"

"Some people are rich. I bet President Hollande is much richer than you. And lots of people are poor. The Arabs who have to live in the *banlieues* are poor, everybody says so, and they do poor jobs like cleaning the streets. And the foreign children who ask for money in the Tuileries, they're very poor. Some of them don't even have shoes. People aren't the same, people aren't kind to each other, people can't choose

23

where to live or what to do. Can they? So what good was the Revolution?"

"It was good, I promise you. It didn't solve everything but it made a lot of things better, and France is a good country because of it. The most important thing is that the possibilities are there. Before the Revolution, for nearly everyone, there were no possibilities. Wait till you're older and you'll understand it all better."

"Grown-up, you mean?"

"That's right."

"Papa?"

"What?"

"Can we wake up maman and Joséphine and go all round the walls once more?"

"Yes of course."

She hadn't remembered that day for years and years. But now, because of yesterday's walk, the beauty of the ruined abbey in the great bend of the Seine, and her sense of Bernard's childish response being somehow close to her own, were as vivid as if the expedition and the picnic had happened a few days ago. She even remembered that Joséphine had been stung by a wasp in the car on the way back to Rouen, with no serious consequences, and how her mother-in-law, full of sympathy, had made her feel that the wasp was her fault.

Bernard. How was he, so far away in Nantes where she had never been? Two and a half years he had been there. Three times he had come home for Christmas, and said almost nothing about his life. His two summer holidays he had spent, with another boy from the *lycée* whom he'd known since they were at primary school, working in a summer camp for children in the Ardèche. She had no picture of where he was living in Nantes, of the new friends he must have made there, even of his work, though it was clear that he was working hard as a university student as he had always worked hard at school. He had said, this last Christmas, that he was writing a book but she had no idea what kind of a book. Occasionally he emailed her, more, she felt, to get an answer saying that she herself was well than to tell her anything about himself. He was a good boy. She missed him. He was more perceptive, quicker to notice things, than either Jean-Claude or Joséphine would ever be, and he had loved her mother since he was a baby. He would have been a real help in her last illness; Joséphine was too young, too selfish, and too afraid of being embarrassed to see much of her grandmother when she was frail and in pain. Once, shortly before her death, Bernard had come to Paris to visit his grandmother, and sat with her for several hours, saying little and holding her hand. A quiet farewell.

Bernard. She wished he were here, with her, to face whatever had to be faced.

The café was empty, had been empty for some time. She looked at her watch. Almost ten o'clock. Hortense came in with a broom, a bucket and a mop.

"All right, madame? Can I get you come more coffee?"

"No thank you. I'll be in your way here. I'll sit outside on the terrace. I'm hoping your husband won't be too busy to . . ."

"Don't worry. He's waiting for the delivery that comes on Monday mornings. It shouldn't be long now."

Hortense opened the door wide, straightened a couple of chairs at one of the little tables outside and gave their seats and the surface of the table a rapid wipe with a duster she took from the waistband of her apron.

"There. It's a lovely day, all the same. The children will be happy—the school holidays start today, you know. When I was at school, this was the holiday, the two weeks at the end of April and in early May, we always enjoyed the most."

Indeed, there were children in the square, three small boys on bikes racing each other, two mothers sitting on a bench in the sun with babies asleep in pushchairs beside them, a pair of girls, perhaps nine or ten years old, walking side by side, heads down, talking and talking, the way girls talk to their friends.

She longed for company. She longed for the silent, encouraging presence of Bernard.

A large tinny van that looked as if it were made of corrugated iron came across the square, scattering dust—one sunny day had dried the puddles as if it had never rained—and some pigeons. The van headed for the café, alarmingly fast considering there were children playing in the square, and slowed down suddenly before turning into an opening beside the café she hadn't noticed before. She heard it stop, clearly in a yard at the back of the building, heard friendly shouts from the driver and the *patron*, a metal door sliding open, and the clatter of crates being unloaded and stacked.

"See you next week."

"'Bye."

More jingling and banging as the *patron* shifted the crates of bottles indoors. Then a long pause. Twenty past ten.

At last he emerged from the café, looking different. No plaid shirt, no apron. A clean white shirt, neat trousers, polished shoes. She smiled, realizing that he had pictured himself escorting a presentable woman in Paris clothes through the village, not a usual event in his life. He smiled back.

"So, madame. Shall we go?"

"Thank you. Yes, monsieur. Let's go."

Now, after all, she was not afraid.

They crossed the square to the Mairie and walked out of the village in the opposite direction from the one she had taken yesterday: she now saw that there were no other roads leading out of the village. The hills and woods began sooner on this side of the houses. They passed a row of cottages, terraced, old, some with pots of wallflowers or red tulips by their doors, each front door opening straight on to the road, and then, after a few newish, ugly houses, each standing by itself, with pebble-dash walls and too-big windows with metal frames, an orchard full of apple trees in lavish white blossom. They came to what was clearly the old garage, where a young man in overalls was lying on the ground underneath a tractor with its engine ticking over. The patron shouted a greeting which the boy didn't hear.

Beyond the end of the village, beyond the sign with the name crossed out, they reached a pretty, old house. It was set back a little from the road behind more apple trees and, beneath them, growing in the grass, a mass of delicate white flowers, little bells in deep green leaves, with a wonderful sweet scent. She didn't know what they were called. The house had rough stone walls and the reddish-brown, steep, tiled roof of all the older houses she had seen. An oak front door with a brass knocker. Windows on either side of the door had their shutters still closed. Upstairs, the shutters were folded back and the small windows open.

The *patron* said: "It might be better if you waited out of sight. He's very shy, as I told you."

She walked a little further along the road. She heard the deep barking of a large dog. Round a bend in the road she saw, also on the right, a pair of old gateposts with much-weathered stone owls on each, and open wrought-iron gates. She walked up to the gateway. A white road from the gateway led through a green field and disappeared behind trees. On a neat board on one gatepost was painted: St Philibert, and underneath, Maison de Santé. The château. The nursing home.

She walked back towards Madame Thomas's house. The barking had stopped. She thought she heard voices, not loud, and not near the road. Silence. She waited, just out of sight of the door.

The *patron* appeared, mopping his brow with a white handkerchief. He smiled.

"It's all right, madame. He will see you."

"How did you persuade him?"

"It wasn't easy. He said he sees nobody. But he asked me to describe you and I said you were perhaps North African. That's true, isn't it?"

"Yes. It's true."

"When I told him that, he thought for a bit and then he said, 'I will allow her ten minutes.' And after that he said, 'And you will go away. You will go home, back to your bar, or I won't see her.'"

The *patron* looked at her anxiously.

"Will you be all right? All by yourself?"

"Yes, of course. And thank you so very much for your help."

"Well, if you're sure. Come straight back to the Paix afterwards, won't you?"

"Of course."

She watched him as he walked back towards the square. Once he turned, and waved, and walked on.

She closed her eyes for a moment and then went back to Madame Thomas's house. There was no one about. She knocked on the door.

"No!" a voice. From where?

"Not the house! Down here! Turn right, left along the path, straight on."

The path was stepping-stones among grass, more fruit trees, more flowers. She saw, under taller trees at the end of the garden, a small wooden hut, a summer house, double doors open, with two steps up to them and a wooden balustrade each side of the steps. All very simple. It was dark inside. The steps were guarded by a large white shaggy beautiful dog, not barking, standing, braced on his front paws, fixing her with a stare. He was nevertheless not frightening. She thought he looked like a dog in a fairy story.

"Yes! Come on! He won't bite you. Nor will I." His voice was much quieter now that she was near. She couldn't see him. She knew he was watching her as she approached the summer-house.

"Stop!"

She stood still, a yard from the steps, a yard from the dog.

"Félix! Lie down!"

The dog obeyed, flopping down to one side of the steps, still gazing at her.

"He's a good dog. He barks only at strangers. It seems he doesn't think you are a stranger." He said this as if to himself.

"Excuse me, madame. I am not used to visitors. No one visits me."

"I beg your pardon, monsieur—I—"

"What is your name?"

"My name is Jamila Charpentier."

"Jamila."

He said nothing for a moment or two. Then he said, "Jamila Charpentier. You are a North African lady. You are married to a Frenchman, Monsieur Charpentier. Is that correct?"

"Yes, monsieur. That is correct."

"Why have you come here?"

"To see you, monsieur. That's to say, if you are Monsieur Jacques Thomas, I have come to . . ."

"My name is Thamar. An Arab name. In my case, a Berber name."

She waited.

"But yes, a long time ago, a very long time ago, my name was Jacques Thomas. How did you know this name? How did you know that you should come to this place?"

"My . . . Someone who was dying, someone I was looking after, asked me to find you, to give something to you."

A long silence.

"Is she now dead? Is she dead at present?"

She had never before heard anyone say this. She swallowed.

"Yes. She died, a few weeks ago."

"What was her name?"

"She was called Tanifa Sadi."

Another long silence.

"Come closer, madame. Come in, to my lair. There is another chair, I don't know what for. No one has ever sat in it. But you may sit in it, if you will."

"Thank you, monsieur."

She went up the two steps and stood for a moment with her hand on the balustrade as her eyes adjusted to the darkness.

The summer house was bigger than she expected. He was sitting at a square wooden table, facing the path through the orchard. His clasped hands rested on the table between two piles of paper. Small, regular hand-writing on the paper. A fountain pen and a bottle of ink. She couldn't see him clearly. He was wearing dark clothes. An old felt hat, pulled to one side, shadowed one side of his face. Spectacles. A small neat white beard. He was studying her with keen attention, not smiling.

"Sit down, madame. Please."

She sat down in a dusty wicker chair at one end of the table. She was close to him now but still couldn't see him properly. He said nothing.

After a while, she said, "Your garden is very beautiful."

"I have lived in the desert", he said, now in a gentle voice. "A garden is a miracle. It needs a little help from the gardener, but not much. And in Burgundy it rains."

"What is the name of the white flowers?"

"They're lilies of the valley. They're wild flowers, flowers of the woods, but if you're lucky they will grow in a garden. The peasants call them the tears of Mary."

She had no idea how to answer this.

He rescued her from her silence.

"Where do you live, madame?"

"I live in Paris. I have lived in Paris since I was a very small child."

"Ah. No tears of Mary in Paris. In any sense, I imagine, these days. Tell me, madame—"

She did not interrupt his silence.

"What did Tanifa Sadi say to you about me?"

"Nothing. Absolutely nothing. A few days before she died she told me your name, Monsieur Jacques Thomas, and the name of this village, and asked me to find you if I could. She said that she knew you were born here, and that someone here might know how to find you. I don't think she expected that you would be here yourself. She said—she wasn't sure you would be still alive."

"Did she explain why she wanted you to find me?"

"She gave me something that she wanted me to give you, if by any chance I were able to find you."

"Ach!" He groaned as if in sudden pain, unclasped his hands and gripped the table in front of him.

"What is it? Do you have it here? Please, madame, forgive me. I am old, to be surprised, after all these quiet years of avoiding surprises, of avoiding, to tell you the truth, very much."

He let go of the table and clasped his hands in front of him again. He took a deep breath.

"I beg your pardon. Do you have it here, this gift? With you, now?"

"Yes, monsieur. It's in my bag."

Her everyday bag was still on her shoulder. She put it on her lap and opened it. She took out the wrapped and sealed package and put it on the table in front of him.

He picked it up, turning it over and over. He tried to unwrap it but his hands were shaking and his fingers could get no purchase on the sticky tape.

"Would you like me to help you?" she said.

At last he looked at her. Now she could see that one side of his face was badly disfigured. A long scar, whiter than his sunburned skin, whiter than his beard, ran down from his ear to his neck and part of his jaw was missing, making his face and the set of his mouth crooked. The eye socket on that side of his face was also damaged, broken and mended long ago.

"I do not accept help", he said. "Since I have lived in France again, I have not accepted help."

He looked away from her, at the orchard and the flowers. "Help can be a dangerous thing. But now—"

He pushed the package towards her.

"Please."

Her fingers were shaking too. But she found an end of the sticky tape and gently, so as not to split the tape, pulled it, round and round, from the paper. She scrunched the tape into a sticky ball and put it in her pocket, pushing the box, now only in its paper wrapping, back towards his hands.

"Thank you, madame."

He unfolded the paper, and held the box in one hand, tracing the carving with two fingers of the other hand.

"Ah. This is Berber carving. Did you know that?"

He was calmer.

"No. What is Berber?"

"The Berbers are the ancient people of North Africa, before the Arabs, before the Romans, before the Carthaginians, there were Berbers in North Africa. They are still there."

He put the box on the table and looked at her again.

"It is possible that I have seen this box before. Possible. But there are many like it. Now."

He opened the box, peered inside it, turned it upside down.

"But there is nothing inside. Nothing."

He looked at her, questioning.

"I'm sorry, monsieur."

"No, madame. You should not be sorry. You have done what you were asked to do."

He bent his head. When he was still, his stillness had an absolute quality she had never seen in anyone else. Not the stillness of sleep, but the stillness of a stone figure.

After some minutes she said, "Would you like me to go now?"

He looked up, as if he had forgotten she was there.

"No. Not at all. It seems to me that the box, this empty box, is not the message. It is a token by which I am meant to be certain from whom the message comes, as in the Middle Ages when a king, or perhaps a queen, would send a message with a ring, say, to show from whom the message had come. In the Middle Ages, or in a story. Is this a story?"

He put his hand on the pile of written-on paper.

She had the impression that he had surprised himself by speaking so many words at one time.

He studied her face so intently that she looked away, back over her shoulder to the path through the apple blossom and the white flowers, the tears of Mary.

"It seems to me that you are the message, madame."

She was afraid again, as she had not been since he asked her to sit in the other chair in his summer-house, his lair.

"Tell me, madame, how did you come to know Tanifa Sadi?"

She looked down at the box, then at her familiar bag on her lap.

"She was my mother."

A long silence.

"She was your mother. I thought so. You look very like her, you know. All the same, with the spectacles, and the clothes, so different, it would have taken me some time to see the likeness if I had met you here in the village—but then, I do not look carefully at the people I see in the village. It is a long habit. And why—" There was a sudden edge to his voice and she looked up. "Why are you a friend of Pierre Chaumont?"

"Pierre Chaumont?"

"The *patron* of the Café de la Paix, so badly named."

"I'm not his friend. That's to say, I met him only on Saturday

32

evening because I'm staying at the café. There's nowhere else in the village to stay. And they've been kind to me, both of them."

"The father of this Chaumont was given the café during the Occupation. By the Germans. The real *patron*—the café was in the same family for generations—was shot by the Gestapo. They found a radio transmitter and some guns in the attic. For the Resistance, you know. Someone in the village tipped them off. People said old Chaumont tipped them off. After that, half the village wouldn't go there. But—the war ended, the Germans left, and worse things happened before they left. People forgot, or pretended to forget. But not everyone has forgotten, even now. I don't remember that time, myself, in my own memory. Or I remember very little. I was not yet five years old when the war ended. But I remember what my grandmother told me. I expect she told me too much. We were alone, she and I, for years in this house, this garden."

She waited, for him to come back to the present. He did.

"Tell me, madame, about your father."

"My father is dead. He was killed in the war, the Algerian war, you understand. My mother told me nothing about him. He was killed before I was born."

A few more minutes of his stillness.

"How did your mother come to be living in Paris?"

"After the end of the war, the Algerian war, her father was murdered. He had worked for the government, so for the French, in our village, our mountains, before the war and during the war. So he was on the side that lost. So he was killed. I was only a baby when we were taken to France so I don't remember the village or the mountains but all the rest of her life my mother wanted to go back. To her home. When her father was murdered, she was in great danger. She was very young, alone with the baby who was me. Her uncle managed to bring her, and me, to France with his children, her cousins. I think it was very difficult. To escape, to find the money, to find a boat. We lived for a time in a camp. It must have been for quite a long time because I remember the camp, a little. It was not a good place to live. Then, I don't know how, she was given a job in Paris, as a maid. The employers were quite kind,

I think. The gentleman had been an officer in Algeria and his wife was good to my mother. I remember them well. But they had an old cook who was not kind to my mother or to me. She wanted to get rid of us and somehow, I don't remember how, she succeeded. There were two or three other jobs. Usually we slept in a maid's room, a room in a line of maids' rooms on the top floor of a house with grand flats on the other floors. By the time I went to school my mother had been lucky to find a good job with a family who liked her and were kind to me. My mother was only a maid but she helped to look after their children, who were older than me, and at weekends we played together in the Luxembourg Gardens. They gave me their daughter's clothes when she grew out of them, and helped me to buy books and things I needed later, when I was at the high school. They helped my mother with some money when I got married. They allowed her to keep her room when she couldn't work any more and when she was ill they let her come back when the hospital said there was nothing more the doctors could do. They even paid for a nurse to help me look after her in the last week. She died in January, when Paris had gone mad because of the *Charlie Hebdo* murders. I didn't tell her about them."

"Your grandfather was a *harki*."

"Yes. You know the word? My husband told me a long time ago that I should never use that word, that it was the same as saying *collabo*. But how can it be the same? In the Second World War my mother's father fought in the French army against the Germans. How is that the same as collaborating with the Germans?"

"Alas, the injustice of people who know too little."

Again, he studied her face.

"Your husband. Is he a man of the left?"

"No. Yes. Not really. He supported President Hollande. He didn't like President Sarkozy. But now he is disappointed."

"As, I imagine, many are. What does he do, your husband?"

"He teaches history in the *lycée* where I am the director's secretary."

"I see. So that's why you look so like the director's secretary."

He smiled, an odd smile because of his damaged face.

"And your poor mother. Would you say she had a sad life?"

She thought about this. She could not describe to this strange man, although he was no longer frightening her, how undemanding, how grateful, her mother had always been.

"I think she had a sad life, but she was not a sad person. She was proud of me—not because I have achieved great things, you understand, but because I worked hard at school and I have a good husband and a good job, and she loved our children, particularly my son."

"Where in Paris is the school where you work, madame?"

"It's an ordinary *lycée*, in the fifteenth arrondissement, which is where we live. Not far from the Champ de Mars. It isn't a famous school but good enough all the same."

"Excellent. I see your life is well organized."

After another silence he leant towards her. She could see clearly the long scar, the damaged face. She looked away.

"Tell me. Was your father French, or Algerian, or perhaps French-Algerian, a *pied-noir*? Not that many of the *pieds-noirs* were truly French. They had come from Spain, Italy, Malta, as well as France, a good Mediterranean mixture, but they spoke French and that was enough. Excuse me, madame, it's so long since I talked, was able to talk, about Algeria. About anything. So. Your father?"

"I don't know, monsieur. I know nothing about him. When I asked my mother, she said, 'He is dead, poor man'. Once she said, 'He is dead, poor boy', so I think he was very young. As she was."

"Were they married?"

She looked at him. He smiled, his crooked smile.

"You think they weren't married?" he said.

"I think they weren't married. I have no birth certificate—we tried to find one when I married my husband—and my mother always had difficulty with documents. In the end, her employers managed to make her a legal person, and so I became a legal person too. They gave me a birth certificate but it had only my mother's name. 'Father unknown', it says. If my parents were married it would have been under some local Muslim

35

arrangement which was allowed, I think, in Algeria then."

"And in France, your mother never married? Never thought of marrying?"

"No. She had me to look after. She always had work to do. I don't think there were many opportunities for her to meet anyone she might have married. And then there was me. Not many men, in those days, would have—Also, she was afraid of men. From something she once said, when she was warning me to be careful, I realised that something very bad had happened to her, after I was born, after the end of the war."

A long silence.

"She was raped?"

"Yes." She felt, rather than saw, him wince. "I know nothing more about it, who it was, how it happened. But I'm sure it did happen."

Another long silence.

"Look at me, madame. You are brave, to look at me, without flinching. You have been brave to find me, and brave to tell me so much when you know nothing whatever about me. Thank you. Now I must ask you this: when, exactly, were you born? And where, exactly, were you born?"

"I was born in a village in the mountains of Kabylia. That's all I know. My mother never told me its name. She said the mountains were very beautiful and the people very poor. As I told you, she always wanted to see it again. Of course it was never possible."

"Of course."

Again he looked at her, long and hard, before looking down at his hand, resting on his pile of paper.

"And when were you born?"

"My birthday is July 20th. I was born in 1962, so I am fifty-two years old. I shall be fifty-three this summer."

"You look younger."

"You are very kind". But he wasn't listening.

A longer silence, heavy and serious.

"Madame", he said, not looking at her. "I think it is possible—no, I think it is probably certain, that I am your father."

This strange old man with his wounded face, his lair, the

tears of Mary in his garden, this strange, solitary old man. Was it possible?

"But—"

"But your mother told you your father was dead. Of course. How could she not? He had disappeared. She knew he had been wounded once. He might have been wounded again. He might have been killed. She may have always believed he was dead. And if he were alive, she would have thought it dangerous to find him. Dangerous for him. She was the daughter of a *harki*. That was bad enough. Worse than bad enough once the war was over. And then there is your name, the name she chose to give you."

"My name?"

"Jamila. Djémila. Yes."

For a few moments he was still, in his remarkable stillness. Then he said, "And the death of your grandfather, what do you know of that?"

"He was killed in the village, with two others, at the end of the war. A punishment for being on the wrong side. In the late summer of 1962, not long after I was born. She told me that. It may have been at the same time that she was herself—attacked. In any case, with her father dead she was very lucky to get to France, with me. She always said she thanked God that she had been saved. And I had been saved. Even though the camp was hard—"

Suddenly furious, he said, "How dared they? How dared they put women and children in camps, with barbed wire and guards, prison camps, when their husbands and fathers had died for France? How dared they? Those camps had been set up by the Vichy government, for Jews, in 1940. But it was de Gaulle, our hero, so-called by himself, who put the *harkis* in the camps. Shameful, shameful, the shadow-history of France. And now, even now, there are helpless people, as you and your mother were, in camps with barbed wire, in France, in Calais, in other places."

"But", she had to bring him back. "But who are you, then?"

"I beg your pardon, madame. I was thinking of your mother. I am ashamed to say I have thought of her very little, for many,

many years. For this I am much to blame. But I never knew she was imprisoned in a camp."

He turned towards her, and put a hand very gently on hers, watching her face. She didn't move her hand or shift her glance.

"And I never knew", he said, "that she had a child."

Tentatively, as if even now she might shrink from him, he added, "that we had a child".

Now she couldn't answer.

Softly, swiftly, he clapped his hands together.

"This is too much", he said. "Too much for my lair. Come into my house and I will tell you the story. We need—"

He looked along the grassy path as if the orchard might give him something. "We need—I know, we need coffee."

For the first time, she laughed.

"I have very little in my house to offer a guest—or rather, to offer you. Guests I never see. They don't come to see me. I have taken good care that they don't. But you. You are not a guest. And I do have coffee. Come."

He got up, moved round the far side of the table, out on to the grass. He gave her his hand to help her down the steps.

She stood in the grass and the blossom, watching him as he went back into the summer house, picked up first the carved box which he looked at again before putting it in his pocket, and then the pile of paper. As he came down the steps this time the dog got up, stretched and shook himself. They walked along the path, Monsieur Thomas, Thamar, leading, followed by his dog, followed by her.

At the back of the house there was a paved terrace with a wooden trellis on each side for walls and widely separated beams overhead for a roof. Different plants were growing in a green tangle, over the trellises, over the beams, over the wall of the house. There were yellow flowers here and there, and differently-shaped white and red flowers just coming out. She didn't know their names. There was a sweet, heavy scent, not the same as the scent of the lilies-of-the-valley. The floor of the terrace, old red tiles with cracks like lines on an old face, gave the shade a cool glow.

"Sit here", he said, and disappeared into the house. The dog lay down beside her chair, his head between his paws. She was sitting in another dilapidated wicker chair with a faded cushion, beside another table. She put her hand for a moment on the dog's white shaggy head and he thumped his tail, twice, in acknowledgement.

As the sound of a hand-grinder and then the smell of very good coffee, much better than Hortense's, drifted from the kitchen, where she could hear this strange old man, whom she had known for less than an hour, putting cups on saucers, pulling out a drawer for spoons, she understood that she hadn't yet allowed the reality of what had just happened to become more real than the beauty of the morning, the garden, the terrace, the flowers, the coffee, the friendliness of the dog. Perhaps because it wasn't more real, but simply as real, all part of the same extraordinary encounter. Arranged—she smiled as she thought this—by her humble, sweet-natured, undemanding mother. But how could her mother have known? Of course, she didn't know. She hadn't known that he was alive, that he was in France, that he was here in the village where, he had told her more than fifty years ago, he was born. But what was it that her mother remembered? What had there been between them, the Algerian village girl who, to the end of her life, had been unable to read French—she could manage the numbers on buses but little more—and could only sign her name, and this mysterious man in his careful loneliness, with the piles of written-on paper that he had put down on the terrace table when he went inside.

He appeared from the open door carrying a black tin tray, painted with flowers. On it were two small cups of black coffee, old-fashioned dark green, twelve-sided cups, white inside with a gold rim. Café cups, almost gone now from Paris. He had changed his hat to a wide-brimmed straw hat, still worn with one side down to keep the brokenness of his face in shadow. He put the tray on the table and said, "One moment", as he went back inside and immediately brought out a wooden kitchen chair.

He sat down.

"How beautiful it is here", she said, after a bit. Her coffee was too hot to drink.

"Yes. It was always beautiful. And these days, I think, it is more beautiful. But that may be old age."

Then he said, "What shall I call you now, now that we have discovered that we—?"

"You could call me Jamila."

A long silence, while he looked at her. She looked down at the table.

"She called you Jamila. She chose your name. Did she—did she ever give you a reason?"

She shook her head.

"No", he said.

Another silence.

"Jamila means 'beautiful'. A beautiful name, as my garden is beautiful. But also—"

He stopped. She saw there was here something difficult for him.

"But also", he managed to go on. "Jamila, Djémila, with a D at the beginning, is a place. A real place where one day—"

He looked past her at the apple trees and the tears of Mary, as if, she thought, his garden were not quite real.

"A magical place, a ruined Roman town high in the mountains of Kabylia. The Romans called it Cuicul. The Berbers renamed it Djémila, for its beauty. It's not far, only a long walk, from the village where—yes, well. I'm glad your mother called you Jamila."

"I didn't know. She didn't tell me any of this."

"Of course. For reasons I can only imagine, alas, your mother had so little she could tell you. She had to make what it was possible for her to make, of her new life in a new country. And look at you: she did well. It will always have been safer for both of you that she thought I was dead. It might have been safer for me if I had been dead. All this time. But of whom is that not true?"

She shook her head. She saw him realize that she couldn't answer this.

"I'm sorry", he said. "You know nothing about me yet.

Nothing about the fifty-two years, the fifty-three years, of my life between then and now. And nor, of course, did your mother, for whom I was dead. But after all she must have wondered—"

"The box."

"Exactly. The box. She wouldn't have sent you here unless from time to time she imagined I might be alive."

"And the box was empty."

"No. The box brought you, Jamila. A little box bringing a great and marvellous gift."

Then he said again "I'm sorry, What perhaps you would like is more of the story?"

She nodded.

"Drink your coffee."

She sipped the hot, strong, delicious coffee.

"I will begin", he said, "at the beginning, which happens to have been here, in this house." He bent down and tousled the ears of the dog, lying between them, which looked up at him briefly and went back to sleep.

"I was born in this house, in a bad time. The house belonged to my grandparents. My grandfather, before the First War, was the village schoolmaster. He was young to be a schoolmaster. It was his first job. According to my grandmother, he loved the work, the children, the Republic, France. As perhaps your husband does?"

"He does. Or he did. He is less sure now, I think, of the things he's always believed in, because, well, at present schools are so difficult in Paris, like everything else."

"Yes. Paris. Twice in my life I have escaped to Paris. Twice I have escaped from Paris. Long, long ago. But the story—

"My grandfather enlisted as a soldier in 1914 when the war began, as soon as they had found an old, retired teacher to replace him in the school. He was killed at Verdun, shortly before my mother was born. So she never knew her father. Like you, my poor child."

It was difficult for her to speak but she said, "Until now."

"Until now. Deo gratias."

A long stillness.

41

"My grandmother didn't marry again. So many widows of that war didn't marry again. Have you looked at the memorial in the village? No. Why should you? When did you arrive here?"

"On Saturday night. The day before yesterday."

"How did you get here?"

"By train, and a taxi from the station."

"How did you know where to come?"

"My mother, before she died, gave me the name Jacques Thomas, and the name of the village."

"Ah. So she could have—never mind, now. What did you do yesterday?"

"Nothing. The *patron*, Monsieur Chaumont, was busy. I went for a walk. A most beautiful walk. I don't know the country. I have never lived in the country."

"That's sad. Because the country is where the hand of man is in the hand of God. This isn't the case in cities, even in beautiful cities, even in Paris. Specially in Paris.

"In any case, you won't have noticed the memorial. Like every village, we have a memorial to the men who were killed in the 1914 war. *'Morts pour la patrie'.* My grandfather's name is on the list in this village, in stone on the memorial, with fourteen others, five of them from two families. Remember the size of the village. Even with the farms. There were no new husbands for the widows. So—"

He drank a little more coffee.

"My grandmother, alone, brought up my mother. And that was perhaps the problem."

"The problem?"

"Wait. Listen."

He paused, as if to set in order what he was going to tell her.

"My grandmother was, in her way, a wonderful woman. I owe her everything. But as the widowed mother of a rebellious little girl with no brothers or sisters to share the weight of her expectations, I think she was something of a catastrophe. She wanted to bring up my mother to be like her dead husband, who in her eyes had been nearly perfect except that he didn't share her faith, and to be like herself only better, even better.

She was deeply Catholic. Do you know what that means?"

"No. I'm sorry. I know almost nothing about the Catholic Church. My mother, also alone bringing up a little girl, was very different from what you say about your grandmother. She didn't expect—she made no demands on me; she was always only pleased when things went well, at school, for example. She was somehow—how can I put this?—always surprised that I could manage to be French, all the way from my learning to read and write when I was little up to my being able to pass my *baccalauréat*. She believed in what she called the will of Allah. She thought, perhaps ever since she managed to take me out of the camp and find a job in Paris, that things would turn out for the best because of the will of Allah. I had no education in religion. My mother had no Muslim friends. Her only friends were other maids, other nannies looking after children. They were Spanish, Portuguese, sometimes French. My husband's family, in Rouen, is Catholic but I think in name only. When we married they minded that I—that I was darker-skinned than a real French girl, that I am obviously North African, but they didn't mind, or perhaps they pretended not to mind, that we couldn't have a religious wedding. And my husband, who's a good man, thinks all religion dangerous, better consigned to the past and forgotten. So, no, I don't know what it means, to be deeply Catholic."

"Like most French people now. Well, my grandmother went to Mass every day, in the chapel at the château with the nuns. She prayed the rosary every evening. She always said grace before meals, even at breakfast when she had just been to Mass. Her friends were two or three of the nuns, particularly one old lady who was, according to my grandmother, a saint. This old nun died before I was born. I think my grandmother would perhaps have been happier if she had been herself a nun. But she had this child, my mother, to look after, and then she had to look after me."

"What is the rosary?"

"Ah."

His hand went to his chest, just below his neck, and rested there, brown on his black shirt, for a moment.

43

"A rosary is a string of beads, arranged in groups of ten and one, with a crucifix—you know what that is?"

She nodded.

"—and five more beads, one, three, one, attached to it. To pray the rosary you run the beads between your fingers to keep you going, stopping at each bead to pray the same prayers over and over again and remember the lives and deaths and new life of Jesus and Mary. The whole story takes you all the way from the angel coming to Mary to tell her she is going to have a child whose father is God to Mary being crowned queen of heaven. Once upon a time"—his hand went back to his chest—" I used to wear a big rosary. It was part of a kind of uniform."

After a short silence, he said, "Never mind that now. Do you know the story that the rosary tells?"

"Not really. I know Catholics love Mary, and Muslims do too."

"Indeed. It's good that you know that. But I'm surprised that you do. Did someone tell you?"

"I have this."

She put two fingers inside the collar of her shirt and pulled out a small silver medal on a thin chain. She showed it to him without taking it off. Mary, looking down, looking sad, on one side; on the other, a cross and the Latin words 'Sancta Maria ora pro nobis'.

"My mother always wore it. I took it from her neck after she died."

"Would you let me look at it, just for a moment?"

She undid the fastening and put the medal and the chain into his hand. He turned it over with the other hand and sat, for some time, looking at it.

"I gave this to your mother when—but we haven't reached that point in the story. My grandmother gave it to me, here, in this house, when I had to leave, when I had to join the army, in 1960. I'd come back from Paris for a few days, to say goodbye to her. She thought the medal would protect me. I thought it might protect your mother."

"Well, it did, didn't it?"

"Or the will of Allah." He smiled at her, his crooked, damaged smile.

"But how much difference is there?" he said. "Unanswerable question. We should get back to the story, mine, your mother's. Would you like some more coffee?"

"I would. Please. It's so very good."

"It's an indulgence. Too late to worry about it. Here." He gave her the medal. "You must put it on again. It's yours now."

She fastened it round her neck and let it stay outside her shirt. No one but Jean-Claude had seen it since her mother's death. The wearing of religious symbols of any kind was not allowed in school.

He took both cups into the house and came back with them filled.

"So. My mother was a headstrong girl. Very pretty, blonde, full of life. I think as she grew up she felt the atmosphere of the sacristy in this house—you won't understand that—the piety and the orderliness of every day and my grandmother almost living like a nun—made the house a prison. And for her, in a way, it was. I think, as I said, it would have been much better for her if my grandfather had survived the war. He was not Catholic. My grandmother tried in their short married life to convert him, but he was, according to her, the soul, if it has a soul, which she denied, of *laïcité*, of educating children as citizens of France and the world, leaving religion to one side because it had been responsible down the centuries for privilege, oppression, every sort of injustice and cruelty."

"Like my husband. I told you he is a teacher too, and that's just what he thinks."

"It's an honourable tradition. Even noble, in its way. But too optimistic."

She didn't understand this. He went on:

"In any case, if my grandfather had been there as my mother was growing up, there might have been more children, which would have been good for her, and he would certainly have—how to say this?—he would have salted the sweetness of the sacristy, loosened the bars of the cage, less Little Flower, more Joan of Arc. Or perhaps Marie Curie."

He smiled at her. She wasn't sure why.

"Never mind. Not Marie Curie, unfortunately. My mother

45

wasn't a clever girl. She went to school, of course, first here in the village and then in Cluny. But when she was thirteen or fourteen she begged my grandmother for a bicycle. My grandmother never had a car, never learnt to drive, so she gave my mother a bicycle as, according to her much later, a grand gesture in the direction of the modern, of independence for this girl who longed for freedom. 'That bicycle was my great mistake,' my grandmother used to say. She gave me one too, but I suppose she knew I would take care not to worry her, so it was different. Anyway, as soon as my mother was old enough for meeting boys after school, chatting on street corners, getting home later than she'd said—all much more shocking behaviour in the 1930s than it would be now—my grandmother fretted, prayed, consulted the nuns, made this house seem more of a prison than ever. I'm deducing all this from what I knew of my grandmother and what she told me as I was growing up myself.

"So, a few years before the war, when she was eighteen, I think, my mother simply ran away. She must have saved up, or borrowed, or even stolen from my grandmother, a little money. She packed up her clothes and said she was going to join a school friend, a girl, which was something, in Paris. This girl, she said, had found some kind of job and was being paid enough for her to live in a cheap room somewhere on the Left Bank. Whether this girl really existed I have no idea, but my grandmother managed to believe that she did.

"For five or six years, silence. An occasional picture postcard, the Eiffel Tower, the Arc de Triomphe, the Mona Lisa, saying she was fine, things were going well. Never an address for my grandmother to reply to. The cards are upstairs, in a drawer in my grandmother's desk, a little bundle tied with ribbon. People have come and gone, lived in this house from the time of my grandmother's death until I came back. None of them took anything that was left here when my grandmother died.

"Then it is 1939. The young men in the village go to fight, as the young men went to fight in 1914. Not so many of them of course—no village recovered from the absence of the unborn sons of those who had been killed in the Great War—and not with the enthusiasm of 1914. But they go, and they fail, and in

46

the summer of 1940 France falls. My grandmother, I'm sad to have to tell you, is at first all for Vichy, all for Marshal Pétain, who had won the battle of Verdun after ten months of fighting and hundreds of thousands of dead including my grandfather. How could France, or what was left of it when the Nazis had occupied so much of it, not be safe in the hands of the old Marshal, so noble and brave, so much approved of by the cardinals and bishops and, no doubt, my grandmother's nuns on their knees, grateful to be here, in our village, by a few kilometres on the Marshal's side of the line dividing France?

"Early in August—we are still in 1940—my mother appears, out of the blue. She arrives in a car from the station—she had no money so how she paid for it it's best not to imagine—as you arrived in your taxi on Saturday evening. She has a suitcase and a portfolio of ugly paintings which no one will ever want to buy—they're upstairs as well—and it's clear to my grand-mother as she walks through the door that she is six months pregnant."

She looked over her shoulder, almost expecting to see the pregnant woman with her suitcase and her portfolio, seventy-five years ago.

"You were the baby?"

"I was the baby."

"And your grandmother?"

"Perhaps, from what I've told you already, it's possible for you to imagine her reaction. I have, myself, had to imagine it. My guess is that she was as much alarmed by what she saw, and angry because of the years of silence, as she was pleased to see her daughter. She did tell me that she saw what she thought was a wedding ring on my mother's hand. But the relief was short-lived. 'It's a curtain-ring. For the journey. We don't believe in marriage', my mother said. 'Another bourgeois institution we have freed ourselves from.' 'Who is "we"?' 'My friends in Paris. Everyone I know.'"

"She said she had come home, and my grandmother wouldn't believe how difficult the journey had been, with thousands and thousands of people leaving Paris, because she didn't want the baby to be born in Paris when Paris was full of

German soldiers, and, without any money, she had nowhere else to go. 'And what about the father of your baby?'

"My mother told my grandmother, then, that first day, that the father of the baby was a Polish Jew, born in Vienna. His parents were from Galicia. I don't think either my mother or my grandmother had any idea where Galicia is. Do you know where it is?"

She shook her head.

"In the Polish east of what was once the Austro-Hungarian empire; after the First War it was in Poland; now, poor devils, the Galicians are in Ukraine with Putin breathing down their necks. There are no Jews now in Galicia, of course. This young man, my father, came from another world, a world that was doomed."

"Have you been there?"

"No. Nor to Vienna. What would be the point? I don't know his name. Even if I did, looking for a Jewish family either in Galicia or in Vienna, would, after Hitler, be next to impossible. And probably not popular, even now."

"Did he die in the war?"

"I have always assumed he was killed by the Nazis. My mother told my grandmother only that he couldn't leave Paris because he had no papers. He was some kind of journalist, writing for a Polish newspaper, when the war began. He couldn't go home: Poland was eaten up by Hitler and Stalin at the start of the war. So he was doing odd jobs in Paris to survive. He had applied for naturalization but there was no more naturalization in France. After the defeat, foreign Jews were rounded up by the Vichy government and thrown to the Nazis even before the Nazis asked for them. He may have been reckoned a political refugee: it was part of the Armistice agreement in 1940 that all political refugees were to be handed over to the Germans. There's no doubt that, one way or another, they killed my father. I only know from my grandmother that my mother never saw or heard from him again after she left Paris. It's possible, from what I know of my mother it's even likely, that he never knew she was carrying his child. So I too have a birth certificate with 'father unknown'. Even my mother had the sense not to put a Jewish name on a birth certificate in 1940."

A long silence.

She held her medal between finger and thumb.

"Yes", he said. "Probably he never knew. As I never knew. That you had been born. That you had lived. That you are alive. But—you must wait until I get to that part of the story."

She let the medal rest on her shirt, and put both hands on the table.

"Are you all right, Jamila? Am I talking too much? You can't imagine—you are too young to imagine—how long it is since I talked like this. In fact, never have I told this story before. But if I'm tiring you—?"

"No. No. Please. Go on. At school I used to say to the other children when they asked about my father, 'He was killed in the war.' 'What war?' 'The war in Algeria.' Many of them had never heard of it. At least, when you were at school, where you must have said the same thing, everyone knew there had been a war. So please, tell me the whole story."

He laughed.

"Never the whole story can be told, can it? Every story of every life is too complicated to be told. Too complicated to be remembered properly, therefore to be really known, by the person who has lived the life, who is still in the thick of it, who, every day, doesn't know what the present will bring, or", he laughed again, "what present the day will bring. As today has brought you, Jamila, my present from the past."

She laughed also, and then said, "I'm afraid that when you know me better, you will be disappointed that I am not very clever."

"Nonsense. How could I be disappointed, in such a—such a miracle from so long ago? And look at you, so brave and good. However, the story, as best I can."

He sipped some more coffee, now almost cold.

"So. I was born, a healthy, cheerful baby, according to my grandmother, and was christened Jacques after my grandfather. My mother, who had expected a girl, was not much interested in me and not at all interested in looking after me. I

49

don't think she was even grateful to my grandmother for being willing, without much reproach as far as I could tell later, to take in a wayward daughter and then a bastard child. So very different from what my grandmother had hoped for. Soon my mother was as bored, constricted and angry as she had been as a young girl. Perhaps my grandmother's Christian charity, even her simple kindness, to my mother and the baby made my mother angrier than ever. Perhaps she was spoiling for a fight my grandmother refused to have. In any case she left again, when I was six months old."

"Do you know what happened to her?"

"Nothing good, I'm afraid. Though of course one can never be certain. The door of mercy is never closed."

"I'm sorry. I'm not sure I know what that means."

"It means it's always possible, this side of death, to turn away from darkness and towards light. And at the same time it's always impossible for anyone else to know what happens inside someone's soul. But the little my grandmother told me about my mother wasn't promising.

"She went to Vichy. Yes, Vichy itself. She said there was plenty of work there, that the Marshal and his friends had had to set up a whole government from nothing and she would easily get a job. I think my grandmother was probably relieved to see the back of her—a kind young woman from the village, whose husband was a prisoner of war, was helping to look after me, and my mother had been the opposite of a soothing presence in the house. Also, as I told you, my grandmother was all for Vichy to begin with."

"Did your mother come back? To see you?"

"Once. She came back in the spring of 1943. Two years she had been gone and my grandmother had heard nothing from her. She didn't come alone. She brought a young man with her, a young man in the brand-new uniform of the *Milice*. Do you know who they were?"

She shook her head. She had never heard the word.

"Vichy soldiers. Not the French army. Not the German army. Frenchmen recruited by the Vichy government, what was left of it when the Germans had occupied all the free zone—here, and by then the whole country—to fight the Resistance, to round up Jews, to help the Gestapo. By the end of the war the *Milice* were hated, by almost everyone, more even than the Gestapo. But this was 1943, not the end of the war, no end of the war in sight."

"What did your grandmother think?"

He laughed, his quick, quiet laugh.

"She was appalled. 'A good-looking boy', she told me, much later. 'So pleased with himself. So healthy and well-fed'. Already in 1943 ordinary people, old people, women and children, even in Burgundy, were hungry most of the time. This young man was getting special rations from the Germans. So, no doubt, was my mother. 'And cruel eyes', my grandmother said. 'You can always tell from the eyes.'

"By this time my grandmother had changed her opinion of Vichy, even of Marshal Pétain himself. The nuns at the château were hiding a family of Jews. No one knew then what was happening to the Jews once they had been delivered to the Germans. But people were beginning to understand that something terrible was going on. Plenty of old-fashioned Catholics like my grandmother would have said automatically, usually without having met a single Jew, that they hated Jews. When a mother with two little girls, from Marseille I think, reached the village, heaven knows how, with nothing but the clothes they were wearing, and were taken in by the nuns for what was intended to be a few days and turned out to be all the years till the end of the war, it was not possible for someone as good, and as practical, as my grandmother to hate them. I don't think she ever knew anything much about the Resistance but she knew that the hunting down of the Jews, and the shooting of French people who helped them, were wicked, and that was enough for her. So the appearance in this house of the *milicien* in his uniform really shocked her. When she talked about this visit later, which wasn't often, I gathered it was the uniform that had upset her most, I suppose because of what it represented.

"They didn't stay long, a few days I think. I don't remember any of it. I was two and a half. But my mother was apparently offended that I didn't know her, as if it were my fault, and the handsome *milicien* frightened me, apparently, playing some game I didn't understand. In any case, they went back to Vichy, or wherever he was sent by the commanders of the *Milice*.

"And that was all, the last time my grandmother saw her daughter, the last time I saw my mother. Years and years later, long after the war was over, and after the next war, the Algerian war, was supposed to be over too, a letter came. From Argentina. It reached me eventually, far away, not here. She had married the *milicien*. They had lived in Argentina since the war; one can easily imagine why. Would Jacques like to visit his mother? Jacques would not. This letter even had an address. I wrote back, saying almost nothing except that I was not able to travel, which was true. She must have died long ago. I had no more connection with her than with my father. Even perhaps less, because my poor father, whoever he was, had not abandoned me.

"So that is the story of my parents. Not, no doubt, the whole story. As much of the story as I have ever known."

"And your grandmother?"

"She died in 1971. May she rest in peace. Which I have no doubt she does. She was seventy-six when she died and I wasn't here. She's buried in the nuns' peaceful little cemetery, at the top of the park at the château, as she wished. At least I look after their graves."

He stopped talking. She didn't move. She wanted the long morning of his trust in her never to end. After some time she said, "You have told me very little about yourself, your life, all the years you were not here."

"Ah, Jamila. It won't be easy for you to understand. It has been difficult enough for me to understand myself, and there's much that still—that even now when I am old, almost as old as my grandmother was when she died—I can't find the words for."

He put his hand, protectively, as if they might blow away, on the pile of papers he had brought from the table in the summer house. There was not a breath of wind on the flowery terrace. She breathed in, sweet-scented warm air, in the shade of the

52

wooden beams and the climbing plants, and looked from the near-darkness at the brilliant sunlit garden, green and white, grass and apple blossom and the tears of Mary.

"I have tried", he said. "In all this writing—" He spread his long delicate fingers, not the fingers of a gardener, over the top sheet of paper. "To find the words. I don't know why. That's to say, I haven't known why. After all, for an old man I have enough to do. I work in the garden of the château, alone because that's what suits me, although it's a big garden and looking after only the grass is one man's job. But it's a beautiful garden I have known all my life and it's good, somehow appropriate, now to share it with frail old people, those who are well enough to sit on a bench under a tree and probably fall asleep to the sound of the birds. Sometimes one of them likes to talk, and that's probably good too. Enough, you might think. But I was trained, for one period of my life, never to waste time doing nothing, unless to pray, which is a use, not a waste, of time, and I have found that the habit doesn't fade. So all this writing, over the years since I came back to this house, is, I suppose, work of a kind, work I have been doing, I thought, for myself alone, a long effort to understand. Now, today, this morning, Jamila, I see that the effort has been for you. Thanks be to God."

She looked at the pile of paper, the thin handwriting—she realized that, because of emails and school records on computers, she hadn't seen handwriting, beyond signatures and the occasional rapid note, for years—and felt daunted, almost afraid.

Now he really laughed.

"You look horrified. Don't worry. I wouldn't ask anyone, but most of all I wouldn't ask you, to read this as it is. One day it might possibly, with a great deal of work, become a book that a person, that you, might be interested to read. But it's at an early stage of its formation as a book, as an adolescent is at an early stage of his formation as a man, growing too fast, all over the place, untidy inside and out. It needs, as the unformed boy does, some discipline, some cutting down to size, but also some growth. Pruning, for stronger growth." He laughed again. "I'm sorry, Jamila. You're not a gardener. You won't know what that means."

53

She shook her head.

"It doesn't matter. But this—" His hand again on the pile of paper. "Even as a first draft, it isn't finished. I had thought—" He looked, as she had, out into the sunlit garden. "I had thought that perhaps by the end of this summer, by the time of grape-picking and ripe apples, I might have reached what would at least seem like the end of a first draft. But now that I have met you—"

His crooked smile that she felt she had always known.

"Now that I have found you, I wonder if there is any reason to try to get to the end, to try to turn all these pages, all this writing, into a real book. Perhaps you are instead of my book."

She saw something new strike him.

"But perhaps—might it be possible?—you and my book are a single gift, a single means of my memory and my old age becoming one. Can you write? Could you perhaps take all this, all these pages—I think there are nearly four hundred pages, here and on my desk in the house—back to Paris and turn them into the book they should grow up to be?"

She shook her head, smiling at the impossibility of what he was suggesting.

"I'm a school secretary. I'm not clever, only adequately educated to be what I am. Since I left school I've never written anything more difficult than the occasional simple letter, as if from the Director, when he's been away. Everything else, more complicated letters, reports on students, reports to the ministry—all are dictated by the Director and checked by him before I press Send. Before computers I typed them out, which took much longer. I don't make spelling mistakes and I don't muddle punctuation and I know how to address envelopes correctly—if I didn't the Director would have sacked me long ago—but I'm not a writer, not capable in any way of even imagining the sort of work your book might need."

"Of course, of course, Jamila. I am an old idiot to have thought of such a thing, even for a moment. I saw that the very idea of reading what is written on this heap of paper was for you a terrible prospect. Perhaps it's time to make a fire at the end of the garden with all the garden rubbish and burn the whole lot, my four hundred pages. Compared with what has happened to me today, they are of no importance whatsoever."

"No. No. You mustn't do that—that would be a dreadful thing to do. All that work. All those hours. You must go back to the beginning and do the cutting and apply the discipline, the pruning—is that what you called it?—yourself, as you planned before, before today."

"I know how to prune apple trees, plum trees, cherries, pears, so that they grow more and better fruit. I know how to prune roses, in the cold weather, so that there are more and better flowers when the summer comes. I even know how to prune vines, severely in the winter, with delicacy through the spring and summer." She looked again at his hands. "But pruning what I have written is a different matter. I'm not a writer, not really, although I have put down on paper all this—foolishness, this old man's probably useless battle with his memory, in order to understand. No. The garden fire, with the dead wood pruned from the fruit trees and the roses, that's where it belongs."

"No. I know nothing about writing. But I know you mustn't burn all this. All this work you have done. I—" She hesitated. She knew him so little, after all. Could she suggest—?

"What were you going to say, Jamila?"

The dog at their feet raised his head and growled. A second later there was a loud knock at the door on the other side of the house. The dog stood up and barked his deep, decisive bark.

Jacques Thomas stood himself.

"Who is that? No one knocks at my door. Stay here."

He disappeared into the house. She heard what sounded like an unfriendly exchange at the front door. She couldn't hear the words spoken. Her father—she found she was just able to think of him as her father—came back, not angry but smiling.

"Chaumont", he said. "He's worried about you. Here for such a long time. What have I done to you? He insists on seeing you, to be sure you are safe and sound. You'd better set his mind at rest. Come."

She followed him through the kitchen and along a short, dark passage that smelt of dog and old wood fires. The dog himself was guarding the closed front door. The old man opened it, holding the dog by its collar.

"Here she is. I have done her no harm. You see?"

"Monsieur Chaumont", she said. "It's very kind of you to be concerned, but I'm quite all right. I've been talking to Monsieur Thomas, that's all. I'll be coming back to the café soon. I have to leave for Paris this afternoon. But thank you for your kindness."

The *patron* had to accept this. He looked at her for a moment, as if to make sure he could believe her.

"Very good, madame", he said, with some doubt. "Then we shall see you later. Goodbye, Monsieur Thamar." He turned towards the road and her father shut the door.

"Come back to the terrace, Jamila."

She smiled as she followed him along the passage, through the kitchen, outside, because she could tell he was enjoying using her name.

"Sit down."

He put the coffee cups on the tray and took it into the kitchen, came back to the terrace and sat on his kitchen chair. The dog had settled down again at her feet.

"Is it true?", he said. "Do you really have to leave for Paris today? So soon?"

"Yes. I'm so sorry, but I should go back today. I have left my husband and my daughter and I promised not to stay away more than two nights. This is the only time—"

"The only time?"

"The only time that I've left Paris without my husband since we were married."

"In that case, it was good of him to allow you to come so far when you could not have known, he could not have known—"

"What I would find? Who I would find? Yes. But, as I told you, he's a good man. Also he was fond of my mother and admired her courage."

"Your mother. Little Tanifa. So long ago." His hand went back to the pile of paper. "There is as much as I could manage to write about her, somewhere in all this. And Jamila, you were going to say something, about this, the writing, when Chaumont banged on the door. It was good of him, I have to admit, to take the trouble to make sure you had come to no harm with me. No doubt I am regarded as an eccentric, perhaps even a freak, in the village, and therefore to be feared. My fault, naturally. But what were you going to suggest?"

"Well. It may be a completely inappropriate suggestion, and I have no idea what his plans are, but my son says he is a writer."

"But this is marvellous", he said, and immediately put a hand up, like a policeman stoppimg traffic. "Wait. We must be sensible. He is very young? Tell me about your son. What is he called?"

"His name is Bernard. He's twenty-one years old. Almost twenty-two. His birthday is in August. He's a good boy, serious—how to describe him?—thoughtful would be the best word. He thinks things out, for himself. He always has, since he was a small child. He did well at school, not brilliantly because he had difficulty with mathematics and was not very interested in the sciences. But he was good at everything that involved writing. History, French literature, English. He chose to do Latin. His favourite subject was the philosophy they have to do for the *baccalauréat*. His father who teaches history himself, I think I told you, was impressed by the time and trouble Bernard put into understanding the difficult philosophy texts they had to read." She laughed. "His father was less impressed when Bernard said that the philosophers who were approved of by his teacher at the *lycée* were too negative. I remember Jean-Claude telling him that that's what philosophy is for, to teach you how to demolish arguments or ideas which are not sound, not logical, so that your mind is cleared of clutter that gets in the way of rational thought. Bernard said something like, 'But when you have cleared away everything that can't be demonstrated logically, is there enough left?'"

"I like the sound of this young man. Very much. Where is he now?"

"He's in Nantes, at the university. He will soon have finished his first degree, his *licence*. We have seen very little of him since he became a university student. He is studying political sciences, and philosophy I think, and journalism because he wants to be a writer and knows that he needs to earn his living if he's to be able to write books which he says won't make any money. He will have been working hard, because he does work hard. He makes contact with us from time to time, to make sure we're all right, but he tells us almost nothing about himself and what else he's been up to in Nantes. He came to Paris once not long ago, to say goodbye to my mother when she was dying. I hope she knew he was there."

"He was there."

"But—" Then she thought she understood. She looked into his eyes, one clear grey eye, one harder to see because of his distorted cheekbone. He was calm, but full of hope in her.

She wanted to help. She also knew that now Bernard was grown up she was a little afraid of her son: she shouldn't encroach on his independence by presuming too much. On the other hand, if she were only afraid of annoying him, that was not a good enough reason to take her idea no further.

"Would you like me to ask him if he would come to meet you?"

"Of course, of course. My grandson. Poor boy. He might not want to meet me. I would understand that. He doesn't know his grandfather exists."

She thought of Bernard's other grandfather, the retired Rouen lawyer, playing bridge after dinner with friends he had known since he was a boy, fussing about the right wine to accompany the dinner that was being carefully cooked by his wife. Bernard had always been polite and attentive to his grandparents in that house in Rouen. He didn't love them.

"It would be a shock for him, perhaps, to discover that his grandfather is a solitary, an eccentric, a freak as I said. He might be afraid of me, as the people in the village are, afraid of what I look like, afraid of discovering what has brought me to this strange old age."

"I don't think he would be afraid of you."

"All the same he might be ashamed? To find that his grandfather is the bastard child of a Polish Jew and a wayward girl who ended up married to a collaborator and ran away to South America. This is hardly an inheritance to be wished."

"I'm not ashamed."

"Ah, Jamila. But you are good, and you are the daughter of Tanifa."

"Bernard loved my mother, remember. And she was a North African maid, a mere Arab, as different as could be from his other grandparents."

"Not an Arab. A Berber."

"I never heard her use the word. Perhaps she thought that in France it was worse, even worse, to be a Berber than to be an Arab. In any case, my husband's parents—my father-in-law is a lawyer in Rouen, a pillar of the community—found the idea of her really difficult: a foreign woman, a domestic servant, becoming their son's mother-in-law. What would their friends think? They met her only once, at our wedding in Rouen. She was terrified; they were doing their best to be carefully egalitarian. You can imagine. It was not a success."

He laughed with her.

"I can well imagine. Well, your parents-in-law need know nothing about me. There are things about my life, things, my poor child, you will learn one day, if this book ever gets written, that would without a doubt stretch their principles to breaking-point. But we needn't worry about them. I do need to worry about Bernard. Perhaps, if you described me to him—?"

"Certainly I would. I would describe you, and your beautiful house, just as you are. But I wouldn't tell him even as much as you have told me today, of the story, the several stories. Bernard is a boy who likes to make up his own mind. But, look—"

She leant forward and put her hand on his arm.

"You mustn't hope too much. This may be only a dream. Bernard has said he wants to go to North Africa when he's done his exams, to work for *Médecins sans frontières*. We're not keen on him going so far away, perhaps into danger. And I don't know whether the plan is definite. I've no idea whether he's thought further ahead, as his father would like him to." She sighed, but not sadly. "It all seems so far away, as we sit in your garden, such a long way from Paris, from Nantes, from students, journalists, the news." She looked again into the sunlit green and white of the garden. "I wish I could stay for a while."

As soon as she said this, she regretted it. It was exactly what she felt but hadn't intended to say.

"I wish you could. But we know you have to go back home, today."

"Thank you. Yes. I must. I'm so sorry. Bernard. I'll find him. I'll explain—", she hesitated. "—what's happened since my mother's death, because of my mother's death, and see whether by any chance he might be able to come down here to meet you. If he can, if it's possible for him, I'm sure he will come. And then—"

She smiled at her father as if she had known him all her life.

"And then it will be up to you. When, if, you meet him, you may think he's too young, too inexperienced to be of any use to you. His father has often found his opinions irritating; you may find the same. But he's older now, older than when he last argued with his father, and I don't know what he thinks. But that he does think I am sure."

"At his age it's best not to think anything with too much certainty. I was older than he is when I thought I had made up my mind about everything, and I was wrong. At least, partly wrong."

"I think you would like Bernard. And I know he would like you."

"And you also have a daughter?"

"Yes. Her name is Joséphine. Younger than Bernard. She's revising now for her *baccalauréat*. Or she's supposed to be revising. I don't think she'll do very well. She's quite different from Bernard. Not serious at all. Always on her smartphone or her computer. She spends hours in her room by herself. She says she's doing school work but I don't entirely believe her. More likely she's wasting time, sending messages to her friends, playing games. I worry about her. She doesn't seem interested in much beyond pop music, clothes, staying out late, getting up late. She's eighteen now so there's not much we can do. I think she can look after herself but whether she will ever have the—what is it you need? Just carefulness of other people's feelings—the capacity to look after anyone else, I don't know."

"You can't tell. She's too young. You mustn't despair of her. One mustn't despair of anyone, ever. And you mustn't, now that you know what I've told you this morning, think that Joséphine has inherited a fatal selfishness from my mother. Joséphine's upbringing has been so different, so much better, and the world she has grown up in is so much better also."

"Do you think so? Really?"

"Until quite recently, I was sure that the world, and in particular the France, in which I am to die was in almost every respect a better world, a better country, than the world, the country, in which I was born. France in the autumn of 1940 was as bad a place to be born as can be imagined. People of your generation perhaps can't quite understand the shame, the disgrace, the fear, that were everywhere during the Occupation, or the lies that were told after it, by the good as well as by the bad. But then, look at where, and when, you were born, my dear. Algeria in the summer of 1962: the end of that horrible war was as horrible as anything that had happened during it. Eight years of war, longer than either of the great wars, and the senseless killing, achieving nothing but misery, going on and on, long after the war was over, and since. Twenty years ago, in the civil war in Algeria hundreds of thousands of people were killed. Very few people in France paid any attention. The government in Paris interfered, of course, but they only made things worse. I was there, and I saw—but never mind all that, now. I don't suppose you knew much about it?"

She shook her head.

"Or your mother?"

"No. She couldn't really read French, as I told you. And she was always afraid of the outside world."

"She had good reason to be afraid of it."

"She wouldn't have a television in her room. When she was ill we tried to persuade her that it would keep her company but she wouldn't agree, I think because she didn't want to see the news. She had a radio, but she only liked to listen to music."

"I don't have a television. Or a radio. Out of old habit. Or a telephone. Or, naturally, a computer. Your daughter would be amazed to hear that I live quite happily nevertheless."

She laughed. "Yes, she would."

"I do read *Le Monde*. So I have some idea of what is happening in the world. And you asked me if I really think it is a better place. When I came back here, to Burgundy, my own Burgundy, in a France that at last had stopped bullying other people, in countries, often not countries until we said they were, which the French should have left in peace from the beginning, I thought the world had become a better place. But now, alas, we find the consequences of the bullying that was done for two hundred years, not just by France but by England too, and now of course by America, have not faded away but become more and more filled with hatred and bitterness and mad fanatical cruelty. So, now, I think the world is again a terrible place. People are not killed in millions as they were in the two great wars. But poor people who are not soldiers, who have themselves made no dangerous or wicked choices, frightened old people, frightened children, mothers with babies, like your mother when you were a baby, are killed by bombs and fire and machine-guns, only for being who they are, where they are. And when they struggle to come to Europe, the Europe that is ultimately responsible for their suffering but which now appears to them as the promised land of safety and work and something like the rule of law, they save and save the money it's so difficult for them to scrape together, give it all to criminals who are waiting for them in Libya, where there is no government, no police force, no one who can be trusted, and then, most likely, the leaky boat capsizes and they drown. While the Europeans argue because their first priority is not to take too many refugees themselves. A world where this happens every week, a world where a million Syrians are in camps in other countries and will never see their homes again—how can this be better than anything? Different, of course, but no better.

"No wonder the young, the very young like your Joséphine, can think of nothing further away than meeting their friends at the end of the street and going to some club to listen to loud music which drowns the cries of the suffering people of the world. No wonder. And I'm afraid that some of the suffering people, whose troubles are also because of the bullying of the long past, are not the other side of the Mediterranean but all too close to Joséphine and her friends. The young Arabs and Africans in the *bas quartiers*, the *banlieues*, the slums we have deliberately built so that the poor don't make the beautiful streets of Paris look untidy, what hope have they of work, of respect, of all that the desperate people risking their lives on the Mediterranean think they will find in Europe? They have no hope, no work, no respect, so they are easily persuadable that all they can do to show the rest of the world, the rest of France, that they exist is to get hold of a gun and shoot someone, a policeman, a soldier, a Jewish child. Then for a day or two they will be someone, a name in the newspapers everyone knows, until everyone forgets it. Better still if, for the cause of Islam, about which I suspect many of these desperate boys in the *quartiers* know practically nothing, they can shoot famous people, the old Algerian Jews who mock the Prophet in their paper which is meant to be funny and is only throwing oil on a fire already smouldering. Of course I have never seen *Charlie Hebdo*. But I read in *Le Monde* that the motto of the paper is '*bête et méchant*', 'stupid and malicious', as it might be the motto of a rebellious child. The whole of France, apparently the whole of the western world, is horrified by the murders at *Charlie Hebdo*. But almost no one bothers to be horrified any more when Christians, not good French Catholics who go to Mass on Sundays, put poor Egyptian Copts, poor Ethiopian peasants, their ancestors Christians almost from the time of the Acts of the Apostles, are lined up and beheaded in wretched Libya by enraged Muslims led to believe that all Christians are crusaders. There have been Christians in Syria always, since there were Christians anywhere, and now they are dead, or in exile, their churches burned, their graves destroyed. They will not return."

He stopped, at last. She had never before heard anyone talk like this, with such passionate feeling. Jean-Claude sometimes came back from the *lycée* depressed, quietly angry after some meeting in which officials from the Ministry had struck him as uninterested and uninformed about the problems facing children, whether French or Arab or black, growing up in Paris.

63

But he never talked as her father just had, either to her or, she was almost sure, to anyone else. His calm, which she had never seen seriously disturbed by any of the ordinary dramas of family life, drove Joséphine, occasionally, into real rudeness, door-slamming, stormy tears. "You don't know how I feel. You don't know how anyone feels. You're supposed to be so clever and you don't know anything." And in any case Jean-Claude, she suspected, history teacher though he was, knew much less about all these painful things than her father knew, though he lived so apparently cut off from the world.

"I am so sorry, Jamila. I have talked far too much. You see—"

He spread his hands in apology.

"I know. You haven't talked to anyone for a long time."

"Exactly. You understand. It's not from you, Jamila, that Joséphine has inherited what looks at present like her selfishness. But she is your daughter. One of these days she won't be so different from you after all. You wait and see. But now—"

He got to his feet and pushed his kitchen chair under the table.

"It must be time for you to go. If you stay much longer, Chaumont will be back at the door to make sure I haven't kidnapped you. And you do have to go, don't you? Back to the café de la Paix—you know, I've never been inside it, in a long life, because of my grandmother's story about Chaumont's father—and then back to Paris. Will you be in time to catch a train today?"

He was talking, saying nothing, she saw, because he didn't want her to go.

She looked at her watch and stood up. There was plenty of time.

"Yes, I must go."

Neither of them moved. His dog stood beside him, wagging his tail as he looked straight at her.

"Is it possible", he said, "that I will never see you again?"

"No. Of course I will come back to see you. I don't know when. It isn't easy for me to leave Paris."

"It is possible. I will be seventy-five in November. I could die, any day. Before you came, before today—everything before today seems so long ago—I used to imagine a sudden death, perhaps in the garden here, perhaps in the garden of the château. A sudden death for which I suppose I have been for many years, many uneventful years, as prepared as one can be. A stroke, a heart attack. And then I would be as little trouble as possible to whoever might find me. But now, I shouldn't care to die before saying goodbye to you, Jamila. So I will say goodbye to you now as if I will never see you again. Perhaps that's how one should always say goodbye. And I want to thank you, for your courage in coming to find me when you had no idea who I might be, or what I might have meant to your mother. And also for—"

"You shouldn't be thanking me. Both of us should be grateful, grateful for the rest of our lives, however long or short, to my mother. And her little box."

"Of course. Peace be upon her. You know, that is a Muslim as well as a Catholic prayer." He smiled. "I don't expect you know much about prayer."

"Nothing at all. Although—" She thought of her walk yesterday, and her memory of the ruined abbey by the Seine. Did both have something to do with praying? Probably not. And she couldn't begin to explain something so vague.

"Although?" he said.

"O. It's nothing."

"It's quite possible, you know, to know what prayer is without ever having learned anything about it."

She didn't understand this, but accepted it from him as if it were a gift.

"Really?" she said.

"Really."

Neither of them moved.

She saw that he couldn't say goodbye. Nor could she.

"Jamila—"

"Yes?"

"I was going to thank you, also, for telling me I shouldn't burn all this."

He put his hand, again, on the pile of paper.

"Will you send me your Bernard?"

"I'll do my best. I can't promise anything. But unless he's going abroad immediately after his exams, and that's quite possible, he'll be anxious, I'm quite sure, to meet his grandfather, someone he's never known was still in the world, before—"

"Before it's too late." He smiled. "And we don't know when that will be. Good. That's the best we can hope for, you and I. Now, Jamila, you must go."

He stood for a moment, looking at her. His eyes, one in its damaged socket, clear and deep behind his spectacles. Then he took both her hands and kissed them, first one and then the other. He held them as he said, "God bless you, my child, and keep you safe. Wear your holy medal."

She bowed her head. He let go of her hands and they walked side by side into the garden, round the side of the house and along the short path to the road. At the gate, he put his arm for a moment round her shoulders and she left him, turning back once to see him watching her. She waved. He waved, and she saw him disappear into the apple blossom.

There was a noisy group of workmen in the café, eating half-baguettes filled with ham and cheese and drinking white wine. Silence fell as she came in, glasses put down on the bar and sandwiches suspended in mid-air.

"Bonjour, messieurs", she said. A murmured, not unfriendly, response.

Monsieur Chaumont, from the other side of the bar, said, "Everything all right, madame?"

"Yes, very good, thank you, monsieur."

As she was walking past the end of the bar to go upstairs, she said, "Would you be very kind, monsieur, and telephone the taxi for me, to take me to the station?"

"Of course, madame."

She packed her few things in her travel bag, sat on her bed and opened her laptop.

There was an email from Jean-Claude.

I hope all is well and I hope you are coming home today. I've had a telephone call from Bernard. He's well but his plans are a bit worrying.

Do I see you tonight?

Love—J-C

She answered at once:

I'm leaving for the station now. Will be home tonight. A lot of things to tell you, all good.

Love—J

She telephoned from the Gare de Lyon to say she would be home in half an hour. When she got to the flat, after eight o'clock, Joséphine was out—" She promised not to be too late" Jean-Claude said—and he was waiting for her, with some cold chicken and salad on the table.

He kissed her. They sat down.

"So. The news." she said. "Tell me about Bernard."

"Shall we do your news first?"

Jean-Claude's politeness was as reliable as everything in his character.

"No. It's too complicated. Tell me about Bernard."

"He says he's definitely going to Tunisia. After his examinations in June."

"Tunisia? How?"

"It seems he's managed to arrange to join *Médecins sans frontières*, working in a camp for refugees in Tunisia. Not as a doctor, obviously, but as an organizer, a helper with transport, supplies, that kind of thing. Logistics, they call it, as in the army. His plan, he says, is to learn first-hand about what's happening in North Africa, so that he can write about it because he thinks the North Africans in France don't have an accurate picture of how things are now, so they continue to hate France and blame France for everything bad. You know Bernard. He wants to make the world a better place and, when you look at the world as it is, it's understandable, I suppose, that he wants to start finding out for himself how Arabs think, how Muslims think."

"Couldn't he do that in Paris?"

"When I suggested that, he said it was impossible. The Arabs here are too miserable, too angry. And if you wanted to find out what French people thought and felt, wouldn't you go to France?"

That was so like Bernard. And actually like his father.

"But isn't Tunisia very dangerous?"

"Bernard doesn't seem to think so. He said it's the only Arab country that's managed to make itself into a better rather than a worse society after the Arab Spring."

"It's all very well him saying that. Weren't there some horrible murders, just recently?"

"Yes, a few weeks ago, at the Roman museum in Tunis. Terrorists killed a number of tourists as they got off a bus. But the Tunisians seem to have acted quickly and effectively. Bernard said there's no reason to be afraid. Also—"

Jean-Claude stopped to eat a mouthful of food.

"Also he said that, since he's half Algerian, it's time he learned about his grandparents' part of the world. He said we had never talked about Algeria in the family, and we should have told him more about it. I imagine he's thinking all this now because he's met some intelligent Muslims in Nantes, or perhaps they've had lectures about North Africa on his course, though, from what I've seen of his reading-lists and essay subjects, I doubt if that's the case."

"Did you tell him he shouldn't go?"

"Certainly not. After all, he's old enough to make his own decisions and he's bound to learn from his experiences in a different country and from senior people working for *Médecins sans frontières*, even if he doesn't learn much from the Arabs, particularly if the charity is looking after refugees and the sick. Talking seriously to earnest young Frenchmen will hardly be their first priority."

"He doesn't know any Arabic. Do they still speak French in Tunisia?"

"Yes, I'm sure the educated Tunisians speak French. And he says he's learned some Arabic."

"Does he?"

She thought for a moment.

"Is he going to Tunisia with a girlfriend?"

Jean-Claude put down his knife and fork and looked at her across the table with an expression she knew well: how is it that you think of these things when I don't?

68

"He didn't say anything about a girl."

"He wouldn't, would he?"

"You could be right, I suppose. If you are, there'll be even less we can do to stop him going."

"I don't think we should try. And you know how stubborn he can be. If we argue against the idea, he'll only produce better arguments for going, to convince himself that he's right. Did he say he's coming home, by the way, before he goes to Tunisia?"

"Yes. He'll be here for a few days after his exams are over, collecting stuff he needs to take with him. And no doubt hoping we can help him with a bit of money."

Jean-Claude started eating again.

"That's good. And we can help him, can't we? Did he say how long he's intending to stay in Tunisia?"

"No."

"You see, I need him to be in France."

This time Jean-Claude looked actually surprised.

"You need him? Why?"

"It's time I told you what has happened to me since Saturday."

"Of course. I'm sorry."

She could tell that, now she was back, he had almost forgotten that she'd been away, taking her mother's little box to find someone in Burgundy who might be dead.

"You must tell me your news. I do apologize. I've been preoccupied all day with the idea of Bernard going to Tunisia. Admirable of course, in its way, to want to help wretched people in trouble, but really he needs to be planning for his career. Doesn't he? I hope he manages a *mention bien* in his exams. But your news. You must tell me all about it."

"I'll make some coffee." She cleared the plates and the remains of the supper, made the coffee and sat down again opposite her husband at the table.

"Well. It's quite a story."

An hour later Jean-Claude said, "You've had a long day. You must be very tired. Go and have a bath. I'll do the dishes." He kissed the top of her head. Then he said, "I think you should go to Nantes, as soon as possible, now, while we have a few

69

days' holiday from work, and see Bernard yourself. You may find he's sufficiently interested in his grandfather to undertake this—writing work, or whatever the old man wants of him—as an alternative project. I must say, I would much rather think of him spending his summer in Burgundy, doing something useful for his grandfather, than think of him facing who knows what in Tunisia."

"So you do think Tunisia might be dangerous?"

"Probably not. But Bernard has led a sheltered life. Paris. School. Homework. Holidays in Normandy. University life in Nantes—not that we know much about that—summer camp with cheerful kids in the Ardèche. But people in distress, in pain, destitute, frightened for their lives: we don't know how he would cope with all that."

"He's a brave boy."

"Of course he is. He gets his courage from his mother. Now, you go and have a bath. What you need is a good night's sleep."

"Thank you, Jean-Claude. You are very good to me."

She had meant it. As she lay in the bath, tired and grateful, she realized that Jean-Claude had listened carefully to her account and in response said almost nothing. She remembered two things he had said.

"How could he have abandoned your mother, when she was so young? I suppose being a soldier explains it. Orders are orders in the army. And he didn't know she was pregnant after all."

Later he had said, "Do you think he is, or was, a priest?"

She had shaken her head. "Surely not." But she knew she had little idea of what it would mean if he had been, or still was, a priest. Could people stop being priests? She didn't know, and, so late, wasn't going to ask Jean-Claude tonight.

She almost fell asleep in the bath. Then she went to bed, pleased to be home.

Chapter 2

Bernard

April to July 2015

His mother had emailed him, saying she was coming to Nantes to see him and asking him to meet her at the station at twelve-fifteen. So she would be in time for lunch, which might make the conversation easier: it was no great surprise that his father, cool but clearly worried on the telephone, was sending his mother to persuade him to drop the idea of going to Tunisia. He decided where to take her, a café he knew on one of the islands in the Loire, with a view of the river and the old city. He had been there once with Syrine. They had eaten couscous and fish stew. His mother liked North African food because it reminded her of her own mother's efforts to give her a little of lost Algerian life when she was a child. Also he needed to get used to couscous at practically every meal, which Syrine had told him there would be in Tunisia.

He sat at his desk, a small stained deal table, one leg of it propped on some folded paper to keep it steady. He had moved from the table the mirror intended to make it a girl's dressing table, and put it in the cupboard where he kept his clothes. He had filled the table's two drawers with paper, pens and spare ink cartridges for his printer, which had to live on the floor. He shut his laptop, on which he had just answered his mother's email. Yes, of course he would meet her train. How pleased he would be to see her, he had written. It was true, up to a point.

He had meant to spend the rest of today doing some more revision of the thesis he had to submit as part of his final examinations. He needed to go to the library, check references, make sure that all the scholarly details were accurate and in

71

place, so that small mistakes couldn't be used as an excuse to mark him down. They—he wasn't sure who they would be, though he had an idea or two—might well be looking for any reason to mark him down that wasn't an explicit objection to his actual argument.

His thesis traced a pattern in French colonial behaviour over three hundred years, in the West Indies, Indochina and Africa. It ended with a section based on articles he had written in the winter for an online student political paper in Nantes. To write these, he had spent a week in February living in a cheap, and miserably cold, room in Belleville. He hadn't told his parents he was in Paris. Belleville was old, poor, immigrant Paris, still with a mixture of people from other parts of Europe but now with many Chinese and also North Africans and black Africans from what had been French colonies. Every day he had gone out to the *banlieues*, the newer, poorer immigrant suburbs beyond the *périphérique*, where flaking concrete blocks of flats seemed to threaten the passers-by, and young men, Arabs and blacks, mooched on street corners with no work and no hope, and shouted insults at girls hurrying past who were not wearing Muslim headscarves. The point of his articles, and now the point of the concluding section of his thesis, was to contrast these two kinds of Paris life, to trace the reasons in history for their existence, and to account, in the present, for the refusal of Muslim children in the *banlieues*, the younger brothers and sisters of the boys hanging about on the streets, to observe the memorial silence for the *Charlie Hebdo* victims on the day of the great march. Why were people surprised by this refusal? There had been a huge *Je suis Charlie* march in Nantes too, three days after the murders. He had watched people running through the streets to join it. He hadn't joined it himself, partly because he hated shouting crowds, but partly because he had felt, while of course horrified by the killings, that there hadn't been any need to provoke Muslims by publishing the cartoons. Why provoke simply for the sake of provoking? No one he had tried to talk to about this seemed to understand what he was saying.

At the end of the first full draft of his thesis he had written about the possible reasons for the defection to Syria, to join

Islamic State, of hundreds of young people including soldiers and entirely French kids with no colonial background declaring themselves to be converts to Islam. What did they think they were doing, the boys who had gone to fight and the girls who had gone, somehow or other, to Syria to be jihadi brides, leaving their families in despair? Had they found a reason for living which their ordinary lives in a prosperous republic had failed to give them? After struggling with this conclusion for days, he had deleted the whole section.

Nevertheless in the rest of what he had written he had done his best to explain, more to increase his own understanding than for the credit on the thesis he needed for his *Licence*, how what was going on in France now was the nemesis that followed the hubris of the eighteenth century, the nineteenth century, the twentieth century. Some of the examiners, particularly if they included sociologists not much interested in history, or Marxists not much interested in people, or feminists not much interested in him, or any professor allergic to any mention of religion, weren't going to like his thesis. But in theory marks were given for a coherent argument properly supported by evidence and this he thought he had produced.

He hoped at least that his prose, sentence by sentence, was clear. His father had brought him up on the saying, he couldn't remember whose, "If it isn't clear, it isn't French."

He looked out of his window. His room was high up at the back of a large nineteenth-century house north of the old centre of the city. He liked it, although in the winter it had been almost as cold as his room in Belleville, because below his window were the trees and grass, the swings and climbing frames and sandpit, of a small park. Today only very young children were in the park with their mothers, or foreign girls who seemed to come from all over the world, looking after them. The children were mostly white and well-dressed. This was solid, bourgeois Nantes. Older children, who last week had been playing noisy games, roller-skating, kicking footballs and skate-boarding with shrieks of enjoyment, were back in school.

Now, because of his mother, work on the thesis would have to wait until tomorrow. Lunch was a good idea. But it wasn't going to be easy to deal with what his mother would say about Tunisia. How could he make his case?

Might Syrine help? Clever, calm, efficient Syrine, who had arranged for him to come with her to Tunisia where she was going to work for *Médecins sans frontières*. While he was there he might be able to write about what they found in North Africa, perhaps for the charity, perhaps for a blog, perhaps even, if he could do it well enough, for the wider world. He knew she wanted to go further than Tunisia, her own country after all, to help people having a difficult and dangerous time in Algeria, perhaps even in Libya, at present the most desperate country in North Africa. Because of the wretched Africans and Arabs drowning in hundreds in the Mediterranean, people, just at the moment, had noticed the horrors of life in Libya. Some of them had even noticed that France had helped to sweep away a monstrous ruler with no thought for the consequences, as America had in Iraq. Their interest, Syrine said, shouldn't be allowed to fade because other things, other terrible places, particularly Syria, were always pushing Libya from the top of the news.

She had recommended him for a minor job with *Médecins sans frontières*, and they had offered him some work, needing only his *bac* and computer skills, because, he guessed, they were very keen to accept Syrine herself. She was a midwife and a paediatric nurse. She had been in Nantes for four years, a year longer than he had, and she had done exceptionally well in all her examinations. She had completed her first two years of training in the biggest hospital in Tunis, where her family lived, and then had won a French government scholarship to continue her education in Nantes, at the big hospital attached to the university. He was still a little afraid of her although, or perhaps because, he so much admired her single-minded dedication to her work. Also, no doubt, because she was a couple of years older than he was.

Should he introduce her to his mother? This afternoon? Would meeting her help his mother to look favourably on the Tunisian idea? Or the opposite? If his mother met Syrine, what would she think?

First, she would wonder whether he and Syrine were sleeping together. His mother was a perceptive person and knew him well, though they had hardly talked, alone, in the last couple of years. She would see at once that he and Syrine were not sleeping together. Would she approve? Or would she think that, particularly if they were not lovers, he was allowing himself to be organized into the Tunisian project by a woman with a stronger character than his own? Was he? Probably. Did this mean that he shouldn't go? Of course not. He wanted to see North Africa. He wanted to learn. He wanted, if it turned out to be possible, to travel from Tunisia into Algeria, to find at least the kind of village in Kabylia where his grandmother had lived, where his mother had been born. He wouldn't say anything to his mother about Algeria, and certainly not about Libya.

No. It would be better if his mother didn't meet Syrine. He could describe her, and make her sound impressive and inspiring without revealing that he was intimidated by her. In any case, she would be sure to be working, on a weekday afternoon.

His mother. He looked at his watch. Nearly half past eleven. Time was going by too quickly. He hadn't prepared what he would say. He got up from his desk, took off his T-shirt and put on his only respectable shirt, with a collar, which his mother had sent for his birthday. He took out of the same drawer one of his two clean white handkerchiefs and put it in the pocket of his jeans, which at least weren't torn. He combed his hair, got out his mirror and looked in it, made a face at himself and put the mirror back in the cupboard. He had shaved this morning, which was good. His mother didn't like the stubbly look that he had most days, and that most of his friends had most of the time.

As he walked, through a bright, windy spring morning towards the station, he wondered whether his mother was perceptive enough to guess that he wasn't sleeping with Syrine not only because he wouldn't have dared to look as if the idea had occurred to him, but much more because he was hopelessly in love with someone else? He hoped not. He very much hoped not

Marie. He stopped for a moment, straightened his back and smiled as he thought of her. He had promised to take her out tonight, to a little café near the château—the medieval castle of the Dukes of Britanny which they both loved—and then perhaps dancing somewhere out of doors. She danced so well that just the thought of holding her, sending her spinning away from him and catching her as she span back into his arms made him feel a little dizzy. She was only nineteen. She had been in Nantes nearly a year, her first year at the university, and she was in love with France. Not yet with him. Perhaps not ever with him, though she talked and laughed and danced with him with what seemed to him like happiness. Or perhaps the happiness was really his, and she would have been as alive, as talkative, would have laughed as easily, with any nice boy lucky enough to take her out. He had kissed her, on the lips but swiftly, as he said goodnight, the last three times he had taken her back to the door of the university hostel where, being only a first-year student and from abroad—though, as she had told him, she was French and not a foreigner—she lived, in a room he hadn't even seen. He longed and longed to make love to her, but he was afraid of scaring her off by taking things too quickly and when he imagined following her into the hostel, or asking her to come up to his high, untidy room with his intention being quite obvious, he couldn't make the picture fit how they were, at present, with each other.

He had often tried to translate the brief affair he had had last year with a student his own age into how he should get Marie into bed with him. But it was all too different. She, Françoise, last year, he realized after the few weeks of their hectic encounters were over, had made all the decisions about when and where and how they had made love. He had been intoxicated by her for those few weeks, but afterwards, very soon afterwards, he found himself wishing none of it had happened. He didn't want Marie to feel this about him, maybe for the rest of her life. Also she was a Catholic, what he thought of as a real Catholic, not like his father's family in Rouen, to whom being Catholic seemed to make no difference to anything. She went to Mass in the cathedral on Sundays. She loved the cathedral. To her it was all of French history in one glorious building, welcoming her, a black girl from far away in the Caribbean, to sit in, kneel in, pray in, stand and sing in, with the soaring white stone of the nave coloured high above her in blue and red and green patterns that the sun shed through stained glass windows. She had, two weeks ago, taken Bernard to Mass with her and was astonished to find that he was puzzled by what happened at the high altar, a long way from where they were kneeling side by side, though he listened carefully to the words. His grandmother in Rouen had occasionally taken him and Joséphine to Mass in Rouen when they were small children but had never tried to explain it to them. Marie was even more astonished when he told her that, after nearly three years in Nantes, he had never before been inside the cathedral. Towards the end of the Mass there was a moment when all round them people were shaking hands; he saw a few couples exchanging chaste kisses so he kissed Marie lightly on the cheek and her face lit with a delighted smile. As she joined the quiet line of people walking up to the altar steps to receive holy communion—she tried to tell him afterwards, in terms he couldn't understand, what this meant—she put her hand on his shoulder to tell him to stay where he was. She came back to him, eyes cast down, and knelt for a while without looking at him.

That he knew that all this was of great importance to her was another reason, perhaps the main reason, for treating her so carefully, for not wanting to upset her confident sense of herself by setting up for her choices which she would find difficult, even painful, to make. He would certainly not tell his mother about her. He had always known that his mother didn't like churches, and wasn't sure how she would react to the idea of his having a black girlfriend.

Marie was the reason for his having done some extra work for his thesis on the history of France's empire. He had thought, like, he suspected, most of his contemporaries, that black people in France were from Africa, they or their families having come from Senegal or Gabon or Mali or the Ivory Coast—he knew there had been several more French colonies in Africa—and he had known nothing about the sugar islands where slaves brought from Africa had made fortunes for Frenchmen in the eighteenth and nineteenth centuries. Marie came from Guadeloupe. He discovered that Gaudeloupe and Martinique were French *départements*, like Loire-Atlantique or Seine-Maritime, where Rouen and Nantes had been cities for two thousand years. That was how Marie was French though she hadn't seen France until she arrived in Nantes.

The French Antilles: so romantic they sounded; so full of misery their story actually was. No one had ever told him about the Caribbean islands at school, or, if they had, he hadn't been listening. Now he had read a bit about their terrible history: French exploitation since the seventeenth century, with Cardinal Richelieu a major shareholder in the company given the islands to farm. Typical, Bernard thought, remembering the handsome, sinister portrait of the cardinal in the Louvre, his arrogant face and flowing scarlet robes contributing to the disapproval mixed with fear of the Catholic Church in which in different ways both Bernard's parents had brought him up. For centuries slaves brought from Africa in cramped, filthy, dangerous ships, like those taking Africans to Sicily now, only bigger and for a journey lasting weeks and weeks, worked the sugar plantations, were bought and sold and beaten and killed by Frenchmen.

Marie, so happy to be in Nantes, so delighted with the beauty of the city, of the château out of a picture-book, of the wide Loire on its way to the sea, seemed to have no idea of this history of her home, no fellow-feeling for the slaves who must have been her ancestors. Nor, apparently, did she know, as he himself hadn't known until his work in the library in the last few weeks, that Nantes was the slave city of France, that the terrible ships had set out from here, had sailed down the Loire to the open sea, down the Atlantic to Africa, were loaded with too many slaves and crossed the ocean, a third of the Africans dying on the way, to the Antilles and the cruel sugar-cane that tore the hands of the slaves into bloody strips. The ships brought back the sugar and later the bananas and the pineapples, and the merchants in Nantes grew rich and built the elegant houses he was passing as he walked towards the château and the station. Since he had learned all this he couldn't any longer take the pleasure in the city that it had given him before. He wasn't going to spoil Nantes or the Loire for Marie, let alone her pride in the beauty of Guadeloupe, which she so much wanted him to see, by telling her any of it.

As he walked into the cathedral square he looked at his watch. Ten to twelve. It wouldn't be more than a ten-minute walk from here to the station. He sat at a café table across from the tall white west front of the cathedral and ordered an espresso coffee which the waiter brought with a glass of water and the bill. For courage, he said to himself to justify the self-indulgence, before meeting his mother.

But here it was the cathedral that was upsetting him, more than the prospect of lunch with his mother. Not upsetting him, exactly. He sipped his coffee. More like demanding thought.

Several times since that Sunday morning two weeks ago, he had realized that he almost envied Marie what that hour in the cathedral, with music and flowers and whatever the priests at the altar were doing in the stillness of everyone's attention, had obviously meant to her. What it meant to her every Sunday morning: he knew she went to the same Mass every week. When, before going with her that one time, he asked her why she went, each Sunday, to Mass, she said, "That's what Catholics do. I can't imagine not going to Mass. It makes everything else seem possible. I can't explain. I'm no good at explaining. Come with me and perhaps you'll understand."

He hadn't understood. He knew he didn't know enough to understand. Information would help, no doubt. Books, libraries, the internet. He had been taught not only at school and at his university but by his father at home to find things out, to organize information, to get topics, subjects, stuff that was out there in the world, under his control so that any argument could be properly based on the evidence. He knew very little about religion in general. He knew very little about Christianity in particular. And even less about Islam, which had become an important topic, theme—there I go again, he thought—in his thesis. Reading about religion, Christianity, Islam, would give him a better-informed view from the outside, so that, for example, he would be able to see the Catholic faith, so important in French history, though no longer, as more than grand old buildings, powerful old cardinals in paintings, pious old women going to Mass early in the mornings, and the conventions observed by his grandparents in Rouen. But he had a strong sense that this familiar kind of learning wouldn't help him really to understand what he saw in Marie: her fidelity to a content, a meaning, a weight that was almost like gravity in her life, keeping her balanced and steady, that the Mass gave her. It was something he hadn't seen in anyone else he knew. Was it something he wished he had? Or was this, as his father would think, some kind of trap, baited with music and flowers and white stone coloured by stained glass, and Marie herself?

He also knew that there was a connection here, somewhere, if only he could find it and describe it, with what he reckoned he had discovered in the course of writing his thesis, and that this was what was demanding thought from him,

But not now. He looked at his watch again, paid for his coffee, and started walking, this time more briskly, towards the station.

"That was delicious", his mother said, putting down her knife and fork, "and what a beautiful place. I should have visited you in Nantes before, but I don't think students are very keen on their mothers suddenly appearing in the life they are making for themselves."

They both laughed.

"I know", he said. "You're very tactful. But it's good to see you here, specially now when there isn't much more time before I leave, and I have—"

"So much work to do for your exams." She laughed again. "Don't worry. I'm going back to Paris this afternoon. I won't take you away from your books for much longer."

Through the hour they had spent over lunch he had explained why he wanted to go to Tunisia, for the experience, to help desperate refugees in any way he could without medical qualifications, and to learn enough to write well about what he found in North Africa. All the time he was talking he had the impression, which surprised him, that she was only half listening to what he was saying. She was looking at him intently, but as if she were trying to understand who he was now rather than trying to find out why he wanted to go to Tunisia and whether she could agree that it was a good plan.

She did stop him once, to say, "Tell me about this Tunisian girl, Syrine. What a pretty name, by the way. Is she really the reason you want to go?"

"Well, she did suggest the idea. And a friend of hers is giving me Arabic lessons, so that I know a little before I get there. He's teaching me for nothing, which is really kind."

"Bernard. Is she—? Are you—? No. I can tell by your face."

He laughed.

"You're right, maman. She's only a friend. Also she's a bit older than me, and—how to put it?—I think she's married to her work."

"Would she be very disappointed if you changed your mind?"

This was easy.

"No. Not at all. It was for my sake that she persuaded them to agree to let me go with her and do something useful, not for hers. She would quite happily go without me."

"Good."

"Why good? You don't want me to go, do you? Why not? I know papa sent you to try to persuade me not to go. I expect he thought that if he came we would just get into an argument. He wants me to sort out what he calls my career, doesn't he? And, honestly, maman, I don't know what I'm going to be doing for the rest of my life. Some of my friends know they're going to be doctors or teachers or lawyers or engineers. That will be for the rest of their lives, and I'm sure papa would like it if I had a clear future like theirs. But I don't. I know I want to write and I know I've got to earn enough money to live, and at the moment that's all I know. On money, by the way, I was hoping that you and papa might be able to help me with a little money for Tunisia. Just enough for the air fare and a few bits of kit? They'll feed me and give me somewhere to live, even if it's only a tent, and once I get there I ought to be able to earn something from writing."

"Yes. We were expecting to help you, keep you alive anyway", she smiled, "until you get settled, and find some sort of job. We're giving Joséphine enough money for her to travel for a couple of months after she's finished her *bac*. She says she wants to do something called interrailing which takes you all over Europe quite cheaply. With a friend from school, a girl, I'm thankful to tell you, though we haven't met the friend yet. So it's only fair for you to have the money you never asked for at her age. But—" He could see that she didn't want to go on.

"Would you like cheese? A dessert?" she said.

"No, thank you. Only some coffee."

But, because of that "good", about Syrine, he was more and more sure that there was something she was holding back, had been holding back all through lunch.

"Come on, maman. You don't want me to go, do you? And not because of my career. Is it because you think it may be dangerous? Syrine says—"

"No. Not because it may be dangerous. Though of course I'd rather you weren't in a part of the world where there are terrorists."

"There are terrorists in Paris. We even had an attack in Nantes, though I think he was only a head case who wanted to behave like a terrorist. To be famous, you know."

"I read about that. What a world, where young men think it's glamorous to seem like terrorists. But I'm not here because Tunisia might be dangerous. Life is dangerous, and of course the people you would be helping have been through dangers we can't imagine. No. The reason I came to see you, the reason I would rather you stayed in France, is quite different. It's a long story. Could we go for a walk, perhaps, after we've had our coffee? In a park or by the river? Then I can tell you properly."

He offered to pay for their lunch, which he could just afford if he ate bread and cheese for the rest of the week.

"Don't be silly, Bernard. You're a poor student and I have a career, remember? A job anyway." She laughed. So did he.

They re-crossed the branch of the Loire near which they had had lunch and walked, saying almost nothing, to the small park in the old city opposite the château which Marie thought so perfectly French. He was unaccountably nervous, perhaps because he felt his mother was nervous herself. He tried to remember the last time they had talked without his father being with them, and couldn't. His father always kept things straight in family discussions and was inclined to interrupt in order to put more clearly things that he thought his wife or children had muddled. Sometimes, Bernard had felt as he grew up, his father actually missed the central point of what he or his mother had been trying to say. Joséphine, when something difficult or demanding was being talked about, and especially when Bernard and their father were arguing, said nothing and either disappeared to her room or sat on the floor by the sofa, her favourite place, playing a game on her phone or texting her friends. He smiled, thinking of his sister, so refreshingly different from him. He had always thought it good for his father that there was one member of the family who didn't take anything very seriously.

"How is Joséphine?", he said. "Working hard for her *bac*?"

"What do you think? Papa gets very annoyed with her. She goes to her room and says she's revising. Papa thinks she spends most of the time messing about on the blessed internet. He wishes it had never been invented."

She looked across the grass at the castle, with its shining moat, its great round towers of pinkish-white stone, its blue slate roofs in the, now quite hot, afternoon sunshine.

"It's very beautiful, isn't it?" she said.

"There are too many people", he said. "Let's walk up to the Jardin des Plantes. It's just beyond the station and much more peaceful."

"This is better", he said, ten minutes later in the city's carefully looked-after park. He took his mother to a quiet bench in a long grassy walk where azaleas, white, cream, orange, pink, the colours of Chinese lacquer, he thought, with their heavy, somehow antique scent, were just coming into flower. They sat down. What could she be going to tell him?

She told him—"The story begins with grand'mère, just before she died"—of her mother's surprising request, and the carved box, so carefully wrapped up.

"So I went, on Saturday, to see what I could find out in this village in Burgundy."

"How extraordinary", Bernard said. "So unlike grand'mère, to be so dramatic. And so unlike you, maman, to be brave enough to go all that way, into the unknown, by yourself."

"I know. Papa was very good. He told me the journey would be easy and if I found no trace of this man, Monsieur Thomas, it would only have taken a couple of days out of the spring holiday. He would have come with me, but we didn't want to leave Joséphine alone in Paris."

"She's eighteen, isn't she? Surely she's more sensible nowadays?"

"Not really. She has these friends we never see. She goes out a lot. And papa's right to worry. What's she looking at on the internet? There's so little parents can do, nowadays. We never worried about you so we weren't prepared for Joséphine, growing up to be so different from you. Anyway, papa, you can imagine, is really anxious about her *bac*. I think he knows too much about exactly what she should be doing, week by week. She might do better at school if her father weren't a teacher."

"I'm sure you're right."

His mother, he could see, was putting off telling him the rest of her story.

"So", he said. "There you are, setting off by yourself to the wilds of Burgundy. What were you wearing?"

"What was I wearing? Really, Bernard, you are a funny boy. What difference does it make, what I was wearing?"

"I'm trying to imagine you on this expedition. You've never done anything like that before."

"No I haven't. I was a bit apprehensive, I must admit. I was wearing my everyday clothes for school. Respectable. Dull. Safe. Easy for you to picture. What I'm wearing today, in fact."

He laughed. "Of course. And what happened when you got there?"

"I found Monsieur Thomas. He's a strange old man who lives by himself, in a house on the edge of a village, with a beautiful garden. He doesn't see people or talk to people. But he did talk to me, and—"

She stopped. Bernard looked at her. She turned towards him on the bench and he saw that her eyes, behind her spectacles, were wide, anxious. Was she about to cry?

"What is it, maman? Were you afraid of him? Was he unkind to you?"

"Not at all. The opposite. This is difficult, Bernard. What I have to tell you will be a shock, in a way, but a good shock. I hope."

"Tell me. What did he say?"

"It turns out that he—that he is my father."

"He can't be! Your father? Are you sure? I thought your father was dead."

"Grand'mère always said he was dead, that he was killed in the Algerian war. But she never said anything else about him. Of course I thought, we always thought, papa and I, that he was Algerian. But he was French, a soldier in the war, and he wasn't killed. He's been alive all this time, and grand'mère didn't know."

"But that must have been because she didn't try to find out...when she knew his name, knew where he lived. Why didn't she go herself to see him?"

"Bernard, think, imagine—she must have been actually afraid that he was still alive. She knew he was French, after all. She had this child, me, an illegitimate child. He had never known she was pregnant. They were both very young. She must have thought he would be married, with a wife, children. How could she upset all their lives by appearing out of his past, with a child he knew nothing about? And in any case, I'm sure she really believed he was dead."

"Was he?"

"Was he what?"

"Married? Did he have other children? Half brothers and sisters of yours?"

She smiled, looking happier now.

"No. That would have been nice, in a way, wouldn't it? Or it might have been. But he didn't marry. He told me very little about his life during all those years—"

"Don't cry, maman. It's good, isn't it? To find your father who you knew nothing about, who you thought was dead? And what kind of a man did he seem to be?"

"It's difficult to say. He's lived by himself for so long. He's not like other people. That's why I so much wish I had known him before now." She was crying properly now. "He's old and perhaps won't live very long. I'm sorry."

"Don't be sorry. How could such an extraordinary thing not upset you? Here."

He took his clean handkerchief out of his pocket for her. She blew her nose and wiped her eyes.

"Thank you." Then she laughed through what was left of her tears. "Well done, darling, a clean white handkerchief. You are growing up."

"On some days."

"I see. And the shirt, specially for meeting me?"

"Of course."

Both of them laughed.

"So, how old is he, my new grandfather?"

"He's nearly seventy five."

"Five years younger than grandfather Charpentier."

"That's right. He was born in 1940, which is another story he told me. Also a very sad story."

"Did he seem frail?"

"No. Not exactly. He talked about dying. But he seems well and he works as a gardener. He is badly scarred, worse than scarred, disfigured I think you would say."

"How?"

"His face. It looks as if part of his jaw and part of his eye-socket on one side of his face were badly damaged, perhaps shot away. He wears hats with brims pulled down to one side to hide that half of his face. But if you talk to him you soon stop noticing it."

He was trying to imagine this stranger, with his mysterious life and his wounded face. It was hard.

"What did papa say about all this?"

She smiled again.

"Well. You know papa. He just accepted what I told him, my father being alive and living alone in Burgundy, as if it were perfectly normal, what might happen to anyone. Just part of the way things are. Perhaps he didn't quite realize—"

"How much this discovery means to you? Your actual father, someone for you to know after all, someone, now that grand'mère's dead, for you to—"

"To love? Almost, perhaps, yes. O it is good to see you, Bernard. I'm so glad I came."

"But did you come to tell me this, finding out who your father is and finding him alive, or did you come to persuade me not to go to Tunisia?"

"Both. Both. You see, they're not separate. I'm sorry. I've let myself get distracted. You're so good at understanding it all that I haven't even got to the real reason for coming to see you."

She blew her nose again and shook her head as if to banish distractions. He looked at her and smiled. He thought he felt fonder of her than he ever had before.

"Poor you, maman", he said. "You've had so much to think about and so little time to get used to this whole new person, a person of great importance, in your life. It's difficult for me to imagine how strange it must be for you, when my parents, both of them, have always been there, like most people's parents."

"But Bernard, you do imagine. I'm so grateful to you for that. Anyway, the real reason that I came to Nantes, inter- rupting your work for your exams and using up a whole day", she looked at her watch, "—my train goes in just over half an hour—nearly a whole day of your precious time, is that my father, your grandfather—it's so difficult even to say that—has been writing a book. I saw it. Piles and piles of paper with thin old-fashioned handwriting, quite neat handwriting as far as I could tell—obviously I didn't have a chance to read any of it—and he says he can't cope with organizing what he's written, pruning he called it, like pruning apple trees, because he isn't really a writer."

"What sort of book?"

"A book about himself, I think. From what he said, which wasn't much, I gathered that he's written about his life, and perhaps what he has thought and felt all this time. He's been living in the house where he is now—his grandmother's house, it used to be, where he grew up—for fifteen or twenty years, though he never said exactly when he came back, but he did say 'came back' as if he'd been abroad, not just somewhere else in France. Though now I come to think of it, he said he'd escaped to Paris twice and escaped from Paris twice, but when that was I've no idea."

"But why should this book have anything to do with me? He hadn't heard of me, because he didn't know you existed, until Monday? Isn't that right?"

"Yes, that's right. Monday. The day before yesterday. It's extraordinary."

She looked down the wide grassy walk between the banks of azaleas, as if, Bernard thought, following her gaze, she might see her father coming towards her. A couple with a little girl were walking away from them, far down the path.

"It seems to me as if I had always known him, or known that he was somewhere, all my life. It's very strange. But you, Bernard. I told him about you. I told him you wanted to be a writer and were already writing a book."

"But I've hardly begun my book. I haven't had time because of the exams and my Arabic lessons and—" And Marie. But he wasn't going to tell her about Marie. "And I've begun to think the book isn't such a good idea. It's supposed to be a story about someone else, someone different from me, but—Anyway, I keep changing my mind about whether it's going to be a sad or a happy book. I've written two first chapters and they're so different that maybe they belong to different books."

It struck him as he said this that what kind of book either of his chapters, or a third version, might become would depend on what happened between him and Marie.

"In any case, I can't afford to sit in my room, here or anywhere, and write a book. I need to—well, do something real first. That's why I'm going to Tunisia."

"I understand. And so does papa. We don't want to stop you going, and you're too old now, in any case, for your parents to be telling you what to do. But listen, darling. Of course you must decide for yourself whether you might like to go to meet him, but I had to tell you how delighted your grandfather was when I said you are a writer. He thought perhaps, if you were interested, you might like to help him with his book."

"But—I'm not a writer, not yet. And I don't know him. I'd never heard of him till today. And there's my exams in June, and then I'm going to Tunisia. Maman, you didn't say I would help him?"

"Certainly not. I don't know whether it's the kind of thing you could do, or would like to try. I don't even know whether you would like him. But I thought I should at least tell you about him and about his book, in case you might—"

She looked at his face and stopped.

"I'm sorry, Bernard, to spring this on you."

All his life, since he was a little boy in his first school, he had been good at organization, at plans, at knowing what was going to happen and when. He was the one who remembered what he should take to school each day, and also what Joséphine needed to take. He had thought for as long as he could remember that getting things done on time, making his life as predictable as possible, was the reason he had done, not brilliantly, but pretty well in all his work so far. "You're so like your father", his mother used to say, although he knew that really he was more like his mother. And so did she.

But even seeing her today had upset the schedule he had made for the week's work. He was going to have to catch up by getting out of bed two hours earlier than usual for the next two days so as to find time for the library work he had planned to be doing this afternoon. And now she wanted him to change the plan he and Syrine had made, together, for Tunisia and *Médecins sans frontières*. The news every day, about the people on their crowded boats crossing the sea from North Africa and often drowning, had made him more and more sure that he wanted to try to help, even perhaps in Libya. And Syrine had, he knew, gone to a lot of trouble to persuade the charity to take him on as nothing more useful than an extra pair of hands. And yet, and yet—this new idea, this new person, his grandfather who, an hour ago, he had never heard of, and his book about a life even his mother knew so little about—.

"No, maman. Don't be sorry. But I don't know", he said.

"Of course you don't. I've told you all this without any warning and it's a lot to take in. That I have a father, that he's still alive, that he's been in the world all this time and we never knew, that he would love to meet you, that he would love your help with his book—it's a lot for you to cope with all at once, I do understand. And I know how carefully you always plan your life and don't like your arrangements being upset. All I'm asking you today is that you should think about it, about my father and his book. The decision's entirely yours. You're a grown-up now and what you do with the next few months of your life after your exams is entirely up to you."

"What does papa think I should do?"

She looked at him and smiled.

"You know your father. He wants you to take sensible steps towards organizing your career. That's his priority. That's more or less what he said yesterday. But he'd be happier with you spending some time with your grandfather helping him sort out his book than with you setting out into the unknown in North Africa. He's worried that you might be in danger, that you might be ill, that you might be gone for years without making any progress towards a settled life in France. That's why—you should see your face, Bernard—that's why he wanted me to talk to you. He knew that if he came and said all this it would only make you more determined to go to Tunisia. And probably my telling you what papa would have said will have just the same effect."

He laughed, thinking again how well his mother understood him and his father.

"Of course", he said. "So papa really sees your discovery of your father and his piles of paper that might turn into a book as a lucky chance because it might stop me going abroad and keep me in France. He'll know where I am and what I'm doing and he likes that, doesn't he?"

"That goes without saying. But any good father would feel the same. Now", she looked at her watch again. "Don't you think we should go down to the station?"

She kissed him goodbye on the platform beside an open door of the train.

"It's been lovely to see you. I've so much enjoyed my day. I know I've left you with a major decision to make. Papa would say, 'remember how long life is', wouldn't he? I know it's difficult to do at your age. If you decide to spend some time with my father helping with his book, and obviously you need to meet him first, to see what you think of him and what he's written, you could join your friend in Tunisia a bit later if that's what you still want to do. In any case, you must make up your mind for yourself. And we'll make sure you have enough money to keep you alive for the time being whatever you decide to do. Don't forget that both possibilities are really good. I'll do my best to get papa to see that. Now I'd better get in and find a seat."

She waved from behind a window as the train left the platform. He waved back.

He could have taken a tram to the end of his street, but he knew that walking for half an hour—and he wasn't going to manage any serious work today—would perhaps help him sort out what he was feeling.

It was nearly half past five. The late afternoon in the city was warm, dusty, almost summery though it was still only the end of April. The streets were busy: people leaving their offices were buying food for supper, chatting over coffee or early glasses of wine or beer in cafés, catching trams and buses. Knowing that the thought was ridiculous, he imagined the strangers he passed to have straightforward, orderly lives in which tomorrow would be the same as today and that was fine.

What was he going to do? For weeks he had been pleased that Syrine had managed to organize the Tunisian venture for him. The work he had done for his thesis had made him feel he knew far too little about the real history of the people whose miserable lives in the *banlieues* were the result of what France had done to their grandparents and great-grandparents. He had read a history of the Algerian war and been horrified by so much, by the behaviour of the French army, the behaviour of the French *colons*, the behaviour of the FLN driven to dreadful cruelty themselves by French treatment of Algerians for a hundred years and more. He had learned nothing about all this in school except that General de Gaulle, after inventing the Fifth Republic, of which everyone was supposed to be so proud, had managed to bring to an end, in some kind of peace, a war that had lasted for eight years, and bringing it to an end was a great achievement. His teachers, including his father, must have been right about that; peace is surely better than war for everyone. He hadn't learned in school that the killing and the torture didn't stop when the war was over, with de Gaulle turning a blind eye. And now Islam, the religion of Algeria, once upon a time of his grandmother, and of the surly workless boys and their families in the *banlieues*, was a word of horror in France. A few of those boys might become fanatics and terrorists, like the murderers at *Charlie Hebdo* on 7th January, like those who had gone to Syria and Iraq, keen to die and ready to kill. "Islamic State", he had read in the last few days, "has no shortage of suicide bombers."

He could understand that the bleakness, the hollow emptiness, of the lives he had observed on the grey neglected edges of Paris might be filled, might be transformed into colour, excitement, hope, by the idea that any Muslim could become a hero, a warrior of God, guaranteed an instant place in paradise. It was harder to understand what was inspiring young men from old Paris, from the French provinces, from reasonably prosperous towns and villages, young men with no upbringing or background in Islam, to join them on the battlefields of Syria and Iraq. And girls too. In the end he had said nothing in his thesis about these wholly French recruits to what now was calling itself the Islamic State: he didn't know enough about them and almost nothing, yet, had been written about them. But he had an instinctive sense, nowhere near so developed or supported that it could be described as a theory, that what was inspiring them to leave France, make their parents miserable, cancel the futures they had worked towards at school, risk their lives, was also the filling of an empty space. He couldn't define the space, but he recognized it because he shared it. He would never, of course, disappear into a war he knew nothing about in order to fight for a bunch of Muslims who believed their barbarous leader to be the new Caliph, and on his orders cut off the heads of Muslims they disagreed with and harmless Christian peasants. But he could see, he thought, why a few of his contemporaries were led into doing this—by what? By propaganda on the internet. By, if they knew about it, the long shame of the west's treatment of Muslims, Arabs, poor people made poorer, their dangerous lives made more dangerous, by politicians down the decades in Paris, in London, in Washington, who seemed to have less and less idea of the consequence of their decisions.

All this was swirling in his head, confused, he knew, needing his time and attention to bring it under rational control, into order, tested against proper evidence. It was because Syrine, a Muslim but what, copying the present Minister of Education, a clever Moroccan lady, she called 'a non-practising Muslim', was intelligent, realistic, well-informed, and above all calm, that he liked spending time with her, that he had been so pleased that she had found a way of getting him to go with her to North Africa so that he could learn, while doing something useful, enough, from her and from the people he would find there, to understand more of what seemed to him the most important mystery he needed to explore: what is Islam really? It, or much of it, must be something quite different from a bloodthirsty drive to conquer and kill Christians, westerners, different kinds of Muslim. And what, come to that, is Christianity? Here he was, an educated Frenchman in a country Christian for seventeen centuries, and he had no real idea of what Christianity was, or still is, except that, like all religion, it was mentioned in school only as dead, as part of history, and was mentioned only with disdain in his university. The students he thought of as friends, who, like him, wanted to be journalists, weren't interested in Christianity. They thought of Catholics as right-wing, anti-Semitic, supporters of Vichy, persecutors of Dreyfus. Even those who weren't Jews wanted to be Bernard-Henri Lévy, on television in a white shirt open to the waist, a lit Gauloise in one hand. Or they read the horrible books of the nihilist Houellebecq—Bernard had tried to, and failed. And yet look at Marie, with her happy love for Christianity and the Mass. Nothing dead about her or about what lit up her life in what she had been given as a child and still felt entirely at home in.

He was glad that he hadn't told his mother about Marie. He knew he could only keep his life moderately clear in his head if he separated it into parts. He hadn't told Syrine about Marie, or Marie about Syrine. He had so much enjoyed falling in love with Marie in the last few weeks that, in the compartment of his life that she occupied, he couldn't look further ahead than the next time he had arranged to see her.

Marie. He looked at his watch. An hour before he was to meet her. He was nearly home. He couldn't face his room, the work he hadn't done and wasn't going to do until tomorrow. He had to think more. He had to decide whether to abandon his plan for an adventure he hoped would teach him more about what he knew he wanted to learn—for what? What, truly, was the alternative? Going to see an old recluse with a damaged face who wanted to turn a pile of hand-written paper into a book. An old recluse who happened to be his grandfather. In his first year in Nantes, he had written an essay on whether genes or upbringing made a person. Would he have something in common with his grandfather just because of genes?

And was it sensible to give up Tunisia, and Syrine—he wasn't in love with her, but he was proud of the trouble she had taken for him because it showed she respected what he had already written and done—for this strange old man who might be difficult, demanding, boring, as the old sometimes are? He thought of his other grandfather in Rouen, familiar, always dressed in a suit and tie, tired, critical but critical only of unimportant things, interested, really, in not much more than expensive wine and bridge.

He could go to meet him, this new, strange grandfather, and then decide not to try to help him but to stick to the Tunisian plan after all. Couldn't he? And—it struck him as it hadn't yet—his mother, moved, as naturally she had been, by meeting her father for the first time, had probably exaggerated his capacity to help with the old man's book. She didn't know whether his journalism was any good. She hadn't read the bits of writing he had done, and if she had she wouldn't have been able to judge them. He couldn't judge them himself, though he thought that, over the three years he had been writing, what he produced was improving. But was it?

And weren't both possibilities, Tunisia and his grandfather's book, actually as pretentious and self-important as each other? Wouldn't it be better, after all, to do as his father wanted, to go to Paris, after he had got his *licence*, live at home for a while and get a job in an internet newsroom or on some paper—there were a few left—that needed a literate office boy who could write the occasional piece? Wouldn't it suit him better to fade himself into the background of an ordinary predictable life until he knew more about the world. More about himself. And most of all more about women. Syrine hadn't been a problem because he was in awe of her and treated her with the respect it was easy to feel for someone older and more experienced than he was. She was an attractive woman but he couldn't imagine himself getting anywhere near her. Marie, on the other hand, was lovely in every way but the idea of getting it wrong, misjudging what there was between them, offending or upsetting her, was quite enough to keep him at what he knew was a ridiculously old-fashioned distance.

With both his ambition and his confidence seeping out of him, he went into a cheap café facing the little park he could see from his room. He often came here for a beer and a sandwich when he was working all day. He sat at an empty table on the terrace. The old waiter came out. They shook hands.

"Good evening, Victor."

"Well, Bernard. Everything all right?"

"Everything's fine. A beer, please. No. A coca cola, that would be better."

"Anything to eat?"

"No thank you."

"One coca cola."

The waiter looked at him.

"Are you really all right, Bernard?"

"Yes. I'm fine."

Over his coke he decided he should make up his mind what he was going to do before he met Marie for the evening. Otherwise she would notice he was thinking about something that was nothing to do with her and that he wasn't going to tell her. Wouldn't she? Perhaps she wouldn't. She was so young, and she didn't know him well. Really, she didn't know him at all. No doubt she could see he liked her, see that he responded to her warmth and enthusiasm. Perhaps she was grateful for his gentle kiss, and no more, when he said goodnight. But she didn't know him. Without saying anything about Syrine, he had told her he might be going to Tunisia after his exams, to work for a medical charity that helped people in trouble, and, although the thought of him going to Norh Africa made her look a little anxious—" You will be careful, won't you?"—she had been full of admiration. "But that's marvellous, Bernard. So many students only seem interested in what they can do to become rich." Then she had said, "Will it be just for the summer?" "I don't know yet."

She was going home to Guadeloupe for the summer holiday. Had he let her think he might be back in Nantes in the autumn, to study for his master's degree? Perhaps he had.

He realized two things as he thought about her. The first was that, whatever he decided to do next, it was most likely that, after his exams, he would never see her again. It was idiotic of him not to have understood this before. This obvious fact was a cloud over the sun: for a moment it chilled him. But it also made him surer than ever that he was right not to have tried to get her into bed. The second thing he realized was that he couldn't possibly describe to her what had happened to him today, still less ask her what she thought he should do about it. What his mother had told him was too complicated for Marie, reached too far back in time. His mother's father had been a French soldier in the war in Algeria, which was only the end of decades of imperial arrogance and exploitation. He didn't want Marie, whatever she knew or didn't know about the history of the French empire in the Caribbean, to see him as the grandson of a bullying soldier, who had got an Algerian village girl pregnant and then disappeared.

All Marie knew about his family was that his father was a teacher in a *lycée*, his mother was the director's secretary, he had a naughty sister called Joséphine, and his Algerian grandmother had recently died. He didn't remember telling her about his grandparents and cousins in Rouen; he had never felt that they had any idea who he was, and their coldness always to his mother had made him angry since he was a small child. Everything he had told Marie was true, and it was enough. After all, until today it had been enough for him.

As he thought this, he realized that he knew what he was going to do. He realized that he had known all along, underneath the noise of the stuff in his head that had refused to settle, since he had waved to his mother as her train left the station.

He paid for his coke—" That's better. Thank you, Victor". "Very good. See you soon, Bernard."—and walked the hundred yards to the door of his house.

Up in his room he opened the window and let in the sounds and now freshening air of the late spring evening.

"Right", he said to himself, "a plan." Light-headed now, with relief, he smiled at himself. He could always remake a plan, absorb something new and unexpected, get the next days and weeks straightened out even if the pattern had had to change.

He wanted to email his mother to tell her what he had decided but she wouldn't be home yet and she didn't have a smart phone. Neither of his parents did, and nor did he, though Joséphine, of course, was texting and emailing her mysterious friends all through the day and probably the night.

Anyway, better to reconstruct his plan first.

He looked at the single sheet of paper on which he had printed his timetable of revision, reading, note-taking, checking every detail in his thesis, for the next two weeks. He found it on his laptop and started to juggle the columns, days, times, hours in his room, hours in the library, two seminars he had to go to, so as to give him one whole day next week entirely free of work, except for some reading on the train, so that he could go to Burgundy to meet his grandfather. Wednesday May 6th. That would be the day, in one week's time. He looked up train times on the internet. If he left Nantes at six-thirty in the morning and changed stations and trains in Paris, he could be in the village in Burgundy by midday. The last train back would get him back to Nantes before midnight. How was he going to pay for the ticket?

He printed out his new work plan, pinned it to the wall beside the window, replacing the old one, and emailed his mother:

Maman—

I have redone my work plan for the next 2 weeks so that I can go to Burgundy for the day next Wednesday. I can't promise I'll be able to help with the book until I've met him. Then I'll decide about Tunisia.

It was so good to see you here.

Love—B

He got his mirror out, combed his hair, thought Marie would like his smart white shirt, looked round his room, pleased, as he had been once or twice before, that, except for his laptop and the printer on the floor, it was a little like the garrets in which he imagined writers in nineteenth-century Paris lived, and went to meet Marie.

He was a few minutes early but she was already waiting for him, wearing a pretty yellow dress he hadn't seen before. He gave her a quick, brotherly kiss on the cheek. "You look very nice this evening", she said, standing back for a moment to admire his shirt, and they set off hand in hand for the café by the château.

They talked, over their meal, about nothing in particular, the class she had been to that morning, on the foreign policy and wars of Louis XIV, about which she now knew a good deal more than he remembered from school.

"It's so difficult to remember the map", she said. "All these places in countries that aren't there any more or are some-where different from where they were. But I would love to go to Versailles. Just to see what it was like, where he lived, the sun king. Imagine calling yourself the sun king. Like ancient Egypt. Our professor said we should go to Versailles to see the *galerie des glaces* because it has been restored and looks so beautiful. Did you know that all the mirrors are still the ones that Louis XIV ordered and when they restored them they didn't break a single one?"

He had been to Versailles twice, once on a school trip, once, later, with his parents and Joséphine. Both times, but especially when he was older, sixteen or seventeen, he had hated Versailles. The scale, the grandeur, the heavy extravagance of the buildings and the park, intimidating because all of it was intended to be intimidating, had really shocked him. For the first time he had understood, for himself and in his heart, not just in his head, the enthusiasm of his father and of some of his teachers at the *lycée* for the Revolution. How could the king and his courtiers live in this frightening luxury, with hundreds of servants cooking and cleaning and washing and presenting things on velvet cushions, while in the slums of Paris people didn't have enough to eat? He also remembered that on the way back to Paris in the train he had thought that working on the building and decoration of Versailles must, all the same, have been a wonderful experience: he found himself imagining the armies of craftsmen who had carved and gilded the rooms, cut and laid the perfect parquet indoors, out of doors in the courtyard cut and laid the polished black and white marble in its great curving patterns, blown and put together the pieces of glass for the huge chandeliers, made and framed and polished the three hundred and fifty-seven mirrors in the *galerie des glaces*, designed and plumbed into the ground the dozens and dozens of fountains. All this must have provided interesting, perhaps decently-paid, work for hundreds, even thousands of people.

He tried to say this to his father, not exactly to defend the *ancien régime*, but to add something to his father's summary of their visit: "Very fine of course, but representing all we did well to overthrow". But his father only said, "Oppression, in every chandelier, every piece of carving, every fountain, beautiful though they are." Bernard actually didn't think them beautiful, but he wasn't sure why, so he kept quiet. "The *galerie des glaces*", his father had said to Bernard, as they stopped in their group of tourists behind the guide to gaze in amazement at its glittering splendour. "A place of humiliation, for France in 1871, for Germany in 1919, deliberate humiliation publicly inflicted by one country on another. Both disastrous. How stupid that was."

"Of course you must go to Versailles", Bernard said to Marie. "It's quite extraordinary and you will love it."

"Perhaps you will take me there one day?"

"Perhaps I will."

She leant towards him over their empty plates.

"You look different", she said. "Not just the white shirt, so chic and old-fashioned. You look happier, as if something good has happened. You have finally finished your thesis? Is that it?"

He was surprised. He was thinking her more attractive than ever and now she turned out to be, also, more perceptive than he had realized. She was a bit like his mother. Not like Syrine, who would never have noticed this kind of thing. Syrine. If his visit next Wednesday went well, he would have to tell Syrine that after all the trouble she had taken on his account, he was going to do something different. Letting her down. He shelved the thought. Too early to worry about that.

"No, not the thesis", he said. "It's very nearly finished, but not quite."

"Well then?"

"Something astonishing happened today."

He had decided not to tell her, but, after all, why not? She had never met anyone in his family.

"What happened, Bernard? It was good?"

"In a way, yes, it was good."

How to begin?

"Shall we have coffee, Marie? Or would you like an ice cream?"

"Coffee, with pleasure, and an ice cream? Would that be all right?"

"Of course."

The girl in jeans who was their waitress took away their plates and went to fetch coffee and Marie's ice cream.

"Are your grandparents still alive, Marie?"

"My father's mother died when I was little so I hardly remember her. My grandfather, my father's father, is a lovely old man. He was a judge and I think he's very clever. You would like him. He has white hair and looks wise and kind, a bit like Nelson Mandela or Kofi Annan. My mother's parents are younger. That grandfather's a doctor—he's still working hard—and my grandmother used to be a nurse. They had five children, and my mother's the oldest. We see them a lot. We have lunch with them after Mass on Sundays. My grandmother is a wonderful cook. Why do you ask about my grandparents?"

"Because today—"

"Today your grandparents came to see you? Or one of them?"

"No. But my mother came. She has never visited me here, never been to Nantes before. She says she didn't want to interfere in my life here, and I suppose she was right."

"Was it good to see her?"

"O yes. You would like my mother. She's Algerian. She notices things, as you do."

"Is she a Muslim? Is it because she's a Muslim that you don't know about the Church?"

"No. Well, not exactly. She's not really a Muslim, at least she never talks about religion, though my grandmother was a Muslim. My mother's not a Christian either, and nor is my father, who is altogether French, but the kind of Frenchman who doesn't like Catholics. I'm sorry."

"Don't be silly. There are lots of French people who don't like Catholics, but I think it's because they don't know anything about the Church. So your mother came. And your grandparents?"

"I've always known my father's parents. They live in Rouen. They're very—correct. Very much the *haute bourgeoisie*." Like your grandparents, he thought, but didn't say, and guessed that such people might be more relaxed in Guadeloupe than in Rouen.

101

Marie laughed. "We hear about the *haute bourgeoisie* in our lectures on the nineteenth century. Professor Stavitsky doesn't approve of them."

"Oh, I remember. I went to those lectures two years ago. He's an old Marxist, you know."

"I suppose he is. I thought they'd all given up being Marxists now that Russia isn't Marxist any more?"

"Some of them will never give up. It's in their academic DNA."

"What does that mean?"

"Never mind. Anyway, what happened today was nothing to do with my grandparents in Rouen. Three months ago my Algerian grandmother, my mother's mother, died in Paris."

"I'm so sorry."

"Thank you, but it wasn't too bad. She'd been ill for some time and she died peacefully in her room. It was sad for my mother, naturally, but she had expected it. So had I. I was probably closest to her, after my mother. I went to Paris to visit her a few days before she died. I don't know if she knew I was there."

"I'm sure she did, but it doesn't matter if she didn't. I'm glad you visited her."

"My mother has always thought that her father died, was killed, in the Algerian war, before she was born. Today she told me that he has been alive all this time, that he lives alone in a village in Burgundy and that she has been to see him."

Marie was silent for a moment. He could see that she understood the magnitude of this piece of news. "But that's wonderful! Isn't it? To discover her father, her own father, who she thought was dead. How extraordinary—why didn't your grandmother tell her before?"

"She didn't know. She always thought he had died."

The girl in jeans brought their coffee, and Marie's ice cream. Marie took a sip of coffee.

"Did your mother like her father when she met him?"

He laughed.

"You are astonishing, Marie. Do you know, I didn't ask her. But yes, from what she told me, I think she liked him. It must have been very strange for both of them, this meeting.

102

He didn't know that he had had a child, the child who is my mother."

"Does he have another family, a wife, children?"

"No, apparently not. But my mother didn't discover much about his life. Certainly he lives alone now. He's lived alone for a number of years, and is a kind of recluse. I think it was quite difficult for my mother to get to see him."

"But you must meet him yourself. Think how interesting, to meet a grandfather you never even knew you had. You might learn things about your mother's character, and yours, things you've inherited without knowing, from this man you thought was dead. It's really exciting, like a book."

"Yes, well, that's another thing. Eat your ice cream, Marie. It's melting."

Obediently, she put her spoon into her ice cream.

"Mmm. That's good. What's another thing?"

"It seems that this old man, my grandfather, has written some kind of book, about his life, my mother says. Only it's piles and piles of paper, hand-written in ink. He says he isn't really a writer and he doesn't have a computer, or, come to that, a telephone or a television or even a radio, and he needs someone to sort out what he's written on these piles of paper, turn it into a book and put it on a computer."

"But that must be you! Obviously, Bernard, it must be you! How thrilling! You say you want to be a writer, so isn't this a perfect opportunity to practise being a writer, helping to organize someone else's book before you write your own?"

"I don't know. I do want to be a writer, but I've only done bits of journalism, and my thesis of course. I have started to write a book, twice actually, but I couldn't get any further with it, and the two starts I made were so different from each other that I realized I didn't know what I wanted, what I was trying to do. I'm probably not good enough, not experienced enough, and probably not clever enough either, to give him the kind of help he needs."

"You won't know till you try. And anyway you won't know whether you want to try till you meet him, will you?"

"You are so sensible, Marie. Eat your ice cream."

She finished her ice cream, and then her coffee. He watched her, loving her.

"I think he sounds very interesting", she said. "Imagine living without a telephone or a television. Isn't that rather brave and good?"

"It could be only cowardly. An old man who doesn't want to face the world as it is now, so he shuts himself away without any contact with anyone or anything. I'm not sure I'm looking forward to meeting someone so odd. He could be a little mad."

"Your mother didn't think he was mad, did she?"

"No. You're right. She didn't."

He tried to remember exactly how his mother had described her father. He couldn't. He was sure she hadn't said she thought he was mad. He remembered her describing the old man's damaged face, but he didn't want to tell Marie about that.

"You haven't drunk your coffee, Bernard."

He laughed. "You're quite right."

He drank his coffee, lukewarm now, all at once.

"So you think I should go and meet him? All the way to Burgundy, and not long before the exams?"

"Of course you must go. You can't just pretend this hasn't happened and carry on with your work as if your mother hadn't told you such an extraordinary piece of news. Can you?"

"No. In fact, I've already decided to go, next week. It may all come to nothing. I may not like him, and if I don't like him I can't even consider helping him with his book."

"Why do you think you might not like him?"

"The few facts I know about him aren't good. He must have seduced my grandmother. She was only sixteen when my mother was born. And he was a French soldier in Algeria when the most horrible war was going on. The French army was doing terrible things to the Algerian people, and he was part of that army."

Marie looked down at the table for a few moments, clearly thinking.

Then she said, "How did your mother know where to find him?"

"Her mother, my grandmother, before she died, gave my

NO! Too Contrived!

mother his name, and the name of the village where he was born, just in case, I suppose, he might be still alive or my mother might be able to find news of what had happened to him."

"Well, there you are. Your grandmother wouldn't have kept the memory of his name and his village all those years if he'd treated her badly, if he'd only seduced her or frightened her or raped her. Would she? And another thing, all those dreadful things France did, everywhere, in Indo-China, in Algeria, in the African countries where my people came from, slaves, you know, to make money for France, in Guadeloupe and Martinique—they were dreadful, of course, but not everyone who was forced to do them was dreadful himself. Do you know how old your grandfather was then, when all this happened, when he and your grandmother met and whatever happened happened?"

He thought.

"My mother said he was born in 1940. My mother was born in 1962."

"So he was twenty-two. Maybe only twenty-one. The same age as you are now. And another thing, weren't people made to go into the army then—what's it called? Conscription, that's it—or did they choose to be soldiers?"

"I don't know.

"I expect he had to be a soldier. I know that for a long time young men in France, and in the empire too, had no choice about it. If he's a good man—and you'll be able to tell, when you meet him—I expect he hated the war, hated what the army was doing. Like there must have been some sailors on the slave ships who hated what they were doing. Horrible people won't have minded the work, but not all of them will have been hor-rible. Don't you think? And the people most to blame were always the powerful people far away, the people in palaces, like Versailles, or in governments, who ordered the wars, the people who got rich because of the work the slaves were forced to do, who didn't care. Some of them were here." She waved, a big, sweeping wave, taking in the whole city though all they could see from the café terrace was the château behind its peaceful moat. "In Nantes. Ship-owners, slave-traders, making lots of money out of Africans who they never saw, Africans bought and sold and dying of overwork so that they could be rich and build grand houses. Did you know that?"

"Yes, I did. I thought you didn't. You seem to love being here, being in France, even being in Nantes, so I thought you didn't know the history."

"How could I live in a slave island and not know the history? And how could I be here and not love France? So old, so beautiful, the cathedral, the château, Paris, though I have only seen a little of Paris when my cousin met me in the airport and took me to the Gare Montparnasse to come here. The Gare Montparnasse, what a beautiful name. And the kind people too, like you. Lots of kind people."

"Marie. How can you forgive, as you obviously have forgiven, this cruel country, this cruel city?"

"But Bernard, France isn't cruel to me now, Nantes isn't cruel to me now. I'm allowed to live here, to be a student, to learn so much, to be your friend. How is this cruel? In any case, it's not for us to forgive things that happened in the past, when all the cruel people are dead. We have to leave it all to God, you know, his judgement, his forgiveness. He takes away the sins of the world."

"I have no idea what that means. You see, I don't know, I don't understand about God. Sometimes I wish I did. And another thing, when the results of all that cruelty are still everywhere, the horrors of Islamic State, the refugees drowning in the Mediterranean, the boys on street corners in the *banlieues* selling drugs because there's nothing else for them to do—how can we leave it all to God, who, even if he exists, doesn't do anything to make any of it better? He doesn't take away the sins of the world. They go on and on. Every day. God doesn't rescue the Christian labourers in Libya from the people who cut their heads off; he doesn't save the good Muslims from the bad Muslims who burn their houses and steal their daughters; he doesn't—"

"No. Because that's not how God does things in the world. But every good deed, every kind action, every time someone is brave enough to help someone else when it's dangerous, that's God working. And the rest of us, who aren't in these horrible places, we can pray for the poor people who are."

"But it doesn't do any good, does it? Praying. Look at Syria, Iraq, Libya."

"It does do good. I can't explain how, but I know it does. Praying for people who've died does good too. When I was little my mother taught me to say my prayers every night and at the end to pray for everyone who died today. So I do. I expect millions of people who believe in God do the same. So if you are killed in one of those places where everything is so bad, at least you are sent to God with lots of prayer."

For a moment, he thought about this. Then he shook his head.

"It's hopeless, Marie. I don't understand a word of all that. Once you're dead, you're dead, surely, and nothing anyone can do will make any difference to you any more."

She laughed and put her hand on his, across the table. She had never done exactly this before and it affected him so much that, looking into her happy eyes, he forgot what they had been talking about.

"Poor Bernard", she said. "You'll understand one day, about God I mean. I'm certain you will."

"Never mind God now. Shall we go dancing?"

"Not tonight. You've got too many things to think about. Let's just walk through the old town. It's a lovely evening."

She was right, and they walked quietly, holding hands, stopping in the cathedral square for her to look up and up at the high west front of the church, floodlit in the dark, for several minutes. He was wondering, after her response to the news about his grandfather, whether to tell her, after all, about Syrine and the definite job in Tunisia she had found for him. He had put off saying much about it because he thought she had assumed that he would be back in Nantes after the summer holiday, to do his master's degree, and he didn't want to spoil the evenings they had together by telling her that when she came back from Guadeloupe he would probably be still in North Africa and would almost certainly never return to university study. Cowardly of him, he thought now. And if he weren't going to Tunisia on account of helping his grandfather with his book, he would be even less likely to come back to Nantes. But he hadn't decided, had he? He'd decided only to go to the village in Burgundy and see the old man. He couldn't decide about Tunisia until he'd met his grandfather. He felt tired and confused and said nothing about Tunisia. Beneath his tiredness and confusion he was more than ever before longing to make love to Marie.

At the door of her university hostel, where about thirty foreign students had rooms, she turned to him to say goodnight. He kissed her, held her close, said into her hair, "Marie, tonight, will you let me come to your room?"

She pushed him very gently away from her, her hands on his shoulders, and said, "No, Bernard. You will go away. And I will be too sad."

Her sweetness didn't help, but he managed to kiss her forehead and leave her, without another word.

Back in his room, he opened his laptop.

Dear Bernard,
I'm so glad you have decided to go to meet your grandfather. Papa is pleased too. He will put some money in your account for the train fare and the two taxis you will need. I will write to your grandfather to let him know that you are coming to see him next Wednesday.
I so much enjoyed my day in Nantes—thank you.
Maman

After this message on his screen was the one he had sent to his mother before he left his room to meet Marie. How calm he had been then. How controlled his email looked: work organized and his trip to Burgundy planned. Simple. But didn't Marie matter to him more than either? More than anything? How could he have thought that he could bear to go to North Africa, perhaps for months, perhaps for years, and not see her, even not see her ever again? Surely some other man, better at dealing with girls than he was, maybe a Catholic, which Marie would like, would have become by the time he came back to France her friend, her lover, even her husband? If she was irresistible to him, to how many other men would she be just as irresistible? But tonight, more than her laugh, her bright eyes, her warmth, her soft dark skin, it had been her goodness and her intelligence, somehow as one in her, that made him love her as he had certainly never loved anyone before.

He groaned aloud as he sat at his desk, looking at the messages on his screen.

He was angry with her too. His day, his plan for his work, his plan for going to Tunisia, had all been upset by his mother's visit and her extraordinary story, and now Marie had upset him more. He wasn't angry with her because she had pushed him away when he so much wanted to go up to her room and make love to her. Or perhaps he was, though he knew she was right: he would, one way or another, go away and she would be more sad, miss him more, if they had become real lovers. Also he thought she was probably a virgin, and it made him angry with himself, as if he had been guilty of something, to think this was partly why she pushed him away. Then he realized that if she had said, "No, Bernard. I'm a Catholic", or "No, Bernard. I'm a virgin", it would have put a cooling distance between them. But she had said "You will go away. And I will be too sad", and that had only made him want her more. It was all bad luck, bad timing, and hadn't he given up too easily? Mightn't they, even now, as he sat miserably in front of his laptop, have been in her room, in her bed, in the dark? It was her goodness he loved and it was her goodness that was now making him angry with her.

He had to move, to do something. He got up from his desk, went down one flight of stairs and along the passage to where a kettle, a cupboard, two gas rings and a small refrigerator sat on a wide shelf, all shared by the five students who lived on the top two floors of the house. He made himself a steaming peppermint tisane in a mug and took it back to his room. He had suppressed the frustration. Poor little Marie. None of what had happened that evening, that whole day, was her fault. She had of course been right to push him away.

Some irritation with her remained. Calmer now, he saw that what had actually upset him most was that she had added to the complications he was trying to sort out in his head by talking about God and praying and forgiveness for things that should never be forgiven because their consequences were everywhere, destroying people's lives. And he didn't want them forgiven until, at least, he himself had understood them properly and done something constructive to make amends.

What did it mean, to say that God takes away the sins of the world? What could it possibly mean?

He could almost hear his father dismissing everything Marie had said. "All that was always for women, children, the poor. A means by which the rich and powerful held down the weak and frightened them into obedience. Marie is a simple black girl from Guadeloupe, her grandfathers and her father were educated, no doubt, but she herself is obviously under the influence of her mother and grandmother, superstitious Catholics. Praying for the dead, indeed! And for dead strangers, not even Christians, most of them. It's simply nonsensical, Bernard, as you know perfectly well."

The imagined words of his father calmed him, but not because he agreed with what he knew his father would say. The words calmed him because they forced him to admit to himself that he knew, somewhere, somehow, that what Marie had said was not nonsensical. He had no idea what it meant, but look at her! Was she foolish and stupid? Wasn't she rather the person he most wanted to be with, to talk to, as much as he wanted to go to bed with her?

She had confused him more at the end of a day which had been in any case confusing ever since his conversation with his mother in the Jardin des Plantes. He hated confusion. He wished it were yesterday still, when his clear priority had been checking the last details of his thesis.

As for the prospect of letting down Syrine, he must try to put it to one side and not worry about it until he had met his grandfather. If he didn't like him, if the idea of helping him with his book weren't interesting after all, he could say that he was committed to going to Tunisia early in July and that would be entirely true.

Why couldn't everyone leave him alone and let him get on with the work he needed to do to get his *licence*? He wished it were not just yesterday but this time last year, when things were straightforward: work, an occasional night out with his two friends Marc and Philippe—he had hardly seen them since Marie had appeared in his life—and the summer holidays with cheerful, naughty kids in the Ardèche, and ordinary study like everyone else in the autumn. Then he hadn't met Syrine, or Marie, and his mother hadn't arrived on her train to upset everything.

Childish, he knew. He finished his tisane, undressed, got into bed and slept like a child.

A week later, he waited until his taxi had disappeared along the road back to the village. Silence. Birds singing. Apple blossom beginning to float down, white petals from the branches. His hands were shaking. The house and the garden, so pretty, and closed, like a picture in a fairy story. Inside the house, or somewhere in the garden, an old man, a stranger, who was also his grandfather. He looked up and down the road, to the village, away in the other direction to the green country. No one to be seen. No cars. No one walking. The hot middle of the day. He looked at his watch. Everyone, no doubt, at lunch, or about to be at lunch.

He was wearing his white shirt, washed and ironed, his newest jeans, a denim jacket, reasonably new trainers. He had shaved, at five-thirty in the morning, and walked down to the station in the dawn light. He passed two noisy trucks, first one and then another, crunching rubbish which men in orange jackets and heavy gloves were tipping into the trucks from bins left on the pavements. Otherwise there were only a few people in the streets, heads down, walking to work, or to tram stops. Early trams were already full. He had never before seen the city at this hour. He wanted to tell someone, anyone, what he was doing, where he was going. Marie knew of course. He hadn't seen her since last week but he had emailed her yesterday to tell her he was going to meet his grandfather today and she had sent him a message back saying "Good luck. I hope it goes well. Marie."

He was carrying a slim case for papers and books that his mother had given him when he was first leaving home for Nantes. On the train to Paris, waiting in the Gare de Lyon with a single cup of coffee for nearly an hour, surrounded by more busy, purposeful people, and then on the train to Burgundy, he had got out the big spiral-bound notebook in which he had written out neatly what he hoped were the essential facts, arranged under likely essay topics, for the first examination paper that he was to take in five weeks' time. He had read nothing.

The roar of an engine broke the silence: in the yard of a big garage and workshop on his right, on the road back to the centre of the village, a mechanic had started the engine of a tractor with the metal engine-cover raised. The mechanic peered inside for a minute or two, and then switched off the engine.

The return of silence seemed like a signal. He walked up the short path to the heavy door of the house and knocked.

From inside the deep bark of a large dog made him step back. His mother hadn't said anything about a dog.

A shout. "Enough!"

The door opened and an old man stood there, one hand on the neck of a shaggy white dog, looking at him from under the brim of a straw hat tilted to one side. The dog growled once and was then quiet.

Bernard had forgotten about the damaged face. He looked down, but then looked up to meet the observant gaze of his grandfather, studying him, through spectacles.

"So you are Bernard. Thank you for coming to see me."

Bernard wanted to say, "Of course I have come", but couldn't speak.

They shook hands.

"Come in, come in. We shall sit on the terrace where I talked to your mother."

The old man turned back into the house, followed by the dog, now wagging its tail.

"Would you shut the door? Thank you."

Along a dark passage with a cool stone floor, through a kitchen unlike any kitchen he had ever seen, pans and china on an old-fashioned dresser, flowers in a jug on a wooden table, then out through an open door on to a terrace shaded with leaves and flowers, the sunlit garden beyond.

"Sit down, Bernard. You will have a glass of wine?"

"With pleasure. Thank you."

The first words he had managed. He had nearly said, "Thank you, monsieur", which didn't seem right, so he left his "thank you" as it was, which didn't seem right either.

There were two chairs at an old table on the terrace, a basket chair with an ancient cushion, its back to one side of the terrace, and a wooden kitchen chair, its back to the house. He sat on the wooden chair. The dog lay down beside him, its head between its paws. In the calm of the house, the terrace, the garden, he relaxed a little. His hands had stopped shaking.

He heard the old man in the kitchen behind him opening and shutting cupboards, uncorking a bottle, pouring some wine. He reappeared with two glasses, each half full, and put them on the table. He sat down in the basket chair.

"Good", he said.

"Thank you." Bernard stretched his hand towards his glass, then rested it on the table because his host hadn't moved.

The old man looked at him again for a long moment.

"Have you read the *Confessions* of Saint Augustine?"

Not only had he not read the book; he hadn't heard of it.

"No. I haven't. I'm sorry."

The old man laughed. "No. It's for me to be sorry. What a question to ask a young man who has been kind enough to come all this way to meet a stranger. Never mind. You will."

Bernard couldn't think of any answer to this.

"You will read the *Confessions*. That's to say, if you are interested enough in my book, in me, to try to understand where I have been all this time, all these years in which your mother thought her father was dead and I didn't know that I had had a child. If you find that by any chance you are interested in me,

113

you will read St Augustine one day. Have you come across him, in your studies, for example?"

"I know the name. There's a métro station in Paris and a big church, Saint Augustin."

"Indeed. A most hideous church. But important for one thing that happened there. Have you heard of Charles de Foucauld? Another saint, though not an official one."

"No. I'm sorry."

These questions were not at all what Bernard had expected. What had he expected? A more emotional conversation. This was easier, and he relaxed a little further.

"I do know Saint Augustine's name. But I'm afraid I know nothing about him. We didn't learn about saints at school."

"Of course not. Or at home, I gathered from meeting your mother."

"Or at home. My father—"

"Your father is a man of the left?"

"Not the real left. My father is an ordinary socialist. Not a Marxist, not at all. He thinks Marxism was a substitute for religion, equally dangerous, and now we've left both Marxism and religion behind and that's good."

"Exactly."

At last the old man reached for his glass, so Bernard picked his up in response.

"Your health!", the old man said.

They touched glasses and each took a sip of wine.

"St Augustine", the old man said, putting down his glass on the table, "was an Algerian, the greatest Algerian who ever lived. You are half Algerian so one of these days you must learn about him, read his books."

"A quarter Algerian." Why had he said this? He was ashamed at once of correcting this strange old man who was, after all, his mother's father.

A sharp look from the one eye he could see. Then a smile.

"You are quite right. Let us be accurate. A quarter only, but still, a quarter is a quarter. I'm sorry. I find, in the last week since your mother came, that when I think of her it's difficult not to think of her as her mother. Because she was so young and I never saw her again." He shook his head.

Into the silence Bernard, for something to say, said, "When did Saint Augustine live?"

"A very long time ago. Before Algeria was invented. Africa, it was called by the Romans, though they knew only the northern part along the Mediterranean, where corn and vines and olives grow, and where the mountains are, the beautiful mountains where—where your mother was born. Soon, to the south, there is the desert, where nothing grows, though traders crossed it then as traders cross it still, and fighters, alas, and now, more than ever before, desperate people trying to escape from the unhappy countries of Africa, also the unhappy countries of the Near East. Augustine died in the year 430. But your mother's people were there long before that, before the Romans arrived, and, in spite of all the empires that came and went, they have not gone away."

Bernard thought he had learned more from these few quiet sentences than he had ever known before, about Algeria, about his mother's country.

The old man took another sip from his glass, so Bernard did too.

"Camus?", the old man said.

This was better: his grandfather wouldn't think him ignorant of everything.

"Of course. We read *La Peste* at school. They told us it was about the Occupation, but I thought it was only about the plague in a hot city. It frightened me, but it was meant to frighten, wasn't it? Later I read *L'Étranger*: a friend of mine in Nantes, where I am studying at the university, told me I should read it to understand that life is meaningless. I didn't like the book. I think I didn't understand it."

"It's more probable that you didn't like it because you did understand it, which would be to your credit, although it is formidably well written. It's a young man's book, the book of a young man in despair, and if you resisted it you were resisting despair. Hope, you know, is a virtue. But Camus grew out of despair, though in his Algeria, his France, the skies became darker and darker, reasons for hope fewer and fewer, as he got older. Not that he was old when he died. But he grew out of his despair in a remarkable way. He was a truly good man, dedicated to truth and to kindness. There are not many famous people of whom this can be said."

"Perhaps I should read more of his work."

"You will. I have in this house everything he wrote. Until he became silent because things were too terrible. As perhaps we all should."

"But—"

Bernard suddenly felt frightened again, trapped. They had agreed nothing, surely. His grandfather hadn't asked him any ordinary questions, knew nothing about him except that he hadn't read Saint Augustine, hadn't heard of another saint, and had read two books by Camus. Yet he had spoken as if Bernard were going to be in his house long enough to read more. Wasn't he taking for granted that he would be here for a long time? How had this happened?

The old man laughed and turned his head so that he was almost facing him.

"You look terrified. Poor Bernard. This is entirely my fault. My apologies. I see so few people, you know. I have lost, a long time ago lost, my familiarity with the conventions of polite conversation. You think I am assuming you will come to help me with my book, when we haven't discussed the book, or you, or what you would like. You are quite right."

Bernard smiled. He didn't know what to say.

"Let's see", the old man said. "You have nearly finished your studies in Nantes. Is that correct?"

"I have a few more weeks, to finish my thesis and to take my final examinations. It will all be over by early in July, and I should have got my *licence*, though I won't hear how I did for a while."

"What is your plan for afterwards?"

"I have been—I am lucky enough to have a friend who has found me some work with *Médecins sans frontières*. I have no medical training but they need people to help with office work, with computers, keeping records, writing reports."

"Where are you going?"

"Tunisia. There are refugee camps which—"

"I'm sure there are. Every country where there is no actual war is having to take in refugees from the countries that war is tearing apart. Lebanon, Jordan, Egypt, Tunisia: thousands of refugees from Syria, Iraq, Libya. Poor Libya. A tragic country that is not a country at all."

He stopped, remembering things, Bernard thought, that he himself knew little or nothing about.

"But Tunisia. It's good that you are going to Tunisia. A country where I lived once, in better times. Tunisia, so far, has almost managed to hold at bay the forces of this new darkness that has come out of Islam. Algeria, alas, has not. But then the French did so much less harm in Tunisia, even, you could say, more good than harm. Perhaps from Tunisia you may be able to visit Algeria. Have you thought of that?"

"Of course. It was one of the reasons, perhaps it was the main reason for—"

"For your managing to find some good reason to take you to North Africa?"

"Yes."

"Good. Excellent. How long are you intending to stay in North Africa?"

"I don't know. I'm hoping to write, while I'm there."

"Ah, now, your writing. That, after all, is why you are here."

Bernard saw this striking the old man as not quite right: he sat back in his chair as if to say something serious.

"No, Bernard. You are here because you were sent to me. By your grandmother, by your mother. Perhaps by God. So that I should meet you, so late in my life."

He couldn't answer.

"Now. Tell me about your writing."

Each of them took another sip of wine.

"I've always wanted to be a writer. I don't know why. I like reading. I wrote stories when I was very young. At school they said they were good, for my age of course. At Nantes I have written pieces for a student newspaper. Only on the internet."

"Ah. Of the internet I know nothing. As you can imagine. What sort of pieces? More stories?"

"No. Not at all. Journalism. I suppose I've been trying to understand why things are as bad as they are, in France now, in Paris in particular, and most of all in the *banlieues*. I spent some time in Paris in the winter, really for my *licence* thesis, just exploring the streets, the cafés, the shops, watching the people hanging about outside the mosques, the schools, asking a few questions, trying not to be intrusive or patronising. I was doing my best to find out how France got to where it is from where it was, maybe a hundred years ago, maybe fifty years ago. And it helped me to write these short pieces for a student newspaper on the internet, and a blog of my own, to get what I'd found in some sort of order, and to explain a few things to people of my age who don't seem at all interested in history, and not much interested in what's going on now either. The dreadful things happening in the Arab world, for instance: the Jews I know, students at Nantes, are keenly loyal to Israel and think all Arabs are potential murderers; the non-Jews think all the horrors are America's, and so Israel's, fault; and that's about as far as they go. The truth is so much more complicated and has its roots so far back in history. Everyone, that's to say all the students, marched in January. "*Je suis Charlie*". Hundreds of them, in Nantes. They never stopped to think what actual good had been promoted by the cartoons in the first place, or bothered to think how serious it was that the Muslim children in schools in Paris had refused to join the silence in memory of the dead journalists. The children got into trouble for their refusal. They were 'reported', it said in the newspapers. To whom? The school authorities? The police? So you see, I wrote about some of these things, some of the Arabs in Paris and their lives, when I had managed to find out a little about how they live, to understand more—"

He stopped, rather than got to the end of what he was trying to say. He was talking too much, he knew. He wanted to sound competent, articulate, adult, and knew he was sounding young, muddled, over-ambitious. Who was he to try to write about a tangle of issues and problems that the governments of France and America and Germany and Britain were finding no means of unravelling? He was just a student, and not as clever, he was well aware, as several of his friends who were concentrating on the narrow objective of getting the precise qualification they needed for the first step in the career they had chosen. As his father wished he would.

The old man said nothing for a while when Bernard stopped talking.

Eventually he looked at him with his one properly set eye.

"Good", he said. "You know how much you don't know, and you write to clear your mind. That isn't common in someone of your age. How old are you, Bernard?"

He could tell that his grandfather liked saying his name, and that pleased him.

"I'm nearly twenty-two."

"So young. You seem to me older. But I haven't known any young people well for many years. I was your age when—yes, well. We will no doubt talk about that another time. Things were so different then, so long ago. And there was a war, though not a war that anyone talks about now."

A long silence.

Bernard said, "And I have begun two novels, or more precisely I have begun one novel twice."

"They didn't go well? It didn't go well?"

"What I wrote was too close to me. I didn't know what to do with the story because I don't know—"

"You don't know how things are going to turn out for you? In a week, a month, a year? Is that right?"

He looked at him in astonishment.

"Yes. Exactly right. How did you know?"

"I guessed. I do remember some things about being young. I suppose you are in love?"

"No."

A questioning look.

"Yes. But—"

"But you don't know what to do about it. That probably means you are in love. Take care of her. Her?"

"Yes."

"Good. Is she younger than you?"

"Yes."

119

"Twice as much, take care of her. Is she in love with you?"

"I don't think so. No. She is happy, always happy."

"Three times as much, take care of her."

The old man got up from the table.

"Enough of love", he said. "It's time we had some lunch. Your mother has told you that I have been writing, for years, but very slowly, what I think has a possibility of becoming a book?"

"Yes."

"And that is partly why you are here?"

"Yes."

"Good. I will fetch you some of what I have written and you can have a look at a few pages, while I find us some lunch. It will be very simple, you understand."

"Of course."

The old man stepped from the terrace into the garden and walked through the sunshine and the grass and the apple blossom petals, fallen on the grass almost like snow. He turned out of Bernard's sight at the end of the path and a minute or two later reappeared with some sheets of paper, not many, which he brought to the table on the terrace. The dog followed him along the path, followed him back.

"This was where I thought the book might begin" he said. "See whether you can read my handwriting."

He went into the kitchen.

Bernard began to read.

It is difficult for an old man, looking back over the changing years to his early childhood, to distinguish what he remembers from what he was told.

The handwriting, neat, level, a thin nib scratching so that he could almost hear it, was easy to read. The first sentence seemed as old-fashioned as the handwriting.

Of the important events of those years, most of them bad for the village in which I was born, I remember little but was later told much. Of the things of no importance, the rhythm of the days, the rhythm of the years, the sun, the rain, the leaves of spring and summer and autumn, the leaves of winter crackling underfoot, fetching the bread from the baker, kneeling beside my grandmother at Mass in the nuns' chapel, I remember much and was told little.

Bernard put down the sheet of paper he was reading and looked out at the garden from the shade of the terrace. He had made up his mind. At the very least, he thought, he would learn to write better from reading what his grandfather had written.

The old man came back from the kitchen carrying a painted tin tray on which were a baguette, two cheeses Bernard didn't recognize, a small sandcastle-shaped cheese with a kind of grey dust on its rind, and a golden-crusted cheese in a round wooden box, a bowl of tomatoes, another of cherries, two plates, two knives, and the opened bottle of wine they had already had some of.

He hadn't realized how hungry he was. Confused by the scale of the decision he had just made, and beginning to imagine the consequences—the difficult conversation he would have to have with Syrine; the chance perhaps of picking up some work with *Médecins sans frontières* later and without her help; the irritation he felt at pleasing his father by not going to Tunisia, but at least his father wouldn't regard helping with his grandfather's book as progress in any sort of career—he ate some bread and cheese and a tomato, and drank a little more wine, poured out for him by the old man, who drank no more himself.

"This cheese—how delicious it is."

"Ah. You haven't met it before? Like me. Two new experiences in one day. Strange, but good, I hope."

A smile, so that Bernard could smile back.

"Very good."

"This cheese, like me, is from the good earth of Burgundy. Unlike me, it is unmixed with anything foreign and mysterious. Unlike me, it is famous. You will not find it in Paris except in very expensive shops. When I was young in Paris, I could afford only the cheapest Camembert, cheaper still by the time it was too ripe to sell to a proper housewife."

The old man's mood had changed, lightened. Did he know without being told that Bernard had made up his mind?

They ate a little more, in silence. Bernard already had five stalks and five cherry stones on his plate when the old man, watching him eat, said, "Did you make anything of my handwriting?"

Now, Bernard thought.

"It's easy to read, very clear."

"And?"

"I read only a little of the first page. But what I read made me want to go on reading, to see, to discover—"

"To discover who this person might turn out to be?"

"Yes. Something like that."

"You might not like the person he turns out to be. His story is not straightforward. There is darkness in it. Much darkness. And some light, here and there. One sees the stars only when the sky is dark, you know. And only in the desert does one see that the sky is crowded, crowded with countless brilliant stars. To believe that the stars are still there when the sun is shining is what is difficult. But you may find the darkness in this story—how to say it?—uncomfortable. Unfamiliar and uncomfortable. You are very young."

"I know. But I need to learn, as you said."

"Have you decided, Bernard, to help me with the book? To sort it out, if it is badly constructed, which it certainly is? To chop bits out of it if it tries to say too much, which I think it does? To make it clearer if it is difficult to understand, by an intelligent young person, such as you yourself?"

Bernard took one more sip of his wine. He could not go back on the promise he was about to make.

"Yes." He had almost again said "Yes, monsieur."

"Yes", he repeated. "I would very much like to help you with the book, if you think I will be able to."

"I do". His grandfather laughed and said, "I told your mother that I don't accept help. That has been true for many years. I never thought I would ask again for anyone's help. But here I am, asking for yours. I suppose it was meeting your mother that changed—well, everything."

Bernard saw him shaking his head, as if to banish too much emotion. Sure enough, his voice had become stronger when he said, "There is one thing I know you can do, type the book on a computer so that anyone else, nowadays, a publisher for example, will take it seriously. Who wants to read a pile of handwritten paper that arrives in a parcel from an eccentric old man of whom no one has ever heard, living in a village hard to find on a map?"

Bernard laughed too. "Of course. But—"

Both of them became serious again.

"But?"

"There is one thing I should tell you", Bernard said. "You are Catholic?"

"Yes. That's to say, I am Catholic, yes. But my life, altogether, has not been an example of a good Catholic life. I was a good child, yes, a good Catholic child. My grandmother didn't consider any other way of life possible."

Like Marie, Bernard thought.

"And that gave me something that I found later was more valuable, more to be valued, in the reality of God, than anything else she might have given me. As a very young man, I thought I had decided that I was no longer Catholic, that it was no longer possible to be to any extent on the left and also to be Catholic. The Catholics I knew or heard about then were either old, like my grandmother and her friends the nuns, who lived in the château up the road in those days, or they were far to the right of anything I thought it possible for an intelligent person to agree with. They had supported Vichy if they were old enough. If not, they remembered Vichy as a noble attempt to preserve France. They didn't know, or perhaps they pretended not to know, what Vichy had done to the foreign Jews in France and to some French Jews as well. As it happens, I am half Jewish myself. Did your mother tell you that?"

"No. She didn't."

"That's a story for another time too. Anyway, these Catholics, when I was young. They supported French Algeria and everything the army was doing there. I suppose, underneath all that, they regretted the Revolution. I didn't think then, and as a matter of fact I don't think now, that it's possible to be a loyal Frenchman of the twentieth, or indeed of the twenty-first, century, and to regret the Revolution. In any case, the Church lost me for a while, and it took me some years, and various things that happened in my life—you will see, when you read what I have written here—", he laid a hand on the pages on the table, "to make me understand that it is possible for many more combinations of beliefs and ideas to be honestly held together in a single person than I knew when I was your age."

Bernard was thinking about this, and didn't answer.

"So, yes", his grandfather said, "one way or another, I am Catholic."

"I'm not Catholic. We, my sister and I, have been brought up with no religion."

"Like most young people in France now, alas."

"So I thought it might be a problem, with your book. There will be many things I won't understand. It might be difficult for you, annoying for you, my ignorance?"

"Bernard, your ignorance is perfect for me. I haven't written this book, which isn't yet a book, for old people like me, who grew up Catholic and may or may not have left the faith, the Church, behind in their lives. I've written it, tried to write it, for young people, if they still read books, for people like you who might be interested to know more about what was, after all, the faith of the French for so many hundreds of years. If you find that what I've written isn't boring, even helps you to understand a whole region of life in which, in truth, every one of us lives even if we don't recognize that we do, then I shall know that the long struggle to write down things that could have stayed in my head, my memory, my soul, until my death, won't have been a waste of time and effort. It isn't easy, writing, as you know, and it's partly because you know this that, when your mother told me you wanted to be a writer, I thought we might, in this enterprise, be able to learn something from each other. What do you think?"

Bernard found he was close to tears. He didn't know why. Was it because what his grandfather had said matched, in some mysterious way, something he had wanted for a long time without being sure even how to describe it to himself?

He pulled himself together, cleared his throat.

"I think that would be very good, the best—perhaps the best thing I could imagine at this moment, exactly when I will have finished my studies at the university."

"And your girlfriend?"

Bernard smiled, knowing the old man would understand.

"She's not my girlfriend. That's the problem. Or perhaps not. In any case she's going home for the whole of the summer."

"Home?"

To tell him or not?

"Guadeloupe."

A long silence.

"Ah. I understand. Do your parents—"

"No."

"Probably wise of you. And who knows, after the summer, where life may take you, both of you? Is she a student?"

"Yes. This is her first year. She's just nineteen."

"I see. And so far you haven't—?"

"No. So far, I have taken care of her, as you said. And that may be, well, as far as there is."

"You are a good boy, Bernard. Tell me, were you baptized?"

"Yes, I was, when I was a baby. So was my sister. My grandmother wished it. My other grandmother, you understand, in Rouen. My mother mentioned it once. It was sad for her because she wasn't allowed to be in the church. I don't remember my sister being baptized, although my mother told me I was there, with my father. She wasn't there, again. My father, I imagine, agreed to this because his mother insisted but he's never talked about it, never explained what it meant or whether it makes any difference to us now."

"It does. But it will take you some time to realize—and that's the right word—the difference it makes."

Bernard saw the old man thinking he should change the subject.

"What time do you have to leave, Bernard? Your mother in her letter said you would be travelling back to Nantes today."

"Yes. The taxi will return for me at four o'clock."

"That's good. We have a little more time."

125

He stood and put the remains of their lunch on the tray. Bernard picked up the tray and followed him into the kitchen as if he had known the house for years. The dog got to its feet and followed them.

"Put that on the table. I will make coffee."

"You have a beautiful dog. What's his name?"

"Félix. He's called after Saint Félix of Burgundy." A smile. "You certainly haven't heard of him. Very few people have. He lived a long time ago, not as long ago as Augustine, but almost. He was a bishop in England, but he was born near here. So they say. Anyway, his name means 'happy'."

"I do know that."

"You know Latin? That's marvellous."

"A little, yes. From the *lycée*."

"Good. Excellent."

He picked up an old black kettle from the side of a stove which looked as if it had been in the kitchen since the house was built, raised the iron lid of a black hot plate and moved the kettle to its centre. Bernard deduced that the stove must be kept burning all the time. The old man tipped some coffee beans into a beautiful coffee grinder of a kind Bernard had never seen, a carved wooden box with a blue and white painted panel, perhaps a tile, on which a shepherdess danced. The grinder had an iron handle. He watched his grandfather turn the handle briskly. This was evidently quite hard work. The ground beans smelt wonderful.

"How old is the coffee grinder?"

"More than a hundred years old. Possibly much older. Like most of the things in this kitchen, it was my grandmother's. Other people lived in this house while I was not here, while I was for many years—elsewhere. My grandmother's things were put in a single cupboard in the dresser and no one touched them."

He poured the ground coffee into a plain blue enamel coffee jug, probably nearly as old as the grinder, and added water from the kettle once it had stopped boiling.

"While the coffee is meditating, I will show you the rest of the house. I hope you will become fond of it, as I have always been."

Back towards the door facing the road. On the left the old man opened the door of a dark room with a low beamed ceiling and the shutters closed. He switched on the light, a brass chandelier with small electric bulbs. A round table covered in a dark plush cloth. Six old dining chairs with faded tapestry seats. Dusty bookcases, some with glass fronts, old books that looked as if no one had touched them for years. "Once my grandfather's study. He was the village schoolmaster. The school has gone. Later this was my grandmother's dining room. There was a good woman in the village, a widow from the Great War as she was herself, who cooked, very well, for occasions. When we were alone, my grandmother and I ate in the kitchen." He looked at Bernard from under his hat. "Perhaps, when you come, you would like to work in here. As my grandfather did, long before I was born."

The door opposite.

"My winter room." This time he opened the shutters, opened the window. A large farm machine rattled by on the road. Then a car. The mechanic was hammering in the yard next door.

"It's noisy sometimes."

The room was more austere than the dining room, and not dusty. Under the window a large desk, actually only a plain deal table, like Bernard's desk in Nantes but four times the size. On it, neat piles of handwritten paper like the sheets the old man had brought for him to look at. A worn leather-bound book, perhaps a Bible. A bottle of ink with the maker's label: Bernard didn't think he had ever seen a bottle of ink. There was a large fireplace, a grate with two heavy horizontal bars, held between stout iron uprights; on the bars big logs; under the bars white ash. All this was as unfamiliar to Bernard as the bottle of ink, but he could see how efficient the wood fire would be on a winter evening. In the centre of the plain oak shelf above the fireplace was a wooden cross a foot high, with a metal figure of the dead Christ, arms stretched out, hands and feet nailed to the cross, head hanging forward. The nails were real nails. There must have been a crucifix, probably several, in the cathedral in Nantes. He had seen paintings of the crucifixion in galleries. He had never seen a figure of Christ that looked so dead, so abandoned.

"Yes." His grandfather had caught his long look at the crucifix. "That was how it was." He paused, and then said, "I asked the metalsmith in the village in Tunisia, where I was living then, to make it for me. He was an excellent craftsman, an old man, my friend. He made tools, locks, complicated hinges for doors and boxes. He was a Muslim. Muslims, you know, are not permitted to make religious images of living beings but for him this was an image only of a corpse and was not religious, so he made it for me. He said it was not for other people to see, and other people have not seen it until today, until you, Bernard."

He didn't know what to say to this, so he said, "Thank you."

There were two black-and-white photographs in plain frames on the mantelpiece, one on each side of the crucifix. One was a nineteenth century photograph of a serious old man with a white beard, a skull cap and a large cross on a chain over his black robes. He was in half-profile, thinking, one bent finger to his chin. The other was a photograph of what looked like a death mask, a younger man's peaceful face, eyes closed, but with even in death a look of intelligence, the mouth nearly smiling.

"On the left, Cardinal Lavigerie, a great man; on the right, the death mask of Pascal, a greater man. You will perhaps learn about both of them in time. If there were a photograph of Saint Augustine, he would be here too."

More bookcases, in this room simple shelves painted white; one ancient armchair with a cloth thrown over it, a red, brown and gold pattern that looked to Bernard like Arab weaving; in front of the fireplace on the wooden floor a small carpet with a dark pattern he thought certainly Arab; a reading light on the desk and a tall brass lamp with a plain white shade by the armchair. That was all.

"There are several rooms upstairs. I use only one, as you can imagine. I will clean up another for you before you come. When can you come?"

"My last examination is on the third of July. I have to pack up my stuff in Nantes—there isn't much—and then I should go home to my parents for a few days. They always go to Rouen, to see my—my other grandparents, for the fourteenth of July and two or three weeks after. When they go to Rouen, perhaps I could come here?"

"Of course. I shall look forward to it." He laughed. He had a soft, tentative laugh which Bernard already liked to hear. He added, "I haven't looked forward to anything, you know, for a long time. Now, coffee."

"What I should like best, Bernard, is that, if you have the patience, and from what I have seen of you, I think you have, you should read through all of what I have written. There is, I'm afraid, quite a lot of it. If you think passages are boring, or difficult to understand, or in the wrong place—it's not, as you will find, exactly a chronological narrative—you should make notes, cross things out, write suggestions on other pieces of paper, and then we can discuss what you have found and what in your opinion could be done to improve the writing in detail and the whole thing as a possible book. How does that sound?"

They were back on the terrace, in the shade, with their coffee, the best coffee Bernard had ever tasted.

He thought before he answered, imagining long summer days at the plush-covered table in the dining room, with the pile of handwritten paper and a large notebook.

"You are thinking it will be hard work?"

"No. Yes. But I like hard work."

"You must not be working indoors all the time. You haven't seen my summer house, a little wooden house I built many years ago, beyond the apple trees" He waved towards the garden. "It's cool, shady, peaceful. Just a table and a couple of chairs. Much of the day I shall be out, doing my gardening at the château. So, when you would like to, you can work in my summer house."

"It sounds perfect."

"Something is worrying you. You think you may be bored, lonely perhaps with no one of your own age to talk to?"

"No. Not at all. I like being alone."

"Good. I shall be here, of course, for breakfast and in the evenings. But I shan't allow you to work all day at the book. It

129

isn't right for anyone to work all day. This is a most beautiful part of France, you know. I shall borrow a bicycle for you. There's one in an outhouse at the château, belonging to the porter. He has a car now and never uses the bicycle. You would be able to explore a little. I think you might enjoy that."

"I'm sure I would. I won't be bored, I promise you. But—"

"But?"

'But won't it be difficult for you? Not to be irritated, even offended, by someone as young as I am, as ignorant as I am, making comments and suggestions, even criticisms, about what you've written?"

This time he really laughed, putting both hands on the table and raising his head so that Bernard saw for the first time the extent of the damage to the side of his face.

"I'm long past the age when I'm likely to be offended. Criticism is exactly what this needs,"—his hand again on the sheets of paper—"all this that I've spent too long writing and now can't read with the unprejudiced mind of someone unfamiliar with it. I'm too close to it, or it's too close to me. It needs someone else, someone with some clarity of thought and some independence of judgement, to look at it as critically as possible, to cut it back where it sprawls and is overgrown. Even to tell me that it has all been a waste of time and I should put it on the garden bonfire."

"No! That would be terrible."

"How do you know? You've read a few lines. If you tell me it should go on the bonfire, that's where it will go. I have to trust you, and you have to trust me."

He looked at Bernard from under his hat.

"Don't be alarmed." Then he said, "Listen, Bernard. If this is all too much, you can change your mind, you know, about the whole idea, and go to Tunisia after your exams as you have planned."

Then he smiled.

'You promise me that you won't be bored here. I promise you that whatever you say about the book, or any part of it, I won't be irritated, still less offended. On the contrary, I shall be delighted that you are taking the trouble to work on the scribblings of an old man you had never heard of until last week but who happens to be your grandfather. You are young, yes, which is excellent, and there is much you don't know, certainly, which is also excellent. I haven't written, whatever it may turn out to be that I have tried to write, only for people—there can't be many of them, and those that are left are old—who have seen and thought about the events, the issues, tbe ideas, the beliefs that have filled my life. It has not been an ordinary sort of life. For this I think I am grateful, though sometimes I am not sure."

"Grand-père." At last, he had managed to utter the word.

His grandfather smiled and said, "That sounds as strange to me as it does to you."

Bermard went on, "I'm looking forward to doing the work, to trying, in any case, and to being here with you."

"Good." The old man sat back in his chair. "There is one other thing I should say."

"Yes?"

"I won't be able to pay you, for your time and for the work. I have just enough money for my simple life, which of course you will share here, but not enough to pay you, as I should like to and as at your age you deserve."

Bernard was relieved.

"O, that doesn't matter. Not at all. My parents said they would help me with a little money for going to Tunisia. They thought it would be fair because they've promised to pay for my sister, who is about to do her *bac*, to travel in Europe this summer. They will be pleased that I'm staying in France for the time being—they didn't like the idea of Tunisia—and I know they'll be pleased, my mother in any case will be pleased, if I can help you with the book. I'm sure they'll be able to give me the money they were expecting to give me anyway. Not that I'll need much money here. But I'll be able to help you a little, with food and so on."

"You are a good boy, Bernard."

A loud knocking on the front door had Félix on his feet, bounding through the kitchen and down the passage, barking his deep bark.

Bernard looked at his watch. Just before four o'clock. His taxi. Usually very aware of time, of not missing trains, of worrying that a plan might have gone wrong, he had quite forgotten his taxi. He stood up.

"Félix!", the old man shouted. "Enough! Come here! Lie down!"

The dog stopped barking, came back to the terrace, lay down, and kept quiet when the knocking started again. Bernard, who had never before properly met a dog, bent and patted Félix's shaggy head.

The old man stood up.

"That will be your taxi. I won't come to the door. Goodbye, Bernard. I hope to see you here in July. You will write to tell me when you will come? And write to tell me if you change your mind and decide not to come. I shall entirely understand."

They shook hands.

"Thank you", Bernard said. He couldn't manage "grandfather" again. "I will come back in July."

"Thank you, Bernard. But both of us should thank Tanifa, for keeping the little box, for keeping the name of this village all those years, and your mother for being brave enough to come to find me. Now you must go. Goodbye and God bless you."

They stood for a moment on the terrace, looking at each other. Bernard was a little taller than his grandfather, who reached up and with his thumb traced a cross on Bernard's forehead.

In the morning he had been too nervous to notice anything about the country the taxi had taken him through. Now, as the car crossed the top of the square, where small boys were playing football and mothers and children were gathered round an ice cream van, and then took him along a wide valley with meadows where cows were grazing, vineyards beyond, and wooded hills rising from the fields on either side, he saw in the deep grass and the trees, the shadows and the sunlight, a beauty and a quietness that delighted him. He wished the next few weeks of revision, notes, learning, worst of all his final examinations, would pass as quickly as possible so that he could come back to live here for a while with his grandfather.

His grandfather. All the way back to Nantes, on the train to Paris, the métro, waiting at the Gare Montparnasse, on the train to Nantes, he hadn't even opened his case to get out the work he was supposed to be doing. He thought. He realized that every so often he smiled. He caught a girl sitting beside him in the train to Nantes looking at him doubtfully, as if he might be a little mad. He gave her what was meant to be a reassuring, a normal, smile but she looked straight down at the smartphone she was playing with.

The day had been extraordinary. He didn't remember feeling so exhilarated except perhaps on the morning after he had first danced with Marie. Ridiculous, the comparison. And yet, perhaps not. Both talking to his grandfather and dancing with Marie had given him the same sensation of an infinitely promising beginning, of possibilities that were indefinite still, too mysterious, too good, to imagine. Now he knew that Marie was a sweet, kind, sensible girl whom he was going to have to leave to her holiday at home, to her studies in Nantes, leave eventually to her own life in France or in Guadeloupe, without, he hoped, having hurt her in any way. He didn't entirely understand why his mother's visit and then his meeting with his grandfather meant the end of possibilities for him and Marie, but he felt that it was so. She would be pleased, it struck him, to hear that his grandfather was Catholic.

But his meeting with his grandfather was the beginning of something that was really going to happen. How was it that a few hours after meeting him for the first time he felt closer to him than he would ever feel to his grandparents in Rouen, whom he had known all his life? They had never been exactly unkind to him, although they had always preferred Joséphine. "She has a real look of Jean-Claude, don't you think? And of course as a child he was blond, like her." He himself had dark eyes and hair, like his mother. He had once overheard a bridge-playing friend of his grandmother say: "He seems a nice enough little boy. I suppose you'll get used to the Arab look." His mother was never not anxious, in the house in Rouen, that the children's table manners wouldn't be good enough, that they would squabble, or be too noisy in the mornings when their grandmother hadn't yet appeared. He, at least, since he was very young, had always tried to behave there in a way that wouldn't let his mother down; he knew that both of them, in that large, tidy house without warmth, were there on sufferance, whereas his father, and Joséphine, always naughtier than he was, belonged to the Rouen family.

And now he had a grandfather who was strange, certainly, unlike anyone else he had ever met, and clearly unused, now, to young people, but who had treated him as his own and talked to him as an equal. He realized that he had never before talked for several hours to someone old, to someone—he struggled to define what he had felt—whose life, whose mind, evidently had a richness and depth that he wanted to share. Otherwise he wouldn't have written, or tried to write, his book.

One small exchange he remembered several times. About Marie. "Take care of her. Her?" "Yes." "Good."

It was hard to pin down what had struck him about his grandfather's "good". It wasn't, he felt, a moral judgement. More something like "that's simpler for you". Remarkably calm, from an old man.

He got back to Nantes after eleven o'clock and walked from the station all the way back to his room, as he had walked to the station in the early morning, that morning, the morning of the same day. Dark when he had left, dark now. He could hardly believe it was the same day. The streets were emptying. A cool wind with rain on it was blowing in from the Atlantic; he thought of his grandfather's sunny, quiet garden, the fallen blossom on the grass, the shade of the terrace, warm with the scent of a flower he didn't know the name of. An inland place.

Tomorrow he must see Syrine when she had finished her shift at the hospital, and tell her that his family needed him to do some important work, which only he could do, during the summer, but that if the charity still had a job for him, he would try to join her in Tunisia some time in the autumn. He reviewed this speech as he walked, and thought it was about right, truthful, if incomplete. He wasn't going to tell Syrine about his grandfather. The story was too complicated and he guessed that if he tried to describe to Syrine the real reasons for his decision, she would think him, or his reasons, sentimental. He had known Syrine, quite well, for more than six months: he was sure that she was wonderful with patients, unruffled, competent and reassuring. How she was with people who weren't ill he was much less sure. A friend of hers, another nurse whom Bernard had met once or twice, had told Syrine she was pregnant and going to marry the child's father in the summer and live near his parents in Bordeaux. "Rather self-indulgent", Syrine had said, "after all that expensive training. Nurses are needed by the poor."

In his room, aching with tiredness, he sat at his desk to send his mother an email.

The day went well. I made up my mind to help with the book and I promised to go back after my exams are finished in July, and after I have come home to see you for a few days. I hope you and papa will be pleased that I'm not going to Tunisia, at least not for a while. I liked him—he hesitated over this, "your father", "my grandfather", and left it at "him"—*and the house and the garden and Félix (Félix is his dog). From tomorrow I must work very hard to catch up with my revision. B.*

Before he went to bed he stood in the dark at his window, looking out over the windy town. He touched his forehead, feeling again his grandfather's thumb tracing a cross on his skin. It was true, what he had just written to his mother: everything he had found in the village in Burgundy had charmed him in ways he wasn't at all expecting when he had, it seemed so long ago, set out. But there was something else that had pulled him into the decision he had made, something more than charm, and more than the promise of learning a lot about how to write from the process of improving a whole book someone else had written. He touched his forehead again.

His grandfather was old, complicated, scarred, very likely, inside as well as in his damaged face. He had chosen to live a secluded and simple life and was lucky enough to have been able to. He was a serious person, clever and well-read, and he was a Christian. Bernard had never met an intellectually impressive person who was a Christian. He thought of Marie and smiled. He knew that Marie's kind of Christianity was already beyond his reach: he was too grown-up, too educated in a particular way, too well trained in respect for rational destruction of statements unsustained by evidence, to be able to do more than admire from a distance, with some envy, Marie's warm devotion to the faith in which she had been brought up. But, after even the few hours he had spent with him, he could see that his grandfather's Christianity was altogether different, very likely at present beyond him for reasons opposite to those that put Marie's faith beyond him. Beyond him because ahead of him.

He shook his head, and shivered. He was very tired and should go to bed. He knew there was something here he couldn't yet put into words, something that deeply attracted him. He felt, only, so far, by a kind of instinct, that he was going to have to grow up much more, and to learn to think in new ways, if he were to understand his grandfather's Christianity. He also felt that he very much wanted to do this, and that this possibility, perhaps likelihood, was the real blessing of the day.

Nearly seven weeks later, Bernard was sitting on the terrace of his favourite café, round the corner from his room, watching the children playing in the park. He was celebrating having just finished the examination paper he was most dreading. At least he had answered the right number of questions, thought, he hoped, of enough relevant information, deployed it clearly, and finished in time, though he could have done with another ten minutes to read through his answers. "Listen to what you've written", a wise old teacher of French literature at the *lycée* had told his class before they took their *bac*. "If it doesn't make sense to you, it certainly won't make sense to anyone else." Well, there hadn't been time and that was that. Nothing whatever he could do about it now. No more exams until the day after tomorrow. So he'd ordered a beer and a *croque-monsieur* for his lunch, a treat he reckoned he deserved.

Only another ten days of work and he would be packing up his few belongings, saying goodbye to those of his friends who hadn't already left, to his landlady, to Victor in the café, to the only one of his professors who knew his name because she had helped him with his research for his thesis before his ideas became too eccentric for it to be fair to ask for her advice. There had been some parties; there would be more. He didn't like parties and had appeared briefly at two or three before going back to his room feeling unaccountably older than his exact contemporaries, leaving the university like him, many to come back or go to another university for further study if their results were good enough.

On the whole he had enjoyed his time in Nantes and liked the city. Even the shadow of slavery in its history had been lightened for him by Marie's unresentful knowledge of it. A few days ago there had been a spectacular fire at one of the biggest churches in the city, quickly described by the police as an accident and nothing to do with Muslims; he hadn't seen the flames roaring from the church roof but later that day he had been to look at the charred rafters like a black rib cage against the sky. Old women were sobbing as they stood watching workmen bring things out of the church. He was glad Marie had already gone to Guadeloupe.

Marie. He had seen her three times since his expedition to Burgundy. Anxious about her first year marks, she had been as busy working as he was. Twice he had taken her out to supper and they had gone dancing afterwards. Marie seemed as happy and relaxed as ever, smiling at him over her ice cream frappé after an energetic dance. But somehow it wasn't the same.

"How was your grandfather?"

"A nice old man. Rather mysterious. He's Catholic."

"O, good. That's very good. Will you help him with his book?"

"I think so. Yes."

And that was all. He found he couldn't begin to describe that day in Burgundy to her. She was used to grandparents as part of a large, warm family; it was too difficult, having grown up as he had, in such a different set of circumstances, to tell her what meeting his grandfather had meant to him. She seemed to have forgotten that he was supposed to be going to Tunisia.

On a hot Sunday early in June they had lunch in the brasserie in the Jardin des Plantes on a white terrace under a white parasol, looking out at the trees and green walks and lush roses of the gardens. This was a much more expensive lunch than he could really afford, but it was her last day, their last day, probably ever, although neither of them said so, or said goodbye as if they might not see each other again, after they had walked for a while in the park, holding hands. He didn't take her back to her hostel that day: she was going to a party on the river with some other girls in her French history class.

"Goodbye, Marie. Have a marvellous summer."

"Goodbye, Bernard. Perhaps you will come to Nantes for a visit some time next year?"

"Perhaps I will."

He kissed her on the cheek, and that was that.

Now, thinking of her far away with her family in the tropical sun of Guadeloupe, he felt a little sad, remembering her supple waist in his arm as they danced, her smile, but also glad, again, that he hadn't taken the relationship any further. He hoped she would be happy, and was sure she would be as long as no one treated her badly.

His one conversation with Syrine had been even more difficult than he had imagined it would be. Two days after Burgundy he had arranged by email to meet her at the hospital at the end of her shift.

"What is it, Bernard? Have you got your ticket for Tunis? Is there a problem with the date?"

"No. But I'm afraid I won't be able to come with you after all."

"Really? Why not?"

"I have to spend the summer doing some work for my family. There isn't anyone else who can do it."

"What sort of work? You mean your parents don't want you to go to Tunisia? So they've found something else for you to do which they say is more important? Is that right?"

"More or less. Yes." This was easier than trying to explain.

"Your family, perfectly all right in Paris, is more important than miserable frightened people struggling to escape famine and wars in Africa and the Middle East? People you could actually help? Well, it's up to you, of course. But I'm disappointed in you, after I persuaded the charity to give you some work."

"I'm sorry, Syrine. I wasn't expecting this to happen."

"Too bad. Perhaps when you're a little older you'll be brave enough to get your priorities right. Goodbye, then, Bernard."

"Goodbye, Syrine. And thank you for the trouble you took for me."

A cold look. Clearly she didn't think that was the point.

He had thanked and said goodbye to the medical student who had been giving him Arabic lessons. Bernard said only that he would be going to North Africa later than he had planned. The nice young man had smiled, shrugged, and said, "It will still be there."

When Victor took away his plate, he asked for an espresso.

"All right, Bernard? You look serious."

"Everything's fine, thanks. I've still got work to do. Just another week and a bit."

"Going well?"

"Not bad. At least, I hope so."

He had stayed up late, revising, the night before. He had arranged with his friends, Marc and Philippe, whom he'd seen in the distance at that morning's exam, to go to the film, *Bande de filles*, about black girls in the *banlieue*, which he'd been meaning to see for months. He paid for his lunch and, so as not to fall asleep in the cinema, decided to go to his room and sleep for a bit.

He opened his laptop, which he'd left on his desk, in case anyone had sent him an email. Unlikely, since Marie had gone and his friends were all working hard.

His mother, who rarely emailed.

Your sister has left Paris. She telephoned this morning from Vienna. She took the night train, she says with a friend called Abidah we've not heard of before. We bought her Interrail ticket last week and now she's left in the middle of her bac *exams. She says she's done too badly to go on and what's the point of the*

bac *anyway. Papa is in despair, you can imagine, and I'm very worried. We both have to go to school now. Please telephone this evening.*
Maman

He answered at once, to his mother's email address at the *lycée.*

Try not to worry too much. I'm sure Joséphine can look after herself. If she thinks she can manage her life without her bac, *she probably can. But poor papa. It would be good to find out what you can about this Abidah. I'll call later. B.*

He also emailed his friends to say he couldn't go to the cinema with them that evening.

His mother on the telephone was shaken, tearful, more worried about his father than about Joséphine.

"I've never seen him so angry. He's gone out. I don't know where. He was so annoyed with me at supper that he couldn't eat. I think he realized that wasn't fair so he went out."

"He'll calm down. He shouldn't be taking it out on you. Can you find out anything about this other girl, Abidah?"

"We don't know where to start. We do know she's not a friend from the *lycée.* There is a girl called Abidah, but she's much younger and she was in school today. I wish I could calm papa down."

"He'll get used to the idea. Plenty of people have perfectly good jobs, perfectly good lives, without the *bac.*"

"You can't blame him for being angry, Bernard. The *bac* is his whole life, preparing the children, getting them through it, and now his own daughter says it's pointless—it's really difficult for him, and he thinks we've spoiled Joséphine, let her do what she liked, not enough discipline at home, he says. He thinks it's mostly my fault because she's a girl."

"That's ridiculous. What were you supposed to do? Lock her in her room with her books and no laptop and no phone? Would that have helped? Some people just aren't made for school, you know. Papa must have come across plenty of them."

She wasn't listening.

"I think it's us who were spoiled, by you, Bernard, because you always worked hard and weren't any trouble. O, here's papa now. Do you want to talk to him?"

"Better not. I'll be home in a couple of weeks. Less. Don't worry about Joséphine. She's got a great sense of self-preservation. She's only travelling about in Europe. Good for her, to see some different places. Tell papa I think my *licence* exams are going quite well. I'll see you very soon, maman."

He put his simple, old-fashioned mobile phone in his pocket, got out his lecture notes on political theory from Rousseau to Rawls, and began some more revision.

Four days later, a man with a gun jumped out of a speedboat and killed forty tourists on a beach in Tunisia. The pictures were horrible. The murderer turned out to be an apparently serious-minded student from Kairouan. Bernard had learnt enough about Tunisia, because he had thought he was going there, to know that Kairouan was an ancient Muslim city with a great mosque, the oldest in western Islam. This was all he knew. The depth of the sadness he felt for the people of Kairouan after such a long, long history, and for the ordinary Tunisians who worked in hotels and shops and needed tourists to come to their country, surprised him. Syrine hadn't yet left Nantes. She would be horrified, of course, that such a blow had been inflicted on her country, trying so hard to keep fanatical Islamists at bay—she had told Bernard that hundreds of Tunisians had gone to fight for Islamic State in Syria and Iraq—but she would be all the keener to go home and help in any way she could.

Meanwhile Bernard's parents would be more than ever relieved that he wasn't going to Tunisia. And he had to admit to himself that, after this, whether or not he was being cowardly, he was delighted to be going instead to Burgundy.

When he got home to the flat in Paris, with, after three years in Nantes, a satisfyingly small amount of stuff—he had carried it all on the métro from the station—they were more pleased to see him than, he thought, they had ever been.

They had heard nothing from Joséphine since her telephone call from Vienna. Her smartphone was permanently switched to receiving messages: she hadn't replied to any of the messages they had left, several times a day. Now the phone was saying the message box was full. Even more worrying was one result of Bernard's father's questioning of Joséphine's class on the last day of the school year, after the students had all finished their *bac*. Bernard could easily imagine the seriousness of his father's request for information, the silence in the classroom, the kids who knew nothing feeling guilty that they knew nothing. One girl, however, after the class had dispersed, had said to his father that she thought that 'Abidah' was most likely a girl called Colette Khider who had been expelled from the *lycée* the year before for doing no work, and was thought to have become a devout Muslim. Someone in another class had invited Colette Khider to go to an end-of-school party. A message had come back saying "Colette no longer exists and her social media accounts have been deactivated". Bernard's father, through the *lycée* records, had tried to find her parents: the concierge at their address told him they were a diplomatic family from Morocco, and had left Paris for Buenos Aires six months ago. She knew that their daughter had stayed in Paris but had no idea where she was living.

Bernard arrived home two days after this piece of news to find his parents worn out by anxiety. His mother, thinner and looking years older than she had looked on that day in Nantes, hugged him at the door of the flat.

"Thank God you've come home, Bernard. We don't know what to do for the best."

His father hugged him too, which Bernard didn't think he'd done since he was about ten years old.

They talked until late that evening, his parents clearly repeating things they had already said over and over again to each other. His father thought that they should report Joséphine's disappearance to the police, to Interpol, to the foreign ministry. His mother, who surprised Bernard by having more of a sense than his father of how news speeds round the internet, thought that this would be a bad mistake: "We don't want to frighten her. We don't want her to think we're so angry with her because of the wretched *bac* that we would even ask the police to find her. That would be most likely to push her into doing something really silly. We don't want her to feel she can't face coming home or even making contact. What do you think, Bernard?"

"But she may be in real danger, don't you see?" This was his father. "If one idiot of a girl can change her name and say she's a Muslim—I remember Colette Khider. She's Moroccan, but her parents are no more Muslim than you are—so can Joséphine. She's got no common sense, we know that. Suppose she's been looking at this dreadful propaganda we're told is on the internet: thugs in black hoods waving severed heads for the Caliphate, heaven on earth, the will of God written in blood. We can all see that it's terrifying, wicked nonsense, but what's Joséphine got in her head to counter it with? We know she thinks her years of education a waste of time—"

His father, who had clearly been thinking and saying all this to himself and to his mother for days and days, broke off and put his head between his hands.

What indeed, Bernard thought, has Joséphine got in her head? But he also thought, and of course didn't say, that young people much more intelligent and much more serious than Joséphine weren't being given, by the kind of education his father had devoted his life to, anything with which to counter the enthusiasm, the fanaticism, of what presented itself as an all-justifying religious cause.

"No.", Bernard said, however. "Joséphine's pretty selfish. I don't think she's likely to be carried away by anything to do with religion."

"Jean-Claude", his mother said. "Listen to Bernard. You mustn't think the very worst. It'll drive you mad. Joséphine's a silly girl, that's all. There are lots of silly girls of her age. There always have been. She's vanished, just for now, because she knows how angry you'll be about her *bac*. She's not interested in anything to do with religion. She knows nothing about it—"

Bernard interrupted. "I'm sure you're right, maman. If she were a different kind of girl, if there were an empty space in her head, waiting for—well, inspiration, an ideal of some kind, it might be filled by a belief that God wants her to do something extraordinary. But that's not what she's like. She never has been, never will be."

"That must be right, Jean-Claude. This is Joséphine we're talking about. Think of her clothes, the music she likes, the money she wastes on all sorts of rubbish, a new bag, a new cushion for her room, a new hairdo, just because some friend has got one and it's what she calls trendy. And I thought travelling in Europe, after her *bac* of course, would settle her down, show her things she'd never see in the middle of Paris, how people have to live in poorer countries than France—And now, where is she? What's she doing?"

"Do you realize, Bernard", his father said. "that the Interrail ticket can take you to Turkey? How do we know she's not trying to get into Syria, trying to reach the Islamic State, trying to offer herself as some kind of sacrifice to these monsters in black hoods? She's probably changed her name to Fatima. Joséphine as a hero's wife, a jihadi bride. Can't you easily imagine it?"

"No. I can't. And you mustn't either. She hasn't been in touch and has switched off her phone because she doesn't want to have you, papa, giving her a lecture about her *bac*, wherever she is. But Joséphine's no jihadi bride. She's not brave enough, for one thing. For another, she's much too keen on having a good time. I bet you anything you like she's on a beach in Greece or somewhere, lying in the sun and enjoying herself."

He was saying all this to reassure his parents. He profoundly hoped it was true.

He said, "How much money has she got?"

His mother, looking grateful for an ordinary question, said, "We bought her Interrail ticket but we hadn't yet given her the money we promised her for the summer. Unfortunately your grandparents gave her a thousand euros, far too much I thought, for her eighteenth birthday, so she's got that. Of course we told her to put it in the bank, in a savings account, but—"

They hadn't given Bernard any money, for his eighteenth birthday or ever.

"Well, there you are", he said. "You must try to stop worrying. She'll be fine for a while. And stop thinking of the terrifying things she might be doing. Imagine it's twenty years ago. Before mobile phones and the internet. People's children went travelling for months, to the Far East, South America, really dangerous places, and no one knew where they were. No news is good news. If she hits problems, or more likely when she's running out of money, she'll be in touch. You'll see."

"O Bernard", his mother said. "You are a comfort. Thank goodness you've come home. Don't you think he's probably right, Jean-Claude?"

"Well, he could be, of course. Let's hope so. If you won't let me go to the police, and you may have a point about frightening her unnecessarily, hoping for the best is all we can do in any case."

Bernard had come home on Monday evening, the sixth of July. The next morning he wrote to his grandfather, "Monsieur Thamar" he put on the envelope, saying he would arrive in the village on Friday afternoon. His parents were going to Rouen for their usual holiday after the weekend and, although they calmed down considerably after that first evening, he felt that a few more days of their fretful company were going to be as much as he could cope with. His mother wanted him to go to Rouen with them—" just for a day or two, Bernard, to have you with us"—but when he said he had promised to be in Burgundy as soon as possible, she said, "Of course. I do understand. And you mustn't let Joséphine spoil your summer as well as ours."

"You know, maman, you needn't say anything about the *bac* in Rouen. Just say Joséphine is travelling in Europe with a friend. That'll be good for both of you. And try to relax a bit. Get papa to take you to the seaside. Or maybe to that abbey by the Seine. Do you remember? Such a beautiful, peaceful place."

"That's a very good idea. Yes, I will. It would be lovely to go there again. Jumièges. I'm so glad you haven't forgotten it. You were only about seven."

Then she kissed him.

"Thank you, Bernard. You've been a real help, these last few days."

She added, "You know, there's one strange coincidence in all this. Joséphine telephoned from Vienna. None of us has ever been there. But one of the things Monsieur Thomas—it's no good, I can't get used to calling him my father—told me was that his father was a Polish Jew who came to Paris from Vienna. Did he tell you that?"

"No. But it explains one thing he did say, about being half Jewish. What happened to his father?"

"The Nazis killed him, almost certainly. But he couldn't find out because he never knew his name."

Both of them were silent for a moment. Then Bernard said, "We are a mixture, aren't we? That's meant to be a very good thing, for brains and so on."

They both laughed.

"Better not mention your Jewish grandfather in Rouen."

"Bernard, I'm not a fool. I don't think we need tell them anything about Monsieur Thomas, and papa agrees. We'll say you have a summer job in Burgundy as secretary to an elderly writer."

"Perfect. And true, which is always good."

So he left Paris on the tenth of July, with, in his rucksack, his laptop, a few clothes, a spare pair of trainers, a second-hand copy of Saint Augustine's *Confessions* which he'd bought in the Boulevard Saint-Michel, and a Michelin map of southern Burgundy.

Chapter 3

Bernard

September 2015

"Thamar", Bernard had said that morning after breakfast, always eaten in silence while the old man read the newspaper, "We need to have a talk."

"By all means."

It was 25 September, late afternoon, a low sun, the air soft, and quivering here and there with clouds of tiny insects. Bernard was sitting in the summer house, on the chair facing the path through the apple trees, the fruit not yet ready to fall. He was waiting for his grandfather to join him. He had put the other chair at one side of his table, so that Thamar would be sitting with the sound side of his face at a right angle to him, which, even after all these weeks, Bernard knew he preferred.

As the old man was leaving for his work in the garden of the château, Bernard had asked him to come to the summer house when he got back in the afternoon. He hadn't done this before.

It hadn't taken him long to fit his days into his grandfather's orderly routine. He very much liked its predictability, even before he was given an explanation for it.

Thamar—on Bernard's second day, his grandfather had said, "Call me Thamar. I would like it. It's just a name, not so old as 'grandfather', and at the same time for me much older"—walked to the village early, to collect bread, yesterday's *Le Monde*, and the local paper, *Le Journal de Saône-et-Loire*. After a couple of weeks, Bernard had offered to go himself for the bread and the papers.

"No, Bernard. Thank you. It's a habit. Habits are good because they limit decision. The clothes that a monk or a nun

147

wears are called habits: did you know that?"

He shook his head.

"So they don't have to decide each morning how to dress, what to choose to put on. No decision necessary. Restful, you see? Every day, in unimportant respects, the same. This is good."

Bernard had nodded, and then laughed.

"Is that funny?"

"No. Not at all. I was laughing at a coincidence. Before I left Paris I bought myself three plain white T-shirts. I thought you might think ordinary student T-shirts with silly pictures and slogans—well—"

"I might think them what?"

"I don't know. Noisy, perhaps?"

"A good word for them, though I'm quite accustomed to seeing them on the lads in the village. But yes, it's quiet in my house. Quiet, thank God, in my life. You noticed when you visited me in the spring. Of course. So that's why you look the same every day? As I do."

Black shirt, dusty black trousers, old working boots, old-fashioned faded blue overalls for gardening. Always a hat. Bernard himself every day wore a white T-shirt, one or the other pair of faded blue jeans, one or the other pair of more or less worn trainers. There hadn't yet been a day when it was cold enough for a pullover, though lately he had put one on in the evening.

His grandfather had added, "Not entirely a coincidence, I would say." Bernard, remembering this later, was pleased.

Every weekday, after breakfast—new bread, no butter, no jam, Thamar's very good coffee—the old man set off up the road to the château, Félix at his heels, and Bernard sat down in the summer house to work, taking with him the next sheaf of paper from the pile on his table in his great-great-grandmother's dining room. Although she had died many years before he was born, and other people had lived in the house after her death, he felt her presence often. A good Catholic lady born in the nineteenth century, in so many ways beyond his experience, but here, definitely still here. A demanding presence. It occurred to Bernard that Thamar had never had a telephone or a television at least partly because he wanted the house to be as it was in his childhood, his grandmother's house.

Bernard now knew that a deeper reason for his grandfather's eccentric resistance to the ordinary world in which everyone else lived was to do with a silence he had once known, in the desert, and had loved. "Did she have a radio, your grandmother?" Bernard had asked him. "Yes, of course. In the war everyone did. Finding the BBC was important. Forbidden, but important. Later, she listened to the news, but little else. I prefer *Le Monde* because it's quieter." Thamar probably had no idea that there were now smartphones in the Sahara, if, indeed, he knew what a smartphone was. Almost everything he had read in *Le Monde* about the internet was negative: social media, pornography, gambling, jihadi propaganda. "Are you happy in this unreal world they call cyberspace, Bernard, and with all this talking and sending messages—what's the word? Connectivity, that's it—I see even here in the village?"

Bernard thought of his abandoned blog, but said, "I'm not. I like your silence better. I don't know why. Everyone I know does social media but it seems to me to waste a lot of time, and a great deal of it is just what you'd call noise. I don't see the point of telling loads of people I don't know stuff about me that's private. And mostly very dull."

Thamar laughed. "So you do know why. And your reasons are good ones."

The summer days were usually sunny, sometimes very hot. Rainy days were not a disappointment: the summer house roof was sound and Bernard liked listening to the tapping of the rain over his head, watching the grateful garden receive water and life.

He worked, or more or less worked, wasting some time watching and listening to the changing garden, every weekday, all morning and most of the afternoon. When it was too hot to work after lunch (bread and cheese or an egg, and fruit, which he ate alone on the terrace) he took an hour off and went to sleep in his bedroom where, if he had left the shutters closed, it was always cool enough to sleep. His room was low-ceilinged, square, not large but with plenty of space because it had in it only a narrow bed, old, heavy and comfortable, a low cupboard, also old and heavy, with two drawers at the bottom for his clothes, one chair with a rush seat, and a table not much bigger than his rickety table in Nantes but solid, steady, and with a pretty embroidered linen cloth, the colour of cream with flowers and leaves in a border pattern of little crosses, which he could see Thamar had washed and ironed for him before he arrived. The walls were powdery white, the ceiling all wood, with big, almost black, beams showing the knots of the trees from which they had been sawn, and dark-stained planks above them.

On Saturdays and Sundays he obeyed Thamar's instructions to stop work altogether and go for a walk or set off on his borrowed bicycle to explore the countryside for himself. On Sunday mornings, because Thamar always went to Mass, some Sundays setting out very early because he had a long way to walk, Bernard stayed in bed until he had gone and then enjoyed, alone, the coffee the old man had left for him. Mass: Bernard could think only of Marie in the cathedral in Nantes and how happy it had made her and how, for him, it was only a man strangely dressed and far away doing and saying things he didn't understand but knew were very ancient. No doubt it was different, perhaps easier to understand, in a small village church, but he wasn't sure. One day, perhaps, he might ask Thamar if he could go to Mass with him. Not yet.

It had taken him almost five weeks to read and make notes on the nearly four hundred pages he had been presented with on his first morning. His notes, he realized when he looked back over them, were no less confused than the manuscript his grandfather had given him.

It was impossible to tell whether Thamar had numbered the pages in the order in which he had written them. Whether or not he had, the story they told was far from easy to deduce. The old man had thought and written in bursts, quickly for a few paragraphs, occasionally for a few pages, and then stopped, not at the end of a section of his story, not even at the end of a passage of reflection or thought, but just stopped, sometimes in mid-sentence, as if in revulsion, or perhaps irritation that what he was trying to say had not been said, had turned out to be too difficult to say. Or perhaps too humiliating. Or perhaps too proud. Bernard was not only getting to know his grandfather's story; he was beginning to get to know his grandfather, which was altogether more complicated. Was understanding this anguished old man, who had tried to think so deeply about himself and yet thought so little of himself, thought himself so insignificant and yet thought his story deserved to be told, always going to be too difficult for Bernard, not only because of the difference in their ages, but because Bernard knew almost nothing about the questions that had troubled Thamar all his life? He found he was asking himself this several times a day.

He had tried various ways of making some sense of the manuscript.

His first idea had been to type the whole thing. For a few days—he couldn't now remember how many—he had typed as he read, starting on page one, putting the text paragraph by paragraph into his laptop. Once this was done, he then thought, he could print out the whole book and go through the typescript with a pen, numbering sections, deciding as he went how to cut and paste pieces of writing until the story became clear and the reflective digressions were fitted into appropriate places. He had asked Thamar to find out whether the office of the nursing home in the château had a printer that the secretary would allow him to use. It did and she would. He told his grandfather that they would have to pay for the ink as well as the paper. "Ink is very expensive. More expensive, if you print a lot, than the machine." "Really? How strange the modern world is."

But when he saw that this wasn't a sensible plan, that the typing of the whole thing would be a waste of time because so much work needed doing on the structure of the book before he could begin to battle with the location of particular passages, he deleted what he had already typed, abandoned his laptop on his bedroom table (plugged in so that he could keep it charged for an occasional visit to the café in the village to email his mother), and just took some pages of his grandfather's neat but chaotic manuscript every day to the summer house.

He had made a chart, a map of the book, on two large sheets of plain paper stuck together with tape, with vertical columns for years and horizontal lines for places. On this plan, as he read, he tried to put dates, places and people in the right relationships to each other. He had begun the chart using one of his usual fine-pointed black felt-tip pens—he had brought half a dozen with him from Paris—but had soon made such a mess of the chart that he had to start all over again with fresh paper and the pencils and rubber that he'd found in the village shop.

Evident here and there in the four hundred pages was a story. There had to be a story: here was a man, nearly seventy-five years old, who in his long life had done and suffered much. Wouldn't this be true, Bernard thought, when he sat back and looked at his plan, towards the end of the process he had embarked on, of any Frenchman born in 1940 and still alive in 2015? But no life was the same as any other. The particular circumstances, particular people, particular ways in which events designed, decided on or blundered into, far away in Paris or London or Washington and inflicted on mere people across the continents, hit, or warped, or transformed, the life of a person whose name was unknown in any capital city: all this combined to push and pull the unique life of one person in this direction or that. Or Rome, he thought as he learned more about the long central period of Thamar's life, the part of his story he understood least.

And then there was the person inside all this, the person himself who suffered what was done to him and did what he could, well or badly, with what he was given to cope with. Bernard's Latin teacher in the *lycée* had said, "*Ago* and *patior*: I do and I suffer. Active and passive, words from those very words, you see, a distinction at the root of grammar, at the root of everything. Don't forget it."

And the result of it all, the suffering and the action, the doing and the—what? allowing? bearing? submitting to? the things that other people did—was one old man, different from every single other person there had ever been. He was, he is,

Bernard thought, his story, the story that he has tried to tell in the fragments that are, at present, what there is of his book. And the story that is also in him, untold, much of it no doubt forgotten as much of everyone's story is.

Memory: what is it? Why is it so patchy? What would be left of a person without it? Where are the moments, the hours, the months and years, we have lived through and forgotten? Memory was something he had been interested in all his life. He remembered—there, how strange—as a small boy thinking "this is happening now, and now now has gone, and will I remember this tomorrow? Probably I won't. Next year? Certainly not." So thinking about memory was always mixed up with thinking about time, and there were no conclusions to be reached about either.

As for Thamar's memory, Bernard knew, from their few long conversations, that Thamar's ability to remember things he had read and learned was deep and impressive. But what about his memory of things he had lived through, noticed, said, thought? Wasn't an old man's memory of his own life, so full of years and days and moments, bound to be shaky, and also coloured, bent even, by how he wanted things to look, to possible readers as well as to himself, now that he was trying to write about them? Bernard, having read hundreds of his pages, had no doubt that Thamar was attempting to recall times and places and people exactly and to write down what was true. But how difficult it must have been for him, to choose what to describe, to fix in words something as it had really been, before he forgot, before he died. And could an account be true even if it weren't exactly accurate?

Might he die soon? Bernard's mother had told him that Thamar had said something to her about his death, but Bernard couldn't remember exactly what. He seemed strong, and well for his age. He was lean and wiry. He never went to sleep in an armchair as many old men do, and his life, moderate, calm, with its measured hours of exercise, fresh air, simple food, one glass of wine each evening, was as healthy as a life could be. Hadn't Bernard's mother said that Thamar was not afraid of dying but was afraid he might die before the book was finished? The implication was that before the day he met her he had thought that his life was already finished, that the world outside his house, his garden, the garden of the château, could no longer reach him, could never again unsettle the peace he had constructed for himself, of himself. And the book, all he wished to leave on the earth at his death, would make sense of everything that had contributed to the construction of his peace. That was it, wasn't it? That was what he had become accustomed to think, in his orderly days, before he knew that he had a daughter, before his daughter was suddenly there, in his garden, in his life. And not only a daughter but now a grandson, sharing his life, his house, his days, sharing in the perhaps unrealizable project that was his book.

Recently Bernard had begun to wonder whether now, after what had happened to Thamar in the summer, the result, which he had never imagined, of something Jacques Thomas had done more than fifty years earlier—the doing so long ago, the suffering now, the suffering then also, Bernard was discovering—it was possible that he had ceased to mind whether or not the book was finished, before his death, or ever.

If that were so, what was he, Bernard, doing here, his own life stalled, North Africa unvisited, its refugees unhelped by him, and his career unfurthered, however much this pleased him because it displeased his father? Well: he was keeping an old man company in a few late months of his life. Good. But he was also working on the book for its own sake, because the story engaged him at levels of his own self he hardly knew existed, and would have engaged him even if the life at its centre had not been his grandfather's life. And that was better than good.

Most of the time, in any case, Bernard didn't believe that the reason for Thamar's silence on the subject of his book wasn't that he didn't any longer care about it. Wasn't it more likely, given what Bernard was learning of his character, that he cared too much, because he was afraid of the answers, to ask the questions Bernard was expecting every day. Was Bernard finding the story interesting? Had he any idea whether someone else, a stranger who came upon it in a bookshop for example, would find it interesting? What did Bernard think of the writing, any of it, all of it? How had he decided to deal with the task he had been given? Bernard much admired his grandfather's restraint in not asking him anything at all about the book.

But Bernard needed to talk to him. The more he worked at the manuscript, the more often he was able to add a name or a date to his plan, sometimes with certainty, usually only as a fair guess, the more daunted he was by the scale of the task he had taken on, and the more radical he thought any solution to its problems had to be.

For instance, thinking, as he had to every day, about Thamar's memory, he was increasingly struck by the difference between memory and understanding. A memory can be shaded, no doubt sometimes distorted, by an interpretation put on it at some point between whatever it was that happened and the present; this point might itself be long ago. The interpretation might have blocked real understanding of that event, that person, that conversation, for years. As Bernard became familiar with a number of things in Thamar's story that obviously held much significance for him, he wondered how well Thamar himself had understood them. Had the very process of writing been part of a movement forward from interpretation to understanding?

Bernard found himself becoming less and less confident about what he was trying to do, more and more uncertain about what his grandfather wanted or hoped he might be able to do. On many days he put down his pencils and rubber, and the pen with which he was making, on a thick student notepad, the notes of his own that he was almost sure increased in quantity as they decreased in usefulness, folded up his plan, took it and the day's pages and his notepad back to the dining room, and walked for ten minutes in the golden light of the September evening up to the château gates and back, almost despairing of anyone, least of all himself, being able to turn all this into a book.

Sometimes he met Thamar and Félix on their way back from the château. "All right, Bernard?" his grandfather would say. "Fine, thank you." That was all. And that was true. Although he had no idea how he was going to deal with the difficulties of the job he had undertaken, and hoped his grandfather didn't think he meant that his work on the book was going well, he loved these peaceful days. He wasn't sure why. Part of the reason, no doubt, was that the time he was spending with his grandfather was limited—Paris, and proper work of some kind, and everyday life would at some not too distant moment reclaim him—and so these weeks, as summer turned towards autumn, were to be consciously tasted and appreciated, like a rare fruit. In any case, he was contented here, as perhaps he had never been before.

In the background of his quiet days there was the continuing question, so painful for his parents, of what had happened to Joséphine. Where was she? Who was with her? Why didn't she get in touch, if only to say that she was safe? Connectivity, he thought: as easy for Joséphine to break as it was for his grandfather to ignore, but in her case the break must have been a deliberate, unkind, actually cruel decision. No doubt she had made the decision, and kept it up this long, because she was furious with her parents—for what? Not just for wanting her to pass her *bac*, but, he felt sure, for much more, however unreasonably—and also felt guilty about hurting them. No doubt she wasn't distinguishing between the fury and the guilt. And the longer she persisted in failing to contact them, the harder it would be for her to face their father's voice on the telephone, their mother's tears. But where was she? What was she doing? Did she have any money left?

Part of Bernard's contentment, and he was sometimes ashamed of this, was the distance he had been lucky enough to be able to put between himself and the whole question of Joséphine. Days passed when he didn't think of her even for a moment. Did he actually care about her, or only about the effect her disappearance was having? The question worried him, but not much. When he did remember her, he was more angry than worried. How could she do this to their parents? Thoughtless, selfish, lacking in imagination: she clearly hadn't stopped to think of the anxiety she was causing. If she had bothered to imagine it, she had decided not to care about it. To hell with her, Bernard thought. And was then more ashamed, remembering the funny little sister he had helped to look after all through their childhood.

Every few days, considerably more often than he had in Nantes, he emailed his mother, answering her answer to his last message. Nothing from Joséphine, she always said. Joséphine's mobile phone had for weeks responded only with an 'out of service' whine, and there was no other way of trying to find her, short of asking the police for help, which they had decided not to do. From the little his mother told him, Bernard gathered that his parents, once they were back in Paris after their visit to Rouen and a short, rainy holiday on the Normandy coast, had become almost accustomed to the worry about Joséphine and her silence. His father's rage had settled into what Bernard could well imagine was actually resentful resignation, though his mother had said, "I know papa feels guilty about her, which he has no need to, but I think that's why he can't talk about her". She herself, probably every day, was clearly making an effort to believe that Joséphine was too frivolous and not brave enough to do anything actually dangerous.

Now that his parents had been back at work for three weeks, perhaps the anxiety was at least a little less sharp. As he had said two or three times in his emails, if anything very bad had happened to Joséphine, they would have been told: she wouldn't be able to manage anywhere without her passport. Meanwhile, he knew it was a comfort for his mother to hear that he was safe and happy working on Thamar's book. She asked after the old man in every message. "How is your grandfather?" or "How is Monsieur Thomas?", never "How is my father?" And he answered, more or less, "Thamar is very well. I think he likes having me here." She didn't ask, and he didn't say anything, about the book.

And, so far, after all this time, Bernard had respected Thamar's silence about the book and held back from asking for his help.

As he waited, patiently because he knew it was early to expect the old man back from the château, he looked again at his plan, full of dates and places and names. He knew all this, about him; but did he really know him, himself, any better than he had known him when he left him on that day in May, which seemed long, long ago, that day when the apple blossom was beginning to fall? He looked out at the ripening fruit. But what he had learned then had been no more than a first impression. And the student he was in the spring, with his exams ahead of him and Marie to lose into her own life, seemed to him someone he scarcely remembered being, not four and a half months but several years younger than he now felt. Nothing, especially not Thamar, was as simple as it had then appeared to be.

For weeks they had been living in the same house, meeting every day for breakfast and for supper, spending each evening together in Thamar's winter room, where there were now a second comfortable chair and a second lamp, on a little table, for him to read by: all three had been brought downstairs by Bernard, obeying his grandfather's instructions, from the third, now unused, bedroom. They had talked about all sorts of things, or rather Thamar had talked and Bernard had listened, and he had learned a lot. But it was difficult to connect this old man who knew so much and was now so calm with the anguished man who had written the hundreds of pages of his book. Where, now, was the muddled boy on the Left Bank? The soldier? The lover? The priest? After spending the day trying fruitlessly, as he went backwards and forwards through the manuscript pages, to find some kind of an answer to one or another of these questions, Bernard would look across the empty hearth where a fire would burn when the weather got colder. There was his grandfather, concentration on his misshapen face as he read, holding his book further and further away as he peered through his spectacles. Impossible to ask him.

Bernard had recently understood that one way in which his grandfather was preparing him to approach the question of the book was by means of improving his education. Alone in the summer house, he smiled as he thought again about this. Two kinds of education were afoot, and he was enjoying them both.

First, the bicycle and the country roads of Burgundy. Bernard and Thamar would look at Bernard's map together before he set off on a Saturday morning. Thamar would suggest a destination, a route, a deviation to see something that might or might not still look the same as he remembered it from fifty years, seventy years ago. "Since I came back I have travelled no further than I can walk." (When did he "come back" as he quite often said? So far the manuscript hadn't given Bernard this obviously important piece of information. No date for his chart.) "So things may have changed. For the worse, very likely. If they have, I don't think I want you to tell me." Another time, after they had planned a long day's ride with, as Bernard's destination, a village that had a ruined castle and an ancient church, the old man said: "I want to hear what has moved you. Only the good news, you understand?" That day Bernard had come back tired, having cycled for miles, and said, "I'm afraid I didn't make it as far as Brancion. It was hot and the forest on the way was so beautiful. I got a bit lost, ate my picnic and went to sleep." "Quite right. Never mind. Another day. You will find it more itself, in any case, after the holidays."

Three weeks ago Thamar had said, "Now that the children have gone back to school and the Parisians and the foreigners have gone back to Paris and whatever countries they belong to, it's time for you to bicycle to the great places of this part of Burgundy. I didn't want you to see them when they were full of families with bored children wanting ice-creams, and even fuller of tourists with cameras, more interested in the photographs they would take than the place they had perhaps gone to much trouble and spent a lot of money to come to. I know about these tourists—what an ugly word, by the way—because the *Journal* is always telling me about them. Not that it can make up its mind whether it loves them, for the money they bring, or hates them for filling the quiet places with crowds and noise. But now they will have gone, the crowds and the noise, and you must set off to Brancion—better luck next time—and to Cluny and Tournus and beautiful Chapaize, to see the marvels of my youth."

This was the point of course, though it had taken Bernard a week or two to see it: Thamar wanted him to learn more about him by looking, with eyes he hoped were not too different from his own, at the trees, the vineyards, the cattle, the stone, the glass, the colours of buildings and woods and fields, that had filled his sight, his imagination, his soul, when he was growing up. So Bernard pedalled up and down hills, as instructed, stopping when he got lost to have a drink of water and to look at his map, folded in the back pocket of his jeans. He took with him, in the basket attached to the handlebars with worn leather straps—this was an ancient bicycle—some bread and cheese, a tomato or a couple of plums or, when he saw them in the market in Saint-Christophe, some cherries. Two or three times, he bought himself a chunk of sausage for a treat. Thamar never ate meat, though every couple of days, on his early morning expedition to the village, he collected from the butcher a parcel of nameless bits of animals which he then boiled for Félix. Enough to put anyone off meat, Bernard thought.

The beginning of his education in Thamar's childhood was learning to enjoy the empty lanes, the deep summer grass of the verges beginning to yellow in August, the tall flowers whose names he didn't know now going to seed. He loved the family parties of white cows and their calves, gathered under trees for shade. He loved the woods. He didn't know the names of the trees either, but he soon found that if he pushed his bike along a stony forester's track until he had left even the lane out of sight and out of hearing he could find such quiet, such sun-littered dark, in the deep woods, that he could sit for an hour or two, listening and looking, happier, he thought, than he had ever been. He loved to sit very still, listening to the small sounds of the woods, the rustles of creatures he couldn't identify moving among fallen leaves, a twig cracking for no reason that he could see. The birds were mostly quiet. He knew, even though he had grown up in Paris, that birds don't sing, except for an odd squawk of alarm, in the late summer, but often he heard the guttural exchanges of wood pigeons, soft pinkish-grey birds when settled on a branch, neat and plump compared to the scruffy pigeons of Paris, and watched them flying, white-collared, black-streaked, silvery wing-beats accurate through the trees.

Twice he had seen deer. One afternoon two does and a fawn—he had to find out later from Thamar the proper terms for them—crossed the path ahead of him, from shade to speckled sunlight to shade. He must have moved his head when he saw them: they bounded away into the trees with surprisingly little sound. Another time, sitting on a hot afternoon with his eyes closed and his back to a tree in a clearing, he felt he was being watched. He opened his eyes. A stag, pale-coloured against the wood behind him, his head up, his antlers poised, was standing, looking at him from the other side of the clearing. Neither of them moved. After a minute or two the stag, unhurried, unalarmed, walked into the thickness of the forest, again with scarcely a sound, and vanished.

The commanding beauty of the stag made Bernard miss Marie, acutely, as he had found he seldom did in his so different life in Thamar's house. Marie would have loved the storybook elegance of the creature from a medieval tapestry, heraldic with his antlers, exotic, almost white as a unicorn. She would probably have worried about the stag being shot by a hunter. Bernard had no idea whether deer were hunted in these woods. He had seen no one with a gun, but once or twice had heard, from far away, what he thought must be a shot, or several shots. Then he laughed, all alone in the wood: Marie would have been worrying not about a gun but about a tapestry huntsman aiming a crossbow, in his belt a dagger with a jewelled handle, riding a horse caparisoned in scarlet and gold.

He had loved her. Or he supposed he had. Enough, anyway, not to press her to sleep with him. He was glad about that. Even dreams of sleeping with her, which he had had several times in his old-fashioned bed in Thamar's house, had left him, calm in the morning, pleased rather than sorry that it hadn't actually happened. Saying goodbye to her after their last lunch in Nantes had been sad, with a sweet kind of sadness: he expected then to miss her more painfully and more often than had turned out to be the case. It didn't seem fair to her to think that she had been for him only a part, even if the best part, of student life, of leaving the library or his desk or some demanding class, and being delighted to take her dancing, to laugh into her eyes over coffee or coca cola or a plate of sliced sausage and salad. But that seemed to be how it was. That life, all of it, was over, and he was glad to feel now that he had outgrown it, was too old for it. In any case, he couldn't have brought Marie with him to Thamar's house, even if she hadn't been going home to Guadeloupe for the summer: the very idea made him smile. Masculine arrangements for everything, for having a bath, for shaving, for washing his T-shirts and under-wear: all were simple and easy for him. But it was impossible to imagine Marie in that house. Even if the rhythm of the days had been less austere, even if Bernard himself had been less busy with the book, it would have been too quiet for her: she had told him once that she couldn't work without music to keep her going. He had never been able to work or even read a book except in a surrounding silence, one reason, after three years of student life, for enjoying the peace, which he felt as a kind of intentness, of Thamar's house. But he would have liked to have had Marie beside him when he saw the stag.

In one high patch of grass, nettles and brambles in the woods, which he reached after pushing his bike uphill for more than half an hour through thick trees on an almost completely overgrown path, he came upon a kind of hut, built of the rough, dark stone of the village houses, not ruined but with an open doorway, no door, two windows with no glass, a black interior. The place terrified him. He had no idea why. He stood for a moment, knowing he was too frightened to look inside the hut, turned his bike and pushed it through the trees as quickly as he could, back to the road a kilometre away. That evening he showed Thamar on the map more or less where he must have been, though he wasn't sure of the direction he had taken once he had left the road.

"Ah. I think I know the place. Once upon a time a wood-man probably lived there, or, more likely, a charcoal-burner. It must have been empty for years, or used for keeping foresters' tools and traps out of the weather. Towards the end of the

Occupation, when the Resistance was getting more organized and more effective. a group of fighters used it for storing guns, ammunition, explosives. It's remote, in that wood, and high up, but it's not far from the railway. Look." A finger on the map. "They were betrayed. Four of them, meeting there one night, walked straight into the Gestapo waiting for them. They weren't heard of again. Tortured for names, no doubt, and then shot. Nobody managed to blow up the railway. The Germans went on using it to the very end."

"But who would have betrayed them? Someone with a grudge? Someone working for the Germans?"

From passages about the Occupation in Thamar's manuscript, he knew that there had been other betrayals, other arrests and disappearances not even yet forgotten among villagers of Thamar's age and older. Jamila, shocked that a piece of treachery more than seventy years ago should still be held against the kind and friendly Pierre Chaumont, born long after the war, had told Bernard the story of the Café de la Paix. In the café to use his laptop, he had met Monsieur Chaumont several times as he ordered a coffee or a coca cola and a hard-boiled egg. "You're the young man staying with Monsieur Thamar?", Monsieur Chaumont had said, the first time. "That's right." "Very quiet, it must be." "Yes. It's quiet, but I like it." "Very good." Madame Chaumont, looking at him carefully across the bar, had said, "You're Madame Charpentier's son, aren't you? The student she's so proud of." "Well, yes, I am." "And Monsieur Thamar was the old man she was looking for?" "He was, yes." "That's excellent."

"Who knows?", Thamar said. "The times were very bad. They may have been Communists, the plotters. There were other people in the Resistance who thought all Communists were foreigners, traitors, Jews. Better got rid of. Particularly towards the end of the war, when it looked as if, once the Germans had gone, France might have a Communist revolution, or at least a Communist government. People have forgotten all this. People were intended to forget it. We were all brought up on the idea that the Resistance was united behind General de Gaulle and the Free French, and between them they defeated the Germans, with hardly any help from England and America. All nonsense, of course. But I remember, from my earliest childhood, and from what my nursemaid told me: she was here every day, looking after me, till her husband came back from being a prisoner of war, and then I used to go to her house for years, for treats my grandmother didn't allow. She told me that it was a competition, the Resistance. Different groups hated each other. They stole each other's guns. Sometimes, yes, they betrayed each other to the Gestapo, so that their group would be the heroes at the end. The Communist Party had to patch things up with de Gaulle for a bit, after the liberation, but only because Stalin ordered them to. It was impossible to tell what side a man was on: there were too many sides. Those were indeed very bad times. In a peaceful region of France, like this one, probably the worst times." He paused before adding, "Later, other things were as bad, in fact much worse, but they were too far away for people to know about them."

Bernard shivered, remembering the stone hut with its sinister door, its sinister windows. Then he said, "But surely you don't think a horrible event like that, the Gestapo waiting for them in the hut, can leave a mark on a place, some kind of shadow, almost like a ghost, that someone who knows nothing at all about the story can years later pick up in some way?"

"Of course. You did. Why not?"

"Because it doesn't make sense. There can't be any kind of rational explanation for such a thing, any scientific basis for—"

He stopped, seeing the expression on Thamar's face.

"No", the old man said.

And that was the end of the conversation.

Exploring the country of Thamar's childhood was one element in his education. The other was reading.

They had had a long talk, about books and other things, one warm evening after supper, when he hadn't been in the house more than a few days.

His grandfather was delighted that he had brought with him from Paris a copy of St Augustine's *Confessions*.

"You remembered. Good. Have you begun to read it?"

"I'm afraid not."

"Also good. I should like you to read it here. Perhaps in the evening, after supper. I read every evening, myself, for an hour or two. I have set myself to read St Thomas Aquinas, the *Summa Theologiae*. For two years, perhaps three—except in the garden, I hardly notice time passing—I've been reading this book. It's a very, very large book, in many volumes if you have the French translation alongside the Latin. My Latin isn't what it was, or, more exactly", he smiled, "what it was supposed to be. A volume comes from the library in Lyon. I read it, make some notes, send it back. Another volume comes. Why do I spend so much time on this one book?" He smiled again, briefly, as he often did. "I don't know. Have you heard of it? Have you heard of Thomas Aquinas?"

Bernard shook his head. They were sitting on the terrace at the table on which they had had supper. Small cups of coffee. The evening was absolutely still. Thamar liked Bernard to sit looking down through the apple trees towards the summer house. He himself sat, as usual, to one side of the table, at a right angle to Bernard, to hide the damaged side of his face. Bernard couldn't now remember how soon this conversation had taken place, but it was certainly very early in his stay, when Thamar was still fitting him into the rhythm of his own days.

"Of course you haven't. Thomas Aquinas, *doctor angelicus*. The greatest of all the teachers of the Church. Once upon a time I had to memorize summaries of his teaching, of his arguments for this and against that. You will find out why I had to do this when you read my book. It was terrible. I understood almost nothing and could see no reason for trying to understand, let alone trying to remember what he was saying."

"When did he live, St Thomas Aquinas?"

"The thirteenth century. Nine hundred years after Augustine. That might sound as if Aquinas were bound to be more modern than Augustine, more like our contemporary. But, strange to say, the opposite is the case. Augustine, as you will discover, might have been writing now; Aquinas most certainly not. This isn't merely because of temperamental differences between two men, though these are great. It's because the world now, our world, is in many ways like Augustine's world and is not at all like Aquinas's world."

"I don't understand, I'm afraid. We learned some classical history at school, but more about the Greeks than the Romans. I don't know anything about the Roman empire as late as when St Augustine was alive. And what I remember about the Middle Ages was mostly to do with wars, wars between the empire and the papacy, the crusades, wars between France and England, Joan of Arc, the wars of religion. Nothing to choose between them, Crusaders and infidels, Catholics and Huguenots, my father says. Cruelty driven by religion. Abolish religion and you will stop the cruelty. That's what he says about the world now. President Bush's crusade. ISIS. The second the consequence of the first. And the boys in the *banlieues* with nothing better to do deciding to be murderers. *Charlie Hebdo.* All because of religion."

As he said this he thought of Joséphine and winced. Thamar didn't notice. Bernard pushed the thought away. Not religion. Not Joséphine. The combination was impossible.

"From what you and your mother have told me about your father", Thamar said. "I'm not surprised that he should think in that way. For two and a half centuries many many Frenchmen have taken that view. And I would agree with him that nothing was stupider than President Bush talking about a Crusade. Except President Bush invading Iraq in pursuit of his Crusade. Alas. Iraq now, you know, is more murderous and full of hatred by far than it was then. It's no good removing a dictator, however monstrous, when you have no idea what to put in his place. Poor Libya, just as bad."

He drank his coffee, put his cup back on its saucer, and went on, "But in general it hasn't turned out to be the case, has it? That abolishing religion abolishes cruelty. Consider the twentieth century, the cruellest century in all the cruel history of the human race. Abandoning faith in God and replacing it with faith in Hitler immeasurably increased cruelty. As for abandoning faith in God and replacing it with faith in History, History with a capital letter, you understand—and I have some idea of this other abandonment because once upon a time

166

I almost chose it—its effects on people's lives, on what they did and what they suffered, was no better than the effects of faith in Hitler. Both turned ordinary people into monsters who believed they were doing what was right when they caused the deaths of millions in famines and purges, killed Jews and Poles and gypsies and homosexuals in more millions. Including, I have no doubt, my own father."

"What happened to him?"

"He was a Polish Jew in Paris when the Germans invaded. Foreign Jews were rounded up first. For death."

"I'm sorry."

"Sorry. Of course, for the millions. And so for him, as one of them. I am most sorry that I never knew him. I never knew even his name. I pray for him, and for the millions."

Marie, Bernard thought.

"And now?", he said.

"Now we see something different. Not the replacement of faith in God with faith in something else—a false religion constructed of lies: worship Hitler; worship History—but a perversion, a turning upside down of faith in God itself, the appropriation of the name of God to justify all kinds of terror and oppression, and torture and murder too, and the suicide of boys persuaded they will be in paradise today. The Islamist fanatics, who thrive on power, are sending young men to their deaths in revenge for the humiliation of Muslims by everyone else, so they say, and the more passers-by, the more women and children and old people, they take with them, the better. This is not Islam. In these desperate places, in wretched Syria and wretched Iraq, there have been for hundreds and hundreds of years Jews and Christians and Muslims, yes, Sunni Muslims and Shia Muslims and other kinds of Muslim too, living side by side, usually in peace, a kind of peace I have known a little of myself, in a distant corner of another desperate country. As for President Bush's so-called Crusade: what was that? The most powerful country in the world bombing and killing hundreds of thousands of people, and torturing and murdering prisoners, also in the name of God. This was, this is, no more Christian than Islamic State is Muslim. And

Islamic State could never have taken hold as it has if America had responded with more intelligence and more knowledge to the attack on America. But then—the behaviour of France and Britain after the Ottoman Empire collapsed was informed with no more intelligence and no more knowledge.

"In these western countries Islamic State is called 'medieval'. This is an insult to the Middle Ages. Mixed, the Middle Ages were, naturally. A mixture of good and bad, like every time in history, like everything human. Like Islam and Christianity and you and me. But they gave us Cluny and Chartres and the village churches of France and Thomas Aquinas's Paris. And the great mosques of Kairouan and Cordoba."

Bernard wished Marie could have met Thamar.

"Forgive me, Bernard. I'm talking too much. So much has happened to the poor world since I last talked. To anyone. I have been silent. I have not been asleep.

"But back to Augustine. What I meant about the worlds of Augustine and Aquinas, one so close to us, the other so far away, was that Aquinas's world was Christian. Some Jews here and there. Muslims beyond the frontiers of Christendom, sometimes the enemy, but also helpful scholars. And there was then, among the learned, considerable respect for both Jews and Muslims. A great abbot of Cluny, in the twelfth century, had the Koran translated into Latin. Remarkable. But everyone Aquinas lived among, his family, his teachers, his students, his colleagues in the Order of Preachers—never mind; I'll explain one day who they are—were Christians. He was born in Italy but he taught and studied in university cities everywhere, in Cologne, in Naples, in Paris. You could in those days think and write anywhere in Latin Christendom because it was in Latin that you thought and wrote and taught. Aquinas spent most of his life in Paris, the intellectual centre of the world, as it has so often been since. No longer. That may be a good thing."

He paused, looking for a moment lost.

"And Augustine's world?", Bernard said, to bring him back.

"Forgive me. Yes. Very like ours. The empire was collapsing, as Europe is collapsing now. Rome itself, the great city, was no longer the centre of everything, as Paris is no longer the centre of anything. The Christians in Augustine's time were mostly peasants, women, enthusiasts, as in Europe they are now. The highly educated were cynical, world-weary, skilled in all the devices of persuasion—that was how Augustine was educated—but without anything of substance to persuade anyone else to think, let alone believe. They were scornful of Christianity, contemptuous of any and all faith in anything beyond their own cleverness."

"Yes", Bernard said.

"Yes?"

"The philosophers we learned about at the university were like that. At least I think they were. Deleuze, Foucault, Lacan, Lyotard, Alain Badiou. Half the time, much more than half the time, I couldn't understand what they said in their books, and I thought some of our teachers were only pretending to understand them."

"I know almost nothing about these philosophers. More or less Marxist? Altogether atheist? Nietzsche is the hero? Power explains everything?"

"That's right. I think. More or less."

Both of them laughed.

"Well, there you are", Thamar said. "The fashionable philosophers in Augustine's time were much the same. Very clever. Very distant from the lives of actual people struggling to understand themselves and their unhappiness."

After a moment, Bernard said, "Thamar, do you think everyone is unhappy?"

"No. Yes." He laughed his brief laugh, and then paused, looking down at his hands folded on the terrace table.

"What I think is that being alive isn't easy for anyone, not even for children. Unhappiness, anxiety, regret, is where we live, until, perhaps, we find acceptance and forgiveness, and until we know, as children can't yet know, that it isn't possible for other people, even from their love of us, to give us the deep, the unconditional, acceptance and forgiveness that each one of us knows he needs. If he does know. Many of us don't. Don't know, or can't recognize for what they are the things we do know. About ourselves, about how we always get things wrong, do things that are wrong, understand things wrongly. Trying to write my book has taught me—Well, you will see."

Bernard wasn't sure he understood this. Thamar didn't give him time to try to understand, but went on, "That was what Augustine had to discover, and it took him years of struggle, and distractions of different kinds, to think and feel his way through the intellectual atmosphere of his time, until he found—well, you will see what he found, when you read his book."

"Are you talking about God?"

"I'm talking about God. Which can't be done."

To Bernard's surprise, Thamar laughed, and then said, "No. Really. It can't be done."

"But—" Bernard began, and couldn't go on. So he said, "And should I try to read St Thomas Aquinas as well?"

A smile. A shake of the head. "No, Bernard, certainly not. Not until you are old and your life is full of empty time. And that, I expect, will never happen to you. No. Not Aquinas."

He gave Bernard one of his searching looks. After only a few days in his house, Bernard knew that his grandfather was more concerned to find out who this unexpected grandson was than to reveal to Bernard who he was himself. Who Thamar was Bernard would no doubt eventually discover from his book. If he could make head or tail of it.

"What do you know about Aristotle?"

"Not much. We learned some elementary logic at the *lycée*. I think that had something to do with Aristotle. In my first year at the university we did a short course on the history of philosophy. Two professors, both going very fast. I managed to hold on to a few things. One of the professors was for Plato rather than Aristotle, but he was getting us as quickly as possible to Hegel who was his hero. The other professor disapproved of Plato, 'the father of all fascists' he called him, and told us that without Aristotle none of us would be able to think straight, reason properly, establish conclusions rooted in evidence. All that."

Thamar's smile.

"No surprises there. Somebody said everyone is by nature

either a Platonist or an Aristotelian. We French are mostly Aristotelians. Paris has been an Aristotelian place since Aquinas's time, since before Aquinas's time. Have you heard of a philosopher called Abelard?"

Bernard shook his head, again.

"He was an Aristotelian. A hundred years, more, before Aquinas. Also a teacher in Paris. The Sartre of his day, king of the Left Bank. He had a famous dispute with St Bernard, a Platonist, though I don't suppose Bernard knew anything about Plato. You see? An ancient, ancient divide."

He stopped, smiled.

"Do you know who St Bernard was? Perhaps you were named after him?"

"I'm afraid not. My grandfather—" He felt himself blush. He had for a moment forgotten who he was talking to. "My other grandfather, in Rouen, is called Bernard."

"It's a good name, however you came by it. One day I'll tell you about St Bernard. A Burgundian. Another shining light of the much defamed Middle Ages. A defender of the Jews, by the way. Where were we? In Paris, naturally. So: Aquinas's book, his enormous and wonderful book, couldn't have been written without Aristotle. That's why it's so clear. That's why its arguments can be summarized and numbered and set out in text books for students to suffer over. And do you know how he learned his Aristotle? From the Muslims in Spain. Aristotle was familiar in Arabic, and much admired by Muslim scholars, long before anyone read him in Latin. He was translated for these clever fellows in Paris from Arabic, not from Greek."

Bernard was thinking he had learned more in the last hour, from this old man who had for years shut himself away from the world, than he had in months and months of study at the university.

"And Augustine?"

"A Platonist. He didn't know much Plato, and various things had been confused for him by later followers of Plato. But he was a natural Platonist. So am I. Mind you, there is a great deal of Augustine in Aquinas. In the end, the truth is the truth though there are many paths that lead to it."

He thought about this later. Much of what his grandfather said on the terrace that evening in the shadows of the climbing plants with Félix, as always, asleep at their feet, had been new to Bernard, a new way of looking, a long view, as if from far away, of things he had learned or heard of, in separate bits and pieces. Of one thing he was sure, or had thought he was sure: his philosophy teachers at the *lycée* and at the university had disagreed with each other about many things but, as far as he had been able to tell, they all agreed that there was no such thing as the truth. There were facts, which could be proved, until they were displaced by fresh facts supported by better proofs. Otherwise there was speculation—the books he was told to read at the university were full of this—in complicated webs of words called theory, set against other complicated webs of words also called theory, beyond understanding, as far as Bernard could see, though he had tried his best to understand.

What was it Thamar had said, about the intellectual atmosphere of Augustine's world? Something like "They were clever, those philosophers. But a long way away from the lives of actual people struggling to understand themselves and their unhappiness." Wasn't this an exact description of all the theory he had read and tried to grasp? Hadn't it been equally beyond the understanding of his fellow-students who in essays and papers reproduced the webs of words as if they meant something that could one day be grasped and translated into straightforward language? Bernard didn't believe it could. I don't believe it, he had said to himself several times: I don't believe this stuff I have to read means anything real. "Believe?" "Real?" Suspect words to his teachers and his contemporaries. At which point he had given up, confused and depressed, and decided that at least politics and history could be written about as if this or that were more or less true, more or less related to reality.

And truth? Let it go, or perhaps let it wait.

When Thamar talked about the truth as something with actual existence, towards which many paths lead, Bernard wanted to explain how unable he felt to set out on any such path, bent over as he was, unstraight, because of the load of doubt he had been educated to carry. Perhaps Thamar could teach him how to undo its straps, how to lift the weight from his back, how to put it down on the ground and leave it behind so as to stand upright and walk easily forward. But Bernard couldn't begin to find the words. Perhaps, one day, it might be possible. So, after that conversation on the terrace, and in the weeks that followed, he said nothing. And in any case he wasn't sure he wanted to lose his load: it was, after all, his education. He had worked hard for it. Also he had always trusted his father's example. His father, after all, was much cleverer than his mother—Bernard recognized that his greater closeness to his mother was a matter of feeling, not thinking—and was a good, kind, responsible man, who had bravely married his mother in the face of his parents' disapproval, and cared for her ever since. And his father certainly thought there was no such thing as the truth.

So he had approached Augustine treading cautiously, peering forward, slowed by his scepticism, and soon found himself more confused than ever. Trying hard to concentrate, he was reading the *Confessions* in the evenings, while Thamar read his Aquinas and made notes in a large black notebook that every so often he picked up from the floor by his chair and then returned to the floor when he had written, quickly but neatly, with his antique fountain pen, a couple of lines or sometimes a whole paragraph. Bernard very much hoped that he was never going to be asked to read, let alone organize, these notes. Sometimes, while Thamar worked on Aquinas, Bernard read that day's *Le Monde*, and sometimes they talked about what was happening in France or in the world, Thamar with a great deal more sorrow than hope for both. But most evenings, Bernard read Augustine, carefully, because his grandfather wanted him to.

The first few pages had made him sure that it wasn't going to be possible for him to read the whole book. Here was Augustine talking to God. Leafing through the pages and reading random paragraphs here and there, he saw that Augustine was always talking to God. Bernard had no sense of God, was certain, in fact—in fact, here in the present, in 2015, where he was alive and breathing in Thamar's house on the edge of a village in Burgundy—that God did not exist, had never existed, and that all ideas of him were illusions acquired or invented for comfort in a comfortless world and then used, abused, as a means to power. He had known this for as long as he had known anything. So how could he read a whole book addressed to a dangerous illusion all rational people had dispensed with? He found himself looking up, quite often, to Thamar's crucifix above the fireplace. There the dead Christ hung, as dead as Bernard felt God to be, the desolation of the figure on the cross only confirming his sense that Augustine was talking to no one but himself, in a great darkness.

On his very first evening of trying to read the *Confessions*, Bernard was brave enough to ask Thamar how he expected him to read a whole book addressed to God when he was sure God didn't exist.

"That's exactly why I want you to read it. You need to be patient. The beginning of the book tells you where Augustine is now, as he writes, a middle-aged man trying to account, before God and for anyone who cares to read his story, for what has happened to him, inside his soul, during his life so far. He has, as he couldn't have known when he wrote this book, a long way still to travel. You'll find as you read more that Augustine for years had in his head, as so many of us in our time do, only a succession of distorted and unappealing pictures or definitions of God, easy to discard, easy to disdain. He was really, all those centuries ago, as lonely as each of us is who knows he is starting from nowhere, starting only from the simple fact of being alive in a time and a place, much though he hopes to discover whether being alive means something or means nothing. As a university student, a boy of your age, he studied Aristotle's logic and read some philosophy just as you did. He found the logic too easy to be interesting, by the way."

Bernard laughed. "I didn't. But I can see how a very clever person might."

"No harm at all in learning some basic logic. It does brush out the cobwebs. But what is there to put into this nice clean space?"

"Yes", Bernard said. He recognized his own sense of a space that needed filling which he had tried without success to explain to his father when he was still at the *lycée.*

"When it came to this question, to the meaning, or not, of being alive, Augustine was for years more confused by everything than sure of anything. As I was, although I had a good, solid, Catholic upbringing from my grandmother, which for a long time I thought a handicap rather than an advantage. Now I am grateful for it, I think, as Augustine was grateful, I think, for the piety of his mother."

He smiled as he said this, and added, "As a matter of fact, I'm not too sure about the gratitude of either of us."

"But you, Bernard", he went on, "had no such upbringing. A secure home, your parents' marriage good, as far as I could tell from meeting your mother, but nothing of Christianity except the not very attractive conventional observance of your father's parents. Am I right?"

Bernard nodded.

"So, then, you are, now, having set out from a different direction, very much as I was at your age. Alone with the great questions. Just as Augustine was, as a student in Carthage. Although, from what I can see in you, as a student in Nantes you behaved much more sensibly, more cautiously, than he did. Or you would never have considered living for a time with an eccentric old recluse in the deep country."

He gave Bernard a long, searching look, facing him with his damaged face, his clear grey eyes, his spectacles.

"Unless, of course, I've been mistaken about you. In which case I can only apologize, ask your forgiveness, and recommend that you give up Augustine's book. There are many other books in this house, as you can see: I'm sure you can find something that interests you."

"I don't know", Bernard had finally said. "I'll think about it."

He felt himself challenged, in a way he didn't entirely understand, by what Thamar had said. Also afraid of not rising to an expectation he couldn't define to himself. That night, perhaps at the end of his first week in the house, he had lain awake for some time puzzling over all this, and wondering whether he had made a serious mistake in coming at all, in raising the old man's hopes that he could measure up, by learning new things and attending in new ways, to the task he had taken on. He slept uneasily and then, towards morning, very deeply. He woke pleased because in the morning light he saw that what Thamar had been telling him the night before was that he thought a lot of Bernard, whom as yet he hardly knew, and was confident that he would, if he persevered, learn a great deal from Augustine's book, and that this would also help him understand his grandfather and what he had written.

So he had persevered, and become drawn, further and further, into the life of this man who lived so many centuries ago. He was taking the book very slowly. He didn't ask Thamar any questions about Augustine himself, knowing that the old man wanted him, by himself, to make what sense he could of Augustine's writing. He had, however, asked if there was in the house a history book that would tell him about the late Roman empire, the empire of Augustine's time.

"I'd like to know more about it, about what you called his world."

"Ah. There is, somewhere in the bookcases in the dining room, the most famous of all works on the later empire. *The Decline and Fall of the Roman Empire*, by an Englishman of the Enlightenment. Edward Gibbon. Have you heard of him? No, why should you have? It's a very great book, a very long book, in one particular respect a rather terrible book."

"How is it terrible?"

"It blames Christianity for the collapse of the Roman Empire, an accusation with which Augustine, who had every reason to know what he was talking about, dealt, brilliantly and comprehensively, years after he wrote the *Confessions*. That book, which is called *City of God*, you must read one day, not yet. But if you can keep your balance, you would learn much about Augustine's world from Gibbon."

"I'm afraid my English isn't good enough for me to read a long book."

"No, no. Why should it be? Don't worry. I don't think my grandfather knew any English; there aren't any English

176

books in the house. Children in French schools when he was a teacher didn't learn English, only some Latin if they were clever enough. In any case, Edward Gibbon's book was translated, into excellent French, very correct, by François Guizot not long after Gibbon finished it. Have you heard of Monsieur Guizot?"

"I think so. A minister of Louis-Philippe? Something about reforming the schools of France?"

"Very good, Bernard. Well remembered. You could say that Guizot was responsible for me, for us, being here, now, in a house full of books on the edge of a village that when Guizot became minister of public instruction probably had no books at all beyond the gentleman's library in the château and the parish priest's missal and lectionary. Every child in France should have at least an elementary education. That was Monsieur Guizot's plan, very remarkable for the 1830s, when most of the country children of France didn't even speak normal French, and, ever since, French children all go to school. Guizot was an interesting man. He was young, not much older than you are now, when he translated *The Decline and Fall of the Roman Empire.* He was a Protestant always but as a young man he was also a true child of the Enlightenment or he couldn't have spent all those months, probably years, in the company of Gibbon. After politics went wrong for him, as they did for nearly everyone of integrity in the middle of the nineteenth century, he retired to the country. He couldn't serve the so-called empire of Louis-Napoleon. He was a great historian himself, of France, and also of England. There are many of his books in the dining room. He must have worked extraordinarily hard, all his life. I admire him greatly. Although he was a Protestant, he was a true Christian, sympathetic to Catholics and to the best in Catholic history. He lived for the last twenty years of his life, simply, because although once very powerful he was, unlike most politicians, incorruptible and therefore not rich. His house, in Normandy, which I have never seen, was the monastery buiding of an old Cistercian abbey—I'll tell you about the Cistercians, St Bernard's Cistercians, one day—which of course had been damaged and looted after the

Revolution. He rebuilt the monastery, though not the church, and lived quietly, almost as quietly as I do, with his books and his writing. I wish I could write a tenth as well as he did. By the way, he outlived Louis-Napoleon, I'm delighted to say, though he was a good deal older."

He stopped talking and looked at Bernard, with his crooked smile.

"I'm sorry. You must forgive me for talking too much, Bernard. Once again."

Bernard smiled back. "No. It's all interesting. There's so much I don't know." He thought of the great ruined buildings of the abbey in the bend of the Seine, which had so impressed him as a small boy and which he had never forgotten. Monsieur Guizot's abbey must have been much smaller. Then he said, "Would you have liked to live in an old abbey yourself, Thamar?"

This time an actual laugh.

"Certainly not. I'm perfectly happy here in the schoolmaster's house. But an abbey for Monsieur Guizot, who had, after all, been Prime Minister and Foreign Minister: why not? A better fate for the building than almost total destruction, like poor Cluny, or, perhaps worse, becoming a prison."

"A prison?"

"A prison. Napoleon, the real Napoleon, emperor of the world, decided that some of the noble abbeys of France should be prisons. Why not? The monks and nuns were never coming back. So Mont St Michel, one of the wonders of Christendom, was a prison for years. Fontevraud, nearer here than Monsieur Guizot's abbey but a long way beyond the Loire, a famous abbey, where the Plantagenet kings are buried, was a prison, still a prison when I was a boy, a cruel prison. I went there once, when I was very young, younger than you because—" Something stopped him for a moment. He went on.

"I was about nineteen I suppose. I was living in Paris. I was on holiday, bicycling in the Loire valley, by myself, you understand. I saw Fontevraud. A prisoner in overalls with a prison pattern, like a prisoner in a newspaper cartoon, was sweeping in the great empty church, the stone tombs of kings and the swish of the prisoner's broom. Dust and fallen leaves on the stone floor. Nothing else. The Vichy government sent resistance fighters to Fontevraud during the Occupation. They were tortured and killed for the Germans, no doubt. In the monastery buildings. And do you know which is now, today, the most secure prison in France, for the very worst offenders?"

Bernard, as usual, shook his head.

"Clairvaux. The abbey of your namesake St Bernard. Perhaps his spirit watches over the prisoners, poor devils. Who knows?"

He looked at Bernard again, with his clear, grey gaze.

"God knows, I dare say. Now, where were we? Why was I telling you about Guizot? Not interesting to a boy of your age, not in the least. O yes, the late Roman Empire. Try Monsieur Guizot's Gibbon. It will give you an idea of that world. But read it with caution."

The next morning, in the dining room, Bernard found the book, or rather the books, because *The Decline and Fall of the Roman Empire* was in three thick volumes. He started at the beginning and was surprised to find himself enjoying what he was reading. Gibbon's admiration for the Roman empire at its highest point of achievement, of peace and order across the known world—as far as Bernard's inconsiderable education in ancient history had taken him—was catching. An ideal, or probably idealized, world. Soon things started to go wrong: destructive emperors, mad, stupid or wicked; treachery, murders, civil wars, rebellions on the frontiers. Bernard knew he wasn't going to remember the names, the places, the detail, but he was still enjoying the writing, clear, sharp, orderly, the writers' eyes (obviously both Gibbon's and Guizot's) never closed to any implication, any loose end, that could be neatly tied into the balance of a sentence. After a few evenings of reading this steady, confident prose. he realized that he was so much enjoying it partly because it made him feel he was in safe hands, and at a measured critical distance from the men and events described, and this was very different, not only from the confusion of Thamar's manuscript, but also from the unpredictable brilliance and astonishing closeness of Augustine's

Confessions. It wasn't difficult to see why Thamar had warned him to be cautious: Gibbon's contempt for Christianity, a set of foolish superstitions which weakened and corrupted what was left of heroic Roman virtue, was evident, almost funny in its negative sarcasm, and as easy to stand back from as the historian's highly skilled, readable but forgettable unravelling of events too long ago and far away to matter any more.

After two or three weeks of reading some chapters properly and skimming through others, he reached, nearly half way through the second volume, Gibbon's brief account of Augustine himself, dying in Hippo as barbarians from the north were besieging the town. Bernard had already discovered, from an old atlas of the classical world among the reference books in the dining room, where Hippo was. He had had to look at the ordinary school atlas on the same shelf to find out which modern country Hippo is in. Algeria. Yes. Hippo was called Bône in the school atlas. Now, no doubt, it had been given an Algerian name. By this time Bernard knew, from his book, that Thamar had spent years in Algeria, at different times of his life. Had Thamar been to Hippo? He couldn't ask him. Not yet.

Gibbon, summing up Augustine in a few sentences, gave him a moment of unexpected praise and then destroyed it, like a child blowing up a balloon in order to puncture it with a pin. The point of the exercise is the bang. Bernard had already acquired a loyalty to Augustine, perhaps really to Thamar; when he read this passage, he returned Gibbon to the shelf and went back to the *Confessions*.

He started again, almost from the beginning, this time reading with a pencil in his hand, marking the sentences that particularly struck him to copy later in a new exercise book he had bought in the village. There was a good deal—at a careful second reading more than he had noticed before—that he didn't understand or found irritating, perhaps as Gibbon had done. But there was also much that he hadn't taken in at his first reading which much impressed him. What he most enjoyed, particularly after Gibbon's dry, sharp but remote account of decades of unpleasant history, was Augustine's extraordinary mixture of directness and complexity.

Augustine was a rebellious schoolboy. He worked hard not because he wanted to but because he was made to. Augustine was critical both of the efforts he made because he was afraid not to, and of the motives of the teachers who forced him to do it. "No one is doing right if he is acting against his will, even when what he is doing is good", he said. And then he said that his teachers had been educating him only "to satisfy the appetite for wealth and for glory, though the appetite is insatiable, the wealth is in reality destitution of spirit, and the glory something to be ashamed of".

Bernard thought hard about this. The second part he would have liked to read to his father because what else, in the end, was his father so anxious for him to achieve in his career, his future, but all that he was neglecting by living this strange hidden life with Thamar? Perhaps this was unfair to his father: ordinary security wasn't exactly wealth and glory. And yet was ordinary security enough as a motive for hard work, for anything?

Augustine's self-criticism puzzled him more. Why did he say that the merit of doing something good was cancelled if a person did it reluctantly, even mutinously like the furious schoolboy he had been (and Bernard, good Bernard, had never been)? Could this be true? Truth again, Bernard thought. He couldn't get away from it. How would anyone observing the person working hard because he was frightened into it, or doing something else good against his will, know the difference between what was done under pressure and what was freely done? Then he saw that behind this one sentence was an idea of goodness not only beyond the goodness of an action, an achievement, but also beyond the perception of another person watching: this was an idea that Bernard had never come across before. It appealed to him. He didn't know why. Did its appeal have something to do with another sentence, a page earlier, that he had copied in his exercise book? It was, of course, addressed to God. Bernard was used to that by now. "Deliver those who do not as yet pray, that they may call upon you and you may set them free." Free from what? Delivered from what? He didn't know. Perhaps he didn't yet know.

One day he would ask Thamar what prayer really was. There was a lot about it in the old man's muddled manuscript, how there had been periods of his life when he couldn't pray although he was supposed to, and although other people assumed from what they saw that he was praying—an example of the good action that wasn't as good as it looked?—and how at other times prayer had been a joy. Bernard thought he was beginning, because of Augustine, to have a vague notion of what the word meant. Obviously it didn't mean, as the word 'pray' suggested, simply asking God for things. Something different, something larger and less to do with the self—he would have to ask Thamar to explain.

As he looked at his watch, Félix, wagging his tail, appeared on the path from the house through the apple trees and came up the steps to lie down beside him. Ten minutes later, after, no doubt, taking off his work overalls and washing, Thamar followed. He had a small cup of coffee in each hand. He put the coffee carefully on the table and said, "Bernard, forgive me. I'm a little late today. One of the old ladies wanted me to wait while she wrote a birthday card for her grandson, for me to post. She took a bit of time to find the address."

"You are very kind to them, the old people at the château."

Thamar shrugged and spread his hands, a characteristic deprecating gesture which always struck Bernard as old-fashioned.

"Why not?"

Then he sat down on the other chair in the summer house, folded his hands together on the table, and said, "You wanted to talk."

Bernard didn't know how to start. He wanted to make one important suggestion about the book, but it was so radical that he was afraid of upsetting his grandfather, who then might not listen to the case he had planned to make. He said nothing.

"You're finding the book badly done? Boring?", Thamar said.

"No. No, not at all."

But Thamar went on.

"Don't worry. I don't think it's any good myself. I don't think it's well done in any respect, at least, not yet. An old man's folly. Self-indulgent. Even self-obsessed. And I am not Augustine. The story of my life can be of no use to anyone else, so I should never have tried to write it down. It was stupid of me, and not kind, to ask you to come and sort it out for me. More self-indulgence, I'm afraid."

He unclasped his hands and put them, palms down, flat on the table.

"You know, I would not have imagined, even in dreams, inflicting all those pages on anyone at all if it hadn't been for your mother's visit. Jamila. My Jamila, of whose existence I had no idea. It was marvellous, that day, but also, you understand, a shock, which—how to put it?—which upset my judgement. And when she said that her son, my own grandson, was a writer, how could I resist the possibility of meeting him, and at the same time the possibility that he might be able to make something of all those years of scribbling? Now I see that I should have recognized the possibility for what it was, a temptation, a test for my judgement. My judgement failed the test."

"No, Thamar. That's not at all what—"

"I shall miss you, Bernard. I hope you will stay a few more days. I want you to see Cluny, and Tournus, before you go home. For your sake, you understand, not for mine. Your parents will be delighted to have you back in Paris."

"Thamar, please."

He managed to stop the old man.

"I'm not going home."

"You're not?"

A silence, during which Thamar sat back in his old basket chair, his hands in his lap, and smiled.

"Really?", the old man said.

"Really. I'm not going home. Being here with you is so good. Quite different from anything I have ever done before, and I enjoy every day. No. I'm not going anywhere. Except Cluny and Tournus."

They both laughed.

"But—the book?"

Now. Bernard picked up his cup of coffee, warm, not hot, and drank it all. Thamar's cup was untouched.

"Your book is not a bad book, as you say it is. I have found it interesting, all of it, very interesting in so many ways, and many other people, I'm quite sure, will also find it interesting, even valuable to them. In your pages there's a remarkable story. But at present, as it is—"

"Yes?" Thamar was looking at him, turned towards him, with his crooked face, his grey eyes shining, waiting.

"It's not actually a book at all. Not yet."

"Of course, of course. I know. It's a chaos. You are entirely right, Bernard. You have no idea how many times some of those pages have been written. I would, one morning, let's say, one Saturday morning when I was not going to the château, when I was not going to Mass, I would write, for an hour, for two hours. I would even be pleased with what I had written. Then the next day, Sunday afternoon, I would read what I had written on Saturday and find that it was awkward, or disconnected, or flat, not at all as I felt it to be while I was writing it. So—tear up those pages and try again. With different results but usually no more success."

"Thamar. May I ask you a question?'

"Naturally."

"When did you number the pages?"

A long, grey look. A crooked smile.

"The Saturday before you came. It took me all day, here in the summer house. No lunch. One pot of coffee."

He remembered his coffee, drank it, and winced because it was cold.

"Félix was puzzled because we didn't go for a walk that day, until he was too much of a nuisance for me not to take him up the road when it was almost dark. Because, you see, numbering the pages meant that I had to make many many decisions about the order in which it seemed best to tell the story, which was very far from the order in which I had written the pages. The decisions were too many, and I dare say many of them were bad."

"Well. That does explain a lot."

Bernard didn't know how to go on. After a silence, Thamar eventually said, "So do you think there is any hope for the book? Can what I have done possibly become a real book?"

"I think it can. It will need a lot of work, and, if you still want me to attempt the work, I will need a lot of help from you. Look."

Bernard pulled out from under a pile of Thamar's pages, where he had hidden it, his plan, his map of Thamar's life, and unfolded it. He pushed the coffee cups to one side and spread it out on the table.

"I made this as I was reading. It's only the dates and places that I was fairly certain of. I'll need you to go through it, and perhaps add some more facts, so that I'm sure of the order of the things you did and the things that happened to you."

Thamar took his spectacle-case out of his pocket, snapped it open and put on his spectacles.

He studied Bernard's plan for some time and then looked up and smiled.

"I don't know how you managed this. My congratulations, Bernard. I'm amazed that you were able to find so much of this—this skeleton of my life, in all the confusion of my writing. I see now, looking at what you've done, that I should have begun with just such a plan, before I wrote anything else down. If I had been a writer, I would have known that this is how one has to start. You have done well, astonishingly well, but now that I see the skeleton I'll be able to add more bones to it, so that it will be properly helpful to you."

He paused, looking at Bernard, and then went on, "You will try, won't you? I know I'm not a writer. Now you know I'm not a writer. But I don't know that you are a writer. Perhaps you don't either. But if you try, and if you succeed, that will be for me the third blessing of my old age, after finding Jamila, and finding you."

"I'll do my best."

Bernard paused, looked down at Félix, asleep, looked up at Thamar.

"I promise you that I'll do my best. But there is one other thing I need to ask you. It was the reason I wanted us to have a talk today."

"And that is?"

"I've been worrying about this. I don't want to upset you—that's the last thing I want. But I don't think I can even begin to write the book, as you have written all that you've written, in the first person. What I'm trying to say is that I can't pretend to be you. I'm sure now that the only way for me even to attempt to write the story of your life, so that it would be something like a real book, and so that you would recognize it as truthful, is if I write it in the third person. From the inside, naturally, from your point of view, writing nothing that you didn't witness or think or feel, but with the distance the third person gives, the distance of a novelist, who is only a story-teller after all, who has made up, invented a character. Of course I won't invent anything. I'm here, in your house. I can show you what I've written as I go along, and you can check everything to make sure I haven't got things wrong. What do you say?"

A long silence. Bernard saw Félix lift his shaggy white head from his paws and look at each of them in turn as if to ask why they had stopped talking.

"I'm sorry", Bernard said at last. "Forgive me, Thamar. I have upset you after all. I was afraid I might."

A shorter silence.

"No. I needed to think about this."

"And—?"

"What I think is that this is the second thing this evening to convince me that you are a writer, that you will succeed with this foolish endeavour of mine, although it will not be easy. The first was the skeleton, your chart of my life, such as it has been. And now you have shown me that you're able to imagine this book as a biography, but written as a novel might be, and not just as the memories, the *Mémoires*, with a capital letter, of an old man of whom no one has ever heard. You're quite right. I've no doubt about this, now that you've shown me how it looks to you: it would be difficult, probably impossible, for you to write as if you were me. 'I came. I saw. I lost.'"

Bernard smiled. "Julius Caesar."

"Exactly. I'm not Julius Caesar, even without the conquest. Whereas if it's your book, written with my help—this is an excellent plan, and I wouldn't have thought of it."

"I will start tomorrow."

"No, you won't. Tomorrow you are going to Tournus, before we get autumn storms when bicycling all that way would be too unpleasant. And I shall spend the day adding some more facts to your chart."

"Thank you, Thamar."

"No, not at all. It is I who should be thanking you, from my heart, for being alive, for being here, for taking such an intelligent view of my wretched scribblings. Now—"

He got up. So did Félix.

"Come on. A glass of wine to celebrate. And it's time we thought about some dinner."

It was almost completely dark in the garden. There were no lights in the house, but there was just enough fading silver left in the sky for them to follow the white form and waving tail of Félix back to the terrace.

When Bernard had studied his route on his map with Thamar, he walked to the village to buy his picnic and send a message on his laptop to his mother. He found an email she had sent him two days earlier.

Bernard, darling,

Papa went to the police two weeks ago to see if they could find any news of Joséphine. I didn't tell you at the time because I thought you would still think it was the wrong thing to do and would frighten Joséphine. This morning they have told papa that the Turkish police have a record of Colette Khider (she obviously couldn't change her name on her passport) having crossed the Turkish frontier into Syria on 4 September. There is no means of discovering where she is now. Imagine how terrible for her poor parents, on the other side of the world!

Neither the French nor the Turkish police can find any trace of Joséphine. The police say this means she is almost certainly still in the European Union, which of course would be good news if we could be sure it is correct. But papa seems to be even more worried about her than he was before. He feels responsible for her running away. He thinks he shouldn't have urged her so hard to work for the wretched bac. *Where can she be? Who is she with? Why doesn't she understand how worried we are and get in touch? All papa is doing is working very hard himself, to fill up his time, and he comes home from school every day later than I do, tired and silent. You know what he can be like. If you could telephone me on Saturday afternoon, I would be so pleased to talk. Papa will be at the* lycée *until six o'clock because he has a meeting.*

I hope both you and Monsieur Thomas are well and busy, and you are not too bored in the middle of the country. I am so thankful you are safe.

Maman

Bernard answered at once:

Dear Maman,

I'm sorry I've only just read your email. Of course I'll call you this afternoon. You must believe that no news about Joséphine is good. Poor papa.

B

He had to go back to the house to put away his laptop in his room, and to charge his little phone which he hadn't used since he arrived in Burgundy.

He didn't go to Tournus that day. He didn't want to spoil an expedition he had been looking forward to by having to call his mother from a strange town, and he didn't want to have to tell her where he was. His father would look up Tournus and find that the only reason for going there was to see its ancient and, according to Thamar, very beautiful church. He thought this might cause new difficulties for his mother: his father hadn't wanted him to go to Burgundy in the first place, and he would regard the news that he was bicycling over the hills and through the woods to look at churches as proof that he was wasting his time. And wasn't it likely that his father was thinking that he, Bernard, no longer a student, not working, should be doing something to help find Joséphine? What could he possibly do?

Bernard wasn't going to tell even his mother how much work lay ahead on Thamar's book, and how much he wanted to do it.

When he got back to the house, Thamar was hoeing in his vegetable patch at the far end of the garden, bending over every so often to pick up weeds the hoe had loosened, and throw them onto a pile. Félix was watching him. When Bernard came into the house or the garden, Félix now never barked, just raised his head and wagged his tail. Today, Thamar didn't notice.

A couple of hours later, Bernard was sitting, his bike beside him on the grass, at the edge of some woods, a place that he had discovered weeks ago and returned to several times. It was a climb to reach it, a steep road with almost no traffic, and then a stony track, still uphill, through a wood. It was worth the effort for the view: long, wide, blue hills in the distance, vineyards where he knew the grapes were ripening though he couldn't see them from so high up, fields, some with a few cows, woods, two villages, each with a church, what looked like a small castle on a hill above vineyards, gold the colour of the light, a road far down with occasional cars, a tractor or a lorry now and then, like silent toys. Everything he could see looked peaceful, prosperous, well cared for. He thought of his sister—who knew where?—and then, because of Colette Khider, he thought of the Arab boys loafing in groups, more or less threatening, on street corners in the *banlieues*, easy to call out of their lives of despair to jihad, their sisters too, gazing at computer screens in flats in dismal concrete housing projects. Wretched kids being promised heaven. He found he was almost crying. France, so beautiful, so quiet, also so cruel. He thought of some of the horrors during the Algerian war, the murdered children and tortured prisoners that Thamar had described in his neat handwriting.

He shook his head angrily, took his phone from his pocket— it was bound to get a signal, this high—and called his mother.

She picked up the telephone after one ring.

"Bernard? How good to hear you."

Then she burst into tears, but quickly pulled herself together.

"I'm sorry, Bernard. I haven't heard your voice for so long. How are you?"

"I'm fine, maman. Everything is going very well. Thamar is remarkable, I think, very quiet, very kind, and he knows such a lot. I'm—yes, well, we are both working on his book. But you needn't worry about me. You and papa have quite enough to worry about with Joséphine."

"O Bernard. It's been such a long time, more than three months now. I suppose you get used to worrying, every day, like you get used to anything else. But it's very difficult. My friend Thérèse, you know, the maths teacher, keeps telling me that if anything terrible had happened we would have heard. The European police and the embassies do talk to each other. An accident would be reported. We would hear. And at least she hasn't gone to Syria with this other girl. I don't think I could have coped with that. And papa—"

"How is papa? Not good?"

"He won't talk about Joséphine. He's hardly talking to me at all. He comes home tired. He's rewriting all his courses—quite unnecessary—just to fill up the time. So he eats dinner, says almost nothing, and then works till I have to go to bed because I'm so tired."

"Poor maman. Would you like me to come home? To keep you company?"

"You are a kind boy, Bernard. Like your grandfather. But no, you mustn't come home till you've finished the work he wants you to do. I'm happy that you're helping him. It's the one good thing that's keeping me going. And—you know papa. I don't think it would help to have you here. He'd start worrying about your career, your future, on top of worrying about Joséphine, and soon you would be arguing, the pair of you."

"I expect you're right. Though it might be good for papa, to be annoyed with me, you know. It might take his mind off Joséphine. On the other hand, it wouldn't be very nice for you. But maman, if you change your mind, you must let me know. And, maman, you must try to remember what Joséphine's like: she'll be looking after herself, I'm sure. She's quite selfish and she's quite tough. She'll come home when she wants to and that could well be quite soon. If there's any news, of course tell me at once. I'm not using my phone, except today, because of

Thamar, but I'll check the emails more often and I can call you any time you want me to."

"Thank you, Bernard. Are you in the house now?"

"No. I'm sitting at the edge of a wood, looking at vineyards and fields."

"You are a lucky boy. I'm glad you're enjoying yourself. Give my love to your grandfather. Goodbye, Bernard. Thank you for calling. Goodbye."

"Tell papa I'm thinking of him. Goodbye, maman."

Now she's crying again, he thought.

"You didn't go to Tournus?" Thamar said, when Bernard got home earlier than the old man expected.

'Not today. I had to telephone my mother."

"Is she all right? Does she want you to go back to Paris?"

"No. She's fine. She—" How to put it? "She's very pleased I'm here with you. She sends her love."

"Thank you, Bernard. Thank you for everything."

The next morning, Thamar left the house early because it was a Sunday on which he had to walk five kilometres to Mass in Saint-Christophe. When Bernard took his coffee into the dining room he found his pencilled chart on the table with a number of corrections and additions in ink, in Thamar's handwriting. Saturday afternoon's work, which the old man hadn't mentioned the evening before. They had, as usual, sat in companionable silence, both of them reading.

For the second time, Bernard was following Augustine as a student in Carthage, through the wild mixture of feelings that tossed him about, lust, love, jealousy, ambition, his passion for watching suffering represented in the theatre, the more violent the better, and his guilt because of this passion. Then the calm he found in a book by Cicero that persuaded him that philosophy would help him fill the space he had been filling for himself with these storms of feeling, although Cicero also showed him how misleading and deceptive most philosophy was.

Was then, is now, Bernard thought, as Thamar had said. He also thought how dull his three years as a student in Nantes had been. He had avoided the constant music, the drugs, the violent computer games, the promiscuous sex going on all round him. As he had told Thamar, he had avoided, completely, social media, to the surprise of his contemporaries. He didn't like any of these things, and he couldn't understand the urge to tell strangers what he was doing, what he thought, or to send them photographs of himself. He hated all photographs of himself and always had. But was he just a coward? Too afraid of being hurt, or getting involved in something he didn't know how to deal with, to lead the ordinary student life of his generation? Neither the weeks of his infatuation with Françoise, nor his love for Marie, had ended too messily, but he knew that this had been not to his credit but because of how each of them, in quite different ways, had managed for him his feelings and now his memories. And what about the philosophy he had studied ever since the *lycée*? Augustine said he read Cicero's book when he was eighteen and it changed everything for him. Bernard was twenty-two and philosophy so far had only made him aware of that empty space, the space Augustine had filled with noise and sex and excitement, and later—how much later? He hadn't read enough to find out—with God. "Our heart is restless until it rests in you". For Bernard the space remained empty. And the restlessness? Perhaps he'd never felt restless enough? But what he had found with Thamar was itself a kind of rest. That he did know.

While both Bernard and his grandfather were reading, that evening, as always in the peaceful quiet of the winter room, he said, "Thamar, can I ask you something?"

"Of course."

"Augustine says he read this book by Cicero, called *Hortensius*, when he was a student and it made a great difference to his life, made him more serious about everything. Have you got a copy of Cicero's book?"

A keen look. A smile.

"No. No one has. It's lost. All we know about it is what Augustine tells us. He must have made many readers of the *Confessions* down the ages wish they could find it."

"Then he says that because of Cicero he tried to read the Bible but it struck him as clumsy and ridiculous. Would—?"

"Would you think the same if you tried to read the Bible? You might, though you're not as confident of your judgement as Augustine was of his, and that's good."

"He was very much cleverer than I will ever be."

"Yes. But, because of his mother, he associated Christian belief with childhood, as so many people have and some do, even now, though less and less. That was why, as a boy of your age, he couldn't make any connection between philosophy and Christianity. It was a handicap for him for years. I shared it with him, because of my grandmother, and you don't, which is fortunate for you in ways you will understand one day. No. You shouldn't read the Bible yet. The *Confessions*, as you read more, will give you a better idea of it than you realize."

Bernard spent the rest of Sunday in the summer house, reading quickly through a lot of Thamar's manuscript again, without looking at the chart, or at the pages and pages of his own notes.

On Monday morning, after breakfast, he looked at his map and decided he was going to bicycle to Cluny, nearer than Tournus and much more important in Thamar's early life. As the old man was leaving for the château with Félix, Bernard said, "I'm going to Cluny today. I'm not just putting off getting down to work. I'm sure I need to see Cluny before I begin."

"You're quite right. It's where I began. That's to say it's where I stopped being a good boy who did what the grown ups wanted, and believed what they told me, and started, very inefficiently it has to be said, to try to think for myself."

One of Thamar's long, appraising looks, across the empty breakfast cups.

"Perhaps because it was when I noticed that the grown ups were telling me different things. I was fourteen." Then he said, "Once upon a time, Cluny was the greatest abbey in France. Alas. But I must let you see it for yourself."

It didn't take him much more than an hour to get there. Hills, empty little roads, woods on either side more beautiful than he had yet seen them, the leaves just beginning to turn, green to gold, in the windless morning, the late September sun.

For the first time, somewhere on the way, he saw a party of four or five men with guns, setting off into the woods from their country cars parked by the road, with a couple of spaniels and a bigger dog not unlike Félix but yellow rather than white, all the dogs purposeful, nosing briskly through the undergrowth ahead of the hunters. Not for Marie, he thought.

He free-wheeled down a winding road from the hills, out of the woods, between sloping fields, crossed the railway and a main road, and, having followed the signs through the little town to the abbey, left his bicycle by the ticket office where a middle-aged lady, looking at him over the top of her spectacles, said, "Student?" "Not exactly." "Student", she said and gave him a cheap ticket. He refused her offer of an audio guide, a recorded voice to hold to his ear: Thamar, he knew, would recoil from such a thing.

Two wide and very grand flights of stone steps led down to what must have been the entrance to a huge church. Then nothing, except grass, pieces of low ruined wall, here and there the bases of enormous columns in lines that must once have reached the single remaining tower, far away, suggesting the great length of the church, and beyond it trees, fields, and the hills he had crossed on his bike. He walked and looked. There was an imposing eighteenth-century building in good order, a formal garden looking autumnal and scruffy, but mostly only neatly clipped and edged grass and fragments of building with metal labels that meant nothing to him. He wandered about, trying and failing to imagine the church, the monks, the lives lived here: he was disappointed to catch nothing of that past, nothing of the mystery he had remembered all this time from the ruined abbey in the bend of the Seine. What had Thamar expected him to find here?

The few visitors there were—he could still hear the scorn of Thamar's use of the word "tourist"—were gathered in small groups in front of the up-to-the-minute touch-screens, placed here and there beside ruined walls or in restored bits of building, obviously presenting the history of the abbey. He preferred to look at what there was, what there had been when Thamar was young, as the old man wanted him to.

Then he came to a complete medieval building, labelled Granary and Museum, and found inside, under a stone-vaulted ceiling, pieces of sculpture from the abbey, and upstairs, in a long room with an even more splendid wooden ceiling of massive beams, an ancient marble altar with, arranged round it in a semi-circle ten carved capitals, blurred by time, on pillars too short for their heavy bulk, rescued, a notice told him, from the ruined choir of the church. He stood opposite the altar. The mystery he had been looking for was here after all. And the model, in the same room, on a table that could be walked round, of the whole abbey as it had been in the twelfth century made sense for him of the tidy desolation of grass and brokenness he had seen. What had happened to Cluny? Why had so much of it altogether disappeared? Where had it gone?

He stayed, looking from the columns, the capitals and the altar, to the astonishing model and back, in a silence he felt was full of the sadness of loss. Then he heard a soft brushing sound, like someone sweeping far away. He thought of the prisoner Thamar had seen with a broom in an abbey whose name Bernard had forgotten, and turned to see, sitting cross-legged on the floor beyond the columns and the capitals, a girl drawing on a pad with a piece of charcoal. Had she been there all along? How could he not have noticed her? He walked round the outside of the semi-circle of columns and said, "I'm sorry. I didn't see you there."

She looked up, clearly surprised.

"That's all right. This is a museum. Anyone can come in."

"Of course. I just—I'm sorry", he said again, and smiled down at her. She didn't smile back. She had long brown hair and large brown puzzled eyes.

"May I look at your drawing?"

"Absolutely not. It's only a sketch, to help me remember the details that matter."

He was about to say something else, anything to keep her attention, when a noisy group of children clattered up the stairs and into the quiet.

"I'm sorry", he said again, and walked slowly back to the staircase, waiting at the top until all the children and, behind them, their teacher, had passed him. Under the oak beams in the half light the children went on talking and giggling, not looking at the capitals or the altar.

Outside the Granary in the sunshine he walked again, back to the flights of steps at the entrance and then all the way round the whole church, trying to imagine what he had seen in the model as it once was, square towers like castle towers on either side of the steps, a long, long nave, some of the lower bits of which were still there in fragments, and then a jigsaw of tall buildings that were the far end of the church, four pointed towers, one of which, with an arched graceful hexagonal top under its slate roof, survived with a smaller tower beyond it. It was too difficult. The mysterious quality of past—what? Substance, meaning, weight, of lives lived in this extraordinary place—had left him. He had felt it briefly in the Granary among those pillars, and now it had gone. He sat on a bench in front of the neat eighteenth-century building that seemed to have nothing to do with the fragments of the church, and ate his bread and cheese and his apple.

Before he left the abbey he went back to buy a postcard in the tourist shop inside the tower next to the Granary. The postcard was a photograph of the model he had seen in the museum, taken as if it were a photograph from the air, or possibly a photograph of a painting, of the church and all the monastic buildings complete and surrounded by trees and the dwarfed buildings of the town. He had walked all the way back through the church to the entrance near where he had bought his ticket, and was standing beside his bicycle, and another propped against it, reading the note on the back of the postcard—" Cluny Abbey. Built from 1088 to 1220; destroyed from 1798 to 1823"—when someone said "Excuse me". The girl who was drawing in the museum.

"Can I get my bike?"

He opened his mouth but at once she said, "Don't say you're sorry again", and this time she smiled.

He had, indeed, very nearly said, "I'm sorry", but he smiled instead, and then said, "Do you have far to go?"

She was tying a flat black writing case, obviously containing her sketch pad, to the rack at the back of her bicycle, which was a lot newer than his.

"Only to the other side of Cluny. Not far at all."

"Would you like some coffee? Before you go."

He was surprised by his impulse, by his courage.

She looked at him for a moment, to assess, as anyone would, whether or not he was someone to have coffee with.

"Why not?", she said.

Side by side, they pushed their bicycles across the Place de l'abbaye and into the narrower and less grand marketplace, full of people, where she chose a café with a cheerful terrace. "This'll do", she said, propping her bike against the railing. He did the same with his.

"So", she said, when they had ordered coffee, "you haven't been to Cluny before?"

He shook his head.

"Are you staying here?'

"No. I'm staying with my grandfather in a village about twenty kilometres away."

"Like me. That's to say, I'm staying with my aunt. But I've been here often before."

He wondered if he could ask her her name, and decided he couldn't.

"Are you an art student?", he said.

"Not exactly. I'm in the second year of my master's degree in art history. My dissertation is on the carving of Romanesque capitals in Burgundy."

Bernard had discovered only that morning, from the notices by the exhibits in the Granary, what a capital is.

"Wouldn't it be easier, and quicker, to photograph them? To illustrate your thesis. Rather than drawing them?"

"O, they've all been photographed. All the good ones are on the internet."

"Well then—"

"It's not a question of illustrating. The carving itself is what my thesis is about. And the carvers. How far did they travel? Who carved what? Not their names but their skills. There were a number of them, obviously. Two generations in Burgundy,

197

perhaps three. What did they learn from each other? Drawing makes you look properly, makes you pay attention, hear the tap of the hammer on the chisel. Taking a photograph doesn't."

"I see", he said. "Sort of."

"I'm quite hungry", she said. "Have you had lunch?"

He kept thinking, how beautiful her eyes are.

"Yes. Well, sort of. I brought some bread and cheese."

"Do you want anything else? I'm going to have an omelette."

"No thanks. Maybe some more coffee."

She summoned a waiter, a boy of about sixteen, with a look. Her eyes. Damn, Bernard thought. She ordered a ham omelette and more coffee.

"Are you a student too?"

"Not any more. I got my *license* at Nantes this summer."

"Why Nantes? Is that where you live?"

"My parents live in Paris. I liked the sound of Nantes. It was OK. Where—?"

"Lyon." Her home? Her university? She didn't explain.

They waited in silence until the boy brought more coffee, a knife and fork, a napkin, a little basket of bread to go with her omelette.

She hadn't asked him what he was doing now that he was no longer a student, but he said, "I'm about to start writing a book. Or trying to write a book. There's a lot of writing that— someone's done. An interesting man, but what he's produced is a terrible mess. I'm trying to understand, almost to hear, through the muddle, what he was intending to write. Rather like hearing the tap of the hammer on the chisel, do you think?"

She broke off a piece of bread, put it in her mouth, and looked at him with something like scorn in those eyes. At once he regretted the pretentiousness of what he had said. She couldn't have been more than a couple of years older than him: he felt half her age.

"No. It's entirely different. The carvers were master craftsmen. Did you look carefully at the capitals in the Granary? Probably not. Have you been to Autun?"

He shook his head, as he did so often when Thamar asked him questions.

"Exactly. The best Burgundian Romanesque carving is in Autun. I'm not trying to sort out someone else's muddle, only hoping to trace some lines of teaching and influence. Time, weather and vandalism have blurred some of the carving I study, not the men who made it."

"I see. I'm sorry. That was a stupid thing to say."

"It doesn't matter. You know, you apologize too often."

Again he almost said "I'm sorry", but managed not to. She hadn't said "too much" but "too often". Better. He said nothing. After a couple of minutes of silence, her omelette arrived. She looked up and smiled at the waiter, and thanked him. She started eating. So as not to look as if he were watching her eat, he said, "Can I ask you a question?"

"Why not?"

She put down her knife and fork and looked at him. He changed his mind about what he was going to ask her, and improvised a question.

"Why were you sitting on the floor to draw, when there were seats in the museum?"

"Why do you think?"

He shook his head again.

"Because the capitals were meant to be looked at from below, far below in fact. But I'm lucky to be able to see them in a museum. I can look at them closely. If they were still in a church the size of Cluny, they'd be practically invisible. In Autun the real capitals are in the chapter house. There are copies in the church. Which is just as well."

"What is a chapter house?"

"A meeting room tacked on to a church. You don't know much about churches, do you?"

"I'm afraid not."

He said nothing while she finished her omelette.

"That was good", she said. She looked the waiter back to their table. "A mineral water. Still. Please." She turned her disconcerting eyes, not smiling, to Bernard. "Would you like anything else?"

He shook his head. "Thank you. No."

Then he said, "It's sad, don't you think, to have only copies in the church the carvings were made for? And even sadder to have no church at all, here, when the church must have been so—so magnificent?" He thought of the postcard in his pocket.

"That depends. I'm studying carving, not architecture."

"Was the other church, Autun, pulled down too?"

"No. Of course not. What would be the point of copying the capitals if it were a ruin?"

"But—the Revolution?"

"Autun wasn't a monastery. Just a cathedral. Guess who was the bishop in 1789?"

Bernard shook his head, as usual.

"Talleyrand. Talleyrand himself. The twister, the deceiver, the great survivor. Brilliant, in his way. Hardly an example of Catholic piety. The Revolution said no more Christianity, so the church at Autun became a Temple of Reason or maybe the Supreme Being. I can't remember which. Then back to a church again, but without Talleyrand who'd stopped even pretending to be a Christian. Not that there's any real difference between the three, God, Reason, the Supreme Being. Useless abstractions, all of them."

"But there is, surely there is, there was, a difference?" Bernard thought of the dead figure of Christ hanging over Thamar's fireplace. He knew he couldn't produce any arguments to support what he'd said.

The waiter brought her mineral water. She poured some into her glass and drank it.

"You're Catholic?", she said, looking at him with her dizzying eyes.

"No. Not at all. It's just that—" He didn't know how to go on.

"Just that what?"

"I don't know. They were Catholic, your carvers, weren't they? And the monks who built the church here were Catholic. It seems a shame to forget that, and only to look at what they made as if, as if—"

"As if they were artists? Like Cézanne or Picasso or Giacometti. But they were, don't you see? The greatest of the carvers put his name on his masterpiece, the tympanum at Autun. *Gislebertus hoc fecit.* That shows he knew he was an artist. He's at the centre of my thesis, how he learned his craft, probably here, by the way, and his students, what did they carve? Where?"

Bernard had no idea what a tympanum was but didn't dare to ask.

She went on, "Their art is what's left now that religion's over. People can make great art in a bad cause."

"I don't know. Can they? And was it a bad cause?"

"Well, false in any case. An illusion for hundreds of years, then lies some people told other people because the lies were useful, to keep them in their place. Talleyrand, for example. Until different lies were more useful."

She poured out and drank the rest of her mineral water.

"Are you Marxist?", Bernard said.

She laughed. "No. Not at all." So he laughed too. "The opposite. No socialist realism for me. I'm an art historian. Or I will be one day. I want to be a museum curator. Art for the sake of art, not for the sake of someone else's ideas. It's obvious isn't it? Common sense. They're all dead, my stone carvers. Religion is dead. We have their art. We're very lucky all of it wasn't destroyed, and so are they."

She looked at her watch, with an air of having won the argument.

"In any case, I must go. I promised my aunt not to be too long."

She summoned the waiter again and asked for the bill.

Bernard got out his wallet.

"Allow me, please."

"Don't be silly." She sounded like his mother. "You only had coffee. I'd have had lunch anyway. You can pay for your coffee if you like."

He could tell that she thought he was a boy who knew nothing about anything. She was right. He didn't want her to go.

"Would you—?", he started. "Shall we—? Will you be here, in Cluny, for a while?"

"One more day. On Wednesday I go back to Autun. I've got a lot to do there."

The waiter brought their bill. They put the right money on the saucer and she added a tip.

"Could I", Bernard said, "see you again tomorrow? For lunch perhaps?"

She looked at him, smiling now. Her eyes.

"I don't think so. I have a lot to get through tomorrow. In the other museum. And you should be getting on with your writing. Is your grandfather the interesting man who tried to write the book?"

"Yes. How did you know?"

"I guessed. It'll be difficult, won't it, with him looking over your shoulder?"

She stood up. So did he. They lifted their bicycles from the terrace railing.

"Goodbye", she said.

They shook hands.

"Goodbye."

"Good luck with the work. I think you'll need it." Her eyes. Her smile.

"Thank you. Goodbye."

And that was that. He watched her as she rode away and disappeared into traffic at the end of the marketplace. He found he was close to tears. Ridiculous, he told himself. The result of spending two and a half months alone with a quiet old man. She was cool, professional, clever. Not for him. But her eyes: she had smiled at him three times. Perhaps she was just organized and efficient, like Syrine. Perhaps not. He would never know.

He shook his head vigorously and pushed his bicycle up to the ticket office at the gate of the abbey.

"Excuse me, madame", he said to the friendly lady. "Could you tell me where the high school is?" It wasn't far from the abbey, but it was a modern building and couldn't have been the school of sixty years ago, Thamar's school.

He bicycled back to the village. He would start writing at once. "Good luck", she had said. And smiled.

When Thamar came back from the château, Félix bounded through the garden to the summer house as if Bernard had been away for a week. Bernard, who had written one paragraph on his laptop, under the heading Chapter I, followed the dog through the apple trees to the house where he found Thamar boiling the kettle.

"Would you like a tisane, Bernard? I'm making one to settle my back. I overdid the digging today, in the nuns' vegetable patch."

"Please." When Thamar forgot that there hadn't been any nuns for years, Bernard understood how the old man's life had contracted, his childhood and his old age become in some ways one.

Thamar poured boiling water into the teapot and looked sharply at Bernard as he put the lid on the pot.

"What happened in Cluny, Bernard? You look happy and a little upset."

"Nothing. Well, not absolutely nothing. I met a girl."

"Excellent. It's time you talked to someone of your own age."

"Yes. No. I'll never see her again. Perhaps that's just as well. She's a scholar. She's working on Romanesque capitals. I knew too little about—about everything, to interest her."

"Nevertheless, you—"

"We spent an hour in a café. That's all. She had lunch. I had some coffee. We disagreed, about art. She said bad ideas, a bad cause, could produce good art, beautiful things. She was talking about Christianity. I disagreed with her, I knew she was wrong, somehow, but I didn't know how to argue with her. She's an art historian, she's working for a master's degree, and I know nothing, nothing about art, nothing about Christianity."

"But you have sound instincts. Some people do. It's possible everyone would have sound instincts were it not—never mind, now. So—you didn't argue, and—?"

"She had to go. She has a lot of work to do."

"And?"

"She has beautiful eyes."

"Ah. Love. A little moment, before things change. That's a gift, a very small gift but a gift. Not to be forgotten."

Bernard couldn't answer this.

"What is she called?"

"I don't know. I didn't dare to ask her."

"It doesn't matter what her name is. Does it?"

Bernard was surprised, but after a moment said, "You're right. It doesn't."

Thamar poured two cups of camomile tea and put them on the kitchen table. They both sat down.

"Now, what did you make of Cluny?"

Bernard pulled himself together.

"It was desperately sad. I couldn't understand why until, in the museum, I saw the model of how it once was. What happened? Why was the destruction so ruthless, so cruel? And so recent, when the buildings had lasted all that time?"

"Ah", Thamar said. "The abbey was sold after the Revolution to a merchant, a trader in Mâcon, for the stone, you understand. Twenty years later nothing was left, nothing except what you see now. Can you imagine the hundreds of labourers, the battering rams to bring the stone down—years before dynamite, this was—the piles of rubble, the noise, the clouds of dust, the loading of wagons, the teams of horses to cart the stone? I wonder what they thought of what they were doing, these destroyers of one of the great buildings of Europe. Earning a day's pay, I suppose. What is known for certain is that nowhere, nowhere in Burgundy, nowhere in Paris, nowhere in the whole of France, was a single objection raised, a single protesting voice heard. It shows—what do you think this story shows, Bernard?"

"It shows what people by then were ready to do for money?"

"Of course. And what else?"

"Hatred for what the buildings represented? Or ignorance?"

"Both. Mâcon has always been a town of the left. And there was plenty of hatred in France for what the church had become, powerful, rich, lazy, corrupt, in the centuries before the Revolution. Richelieu was abbot of Cluny. So was Mazarin. A grand title and a handsome income, no doubt, among many others for each of them."

Bernard saw him again, the clever, contemptuous, flattered face, the crimson robes, Richelieu in the Louvre.

"Well", Thamar went on. "The last abbot of Cluny, before the monastery was shut down by the Revolution, was Cardinal de

Rochefoucauld, Archbishop of Rouen. I don't suppose he ever came down here. The hatred goes back a long way, and hasn't disappeared. And as for ignorance—the rich, corrupt church the Revolution was out to destroy hid from view the noble past, the great abbots of Cluny in the tenth, the eleventh, the twelfth centuries, several of them saints. As it still does. And it was their church that was taken to pieces, stone by stone."

"But there's another thing. Nobody said it was dreadful to destroy something so beautiful. Isn't that strange? The girl I met today didn't care a bit about Christianity, actually despised it, and probably didn't know about your abbots, so long ago, except that they must have hired the builders, the stone masons, the carvers she's studying. But she cared very much about their craftsmanship, about the beauty of what they made. That's her life. Why didn't anyone protest at the destruction of so much beauty?"

"Imagine, Bernard. Imagine the first twenty years of the nineteenth century."

Bernard took out of his jeans pocket his postcard, a bit crumpled from his bicycle ride. He read from the back, "Destroyed 1798 to 1823".

"Exactly. The Directory, the Consulate, the Empire, the Restoration. Political chaos. Financial chaos. Wars, victories, defeats. No one in Paris had time to care about the beauty of buildings they all agreed had no further use. Also, consider the powerful people in those years, most of whom stayed in power for five minutes in any case: children of the Enlightenment, all of them. If it didn't look Greek or Roman it couldn't be beautiful. Romanesque buildings were primitive and Gothic buildings ugly. Alas."

He got up, poured himself another cup of tea, and sat down again.

"Your friend", he said, "is a fortunate girl. A society needs a bit of calm and some spare money for universities to produce art historians. France doesn't have much of either at present, but she is peacefully working for her master's degree. That's good."

"I wish she were my friend. She could never be. She thought I was stupid. She's quite right."

"Bernard." Thamar sharpened his voice. "You are not stupid. You are intelligent in ways she may have no perception of, that's to say, ways she has chosen to exclude from her idea of the world. If, as you say, she separates beauty from goodness and truth she may find, as time goes by, that her career as an art historian presents her with difficulties she has at present no idea of. Not professional difficulties but difficulties for her as a person, a person alone on the planet as each of us is."

"I don't know."

"You don't yet know."

Bernard also poured himself a second cup of tea. When he sat down again, he said, "Thamar. You are trying to convert me. To God. Aren't you?"

"Naturally. Yes. To turn you round—that's what conversion means—so that you are looking towards the light, not towards the shadows cast by the light."

"Plato."

"I told you I was a Platonist."

"Yes." Bernard felt trapped by a set of things he didn't understand. Perhaps the girl had been right, about Christianity, about art and her carved capitals, about everything. Why hadn't he asked her what she was called?

"Don't be afraid, Bernard. Or, don't be afraid of me. Often, already, you are looking towards the light, more of the time than you realize. But I know the light can be frightening. Too bright. Even blinding. It's always easier to turn back towards the shadows. Plato knew that too. Never mind for now. There's work to do on my so-called book. I hope the work won't be too much for you but if it is, you must tell me, and we can forget, both of us, all about this old man's folly. Getting to know you has been infinitely more important to me than anything that may or may not come of the book."

Bernard couldn't answer.

"Show me your postcard", Thamar said.

He looked at the photograph for a long minute.

"No one had made this model when I was a boy. Cluny was a wonder of the world, nine centuries ago. In what they like to call the Dark Ages."

He stood up and put the postcard on the dresser, in front of one of the old painted plates he never used.

The next morning, Tuesday September 29th, Bernard took his laptop to the summer house when Thamar and Félix had left for the château, deleted the page he had written, and started again.

Chapter 4

Jacques

January to November 1960

As he opened the street door of the bookshop, the freezing air hit his lungs. He held the door for Mademoiselle Gaillard to go out ahead of him, and shut it quickly behind them, so as not to let more cold than he could help into the shop, where people would still be buying and selling books, journals and magazines for another half-hour.

The Boulevard Saint-Michel was busy in the dark, icy evening, crowded buses waiting at the traffic lights, cars, taxis, people on the broad pavements, their heads down against the cold, making their way home from work or out for the evening.

"Which way are you going, Jacques?"

"I'm meeting a friend, the other side of the Panthéon."

"Very good", she said. "I'll say goodnight then. I'm going down to the Métro. My goodness, it's cold this evening."

"Goodnight, mademoiselle."

They shook hands, as every day. Her hand was small and neat in its woollen glove, as she herself was small and neat. She was, as always, formal, correct, but kind. She fussed over every detail, every bill and receipt, in the shop, but that was what, as the bookkeeper, she had to do. The other young assistants mocked her behind her back but she had helped Jacques to learn how to do his work as it should be done when he started his job eighteen months ago, and he was fond of her. "Poor old thing", Henri, two or three years older than Jacques, had said one day, although Mademoiselle Gaillard couldn't have been more than forty. "Apparently she was engaged to be married just before the war, to a soldier. The Germans captured

208

him in 1940 and put him in some prisoner-of-war camp and she waited for him all through the war. Then he came back in 1945 and didn't want to marry her after all. Tough, don't you think, after she'd written him a Red Cross letter every month for five years. No wonder she's a bit dried up and pernickety. What else has she got to care about beyond getting the numbers right?" "A cat, at home in her flat, I bet you", said Marcel, Henri's friend. "A pampered, smelly cat. Anyway, how do you know she wrote him a letter every month?" "Well, look at her. She would, wouldn't she?"

But Jacques liked Mademoiselle Gaillard, with her neat grey suit and her high-necked cream blouse, fastened with a cameo brooch with some kind of Greek nymph, white against a grey background, in a small oval gold frame. Sometimes, when a customer was being difficult about a bill or the price of a book, she would give him a quick look, almost a smile, of understanding and encouragement. Because of her, he felt less lonely in the shop.

He turned left, up the Boulevard, in the opposite direction from the Seine. It was so cold that after a few yards he stopped, pulled off his scarf and rewound it so that it covered his mouth as well as his neck. It wasn't exactly snowing but there were splinters of ice in the air; he could see them, tiny needles catching the light from the shop windows and the street lamps, and feel them sharp on his face.

He had promised to meet Mathieu in the bistro on a corner of his own street, the Rue Mouffetard, where he lived in a little room up the rickety stairs at the back of a charcuterie. Mathieu had appeared in the bookshop at lunchtime and said: "They say the General's going to do a broadcast on the television tonight. It's going to have to be good. There's a hell of a mess in Algeria. He probably can't sort it out but at least he's got to sound as if he can. We'd better watch him. Meet you at the bistro at seven? We can have a bite to eat."

Jacques turned left into the wide street that led to the open space of the Place du Panthéon. Across the square he saw the backs of a line of half a dozen policemen, watching a few demonstrators holding above their heads a white banner with writing on it. He couldn't see but knew what it said: *Algérie française*, painted as if in blood, the sloping letters jagged, bleeding into the white background. Not, or perhaps not yet, an alarming demonstration. Perhaps it was too cold, or perhaps the demonstrators were waiting to see what the General said.

The Panthéon was entirely dark. He disliked it very much, for no good reason that he could think of. When he first arrived in Paris, and was trying at the weekends to see as many famous buildings and museums as he could fit in to his days, he went inside the Panthéon just once. The heavy white columns and the grand tombs and memorials he found only oppressive, suggesting nothing of people who one by one, after all, had died, on a particular day in a particular place. The grave he was used to was the one in which the old nun his grandmother had loved was buried. He had regularly visited it with his grandmother when he was a little boy, carrying a bunch of flowers to lay on the grass at the small headstone, among others in a distant, shaded part of the château's garden. A grave in the grass was good. Or a name on a list, like his grandfather's name on the village war memorial. Every time they walked past it, which was almost every day, he and his grandmother stood for a moment and bowed their heads. A couple of times, children playing in the square had laughed and pointed; a look from his grandmother had sent them running.

And the Panthéon was a huge church that was no longer a church. In the place where there should have been an altar was a large white sculpture, a number of figures hailing a tall woman with a sword, and the bold letters of an inscription: The National Convention. 1792, he remembered being told. The First Republic. Intended to last for ever. And now General de Gaulle had proclaimed the Fifth Republic, on the ruins of the Fourth which had lasted twelve years. What was there to be so proud of? And why in a church, or what had been a church, when all the Republics had hated the church?

Why should he mind, now? And in any case, he had disliked even more the Sacré-Cœur, high on its hill at the other end of Paris, and that was definitely still a church.

There they all were, in the Panthéon, gathered together, Voltaire, Rousseau, Victor Hugo, Zola, heroes of France he had learnt about at school. No soldiers. He liked much better the Invalides, where the generals and the marshals of France were buried near the ashes of Napoleon. Soldiers and glory, under their golden dome: that seemed right. But here were writers and philosophers, in their unchristian, their anti-Christian space. However unchristian they had themselves been, it seemed wrong. He couldn't have explained why, and, perhaps because he couldn't, was ashamed of what he felt.

Voltaire, for example.

Monsieur Fouchet, who had taught the clever boys French literature and philosophy in Jacques's last year at the *lycée* in Mâcon, read *Candide* with them and said, "The Lisbon earthquake destroyed the faith of intelligent men in a just God. You are supposed to be going to become intelligent men, so don't you forget there is no just God. If there is no just God, there is no God. Whatever anyone tells you. You can rely on Voltaire. He knew how to think."

Jacques found Voltaire's tomb in the crypt, behind a statue of the philosopher as an old man dressed as a Roman orator, pen in one hand, book in the other. The tomb was a grim marble casket, inscribed "Aux Manes", "to the shades". Not even "to the holy shades". Jacques remembered a little drawing of a Roman gravestone in his Latin textbook at school, "D M" before the dead man's name: "Dis manibus", "to the holy shades". "Voltaire couldn't say he was an atheist", Monsieur Fouchet had told them, "because atheism before the Revolution was against the law. But he was the father of atheism. We owe him a great deal."

Monsieur Fouchet was a Communist. According to him, it wasn't advisable to say so in the classroom, just as it wasn't advisable for Voltaire to say he was an atheist. This he explained to Jacques and the other two boys he sometimes took to a café after school, to talk to them, to lend them books, to make sure they were, at seventeen, clearing out of their heads the "superstitious nonsense" they had been brought up to believe since early childhood. They discussed the *Communist Manifesto*: each of them in turn had read a dog-eared copy which had, in pencil on the title page, "J-M Fouchet Paris 1935". J-M, probably Jean-Marie. So, very likely, he had pious parents, which meant he knew what he was talking about. When did he abandon the "-M" from his name? Notices and chits in the *lycée* he always signed "J. F." And another, slightly less dog-eared, book that the three boys read in turn, Sartre's novel *La Nausée*, had "Jean Fouchet Paris 1938" on the title page.

Jaques was impressed by the *Communist Manifesto*. It made sense of much that was obviously unjust in rich countries like England and Germany, and still in France, even after France had had one great Revolution and then plenty more. But he couldn't translate what Marx had said about class warfare into what he knew best: life in a village in the middle of Burgundy. There hadn't for a long time been a powerful landowner. Could a few shopkeepers and farmers, and the priest and the mayor and his grandmother, and the nuns in the château, be described as the oppressive and doomed bourgeoisie? If he lived in a city he would no doubt understand Marx better. But the ideal of a new, free, equal society appealed to him anyway.

He hated *La Nausée*. It seemed intended, deliberately intended, to destroy his love for the fields and woods and vineyards and cattle of home, the little castles and churches, so as to replace this love—but with what? Not only disgust, but some kind of liberation that Jacques didn't grasp: it wasn't a question, in Sartre, of religion or no religion, but somehow of ordinary security in the world or none. As if none were better. But he didn't trust himself to get this right if he tried to say it to Monsieur Fouchet. There wasn't anyone else.

Jacques would go back, in time for supper, to the big, chilly presbytery where, with a couple of other boys from the country, he lodged with the four priests, one of them over eighty, from Monday to Friday. Of course there, eating the very good food cooked by the priests' crotchety old housekeeper while the priests chatted about this and that, he never uttered a word about Monsiuer Fouchet, let alone Voltaire or the *Communist Manifesto* or Sartre.

To Jacques, Monsieur Fouchet was a hero. He was known to have been a brave Resistance fighter in the war, to have been captured by the Gestapo and to have escaped by jumping from a moving train somewhere in Belgium on his way to prison, and probably execution, in Germany. He had managed to get back, all the way to the Mâconnais, through fields and woods and along river banks, keeping out of sight in the daytime. This, at least, was the school legend, which also reported that he had killed with a shotgun an important Nazi colonel while a group of German officers, out hunting in the woods above Cluny, were so busy shooting at birds that they failed to notice Monsieur Fouchet's shot until they saw the colonel lying dead. Perhaps all this was an exaggerated version of what had happened, but Jacques didn't care. He loved Monsieur Fouchet because he took seriously what his boys tried to say, and because Jacques knew that the schoolmaster had freed him from the habits instilled in him by his grandmother, who was so devoted, no doubt partly because of his mother's chaotic life, to the task of making him a good Catholic boy.

Did this new freedom have anything to do with what Roquentin decided at the end of *La Nausée*? He had an idea that it did, though he very much hoped that it didn't. Surely he could decide for himself what to think about all sorts of things without having to hate everything real? He knew he could never hate his own countryside, his own piece of France. He knew he could never hate, for example, the weather. Every kind of weather he had loved all his life, however unpopular it was with the grown ups.

When he left the *lycée* Monsieur Fouchet had given him, and each of the other two boys from the sessions in the café, a copy of Camus's *L'Étranger*. "I want you to read this. Existentialism in a nutshell. A great book." Jacques had disliked the book even more than he had disliked *La Nausée*. He couldn't see what they were supposed to have in common, but he could tell that *L'Étranger* was much the better book because he couldn't forget it: the hot beach, the pointless murder, the prison cell, Meursault raging at the prison chaplain. Even remembering the story made him miserable. He had found leaving his Catholic childhood behind calm and encouraging, not enraging. But then, he hadn't killed a wretched Arab for no good reason, really for no reason at all.

As for existentialism, neither Sartre nor Camus had given him any clear idea of what it meant.

When at last, in the summer of 1958, a few weeks after he had left school, he reached Paris, he had one more fence, raised round him by his grandmother, to climb over. She and Père Bonnard, Monsieur le Curé, the parish priest in the village who always did as she asked, had arranged for Jacques to stay in a hostel for students run by nuns in the Latin Quarter. He wasn't a student. He had found his job in the bookshop by writing to twenty bookshops on the Left Bank—a secondhand bookseller in Mâcon had lent him a list—and asking each one if they would give him a job as a trainee in their shop. A few of them replied, saying they had no vacancy on their staff. Only the big shop on the Boulevard Saint-Michel offered to take him on for a trial period of three months, paying him, to begin with, almost nothing. So the nuns let him have a room, paid for by his grandmother. As soon as the shop gave him a real job and a real wage he left the hostel, saying the nuns would need his room for a proper student, and found his tiny room, with a bed, a washstand with an enamel jug and basin, an ancient straw-bottomed kitchen chair, a chest of drawers, and a peg on the back of the door for his coat, in the second-floor attic above the charcuterie in the Rue Mouffetard.

At last, at last, he could decide things for himself. He was cold most of the time, that first winter, until he saved enough money to buy an extra blanket and a warm scarf. He was often hungry, until he learned how to eat enough bread and cheese and eggs to keep going, and discovered that when he came home in the evenings the fruit and vegetable sellers in the street market in the Rue Mouffetard would let him have, for a few francs, a lettuce, a couple of tomatoes, a peach or a pear, from what they hadn't sold at the end of the day. Those were still the days of old francs: they were centimes now that the General had confused everyone by announcing, just this month, the New Franc, worth the same as a hundred old francs.

He might be cold, he might be hungry, but he was free.

The charcutier, a tough little man from the Auvergne, and his wife, who laughed at everything, didn't mind when he came and went—they lived immediately above the shop and could hear him come in and go out on the wooden stairs—or for how long he stayed in bed when he could. There was no grace at his meals, in any case more or less picnics wherever he happened to be, no rosary after supper, no need to go to Mass when the churches of the Left Bank rang their bells on Sunday mornings. No need even to say his prayers before he fell asleep. This was one habit, however, that he found he couldn't quite break: he stood for a moment every night beside his bed before climbing into it, and said a prayer for his grandmother, who after all deserved an acknowledgement of what she so strongly believed herself, and for the soul of his father because he didn't know his name and didn't want him altogether forgotten. He knew this was ridiculous. He didn't believe in any of it any more. There was no God to receive his prayer. But no one would ever know he was, once each day, being a child again. Certainly Mathieu would never know.

Jacques thought of him as the first real friend he had ever had, and he wanted, more than he wanted anything else, Mathieu to take him seriously.

His name was Mathieu Rostand. He was a medical student, almost a doctor, five years older than Jacques. They had first met in a bar one evening in September, more than four months ago, when both of them had been at a Left Bank meeting of the Communist Party. Most of the people there were students. Mathieu, standing next to Jacques afterwards, as they waited to catch the barman's eye, had offered him a cigarette and said, when Jacques shook his head, "You were at the meeting weren't you?"

"Yes."

"Member of the Party?"

"No. Or perhaps not yet."

"Ah. You're a student?"

"No. I work in a bookshop in the Boul'Mich."

"Good for you. Did you hear the old man on the radio last night?" Rostand, Jacques soon discovered, always called General de Gaulle, President of France since January, "the old man".

Mathieu was now facing the barman. "A beer?", he said to Jacques.

"Yes. Thank you. Let me."

Mathieu, looked at him to see, Jacques thought, what he was likely to be able to afford, and said, "No. Have this one on me."

"Thanks."

They took their beers outside and sat on the narrow terrace, a strip of pavement with three small marble-topped tables, up against the windows of the bar.

"No", Jacques said. "I didn't hear the general last night." He didn't possess a radio. Sometimes he heard through the floor-boards a blurred voice or dance music coming from the radio in the charcutier's kitchen. "I read in the paper about what he said. I wish I understood Algeria. These three choices he's talking about. Which does he want? Which do they want?"

"It depends on who you mean by 'they'. Two choices are impossible for the Arabs, especially for the FLN—you know who they are?"

"*Front de Libération Nationale*?"

"That's right. Terrorists, or liberators, depending on who's talking. They've lost so many killed in the war, they have to go on fighting; two choices, but not the same two, are impossible for the wretched *colons*; all three are probably impossible for the army—why should they go on killing, and dying, if Algeria is to be abandoned? Even if they were to win the war, which they're not going to, and then leave. But that's the whole point. What the old man wants himself is pretty clear: he wants them all to realize the situation is already impossible before any of them think it's his fault."

"Really?"

"Really. He's a clever old bastard. What's your name, by the way?"

"Thomas. Jacques Thomas."

"From the country?"

Jacques laughed. "Yes. I'm afraid it's still obvious, though I've been in Paris for more than a year."

"It doesn't matter. I'm not a Parisian either. My name's Rostand. Yes. Like the terrible playwright. No relation, I'm happy to say."

Jacques got the feeling he always said this when introducing himself.

What Rostand had said about Algeria only added to Jacques's confusion. The meeting, the first Party meeting he'd been to, had made him realize how little idea he had as to what was going on in Algeria or, come to that, in France. No one at home, not even Monsieur Fouchet, and no one in the bookshop, had ever said more about the war than that it was terrible and that only the General could end it. He didn't know enough even to understand Rostand's distinctions, let alone to argue. So he said, because it was an easy question, "Do you think the General is a dictator?"

The most vehement of the speakers at the meeting had called the President a fascist dictator. "We have to plan for his downfall. We don't need to help the FLN. They're not going to help us. Let them and the army go on tearing each other apart. We need our own revolution, in France. Do we want to be ruled by the second fascist, the second old soldier masquerading as the saviour of the nation, the second old Catholic, the second old fraud, in twenty years? Less than twenty years. Pétain and de Gaulle. What a pair!" Roars of approval from the meeting.

"You mean like Hitler or Mussolini?" Mathieu said. "No, I don't. They're too recent and he's too clever. He's not going to behave like them, look like them. Also, unlike them, he's not deranged. Far from it. Nor is he at all like Pétain, whatever the out-and-out Communists say. He's by no means too old to think straight, and he's a real politician which that old fool Pétain never was. But what he's managed—to be ruling France more or less single-handed, without a revolution, without barricades and flying paving-stones and blood in the streets— is too close to dictatorship for comfort. Look how he did it! Waiting and waiting until he was asked to rescue the country. By then he looked like a better option than any other, except to the Party of course."

"I don't understand why the Party hates him so much."

217

When de Gaulle had appeared, a bit more than a year ago, to save France from what looked like being a coup by the army, or even civil war so the newspapers were saying, Jacques had been seventeen, at the *lycée* in Mâcon. The priests in the presbytery were delighted; his grandmother, when he went home for the weekend, was delighted. Even Monsieur Fouchet, though grim-faced, was grudgingly relieved. "De Gaulle as the saviour of France is not good news", he had said to the whole class. "But any other news at this moment would almost certainly have been worse. Time to draw a line under the Fourth Republic in any case: twenty governments in twelve years is no way to run a country."

"It's history, recent history", Rostand said. "The Party will hate him forever because after the war he wouldn't give us credit for what we'd done in the Resistance. He pretended that everything that anyone, any group, had done to disrupt the Occupation had been organized from London, by him. Then he fought tooth and nail to keep Communists out of the government in 1945, though the PCF won the first election after the war. De Gaulle said all Communists were enemies of France which they certainly weren't. Not then."

"And now?"

"Well. It depends, doesn't it? On what you mean by 'France', for a start. The Party will never, as long as it fights for French workers, for the little people of France as of everywhere, be the enemy of their France. During the war, after the war, we were all on the same side, the side of the little people. De Gaulle and the Party, even if not together, had both done all they could to free France from the Nazis, from the Vichy fascists. We should have been able to stay on the same side, but de Gaulle wouldn't have it. Now—well, look at the world."

Rostand, who clearly enjoyed talking, took a long drink of beer. Jacques was pleased that there was no need to say anything.

"What do you see?", Rostand went on. "Desperate people struggling to free themselves from imperialist powers that should never have been in their countries in the first place. The Party should always be on their side. The people of Indo-

China, the people of Algeria, the people in most of Africa. But France, the France the world sees, de Gaulle's France, is on the other side, the side of oppression, exploitation, cruelty, injustice. So is America. Look at Indo-China. France gets beaten. Dien Bien Phu: a disgrace for the army, not a huge disaster like 1940, but symbolically almost worse. No wonder the army is so edgy about Algeria: if that's lost too . . . well! What price the *grande armée* then? And now the wretched people of Indo-China have got the Americans on their backs instead of us, no less determined to keep them down, keep them from the freedom they deserve. The Americans will lose Indo-China, just as France did, you wait and see."

"And is that what you think, what the Party thinks, about Algeria too? France on the backs of the people, fighting battles we can't win? And we'll lose Algeria as well?"

"All of that, yes. We'll lose Algeria for sure. The old man knows it, though he can't say it. But Algeria's a different kind of problem from Indo-China, and the Party can't make up its mind, mostly because Moscow doesn't like the FLN, whereas Moscow loves the Viet Cong. We shouldn't ever have been in Indo-China, but at least when we lost the war, we left. Soldiers, officials, tax collectors: they all cleared out, bar a few traders and nuns and archaeologists. But Algeria's another thing altogether."

Rostand lit another cigarette. Jacques, after a year and a half of hearing no one talk seriously, felt he was back in the café in Mâcon after school while Monsieur Fouchet explained the world. This was better because Rostand wasn't much older than he was himself, and he wasn't a teacher.

"Algeria's much, much more difficult. Losing the war won't be the end of the story. There are a million *colons* in Algeria, a million people who all their lives have been told they're French, French citizens, part of France, to be defended in all circumstances against the despised Arabs. Mind you, a lot of them aren't, properly speaking, French at all. They're a ragbag of people from all over the Mediterranean. Always have been, for more than a hundred years. Useful labourers for the *grands colons*—they're the ones, most of them actually not in Algeria but in France, who make stacks of money out of Algeria and won't hear of us leaving it—or the children and grandchildren of useful labourers. But there are nine million Arabs, nine million real Algerians, whatever that means. People who were there before we arrived in any case. So you can't have any kind of independence, any kind of democratic elections, in Algeria without the *colons* being swamped by the Arabs. The *colons* will never agree to that. But the real Algerians, now, will never agree to being ruled from France or being ruled by the *colons*. That's why the old man's other alternatives are nonsense and he knows it. The only choice that's possible is also inevitable: France abandons Algeria. The old man threatens bloodshed and chaos if Algeria is abandoned. But what is there now? Bloodshed and chaos for five years already. Nearly six."

"I had no idea it was so complicated. Would you like another beer, by the way?"

"Sure."

"I'll get it this time."

Another look. "OK. Thanks."

"So", Jacques said, putting two more beers on their little table, and sitting down. "Have you been there, in Algeria? Did you have to do the army?"

"Medical students are exempt, thank the Lord. No. I haven't been to Algeria. You won't find many people in Paris who have, apart from soldiers of course. And they, in my experience, won't talk about it. It makes you wonder why. But we know why." He looked at Jacques over the beer and his full ashtray. "How old are you?", he said.

"Nineteen. Nearly. I'll be nineteen in November."

"Ah. Anything wrong with you? Bad feet, bad eyesight, fits?"

"No."

"Then you're for it, my lad. This time next year they'll call you up and you'll have to go."

Jacques knew this, had known it for a long time. He had always pushed the thought of it to the back of his mind, hoping that the war, perhaps even conscription, might be over before it was his time to join the army. He had little idea of what that meant. One boy from the village had been killed in Algeria, while Jacques was still at school. He had known him a bit, from kicking a ball around in the square when they were much younger. The soldier's parents had wanted his name put on the war memorial with the names of the soldiers killed in the Great War. The mayor had refused permission. Jacques had heard his grandmother say to Monsieur le Curé that everyone knew the mayor was a Communist and this proved it. The soldier's family had left the village.

Now, more than four months after that conversation on the evening they met for the first time, Jacques was waiting for Mathieu in the bistro on the corner of the Rue Mouffetard. He was early; Mathieu would be late. He always was.

His father was a cardiologist in a big hospital in Lille, where Mathieu had been born and grew up. "Don't bother", he had said, three weeks after the Party meeting, when Jacques said he'd never been to Lille. "It's a shocker. I'm fond of it, I sup-pose, but there's no point in going there if you haven't got a reason. It's just a worn-out industrial city going backwards. The Occupation didn't help. The Nazis were very heavy-handed, so far north. They governed Lille as part of Belgium. Imagine: Lille, a left-wing French city being told it was Flemish, part of the greater Reich or whatever. People went along with it, or not. There were a lot of recriminations and resentments after the war. There still are. Outside the centre the city's still very poor, industrial slums and a bit of low-grade new building where bombs fell, and no one's thought about how to provide work for the people the mills and the foundries don't need any more."

"Is that why you belong to the Party?"

It was early in October 1959, a sunny autumn day, the leaves still dusty green on the plane trees along the *quais*, most of the foreign visitors gone, warm enough for the *bouquinistes* to be still dozing on their chairs by their long boxes of books. For the second time, Jacques and Mathieu had met for lunch. Because of the weather, they had bought ham sandwiches, crossed the bridge to Notre-Dame and were sitting on a bench in the little park behind the cathedral. They were beginning to find out about each other's lives.

Mathieu munched his sandwich. "I don't, as it happens. I was going to join it when I got to Paris. The left is a family tradition. My father's always been a socialist. His great hero was Salengro. Roger Salengro? You haven't heard of him? Of course not. Why would you, in Burgundy? He was the socialist mayor of Lille for years. A real champion of the poor, the unemployed, the little people. He was in Blum's government, you know, the Popular Front, 1936. The far right hounded him, to his death."

"What? Literally?"

"Literally. *Action française*, *Croix-de-feu*, fascist monsters, the lot of them. Catholic fascist monsters. You're not Catholic, are you?"

"Not any more", Jacques said.

"Good. Anyway. Salengro. They said he'd been a deserter in the Great War, when he'd been a prisoner-of-war in Germany and nearly starved to death. Of course they hated him mainly because he was a Jew, like Blum. He was cleared of all the lies, officially exonerated, in the *Assemblée*, but he killed himself two days later. A million people turned out for his funeral in Lille. My father's always said it was the proudest day of his life."

"When was all that? Before the war, obviously."

"1936. The year after I was born."

"Was your father born in Lille too?"

A long look from Mathieu.

"Ah. You guessed. People do sometimes."

Jacques had no idea what he was supposed to have guessed.

"No", Mathieu said. "My father was born in Alsace. His family were Alsatian Jews. Heaven knows for how long. Perhaps centuries. They moved to Lille after 1870. They preferred being French to being German, even though the French were more anti-Semitic than the Germans in those days. My grandfather changed the family name in the Great War. Rosenberg to Rostand."

Jacques thought back to what, as a child, he had heard about Jews, because of the family the nuns looked after in the château. He had hardly ever heard Jews talked about since.

"What about the Nazis?", he said. "During the Occupation?"

Mathieu shrugged. "We were lucky. As you see. My father

kept his head down. He was called Rostand. He was a doctor. The Nazis needed the hospitals to function. The family hadn't been religious for generations. My mother isn't Jewish. We all survived. Fate on our side. Chance, more likely."

"My father was a Jew."

"Really?" Another long look. "I can't see it. I thought—the deep country? Catholic Burgundy?"

"I was brought up by my grandmother. She is all of that. My mother left when I was a baby. She couldn't do Catholic Burgundy."

"So, your father? What was his name?"

"I don't know."

"You don't know? Then—Thomas?"

"My mother's name. My grandmother's name."

A pause, while Mathieu crumpled the paper his sandwich had been wrapped in, got up to throw it in a bin, came back to their bench and lit a cigarette.

"I see. Then how do you know—"

"He was a Polish Jew. That's all my mother told my grandmother. My mother left Paris in the summer of 1940, in the panic, alone. I was born that November, in my grandmother's house. No doubt the Nazis killed my father. I don't know if he ever knew she was pregnant."

Mathieu took a pull on his cigarette.

"Alas", he said. "Another sad story, of the war, of the Jews. I wonder if he was a Communist, your father. The Nazis, and Vichy, naturally, thought, among other things, that all Jews were Communists and all Communists were Jews. Idiotic. But of course some were. Some are."

Jacques finished his sandwich.

"But not you."

"No. I've been to plenty of meetings. Some of the speakers talk a great deal of rubbish. And the PCF, the *Parti Communiste Français* that they're all so proud of, is too much in Moscow's pocket. I've heard them defend what happened in Hungary, which was diabolical. Marx would have been on the side of the revolution in Hungary. Just as he would be on the side of the FLN—if ever there were a case of the oppressed proletariat rising up against capitalist exploitation, the FLN is it. And all its leaders are proper socialists, as *laïque* as you or me, educated in French, French soldiers, some of them, but Moscow thinks they're religious because they're nominally Muslim, and nationalists who won't obey Moscow, so it won't let the PCF be on their side."

Mathieu, who had been talking with his usual eloquence, watching the pigeons at their feet, turned to Jacques.

"Sorry", he said. "Too complicated. What about you? Have you made up your mind to join the Party?"

"No, I haven't. In fact, I think I've made up my mind not to."

"Good. Better to make up your own mind about each thing that comes along. It's your own life, after all."

"I've only in the last year or two managed to leave the Church. Not that I ever joined it, but my grandmother had me in it from when I was born. But I don't want to join anything else. Not for the moment."

"Very sensible. I joined the youth wing of the Party in Lille when I was still at school. My father wasn't pleased. 'No need to go to extremes, even at your age.'"

Jacques laughed at Mathieu's imitation of a heavy father: he could tell that Mathieu loved his father.

"I chucked a couple of years later", Mathieu said. "Over Hungary. I still go to meetings, to see what they're up to. But joining things when there's no need—never a good idea. And you're going to have to join the army."

"Don't, Mathieu, don't remind me. I keep hoping the old man will have managed to end the war before then."

"He may. He may not."

"If he does, they won't need any more soldiers, will they?"

"Perhaps. Perhaps not."

Jacques laughed again. "Mathieu! It's your medical training. They're making sure you know how not to commit yourself to a diagnosis if you haven't a clue what's wrong with the patient."

"Perhaps."

"Perhaps not."

Now Mathieu laughed, as he looked at his watch. "I've got to go. Neurology lecture at 2. See you next week?"

"Of course."

Jacques walked back to the shop as if it were spring. He was pleased, without any real idea why, that Mathieu's father, like his, was Jewish, and also pleased that Mathieu had joined the party as a schoolboy and then left it, so certainly wouldn't press Jacques to join it. It turned out that Mathieu, unlike Monsieur Fouchet, had refused to put his loyalty to the Party above his shock at what Russia had done in 1956. Jacques hadn't yet been in Monsieur Fouchet's class when, three years before, the Red Army tanks had rolled into Budapest and Red Army soldiers had shot people down in the streets. Later, Monsieur Fouchet had told his boys in the café after school that this Soviet invasion was the only thing that had ever seriously threatened his faith. "But look—peace is restored to the Warsaw Pact. Compare the disgraceful deal we did with England and Israel to attack Egypt, at just the same time. Compare the mess that France has made of so much since then. Perhaps the Russians were right."

At seven-thirty, Mathieu appeared in the bistro, bringing with him, though he shut the door quickly, a breath of the bitter cold outside.

"Sorry, sorry", he said. "I had to go back to the ward with my chief to look at a patient. What shall we have?"

With some difficulty, Jacques had kept a chair for Mathieu at a table from which they could see the television, which was why they were there. A football match was taking place on the screen with the sound turned down. No one in the bistro was watching it.

"A beer?" Jacques said. He had had some rather unpleasant lemonade while he was waiting. "A *croque-monsieur*?"

"Excellent. I'll have a couple of eggs too. I'm starving."

The bistro, cheap, basic and old-fashioned, was very full, with a dozen men crowded round the bar, because of the general's broadcast. Eventually a waiter, carrying a tray of glasses at shoulder height, noticed Mathieu's signals and put the tray down on their table long enough to scribble their order on a pad.

"What's he going to say?"

"It'll be a call to order", Mathieu said. "He's really got to pull something pretty impressive out of the fire this time. You realize there's been total chaos in Algiers for a whole week. Ghastly. Corpses on the streets. If it were Paris everyone would be saying it's the Commune all over again. The *colons* seem to have got it into their heads that they could start a rebellion of their own. That was how the chaos in May '58 started, if you remember."

Jacques didn't, because the crisis from which de Gaulle rescued the country was much too complicated for him to understand at the time.

"So this time the FLN took advantage. The army, which seems not to know whether it's coming or going, held back. Result: a massacre. French soldiers killing French policemen. FLN fighters killing both. *Colons* running amok, killing and being killed. The army, or the generals anyway, want it to look like old man's fault. And sacking Massu probably was the spark that lit the blaze. But what else could he do? Massu obviously told the truth in the famous interview."

"I don't understand about these generals. I thought they all worshipped de Gaulle."

"They do. Or they did. That's why they're so disappointed, so angry. They thought they were bringing him back to save Algeria, save the army, save France. And now it's clearer and clearer that Algeria's going to be dumped to save France, which means, actually, defeat for the army. Again. Defeat in 1940. Defeat in Indo-China. And now, staring them in the face, defeat in Algeria. That's why—did you read about Massu's interview?"

"Yes, of course. I thought maybe the journalist had made up half of what Massu was supposed to have said?"

"Not at all. He couldn't have printed stuff Massu hadn't said: he was the commander-in-chief in Algeria, after all. But to say the army now thinks de Gaulle is a man of the Left—ridiculous idea, though one can see why the generals might come to that conclusion, and anyway 'the left' is for them just an all-purpose insult—and then to say that the army might not obey the president of France if they don't like what he tells them to do:

well, that amounts to a call to mutiny. And all in a German newspaper, for heaven's sake. That must have been the last straw for the old man. Of course he sacked Massu. And then of course there was mayhem on the streets of Algiers."

"So what can he do now?"

"We'll see."

The waiter dashed up with their supper and at high speed put it, and their scribbled bill, in front of them.

"If one were to be cynical—", Mathieu said, knife in one hand, fork in the other.

"Which you are", Jacques said and they both laughed.

"Sometimes. Well, a cynic might say the old man's got them where he wants them: everyone except him is evidently in the wrong. That suits him fine."

Suddenly the blare of the Marseillaise, from the television with the sound now on, quelled all the noise in the bistro and everyone, sitting or standing, turned to look up at the small screen, on a shelf above their heads. Most of the lights were switched off so that people could see the television better.

There he was, the general, in his wartime uniform, glaring imperiously at the nation. Jacques had never seen him before, except in photographs in the papers, let alone heard him speak. "*Françaises, français*", he began. No one moved in the crowded café for the few minutes of the speech. At its end there was an impressed, even stunned, silence in the café. Then five or six men clapped; the rest didn't join in as, from somewhere close by in the Rue Mouffetard, there came the sound of a few people cheering. The *patron* switched on the lights and switched off the television. Jacques saw tears on the cheeks of two or three of the older men. One blew his nose so loudly that others laughed and began to talk.

Afterwards Jacques would have found it difficult to give to someone who hadn't heard it a summary of what the general had actually said. It was easy to tell what had made the old men cry. Perhaps they had been soldiers. One or two were old enough to have been soldiers in the Great War. "My old and dear country", the general had said, "So here we are together, once more": Jacques had almost cried himself. But what else had he said? That for Algeria, "self-determination is the only policy worthy of France" and that there must be no question of disloyalty in the army. "It is I who bear the country's destiny. I must therefore be obeyed", he had said. That was all Jacques, as the speech ended, could remember. He looked across the table.

Mathieu, waiting for his look, was smiling.

"Well?" he said.

"That was pretty terrific, don't you think?"

"Of course. He knows what he's doing. He wants everyone eating out of his hand, the Algerians, or the *colons* in any case, the army—they'll all have been listening on radios—and everyone in France. It'll work, for a while. 'Trust me and I'll sort it all out.' That's what the speech amounts to. But he can't, because no one can."

"But—"

"But what? Look, Jacques. It doesn't add up. Self-determination for Algeria: it sounds all right but what happens to a million *colons* whom the Arabs want determined out of existence? As for the army, naturally obedience is what armies are all about. Massu's been sacked. A few other generals may be sacked too. But half the army, I should think, agree with what Massu said in the interview. How does anyone, even de Gaulle, persuade people to go on fighting in a cause they've just been told is lost? It's all going to get worse before it gets better."

"Don't you trust the old man, yourself, to work something out?"

"We all have to, up to a point. Who else is there? But there are horrors ahead. You'll see when you get there. My poor Jacques."

Jacques was again close to tears, not because of the general's speech but because the way Mathieu had said those last three words had made him realize—what? How much he depended on him? How pleased he was to see him, once a week for lunch? How sad he would be to have to leave him, and to leave him to fight in a dreadful war he was sure Mathieu was right about? He felt sorry for himself, like a small boy left out of the game in a school playground, and ashamed, at nineteen, of feeling like a small boy.

228

"It's not fair", he said, like a child. "You can get on with your life. You can stay in Paris, learning how to be a doctor, just reading about all these things in the newspapers. But I'm going to have to go there, later this year or next year. And the army are doing horrible things, everyone knows that. What can I do, Mathieu?"

"I know. I'm sorry. It's not fair. But what is?"

He pushed away his empty plate, put his elbows on the table and clasped his hands under his chin.

"Listen. I wasn't going to tell you this, and you mustn't say a word about it to anyone else."

"Of course I won't."

Who else was there?

"We have a couple of very badly wounded soldiers on the ward. One's been blinded by a grenade going off in his face. We'll patch up his face and he'll recover, but he won't get his sight back. He has some brain damage too. The other fellow was shot in the back and his spine's in bits. He's paralysed and he's not going to make it. It would have been better for him if he'd died straight away. Over there. Anyway, I'm not telling you all this to frighten you more. My professor, who belongs to the Party by the way, is furious about these soldiers. They're not the first we've had, of course. He'll be even more furious tonight, after the speech. He wants the old man to call off the war, bring the army home now, and let the FLN sort out Algeria. He thinks they'll need the *colons*, the *petits colons* in any case, to keep things going, and once the army and the *grands colons* have left, they'll find the common cause of the working man and between them pull the country together. Not Moscow's line, but good Marxist stuff. As a first step, he and a few other important people in the Party, with the big names of the left, Sartre and de Beauvoir, Claude Simon, Truffaut, lots of others, want to produce some kind of public manifesto, to start a campaign to encourage conscripts to desert."

"You get shot if you desert."

"The idea is that you never join up: you say you have conscientious objections to the war. They can't force you to fight in a war you believe is wrong."

"Want a bet? How much do they care what someone believes or doesn't believe? And I'm not brave enough to get myself into a lot of trouble because Sartre and his highbrow friends think I should. They wouldn't be the ones to be punished."

"No. I expect you're right. Typical of these famous intellectuals. 'Desert', 'refuse', 'paralyse the army', they say, expecting ordinary people to risk their necks for their Left Bank ideas. It's like their Communism: they're all for Moscow, but do they go and live there? They know they'd never manage without the *Deux Magots*."

Mathieu looked at their bill, put some change on the table, saying "I'll do this. My idea."

"Thanks. I'm broke. End of the month."

"Another interesting thing", Mathieu said, as they waited for the saucer to be collected. "My professor also told me that, just before he died, Camus refused to sign this manifesto."

"Why? You'd think that, being an Algerian, he of all people would want the war to stop."

"Of course he wanted the war to stop. But he'd given up in despair. A few years ago he went back to Algiers—he'd been forced to leave Algeria because he'd pleaded for the Arabs to be treated fairly—to make a speech begging for a truce, begging for all the violence to stop, and he was shouted down and threatened with death by the *colons*, his own people. After that he never went back and never said another word about Algeria. And now he's dead. So stupid and pointless, a car crash. And he wasn't even driving."

"But he wrote *L'Étranger*. About Algeria. That's not exactly about treating Arabs fairly."

"Of course he did. But that was years ago, when there wasn't a war in Algeria, and when he thought he was an existentialist."

The waiter came and took away the saucer. Mathieu found some more change for a tip and put it on the table.

"Mathieu", Jacques said. "What is existentialism?"

Mathieu laughed.

"Your guess is as good as mine. How to live, what to do, the usual questions, and you make up the answers as you go along. You are what you do. Perhaps there's not much difference between existentialism and existence."

"You are what you do? Is that all? I don't mean is that all that existentialism is; I mean is what you do really all you are? Really?"

"Ah. That's what they say, Sartre and company. Do I agree with them? Who knows? You are what you do is OK for a doctor, I suppose."

"But for—"

"Come on, Jacques. Let's go to the jazz club. We need some cheering up."

"I don't know."

"Try and forget it all, Jacques. It's nine and a half months till your birthday. Anything could have happened by then."

They went out into the freezing cold. In the dark smoky crush of the jazz club, in a basement near Saint-Germain-des-Près, Jacques, watching the terrifying girls with their white faces and tight black clothes, could think only how pleased he was that Mathieu had remembered the date of his birthday, and that he'd called him "my poor Jacques".

Almost exactly nine months later, on 27 October, Jacques left the shop at seven-thirty in the evening, later than usual because he had a lot of paper to sort out at his desk and only two more days to get everything straight for whoever would be doing his job next week.

He was going to turn right instead of left on the Boulevard Saint-Michel because he and Mathieu had arranged to meet for a last meal, in an Alsatian brasserie on the tip of the Île Saint-Louis, which they had always reckoned was too expensive for them. Mathieu had said, "We'll have a really good dinner before you go. I shouldn't think army food is up to much."

On Sunday, three days later, Jacques was going home to spend two weeks with his grandmother before joining the army. He had, a month earlier, received a letter, forwarded to Paris by his grandmother, ordering him, "unless there are any particular circumstances you wish to discuss"—he knew that there weren't—to report to the barracks in Lyon to start his basic training course on Monday 14 November, the day before his twentieth birthday. He had already had the army medical examination in Paris, and had been told that he was fit and healthy. He and Mathieu couldn't meet on Friday or Saturday because Mathieu, now working hard in a different department in a different hospital, Cochin, the big old hospital on the Left Bank, was on night duty for the whole weekend.

As soon as he shut the shop door behind him Jacques saw that something odd was going on. The Boulevard Saint-Michel was full of people hurrying towards the Boulevard Saint-Germain and the Seine. Jacques walked with the crowd; it would have been difficult to go in the opposite direction even if he'd wanted to. When he and a number of others reached the crossroads with the Boulevard Saint-Germain, four police vans one after the other came towards them very fast, lights flashing and sirens shrieking, across the Pont Saint-Michel from Police Headquarters on the Île de la Cité, crashed the traffic lights and turned, with a squeal of tires, eastwards along the Boulevard Saint-Germain. He turned on the pavement in the same direction: another, denser crowd of people was running towards him, away from the Place Maubert where, in the distance, he could see more flashing lights. The ordinary traffic had stopped because of the police vans. And he realized that he could hear a dull roar, the sound of shouting and the odd bang like a gunshot, from the Place Maubert, as more and more people came running, along the road as well as the pavements.

A girl had stopped beside him, frightened, the knuckles of one hand in her mouth, her other hand on his arm.

"What's happening?" he said.

"I don't know. Something bad. I'm late. I was going to the rally in the Place Maubert but my bus didn't come. Now—well, I can't get there, can I?"

"What sort of rally?"

"Didn't you know? Aren't you a student?"

He shook his head, put his arm round the girl's shoulders and pulled her back from the tide of running people so that they both had their backs to the railings of the Musée de Cluny.

"A rally for peace in Algeria. Everyone was going. All the students I know. Now—look! Something dreadful must have happened."

She looked, with panic in her eyes, at the people running towards them, past them, mostly young, mostly no doubt students. It was obviously impossible to stop someone and ask what had happened.

Another three police vans came screaming from the bridge and stopped, their lights flashing as policemen jumped out, in the middle of the Boulevard Saint-Germain. At the same moment they heard, over the distant noise of whatever was going on in the Place Maubert, a rhythmic chanting getting louder and louder from behind them, from the Boul'Mich itself. Three short sounds, two long, over and over, louder and louder. *Algérie française. Algérie française.*

"My God", the girl said. "You hear that? Now there'll be a fight."

Four big vans, not ordinary police vans, came towards the crossroads, along the Boulevard Saint-Germain from the other direction, the west, and stopped. Riot police in shiny helmets and black capes, with long clubs in their hands, jumped down.

She was holding his hand. She pulled him a few yards along the pavement, back to the corner of the Boul' Mich, to look.

They looked and shrank back. Coming down the Boul' Mich was another dense crowd, more orderly, walking not running, some of the leaders carrying flares which eerily lit grim faces, marching in step to the chant of *Algérie française*,

"Get back! Back!" They were pushed against the railings by a hefty policeman whose face they couldn't see, backwards into the Boulevard Saint-Germain, into the crush of students which, heavy with moving people, had stopped. To their left, a line of riot police, more like soldiers than policemen, had formed up to block the whole intersection so that the crowd running from the Place Maubert was dammed, with people backing up in the Boulevard Saint-Germain, a furious mob more and more closely packed together.

Holding his hand more tightly as they were squashed against the railings by the crush of students halted by the riot police, she said in his ear, "You see that? You see which side they're on?"

"We should get out of this", Jacques said.

"How can we?"

It was impossible to run, indeed impossible to move. Against the mass of people they couldn't have crossed the Boulevard Saint-Germain to the little streets on the other side, and the Boul' Mich was out of the question.

Jacques remembered suddenly that in a few minutes he was supposed to be meeting Mathieu on the Île Saint-Louis. He couldn't even look at his watch. He couldn't move. He groaned.

"Are you hurt?" She looked up at his face, her eyes a few inches from his.

"No. No, but I've got to get out of here."

"You can't. Look!"

Out of the crowd of students something was thrown at the line of police, he couldn't see what. A bottle? A stone? A cheer from the front of the crush, which echoed back along the Boulevard Saint-Germain. More objects were thrown, and a surge forward broke the line of policemen, just as the *Algérie française* march reached the intersection.

Suddenly there was fighting all round them.

"Get behind me! Get down!"

She crouched against the railings and he crouched in front of her as the riot police with their clubs raised tried to push the mob of students back. Very close to them a police bludgeon came down so hard on the head of a boy, an Arab boy, as his arm went back to throw what looked like a lump of stone, that they heard the crack of the weapon on his skull. He crumpled and fell to the pavement in front of them. "Look out!", someone yelled. "Don't trample him!" Three students immediately bent down, picked him up and started dragging him against the crush and shouting "a doctor, a doctor". Jacques saw the crowd open enough to let them through, the injured boy's feet dragging behind them, and then close again. Further across the road two tall, heavy policemen were beating the backs of a young man and a girl who were clinging together as they tried to get out of the way of the blows. Two more policeman were dragging a boy between them in the opposite direction, towards the parked police vans. Shouting, fighting, hitting, screaming people were all round them. A student with blood streaming down his face appeared in front of them, shouting "Thugs! murderers! scum!", then stopped, swaying, and just before he fell, said to Jacques in an astonishingly quiet voice: "Get her out of here—there shouldn't be women here! It's war!'

Jacques stood up and looked all round him. The worst of the fighting seemed to be moving up the Boulevard Saint-Germain towards the Place Maubert. The riot police with their heavy clubs were no longer in anything like a line but were hitting out at students' backs as they chased them. So many had run away that the crush of the crowd had much loosened. But it was impossible to move in that direction without having to pass policemen who seemed to be hitting out at anyone they could reach. From their patch of pavement by the railings, he couldn't see round the corner into the Boul' Mich but he could hear more shouting, obviously more fighting. Nevertheless, if they were going to get out of the battle they had to move to the corner to look because only from the Boul' Mich could they possibly escape.

The girl was cowering, sitting on the ground, her arms round her knees, her face hidden in her arms, her body shaking. Jacques bent over her and took one hand. She let him pull her upright. She lost her balance and he caught her briefly in his arms, to stop her falling forward. He held her for a moment by her shoulders to steady her, and then again took her hand.

"Come along", he said. "We can't stay here. We've got to try the Boul' Mich."

"But—", she whispered, looking up at him with terrified eyes. "All right."

They crept round the corner, holding hands. In the Boulevard Saint-Michel, as far up as they could see, in the dark lit by headlights from stationary police vans as well as light from the street lamps, there was chaotic fighting, clubs flailing, injured people on the ground, shouting and cursing, some riot policemen swinging their heavy capes at fleeing students. Jacques, leading the girl by the hand, edged along the railings and then along walls and shop fronts, until, as soon as he could, he pulled her into a side street that led towards the Sorbonne. Now free of the fighting, they turned towards the Panthéon until they reached the square, emptying as people crossed it, most of them running, like them, to get as far away from the battle as they could, as quickly as they could manage.

They ran past the Panthéon, huge and dark as always, and stopped, panting for breath, the girl shivering and sobbing, under the carved wall of Saint-Étienne-du-mont. There was some dim light in the church. They could hear quiet singing inside, but also, much louder, the noise of shouting and fighting and instructions barked from loudspeakers, in the Place Maubert, now only two side streets away.

"Shall we go into the church? They'll let us, won't they?", the girl said.

"No. We're nearly home."

"Home?"

"Where I live. In the Rue Mouffetard. Down the Rue Descartes. The other direction from the Place Maubert. Heaven knows what's going on there."

She was sobbing, and still shivering.

It struck him that he had no idea who she was or where she had come from, trying to join the rally that seemed to have been what started the whole nightmare: no doubt it was the prospect of the peace rally that had provoked the *Algérie française* demonstration.

He took her hand again. It was very cold and he rubbed it between both of his to warm her a little.

"Where do you live?", he said.

She took her hand from between his hands and rubbed both of hers together. Then she sniffed hard, pulled a handkerchief from her pocket and blew her nose.

"I'm sorry. Thank you. You saved me from those horrible policemen, soldiers, whatever they are. I live on the Right Bank, in a little street off the Boulevard Voltaire. The Métro—" She looked round as if she might see a station; obviously she didn't know these streets.

"The nearest Métro is Cardinal-Lemoine but—Let's go and see."

It was five minutes' walk. But the Métro station was closed, the heavy iron gates shut, with four policemen, these at least ordinary gendarmes, guarding them. The girl began again to cry.

Jacques stood holding her hand and thinking. He looked at his watch. He should have been at the brasserie on the Île Saint-Louis half an hour ago. He led the crying girl up to one of the gendarmes and said, "Is it possible to get to the Right Bank, or to the Île Saint-Louis?"

"Can't you hear them, monsieur?", the man said, jerking his head in the direction of the Place Maubert. "It's not over yet. The Métro is closed. The bridges down here are closed."

"So I can't walk to the Ile Saint-Louis?"

"Certainly not."

"For how long?"

The man shrugged. "That depends. The Chief will decide. When the students have stopped fighting."

"It's not—O, never mind."

Jacques remembered what Mathieu had told him about Maurice Papon, the Chief of Police. "He's a monster. He looks like the soul of bureaucratic respectablity and the old man loves him. But he's Vichy through and through. After the war, before de Gaulle gave him the Paris job, he was some kind of governor in Algeria. The Party's contacts there say he's a torturer and a murderer."

Mathieu. He would be waiting in the brasserie—but, if he was coming from Cochin, how would he have got there? Before the riot? Through back streets? Jacques gave up wondering as he realized that he might not see Mathieu again, not before he left Paris, perhaps not ever. Now he was almost crying himself.

He shook his head to pull himself together. What was he going to do with this girl?

"You heard all that?", he said.

She nodded miserably.

"I'm so sorry", she said.

"Don't be silly. None of this is your fault. Come along. You need something to eat."

She smiled for the first time.

"So do you."

He took her down the Rue Monge and across to the Rue Mouffetard, avoiding the Place de la Contrescarpe, where there was often trouble at night anyway, and from which he could hear shouting. They reached the bistro on the corner of the Rue Mouffetard where with Mathieu he had watched the general deliver his call to order on the television in January.

Inside, it was warm, crowded and quiet: everyone was peering up at the television, on its shelf, which was showing news film of the riot. Black figures in moving beams of white light struggled on the little screen. Some were being dragged across the picture by pairs of policemen. It was impossible to tell whether this was a recording or live filming of what was still going on. As they watched, a black-helmeted policeman filled the picture, club raised above his head: the picture dissolved in a blur and then the head and shoulders of a news reader appeared, in a suit and tie, sitting in a studio: "And that's all we have for you for the moment. Our cameraman was injured and we can report that a number of journalists, some of them also injured, are among those who have been arrested." Some music followed, the screen blank. Then the news reader was back, reading from a piece of paper: "We have just learned that the Paris police have made more than three hundred arrests this evening, as rioting broke out in the Place Maubert and spread to the Boulevard Saint-Michel. Calm is now being restored to the Latin Quarter, where the Métro stations remain closed. It is hoped that the bridges from the Pont de Sully to the Pont Neuf will reopen to traffic in the next half hour. We shall now resume our normal schedule".

A dance band replaced the announcer on the screen and someone emerged from behind the bar to turn down the sound. Everyone began talking loudly, some blaming the students, some the police, some the "march of the Right" for the riot.

Jacques, who remembered he had saved some money to share the cost of his farewell meal with Mathieu, saw that it wasn't a good idea to ask the shocked girl what she would like, and ordered soup, and cheese omelettes and a half-carafe of red wine.

"Why are you so kind?", she said when their food arrived. "It was all so horrible."

She looked as if she were about to start crying again.

"What's your name?", Jacques said.

"My name's Sylvie", she said, managing not to cry.

"I'm called Jacques Thomas." They shook hands across the table, and both of them smiled. She got out her handkerchief, mopped up her face again, and blew her nose.

"Eat your soup", he said. "You need something to warm you up. And drink a little wine. It'll make you feel better."

"This is a good soup", she said, after a few mouthfuls. "If you're not a student, what is your work?"

"I work in the big bookshop on the Boulevard Saint-Michel. But only for two more days."

She looked shocked. "Why did you lose your job?"

"I didn't. I have to join the army."

She put down her spoon, and looked at him, her eyes frightened again. "O no!", she said. "But that's terrible. Isn't it because of the army that we, that France, can't make peace in Algeria? Surely we should just leave it to the Algerians? And you have to go and fight, and kill people who only want to be free?"

"I think it's a bit more complicated than that. And it's hard to tell what the Algerians want. Different things, and not just peace I'm afraid. But in any case, I have to go. I've got no reason to be excused the conscription."

"I'm so sorry. And your poor parents."

"Yes. Well—" He couldn't begin to explain. "It's the same for thousands of families."

"That doesn't make it any better."

"But it's bound to be interesting, even if it's very unpleasant. It's Africa, after all. A new continent." This was something Mathieu had said, to cheer him up. Ah, Mathieu. He looked at his watch. Nearly nine o'clock.

The waiter took away their soup bowls and brought their omelettes and a salad. Jacques was trying to think, as they ate. When they were escaping from the riot he realized now that he had been intending to take her to his room in the Rue Mouffetard, for safety. And even, he now understood, to take her in his arms, to push her gently down on to his narrow bed—What had he been thinking of? He glanced across the table. She noticed, and smiled again. He went on eating, though it was suddenly difficult.

She was sweet and pretty and trusting. He had never made love to a girl and there was nowhere else for her to sleep in his house. But it would be worse than unkind to make a selfish triumph out of the riot and her vulnerability. She had probably never slept with anyone either, and she had been seriously frightened and upset. How could he, even for a moment, have pictured such a thing?

He banished the picture, the very idea.

"What are you studying?" he said.

"Music. The flute and composition. At the Conservatoire."

"Really? Good for you. That doesn't sound very political."

"No, but a lot of us worry about the war, particularly the boys of course. And people have brothers who are soldiers. Some of the girls have boyfriends who've had to go. We all thought, I thought myself, that the rally was a way of showing support for peace, and so we decided to go. There've been posters up for days. It was all meant to be about peace, and look what happened!" She was almost crying again.

Jacques checked the time.

"Now, listen", he said. "According to the television, the Pont de Sully should be open very soon. We'll go back to the Rue Monge and find a taxi. I'll get out at the Île Saint-Louis, where I should have been an hour ago, and the taxi can take you home to the Boulevard Voltaire."

"But I can't afford a taxi."

"Don't worry. I have enough money to get you home. I was meant to be having supper with a friend, to say goodbye in fact, because he's a doctor, and now it's too late. You've had a very upsetting evening and you deserve a taxi tonight."

Had she noticed that this was a muddled little speech? Probably not.

240

"Thank you", she said. "Thank you so much."

The traffic was slow and bad-tempered but the Pont de Sully was open. The taxi stopped on the bridge, at the tip of the island, for him to get out: the result was more hooting and shouting from other taxis and cars. He had given her plenty of money to pay the taxi when she got home. As he opened the door he turned, took her hand, kissed it, said, "Good night, Sylvie. Sleep well", and immediately got out and shut the taxi door.

He walked the length of the Île Saint-Louis, towards the Île de la Cité and Notre-Dame. The perfect streets with their old lamps were as quiet as if nothing out of the ordinary had happened in Paris that evening. The brasserie was full of people eating, drinking, and discussing the riot. Mathieu had left a note for him.

In case you make it after all—sorry, I had to go. I rang the hospital and they're calling everyone in to help with casualties. What a night to choose for our dinner. I hope you weren't arrested. See you when you're in Paris on leave. It will be worse and better than you think. Good luck. M R

When he got back to the Rue Mouffetard, the charcutier's wife was waiting to hear him come in.

"Jacques? Thank God you're all right. What is happening to Paris? It's worse than the war."

She insisted that he drank a little glass of marc in the kitchen. He went up the narrow stairs to his room, sat on his bed and cried. Because he had been frightened. Because he had to go to beat people, shoot people, kill people in Algeria. Because of the girl and her soft, slight body for a few seconds in his arms. Because of Mathieu.

He never afterwards forgot the peculiar quality of the two weeks he spent with his grandmother before he arrived at the barracks in Lyon and began his three months of basic training and fierce exercises in the cold hills of the Cévennes, which he tried hard not to remember.

His grandmother cosseted him: "You're so thin, Jacques. You haven't been eating properly in Paris. You should never have left the nuns' hostel. Living alone in Paris—what an idea, at your age!"

Although it was November, often chilly, sometimes wet, he walked in the country as much as he could. Baron, his grandmother's dog, a gentle German shepherd dog who loved a long walk, kept him company and occupied himself disappearing into the undergrowth and coming back looking pleased with himself, over and over again, covering twice as much ground as Jacques.

Sometimes there was a fine day. In cold sunlight the woods were as beautiful as he had ever seen them, a few leaves left on the trees, transfixed when there was no wind, gold and russet and brown, the colours sharp, the shadows sharp, in a silence broken only by his tread on fallen leaves, on stony paths, and the rustle of Baron's expeditions into the brushwood. When he stopped walking to listen to the quiet, Baron would sit beside him, still and attentive, as if he would leap into action at any movement in the woods. Jacques breathed the silence and the clear air with deep delight.

Only days had passed since the riot but he found that it was now possible to think of it as much longer ago. In the stillness of the woods he could look back, as if to a film he had watched, to the terrifying fighting at the intersection of the boulevards: the noise, the scream of sirens, the shouting of the police through their loud-hailers, the thump of their clubs—the newspapers next day had written of "a baton charge", which gave no sense of the chaos—the crack of the Arab boy's head hit in front of him and Sylvie, the sinister weight of the capes, lined, the papers said, with lead, which the riot police swung at the students. The papers also explained the start of the trouble: the packed student meeting in the Place Maubert, to demonstrate support for "a negotiated peace", into which *Algérie française* demonstrators had thrown smoke bombs intended to cause panic and, once those running away met those marching, certain to cause fighting. *Le Monde* wrote of the "visible pleasure" with which the police were attacking journalists and politicians. And students: he had seen it.

The film his memory ran over and over again ended with the silent shambles on the Boul'Mich when he went to work the next morning: the street cleaners, dozens of them, sweeping together piles of debris, broken glass, bricks, torn clothes, dropped briefcases, scarves, papers, and shovelling the piles into their handcarts. Three or four of the Musée de Cluny's iron railings had been torn from their concrete footing—how had anyone been strong enough?—and three or four more had been bent in vain. Here and there on the pavements of the Boul'Mich and on the road were stains, bloodstains: seeing them made him feel sick. How was he going to deal with being a soldier, in a real war?

"Jacques, how much do you know about Algeria? It seems they will send you there as soon as your training is over." His grandmother, in the kitchen, was clearing the table after dinner on his second evening.

"Not much. Only what I've read in the newspapers. The war seems to be getting worse."

He hadn't told her that he'd been caught up in the riot.

"Worse for whom? According to the news on the radio, France is winning the war."

Jacques knew what Mathieu would say to this.

"They can't very well say France is losing the war, can they?"

"That's very cynical, Jacques. You don't think France is losing the war, do you? Losing Algeria? After all these brave young men have gone to defend it?"

"I don't know, grand'mère. I really don't know, and I'm not sure anyone knows."

At the sink, she was scraping and rinsing their plates before washing them properly. "Jacques", she said, her back to him, "you will be careful, you will come back, won't you? To lose your grandfather, all those years ago, and then your mother, though that was a different thing—that is enough loss for one life."

"Of course, grand'mère, I'll come back. I'm sure I'll be fine."

"I shall pray."

She clattered the dishes in the sink, ran the tap, turned it off, cleared her throat and came back to the table.

"I'm sorry, Jacques, you must forgive an old woman. After all, only a moment of weakness."

She sat down and put both fists on the table, signifying resolution: she had done this all his life. "Now. I have two books for you to read, while you're here. One belonged to your grandfather; it's about one of his heroes of the last century. The other comes from the nuns' little library, about one of their heroes. Don't make that face, Jacques. Both of them are about Algeria. Perhaps it would be good to know a little about the country and its history before you go?"

"Of course. Thank you, grand'mère, for going to so much trouble."

"Silly boy. It was no trouble. I was thinking of what you might like to do, while you're here, and it was difficult. You don't have any friends in the village any more, do you? Since you went to Paris—"

She hadn't wanted him to go, no doubt because of his mother.

Now, reading his thought as she often did, she said, "At least I always knew where you were. And that you had a good, sensible job, even if it was only in a shop. Thank you for that, Jacques. Anyway, these books—" She got up, brisk now. "I put them in the dresser drawer for you. Here they are."

He took the books, one in each hand, and weighed them against each other. He looked at the titles and opened them to see their publication dates: he was used to cataloguing secondhand books. The heavier and older of the two was a biography of a soldier whose name was Marshal Bugeaud "from his private correspondence and unpublished documents"; the date of the book was 1882. The other book, published in 1921, was called *Charles de Foucauld, Explorer*. Jacques had never heard of either of them.

"They do look interesting", he said. "I think I should read about the soldier first, don't you? Since very soon I'll be a soldier. I might like the explorer better, all the same."

"Ah", his grandmother said. "According to the nuns he wasn't only an explorer. But you'll see."

When it rained all day, and in the evenings, he read both books.

He discovered quickly that Marshal Bugeaud, much admired by the author of his biography, someone called the Comte d'Ideville, was an efficient and resourceful general who had begun his military career fighting with Napoleon and was later more responsible than any other man, at least by this account, for the conquest of Algeria by the French army in the 1830s and '40s after a muddled and almost accidental beginning: Jacques hadn't realized how long ago all this happened. He also discovered, as he read on, that Bugeaud became a cruel and treacherous bully, though still much admired by Monsieur d'Ideville. His method in what Jacques increasingly understood to be the theft for France of a huge area of north Africa, not exactly from the Ottoman empire which had given it up without a struggle, but certainly from its own people, was to terrify and to destroy. Bugeaud's declared policy was to chase farmers and their families off any half-way productive land and replace them with *colons*, from France or anywhere else, who might grow more corn or olives or fruit, than the Arabs had grown. If the people whose land it had always been resisted, they were killed or tortured to make them say where they had hidden grain or jars of olives or herds of goats or sheep. Reading this story with horror, Jacques met a word that was new to him: *razzia*. This, explained in the book as an Arabic word, seemed to mean a swift, violent raid that swept the people out of a village or even a town and often killed the men, leaving homeless women and children to fend for themselves.

Bugeaud was actually proud of saying to the *Assemblée* in Paris in 1840: "Wherever there is fresh water and fertile land, there one must locate *colons*, without concerning oneself to whom these lands belong." Some of the *colons* were French soldiers, rewarded with land for their brutal campaigning. Like the Roman soldiers Jacques remembered being told about at school, given land that had belonged to peasants, to keep them loyal to Julius Caesar or Augustus or whoever.

When Jacques read about these military colonies he remembered something the general, de Gaulle, not Bugeaud, though he was finding it difficult to keep them separate in his head, had said in one of his speeches: there had never been an

Algerian state, only invaders, Carthaginians, Romans, Vandals, Byzantines, Arabs, Turks, finally the French. He might not have remembered the whole list, but he did remember that de Gaulle hadn't concluded that therefore the French should leave, give up the war, let Jacques Thomas go back to his bookshop and his lunches with Mathieu, and perhaps to Sylvie, who might come to find him one day in the Boul'Mich.

He also discovered in the Bugeaud book a hero, Bugeaud's enemy naturally, an Arab Emir called Abdel Kader, brave and truthful. Bugeaud made a treaty with Kader, then broke it, then over several years fought and defeated Kader's tribesmen with the heavy guns of the French army until they were broken and scattered.

Jacques was appalled by this story, this life, this man, and not surprised to find that one of the last things the famous Marshal did before he died, by this time made a Duke for all his victories over the wretched Arabs in Algeria, was to command troops repressing the ordinary people of Paris in the 1848 revolution. Like Chief of Police Papon. Torturing and killing people in Algeria was training for torturing and killing people in Paris.

Jacques had spent two years listening to Monsieur Fouchet at the *lycée*, and more than a year listening to Mathieu—Mathieu: every time he thought of him, Jacques winced miserably at the loss of that last evening in the brasserie on the Île Saint-Louis—but neither of them had explained the long history of the conquest of Algeria. He sat at the table in his grandmother's dining room, the closed book in front of him, and felt younger than he knew he should feel, scared, resentful and despairing. In a week he was going to have to report to the barracks in Lyon, put on the uniform he would be given, and start learning to do, without question, what he was ordered to do, however unjust or cruel, as a member of the very same army he had been reading about, described with pride by Monsieur d'Ideville.

How much had the army, how much had Algeria, changed since the days of Marshal Bugeaud? As far as one could tell, from the behaviour of Papon's police in the riot, and the appearance, at last, of the Manifesto of the 121, in a hundred years it hadn't changed at all. The Manifesto was the document Mathieu had told him about in January. Every famous left-wing figure in Paris seemed to have signed it. Several had been arrested, because the document did indeed urge conscripts to desert rather than be made to torture and kill in Algeria.

How could Jacques desert the army before he had even joined it? He knew he didn't have the courage, to make himself conspicuous, to get into kinds of trouble that he couldn't even imagine. And how could he tell his grandmother that he was a deserter when she had for more than forty years revered the memory of his grandfather, *mort pour la patrie*, killed at Verdun, defending the soil of France? Which, according to half the people in France, and all the *colons* in Algeria, and Marshal Bugeaud, Algeria was too.

"I've finished grandfather's book about Marshal Bugeaud", he said to his grandmother that evening.

"Did you learn a lot from it?"

"I learned a lot, yes."

A sharp look.

"And?", she said.

"It's a pretty terrible story, the way the poor people in Algeria were treated."

"They didn't know what was good for them, did they? They're Muslims, you know, primitive people. Wild tribes. To be made part of France, given civilization, the example of Catholic life—they should have been grateful. France has so much improved a very poor country, their farms and vineyards and so on. And now they want to get rid of us, when we have educated them, built cities and schools and roads for them, even railways, I believe. So ungrateful."

"You can understand—"

But she wasn't going to listen.

"At any rate", she went on, "President de Gaulle—such a comfort to us all that he's in charge again, you must agree, Jacques—has to look after Algeria. As he looked after France when everything seemed lost. You have no idea, Jacques, what 1940 was like, even without—yes, well. You should be proud to be joining the army, you know. You're going to be defending

247

Algeria, and defending Algeria is defending France. Isn't that the truth?"

"It seems so."

"Well, then."

He gave up.

He gave up thinking about the marshal, and the general, and next morning started reading about the explorer, whose life, though eighty years later, began, he noticed, just as the marshal's had: a noble family of Périgord; a good education; the army. He discovered that, like Jacques and unlike the marshal, de Foucauld as a schoolboy decided that he had left behind the Catholic faith of his upbringing. As a newly-commissioned lieutenant, which Jacques would never be, he was sent to Algeria, aged twenty-one, in 1880. The army was suppressing a revolt. Jacques groaned when he read this. The marshal had suppressed revolts, killed Arabs, burned their villages, stolen their land, for decades. This young man in 1880 was being ordered to do the same. Just as, in 1960, he himself was about to be.

"It's against the logic of history, to fight for the *grands colons*." This was Mathieu on the subject of the war. "Who are the proletariat in this revolutionary struggle? The Algerian people, oppressed for all these years. Who are their champions? The FLN. Who are the bourgeoisie growing fat on their labour? The *colons*, especially the *grands colons*, who oppress the *petits colons* almost as much as they oppress the Arabs. And all the rest of us, in France, making bread out of their cheap wheat, cooking with their cheap olive oil, drinking their cheap wine. Do you realize that the Arabs, in thousands, good Muslims, toil in the hot sun growing vines for French wine-merchants when Muslims themselves don't drink any alcohol?"

This conversation had taken place months ago, at the time when Jacques was finding Mathieu's Marxist ideas most convincing. "If you're right, and I'm sure you are, I don't see why the Party doesn't support the FLN. Doesn't history have to be on the FLN's side?", he had said. He knew he had asked Mathieu this question before, but couldn't remember the answer.

"The Party won't support the FLN because Moscow has decided that history is only on the side of Moscow. And the Party in France is too feeble to stand up to Moscow. But any decent Marxist has to be on the side of the FLN. Any decent socialist, my father would say. But socialism supposes some kind of society set up for peaceful change, for party politics, for gradual improvement. What the FLN are running is a revolution. They have to start from scratch once they've won and the dictatorship of the proletariat is the way to go. Not the dictatorship of the old men in the Kremlin."

Jacques had wondered what Monsieur Fouchet, who had never, as far as he could remember, said anything about the future of Algeria, would have made of what Mathieu said.

Now, in the peace of his grandmother's dining room, Baron asleep beside him on the old Persian rug, with no one to talk to about what he was learning, Jacques read on, keen to see what this young soldier, de Foucauld, no longer a Catholic, would make of what was eighty years ago, what had already been for half a century, what still was, the unjust war.

Well! Only two years after he arrived in Algeria, de Foucauld resigned from the army: unlike Jacques, de Foucauld was not only an officer who had been to Saint-Cyr, but a proper soldier who could resign, not a conscript who couldn't. He left the army but he stayed in north Africa, to explore Morocco disguised as a Jew.

As a Jew? Jacques was pleased to discover that it was for safety that de Foucauld travelled as a Jew. Christians were hated because they were French and foreign and the colonial power. De Foucauld couldn't pretend to be an Arab among Arabs. But Jews were tolerated everywhere, could come from anywhere, spoke all sorts of languages, always helped each other. But that was then. What had happened to the Jews in Vichy Algeria? Jacques had no idea, but was sure that whatever happened must have been bad. He thought of his unknown father.

In one marketplace de Foucauld was sitting in the shade, eating with a real Jew, the Syrian rabbi who was acting as his guide and protector. A group of young officers whom he knew from Saint-Cyr and his regiment walked past, looking scornfully down at the two Jews sitting in the dust. One spat. This was the army that, a bit later, condemned Dreyfus as a traitor because he was a Jew.

De Foucauld learned Arabic. He learned Hebrew. He spent a year in Morocco and wrote a book about it. He spent four months with one Arab companion crossing the whole thousand miles of the Algerian Sahara from west to east. He wrote that he thought of becoming a Muslim because the days of the Muslims were full of God. So were the days of the Jews. "And here am I without religion!"

At this point, still early in the story, Jacques put the book down on the dining room table, marked his place with a folded piece of paper torn from yesterday's *Journal de Saône et Loire*, and set out to walk, Baron beside him, along the road out of the village, through the fields, anywhere. His grandmother was already out: she had gone, as on every weekday, to the nuns' Mass at the château. Often she stayed for most of the morning, reading to the old nuns in the infirmary, giving embroidery lessons to the novices, talking to the prioress.

Were her days full of God, like the days of the Muslims and the Jews Charles de Foucauld had met in Africa? Or were they full of the Church? He didn't know whether there was a difference: the question had never before occurred to him, and if there were a difference he didn't know what it was.

He walked briskly. The day had started wet. He had woken in his room, the room of all his childhood, and listened to the rain before he got up, wishing he could stay here, not just stay in his warm bed but stay at home, stay with his grandmother, just for a holiday, a change from Paris, and then go back, to the Rue Mouffetard, to the bookshop, to his weekly lunches with Mathieu. Even after the riot he wanted to be in Paris, to see what was going to happen, to hear what Mathieu would say about whatever did happen. How was he going to understand Algeria, Africa, Muslims, the desert, with only the eyes of the army, the cruel, bullying army, to see through? Would he be able to look through his own eyes as de Foucauld had? Would he understand what he saw?

The rain had stopped while he was reading. The sky had cleared, and as he walked the sun came out and drops of water glittered on the grass, the seedheads, every frond of the tawny dead bracken, at the side of the road. Baron, in and out of the grass, was getting very wet.

Jacques was walking between the fields, along the road that had left the village in the opposite direction from the château. He didn't want to meet his grandmother. Before he reached the wood through which the road twisted uphill for a mile or so, he heard the sound of hoofs coming down through the wood towards him, slowly, the sound of one horse at a careful walk, a hoof slipping now and then on the slope. The horse appeared, pulling a cart, a young man walking at the horse's head.

"Good morning", Jacques said, holding Baron's collar—he never barked but he might growl at the horse—as the young man approached.

"Good morning." Then the young man stopped, beside the horse, and looked carefully at Jacques and then at the dog..

"That's Madame Thomas's dog. Ah—you're Jacquot, aren't you?" His nickname at primary school.

"I'm sorry—", Jacques said.

"You've forgotten me! You can't have! That's what comes of going to the *lycée* all the way over to Mâcon. And then Paris, isn't it? Where you live now?"

"I've got it—you're Benoît, from the farm on the Saint-Roch road."

They shook hands as, when they were little boys, they had shaken hands every morning as they went into school.

"Very good, Jacquot. Of course I'm Benoît. Same as ever. How's it going?"

"I have to go to Lyon, to join up, next week."

Benoît crinkled his face in sympathy and put his free hand on the horse's neck. "No! You can't be old enough—but maybe I'm a bit younger than you. That's really bad luck."

"And you?"

"As you see. I have the farm, the vines, to run. Reserved occupation, thanks be to God. My dad's never been well since the war, not right in the head, you understand? The Vichy government got prisoners of war who'd been farmers out of Germany in 1942, only a few. They were swapped for forced labourers. 'The relief of prisoners', it was called. Heard of it?"

Jacques shook his head. "Three slaves sent, for one prisoner allowed back. They hated my father in the village, for getting home when the others had to go. He's not been right since, can't work, you know, and I've only got sisters. You remember them?"

Jacques, in the same class at school as Benoît, had known nothing of all this.

"I think I do. Older than you?"

"That's right. Yvette's married. She lives in Cluny. She's expecting a baby. I'm getting married myself in the spring."

"Are you? Really? Well, congratulations."

"Thank you, monsieur", Benoît said, with an ironic bow. "And you? Girlfriend in Paris?"

"Not exactly."

"O, come on, Jacquot! Paris, after all!"

To change the subject, Jacques, looking into Benoît's cart, said: "What've you been doing with that lot?" Stacked in the cart were bundles of hefty stakes, a huge mallet, coils of strong wire.

"I'm planting some new vines next week. The ploughing's done. Today I'm setting up the frame. I've been fetching the stakes from the sawmill. It'll be just a small addition to the vineyard. Wine's doing well here."

"Good. That's good to hear."

"I must be getting on. Good luck with the army. I suppose you'll have to go to Algeria? That'll be tough. See you when you get back—perhaps we'll have a baby by then."

"Goodbye, Benoît. I'm glad we met."

"So long!"

Another handshake.

Now on the flat, Benoît threw the reins back over the horse's head, jumped up on the cart and drove off towards the village at a trot.

Jacques felt like crying. It wasn't fair, he thought, again. It wasn't fair that Mathieu didn't have to go. It seemed even less fair that Benoît could stay in the village and plant his new vines while he—

He hadn't the heart to walk up the hill through the wood.

"Come on, Baron. Home."

He was relieved that his grandmother was still out. He made himself some coffee, returned to the dining room with Baron, shut the door and sat at the table where he had left the book open, to find out what happened next to the explorer.

He was still reading when his grandmother came in. When she called him to the kitchen for lunch—grace, of course, as always, and then soup and the rest of the chicken they had had the night before—he was so deep in the book that he found he was looking at her blankly across the table, not listening to what she was saying.

"What's the matter with you, Jacques? You look as if you'd seen a ghost."

"Perhaps I have."

"What?"

"No. I beg your pardon, grand'mère. I'm talking nonsense. I'm finding the book you borrowed from the nuns, about Charles de Foucauld, very—". Very what? "Very impressive. I like him much better than I liked Marshal Bugeaud."

"That's good, I suppose. Are you learning more about Algeria?"

"Yes. No. Not about wars and revolts. Not about Algiers, the city. Not about the army. But something about the Arabs and the Berbers, something about the desert, a lot about an extraordinary man."

"Who are the Berbers?"

"The people who have always been there."

"Really? I've never heard of them. Eat your lunch, Jacques."

He finished the book that afternoon.

That evening and for days afterwards he could think about nothing else, which was good, because, for a time, the book, above all the strange figure of Charles de Foucauld, displaced for him his dread of leaving the house, the village, Burgundy, on Monday 14th November, only days away.

After de Foucauld's travels in north Africa he went back to

253

Paris, became again a Catholic, though now with a passionate single-mindedness that struck Jacques as entirely understandable: if you're going to take seriously the existence of God and the demands made by believing that everything you do and feel and think has meaning in God's sight, in God's knowledge, then the only sensible path is the most direct. But de Foucauld's path was too direct for anyone else even to accompany him part of the way—at least, this was how the story of the rest of his life, Jacques thought, was to be explained. He was a Trappist monk for seven years, but he couldn't cope with being told what to do, and the other monks couldn't cope with him. He lived for a while in a gardener's hut near a convent of Poor Clare nuns near Jerusalem. He prayed, alone. He did odd jobs for the nuns, not very efficiently. Something in this solitary, marginally useful life appealed to Jacques. He didn't know why.

The nuns persuaded him to go back to France and become a priest, at which point Jacques's sympathy for him drained away: wasn't this the Church rather than God, a deflection in that straight path? But no, as it turned out, it wasn't. Once he was ordained, de Foucauld returned to Algeria and lived for the rest of his life in the Sahara, hundreds of miles from cities, from Frenchmen, from soldiers, though a few occasionally passed by. He lived alone in a kind of hermitage where the tiny chapel he made was for the Blessed Sacrament, for him to pray in, and for any Christians who might come, and where the Arabs and the Berbers and the Tuareg tribes of the desert loved and respected him as a *marabout*, a new word to Jacques. It was an Arabic word and it meant a holy man; this was all as far as it could be from the *razzia*. He worked to learn the Tuareg language, which no European had ever before bothered to do. No one came to join him. Except very occasionally, no one helped him.

Then he was killed, while he prayed, in 1916, in a muddled attempt to kidnap him as a hostage, by Tuareg tribesmen pushed, in the middle of the Great War, by the Turks, themselves pushed by the Germans, to attack Frenchmen in north Africa. So he became a casualty of the war, among the millions of Frenchmen who died, including Jacques's grandfather, killed in the same year.

But de Foucauld the *marabout*, better understood, as far as Jacques could tell, by the Muslims than by the Christians, was happy during those years in the wilderness. Was this because he had filled his days with God? Was it also because of the presence of the Blessed Sacrament in his little chapel hundreds of miles from a church—which he thought of as his reason for living, a priest, in the desert? For years he could only say Mass, and so receive and renew the Blessed Sacrament, if a Christian, perhaps a trader or some French soldiers, came to his hermitage. Then a community of priests called White Fathers, of whom Jacques had never heard, obtained in Rome permission for de Foucauld to say Mass alone, which, for the last few years of his life, made him happier than ever.

What did all this mean?

Hadn't Jacques decided, with the help of Monsieur Fouchet and Mathieu, that it meant precisely nothing? That de Foucauld's veneration of a piece of bread in a little box kept in a hut in the wilderness was a particularly pure example of superstitious nonsense, no sense, without sense or reason? The presence of Christ in the consecrated host: he had been brought up to believe that this was something real, something true. He had been brought up to genuflect, to go down on one knee, like a courtier before a king, before the Blessed Sacrament in a church. It was one of the things he had, in Paris, been delighted to leave behind in his childhood, like going to Mass on Sundays and grace at meals, so that the horrible Sacré-Coeur was no different from the horrible Panthéon.

So why couldn't he get out of his head the sense—not perhaps after all nonsense—that there was something beautiful and true about de Foucauld alone in the wilderness with the presence of Christ that he had brought?

There was one paragraph in the book, nothing to do with these questions, that had had him for a moment actually looking forward to the new, hot country he had never seen. De Foucauld, on his way home for a brief holiday in France, stayed with his friends the White Fathers in their house in Algiers.

In the garden were orange and lemon trees, locust-trees, asphodels, African marigolds, and in the distance the violet mountains of Kabylia. Jacques had never seen these plants. He had never seen the Mediterranean. He had never heard of Kabylia and its violet mountains. He looked out of the dining room window at the November rain falling on Burgundy and wondered what a locust-tree looked like.

Even fighting in a war, whatever that was going to mean, might he get the chance to see a locust-tree, or asphodels?

Jacques was struck forcibly by the fact that the man who wrote the book, whose name was René Bazin, obviously himself a serious Catholic (or his book wouldn't have been in the nuns' library), was, in 1921, far from hopeful for the future of *Algérie française*, the drumbeat of the marchers who had a few days ago in the Latin Quarter turned a demonstration into a battle. Monsieur Bazin admired de Foucauld, and also the White Fathers, for being, among devout Muslims, not preaching missionaries but a quiet, kind presence and example. But he had also understood that this very quietness was made inaudible by the noise of roads and railways and pneumatic drills, the bargaining of dishonest traders, and the guns of soldiers. De Foucauld himself wrote that the Muslims were seeing "as self-styled Christians, only unjust and tyrannical speculators giving an example of vice". Monsieur Bazin said in his book that Cardinal Lavigerie, who seemed to have been the founder of the White Fathers, had expected it to take a hundred years for his gentle evangelization to convert the Arabs, but that the attempt was altogether failing, so that "within fifty years we shall be driven out of North Africa". 1921 to 1960: not yet forty years. But if only it could have been sooner.

There was one passage which made Jacques think so hard that he copied it out on a piece of paper and took it up to his room. He took the china jug and bowl off his washstand and put them on the floor. He sat at the little table, with its cloth embroidered by his grandmother, and wrote a letter to Mathieu.

Dear Mathieu,
I was so sad not to see you on the night of the riot.

He crossed out "I was so" and replaced it with "It was", and then started again on a fresh sheet of paper.

I came across this in a book about Algeria my grandmother produced for me to read. It reminded me of you because I remember you saying that we can't expect the clever people we've educated in the countries we've conquered not to want what we've taught them are the fruits of French civilization. Look at Ho Chi Minh, you said. Look at the FLN. The author of this book says, in 1921, that in Algeria France made a terrible mistake: "We have taught them to exalt 'liberty, the rights of citizens, the electorate, and the whole considered as the supreme good'; an ideology baneful in France, and still more so between the sea and the desert." "Baneful in France" is nonsense—isn't this how we were all brought up?—and he says it only because he's a keen Catholic and obviously hates the whole laicization campaign. But otherwise spot on, don't you think? On the same page he says: "The more the natives have acquired French culture, the more they have a tendency, in secret or openly, to hate us." QED

Now I'm supposed to go and kill them for wanting what we've told them every human being deserves.

Wish me luck, Mathieu. I'll see you in Paris when/if I get back on leave.

Till soon,

Jacques

He read the letter through, hoped that Mathieu would approve of his capacity to put two and two together by himself, addressed the envelope to Mathieu's ward in Cochin hospital, and went out to post the letter in the village.

As he walked back he couldn't stop thinking about the book. There was something still puzzling him, something missing in the connection between what he had learned about de Foucauld and the White Fathers and what Monsieur Bazin had written about French education. At his grandmother's gate, he saw that what was missing was that it wasn't the Muslims who needed conversion to the gentle Christianity the book described, but the French, and that it was already in the time of Marshal Bugeaud, and even more, half a century later, in the time of de Foucauld, too late. As for now, in 1960, after the war, and the Occupation, and Marshal Pétain whom the Catholics had seen as restoring the faith to France, and *Algérie française* being the cause of the right and the Church—he pictured again the marchers with their chanting and their flares in the Boul'Mich—how much more too late was it now?

He hadn't thought of this in time to put it in his letter to Mathieu. But as he realized that it wasn't an idea for Mathieu, he wondered all over again how much Mathieu actually cared about him. He was used to this question, and used to pushing it away before allowing himself to answer it. Now, when he might never see Mathieu again, he knew he had to face the fact that he didn't know what Mathieu really cared about. His career, his patients, no doubt. But it was perfectly possible, for example, that Mathieu had a girlfriend about whom he, Jacques, knew nothing. Whether or not this was the case, the fact was that Mathieu cared about him a bit, but not much: "MR" at the end of that note on the night of the riot. And he, Jacques, probably had the rest of his life to get used to this fact.

That evening at dinner in the kitchen, he asked his grandmother whether she knew any White Fathers.

"White Fathers? Of course not. They live in Africa. Very holy men, I believe."

As she helped him to some more potatoes, she said, "Now I come to think of it, a White Father visited us once, a long time ago. He preached at both the Sunday Masses. He was asking us for money, of course, for schools and hospitals in Africa. All very worthy and good, no doubt. He gave out prayer cards with pictures of little black children. He had a beard and a white habit, with a big rosary round his neck, and a dark brown face. But he seemed to be French. Why do you ask?"

"The White Fathers are mentioned in the book about Charles de Foucauld."

"Well, they would be. Did you like the book? You seemed to be very wrapped up in it."

"I found it interesting, yes. Did you know that de Foucauld was killed in 1916?"

"Père de Foucauld, if you please. No, I didn't know. In the war, I suppose?"

"Alone in the desert, though as a kind of side-effect of the war."

"How strange. I thought he lived much longer ago. The nuns seem to think he was some kind of a saint. Perhaps I should read the book."

She wouldn't, he knew. She didn't read books.

Having arrived in the village on the Sunday evening after the riot, Jacques was at home for the two following Sundays. He had last been home, for a few days including one Sunday, fifteen months ago, in the summer of 1959, after a bicycling holiday in the Loire which had taken him to half a dozen of the grand châteaux, which had depressed him, and to the prison abbey of Fontevraud, which, for its sadness, he had loved. That Sunday, he had gone with his grandmother to Mass, and even received Holy Communion, though he had definitely concluded, after he left the nuns' hostel in Paris, that he didn't believe in God. This was something he could never tell his grandmother. It had been easy to go to Mass, to behave properly, to pretend.

Now things were more complicated. On the Saturday evening before his first Sunday morning, he decided that he couldn't do this again. The reason was something to do with Mathieu: he had told Mathieu that he had left Christianity behind, that he recognized it for what it was, that he had grown out of its blandishments and threats, for good. It worried him a little, but not much, that he had said all this to Mathieu knowing it was what Mathieu wanted to hear. But it was true, wasn't it? And since truth was more important than the hazards of upsetting his grandmother just as he was going off to the war, he couldn't now pretend.

When it came to Sunday morning, however, the idea of any kind of explanation still seemed beyond possibility, so he put on a tie and his respectable jacket and went with her to Mass in the village church. At the time for receiving Holy Communion he stayed on his knees. His grandmother, after a quick look which he felt rather than saw, joined the line of the faithful approaching Père Bonnard at the altar steps and returned to kneel beside him without even a look.

At lunch that day, she said: "Jacques, you have only eight more days here. I must speak to you seriously."

Not surprised, he said, "Yes, of course, grand'mère."

"Next Monday you are setting off to be a soldier. You will be fighting in a war. Your life may be in danger. I don't have to tell you how anxious I am about you: after all, you are everything I have in the world. But my anxiety would be greatly relieved if I knew that before you go you had been to Confession and returned to a state of grace. I could so easily ask Monsieur le Curé to give you a time one day this week when he would be in the Confessional in the church just for you, so that no one else would know. Not that it would matter in the least if they did."

He knew that she would like it if they did. One of the old busy-bodies in the parish, seeing him enter the church on a weekday afternoon, would tell all the others that Jacques, so soon to be a soldier, was still a good Catholic. "I'm glad for Madame Thomas, aren't you?"

"No, grand'mère. It's kind of you to think of it, but I would prefer to make my confession to a priest who hasn't known me all my life. You understand?"

"Yes, of course, Jacques, I quite understand."

She smiled, but then looked keenly at him.

"But you will—"

"Yes, grand'mère, I'll do what's right."

This seemed to satisfy her. Even if it didn't, it was as far as he was able to go. He wasn't going to make a specific promise he didn't intend to keep. Once he'd left for Lyon, after all—the phrase she'd just used herself—he might never see her again.

In the afternoon, with Baron beside him, ahead of him, briefly vanishing and always returning, he went for his favourite walk, out of the village on the road to Saint-Christophe, up the hill through the woods, and then, turning left off the road, along the top of the hill at the edge of fields and through another wood until he could turn downhill, walk through the park of the château, and join the Saint-Roch road back towards home.

As he walked he wondered why he had found it impossible to say to his grandmother, "Yes. I'll go to confession when I get to Lyon". Or perhaps, "There'll be an army chaplain who'll hear my confession". If there were no God, what was wrong with a lie to make someone happier? Hadn't he already lied by going to Mass and not receiving Communion, so that his grandmother would think he had committed a serious sin, which wouldn't worry her unduly, rather than that he didn't believe in the existence of God?

What would Mathieu say? He was used to referring things he didn't understand to Mathieu, because Mathieu was older and cleverer and always seemed to have decided, before Jacques asked him, exactly what he thought. He realized that he knew Mathieu would think this anxiety about lies and truthfulness was nothing more than a consequence of early conditioning to superstition and falsehood. "Time to grow out of all that, Jacques." Was it? Somewhere, somehow, he felt, perhaps he even hoped, that it wasn't.

"Conscience is an illusion. Dump it. Forget it. The only thing worth fussing about is the consequence of what you do, what you say. If the effect of a lie is good—setting your grandmother's mind at rest, for example—then the lie is fine, has improved someone else's life a little. What could be wrong with that?" He could hear Mathieu saying this, or something like it. If he'd been in Paris, sitting across a café table from Mathieu as they finished lunch and before Mathieu looked at his watch and said he must dash back to the hospital, Jacques would have accepted Mathieu's advice without questioning it. But didn't it only amount to "you are what you do", how Mathieu had summarized existentialism for him? And hadn't he been sure, ever since Mathieu first said this, that it wasn't enough, as a description of him, or of anyone else?

The second Sunday was his last day at home. In the week since the first Sunday, he had read Monsieur Bazin's book about Charles de Foucauld. Now he didn't want to go to Mass at all. He thought of saying that he was ill, but the certainty of the fuss his grandmother would make, with him leaving for Lyon the next morning, made him drop the thought at once.

It was raining, and cold, when they walked to the village. He held her umbrella over his grandmother's head. In the porch of the church she would take off her hat, put it in her capacious handbag, and replace it with her black lace mantilla. He was wearing his winter coat and an old-fashioned hat that had belonged to his grandfather. He never wore a hat in Paris; when it rained, he got wet.

Kneeling beside his grandmother in her usual pew, after the altar boy had rung his bell three times for the Sanctus, Jacques was watching Père Bonnard's back at the altar, and dreading, as he had known he was going to, the consecration. Last Sunday the Mass hadn't upset him at all. Nor had letting his grandmother think he was in a state of sin. Which no doubt he was, whichever way you looked at it.

Now, as the priest spread his hands in prayer over the altar and raised the Host and then the chalice, and the altar boy rang his bell once and then three times, and again once and then three times, as Jacques had often rung the same bell, kneeling at this same altar, he tried to see what he was watching as he had seen it last Sunday, except that last Sunday he had paid it little attention. There was a middle-aged man in antique clothes with a round, flat piece of bread in his hands, and then a silver cup with some wine and water in it, reminding the people on their knees behind him that two thousand years ago a man called Jesus had used some strange words to make sure that his last meal before his arrest and execution would be remembered by his followers. Perhaps he had. Perhaps, as Mathieu would say, he hadn't. And that was all it was. Wasn't it? A ceremony harmless in itself, a comfort to old ladies like his grandmother, but meaning nothing to a rational person beyond its survival as a quaint and, even in a small village church of no distinction, a decorative relic, with its altar silver, its candles and flowers, of the past. He knew that this was what he thought. But, haunted by Charles de Foucauld, alone in the desert with the Blessed Sacrament as the heart and soul of his simple life, the reason for his existence, Jacques couldn't regain, put together again, his familiar conviction. His familiar emptiness of conviction.

At lunch he was silent, letting his grandmother think he was apprehensive about travelling to Lyon and joining his military training course the next day. Which, after all, her favourite phrase, he was.

In the afternoon, with Baron, he went, as he had the Sunday before, for his favourite walk, for the last time. Perhaps for the last time ever.

He stopped at the highest point of the path along the top of the hills above the village and the park of the château, and looked westward at the fields and vineyards, several farms and two small villages, spread below him. It had rained all day yesterday and most of the morning. The grass at his feet was too wet to sit on. He watched the lines of grey and purple cloud in the sky, and the streaks of light, gold, orange, red, as the sun, nearly setting, lit the landscape with a weak, wild light. Behind him the sky was almost black, but there was enough light left to see his way home.

For a few minutes he watched the sky changing, both brightening and darkening, trying to consider properly the idea that he might never again stand here and look at the country of home.

What if he were to be killed, quite soon, in Algeria, before he had time to make up his mind—about what, in any case? About whether Christ was present on the altar? How much did it matter? Either not at all, or a very great deal. He had to decide which. He couldn't.

It was hard to face the idea of being killed, as so many young men of his age had been, in all the wars, in the Great War like his grandfather, before they had time to become who they might have been. Dying in old age was one thing, giving up life when it was time: being killed, having your life taken away, before it was time, was different. His grandmother wanted him to put his soul in order in case he was killed in Algeria. She wanted him to go to a priest, whom he wouldn't be able to see, and confess, so as to be given absolution. So as to be in a state of grace when he was killed, if he were going to be killed. But confess what? And did any of these words mean anything to him now? "Absolution": a formula spoken by a priest who

263

might be a more serious sinner than he was. "A state of grace": how could anyone whose mind was as confused as his be in anything as simple and pure as a state of grace? He knew he was a long way from any real understanding of what the phrase meant, what it had meant to Charles de Foucauld, for example. But he wasn't going to go to confession: if he did, he would be admitting that he couldn't sort out his own soul, whatever that was, if anything, for himself, by himself, as Mathieu, or Monsieur Fouchet, if they would allow the word "soul", which of course they wouldn't, would tell him that he could. That he should. He was suddenly furious that he had allowed himself to be so rattled, so upset and muddled, just at this moment when he wanted to be calmly saying goodbye to the only place he loved, by reading about an eccentric, to some people clearly irritating and difficult, man who had left everything ordinary for a confidence in Christ that Jacques didn't understand, let alone share. Forget de Foucauld, he told himself. Concentrate on dealing with the next bit of life, with the army about which he had no choice, with being brave enough to do whatever he was ordered to do. After all—his grandmother again—this was enough.

He gave up thinking and watched the light change until the barred blaze of the setting sun had faded and gone. Then he said, "Come, Baron", to the dog sitting on the hilltop quietly beside him, and they walked home in the gathering dark.

"There you are, Jacques. I wondered where you'd got to."

"I went for a walk."

"I see." She put down by the grate in the dining room fireplace the bundle of kindling she was carrying. "Make the fire for me, Jacques, there's a good boy."

This meant company. He gave no sign of disliking the prospect, although he disliked it very much.

"Of course", he said.

"I've invited Monsieur le curé and Père Louis to dinner, and I've asked Madame Marchand to cook. She'll be here at any minute. I thought we would have a little celebration before you leave us, for you to remember."

"That's kind of you, grand'mère. Thank you."

He thought of all that she must have done while he was out. Had she walked to the village to find Père Bonnard, and to the château to find Père Louis, the nuns' chaplain, who lived in the old coachman's cottage in the park? More likely, she had found someone to take them notes and wait for answers. As for Madame Marchand, a widow who lived alone on the far edge of the village and was its best cook, his grandmother must have gone to see her. She wouldn't have been easy to persuade to come and work for the whole of a Sunday evening in winter, and there must have been a considerable discussion about how, so late, they could put together a good dinner. At least, as he knew his grandmother would have promised, Père Bonnard could fetch Père Louis in his car and after dinner take the old priest and Madame Marchand back to their houses.

The table was laid with the best silver and glass and linen and candlesticks: on his knees, making sure the fire was burning properly before the guests arrived, Jacques turned to look at the table, so different without its old red plush cloth, and thought of the altar that morning in the church, looking much the same. He shook his head to get rid of the thought, and wished he were going to eat with his grandmother in the kitchen as usual.

The meal was very good. Madame Marchand, in a black dress and a white apron, came in and out with dishes and plates. Jacques hardly noticed what he was eating—the rich main course was veal escalopes, mushrooms, cream—but he saw how much both the priests were enjoying their food, and an old bottle of Burgundy his grandmother had brought up from the cellar where she kept a few good bottles for this kind of occasion. Jacques and his grandmother, like children, both drank water with a dash of wine in it.

Jacques said almost nothing throughout dinner, answering politely when he was spoken to but otherwise watching the priests, both of whom knew his grandmother well and were clearly in awe of her.

Père Bonnard was middle-aged, perhaps between fifty-five and sixty. He had arrived in the village as a young priest before Jacques was born, seeing himself, so Jacques's grandmother had often said, as staying for a few years and then moving to higher things in the Church, perhaps to a city parish from which he might in due course join the clergy of a cathedral, be given an important post, even become a bishop. None of this had happened. He had stayed in his country parish, become a familiar local figure, perhaps had to get over some resentment about his failure to achieve an ecclesiastical career, and then, Jacques suspected, become both rather lazy and rather pleased with himself. He had been jovial, and somehow false in manner, to Jacques as a child in the first communion class, as an altar boy, as a confirmation candidate. This morning at Mass, Jacques now realized, was the first time in his whole life in which he had taken Père Bonnard seriously, as a priest who held in his hands—what? Christ himself? Jacques looked across the table at this unimpressive man he had always known. No. He had been right for years. It wasn't possible. The whole thing was a charade, preserved down the ages by the Church, for the Church, to impress and scare people into respect for ordinary men who enjoyed a little power and a little indulgence.

Père Louis, twenty years older, was quite different, quieter, more untidy, with sharp, observant eyes, and a smile that came and went unpredictably in response to what others, Père Bonnard and Jacques's grandmother, were saying. He had a gardener's hands, strong and scarred, and he smoked a pipe. Jacques scarcely knew him and had never before seen the two priests together.

"So, Jacques", Père Bonnard said, when Madame Marchand had taken away their dirty plates and brought them each a dessert, of little caramel custards with some hot, buttery slices of apple. "At your farewell dinner we wish you every success as a soldier. It's a noble profession, you must remember, even if you haven't chosen it, and even if it's only for two or three years."

Twenty-seven months, Jacques thought with bitterness.

"And the cause", Père Bonnard went on, "of preserving Algeria for France is a noble cause. Is it not, Madame Thomas? You must be proud of your grandson, at this great moment in his life."

"Naturally. I'm very proud of Jacques. Thank you, Father", she said.

"My poor boy", Père Louis said. "I was a young priest in the Great War. I will pray for you and for your comrades. And for those you will see suffer."

"Thank you, Father", Jacques said.

Père Louis bent his head for a moment. "I'm sorry that we can't do more", he said. "But we can pray, which is not nothing."

"Ah", said Père Bonnard, looking pious, "the power of prayer."

Looking at Jacques and not at Père Bonnard, Père Louis said, "There is always a better way than war. Everyone knows this but almost everyone forgets that it is so. Down the generations, therefore, down the centuries, boys like you are sent to fight. It is tragic. But then, life is tragic. The pride and the fall. In war it will sometimes seem that it is their pride, whoever they are, in government, in command, and your fall. But no. It is always more complicated. In every soul there is pride and there is falling. In every soul there is always the possibility of truthfulness and kindness as well as of courage, and for every soul there is always the mercy of God. Look about you, Jacques, when you are there, and see, really see, what you are looking at. Then you will be safe with God, whatever harm may come to you, which we will pray for you to escape."

"Amen", said Père Bonnard, too loudly, to stop the old priest talking, Jacques thought.

"Amen", said his grandmother, as Madame Marchand came in from the kitchen with the cheese. Jacques hadn't touched his dessert. Madame Marchand took his plate with a disapproving sniff.

After they had had coffee, Père Bonnard stood up, said a swift Latin grace while the others were still getting to their feet, and then said, "Time for bed. I'll drive Père Louis home and then come back for Madame Marchand so that she can finish tidying up for you, madame."

"One moment, Father", she said. "I have a holy medal for Jacques. To keep him safe, you know. I asked my husband if he would wear it, when he went to the war in 1914, but he said I shouldn't part with it because it had belonged to my mother.

Perhaps, if he—Well, in any case, I should like Jacques to wear it now. Would you be kind enough to bless it for us?"

"Gladly, madame. A beautiful intention."

She took from the pocket of her long black skirt a small box, and from the box a silver medal on a chain. It shone in the candlelight: she must have polished it recently, perhaps this afternoon when she polished the candlesticks.

Père Bonnard held the medal in his left hand, made the sign of the cross over it with his right hand, muttered a few Latin words, and gave it to Jacques. "There you are, my son. May Our Lady bless you and guard you with her medal."

"Amen", his grandmother said. "Here, Jacques, let me put it on." She took the medal, hung it round his neck and fastened the clasp at the back. "There. No one need see it, you know." Jacques put the medal under his shirt and his pullover. It was cold.

"Thank you, Father", she said again, to Père Bonnard.

"Now we must be going", he said.

They left the dining room. Jacques stayed in the doorway as both priests, in the narrow passage, put on their coats and black berets, and his grandmother went to open the front door.

"Goodnight, madame. Goodnight, Jacques. Thank you for a delightful evening, God bless." Père Bonnard disappeared into the night with a wave, Jacques's grandmother holding the door open for him.

Père Louis turned back to Jacques. "I shall pray for you every day, my son, before the Blessed Sacrament." He took Jacques's hand in both of his, and held it for a moment.

Later, in his room, Jacques was almost angry. Why had the old priest said that, exactly that, to confuse him all over again when at dinner it had been easy for him to see that Père Bonnard, as he had known for years, was not much more than a decent actor with a part that pleased him no end. But—but—Jacques had had quite enough of a Catholic upbringing to know that the quality of the priest has nothing to do with the reality of a sacrament, the truth of—He groaned with frustration at his inability to think clearly, to decide, got into bed and slept soundly.

The next morning, after he had patted Baron for the last time, his grandmother went with him in the village taxi to the station in Mâcon, said nothing on the way, didn't cry, kissed him on both cheeks, and waved on the platform as the train left for Lyon.

The soldier's widow, he thought as he sat down, his hand going up to his neck, where the holy medal was under his clean shirt and his tie. She had known how to do this all her life. And he knew nothing.

Chapter 5

Thamar

August to November 1961

"Shh—shh—It'll be all right. Shh—"

It was only when he heard her voice, a young girl's voice, very quiet and close to his ear, that he realized he was sobbing. She lifted his head a little from the hard, spiky ground where some time ago, he had no idea when except that it was still dark, he had collapsed. She eased her arm under his head so that his cheek lay on her arm in its thin sleeve.

"Shh—", she said again, and gradually, like a small child, he stopped crying, his sobs turning to convulsive sniffs, jerking his chest less and less until they faded altogether and he nearly fell asleep.

"You are hurt?", she said.

He opened his eyes. It was light, bright, not yet hot, so it must be early in the morning. The air was soft and smelt clean. Mountain air. He saw a very young face, brown worried eyes, a white headscarf with a red and blue pattern. He took a deep breath in order to talk.

"My leg", he said. "They threw me out. It was dark. I can't stand up. I crawled as far as—as I could."

"Who threw you out?"

"I don't know. The FLN. They attacked us. They must have been waiting for us. We were meant—we were meant to be—I can't remember."

"Do not talk. It is too difficult. You are safe now."

She spoke French, simple French with an accent. French was not her first language. If she were an Arab girl—he tried and failed to think what this might mean.

She sat still, her arm under his head. He guessed she was deciding what to do.

His eyes closed. He again almost fell asleep. Then she took her arm gently from under his head. He felt again the spikes of mountain plants under his cheek.

He saw her loosen the scarf she wore and her dark shiny hair fall round her face.

"No. You mustn't", he said. He had an idea that Muslim girls could be in trouble if they weren't wearing a scarf over their hair.

She laughed.

"Don't worry. My scarf is for the sun. Only for the sun."

She folded the scarf and, lifting his head once more, put the soft cotton under his cheek.

"I'm going to fetch my father", she said. "He will bring someone to help him. To carry you."

"No. You can't. It's too dangerous. For you. For your father."

"Shh . . .", she said. "Everything is all right. My father is a *harki*."

He hadn't heard the word before.

"What? I don't know—"

"He fought for France. He was a French soldier. Like you. You understand? He is trusted. In our village he has—" She stopped, as if she didn't know the right word.

"Is there some water?"

He saw her look round at the hillside. It was still early, with the sun not yet high, but the heat was gathering.

"We shall bring you water. We shall come soon. The FLN move at night. They will not find you here."

She touched his forehead with the middle finger of her right hand, in farewell, and left him. As she went away he heard her calling—calling animals? Goats? Sheep? Her calls faded. Sunlight. Silence. Cicadas.

He remembered the sergeant on the troopship that had brought them from Toulon to Algiers saying: "Don't you forget, you boys, never trust an Arab. They'll lie and cheat their way out of anything you try to pin on them. The *pieds noirs* aren't much better but at least they're supposed to be French. Some

271

of them are, more or less, and they do talk French. But if you find you're on your own, you'll have nothing to fall back on but your own gumption. Most of you haven't got a lot of that, so you'd do well to take care not to find you're on your own."

Was the girl lying? Was it some kind of trap, like the ambush, the men with guns suddenly shooting, out of the darkness, at their trucks? The trucks had lights. The men with guns didn't need lights. Simple.

Whether or not she was lying he had no idea and in any case it made no difference: he couldn't move. The pain in his leg was too bad for him even to try to crawl, and he had no idea where he was. Their little convoy of three small trucks had driven out of Sétif towards the mountains, "the violet mountains of Kabylia" that he had read about, it seemed long ago, in his grandmother's dining room in Burgundy, that he had for weeks seen in the distance. They had driven, mostly uphill, on a road that was soon a stony track. For how long? Perhaps two hours, perhaps more. Then, another hour or two after darkness had fallen, suddenly as it always did in Africa, out of the night the shots. He tried to fit together what he could remember of what had happened, and couldn't. He thought the first truck had got away: he heard it accelerate with a wrench of gears. He was in the middle truck, which lurched and stopped, probably because a tyre had been shot. All eight of them jumped down and ran into the darkness. There were bangs and flashes from guns on all sides. He was quickly shot in the leg and fell. He hoped some of the others got away. Two Arabs, looking with a torch, turned him over. One said something he didn't understand to the other, and they picked him up and put him quite carefully into the open back of a pick-up, with another wounded man. They drove, fast, still uphill, for some time, his leg hurting more and more with every jolt. The other soldier, beside him, was silent, didn't move at all. Was he breathing even? Quite soon, Jacques realized he was dead. At last the pick-up stopped. More Arabs, or the same two, pulled down the back of the truck, exchanged a few words, and then threw first Jacques and then the dead man on to the ground and drove away.

Jacques knew at once that his fall had further injured his leg: he heard his shout of pain and protest fail against the noise of the pick-up's engine fading into the great silence of the night. After a while he began to crawl, at least away from the track.

That was all he could remember.

And now? Someone would come. The girl, or someone else. He believed her. Someone would give him water. If no one came he would die, in the end, in the heat. Or because his wound would fester. Perhaps to die would be best.

Without moving his head, he opened his eyes and through the dazzle of the morning looked up. Far away, high in the silver blue of the sky he saw a poised bird, a great and distant unfamiliar bird. Was it an eagle? A vulture? A vulture waiting for him to be a corpse to be swooped on, pecked at? He thought of the dead soldier flung on the ground by the track. He didn't know who he was. He couldn't see in the darkness of the jolting pick-up.

No. Not a vulture. Not that he knew what a vulture high in the sky would look like. It was an eagle, he decided, a Roman eagle: he had discovered from the books about General Bugeaud and Charles de Foucauld that the Romans had been in Algeria for hundreds of years. So far he had seen no trace of them. But here, way up in the sky, balanced and still, a Roman eagle was observing him, so that, being observed, he was less alone. The light was too bright. He shut his eyes.

Lying on the hillside, his cheek on the girl's folded scarf, he breathed in the scent of the herbs growing on the rocky ground. He didn't know their names. As the sun and the silence beat on his turned head, his closed eyes, the scent of the herbs kept him company. Two or three times he saved the saliva in his mouth to give him something to swallow. He fell asleep.

Water splashing on his face woke him. He came to, remembering nothing for a minute or two, then—he must have moved a little—remembering the pain. He groaned. He heard water being poured. Someone, not the girl, raised his head and put a tin mug to his lips. With relief, he drank. The water was warm and tasted of metal. But it was water. Drinking too fast, he almost choked.

He tried to focus on the faces leaning over him. He saw the girl, her hair now covered by another scarf. A middle-aged man, an Arab with a beard flecked with grey, his eyes concerned, must be her father. On her other side was a younger Arab, also bearded, his eyes colder but interested. He was wearing some kind of army uniform that Jacques hadn't seen before.

The older man spoke to the younger man, in a language that Jacques didn't know, but thought wasn't Arabic, and very gently they straightened Jacques's arms and his uninjured leg so as to pick him up, the older man lifting his head and shoulders, the other taking his feet. This was so painful that he yelped, and then apologized. He realized he was trusting them. What else could he do?

He saw the girl bend to pick up the scarf she had folded and put under his cheek.

Suddenly, as the two men lifted him clear of the ground, he said: "Where's my gun?"

The conscripts had been told over and over again to lose anything rather than their guns. "Lose your pack. Lose your rations. Lose your boots. Lose your head for God's sake, but don't lose your gun. Nothing else you've got will be any use to the FLN for more than five minutes. But a gun's a gun and they're short of them."

"Have you got my gun?"

The two men paused before beginning to walk, and moved their heads, looking at the ground near where he had been lying.

"No gun", the girl said. "You said they threw you out—of a truck? A cart? They will have kept your gun, won't they?"

Of course. He relaxed. Nothing he could do about his gun. As he relaxed the pain shot from his injured leg all over his body. He managed not to cry out again. The older man said something else, perhaps to go more slowly, more carefully. But the ground was rough and the hillside steep: they were carrying him sideways so as to keep him as flat as possible, but he could feel every step they took. The girl was walking between them, facing up the slope so that he could see her face. She smiled at him. The younger man stumbled slightly, jolting his leg. A new wave of pain swept up his body from his leg and, as they carried him into the cool shade of chestnut trees, he lost consciousness.

When he woke again, he was lying on a bed of hay or straw of some kind, sweet-smelling, that was covered with a woven cloth. Another cloth was loosely spread over most of his body. The girl was kneeling beside him on the floor of what must have been the house where she lived with her father, a simple baked-earth house with two open windows—did the windows have glass? He couldn't see.

"You have woken up", the girl said. "That's good. Can you drink some milk?"

He tried to raise his head himself, and almost succeeded. She helped keep his head steady on her arm and with the other hand held a pottery beaker to his lips. The milk was warm, thin, unfamilar. Perhaps it was goat's milk.

He thought his leg was hurting much less. As soon as he tried to move it, a very little, the pain returned. He flinched but didn't cry out.

"Don't move. My father has gone to fetch the nurse. She is the midwife. She has some training, some education, you understand, in a hospital in Constantine. She will help your leg."

He drank a little more milk. She saw he had had enough and laid his head gently on the bed.

"Thank you", he said. "If you hadn't come back, I would have died, I think."

"No", she said, and smiled. "You are too young to die."

She straightened the cotton blanket that covered him. "It is a hot day. But you mustn't get cold, because of your wound, my father says. He will come soon, with the nurse. Now, rest. I have some work to do."

She touched his forehead with her finger, as she had when she left him on the hillside, took the beaker, stood up, and walked, barefoot he saw, to a doorway he noticed for the first time. In the doorway she turned and raised her hand, smiling again, and then disappeared.

As long as he stayed absolutely still, his leg wasn't hurting, or was hurting only in a dull, warning sort of way.

Someone—who? Surely not the girl—had taken off his boots and his socks, undressed and washed him, and covered him in something like a white sheet, cool and light. There was no weight on his leg. He winced as he realized that his clothes must have been soaked and soiled. These were good, good people.

He moved his head, a very little, to look at the room he was in. Bare and clean. A table with a cloth. On the table a complicated oil lamp, and three small carved wooden boxes with intricate patterns. Some wooden chairs. A very beautiful carpet, not as large as the Persian rug in his grandmother's dining room but wonderfully patterned, was on the floor.

If his leg got better, what would they do with him? The girl had said that her father had been a French soldier; wouldn't he return him to the barracks in Sétif as soon as he was well enough to get there? As this thought struck him, he must have moved again because the pain from his leg spread all over him and he groaned. Perhaps he was wounded badly enough to be sent back to France. Perhaps his leg would become gangrenous and have to be amputated. Then he would be discharged from the army altogether. *Mutilé de guerre.* One of those phrases from the Great War, like *mort pour la patrie*, that everyone in France had known since childhood. Then he would be an evident casualty, even a bit of a hero, for the rest of his lfe.

That would be ridiculous, though his grandmother would like it.

He wasn't and never would be a hero. He wasn't brave. He had done what he was told to do since he arrived in Algeria, six months ago now, when over and over again he knew that the brave thing would have been to refuse. No one refused. They had been trained, on the winter barrack square in Lyon, on the exercises in the mountains when they had been shouted at again and again to carry on, however wet and cold and exhausted they were, to obey orders, always to obey orders, to shoot, to go on shooting, at hanging sacks stuffed with straw as if the sacks were people who would die if one shot were correctly aimed.

Once they got to Algiers the targets were no longer stuffed sacks. They were people who ran away, who were stopped by bullets, who fell and twitched and bled and died.

He hadn't been directly ordered to shoot a particular person, although he was supposed to be ready to shoot anyone who looked like an enemy, anyone who aimed a gun at the patrol marching along the pavement or being driven slowly down a street watching from each side, and from the back, of an armoured car. Many times he had sat in one of these jeeps, his gun loaded and poised to shoot as he and another soldier, their backs to the driver, looked along the street they had just driven down, at the shops, the houses, the cinemas, the cafés, specially the cafés, where they had been told that pretty girls were ordered by the FLN to plant bombs.

The patrols weren't the worst of it: even if there were shooting, you could aim badly, shoot but fail to hit anyone, look brave by not ducking the bullets whizzing at the armoured car. He had had to do this only twice.

"You lads don't know you're born. Algiers is a holiday camp compared to what it was like four years ago. Shoot or be shot, it was then. Every day for months." This was their own sergeant, in their wretched sleeping hut in the prison, months ago. He was a regular soldier from Lille, like Mathieu but nothing like Mathieu; he looked as if he had once been a prize-fighter, and he'd lost an eye in the Battle of Algiers. "We had them holed up, like rats they were, in the Kasbah. We beat them hollow in the end. Why didn't they give up then? Why wasn't that the finish of the war? All go home, call it *Algérie française* if you like—it's not France, is it?—any fool can see that—and let the sodding Algerians cut each other's throats without us. Not a lot to choose between them, the Arabs and the *pieds noirs*, if you ask me. Clear out and let them get on with it, I say. That's what should have happened then. That's what should happen now. General de Gaulle's a soldier after all. We believed he would know what to do. Call it a victory and pull us out. Let you boys go back to your factories and your families. You'll never make soldiers in any case. Of course the top brass won't hear of it. The honour of France. The honour of the army. All that crap. How many of them get blown up, shot to bits, lose legs, lose eyes?"

The sergeant had made this speech one evening as the conscripts sat around playing cards and throwing dice before it was time for bed. Only a few days later something happened that made Jacques remember the sergeant's words.

What, exactly? He never properly understood what was going on in Algiers towards the end of April.

He had been in Algeria nine weeks. Each week had seemed so long, so full of dreadful things which he saw, which he heard about, which he had to do, that he could not imagine himself being able to bear another twenty-five months.

When the crisis, whatever it really was, overtook the army in Algeria, he was in his second week as a guard, not even a guard, just one of eight conscripts detailed to fetch and carry for the real guards in an army prison for FLN suspects. The real guards were paratroopers, tough, joking amongst themselves, almost as contemptuous of the conscripts as they were of the wretched prisoners.

The Arabs were brought in at night, two or three at a time, sometimes only one, hand-cuffed, with their feet tied together, and dumped on the floor in front of a tin desk where a sergeant was supposed to take their names. They were shouted at until they gave a name, real or invented. Date of birth? Some of them knew French and gave a date. Some didn't, or pretended not to. Then their feet were untied and each was marched off between two guards to the cells, a couple of huts each holding twenty or thirty prisoners crammed together. The huts stank. The prisoners weren't given any water to wash with. In the corners of each hut were toilet buckets, usually overflowing. Two swinging light bulbs, always switched on, hung from the ceiling and a guard with a gun peered every minute or two through a spy-hole in the door.

Jacques and the other conscripts took it in turns to brave, in pairs, the crowd in the cells, carrying in trays with stale chunks of bread, sometimes not as many as one each for the prisoners, and buckets of water with half a dozen tin cups chained to each bucket. Fights, quelled by shouted threats from the guards, would quickly start, While the prisoners were squabbling over the bread and water, the conscripts had to pick up the filthy toilet pails, take them out past the guards in their clean uniforms at the cell door, and empty them in a deep ditch at the end of the yard round which the huts had been built. The first time he did this he was sick before he got back to the cell with the empty buckets. The second time he managed to deal with the nausea without throwing up. After that he got used to it, though not to the desperate eyes of the prisoners who, he was sure, would have sprung at him in fury and misery if it hadn't been for the guns of the guards at the door.

But taking in rations and taking out slop buckets wasn't the worst.

At night the conscripts who weren't on duty inside the gates slept in a small hut of their own, nearly as dirty as the cells but at least dark at night and without slop buckets because they weren't locked in. One night near the beginning of his time at the prison, Jacques was woken by a terrifying cry, a howl of pain, from not far away. He jumped from his bed, a thin mattress on a sleeping mat with a single blanket over him, and shouted: "What was that? Who was that? Should we do something?"

"Go back to sleep, Thomas", the sergeant said, annoyed at having been woken himself. "You'll get used to it."

The howl came again, higher-pitched, more desperate.

"But what is it? Who is it?" Jacques said, quietly, to the sergeant, so as not to wake any more of the sleeping soldiers.

"Interrogators. Trying to get information out of them. Who did what, where, when, who's planning the next bomb, all that. They've got a job to do, like we have. Let them get on with it, I say. In any case, what can we do if we don't like it? I don't like it. Nobody likes it. Though I wouldn't be surprised if some of the paras like it. In any case, it's got to be done."

Another howl, while the sergeant was talking, which disintegrated into sobs. Then silence.

"You mean torture? They're torturing prisoners in there?"

Before the sergeant answered, Jacques heard two shots, one, then a pause, then another.

"Poor devils", the sergeant said. Jacques saw him quickly cross himself in the dark.

Then the sergeant said, "Now, you listen to me, Thomas. Nobody's allowed to use that word. Don't let me hear you ever use it again. Never. Now, go back to sleep, and let me do the same."

Early next morning, before it was light, before the horrible coffee and piece of bread that was their breakfast, Jacques and three other conscripts were called out of the hut where they slept and ordered to carry two bodies, two dead prisoners, out of the main block of the prison, across the yard with the latrine pit at the end, through a door unlocked for them, and into a piece of waste ground enclosed by a high mud wall with barbed wire coiled along its top. The man Jacques carried, with another conscript, was still warm, limp, broken, blood-stained, a bullet hole in the back of his neck.

"Get them buried. As quick as you like. There, and there, side by side."

The young paratroop officer stood a little way off, looking at anything rather than the two bodies lying on the ground, as the conscripts laboured with picks and shovels to dig something like graves in the stony sand. Who are they? Who were they? Jacques kept thinking. Does anyone know? Who will tell their parents? The dead deserve names. He didn't dare to say anything. It was light before they had finished. Jacques saw that there were twelve, fifteen—he couldn't count because the officer shouted at him to get on with his work—other recently dug graves nearby.

The prison was in a suburb of Algiers, a poor suburb, the people mostly *colons*, but the scruffy, busy main street with some Arab shops and cafés. There were very few cars and no buses, but plenty of young men and boys bumping along on rickety bicycles. There were dogs, laden donkeys, an occasional camel being led. Where to? Why? There was no telling. That afternoon Jacques and one of the others who had dug the graves were given two hours off to leave the prison, with their guns, to walk down this normal street and sit at a normal café table for a good coffee that they could just afford once or twice a week.

"Did you know they're torturing prisoners?" Jacques said, across the café table on the unpaved street.

"Shut up", the other conscript said, looking round to see if anyone was listening. His name was Paul Mercier. Jacques had met him only in the prison. He had asked Mercier if he wanted to join him that afternoon because he had seen the anger in Mercier's face as they buried one of the wretched corpses.

"Everyone knows", Mercier said. "It's bloody disgusting. I hate it. But it's absolutely forbidden to talk about it."

Jacques remembered Mathieu, months ago, saying that soldiers who'd been in Algeria didn't say anything about it. Mathieu thought the reason for their silence was obvious. Jacques hadn't known what he meant.

"OK, it's a war", Jacques said. "But once they're prisoners—aren't there rules, laws even, about treating prisoners properly?"

"There used to be, I think. Not any more. It's tit-for-tat isn't it? You know what the FLN do to soldiers? Even when they're dead. Cut up their bodies, stuff their—"

"I know. I know. But we're the French army. Aren't we supposed to stick to the rules even if the FLN don't?"

Mercier shrugged.

After a minute or two of silence, Jacques said, "And why shoot them? As well as—"

"They're evidence, aren't they? Once they've been messed about, beaten, electrocuted, nearly drowned but not quite. Nobody wants them talking about what's been done to them. Get rid of the evidence as fast as possible, shoot them, bury them, forget about them. That's the idea."

"Electrocuted?"

"Enough to hurt them, a lot. Not enough to kill them. To make them talk. And to terrify them. One of the sergeants told me when he was drunk that some of them, picked up from the villages, don't know what electricity is, have never met it before, till it half-kills them. It doesn't leave scars, The near-drowning doesn't leave scars. The Gestapo used to do it, during the Occupation. No scars was the point in the first place. But now that they shoot them afterwards it doesn't make any difference. It was a lot worse in Barberousse. I was there for months. They guillotine them there. In front of the others."

Mercier was older than Jacques and had served in Algeria for perhaps a year longer.

He pushed toward Jacques a plate of *baklava*, delicious Arab pastries with honey and nuts. Mercier, who must have saved a bit more money than Jacques, had ordered the *baklava* to go with their coffee. Jacques looked at the pastries and shook his head.

"I can't", he said.

For two or three minutes he watched Mercier eat.

"Isn't there anything we can do?" Jacques said.

"How do you mean, 'do'?"

"I don't know. Write to a senior officer? One of the generals? They can't know what's going on. If they did, maybe they'd stop it? "

Mercier looked at him as if he were six years old.

"How long have you been here?"

"Two months. Since the middle of February."

"Exactly. There's a few things you're going to have to learn, mate. Of course the generals know. In fact, it'll be on some general's orders, all this, bound to be. How do you think General Massu won the Battle of Algiers? Not by pussy-footing around with nice comfy beds for prisoners, that's for sure, when every second Arab in the Kasbah was out to get us. FLN headquarters, the Kasbah was then. Bombs, guns, grenades, booby-traps, you name it, made there, stored there, bought and sold there, for dollars, for girls. And they were all hiding each other, lying for each other. Spying on each other too, naturally. That was the point of the—interrogations. And we won, didn't we? We won the Battle of Algiers. And we've nearly won the whole war. Or so they keep telling us. They've got to cheer us along somehow, haven't they?"

Jacques, in a small troop of newly-arrived conscripts, had been marched along a street past the Kasbah when he first arrived in Algiers. The Kasbah was the centre of the old town and an ancient fortress. Through the tall gates in the walls a jumble of buildings, flaky walls, windows mostly shuttered with iron grilles, narrow winding streets, balconies strung with washing almost meeting across the street, some with beautiful carpets draped over them, the lanes crammed with Arabs walking, arguing, buying and selling. A smell of spices, coffee and drains was evident in the road outside the walls, even on a winter afternoon. "You're never to go in there unless you're sent. Never. Do you hear?"

"You don't think we're winning the war?", Jacques said to Mercier. "Nearly seven years since it began, and if we're not winning it, what's ever going to end it? They're not going to give in, the FLN, the Arabs. Why should they? There are more of them than us, even with all these soldiers, even with conscription. And the worse we treat them, the more we—well, what I heard last night, what we saw this morning—the more of them there'll be, willing to fight, willing to die. And the harder they'll fight. Wouldn't you, if it was your country?"

"But it is. Our country. Didn't you listen to the lectures they give you when you're training? I don't expect they've changed much. That's why we're here. The FLN are a bunch of rebels in a part of France. A bunch of Communist rebels, what's more. And the French army's bound to win in the end."

"I don't think so. And nor does President de Gaulle."

"Hey, steady on, Thomas. Saying that is something else that's strictly forbidden. You'd better watch out, you know, and watch who you're talking to. I could report you for what you've said already. Using the word 'torture'; defeatism; saying the President thinks we're losing the war. That could make quite a charge sheet."

Jacques, suddenly cold, looked at Mercier over the café table. He didn't know him. Perhaps he'd imagined the look of fury on his face as they buried the prisoner.

"Will you? Report me?'

Mercier laughed.

"Don't be ridiculous. It's all right. I won't report you. Not this time."

Mercier was watching Jacques's face, and laughed again.

"Not ever. I hate it all too. But you need to take care, Thomas, or you could be in serious trouble. I mean it."

Jacques relaxed, and thought some more.

"What about the papers?", he said.

"The papers? How do you mean, the papers?"

"I don't know. A letter to *Le Monde*? Telling them exactly what's going on here, in the prison. I got mixed up, just by accident, you understand, in the riot in Paris last October, and I saw what the police were doing. Very unpleasant, it was. *Le Monde* next day made it clear whose side they were on. Not the side of the police. Important people read *Le Monde*."

"You're off your head, Thomas."

Mercier, having eaten the rest, had picked up the last of the pastries. He put it back on the plate and leant forward, both elbows on the table.

"In the first place, if you wrote a letter like that it wouldn't get past the censors here, so it wouldn't ever reach Paris or the snooty papers. In the second place they'd put you in prison for writing it. Once the military police have got you in their cells, I don't suppose they treat you much better than the paras treat the prisoners we buried this morning. I mean it, Thomas. You keep your mouth shut if you want to stay in one piece over here."

He ate the last pastry, clinked his spoon on the side of his cup, and, when the waiter brought their bill, split it two thirds and one third with Jacques who had had only a cup of coffee.

"Thanks", Jacques said, as they shook hands inside the double doors of the prison.

Ten days after this, when Jacques had had to hear more dreadful sounds at night from the prison kitchen where the torture was done, and deal with more makeshift burials before dawn, the conscripts began to pick up scraps of news about some kind of rebellion in the army. In the other ranks' mess hut, they ate, at midday and in the evening, with the ordinary para soldiers, sitting at different tables. The paras almost never spoke to the conscripts, but the conscripts could hear the paras talking to each other.

"Well—what do you reckon?"

"If the generals can do what they say, we'll have a chance at last."

"Chance of what?"

"Winning this bloody war. Smashing the Reds once and for all. Can't you see? We're not supposed to know anything about it of course. Not yet. But I heard the colonel say to the captain this morning—"

"Not here. Walls have ears. So do the conscripts."

The next morning, Saturday morning, April 23rd, after a peaceful night with no cries of pain and no burials, the one-eyed sergeant in Jacques's hut woke the rest of them up.

"Hey—come over here all of you and listen to this."

With a good deal of grumbling the sleepy soldiers gathered round the sergeant's crackling transistor radio.

"—is not dead", Jacques heard an official-sounding voice say. "There is not and never will be an independent Algeria. Long live *Algérie française*, so that France may live."

There was a cheer from the paras' hut.

Immediately the radio played a march. Then another announcement: "'*Radio Alger*' will from now on be called '*Radio France*'." More cheering from the paras.

The sergeant turned off the transistor.

"What's happened?" "What's going on?" "Come on, sarge, you heard it all."

"Shut up, the lot of you, and listen."

Silence. They were still close together round the sergeant's bed.

He stood, looking solemn, and they backed away a little.

"The army has taken charge of Algeria. What was it they said, exactly? Yes. The army has assumed control of Algeria and the Sahara. *Algérie française* is not dead."

Silence.

Eventually someone said, "But what does it mean?"

"It means the generals are defying President de Gaulle. They're saying they're in command, and he's not, of what happens here, even maybe of what happens in France. This is very serious. It's what's called a putsch. Perhaps it's even a *coup d'état*."

"Like a revolution?", one of the conscripts said.

"Sort of like a revolution", the sergeant said. "But, call it what you like, it won't work, it can't last."

"Why not?"

"I'll tell you why not. Because the whole of France isn't going to rise up to support the army in Algeria, against General de Gaulle. Is it? Can you imagine such a thing? Our generals are mad if they think that's what's going to happen. France is sick to death of this war, of sending its sons to risk their necks for nothing. How many of your parents were pleased, proud, to let you come here?"

"But we can have a revolution here, can't we, whether General de Gaulle likes it or not? Join with the *colons* and finish off the FLN once and for all? Put the Arabs back in their place and make Algeria how it used to be? Can't we? I bet the paras think we can."

The boy doing the talking looked about sixteen, though he must have been the same age as Jacques. He was a clever boy from a Paris suburb and he had told them all one night that he had wanted to be a soldier since he was ten years old.

"Paras don't think", the sergeant said. "It's not what they're for."

A laugh, a nervous laugh, from the conscripts.

"Now, you lads listen to me", the sergeant went on. "This concerns you all. You are soldiers of France, however wet behind the ears some of you may be. I've been here a long time, five years on and off, and I promise you I know what I'm talking about. Look what happened last year when Massu was sacked. Nearly a mutiny. Chaos here in Algiers. How long did it last? Three days. Four days."

Jacques remembered de Gaulle's broadcast which he had watched in the Rue Mouffetard with Mathieu. A thousand miles away. A thousand years ago.

"It'll be the same this time. You wait and see. These generals aren't Massu. The paras may be cheering, but most of the army won't be."

"But—" The same boy objecting.

"But nothing, sonny. If France cuts Algeria off, no ships, no planes, no supplies, how long would the army here last? Two weeks? Three weeks?"

The conscripts were silent.

"Now, come along. Get washed. Get dressed. Outside for roll-call in fifteen minutes."

Four of the conscripts, including Jacques and Mercier, had two hours off duty that afternoon. They found the streets of their suburb full of celebrating *colons*. Tricolour flags were hanging from windows and red-white-and-blue bunting was strung from one side of the main street to the other. Arab shops and cafés were closed, shuttered, barred. As they walked, Jacques and Mercier were applauded by *pieds noirs*, standing in the street and clapping. Two girls came up and kissed them. A scruffy procession of half a dozen old cars came slowly down the street, their horns blaring out the *Algérie française* rhythm of the march in the Boul'Mich on the night of the riot. A few *pied noir* housewives were out in the street beating the rhythm on pans with wooden spoons.

"Anyone would think the war was over", Jacques said.

"Anyone would think the war was won", Mercier said. "Poor sods."

"Do you think the sergeant's right?"

"Of course he's right. As he said, wait and see."

On the next day, Sunday, as far as the conscripts in the prison could tell, almost nothing happened. Jacques had no idea what was likely and what was impossible. Everyone, including the paras, seemed only to be waiting.

One captured FLN fighter was brought in. Very young and defiant, he wouldn't give his name, any name, and shouted the same thing in Arabic over and over again. The desk officer, who knew some Arabic, said, "He wants to see his chief, who's here apparently." "He'll be lucky", someone else said as two paras half-carried him, still shouting, to the prison huts.

At supper in the mess hut, the conscripts were complaining about the grit in their eyes and throats from the *chergui*, the hot sand-laden wind from the Sahara, blowing through Algiers that day. "You'll get used to it", Mercier, sitting next to him, said to Jacques. "It's worse in the summer."

As they ate, Jacques noticed that the paras were paying the conscripts more attention than usual, looking across at them, not with their usual bored contempt, but with something more like distrust, even fear.

"What's the matter with them?", he said quietly to Mercier.

There was enough noise for Mercier to answer without being overheard, even at their own table. "Come along, Thomas. Think. They're the putsch, the coup. The generals are counting on them. The paras will do anything their officers tell them. But if the rest of the army doesn't join in, they're sunk."

Jacques looked round the familiar hut.

"Eight of us. Useless conscripts as everyone keeps telling us. Twenty of them, real soldiers. What can we do against them?"

"Nothing. Absolutely nothing. But we don't matter a scrap, whatever happens. Just think of the size of the army in the rest of the country, the navy, the air force. From what I overheard this afternoon, they're not keen on any of it."

An officer came into the hut, stood at the paras' table. All of them, silent now, looked up at him.

"Good news, boys", he said. "General Salan has arrived."

Most of the paras cheered and banged out on the table with both hands the familiar rhythm, *Algérie française, Algérie française*. A few looked doubtful but then joined in. The conscripts didn't join in.

"General Salan?", Jacques whispered to Mercier.

"Used to be C. in C. here. Top brass. Loathes de Gaulle. Snake in the grass."

"Now we'll be getting somewhere", the para officer said to his men as the drumming died down.

Jacques couldn't ask Mercier any more questions. In near-silence they sat eating the bread and poor cheese that filled them up at the end of every meal, until, at the end of their table, their sergeant looked at his watch, got to his feet and said, "Right, you lot. By your beds in five minutes."

Jacques looked at Mercier. Mercier shrugged.

Round the sergeant's transistor again, the conscripts heard

President de Gaulle attack with tremendous force what was going on in Algeria. Jacques, listening hard, as they all were, through the static on the radio, shut his eyes and imagined the figure in uniform that he had watched that evening in the Rue Mouffetard. The general sounded even more emphatic, even calmer, even more sure that France would remain loyal to him, than he had then. "Alas, alas, alas", de Gaulle said, mourning the revolt of soldiers, his soldiers, soldiers sworn to serve and to obey. He called the leaders of the putsch, with scorn, "a handful of retired generals", and commanded every Frenchman, "and above all every soldier" not to carry out any of their orders. No excuses whatever would be accepted for disobeying him, General de Gaulle.

At the end of the speech, the Marseillaise. The sergeant switched off the radio.

Silence in the hut.

"Well, lads, that's that", the sergeant said after a moment or two. "What did I tell you? Every soldier in Algeria will have heard the general."

No one said anything.

"You're not leaving this hut tonight. God knows what sort of mood the paras will be in. I don't want them having a go at you lads just for something to do."

Three days later the paratroopers in the prison formed up in the street outside the prison wall, saluted their commanding officer and marched away. They were replaced by a detachment of regular soldiers from an ordinary infantry battalion. About half the prisoners were moved to a different prison, no one knew where, and the rest began to be rather better treated, allowed into the yard for exercise for an hour every day, and fed basic couscous, sometimes with onions and carrots, in tin bowls, as well as their usual bread and water. The interrogators hadn't gone away with the paras, and in the next week three more prisoners were tortured, and shot, and had to be buried by the conscripts.

The sergeant's radio said nothing more about the attempted coup, but the sergeant picked up from somewhere the news that the rebel generals, except for the leader, General Challe, who had given himself up and gone to France to face punishment, had disappeared. They were still in Algeria, but in hiding.

The next, the last, time Jacques and Mercier walked down to the main street of their suburb, all the flags and bunting had disappeared, the Arab shops and cafés were open, and the passers-by, poor *colons* and Arabs, were subdued, nervous, avoiding each other. No applause now, no kisses for two off-duty soldiers, only shifty looks and boys ducking down side streets or into tiny shops to get out of their way.

On the walls new posters had appeared, each showing a map of France with a huge dagger emerging from it, the dagger cutting to pieces both the FLN's crescent and star and President de Gaulle's Cross of Lorraine.

"What on earth is that?", Jacques said to Mercier.

Mercier pointed at a wall a little further along the street, where a huge pair of eyes was crudely painted on the plaster, with, above the eyes, the words "The OAS sees everything".

"What's the OAS?" Jacques said.

"*Organisation Armée Secrète*. Not that they're trying very hard to be secret, as you can see."

"Who are they?"

"The remains of the putsch."

"So soon?"

"The OAS has been going for a couple of months. It started with *pied noir* ultras, fascists the lot of them. And now there are sacked or demoted paras joining in, Legionnaires, officers who hate de Gaulle and seem to think they can run Algeria by themselves, for themselves."

"But that's ridiculous. Isn't it?"

"I've no idea how ridiculous it'll turn out to be. But they're serious. They're a pretty frightening bunch. They seem to think a lot of people at home will support them. Look at the poster. I don't suppose that'll happen, but you never know. White this. White that. No giving in to Communism. All for French civilization. The Church. There's a lot of Vichy still about, you know."

"The Church?"

"Well, look how the Church loved Pétain. And plenty of officers in the army have never forgiven de Gaulle for being right in 1940. Now they think he's going to sell Algeria down the river so as to stay in power."

"How do you get to know so much, Mercier?"

Mercier laughed. "One keeps one's ears open."

Four days later the little band of conscripts working in the prison was split in half. Four of them, including Mercier, were posted to somewhere near Oran, miles away to the west. As they left, Mercier, in the back of a jeep, cheerfully signalled farewell to Jacques in a casual gesture between a salute and a wave. Jacques waved back. He was going to miss Mercier, not because he liked him—he seemed to care about almost nothing—but because he knew a lot Jacques didn't know.

After Mercier had gone, Jacques thought sadly, as he often did, about Mathieu, busy in his hospital in Paris. Did Mathieu ever remember him? Did he bother to wonder where he was or how he was getting on? Jacques had sent him from Lyon the address by which he could be reached in the army. His grandmother wrote every two weeks, saying little beyond how proud of him she was and how life in the village was going on as usual. There hadn't been a word from Mathieu.

Sometimes Jacques thought of Père Louis, kneeling in front of the Blessed Sacrament in the nuns' chapel. Would he remember his promise? He was old; perhaps he had forgotten all about Jacques and that meal in his grandmother's dining room. Did it make any difference to anything, whether he had remembered or forgotten? Jacques felt Mathieu's scorn for the very idea that it did.

On the day Mercier, with his mock salute, disappeared round the street corner in his jeep, Jacques and the other three conscripts, whom he knew only by name and had never talked to, also left the prison, sent east in a military truck with ten others who had several months' more experience, to a barracks in a place called Aghribs.

At first he was pleased to be in a small town, not much bigger than a village. Things must be quieter, better, less horrible than in Algiers. They were not, as he soon discovered, although he was lucky, himself, to see less of them.

The whole village had been taken over as a barracks by the army. This meant that the soldiers, about half of them conscripts and half regular infantry soldiers, lived not in huts but in Arab houses. In the centre of the village was a little Mairie, as in a French village, now the command centre for Aghribs and the surrounding countryside, and a building, obviously once the school, with a high wall of mud-bricks and the coiled barbed wire which almost made Jacques cry when he saw it. Another prison.

"Where are the Arabs?" he said, on his second day, to one of the regular soldiers who was taking a group of conscripts through the routine of sentry-duty and patrols beyond the edges of the village.

The soldier shrugged, Mercier's shrug.

"Gone. Dead, most of them, no doubt. *Ratonnade. Razzia*", he said. "Whatever you want to call it."

Still? Jacques thought. Now?

"Really? When?" he said.

Another shrug.

"Whenever. Aghribs has been a barracks for some time. You can see."

Jacques was given no duties in the prison, and no one ever talked about what was happening there. He knew, however. He was, two or three times a week, sent out on patrol in a convoy of armoured cars, bigger and more solid than those the army used in his Algerian suburb. They would be given the name of a village, and two or three names of suspects to be "brought in for questioning". It was always difficult to find the right men; more often than not, they failed to bring anyone back. On most of these expeditions, they would rattle into some poor village in the hills—Aghribs itself was high on a windy, often sand-swept, hillside—and discover that there were no men of fighting age to be seen, only women, children and old people. Someone who spoke French usually appeared to explain that the men had gone, were in prison, had disappeared, were dead. Jacques could see how long all this had been going on, with how much experience of searches and questions, and how much controlled fear of what would happen to men taken away, the villagers talked to French soldiers, and, no doubt, knowing by now exactly how to do it, had warned and hidden the men who were certainly somewhere not far away. Sometimes a woman, a wife or more often a mother, dressed in dusty black, would emerge from a group of silent people watching the French, with their guns, looking in vain in houses and yards, and throw herself down at the feet of a soldier, crying, beating her breast, pleading for her son to be returned to her. Jacques could understand only that she was repeating over and over a single name as she wailed.

He knew perfectly well that the prisoners had no names or the wrong names, that the old woman's son was unfindable, even if anyone thought of the possibility of finding him, which they wouldn't, and was anyway probably dead.

These villages, where even the children stood quietly and watched the soldiers, where a group of women squatting as they milled grain for couscous got to their feet and watched, and then gathered round the weeping mother to comfort her, where the hot silence was broken only by chickens pecking in the dust, by the bray of a donkey somewhere, by half a dozen sheep or goats pattering along the street, seemed to Jacques stricken by an ancient, biblical desolation. They were being punished, they had for years been punished: why? Because some of the young men had wanted to rid their country forever of French soldiers and of the *colons* who were given the best land, with the result, of which General Bigeaud had been so proud, that they and their fathers and grandfathers had been turned into poor labourers, almost slaves, on land that used to be their own. They had got hold of guns, had obeyed FLN chiefs, had perhaps shot and mutilated French soldiers and helpless *colons*. If they had been captured they had most likely joined nameless prisoners somewhere, in fear, pain and death.

Jacques was in Aghribs for three months. It could have been worse; it had been worse in Algiers, but only for him, only because of what, by chance, he had been ordered to do. He suspected that what was going on in the old school building— presumably built by some good French official to educate the local Arab children: what had become of that enterprise?—might be more cruel, more ruthless, than what had been done in his prison in Algiers.

Although he was never alone, because it wasn't allowed, he was lonelier here than he had been in Algiers. There was no friendly sergeant, and no Mercier to mix the news he had somehow got hold of with mockery of Jacques's ignorance.

Aghribs wasn't far from the sea. On hot, hot afternoons—it was now June, then July—groups of soldiers, with old bicycles lent from the barracks, bumped off down a terrible road the few miles to empty dunes with tufts of fierce grass and then the astonishing blue of the Mediterranean. Jacques joined one of these rides to the sea. The others threw down their bikes, stripped off, and ran into the water, shrieking and splashing like children. Jacques, imagining and longing for the coldness of the sea, had never learned to swim. He sat, in his clothes, watching. Someone noticed.

"Come on, Thomas! Scared of the water?"

Four or five of them clambered up the sand, picked him up and carried him far into the sea where they plunged him into the water, once, twice, three times until he lost count, couldn't breathe and had salt water streaming from his mouth, nose, ears, eyes. Then they dropped him and swam away laughing. He managed to think that, if they had been standing, he must be able to stand too, and then he managed, no doubt quite quickly although panic was weakening him, to stand, to shake the water from his head, to see that they were too far away to push him down again, and to wade slowly to the edge of the sea.

In his sopping clothes he sat and shivered, though the sun was high in the glittering sky, and thought of the prisoners plunged and held down in water over and over again until they were sure they would drown. He was crying, for them, for himself. No one noticed.

His clothes dried. The other conscripts eventually came out of the sea, unpacked the bread, sausage, cheese, and a couple of bottles of wine three of them had brought from the barracks in canvas bags slung over their handlebars. They ate and drank on the sand close to the sea.

"Here, Thomas!"

One of them threw towards him a chunk of bread. It arched through the sky, came out of the sun at him, and he failed to catch it. He picked the bread out of the sand, and threw it into the water. They all laughed.

He didn't go to the sea again.

Early in August a dozen of the conscripts, including Jacques, were sent to the barracks in Sétif. No one ever explained why these changes were made.

Jacques was pleased with his new posting. Higher, cooler and much further from the sea than Aghribs, Sétif wasn't a village stolen from its inhabitants but seemed almost like a French city. The streets in the centre, where soldiers, with their guns, regularly walked in pairs, looking for trouble that they didn't find, were French streets, perhaps a hundred years old, with trees down each side. The people, both *pieds noirs* and Arabs, looked more prosperous than the people Jacques had seen in the poor suburb of Algiers, though the atmosphere was more tense, more sullen. No one seemed to smile at anyone else. Certainly no one smiled at a soldier.

Jacques remembered that Charles de Foucauld, as a young officer, had served in the barracks at Sétif, eighty years ago.

On their first night in Sétif, an officer had spoken to the conscripts, gathered in a kind of lecture room in the barracks, which was a large, dark fortress obviously built, also at least a hundred years ago, on ancient walls.

"Some of you have recently served in the big cities. Sétif is not Algiers. Sétif is not Oran. The streets here are not so dangerous. We haven't had the Muslim demonstrations, the assassinations. Our gendarmes are not so afraid to answer a call for help, to intervene themselves if there is minor trouble. This leaves us freer to deal with anything serious that may arise. But you need to be watchful at all times. You will know what happened here at the end of the war. This you must never forget. French soldiers will never be popular in Sétif. But we have a job to do here, as everywhere in Algeria, and it is our duty to do our job to the best of our ability, to keep order and to make sure that rebellion from any side is not permitted to take hold. Any questions?"

There had been no pause before the last two words: the officer wasn't expecting questions.

"Sir", someone said.

"Yes?" The officer was clearly irritated.

"What about the OAS, sir?"

"What about the OAS?"

"Sir, in Algiers—"

"Haven't I just told you? Sétif is not Algiers. What's your name?"

"Dubois. Sir."

"Now, listen to me, Dubois. I don't wish to hear those initials mentioned again in this barracks. Do you understand me?"

"Yes, sir."

"Right. I should add—and I hope all of you are paying attention to what I say—that the army of France does not acknowledge the existence of the supposed group to which those initials refer. Indeed, you should all take note of the word signified by the third initial. And if you want to get to the end of your service, however much of it remains, with your military record intact and creditable, keep your mouths shut on this and all related topics. Dismiss!"

The officer left the room almost before they had time to stand up and salute. They looked at each other and didn't dare to say anything.

The next morning, Jacques found himself next to Dubois, though surrounded by other soldiers, when they were towelling themselves dry in the old but efficient shower room. (There had been no showers in the Algiers prison, let alone in Aghribs.)

"Why did you ask about the OAS last night?"

"Keep your voice down", Dubois said, very quietly. "Come out to the toilets a minute."

There was no one else there.

"Keep the water running in the sink", Dubois said. "I wanted to know if they're here too. Have you had a posting in Algiers?"

"For a few weeks. It was horrible. But it ended three months ago, a bit more."

"Lucky for you. I've just come from Algiers. It's a shambles. Nobody knows who's OAS and who isn't. They kill people, Muslims of course, Jews, anybody they don't like. Even French officials sometimes. And nobody stops them. The gendarmes are on their side, and plenty of the soldiers I think. They're called Delta Commandos, don't ask me why. They've been killing people in Paris too. Somebody told me they want to kill de Gaulle."

"Really?"

A soldier came in to use the urinal. They busily washed their hands until he had gone.

"Do you know", Jacques said, "what happened here at the end of the war?"

"No idea. Something bad, obviously", said Dubois. Two more soldiers came in to use the toilets and they had to go back to the shower room to collect their clothes.

Jacques and Dubois were assigned to different troops. In the next four weeks they didn't meet, and Jacques didn't dare to look for Dubois to talk to him again.

There was no prison in the barracks at Sétif. Apart from the normal duties which, Jacques understood, the army had to impose on soldiers to keep them busy when nothing was happening, the conscripts were regularly sent out into the mountains on patrol.

These patrols lifted Jacques's spirits as nothing else had since he had joined his group of conscripts for training in Lyon in November.

The country north-east of Sétif was like nowhere he had seen near Algiers or Aghribs, like nowhere he had ever seen in France. These were, at last, the violet mountains of Kabylia, real mountains, not, as far as he could tell, very high but more beautiful than he could have imagined, pale, steep mountains that caught the colours of light as they changed, deep valleys, some almost ravines, with wheat growing in the bottom, terraced slopes with olive trees, fig trees, higher up peach and apricot trees, thin goats and sheep on their narrow paths. Sometimes in the mountains it rained, briefly and violently: sudden streams rattled down hillsides; the green of grass and more trees than he had seen anywhere in Algeria was explained. The villages were high up, almost invisible against the rocks from which they seemed to be made, poor, stony. When they were too difficult for the soldiers' jeeps to reach, they didn't try.

"We're not climbing up there on foot. Easy targets, we'd make. Brigands' hide-outs, these villages, always have been. Let sleeping dogs lie, I say. They're not doing us any harm while they daren't come down."

The point of the patrols seemed to be simply to demonstrate that French soldiers were still there, still in charge, had guns, could shoot. So they drove slowly, on stony tracks that weren't roads, in daylight, to be seen.

Then there was last night: was it only last night?

They had set off after dark, to reach before dawn somewhere in the mountains; Jacques couldn't remember or hadn't been told the name of the place they were supposed to search, or impress, or frighten. There must have been some objective, some plan. Then the ambush, the shooting, the back of the pickup, the much worse pain in his leg as they drove away. Had they thought he was dead, like the other soldier they threw out of the pickup? Or perhaps they decided that a young conscript already wounded wasn't worth the trouble they'd have to go to to keep him alive. Did the FLN take prisoners? Keep hostages? He didn't know. If the stories he'd heard about what they did to French soldiers were true, he'd been extraordinarily lucky.

He remembered again, as he did every day, and, often, worse, in dreams, the limp, warm bodies of the tortured prisoners he had had to bury. Since the horseplay on the beach near Aghribs, he had several times dreamed that he was drowning and woken struggling to breathe. He had also dreamed that he was pushing someone else down into water, over and over again. And now he was in this quiet, cool house, in a mountain village that didn't seem to be full of bandits, with a kind Arab girl caring for him.

Perhaps, somehow or other, this would mean he could go home, to his grandmother's house, to Baron, to the village, to Burgundy, so that his grandmother could look after him until he was better, and then he could go back to Paris, to the Rue Mouffetard, to the bookshop, to Mathieu. But Paris—was Paris now terrifying too, with those riot police swinging their heavy capes at students and Arabs, with the OAS murdering people? What was happening to France?

And wasn't it all, here in Algeria and there in the streets of the Left Bank, because of what France had done in this wild and beautiful country that wasn't and never would be France, in the days of General Bugeaud, and ever since, and was still doing now?

He groaned, turned his face away from the sunlight outside the windows, and fell asleep.

In a dream he was running and running away from a huge man, a giant who was also a general, blundering after him with long, long strides and holding a weapon that was going to electrocute him. He didn't see the barbed wire and crashed into it, the spikes piercing his leg. His own gasp woke him. Someone was holding steady his leg, raised now on some kind of pillow or cushion. Someone else was bending over it with a sharp tool in one hand, a blade, a knife, scissors, he couldn't see which, and a cloth, stained deep purple, in the other hand.

"What are you doing?", he managed to say.

"Stay quiet. Keep still. The nurse must explore your wound." This was the girl's father, his deep, soft voice. He was holding Jacques's leg still as a woman dressed in a white robe with a blue pattern at her neck and on her sleeves probed the wound in his leg, dabbing it often with the purple-stained cloth. Each dab of the cloth was piercingly painful, the barbed wire of his dream. He shut his eyes, screwed up his face and clamped his jaws together so as not to cry out. He tried to remember the name of the purple stuff: when he was a child, his grandmother used it to clean his grazed knee or elbow. Iodine. Remembering its name was a small victory over the pain.

The woman raised her head and said something Jacques didn't understand to the girl's father. She dabbed the wound again with the iodine. Then she covered it with a weightless white cloth and pulled the cover over his leg as it had been before.

The girl's father took another white cloth from somewhere and wiped Jacques's face, which was wet with sweat.

"Be careful", the woman said to Jacques in French. "Do not move your leg. A bone is broken and I need to tie your leg to—to—something that will prevent all movement."

"A splint", the girl's father said.

"Exactly. A splint. I do not have plaster. A splint will permit the bone to mend. In a while."

"Thank you", Jacques said.

The nurse said something else, at more length, to the girl's father, and he translated it for Jacques.

"Mademoiselle says that there is shot in your leg, lead pellets from a shotgun, you understand, but that it is too difficult for her to remove them. They may stay in your leg without harm, if infection can be prevented. But the bone must be healed."

The leg, already shot, must have broken when they threw him out of the pickup.

Another sentence or two, with an apologetic look, from the nurse, and the translation:

"We are sorry we have nothing to help the pain. You are a brave young man."

Jacques shook his head.

"Now we shall leave you for a while. Tanifa will bring you something to eat. Mademoiselle and I will return to place your leg in a splint. Then you should be able to stand up, even to walk a little way, with a stick to help you."

"Thank you, monsieur. I am so grateful to you."

"Not at all. You are a wounded French soldier, and, without doubt, you have not chosen to be here. Isn't that so?"

"Yes, monsieur."

"This terrible war. It has killed so many young men. And sent so many people to where they do not wish to go. With the will of Allah it will be ended soon."

Both Tanifa's father and the nurse, with little bows of the head, left him.

300

That afternoon, Tanifa brought him some couscous and some ripe and delicious figs, which she helped him to eat by propping his back on another pillow.

"What is your name?", she said, when she had given him a drink of cold mint tea.

"My name is Thomas, Jacques Thomas."

"Thamar", she said. "This is a Berber name?"

"No. I am French."

She laughed. "I know that. I will call you Thamar. Berber or French, it doesn't matter."

Later the nurse and Tanifa's father bound his leg to a solid, straight piece of wood. They soon had him sitting—his knee was uninjured so he could bend his leg—and the next day, with the help of a crutch, an old crutch from somewhere in the village, he stood, briefly, not putting any weight on his wounded leg.

The next few weeks, in which Tanifa and her father, whose name was Monsieur Sadi, looked after him in their house, was for Jacques an enchanted time. He was in Algeria; he was a French soldier; it was the late summer and then the early autumn of 1961 and the FLN and the OAS, he later discovered, in Algiers and all over the country, were more and more desperately assassinating targeted enemies, flinging bombs into places where innocent people were certain to be killed, the FLN trying to settle scores and eliminate people they reckoned to be traitors before peace was somehow or other imposed by President de Gaulle, and the OAS trying, by any means, however brutal, to prevent that peace being imposed.

In the village in the violet mountains of Kabylia, however, there was a blessed tranquillity. Jacques's leg, strapped to the splint, gradually healed, the pain faded, and soon he could walk, slowly and carefully, using his crutch instead of his broken leg, between the mud and stone houses, none of which had more than one storey. He was surprised that there seemed to be no mosque in the village, less surprised, after what he had seen near Aghribs, that there were so few young men.

As he walked a little further day by day, in the mountain sunshine, not oppressively hot and punctuated every so often by sudden storms of rain that stopped as quickly as they began, he realised that once there must have been many more people in the village. Perhaps half the houses had no one left, no grandmother sitting sewing in the doorway for the light, between earthen pots of brilliant flowers, no girls in bright clothes like Tanifa's grinding wheat, cooking couscous, going to the pump for water with their jars, no washing spread on windowsills to dry in the sun, no children.

The children there were, to begin with stopped playing as he limped by, studying him warily with their wide brown eyes. He smiled at them. They didn't smile back. But soon they adopted him as something new, something different, a one-man show in the dusty streets of the high village protected by rocks at its back and rocks, with a low wall on top, from which the deep valley, every terraced surface with fruit trees or olives or fig trees, could be watched without, probably, the watcher being visible from anywhere.

The children, chattering among themselves in a language of which Jacques understood not a single word, followed him in little groups, made fun of him, waited for him outside Tanifa's house and bowed with broad smiles when he appeared. One boy, perhaps eight years old, an obvious leader of mischief, got his leg tied to a splint, and, using a bent piece of olive wood he must have looked hard to find as a crutch, limped beside Jacques, copying his walk exactly, to the delight of the others. The second time this happened, Jacques stopped, knowing his shadow would stop beside him. Jacques turned to the boy, who turned to face him. Half a dozen children stopped to watch.

"I am Thamar", Jacques said, pointing to his chest with his free hand.

"Adjel", said the boy, copying the gesture.

They shook hands. The other children clapped. Then Adjel pointed to them one by one and each in turn said his or her name—Jacques hadn't seen boys and girls playing together in the Algiers suburb—and shook Jacques's hand.

After this, the children, joined by a few others who were

made by Adjel to introduce themselves properly, became Jacques's band of devoted followers. Sometimes mothers watched, smiling, from doorways. There was evidently no school in the village. And there were few fathers.

On some days the children brought him things they thought he would like, or would like to see: a couple of eggs in a little basket lined with wool; a billy goat, brown and white, a thin rope round its neck; some figs; a wonderful bunch of flowers, scarlet geraniums and small white flowers like lilies; once, brought by one of the girls, a baby, wrapped in white cotton, that couldn't have been more than two or three days old. The children watched his face for his delight, and clapped again when he smiled.

But when one morning Adjel's sister, who must have been five or six years old, took Jacques's hand as he and his following of children walked along beside the wall that he thought of as the rampart of the village, Adjel angrily pulled the little girl away, ticked her off, glared at Jacques and, with three or four furious words Jacques didn't understand, led his band away. That was the end of his connection with the children.

So he walked alone, going each day a little faster, a little further. On some days, when she wasn't too busy—she did everything in the house, grinding wheat, cooking, washing, sweeping, for her father and for Jacques—Tanifa walked with him. Her father was out most of every day. With some of the few men left in the village, and more women, he would set out for the terraces where olives and fig trees grew, ancient and bent against the hot white rocks, peach trees and apricot trees close to where clear, rapid streams ran after rain and quickly vanished. On little flat fields, gardens rather than fields, potatoes grew and were harvested, a few every day.

Once Monsieur Sadi went away for three days and two nights, to Sétif, he said, on village business. The nurse who had dealt with Jacques's injured leg stayed in the Sadis' house for those two nights. Obviously for reasons of respectability, which Jacques entirely understood. He was afraid that Monsieur Sadi would report his survival, his presence in the village, to the barracks in Sétif, but when he came back he said nothing.

Jacques and Tanifa talked little, though her French was improving with the effort to tell him about the village, and he was careful, after the incident with Adjel's sister, not to touch her.

He gathered from the little she said that in the winter of last year, "before the spring, you understand", there had been a devastating attack on the village. "They came over the mountains, with guns. They shot the boys, the young men. Many they took, many."

"Who came, Tanifa?"

"Soldiers, French soldiers. My father was so sad. He is now so sad, because of what they did. The men who are left, they are not enough, to take care of the olive trees."

"But why?"

She shrugged.

"The war", she said.

One day as they walked downhill on a winding goat path towards the green bottom of the valley, Jacques dared to ask:

"Tanifa. Your mother is dead?"

She stopped, looking at him with her dark, beautiful eyes. She nodded.

"Of course. I do not remember her. She died when I was very little. The baby, my brother, died also. My father says that if there was a doctor—once there was a doctor—she would not have died. She died before the midwife, you know her, came back to the village from Constantine."

Jacques had had no serious conversation with Tanifa's father. Monsieur Sadi treated him with great courtesy, as an honoured guest, every so often congratulated him quietly on his progress, and asked him no questions. Two or three times, over their evening meal of couscous, sometimes with meat, always with vegetables, Jacques noticed Monsieur Sadi looking from Jacques to Tanifa and back, as if to detect something between them that might make him anxious. Once Jacques saw him nod his head a little, smile almost imperceptibly, as if he were satsified that all was well. Which of course, Jacques thought, it was.

Seven weeks after they had carried him up the mountain, the nurse came to Monsieur Sadi's house and said it was time to take the splint off Jacques's leg. Very carefully, she unwound the strapping and removed the piece of wood. The process didn't hurt but the appearance of his naked leg, thinner than the other though swollen at the ankle, the skin purple and white, wrinkled, dead-looking, gave him a shock. The nurse laughed.

"That's good, very good", she said. "Now try it. Gently, gently."

He put his foot to the floor and sat for a moment on his bed, his legs side by side. They looked unnervingly different from each other. The leg unwrapped from the splint didn't look or feel as if it belonged to him, to the rest of his body.

"Stand", she said. "Gently. Here." She gave him his crutch.

Using the crutch to balance, he stood up gingerly and allowed his injured leg to take half his weight. It did. He understood at once that he had been hoping—what? That the leg might crack, buckle under his weight, break again, so that he could go back to the splint, back to the beginning, not have to face his recovery, his return—to what?

As he took his first few steps and realized that he didn't need the crutch to keep him upright, he almost wept.

"My congratulations, Monsieur Thamar. Now you must practise, at the beginning with care—you must not fall—and soon you will be walking as always."

Jacques pulled himself together.

"I am so grateful to you, mademoiselle. Thank you."

They shook hands.

"You have been an excellent patient", she said. "Thank you, and goodbye."

Goodbye?

That evening, after Tanifa had taken away their empty bowls and brought them coffee, her father said, "Now Tanifa, I must talk to Thamar.", and she went out into the village street. It was dark but she would go, Jacques knew, to the house of one of her girlfriends to chatter, and perhaps sew, which they all did, until her father fetched her.

"Now that you are better, Thamar, not completely as you were, I understand, but nearly so—another few weeks and you will be—it is time for me to ask you some questions."

"Of course, monsieur."

"I know that you are a conscript."

"Yes."

"To which regiment do you belong?"

Jacques told him.

"Where were you serving when your patrol was ambushed?"

"We were stationed in the fortress at Sétif."

"And before that?"

"In Aghribs, and before that in a prison in Algiers."

"A prison. For FLN captives, FLN suspects?"

"Yes."

"My poor boy. Were you—? Were they—?"

"Were they being tortured? Yes, they were. Then they were shot. I had to—"

He couldn't go on. He felt the limp, warm bodies of the dead prisoners, the weak spade in his hands as he and the others tried to dig graves in the baked ground as quickly as they could.

"I'm sorry", Jacques said, tears running down his face.

Monsieur Sadi got up, opened the only cupboard, a space in the wall with a wooden door, found a handkerchief, and gave it to Jacques.

"You had to bury the prisoners?"

Jacques nodded.

After a long silence during which Jacques stopped crying, blew his nose and apologized again, Monsieur Sadi said:

"I don't know what has happened to the French army. Something terrible has happened to it. When I was a French soldier, in 1944, you know, we did not torture prisoners. We were fighting for the liberation of Toulon, of Marseilles. We were victorious. We defeated the Germans. We took many, many German prisoners. Did we torture them? After what the Germans had done to France through four whole years of occupation? After everything we had harvested in Algeria during the two years of Vichy, our olives, our wheat, our fruit, had been taken from us and given to the Germans? No. We did not. We were the Free French and we behaved as General de Gaulle would have wished, though plenty of the *colons* had really preferred Vichy and the Germans. And now, look, General de Gaulle is President of France and French soldiers are torturers. I find it impossible to understand." He paused, and added, "As I found it impossible to understand that after the war we Algerians who had fought for France were still not counted as citizens."

Jacques, who had known nothing of Arab soldiers fighting with the Free French, and nothing of Vichy rule in Algeria, had never heard Monsieur Sadi speak at such length, and knew that, in front of Tanifa, he wouldn't have said so much. Perhaps, if he asked Monsieur Sadi some questions, he would not only be able to postpone the discussion about what Monsieur Sadi planned to do with him, the discussion that he so much feared, but also find out more about the complicated story of Algeria. The couple of talks given to the new conscripts in the barracks in Lyon, by a bored middle-aged officer who clearly thought he deserved a more interesting job, had told them only that the *colons* were French, "more or less", while the Muslims were not: "most of them don't speak French, most of them can't read and write". The Muslims conspired to hide the fighters, "the *Front de Libération Nationale*, FLN, you see; *fellagha*, the fighters are called", who were determined to kill as many *colons* and as many French soldiers as possible. "You will be there to defend *Algérie française*, which means you will be there to defend France, to defend your families, your villages, your towns and cities. From the march of Communism. The FLN are all Communists. Nasser pulls the strings everywhere in the Arab world, on the orders of Moscow." The officer, who had obviously given this lecture many times before, sounded unconvinced by his own rhetoric.

"Would you tell me, monsieur," Jacques said, "What happened here in the village? Why there are so few young men."

"Ah. It was a catastrophe. A year and a half ago, in the winter, French soldiers came, cruel, hard soldiers, not conscripts like you, not *harkis* like me. Paratroopers. Apart from a tax collector once a year, most people in this village had never before seen a Frenchman. They were looking for FLN fighters. There were none here. A few young men, who had got out of the village to go to school, as, many years ago, I did myself, had stayed in the towns, in Sétif or in Tizi Ouzou, or had gone to Algiers, to join the FLN. There were none here. That didn't stop the soldiers. They killed some young men, boys too, one or two older men, for arguing, for trying to hide, for nothing. We were two days burying the dead. And weeks, already without a doctor, as you know, caring for the wounded. Two of them died. And many more than they shot they took away. We have heard nothing from any of them since."

Jacques thought for a moment, and then said, "Was there once a doctor in the village?"

"There was. Ten, perhaps fifteen years older than me. He was a Jew from Algiers. He liked the Berbers, liked Kabylia, so far from the cities. The government in Vichy did not allow Jews to be doctors, to teach in schools, to hold official positions. He left, in 1941 I think. I was away, in the French army. I don't know where he went. I don't know if he is alive. If he had been here, my wife and my son might have lived."

The Berbers. Jacques had gathered from reading the book about de Foucauld, Père de Foucauld, as his grandmother would have said, that the Berbers lived in the desert. If this were a Berber village, he understood why the language he heard them speak wasn't Arabic.

"I'm so sorry", he said.

Monsieur Sadi waved a hand, in both acknowledgement and dismissal. "That is life. Life here, in Kabylia. There were always Jews, you know, in Algeria. Before the Romans came, there were Jews. Now—well, you know what happened in the war with Germany."

Jacques remembered that de Foucauld had disguised himself as a Jew because to be a Jew was safe. After a moment, he said, "And you, monsieur. When the paratroopers came, how did you manage to—?"

"How did I escape? Why was I not shot or taken away? Because I am a *harki*. Because I have been a French soldier. Almost I was ordered to go to Indochina to fight against the

Viet Cong. By the mercy of Allah I was permitted to stay here because my wife had died, so that I could look after Tanifa and our olive trees and orchards. When the paratroopers came I put on my old uniform and went out in the village to protest. Useless, of course, but they didn't shoot me. Hani, the young man who helped to carry you to the village when you were wounded, is also a *harki*. He did fight in Indochina. We are not liked in the village since the *razzia*. But we stay because it is our home. And there are women and children here who think we can protect them from the war, although we could not, we cannot."

How much there was that the officer lecturing the conscripts in Lyon hadn't told them. Or, most likely, didn't know.

"My I ask you another question, monsieur?"

"Of course, Thamar. I will try to answer it."

"What happened in Sétif at the end of the war?"

"They didn't tell you? No one told you about Sétif before you came to Algeria?"

Jacques shook his head.

"They should have told you. It was another, a far greater, catastrophe. On the very day of victory over Hitler, in May 1945, there was a procession in Sétif. To celebrate victory, you understand. Very soon it became a demonstration for freedom, for the freedom of Algeria, for the Arabs, the Berbers, all the Muslims, to be free of the French, free of the empire, the *colons*, the officials, the tax-collectors, the soldiers. That demonstration was the first time in a hundred years that the flag of Abd-el-Kader, the flag, now, of the FLN, was seen in the streets. Some *colons* were killed. About a hundred, I think. That was terrible, wicked, above all foolish. The revenge of the French was much more terrible, much more wicked, and in the end much more foolish. Thousands of Muslims were killed. No one knows how many thousands. Soldiers like me, coming back from the war in France, had nothing to do with any of it, but were suspected, of course. Some of us were arrested. I was lucky. I got home. But that was the beginning—of all this, of this war, of all the cruelty and despair, though nine years of peace, more or less, lasted until this war began."

After some moments of silence between them, Jacques said, "I never knew. No one told us. There's so much no one told us. I am sorry."

"Thamar. The sins of the past are the sins of the past. Unfortunately their consequences persist."

"Until when? When will it all be settled?"

"The general will end the war, perhaps sooner than anyone expects. But that will not be the end, of the cruelty and the despair. Not for Algeria. Not for France."

Jacques couldn't answer this. So, after another silence, he said, "Monsieur Sadi, may I ask you one more question?"

"By all means."

"Is your village a Berber village? You and Tanifa and everyone here, you do not speak Arabic?"

"That is correct. We are Berbers. We are called in our own language *Imazighen*. This means "free people". We are free in ourselves, in our souls, in our mountains, but the time when we were truly free people, that's to say free of other people ordering our lives, is too long ago for anyone to know when it was. The language we speak is Tamazight. One of the most ancient languages in the world, they told me when I learned French, at school. We have recounted to each other, father to son, grandmother to granddaughter, for more time than we can measure, that we have always been here. Always. North Africa is our home. The Phoenicians came." He stopped, looked at Thamar instead of deep into his memory, the memory of his people, and said, "Did you go to a *lycée*, Thamar?"

"Yes, I did. In Mâcon, in Burgundy."

"I too. I went, by a series of chances and by good luck because I was a clever child, to the *lycée* in Tizi Ouzou. So you will have read some Virgil at school, and learned, no doubt, about Dido, Queen of Carthage?"

"Of course."

"And she was the only North African you ever heard of at school?"

Jacques tried to think of another and couldn't. "Well, yes."

Monsieur Sadi laughed.

"There you are. A classical French education. Like mine. *Algérie française.* The Algerian children thought to be worth educating were to learn all about France. They were to become as French as possible without, of course, being citizens of the Republic. Fair representation in the *Assemblée* would have meant fifty or sixty Muslim deputies: whatever next? Meanwhile, what were French children to learn about Algeria? Nothing whatever. I put this in the past tense, you understand. All of it will soon be over, finished. We were supposed to love France. That was always the plan. And look how we have ended hating her. Because she says one thing and does another."

For a moment sadness collapsed his face. Then he smiled.

"But it's not too late for you to learn a little about our land, which I hope for your sake you will soon be able to leave. Look: we talked of Dido. She was a Phoenician queen, already an invader: Dido and her faithless Roman lover—faithless as the French have been to us—is a story, certainly, but the invasion was real. They always are. The Phoenicians built Carthage, as you will remember. The Carthaginian empire was a foreign power with its capital city, Dido's city, here, in North Africa, where the city of Tunis was later built. The Berbers did as they were told, no doubt, as, more or less, they have always done. The Romans came, defeated the Carthaginians, demolished and rebuilt Carthage, and here we were, the Berber people, on the edge of another empire, for more hundreds and hundreds of years. Have you seen anything Roman since you were in Algeria, Thamar?"

Jacques thought of the eagle he had seen high above him when he was lying wounded, and shook his head.

"You must. You must."

How? This would mean leaving the village. This was where this conversation was leading. This was what he most dreaded. Jacques shook his head, and instantly regretted doing so, hoping Monsieur Sadi would go on talking without noticing. He did.

"No doubt the Romans, like the French, were oppressive and demanding masters, but they were not so unjust as the French have been. What did we learn at school, you and I?

311

Liberté, égalité, fraternité. The great ideals, the watchwords of the French republic. There has been very little of any of them in *Algérie française*. In Roman Africa, on the contrary, all kinds of things were possible. A Berber—the name means "barbarian", what the invaders thought of us, you see—could become one of the most impressive emperors of Rome. Imagine an Algerian becoming president of France. You can't? No. Exactly.

"After the Romans, the Vandals. Then the Romans again. Then the Arabs. More empires. The Ottomans, not Arab but a Muslim empire. Then the French. Every time the Berbers fought, with the Carthaginians against the Romans, with the Romans against the Vandals and the Arabs, with the Arabs against the French, even, some of us, with the French against the enemies of France. And as for—Are you a Catholic, Thamar?"

"No. Yes. I don't know."

A long, steady look from Monsieur Sadi.

"What does this mean? You were given a Catholic childhood. Someone gave you the Catholic medal that you wear. Your mother?"

"My grandmother."

"Your mother is dead?"

Jacques nodded. He could not explain.

"I am sorry", Monsieur Sadi said. "You are a motherless child. Like my poor Tanifa. Your grandmother is a good Catholic, I suppose?"

Another nod.

"So", he said, "now that you have left your childhood—what? You haven't had time to make up your mind. Is that it?"

Yes, that was it. Since the day he had said goodbye to his grandmother in the station at Mâcon, except for sometimes imagining old Père Louis remembering him before the Blessed Sacrament in the nuns' chapel, he hadn't returned to the questions he had recognized during his two weeks in Burgundy as so demanding of his thought, his decision. There was a chaplain and a chapel in the barracks in Lyon. A few of the conscripts went to Mass on Sunday. Jacques didn't.

Those questions had been too demanding. And being a soldier was first both too tiring and too dull, and then, in

Algeria, too horrible for him to think, to worry, about anything beyond getting through each day. He had put off the questions to another time. But if they mattered, didn't they matter more than anything else? He shook his head to banish the whole subject, for the moment. Hadn't he failed to think about them only because it was easier, lazier, not to?

"Yes", he said. "That's it."

Monsieur Sadi smiled.

"You are very young", he said. "There will be time. We hope."

Then he said, "I know how it is. We Berbers in our mountains are Muslims. In theory. Do we fast in Ramadan? No. Have I travelled to Mecca? No. Do I pray? Sometimes. Do I believe in Allah and his mercy? Yes, I do. So must you. So must we all. There must be mercy for the poor, the beaten, the despised, where there is no freedom, no fairness, no kindness given by the men with wealth and weapons, so the mercy must be Allah's. You understand?"

Jacques sat very still, looking into the thoughtful, intelligent eyes of Monsieur Sadi, and thought, as he hadn't since he left home, of Charles de Foucauld in the last years of his life, praying alone in the desert. Did he, Jacques, understand, or not?

"I think so", he said.

"That's enough", Monsieur Sadi said.

What did he mean?

"I asked you", Monsieur Sadi went on, "whether you are a Catholic because I wonder if you have heard of Augustine?"

"Who is Augustine?"

"A Catholic, a Roman, up to a point, but not a man of wealth and weapons. He was born in Souk Ahras, east of here, towards Tunis, when the Romans were the masters, He was a wise and holy man, and he was a Berber, some people say the greatest Berber who ever lived, and perhaps they are right. One day when the war is over, if ever the war is over, and you are back in France where you belong, you must find out about him. Now—"

Monsieur Sadi's tone had changed with his last word. He leant towards Jacques with his hands clasped on the table.

"Now that you are almost recovered, we must decide what I should do with you."

So. It had come, as it was certain to do.

"They must think I am dead", Jacques said. "Like the other soldier they threw out of the truck. They won't have known anything about what happened to either of us when the ambush was reported."

"That is true."

Jacques swallowed, looked at Monsieur Sadi's thoughtful face, and said, "So couldn't I—would it be possible for me to stay here, quietly, in the village? As if I were really dead? Now that my leg is better, I could help with the work, with the olives, the orchards, the goats?"

A long silence. A smile from Monsieur Sadi.

"No. Thamar. This is not your village, your home. And I have been a soldier of the French army. I cannot hide you here, as if, as you say, you were dead. I must take you back to Sétif and return you to the barracks so that you can rejoin your unit. Risen, as the Christians say, from the dead."

Jacques forced his lips together so hard that he felt his front teeth piercing the inside of his mouth. But it was no good. Tears overtook him and he sat at the table, his forearms pressed into the wood and his head pressed into his arms, and sobbed.

Monsieur Sadi got up, came round the table and put one hand on Jacques's shoulder.

"You must understand, Thamar", he said. "There is nothing else I can do."

He left the room for some minutes, giving Jacques time to stop crying, blow his nose, shake the tears from his head.

Monsieur Sadi came back with the two patterned pottery beakers Jacques knew well, each filled with steaming mint tea.

"Thank you", Jacques said. "Forgive me. I know you can do nothing else. You have done so much for me. You saved my life, you and Tanifa. I shall be grateful to you forever." He looked at Monsieur Sadi and managed to smile. "I hope."

"You hope you will not wish that you had died?"

"Yes."

"For that you must pray, to Allah, to the good God, as the French say, who is Allah the merciful." As he said this, Monsieur Sadi returned Jacques's smile. "Drink some tea."

The tea was very hot, and for a moment it was all Jacques could think about.

"Now listen, Thamar", Monsieur Sadi said. "You know that I have to go to Sétif every so often, on village business. Next time I must go is in about fifteen days from now. Then I shall take you with me. We shall have to walk quite a long way before we reach the road, where there is a post bus. Between now and then you must practise walking so that you will be able to do this. You understand?"

"Yes, monsieur. I understand."

"Before I take you to Sétif, however, I want you to see something Roman, something beautiful in our past, and our present, which neither the Arabs nor the French have been able to take from us. If you are a good boy, a brave soldier, and walk further every day to strengthen your leg, I will take you to Djémila before we go to Sétif, and perhaps Tanifa will come with us because she loves the place as I do. Will you promise to do this?"

"Of course."

"Good. Now I will go to fetch Tanifa from her friend's house. Drink your tea."

The day before the expedition to Djémila was to take place, two days before Jacques was to set out with Monsieur Sadi to leave the village for ever, there were violent storms in the afternoon and the evening.

"There are always storms in October", Tanifa said. "Don't worry. If there are storms today, the sun will shine tomorrow."

The sun did shine. Through a glittering morning, not hot because it was autumn, they walked for two hours, Jacques using a stick to help him, on goat paths through rocks, bushes, trees gnarled by age and bent by winds, after they left the olives and orchards behind. They walked mostly uphill, though down also, sometimes steeply, crossing streams that were already drying after the storms. Jacques, by himself, had been walking further each day to strengthen his leg, but as the path, still uphill, led them into a strange wood of trees he didn't recognize, with crackly autumn leaves, he was so tired that he said

315

to Monsieur Sadi, "Is it much further?"

"Only a little further. Wait and see. You are doing well, Thamar."

They left the wood behind them and at once came out on to a narrow rocky height, in sunshine and a gentle wind, looking down on an astonishing breadth of white stone, roads and walls and columns, a victory arch, the ruins of halls and temples, spread over a promontory of land with deep valleys, almost ravines, green and sounding with yesterday's sudden streams, on either side. Between the rushing waters, invisible in the narrow valley, the stone made a great silence.

"Sit down, Thamar, and look."

Far down, a few brown goats were grazing on low plants growing in the marble pavement of a straight road between the walls of what once must have been houses, shops. Down each side of the white road ran neat stone channels, drains, just visible from their high vantage, and the road was crossed, at regular intervals, by more roads, straight and parallel to each other, a neat grid pattern of roads, on such a difficult piece of land. Away to the right, built into the slope of a hill, was a big semi-circular arena, tidy stone rows of seats in a perfect curve, a flat white space at the bottom, behind it wide steps and the ruins of a complicated wall with doorways.

Monsieur Sadi, standing beside Jacques and following his wondering eyes, said, "The theatre".

"For so many people?" Jacques said.

"For so many people. Who knows what they watched?"

After some minutes, during which he tried to imagine the streets full of people, traders, soldiers, children playing, Jacques said: "So. This is a Roman city."

"The Roman city of Cuicul. Four hundred years of Roman life was lived here. Imagine: that was four times as long as French life has been lived in Algiers or Oran, that's to say, in some parts of Algiers and Oran."

"The arch?"

"In honour of the emperor Caracalla. A horrible man, a Berber, I'm sorry to say, like his much less horrible father the emperor Septimius Severus. You see the space beyond the arch? That's the forum, for speeches, for business, for buying and selling, for gossip, the *grande place* a Frenchman would call it. Picture to yourself the scene—"

"But up here in the mountains, so far from anywhere, why such a wonderful city?"

"First, to show power: when the Romans came to Kabylia, they built a garrison town here. Then to show glory and wealth: Caracalla's arch, temples, baths, the theatre. Then, no doubt, it was a beautiful place to live, as you can see. There were big houses here, mosaic floors, statues, once. Over there—"

Monsieur Sadi pointed to their left, where the promontory of land on which the city was built became a little lower, a little wider, more fallen stones among the grass, and the ruins of a large building with columns, some tumbled, and a marble floor.

"The Christian basilica."

"Really?"

"Really. People say the Berbers were never Christian. They were. Or some of them were. Look—those broken walls are the remains of a church, a baptistery, a fine house for the bishop. Cuicul was a Christian city with a bishop of its own for two hundred years, probably more. When the Arabs came, they changed its name to Djémila. Djémila means 'the beautiful.'"

Jacques looked and looked. Why were the ruins of the city, white under the midday sun, with green trees and bushes here and there where they had found somewhere to take root, grass between the great stones of the pavements, beautiful and not sad? The streets and squares were, except for the goats, deserted, but somehow they were not desolate.

"Look, Thamar", Tanifa, who had been sitting a yard or two away from him on the grassy brim of the hill, had jumped to her feet and, with her head right back, was pointing at the sky.

He looked up. High over the stones of Cuicul, high over the three of them as they watched, were two eagles sailing in the sky. He smiled to himself. He had been right about the eagle he had seen as he lay unable to move where the FLN had thrown him out of the truck. Eagles were Roman and hadn't gone away when the Romans left.

He looked at Tanifa. Flushed and happy, she smiled at him. "The eagles, you see, they are so—" She couldn't find a French word that would do. She swept her arm wide, indicating everything they could see below them.

"What do you think?", she said.

"I think it is a marvel, all of it, the city, the eagles, the mountains. Like nothing I have ever seen before."

Monsieur Sadi translated this for Tanifa. She smiled even more and gave her father a quick hug.

"I'm glad", she said.

"Now", Monsieur Sadi said. "I think we deserve something to eat." He had a canvas bag, a smaller version of a soldier's kitbag, strapped to his back. He hoisted it to the ground.

"Ah—", Tanifa bleated, like a small child, and said something Jacques didn't understand.

"Tanifa wants to go down to Cuicul. But look, the path is too steep for your leg. You will need all your strength to get back to the village, don't you think?"

Jacques was relieved. He was already tired. The walk back to the village would take at least two hours. And he wanted to remember the city as he could see it now, from here, their grassy terrace in the mountains.

"Yes, monsieur. Thank you", he said.

Sitting side by side, and looking down at the ruined city, they ate the delicious flat bread Tanifa had made the day before, with some goat's cheese and olives, and drank cold mint tea from an old kerosene tin.

A flock of sheep, the creamy long-legged sheep Jacques was familiar with from Aghribs as well as in the village, appeared at the top of the hill, followed by a boy with a staff, and a shaggy white sheepdog, fussing at the heels of the sheep when they took fright at the sight of strangers. The boy and Monsieur Sadi exchanged friendly greetings. The dog stopped, front paws braced, glared at all three of them, and growled briefly before chivvying the sheep down the steep path toward the ruined streets. Jacques watched the sheep, the dog, and the boy thread their way through the trees and bushes until they were out of sight below the hill.

"Now we shall have a short rest", said Monsieur Sadi, lying back in the grass and folding his hands on his chest.

"Thamar", Tanifa whispered, holding a hand out to him. She looked happy, excited, as he had never seen her before, this sweet girl who had helped to nurse him, had fed him, had washed his clothes and the cotton sheets from his bed, for weeks and weeks.

He was suddenly afraid, of something that had never occurred to him before.

He put a finger to his lips and shook his head. "I must sleep, Tanifa. So must you." He lay back in the grass like Monsieur Sadi, and closed his eyes against the sun, and couldn't sleep. When he opened his eyes, a few minutes later, Tanifa had disappeared. He stood up to look for her, and saw her some distance away, on the path by which they had come, walking slowly towards him and her father, trailing a long stick through the shrubby grass. Jacques quickly sat down, hoping she hadn't seen him stand, and, when she got back, was sitting facing Cuicul and the distant mountains which, as the sun went down the sky, were beginning to change colour. "The violet mountains of Kabylia": the phrase had haunted him; he had had no idea that it was preparing him for this moment, this miraculous place.

Tanifa sat down where she had been sitting earlier. Neither she nor Jacques spoke. Soon Monsieur Sadi sat up, looked round to check that his daughter and Jacques were there and awake, and said, "It's time we started to walk home."

They walked, as they had in the morning, in single file, Monsieur Sadi leading, then Tanifa, then Jacques with his stick. Every so often Monsieur Sadi looked back to make sure that Jacques was keeping up. The walk, particularly when it was downhill, Jacques was finding much more difficult now, his knees sometimes trembling with the effort of not falling. Monsieur Sadi saw how tired he was getting and ordained a rest for all of them three or four times when he saw a good rock or a fallen tree for Jacques to sit on and have a drink of mint tea. All the time on the long walk home Jacques, following the neat figure of Tanifa, picking her way nimbly over stones and the roots of trees, now and then looking back to him with an encouraging smile, had the beauty of Cuicul, which probably he would never see again, and the beauty of Tanifa, whom he would leave tomorrow for the fortress in Sétif, mixed up in his mind, in his soul, in an anguish he couldn't have put into words.

At last they got back to the village, to the house.

"Now, Thamar", Monsieur Sadi said. "You have done well today. I hope you thought the long walk to Cuicul, to Djémila, was worth what it has cost you. You look now very tired."

"It was a marvel. Thank you for taking me there." Jacques was sitting on his bed.

"Tanifa will find you something to eat. Then you must sleep. We have a journey tomorrow, but, don't worry, not so far to walk. I have to go out for a while. I have some business to do in the village, some papers to collect to take to the district governor's office in Sétif. I shall be back in an hour or so. I hope to find you asleep when I return."

He left, taking with him the old attaché case that seemed to be all there was of the village office.

A few minutes later Tanifa brought in from the other room, on a little wooden tray, two bowls of couscous and some bread.

Jacques stood up, stronger now, strangely strong, took the tray from her and put it on the table.

"Tanifa", he said, his arms open to her.

She came into his arms, put her hands on his shoulders, and then clasped them round the back of his neck and pulled his head down towards her face so that he began to kiss her face and then her mouth as if he had been wanting to kiss her for two months although until today he had never known it. He didn't think anything. She was the kindness of the village, the sadness and tidiness of the olive groves, the apricot trees, the little fields of wheat, carefully tended in a country of war and death. Above all she was the beauty of the day, the Roman city, the eagles, the violet mountains of Kabylia. He hadn't ever held a girl close, close, except for a moment Sylvie when they had escaped the riot, and Sylvie was terrified. Tanifa wasn't.

320

Afterwards, lying with her on the carpet, his limbs woven with hers, he watched her face for a long moment until she opened her eyes and smiled at him. "Thamar", she said, very quietly.

Then he panicked. What had he done? How could he have done it? Her father, any minute, would come back and see, and know—

"Tanifa. Quick." He pulled himself free of her, as gently as he could, and began tidying his clothes. She lay, looking up at him, happy and at peace.

"No", he said. "Your father will come. Quick."

He took her hand and pulled her to her feet. She seemed to wake into ordinary consciousness as if from a dream. Her eyes lost their shining delight and she fastened her dress, shook her hair and found the scarf she had been wearing all day as they walked to Djémila and back. She put it on, looked up at him and said, "All right?"

"All right", he said.

She looked round the room as if she had come back from a journey. Perhaps she had.

"The couscous", she said when she saw the tray on the table. "We must eat."

So they sat at the table as they should have been sitting half an hour before, and ate their couscous, Jacques not hungry but understanding that eating was necessary. They avoided meeting each other's eyes.

When they had finished, Tanifa put the bowls back on the tray and took it into the other room. She came back to the doorway, looked at Jacques, and put her finger to her lips as he had on the hilltop above Djémila.

"Tanifa, wait." He wanted to give her something, something to keep. In the morning he had to go. He looked round the room where he had slept for so many weeks. He had nothing. "Tanifa", he said, his hand to his chest in a kind of promise. Then he remembered his medal. He undid the chain and gave it to her. "Take this. Wear it. It will keep you safe. Until I come back."

"You will?"

"I will."

321

When Monsieur Sadi returned, shortly afterwards, Jacques, under his cotton blanket, pretended to be asleep.

He and Monsieur Sadi left before it was light. Tanifa did not appear, from her little room which Jacques had never seen.

The next few weeks Jacques tried for the rest of his life to forget.

At the fortress in Sétif he wasn't given the opportunity to say goodbye, to say thank-you, to Monsieur Sadi for all his care and kindness, for the day at Djémila, for Tanifa. They were separated as soon as the sergeant at the gate had understood who they were

For a week, Jacques was kept in a cell, a prisoner, taken out only to be questioned by different officers, finally by three senior officers sitting at a table while he stood in front of them with an orderly on each side of him as if he might try to escape. They were deciding whether he should be court-martialled as a deserter or further punished in the barracks for being absent without leave.

"This so-called injury, Thomas." The colonel said, looking down at an open file of papers in front of him. "How severe was it?"

"I was shot in the leg, sir. Then the leg was broken when I was thrown out of a truck on to the side of a road. Not a road, a track through rocks. I couldn't walk for several weeks."

"Walk round this room."

Jacques obeyed.

"Nothing wrong with your leg now."

"No, sir."

"Witnesses to this story? I see—" He turned over a page or two in the file. "I see you claim to have been picked up with another soldier, after an ambush. Who is he? Where is he?"

"He was already dead, sir, when they threw us out. I suppose they thought I was dead too, or dying. I don't know who he was. It was dark."

"How convenient. And this Sadi, a *harki* I gather, or once a *harki*, who brought you in, he found you?"

"His daughter found me, sir. Monsieur Sadi and another man came to carry me to the village."

The colonel turned to the officer beside him. "Do we have a statement from this daughter?"

"No, sir. She is sixteen. An illiterate peasant girl. There seemed to be little point in fetching her here."

"Quite right. In any case, the *harkis* are all frightened out of their wits now—they think they'll be slaughtered if we abandon them to the FLN, and they probably have a point. No good expecting them to tell the truth about anything. Trying to save their own skins."

The other officer said: "Sadi did bring Thomas back here, sir. No particular reason for him to lie about what happened."

"Did he ask for money, for looking after this young man in his house for a couple of months?"

"No, sir, he didn't."

"Astonishing."

The colonel shut the file with a bang.

"There's something fishy in this business but I'm damned if I know what. Benefit of the doubt, I suppose: we've got more important things to worry about in any case. Give him one more week in solitary. That'll teach him not to disappear into the blue another time. After that, back to the ranks. Got that?"

This was addressed not to Jacques but to the other officers.

"Sir", they said, as one.

"And you, Thomas", the colonel went on. "Once you're returned to the ranks, not a word about this—episode—to anyone. Not a word. Understand?"

"Sir", Jacques said.

"And this will be a black mark on your army record."

The colonel stood. So did the others.

"Dismiss!"

For a week, alone in his cell, Jacques had just managed to hold himself together, before this hearing. Guards had fetched him for questioning on some days and not others and at unpredictable times. He knew it was necessary to keep his head, to tell the truth, not to get confused by officers who seemed to want him to incriminate Monsieur Sadi in some way. And he was sustained by anger: why was the army punishing him already,

323

and, as far as he could make out, deciding whether or not to punish him more, only for being alive and not dead?

At the same time, beneath his anger and his resolve to keep his head, the glow of Tanifa's gift to him, at the end of a day which had clearly moved her as much as it had moved him, partly, he now saw, because she had watched it move him, lasted for days and days. He had promised to come back to her. He would, wouldn't he? When? When the war was over. How? He had no idea. Gradually, the warmth and light of Tanifa's body, eyes, voice, disappeared into the darkness of anxiety for her—what would happen to her if he couldn't get back to the village to find her? Soon? Ever?

Then, today, he had been taken through the corridors of the fortress to the disciplinary board, or whatever they called themselves. Another week alone in this cell. After that, they would return him—to what? To where? Whatever, wherever it was, the prospect terrified him. He knew he had lost whatever resolve he had had, to survive as a soldier obeying orders. Because of his injury? Because of Tanifa? Because, in the village recovering, he had had time to think, and Monsieur Sadi had told him things that made him understand Algeria better, and so made him more ashamed, even more ashamed, of France.

In any case, whatever had got him through burying the tortured prisoners hadn't been courage but almost the opposite of courage: the kind of obedience that soldiers were drilled to deliver, whether or not they understood the reasons for what they were told to do, and especially if they understood them only too well, and hated them.

If they sent him back to Aghribs, with nothing much to do, he would survive. If they sent him to Algiers and he had, again, to—He couldn't even look at the thought, the memory.

He tried to think about Tanifa instead. But suddenly this memory wasn't a happy dream, a consolation.

He would never get back to the village. How did he ever imagine that he could? So—

Weren't all Muslims very strict about girls and honour and virginity? What would become of Tanifa if her father somehow discovered, perhaps when she married, that she was no longer a virgin? What if he were to find out sooner—she might be too upset not to tell him—and then she were to be forbidden to marry at all? What if she became some kind of despised, disgraced outcast in her own, her flower-filled and hard-working village, so beautiful and so sad?

Had he, Jacques Thomas, meaning no harm, destroyed, in one reckless moment, the whole life of a gentle girl who, by herself, had found him by that track and rescued him from a slow and painful death? How monstrously he had abused the care, the hospitality, the kindness of Monsieur Sadi, who on that last day had taken him to Djémila to show him the wonder of his country, the country which Frenchmen had stolen and bullied and tortured and raped—

There was nothing in Jacques's cell in the fortress but a pile of straw, a blanket, a can of water and a tin mug, a bucket, a small, high, barred window out of which he could see only the sky. Twice a day a guard, not a conscript but a lame old soldier, brought him a bowl of indeterminate soup and a chunk of bread, filled his water can, took the bucket and brought it back emptied. When it struck him that Monsieur Sadi, who had trusted him, might think that he had raped Tanifa, as France for a hundred years had raped Algeria, he collapsed to his knees on the floor of his cell and howled.

Someone banged on the door and shouted, very loudly, "Shut up, you in there."

He stopped howling and, sitting on the floor with his back against the wall, sobbed for some time into his arms, folded across his knees.

His sobbing, in the end, exhausted him. Quiet now, still sitting with his back to the wall, he raised his head and looked, not at the wall of his cell but as if through it and far away into the mountains to the village. He tried to think. They had saved his life. They had looked after him for more than two months. They had encouraged him to walk, and so to learn a little and to love their village high in the violet mountains. They had taken him to Djémila. And he had spoiled, sullied, betrayed, all they had done for him, endangered Tanifa in ways, because, really, he knew so little about their lives, he couldn't even imagine. It would have been better, much better, if the FLN had shot him dead, or if someone had found him dead by the side of that track once his wound and the August sun had killed him.

Over and over again he longed to go back to that evening, to get it right, to kiss her, just to kiss her and say goodnight.

He hadn't made her unhappy. Not then. But now? Could it be that she was unhappy now only because he had gone away? That wouldn't be bad. That would be how things go. But if she felt ashamed, dirtied, violated, he couldn't forgive himself, now or ever. And he didn't know what she felt and had no way of finding out.

In the week that followed nothing happened. Only the old soldier appeared each morning and each evening with his food and water. No one fetched him for more questions. No one told him whether he would stay in the Sétif barracks or, if not, where he would be posted.

Once the guard came in and found him crying.

"Cheer up, lad. Only another couple of days. You've got off light, you know."

But Jacques, by then, five days after the hearing, was, he knew, somehow broken. No one had hurt him. No one had even hit him, let alone tortured him with electric shocks or near-drowning. But somehow he had lost himself in misery and fear.

He made himself eat his soup, kept some of his bread for later, when he might be hungry, and wasn't. He cried a lot, slept so restlessly that the nights lasted and lasted until he ceased to believe that it would ever again be light enough for him to look at his watch.

When two guards came for him on the seventh day, he crouched in a corner of his cell, shaking so much that he didn't think he could stand up. The guards looked at him, went away, locked the door and came back with one of the officers, not the colonel, who had been at the hearing.

"Pull yourself together, Thomas. What's the matter with you, man? You could have been sent to a military prison in France, you know. Absence without leave is a serious offence. What would your parents have thought then? Their son a coward?"

Jacques couldn't move. He was trying as hard as he could not to cry.

"This is ridiculous", the officer said. "There's nothing wrong with him. Get him up."

The two guards took one arm each and pulled him upright. He made himself take his weight on his feet, and succeeded.

"Good", the officer said. "Take him to the truck. Make sure he doesn't try anything. Has he got possessions to collect? Kitbag? No, he wouldn't have. Come on, Thomas. Get going."

The journey he remembered afterwards as a long nightmare in reverse: sleep was patchy and uncomfortable; being awake was much worse. He slept now and then but every time he woke the jolting truck, the cold—he was wearing his now filthy summer uniform that Tanifa had washed and mended for him—and the dark, because the back of the truck with its canvas cover let in almost no light, were still there, as if they would never end. He was stiff, and shivering, and felt bruised as if he had been beaten, though he had not. There were seven other conscripts in the back of the truck. He didn't know any of them. They knew each other and he gathered that they had arrived in Algeria only in the summer and had been bored in Sétif for three months.

"A bit of action", the sergeant said. "About time too. What's the point of being a soldier if they don't give you anything to do? Let's get at 'em, I say."

"It's all very well, saying that. If we get near enough to shoot them, they'll be near enough to shoot us."

They ignored Jacques, sitting in a corner of the truck with his head on his knees, until the chattering of his teeth made one of them say: "What the hell's the matter with him?" And another said, "He's freezing cold, can't you see?" and found in his kitbag some kind of blanket. "Here, you. Put this round your shoulders."

When he could speak, Jacques said, "Thanks. Do you know where we're going?"

"Algiers", the sergeant said. "Bound to be a bit more lively than the old barracks. Dead, Sétif. There'll be more to do on an afternoon off, in Algiers. Girls, maybe. Cinemas, anyway."

327

Almost, he started crying, again, but managed not to.

Twice on the journey the truck stopped, the first time, in a wood on a mountain road, only so that all the conscripts and the driver and the junior officer sitting beside him could relieve themselves as quickly as possible; it was pouring with rain and very cold. As they got back into the truck the young officer gave each of them a chunk of bread and a chunk of sausage. There was water in the usual can in the back of the truck, and a couple of tin mugs.

The second stop was in a village. Jacques was now so cold, shivering so much, that he didn't move out of his corner until one of the others pulled him up and pushed him off the tail of the truck. "Come on, walk about a bit. Warm you up."

It wasn't raining. The sun, cool and bright, was shining.

"Dear God", one of the conscripts said. "What's happened here?"

A small village, an Arab village, empty, silent except for an old woman in black wailing in her open doorway. A large dog appeared and stood barking at the soldiers. A younger woman came out of a house and stood a little way off, screaming at them, both arms in the air, fists clenched. A small child was clinging to her clothes.

"Looks like after a *razzia*", the driver of their truck said. "Better clear out. You never know."

Two or three of the conscripts had disappeared round corners. Jacques made himself walk a little way from the truck, trying to warm up. The houses were meaner and poorer than the houses in Tanifa's village. As there, hens scratched in the dust. Outside one house a big clay pot, broken in pieces, lay on its side in a dirty pool of precious olive oil. The dog was still barking at the truck. He heard, behind one of the houses, the sound of someone working, the knock of a tool of some kind, rhythmic but wth a long pause between knocks. He walked three more steps and saw a man with a pick, breaking the clay, each blow making very little impression on the hard ground. Behind him, lying on the clay, was the body of a child, four or five years old, her face covered in a thin cloth, her white clothes stained with blood. Over and over again, the man raised the pick with both hands above his head, and brought it down on the just-broken ground. There were tears running down his face.

A shout. The officer at the truck, calling the conscripts back. Very quietly, crying now himself, again, Jacques turned and joined them.

It was dark when they reached Algiers, but not too dark for Jacques to recognize the prison. Two of the other conscripts had to pull him out of the truck in the yard.

He quickly understood, from listening to what was said at meals—he sat at the table, barely able to eat—that, in the months since he had been away, the soldiers' work in this suburb of the city had changed. He gathered that suspects were still being brought in for interrogation. He realized that some of these were now French when one of the new conscripts who had arrived with him asked, at the midday meal on Jacques's first day, why French soldiers were being arrested.

"OAS suspects. They're murdering people every night, you know. They kill people in the evenings. The FLN kill people in the mornings. Every day. It's not much fun here at present." This was an older conscript, who must have been in the prison for some time.

"What is this, OAS?"

"Haven't they told you anything? It means 'secret army organization' but it's not secret any more, if it ever was. They want a white Algeria, with all the Arabs slaves. Most of all they want to kill the general. They keep trying."

"What general?"

Two men laughed, and at once stopped laughing.

Into the silence of the mess hut, the know-all said, "The general himself, of course. General de Gaulle. The President of the Republic."

"Really? They want to kill him? Whatever for?"

"For screwing Algeria. Screwing the *colons*. Most of all, for screwing the army."

"That's enough", a sergeant said. "You stick to doing what you're told, my boy. Never mind the questions."

On his second morning, Jacques, now very weak because

he couldn't eat without, almost at once, throwing up, was sent out on patrol in one of the armoured cars he was familiar with. The soldiers had guns. He had a gun. Without being told, he quickly discovered that they weren't, as in the spring, watching the streets for possible fighters. They were looking for bodies. In a couple of hours, driving slowly through the poor streets of the suburb under a grey winter sky, they found three. Two soldiers had to jump down and pick up the corpse; the other two covered them with guns to their shoulders. Jacques managed to stay in the jeep and hold, his hands and arms shaking, his gun. The bodies, two Arabs, one an old man, and a *colon* boy of about fifteen, were slung on top of each other inside the jeep. As they drove, a few *colons* in dilapidated old cars sounded their horns in the familiar *Algérie française* rhythm.

"Why the demonstration?", one of the soldiers said.

"Eleventh of November, dope. Armistice Day", another said. "Very patriotic, the *colons*. Though it's bit late for all that." He looked down at the dead boy at his feet.

By the time they got back to the barracks, Jacques was sobbing and couldn't stop.

The next morning, when he had been unable to eat, unable to answer questions, almost unable to fasten the buttons on the winter uniform someone had thrown at him, he was taken to the small infirmary hut to be examined by an army doctor.

He had been sick, again, after swallowing some coffee. He was trembling and thought he might at any moment fall.

"Sit down." The doctor, who was sitting at a tin table with a pen in his hand, looked at a form in front of him. "Thomas."

Jacques sat down, and put his head in his hands.

"How long have you been like this?"

He shook his head, cleared his throat, looked up, at the doctor's stern face. He made himself answer.

"Not long. Some days. I was in prison."

"I know all that. Absent without leave, I see. Did you run away?"

He shook his head again.

"No. No. I was injured. I couldn't move. They saved my life."

"Who?"

"A Berber family. In Kabylia."

"Good of them. I wonder why they bothered."

The doctor studied the form.

"Your injury?"

"My leg was shot, and broken when I was thrown—"

The doctor interrupted: "And now?"

"It's better."

"Then what's the problem?"

Jacques began to cry.

"Pull yourself together, lad. You're not a baby."

Jacques took a breath, sniffed long and hard, and shook his head yet again.

"It's the bodies. I can't do it."

"Bodies?"

"The prisoners who were shot here. We had to bury them. The bodies in the streets, yesterday. A dead boy, in the jeep, like the man I was next to in the truck. And an old man. The little girl."

"What little girl?"

"In the village where we stopped. A little girl dead. Her father had a pick, but he couldn't break the ground for the grave."

"You're not making sense, Thomas. This is a war. You expect bodies in a war. People get killed. We all have to cope with bodies. What's the matter with you?"

"I don't know. I can't do it."

The doctor wrote something on the form.

"When were you last on leave?"

"I've had no leave since I joined up."

"When was that?"

"A year ago. Almost exactly. My—"

"Ah. I have it here. Yes. 14 November last year. What's the matter now?"

Jacques was crying again because in three days' time it would be his birthday. Not that it mattered, he knew. The doctor was right. He wasn't a baby. But the idea of his birthday was too much for him, as if he were a small child.

"I'm sorry. It's nothing. It doesn't matter."

The doctor waited, and then said, "What kind of effect do you think the state you're in will have on the new recruits who've just finished their training?"

Jacques looked up at the doctor and, this time, nodded miserably.

"I'm sorry", he said again.

"You're a disgrace to France and to your family. Where do your parents live?"

"What? I'm sorry."

"Your parents. Where do they live?"

Jacques had stopped crying. He looked at the doctor again. There was not the slightest suggestion of sympathy in his face.

"My parents are dead."

"Ah", the doctor said. "Have they been dead a long time?"

"I never knew them. Either of them."

"Who brought you up?"

"My grandmother."

"Still alive?"

"Yes."

"Where does she live?"

"In a village in Burgundy."

Very nearly, he began to cry again.

"Good. I'm going to order some leave. You're not the slightest use at present to an army fighting a war. You will go home to your grandmother for three weeks, and during that time you will sort yourself out so that you can deal with the normal demands of military life. Understood?"

"Yes, sir."

"Dismiss!"

As Jacques left the hut the doctor shouted "Next!" An orderly was waiting outside with a soldier who had a bandage over his eyes. Jacques held the door open. The orderly led the wounded soldier by the hand into the hut. Jacques, feeling, for the first time, ashamed of what seemed after all, in his grandmother's phrase, no more than sheer weakness, shut the door behind them.

He was sick in the jeep on the way to the port, and sick several times, through a night and most of a day, in the troopship that took him and hundreds of other soldiers across the stormy sea from Algiers to Toulon. Shivering and exhausted, he couldn't sleep on the night train to Paris, which he was supposed to leave in Lyon station so that he could catch an early morning local train to Mâcon.

Huddled in his seat in a waking nightmare of memory, guilt and indecision, while around him soldiers he didn't know joked, drank, smoked, and eventually snored, he realized that he couldn't face going back to his grandmother's house, to the village, to Monsieur le curé and to what his grandmother would regard as disgrace. He needed to tell someone everything, about burying the prisoners, about the bodies in the streets in Algiers, about the little girl and her father, and about Djémila and Tanifa and—and how could he tell anyone what had happened with Tanifa?

Mathieu. He had to find Mathieu, who would listen, who wouldn't think him a coward, or, if he did, would understand what had broken such nerve as he had once had; who would understand, too, about Tanifa.

He would, he must, find Mathieu.

He stayed on the train in Lyon—the soldiers all had railway passes so he didn't have to worry about a ticket—and arrived in Paris with most of the others on leave, in the chill drizzle of a November morning while it was still dark. On the train, once they woke up, most of the others had changed out of uniform into what they had of civilian clothes, though their overcoats were evidently military. Jacques watched.

"You got any civvies?" someone asked him. He shook his head. "You'd better watch out, then. They don't like us in Paris. They send us off to die and kill people in Algeria but they don't want to see us in the streets. They like soldiers in shiny uniforms marching down the Champs Elysées on the *quatorze juillet*. That's why they get us here in the dark. That's why all the troop trains leave in the dark."

He had his kitbag, which they had given him on his first day back in Algiers. He had some money, not much because they had taken out of his pay what he should have been paid for the weeks he had been absent without leave.

He stood outside the Gare de Lyon in the rain. It was after seven o'clock in the morning, the day showing no sign of dawning. He stood like a stone in a river among the hurrying people who had arrived on suburban trains and were joining bus queues or disappearing into the Métro. No one even glanced at him. He could have caught a bus to Mathieu's hospital but he shrank from the prospect of being in another enclosed space with strangers crammed against him, so he started to walk.

He walked along the quai on the Right Bank until he reached the Pont de Sully at the tip of the Île Saint-Louis where a bit more than a year ago he had got out of the taxi which was to take Sylvie home. He stood on the bridge for a long time, looking south-east, the river flowing towards him, until the sky began to streak with the beginnings of the day, the rain stopped, and at last the light dimmed the electric glow of the street lamps. People passed him, hurrying to work in both directions, paying him no attention as he stood, his back to them, a stone in the water again. At last he turned, crossed the road and looked down the straight, elegant street that led to the Alsatian brasserie where he had failed to meet Mathieu on the night of the riot. Today, whenever Mathieu finished work, perhaps they could have a meal, a long talk.

To his astonishment, the idea of this meal with Mathieu made him feel hungry, actually hungry, for the first time since he had arrived in Sétif with Monsieur Sadi from the village. He crossed the other branch of the Seine to the Left Bank and walked to a workmen's bar in a little street off the Quai de la Tournelle where he used to have breakfast when he walked from the Rue Mouffetard to the bookshop.

A silence fell as he went in, but the *patron* remembered him.

"You on leave?"

"Yes."

"You look terrible. Algeria?"

"Yes."

"Sit down. *Café au lait*? Croissants? A dash of *marc* in the coffee?"

His stomach turned. "No *marc*. Thank you. Coffee and croissants please."

It was warm in the bar, and the atmosphere not unfriendly though no one except the *patron* spoke to him. He drank two big cups of milky coffee and ate three croissants. He didn't feel sick. His clothes dried. He pulled himself back from falling asleep on his hard café chair, and looked at his watch, which had survived everything. Nearly nine o'clock. Mathieu.

He bought a cheap writing pad, a pencil and a small packet of envelopes, sat on a bench on the *quai* and wrote a note to Mathieu. Then he crossed the Latin Quarter through back streets, avoiding the crossroads of the riot, the Panthéon, and the Rue Mouffetard, and emerged into the Boulevard Saint-Michel opposite the Luxembourg Gardens. Three students, walking arm-in-arm along the wide pavement, stopped when they saw him.

"Look!", one of them said. "A soldier!"

"Where've you been, soldier? Torturing Arabs? Murdering children?"

He shook his head miserably as the tears came. One of the students spat, at his feet, on the pavement. They laughed, and left him there. He was shaking, again, even after his breakfast.

He managed to walk, steadily enough, for the ten minutes it took him to reach Cochin Hospital, the huge old hospital after the Port Royal crossroads.

At the reception desk he waited in a line of people, his note to Mathieu in his hand. When his turn came he said to the man at the desk, middle-aged, grey-haired, "May I leave a note for Doctor Rostand? I don't know the number of his ward."

"Rostand. Rostand.", the man said, looking at a long list. "No Doctor Rostand is working here."

"He must be. He was—he was working here, last year."

The man looked more carefully at Jacques.

"You're a soldier on leave?"

Jacques nodded, again on the edge of tears.

"You don't look well, mate. I know what it's like. Go round to the emergency department. Out of the main door. Turn right and right again. They'll sort you out."

"No. No. I'm not ill."

"You're not well, all the same."

"I must find Doctor Rostand, find out where he is now."

"Look. Sit down over there. When it's a bit quieter I'll see what I can do."

"Thank you, monsieur."

Nearly an hour later, when Jacques, in the visitors' toilets, had thrown up his breakfast, washed his face, and done his best to calm down, the man, at last, beckoned him back to the desk.

"Your Doctor Rostand. I've managed to find out where he is. He's in Djibouti."

"What? Where?"

"Djibouti. French Somaliland. East Africa, you know. Hey! Don't fall. You'd better sit down again."

"No. Thank you. It's all right."

Jacques, unsteady on his feet, left the hospital and walked some of the way back along the Boulevard Saint-Michel. A few passers-by looked at him doubtfully, thinking, no doubt, that he was drunk. Making sure that there was a big enough gap in the traffic for him to get across the Boulevard safely, he found his way into the Luxembourg Gardens and sat on a damp bench under some leafless trees.

What should he do? Where could he go? He had no other friends in Paris. He hadn't thought ahead as he changed his mind in the train: only the idea of seeing Mathieu had brought him to Paris, and had been a way of avoiding going home to his grandmother.

He must have fallen asleep on the bench because when, stiff and cold, he sat up straight and looked at his watch, it was nearly four o'clock and getting dark.

He picked up his kitbag, clammy from lying on the grass for hours. He walked to the bookshop because he couldn't think of anywhere else to go. He tried to look through the window to see who was there, but the window was too steamy. He opened the door cautiously, and saw no one he knew. The shop was busy, as always at this time of day, and he went to a dark corner in the second room and took a book out of a shelf at random, and opened it, facing the shelves so as not to meet anyone's eye.

After perhaps twenty minutes, as he was reading an account of nineteenth-century travels in the Himalayas, which was calming him, someone tapped him on the shoulder. He jumped, dropped the book, and turned. Mademoiselle Gaillard.

"Jacques. I thought it was you. What's happened to you? You look dreadful."

"Mademoiselle. I'm sorry."

They shook hands.

"What is it, Jacques?"

"The war—" He couldn't go on.

"Come into the office. Bring the book. I saw you reading it. Read some more."

He picked up from the floor the book about the Himalayas. She took him into the office at the very back of the shop, where he had been only to collect his pay at the end of each month. There was no one there.

"Sit here and wait for me", Mademoiselle Gaillard said. "Until it's time for me to go home."

Someone kind was telling him what to do, so he did what she said.

At six o'clock she came to fetch him.

"Where are you staying, Jacques?"

He shook his head.

"Have you any friends in Paris?"

Beginning to cry, he shook his head again.

"Come home with me for tonight. I have a couch for when my sister visits me."

She took him down to the Métro and stayed close to him in the rush-hour press of people. He made himself and his kitbag as small as he could, and looked down all the time at his feet. The familiar reek of the crowded Métro, garlic, sweat and Gauloises, almost made him sick, again. It was a short journey, half a dozen stops, to La Motte-Picquet Grenelle. He remembered where that was, just beyond the Champ de Mars. Respectable bourgeois Paris. Her flat was exactly as described by Henri and Marcel who had never seen it: small, neat, warm, faintly smelling of cat, because of the white Persian which greeted them when Mademoiselle Gaillard opened the door.

"Take off your coat, Jacques. Put your bag by the door. Sit down. That's right. You look as if you need a glass of spirits, but I'm afraid I haven't any. When did you last eat a proper meal?"

He shook his head.

"I have some soup, good soup, and some cheese. Stay there."

She left him by the gas fire, which she had lit, and a few minutes later came back, an apron over her grey suit, and laid the little table by the window.

He managed, slowly and carefully, to eat some soup and some bread, but shook his head at the cheese.

"Now, Jacques", she said when they had eaten. "You are on leave?"

"Yes, mademoiselle."

"You have been in Algeria?"

"Yes."

"It was—very difficult?"

"Yes."

"But why have you come to Paris? You have no family here?"

"No. I came to see a friend. He's not here. He's in Djibouti." The threat of tears, avoided.

"That's sad. I understand."

She waited for a few moments and then said, "Where does your family live?"

"I have only my grandmother. She lives in Burgundy, in a small village not far from Mâcon."

"In that case, that's where you must go. Your grandmother will look after you, feed you properly, make sure you sleep. That's what you need, Jacques."

He looked at her kind, serious face. Could she be right? Might he get better without having to tell his grandmother, or Monsieur le curé, or anyone, about anything that had happened in Algeria?

"Really?", he said.

"Really."

Later, she brought him a quilt and a pillow.

"I'll wake you early and I'll come with you to the Gare de

Lyon before I go to the shop."

He was so grateful to her for not asking him any questions, and for offering to take him to the station, that he slept for most of the night, though he was awake at six when she brought him coffee.

"You know, Jacques", she said, as they walked to the Métro through dark, early streets, "I'm glad your friend isn't in Paris. You shouldn't be in Paris when you're not well. The atmosphere has been very bad lately. People are afraid and shocked, and we're not told enough, not told the truth, I'm sure. I'm leaving Paris myself at the end of the month. After twelve years in the shop, I'm going to Blois to live with my sister. I've been fortunate enough to find a job in a well-thought-of notary's office, with several partners, you understand. I believe I shall be happier in the country."

"Why? What, in Paris—?"

Mademoiselle Gaillard looked both ways along the empty street. There was no one in earshot.

"Last month there was a big Arab demonstration, against a police curfew which had been ordered only for Arabs. It started in the Grands Boulevards, quite peacefully, a student who was there told us in the shop. Well, it turned into a nightmare. Much worse than the riot in the Latin Quarter last year. No one knows how many Arabs were killed. There were dozens of bodies fished out of the Seine. The students were saying the police at headquarters on the Quai des Orfèvres were throwing them into the river in the middle of the night. Horrible, horrible. And there's some kind of concentration camp for Arabs in the park of the Château de Vincennes. People have seen Arabs hanged from trees. It's hard to believe that General de Gaulle allows the police to behave in this fashion, when it's not the Arabs who are trying to assassinate him but the OAS, whoever they are. I suppose you have met them in Algeria?"

She looked at him under the street lamp. He saw that she was suddenly a little nervous.

"You don't—You're not—?", she said.

"Absolutely not. Everyone knows they exist. No one knows who they are. I think for the poor *colons* they are the last hope—There were paratroopers who—never mind. It sounds as if the Paris police—I don't know."

"But you see why I have decided to leave Paris?"

He nodded.

"I'm glad I was still here when you—Come along, Jacques. The Métro."

At the station they found the first slow train to Lyon that stopped at Mâcon.

Jacques began to tremble.

"Goodbye, mademoiselle. You have been so kind."

She put a hand on his arm.

"Get yourself home, Jacques. Your grandmother will look after you."

She looked at him for a moment.

"How old are you?" she said.

"I am twenty-one. Since yesterday."

"Yesterday was your birthday?"

"Yes."

"My poor Jacques. But you are very young. You must look forward. To the future. All this—all these horrors—can't last much longer. The General will see to it, I'm sure."

"No, mademoiselle. The horrors will last much longer. Much longer than the war."

Chapter 6

Bernard

January 2016

Bernard had written a postcard, with a picture of the blue and gold interior of the Sainte-Chapelle, saying that he would arrive at about eight o'clock in the evening. It was ten minutes past.

Thamar must have been waiting, no doubt at his desk in the winter room, to hear the taxi stop outside the house. He opened the door and stayed out of the rain while Bernard paid the driver. As Bernard came up the path, its stone slabs wet and gleaming in the light from the door, Félix pushed past the old man, wagging his tail, and greeted Bernard first.

"He's pleased his friend has come back. Quite right. Bernard, my dear boy. How good it is to see you."

Thamar took Bernard's free hand—in his left hand he was carrying his backpack by its strap—and held it in a warm, firm grip for a moment or two.

Bernard realized that he had been expecting a hug, and then realized, before the old man released his hand, that his grandfather, who, on the day they first met, had made the sign of the cross on his forehead, had never touched him again, except that, now, he was shaking his hand.

"Come in, come in. Have you eaten?"

"Yes, thank you. A sandwich on the train."

He took off his donkey jacket and dumped it in the passage on top of his backpack.

In the winter room the fire was crackling and spitting—raw logs, Bernard saw—and on the painted tin tray on the desk was an unopened bottle of red wine and two glasses.

"A moderately good Mâcon, for once", Thamar said, following Bernard's look, "to celebrate. Wednesday's feast and your return."

"Wednesday's feast?"

"The day of the kings. I always forget how little you know of the Christian year. Secular France made us celebrate it on Sunday but the day before yesterday, the sixth of January, was the real day of the kings, the kings from the east who brought gifts for the infant Christ. Never mind. Let's celebrate, in any case, your return, a gift to me."

Then, apologetically, he said, "I know you've only been away two and a half weeks, and I am accustomed to life alone with Félix, but I have missed you."

"I'm glad to be back. It's wonderfully warm in here. Paris was freezing, and Mâcon station not much better."

The old man looked at him carefully, through his spectacles. Bernard had forgotten how crooked his damaged eye-socket was.

"How were things at home? How is your mother? You look tired."

To tell him, or not? All through the autumn he had said nothing about Joséphine.

He had gone home for Christmas and the New Year, not because his parents ever made much of either, but because he felt he should, and because he knew that his mother, however hard she tried not to say so, was longing to see him.

"No. They're fine. My parents are fine."

"Bernard. Something was wrong at home. They didn't want you to come back to me? No doubt your father is anxious about your career. I can easily imagine he thinks you're wasting valuable time writing a book for me which will be of limited interest, if it's of interest at all, to anyone else. He's probably quite right. I understand. Perhaps you have come to say goodbye?"

The old man was talking more volubly than usual. Bernard saw his anxiety.

"No, no, Thamar. It's nothing like that. I've told my father I shall need a full year, until the summer, to finish the book. And now that I've started, of course I must finish. He's accepted that

I'll be here till then. And I've promised him that afterwards I will go back to Paris and find myself some kind of job. It won't be easy but it should be possible."

Also more words than were necessary, to cheer him.

"Thank you, Bernard. You know I am more grateful than I can tell you."

But the old man looked at him again.

"All the same, there's something wrong. Open the wine and tell me about it. Only if you want to, naturally. I think you are worried about your mother. Perhaps it is she who would like you to be at home?"

Bernard opened the bottle with the familiar ancient cork-screw, and poured some wine into each glass. He gave one to his grandfather who had put two more logs on the fire and was now sitting in his usual chair. Bernard sat down opposite him, the fire between them.

He had to tell him.

"My parents are worried, it's true. But not about me. On the contrary. My mother is pleased that I'm here, helping you. My father is resigned. But—"

"But?"

Bernard looked away, at the spitting fire.

"My sister Joséphine has disappeared, vanished."

"What? But Bernard, how can this be true? What does this mean, vanished?"

"She left Paris months ago. Six months ago. In the middle of her *bac* exams. She knew she was doing badly. She hadn't done enough work. In fact, I think she'd done hardly any work in her last year at school. So when the exams came and she couldn't do them, she was afraid of what my father would feel—no, that's wrong: Joséphine isn't good at imagining what anyone might feel. She was afraid of what my father would say and do when she failed her *bac*. You will understand. The *bac* is his whole life. Preparing students, getting them through, being pleased when the most unlikely candidates manage to pass because of the help he has given them. Grateful parents coming to thank him, giving him presents. Perhaps Joséphine has more of an idea of all this than I give her credit for. In any case she knew he would be very upset, and furious with her. And with reason. She isn't stupid. She's been taught in a good *lycée*, his *lycée*, where he's worked for twenty years. So the failure would be entirely her own fault. He would have told her she must retake the year, retake the exams. And she couldn't face that. She couldn't face him. She couldn't face any of it. So she left home, left Paris, before the *bac* exams were even over. And no one has heard anything of her since."

"Surely that isn't possible, in these days? The telephone? The ways of reaching people on the internet? I read about them, though naturally I don't understand them."

"In fact it's as possible as it ever was for someone to decide to break all communication. Just by cutting off the phone, maybe losing it and not replacing it, and making no contact. That's what Joséphine has done."

"But your mother—how terrible for her."

"Exactly. I'm more angry with Joséphine than I'm worried about her. But there's plenty of cause for worry. She left Paris with a Moroccan girl who had changed her French name to a Muslim name. After a while the police traced the Moroccan girl to the Turkish frontier with Syria. The Turkish police turned her back, didn't allow her to cross the frontier. There's been no more news of the Moroccan girl, and no news at all, no scrap of information, about Joséphine, though the police have her on their list of people who are missing."

A silence, while the old man took this in.

"This is terrifying." Thamar got up from his chair, fetched the bottle of wine from the desk and poured some more into Bernard's glass. He sat down again, leaning forward with his hands clasped.

"This is truly terrifying." He lowered his head for a minute or two, and then raised it, looking again at Bernard.

"Is Joséphine interested in Islam? Because of her grand-mother perhaps?"

"No. Not at all. Not, in any case, that either of my parents could see—I was in Nantes myself for most of the last three years. But I don't remember, and more to the point they don't remember, Joséphine ever raising the subject of religion at home. My parents, as you know, don't have any interest themselves in religion, in Christianity, let alone Islam. They say Joséphine never asked questions about Islam, or talked about it. Nor politics. And she wasn't close to our grandmother. If anything, I think she was ashamed of her. A North African maid, who couldn't read or write—" He saw his grandfather wince. "I'm sorry, Thamar."

A half smile.

"It's all right, Bernard. I know you loved your grandmother."

After a moment, he went on, "But your sister. What could have happened? Who could have persuaded her to leave, not just to get away from home and your father, but to set off for this terrible war in Syria?"

"If she really did. If it's true that she did, I've no idea what could have so changed her. Although—According to my parents, she spent a lot of time alone in her room playing with her laptop, her smartphone. They thought she was messing about with pop videos, films, chatting to her friends. Perhaps she was watching propaganda? Perhaps she was believing lies and promises from Islamist fanatics? Who knows what friends she was making when she wasn't at home? But I find all this almost impossible to believe, of her. She's a silly girl. Just a silly girl."

Thamar thought for a moment, looking at the fire. Then he said, "Did she have money, when she left?"

"I'm afraid she did. Enough to keep her going for quite a while."

Bernard didn't explain. In all the time he had been in Thamar's house, he hadn't mentioned his other grandparents.

Thamar sat very still, this time for a few minutes. Bernard, used to his silences, waited.

"I've read in *Le Monde*", the old man said at last, "that young French boys, and girls too, from good families and with a good education, have been declaring themselves to be Muslim converts, and then, immediately, they say they are jihadists and go to Syria or Iraq to try to—to try to what? To fight for the Caliphate. To kill. To die, best of all, and go straight to paradise. This is appalling. This is a travesty of Islam, you know. The Koran forbids suicide in any circumstances whatever. And in the Koran it says that he who takes a single life has destroyed all of mankind."

"Does it?", Bernard said, "Does it really? Then how can—?"

It wasn't the moment to go on. So he said, "In any case, I can't believe any of this interested Joséphine. I don't think she's ever given a single thought to the next world, or to this one, come to that. She's too selfish. I'm as sure as I can be that she won't have got anywhere near Syria, whatever her friend was telling her to do. I think she'll have been on a beach somewhere all summer, maybe in Turkey or Greece, enjoying herself. And then, who knows? She doesn't want to come home and face the consequences, not only of messing up her *bac* but of running away and leaving my parents to worry. The longer she's away the more difficult it gets. And her money's running out. So she gets a job in a bar or a hotel. Or worse: she's pretty enough and confident enough—"

"My poor Jamila. She must be ill with worry."

He paused.

"Is she? Is your mother ill? It wouldn't be surprising if she were."

"No. She's not ill. She looks tired, thinner, older. But she's—how to describe how she is? She's brave."

"I know."

"She goes to work, as always, in the *lycée*. She keeps house, shops, cooks, irons my father's shirts. It keeps her going, her ordinary routine. She quite enjoys it all and has never resented it. In a way, I suppose she's become, over all these months, accustomed to worrying about Joséphine, every day but at a low level. I remember her saying about other things that human beings can get used to anything. And in any case, what can she do? What can they do? They had to go to the police to report her disappearance, after a month or so. The police have her on every missing persons list. They suggested that my parents might like to talk to other parents with missing children who have tried to reach ISIS. But my father would never do that. The other parents might be Arabs in the *banlieues*. He would have no idea how to talk to them. And of course they want as few people as possible to know, about Joséphine."

He had asked his mother at Christmas what she or his father had said in Rouen. "Nothing. Can you imagine your grandparents' horror? They think Joséphine is travelling in Europe, on her Interrail ticket, sightseeing and enjoying herself."

"I expect she is", Bernard had said.

Now he said, "They tell themselves that if anything really bad had happened to her, they would hear from the police. That's all they have to hold on to."

"Bernard". Thamar looked at him, again the acute grey eyes. "I am so sorry, so very sorry to hear this."

Bernard waited.

"You know", the old man said, now looking down again, at his clasped hands, "for this, for these unholy and apparently unstoppable waves of hatred and fear that have overtaken France, and some, only some, in Islam, I am myself in a way responsible. You have read what I have written, or tried to write, in my book. You will understand. If there is even a remote chance that my own granddaughter, whom I have never met, has left her parents, her home, to join these wicked murderers—then for what has overwhelmed her, seduced her, and all the other children who have been led into these horrors, I am in a way responsible. Answerable, that means, to God."

Bernard could see that it wasn't time to say anything.

"For I, the Lord your God," the old man said very slowly, "am a jealous God, and I punish the sins of the fathers in the children, the grandchildren—"

Bernard took this in. He had never heard these words before.

"Thamar", he said. "That is dreadful. Who wrote it? I thought that God, if he exists, was supposed to be good. And just. I thought that goodness and justice are part of the definition of God. There's no justice in punishing the children and grandchildren for what the fathers have done. How can there be?"

"Ah. Those words are among the words Moses hears from God when God is giving the people of Israel the commandments which God is telling them that they must obey if they are to remain his children. God explains that the sins of the fathers, for which the children will suffer, were sins of idolatry.

That means calling things other than God divine and worshipping them instead of worshipping God."

"I don't understand at all. What sort of things?"

"History, in the case of Marxists. But always power. And money. Fame. Conquest. Empire. The things for which the sins of the fathers were committed in Algeria, and in Syria, and everywhere in Muslim lands where the French competed with the English for a hundred years. And these sins, all these sins, were committed in pride, in pride and for the sake of pride, by men who didn't stop for a moment to consider with any intelligence or imagination what was bound to follow. The results of what they were doing were and are evident in the history of Algeria, and are here and now, in 2015—I'm sorry, in 2016—evident in Syria, and Iraq, and poor Libya. They are also evident in France. The warning, you see, is that some sins, some kinds of turning away from what is good, will have consequences for which the children and grandchildren of those who turned away from God will suffer. The words are a description of what happens, no more and no less."

"But—but—" Bernard was struggling. Now Thamar, in his turn, waited.

"But the children and grandchildren of those to whom wrong was done also suffer, don't they? There is even less justice in that."

The old man was now looking at Bernard across the space between them with an intensity Bernard had never seen in his crooked face before.

"You are right. The suffering which is the consequence of sin is universal, as sin is universal. Nevertheless that God is just I believe, and that God is merciful I also believe, as do, by the way, all Muslims who have not been led by crazed fanatics into crazed fanaticism. I realize that the justice and the mercy of God seem to clash, to be inconsistent, even to cancel each other out, but that both are in the being of God, together, is a mystery, in which I believe. Of course the injustice, to each other, of human beings, and the consequences of this injustice from one generation to the next, are facts, evident facts, which

I know and you know. This is knowledge, ordinary knowledge, and between knowledge and belief there is a difference. They ask of us different responses."

He paused, looking down at his hands, and then looked up at Bernard again.

"How to put it? Knowledge asks for our recognition; belief is already a response, our assent to what can never be rationally proved to be the case. Both justice and mercy. Both. And. There are other such pairs, which seem to contradict one another, in what Christians hold, hold to, as true. Both knowledge and belief: perhaps they are such a pair. Both are necessary but they are different."

There's not just a difference, Bernard thought, but a gulf, an abyss across which he knew—knew?—that he couldn't follow his grandfather. He said nothing.

"So" the old man went on, "France has heaped on Muslim peoples a mountain of injustice, and I have been guilty of adding my grains of sand to that mountain; for a part of it I am to blame. If your sister is killed or harmed beyond healing in the madness of violence and revenge and cruelty that is the Syrian civil war, it will be partly because of my own sin."

"You can't say that, Thamar. How long have you lived here, out of the world, out of all those worlds, almost even out of France? Years and years. You have never been to Syria or Iraq, where this dreadful Caliphate has arisen."

"The Crusaders humiliated Muslims in Syria and Iraq. The Crusaders were French, not all of them of course, but the Crusades were inspired and driven from France, from Christian France. The Arabs have always called the Crusaders 'Firangi'. Frenchmen."

"That was all centuries and centuries ago."

"In memory and resentment, particularly, alas, in resentment, centuries are short. And President Bush was not centuries ago."

"But you—you, yourself?"

"Listen Bernard."

Bernard sat back in his chair and, in his turn, clasped his hands.

"There are levels of sin, levels of guilt. At the deepest level, where we all have to begin, I am a man. Do you remember what my old friend Augustine says about the jealousy and rage of babies? The lies told by little children? I am a man. Therefore I am already implicated, folded, merely by being alive, into the sinfulness of the whole human race, into the sticky web of greed, laziness, selfishness, dishonesty, and pride, pride above all, that entangles human beings in cruelty to the weak and defenceless, the poor, the hungry, those with no hope. All of us are to blame to one degree or another, I, and you, and even the saints who have had to struggle with their own sinfulness until they are able to receive the mercy and love of God. And even then, perhaps, they must struggle with their pride. Augustine knew this well. It took him all his life to know, really to know, that the best in him came not from himself but from God."

"I wish", Bernard said, "that I understood. I've read the *Confessions* twice now, and I see why you love him as you do. What he says about time and memory is marvellous and marvellously intelligent. But so much that he says, that he knows, still seems far away from me, impossibly far away, as if it were the other side—the other side of the gulf that separates knowledge from belief. Or the other side of ranges of mountains I'm not strong enough to climb, though I can see that you reached the other side, of the gulf, of the mountains, years ago."

"It's there, Bernard. It's there, not the other side of a gulf or of ranges of mountains, but in you and for you, for you to discover when you turn a little further, from the region of unlikeness into which each of us is born, towards the light, Plato's light which Plato didn't know was the light of Christ, but Augustine did. You will do it. You will turn a little further, one day."

Thamar looked up for a moment at the figure of Christ on the cross that hung over the fireplace. Bernard followed his look.

"He's dead. Look at him. Darkness, not light", Bernard said. "Why can't God be as you say, somehow holding both justice and mercy together, while Christ is simply a good man who was killed?"

"Ah, Bernard. That's what Muslims believe. And plenty of Christian heretics down the ages. But if Christ be not raised, our faith is in vain and we are still in our sins."

"But we are still in our sins, aren't we? You have just said so. Someone else told me once that he takes away the sins of the world. But he doesn't, does he? Look at the world. Where is the light in Syria? In Iraq? In the *banlieues* where these kids become jihadists because they have, as you said, no hope?"

"Who told you that?"

"What? I've seen them for myself."

"No, Bernard. Not the children in the *banlieues*. Who told you he takes away the sins of the world?"

"A friend. In Nantes. Well, the girl I thought—"

"The girl you took such good care of? The girl from Guadeloupe?"

"That's right."

'She is a Catholic."

"Yes. It all seemed so straightforward for her. She loved everything about it."

"She is very young." Another half smile. "So are you."

Thamar got up from his armchair, rearranged the fire with the poker and put on another couple of logs. He took his glass to the desk.

"I shall have another small glass. For once. And you?"

Bernard shook his head.

"She was right", Thamar said, back in his chair, holding his glass between his hands. "About the sins of the world. But this, like much else in the Christian faith, like the justice and mercy of God, is a mystery in which we may only believe. He takes away the sins of the world. What he has done for us, what God, in Christ and through Christ has done for us, is done. In eternity the sins of the world are taken away. In time the sins of the world are as dreadful as they ever were, as, most likely, they always will be, for the very reason that sinfulness is in every one of us."

He took a sip of wine and put the glass on the little table beside his chair.

"So I am not blameless. None of us is blameless for the

sins of the world. But that, I know, becomes a bland thought, something, as your mother would say, that one becomes accustomed to as soon as one accepts it as true. It remains true, however. What can one man, one human being, do about it? Almost nothing. But I meant something more specific than my implication in the web of sin common to us all.

"I am old. I am a Frenchman. I have been a soldier in Algeria in a horrible war which happened because the French refused to understand what they were doing, to people they refused to recognize as people, for a hundred years. I have heard through a wall men being tortured and I said and did nothing. Obediently I buried the bodies of these men, whose graves were given no names. I have watched a Berber peasant digging in the baked earth a grave for his child whom French soldiers had killed. I have been kindly treated by a good man, also a Berber, who had fought and worked for France because France had educated him to believe that French civilization is a noble cause, worth dying for. France abandoned him and he was murdered by men who had been educated by France to believe that liberty, equality and fraternity are a noble cause worth killing for. And I betrayed that man's trust in me, in one moment of love for your grandmother."

"I know", Bernard said. "I know all this. But Thamar, you yourself can be blamed for so little. For that moment of love, perhaps. But how old were you? Younger than I am now, and you know that, for all my supposedly good education, I know nothing about anything."

The old man had shut his eyes.

Without opening his eyes he said, "God, be merciful to me, a sinner."

He opened his eyes and smiled. "The shortest prayer. And the best. The prayer of another agent of empire hired to oppress the poor for the sake of the rich."

"Another agent of empire?"

"A tax collector for Rome. It's a story Jesus tells."

"I thought you admired the Romans?"

"They were better than most. They treated the people they conquered as human beings. Except for the slaves. And even their slaves they often treated quite well. But Augustine knew that the empire, like all empires, was founded on *libido dominandi*—"

He looked at Bernard to see if he understood.

"The lust for power. There you have it. No doubt the poor tax collector was only doing a job, but he was right to call himself a sinner. Like me."

Bernard wondered if he should add something, and then did: "But, Thamar, imagine: without that moment, there would have been no Jamila, no me. Our lives are—well, our lives are lives, aren't they? Not nothing?"

"They are precious in the eyes of God, as is every human life. Of course, Bernard. But—but I shouldn't have been there at all, in that beautiful village being cared for by people who had suffered already, and who were to suffer much more, because of what France had done and would do. Did you know that Jamila as a small child was shut up in a prison camp with her mother, a camp in France, built by the Vichy government for Jews, with barbed wire and filthy water and rations barely enough to live on? Did you know that?"

Bernard shook his head. "She has never said anything about her childhood except to tell us about the families in Paris her mother worked for."

"Well then. You see? How can a Frenchman of my age not feel to blame? The *harkis* who were left alive fled to France, this France, for which they had bravely fought, and we failed to treat them even as human beings. We are to blame for so much wrong done, for so many seeds of resentment and rage sown like dragons' teeth for the future. Now, as we sit by the fire in a peaceful village, look at what is happening to the world, to France. Look at the horrors we read are being perpetrated in Syria, in Iraq, in Libya, and now also here. Until very recently, we could not have imagined such things taking place in France Look at the killing of all those young people and harmless visitors enjoying themselves in Paris just a few weeks ago: more than a hundred people are dead; another hundred people were badly hurt. The killers were boys from the *banlieues*, French, Belgian, educated here, but Arabs, even Berbers, I dare say,

353

full of bitterness and rage for what was done to their families in their own land, in their own villages and farms. And all of that was done in the name of French civilization. In the war to preserve it I was given a contribution to make, a part to play, and I did as I was told. How am I not to blame?"

"But—" Bernard, remembering what he had discovered when he was doing the research for his thesis, was going to say that the dragons' teeth were sown generations before Thamar was born, and that he had had no choice about being a conscripted soldier or about the things he was ordered to do in Algeria. But the new picture Thamar had just put into his mind, the picture of his mother as a small child, stopped him. No wonder he had never seen a photograph of her when she was younger than the six-year-old going to school for the first time in her pinafore, with her satchel, holding hands with the little girl who belonged to the family employing his grandmother. Now he saw her, three, four years old, in a prison camp built for Jews herded behind barbed wire like animals before being taken to the slaughterhouses of Poland, with his frightened, uncomplaining grandmother, very young, doing, no doubt, everything she could to feed and keep warm and comfort her child. He wondered whether his father knew about the camp. Then he thought of the refugees from Syria, from all over the Muslim world, now, in Calais, in a camp with barbed wire round it and mothers struggling to look after their children and French policemen trying to stop them escaping. Beating them. He said nothing.

"Forgive me, Bernard. There was no need for you to have to think of Jamila and—and her mother in such a place."

"No. To know the truth, more of the truth, is always good. Isn't it? But I wish—"

He stopped again. He had no idea what he wished.

"You wish? That you could help your mother find your sister?"

"No. Yes. Of course. I've thought about it a lot. I can't see anything I can do. But that wasn't what I was going to say."

"Which was?"

"I wish I understood—anything."

354

"Bernard. You understand more than you think. You understand as problems things that most boys of your age, probably now more than when I was young, are not even aware of. I am certain that this is so. Above all, you know what you don't know. That is true of few people always. Now—"

With a sudden briskness, Thamar stood up. As he did, his eyes shut and a hand went to his chest. With the other hand he clutched the arm of his chair.

Bernard got to his feet at once.

"Thamar! What is it? You're not well."

The old man opened his eyes, stood up straighter with a push on the arm of his chair, and took a deep breath.

"No. It's nothing. Just occasionally I feel—a little dizzy. That's all. It's nothing."

"Really?"

"Really." His smile, almost reassuring.

"Now, Bernard. I have some soup on the stove. I made it in case you were late, and cold. I have been talking too much. I am so pleased you are back. Come into the kitchen."

Bernard sat down at the table and looked round the kitchen as if he were putting on a favourite old coat. From a black pan keeping warm at the side of the iron hob Thamar ladled into bowls his thick leek and carrot soup and broke in pieces half a baguette. Bernard was hungrier than he had realized.

"What are those beautiful flowers, in the middle of the winter?"

On the kitchen table the usual blue and white jug had in it, among spiked, shiny deep-green leaves, half a dozen white flowers, with faint red lines on each petal, each flower so perfectly symmetrical that it might have been painted on a tile. An Arab tile.

"Ah. They appeared just after you left. Christmas roses. They grow in the shade of the trees at the end of the garden. They're called black hellebores, although, as you see, they are white, with streaks of blood."

He looked across the table at Bernard. "Like our souls", he said.

355

They ate.

"Your soup is very good", Bernard said. "Thank you." In Paris he had found it difficult, accustomed as he was to Thamar's food, to be enthusiastic enough to please his mother when she cooked rich dishes of lamb or beef or chicken with bacon and wine. His father thought that a meal without meat didn't count as a meal.

Thamar put down his spoon and said, "You haven't asked me about your book. Your patience with me is very impressive."

Bernard was so anxious to know what his grandfather thought of what he had written, hour after hour all through the autumn, that he had been pleased, when he arrived, to talk about anything else, everything else, by the fire in the winter room. Before he left for Paris he had been to the château, with a new ink cartridge he had bought over the internet, and, with the help of the secretary in the nursing home office, printed what he had written, nearly fifty thousand words, to leave on the dining room table for Thamar to read while he was away.

Now he said, "So Thamar, what do you think?"

A long silence. Then a smile.

"I haven't read it."

"You haven't? Really?"

Bernard managed not to burst into tears like a disappointed child. While he was in Paris he had kept wondering what his grandfather was making of what he had written, kept hoping he would be pleased—Bernard thought that quite a lot of what he'd done wasn't bad—or at least would have suggestions for improvements, more accurate descriptions of what had actually happened. Hadn't he come back for this response?

He picked up a piece of bread from beside his empty soup bowl and put it down again. He didn't know what to say.

"I'm sorry, Bernard. I can see this is a shock for you. The truth is that I don't want to read what you have made of my life until it's finished—that's to say, until your book, not my life is finished. Because it is your book, not mine. On the other hand, it's always possible that my life may be finished before the book."

"No, Thamar. Don't say that. You're not going to die, not yet."

"Who knows? *notum fac mihi, Domine, finem meum, et numerum dierum meorum.* Lord, let me know my end, and the number of my days. It's a good prayer, but often the wish is not granted."

He smiled.

"You mustn't worry about my death, Bernard. I don't. But I want you to finish the book before I read it. I'm looking forward to seeing what you have made of my life, so long, so confused. But I want your confidence that you can write the book to be safe from the harm I might do it by saying anything before you have finished the work."

Bernard made an effort to smile back.

"I understand", he said. "I think I understand." He took a deep breath, looked down and then up again, and made himself dare to say, "But I need your help. With the book. Not only with the book, of course. But I need your help with the book before I can go on."

A piercing grey look across the table.

"You need my help with the book? You shall have it, of course. But not tonight."

The old man got up, took the soup bowls to the sink, and tidied the table as he went on, "You must be tired, Bernard. You've travelled from Paris where it can't have been easy trying to help your parents with their anxiety about your sister, and you've kindly listened to me talking too much. You must go to bed now, and sleep soundly before we talk about the book. It's Saturday tomorrow so I won't be going to the château. I lit a fire in your bedroom. I thought it was very cold when I went to close the shutters, too cold for a boy from Paris where, no doubt, your parents have central heating in their flat. I hope you will be warm enough."

Too many words, Bernard thought again. He's hiding how pleased he is that I've come back. He got up and almost put an arm round the old man's shoulders, thought better of it, and said, "You're right. I'm tired. I'm sure I'll be warm enough. It's warm—just being here."

"Thank you, Bernard. And goodnight."

The next morning they sat at the plush-covered table in the dining room, Bernard at his usual place, facing the window, with his laptop shut on his right, a notepad and pens beside it, and in front of him the pile of paper he had put there for Thamar to read. Thamar sat to his left facing the door, so that Bernard would mostly see the undamaged side of his face: this was his instinctive position, as a deaf person presents his better ear to someone he is talking to.

Each of them had beside him a second cup of breakfast coffee that he had brought from the kitchen. Bernard had lit the fire before breakfast, with dry logs he had brought in and stacked before he went away. They were burning quietly.

"How can I help?", Thamar said.

"I don't understand what happened next."

"Next?"

"I'm sorry. Of course, you don't know where I've got to. You have just been sent home from Algeria. You have left Paris after one day and one night. You have failed to find Mathieu at the hospital. You come home to your grandmother. And then? In all the pages you wrote I could find only a long gap, a gap of years, a blank on my chart."

Thamar looked at him, and said, "My poor Bernard. Is that as far as you've got? Your book is going to be very long."

He paused for some time, now looking down at the table, his hands clasped on the plush cloth.

Eventually, he said, "Well. When I came back to my grand-mother, I was still a child, a wretched scarred child." His hand went to the left side of his face. "Not scarred like this. Not yet. Scarred all the same.

"It took years, a lot of years, for those scars to—what? Not to heal, exactly. I suppose to become invisible, even, much of the time, to me. Dull is the word, for me, for my life, during most of those years, although they began with a short period—they sent me back to Algiers—too terrible for me, in the condition I was in, to suffer much. If you can imagine such a thing. Then nothing of interest happened for a long, long time, and I was of little interest to myself. Hence the gap in your chart. I must have appeared to be better, to be alive, to be capable of carrying

358

out orders, instructions, whatever life was requiring of me, but that was all. Let me try to explain."

Bernard pulled his notepad towards him and picked up one of his felt-tipped pens.

"No." Thamar raised a hand. "Don't write anything down. Just listen. It won't take long."

Bernard put down the pen, pushed away the pad, and rested his right hand on the pile of printed paper as if to keep it steady.

"The army had given me three weeks' leave to pull myself together. It was too short a time. As each morning came—I was sleeping, or not sleeping, in the bedroom that's now yours— the day on which I had to report to the barracks in Lyon got closer and closer in a rush I couldn't stop, and I could manage less and less. Manage what? Manage just to behave in a normal fashion, to put on a clean shirt, have breakfast with my grand- mother, go for a walk with Baron, chop wood for the fire and bring it in.

"I remember those weeks as if they were a single miserable day. I cried a lot. I couldn't eat. I was afraid of going outside. I shivered with cold all the time although my grandmother made sure the fires blazed and I wore my winter clothes. She did her best, of course. She thought I was ordinarily ill, had caught some foreign disease in Africa. She sent for the doctor. He listened to everything, tapped everything, and said there was nothing wrong with me that rest and good food wouldn't cure. I would get better because I was young and strong. Then she decided I was ashamed of being sent home because the other soldiers I had been with, and people in the village—much more serious from her point of view—would think I was too weak or too much of a coward to do my military service, as the conscripted sons or brothers of other people seemed to be doing, without fuss. When she asked me, kindly at first but more and more impatiently, what was the matter with me, I couldn't tell her. She sent for the curé, Père Bonnard.

"I heard her talking to him out there"—he nodded towards the passage—" when she opened the door and let him in. 'Thank you for coming, father', she said. 'He won't tell me any- thing, poor boy. He needs a priest. I'm sure of it.' I was waiting

359

in here, standing there, by the fire, cold, cold. He came in and shut the door behind him, on his face a concerned and interested look that I didn't trust. I can see it now."

He shut his eyes for a moment or two.

"'Now, Jacques, how are you?' he said, holding out his hand. My stomach turned. I bent over, rushed past him, through the door, then the kitchen where my grandmother, a knife in one hand, an onion in the other, stood looking horrified. I was sick in the garden. At the end of the garden I stood crying by the fence until I was so cold I had to come back to the house. I suppose it was only a few minutes. When I came back, Monsieur le curé had gone. My grandmother was furious with me.

"A day or two—I can't remember exactly—before I was to go to Lyon, I was worse than ever. I couldn't, or wouldn't—I don't know how much I was really to blame for all this—get out of bed. My grandmother sent for the doctor again and this time he said that, whatever was wrong with me, he couldn't be responsible for allowing me to go back to the army. He was talking to my grandmother out there in the passage, where she had talked to Père Bonnard. I'd got out of bed to listen from the top of the stairs. I heard the word 'breakdown' and also heard the doctor say, 'There's a serious risk of him doing himself harm, Madame Thomas. You must keep an eye on him at all times. I shall telephone the authorities in Lyon tomorrow.' Then he left.

"I went back to bed and pretended till the next day that I hadn't got up except to go to the bathroom. The doctor returned that afternoon and said that the army medical corps doctor in Lyon had agreed that my compassionate leave should be extended for two months."

He paused and drank his cold coffee.

"Did you get better?" Bernard said.

"Of course."

"Of course?"

"The doctor had been right in the first place. I was young and strong, and terrified of going back to Algeria. That was all. So my grandmother decided that I had simply succeeded in putting off my return to duty, and probably that was at least

360

partly true. In any case, from then on she treated me firmly, as if I had been still a small child. 'We're not having any more of this nonsense, Jacques.' I can hear her saying it."

He looked at the door as if she were about to come in.

"She was right, in her way, and her character was always stronger than mine. She made me get out of bed, get dressed and have, at least, some coffee before she set off for Mass with the nuns. She made me eat lunch and dinner. She made me take Baron for a walk every afternoon, however cold and wet the weather—this was the winter of 1961 into 1962, a bitterly cold winter even in Burgundy. She clearly paid no attention to what the doctor had said about watching me in case I harmed myself, or worse. She was right about that too. Although—"

"Although?"

"What he said had given me the idea: I remember, a few days after his second visit, looking at the knives in the kitchen drawer and wondering if I were brave enough to cut my wrists, far away from the house where no one would find me until I was dead. But I also remember that the idea struck me as self-indulgent, over-dramatic, silly. Also it made me realize that I didn't want to die. I wanted, one day when the war was over, to go back to the village in the mountains of Kabylia, and find Tanifa and ask her father's permission to marry her. I think it was at that moment, when I looked at the knives in the kitchen drawer and was almost able to laugh at myself, that I understood that the only thing wrong with me was fear. Fear of going back to Algeria, not because I was afraid of being killed but because I was afraid of what I would have to do, and see."

"I was right to be afraid of what I would see, but it turned out that I was wrong to be afraid of my own fear, of collapsing again into tears and shivering and not being able to eat without being sick."

A long pause.

"It turned out?" Bernard said.

"Yes. I went back to Lyon after my two months of extended leave. I don't remember the date. Early in February 1962, in any case. They put me with a bunch of new conscripts 'to get me back in shape', they said. The new conscripts had nearly got to the end of basic training. A couple of weeks of drill and target practice, and lectures from officers delivered with even less conviction that those we were given a year earlier. Then we were sent off, troop train, Toulon, troop ship, Algiers, just like the time before. We were put in barracks in the middle of Algiers, not far from the Kasbah."

He stopped, and looked at Bernard, his old eyes now creased with memories he didn't want to face.

"Go and make some hot coffee, Bernard. I never tried to write about those few weeks because I couldn't. They were the very worst. But you need to know that I was there."

Bernard picked up the cups, his own untouched, went to the kitchen, put the kettle on the stove, washed the coffee pot and the cups, measured out coffee as for breakfast, poured in water which he had allowed, according to Thamar's rules, to stop boiling, and waited for five minutes before pouring coffee into their cups. He heard the old man go upstairs to the bathroom and come down again, slowly.

Thamar took a sip of coffee, winced at its heat, and said, "Yes. That was the end of the war, but it was also the most chaotic, the cruellest, time of the whole war.

"Algiers during those few weeks was like the worst nightmare you ever had, going on and on without the possibility of waking up. I suppose it was like how people have always imagined hell.

"There were negotiations going on, between President de Gaulle and the FLN. We didn't know anything about that. All we knew was that every day more and more people were being killed, anyone, everyone, soldiers, *colons*, Muslims, Jews. The OAS were killing more people than the FLN. I don't suppose you know—most French people have never known—that in those six months, before and after what was said to be the end of the war, the OAS killed more civilians in Algiers than the FLN had killed in six years. The OAS. The French army, or, more exactly, the fascists in the French army, had gone mad. Why? Humiliation. Defeat. One defeat after another, defeated by the Germans in 1940, defeated by the Viet Minh in 1954, humiliated by the Americans in 1956, now humiliated by the FLN. The pride that had originally been curdled by humiliation in the war of 1870, so long ago, had become dreadful cruelty. Resentment, you see, as we were discussing last night, at the root of it all. *Ressentiment*. Nietzsche. Never mind.

"I was there only for a few weeks of this horror. After we'd been in Algiers about a month, a month of occasional patrols through the streets, dodging snipers' bullets, stopping to pick up corpses, mostly sitting in the barracks listening to gunfire, we were told that it was all over. There had been an agreement, between de Gaulle and the FLN. This agreement was supposed to mean peace, the end of the war. We were also told that most of the army, the obedient army to which the confused and frightened conscripts belonged, would soon be going home. That at least was good news that turned out to be true."

"The peace", Bernard said, "didn't turn out to be peaceful?"

"It's hard to believe what happened next. We found it difficult to believe then, what we were seeing. The so-called peace was even worse than the war. I didn't understand at the time. None of us ordinary soldiers did. The fact was that the upshot of de Gaulle's peace was this: the FLN had got everything they had wanted right from the beginning, after half a million Algerians had died and half a million young Frenchmen had wasted two years of their lives. When this fact became known, the result was the blind rage of the OAS, stoked by the misery of the *colons*. In the poor streets of Algiers the old rhythm, *Algérie française, Algérie française*, was beaten out on saucepans by desperate women every time French soldiers went by. We seemed to hear it all the time, day and night."

Thamar drank some of his coffee. Bernard, waiting for him to say more, did the same.

"Two or three days after we were told about the agreement, we were ordered to join forces with the FLN—can you imagine that? All of a sudden we were to fight alongside the FLN, who had done unspeakable things for years to French soldiers, who had nearly killed me in Kabylia, to stop the OAS and the most furious of the *colons* murdering Muslims. They were shooting every Muslim they came across. There was something like a massacre. We were French soldiers. We did what we were told, and fought beside Muslims to save defenceless Muslims from French soldiers. I was lucky. I wasn't in the place where the OAS killed eighteen conscripts, wretched boys obeying orders without any idea of who they were fighting or why. Our officers, particularly the sergeants looking after the lads who had just arrived from France, were so enraged that there was a battle, in a *colon* slum called Bab-el-Oued, north of the Kasbah, close to the sea. It was a kind of siege, but chaotic. The OAS were inside the district. We were outside in our jeeps, guns at the ready to shoot. Helicopters overhead. Tear gas. Naval ships, including the one that had brought us across from Toulon, with guns trained on Bab-el-Oued. I never discovered how this became a victory for us and the FLN and a defeat for the OAS. In any case, once more I was lucky. I never fired my gun.

"It ended horribly, with a lot of *colons* from the poorest parts of the city demonstrating against the peace. They were held up by army road blocks outside the Grand Post Office, and then they were shot down by French soldiers, panicking, I imagine. Many of them were killed. I wasn't there, so, again, I was lucky. By then, we were back in the barracks. We heard the drumbeat of the march, *Algérie française, Algérie française*, and then the shots and the screams. The wretched *colons*: they had been left with nothing. Algeria was the only home they had ever known and now France which had always promised to defend them had not only abandoned them but was killing them on the street.

"You know, the ends of wars are always terrible. The defeated lashing out in rage. It was like that here."

"Here?"

"Here. In the summer of 1944. I was not quite four years old, so I don't remember anything of that summer. But dear old Père Louis, the nuns' chaplain, told me after, at last, I came home from the army, that the Germans, knowing they were losing the war, had set themselves to round up every last Jew in France to finish the killing before the war ended. Someone must have told the Gestapo that the nuns were hiding Jews in the château."

"Someone local? Why? How could they?"

"Remember the story of Chaumont's father and the Café de la Paix? Remember the charcoal-burner's hut you came upon in the woods? Afterwards, everyone tried to forget the Occupation, but there were people who would do anything, betray anyone, for a little advantage, a bit of money, some real coffee, a blind eye turned to some black market venture. In return for an important betrayal you could get a railway ticket to Switzerland.

"In any case, the Gestapo came to the château to find the Jews. A boy on a bicycle warned the nuns—there were good people here too—and Père Louis assembled the whole community, including the old ladies, the girls who worked in the kitchen and the laundry, everyone, for Mass in the chapel, which they didn't begin until they heard the Gestapo jeeps roaring up the drive. The Jewish mother and her children were hidden under the altar. They kept the Mass going for as long as they could, with lots of singing, and then started the midday office—you won't know about the office: prayers and psalms nuns and monks say or sing seven times a day—until the Gestapo major came into the chapel and shouted 'Where are your Jews?'

"Père Louis said, 'This is a Catholic monastery. There are no Jews here.'

"'We'll see about that. Everyone outside! Everyone!'

"They lined them up outside, checked their names against a list, made each nun, each servant, fetch their papers: the whole building had been ransacked, every cupboard left open, every bed left pulled apart, while they were in the chapel. No identity card, no food ration card, had 'Jew' stamped on it. Eventually the Germans left, roaring the engines of the jeeps in rage. The mother and her daughters were saved."

A long silence.

Then Thamar smiled and said, "We have to believe that even in Algiers at the end of the war such things did happen, such saving grace was given to a few. I heard of poor Jewish families kept alive in the chaos by small boys, Muslim boys, smuggling them bread in dirty bags because Jews might be shot by the

FLN or the OAS if they ventured to the baker's."

Another silence.

"So. Two weeks after the shootings at the Post Office, they sent us back to France."

Thamar finished his coffee. Bernard saw that he hadn't finished talking.

"Back on the troop ship. Back to Toulon. Back to Lyon. After a few weeks my group of conscripts was packed off to Berlin."

"Berlin? You haven't mentioned Berlin in your book, Thamar."

"No. Nothing happened there. Or nothing happened that penetrated the numbness which was making it possible for me to get through the days. We patrolled the streets in the French quarter of the city. Quiet. Peaceful. Spies were busy, not soldiers. The wall had just been built. Everyone seemed relieved rather than horrified. The Germans were busy rebuilding West Berlin, building sites, scaffolding, cranes everywhere. We spent our time doing the things soldiers do when there's nothing going on. I was—how to describe how I was?"

He thought for a few moments.

"I was as if half dead, thinking nothing, feeling nothing. I suppose I was in some kind of long-term shock, grieving for Tanifa, for her father, for the village, though I knew nothing, then, of what had become of them. The dreadful weeks I had lived through in Algiers that year I remembered as if it had been someone else, not me myself, witnessing the deaths, the rage, the misery, perhaps because there was no one, no single person there, to whom I had any attachment. Or perhaps because the things I had seen and done the year before had destroyed something in me, my sensibility, my feeling for other people, at least for a while. That did return, much later. As you know."

He looked at Bernard, intently, without smiling.

"Isn't it always the personal that causes real suffering? When my ability to feel things at last returned, it was, eventually, my undoing."

Bernard wanted to steer him back to the distant past.

"Did you know anything about what was happening in Algeria after you left?"

"At the time, I knew very little. We were told in the middle of the summer that a plot to assassinate President de Gaulle as he drove with his wife out of Paris had almost succeeded. The next evening we were given glasses of schnapps and we all stood up to sing the Marseillaise to celebrate the general's survival. In the army, you know, he was always called 'the general', not 'the president."

"Who tried to assassinate him?"

"Who do you think? The OAS of course. A number of times they tried, but that was the closest they came to succeeding."

He paused again, looked down at the table, and went on, "I didn't find out until many years later, when I was again in North Africa, how terrible had been the immediate aftermath of the war. The massacre of the *harkis* by the FLN, the deaths of thousands like Tanifa's father, your great-grandfather, was shocking, but it was probably inevitable after France had left the *harkis* to their fate. They were faithful to France, so they were traitors to Algeria.

"Worse, if anything could be worse, was what the OAS did after they saw that their resistance to independence was hopeless. They decided that as they had failed to win the war, they were going to do everything they could to destroy what they had lost. Their aim, they actually declared, was to return Algeria to the condition in which France had found it in 1830. They couldn't do that of course. The FLN leaders, quarrelling among themselves though they were, were educated in French; many of them were trained as soldiers in the French army; all of them had been given by France the ideals for which they had fought the war. There was too much of France in Algeria for all of it to be uprooted. But the OAS wrecked what they could wreck. They set themselves to murder the teachers, the doctors, the lawyers, any Muslim wearing a tie they said, everyone they could find who had been educated and inspired by France. They burned down schools and hospitals. The library of the university was burned to the last book. Imagine how terrible for the future of this poor country—"

Bernard looked at Thamar's stricken face beside him and immediately looked down at the pile of paper in front of him.

"Let me give you an example of the depths of wickedness to which the OAS descended. Have you ever heard of Mouloud Feraoun?"

Bernard shook his head. "I'm afraid not."

"He would be next door, alongside Pascal and Cardinal Lavigerie, if I had ever had a picture of him."

Bernard waited.

"He was a Berber from a village in Kabylia."

Bernard saw that it was difficult for his grandfather to go on, saw him swallow, take a breath, regain control.

"I can't remember when he was born. He was in his forties during the war, like Tanifa's father, your great-grandfather, and like him he went to the *lycée* in Tizi Ouzou. So he was a clever boy, much cleverer, in fact, than Tanifa's father. He was given a scholarship to the École Normale d'Alger, the best, the most French, university in Algeria. He became an excellent writer. He was a friend of Camus and the other French-Algerian intellectuals, not that there were many of them. He was a teacher all his life, and worked against ever-increasing difficulties, and all through the horror of the war, to preserve some good schooling, where it was possible, for children, even for girls, without privilege and without money. Three days before the peace agreement, the OAS killed him, with five other senior education officials, three Frenchmen and two Algerians, as they came out of a meeting. Why? Because they represented the best of French Algeria. Because they were trying to save what could be saved from barbarism and destruction. Because they were wearing ties."

Again, Bernard allowed Thamar's account to end in the stillness it seemed to need.

Then he said: "What did he write?"

"He wrote several books, always in French. He spoke Tamazight, the language of the Berbers, you know?"

Bernard nodded. "Of course. From your book."

"So, his languages were Tamazight and French. Not Arabic. His greatest book is the journal he wrote all the way through the war, watching the crimes committed on both sides, the murders and rapes, the ruin of what he had grown up with and loved, ancient Berber tradition, peaceful and orderly, French civilization, rich and liberating: both destroyed by the war. He saw the FLN and the French army locked in a hatred of the other in which people on neither side, peasants wanting nothing but to get on with what were already hard lives, were falsely accused, framed, betrayed, killed, their olive groves and fig trees burned, their villages left abandoned. He always understood that violence breeds more violence, that violence solves no problems but generates more problems. Look at Syria now, Iraq, Libya—"

"Why isn't he more famous?"

"Because the voice of moderation, then as now, was too quiet to be heard. Loud voices always prevail, alas. You see—"

Another long pause while Thamar, looking down at his clasped hands on the plush tablecloth, gathered together what he was trying to say. Bernard wanted to put two more logs on the fire but didn't dare to move.

"Extreme opinions, or summaries of how things are and how they should be, are simple. They can be shouted into the world and understood by everyone. Mouloud Feraoun's understanding of the Algeria he knew was deep and subtle. He saw, for example, that the respect for things French, to which he had been brought up and which he profoundly felt, reinforced the patronising superiority with which actual Frenchmen, with few exceptions, treated educated Muslims like himself. So French Algeria was both beneficial and inimical, both, and, not either, or. Like more, even more, important things we were talking about last night.

"Such complexity was beyond the noisy simplifications of the extremes. The right, at the time, not only the OAS but the political right in France and much, I'm sad to say, of the Church, thought that Christian civilization must be preserved in Algeria at any cost. This whole idea was not only, by the end of the war, impossible; it was based on a false premise. Frenchmen in Algeria, with very, very few exceptions, Cardinal Lavigerie and the White Fathers, Charles de Foucauld, had never behaved as Christians, nor was what they had brought to an old Muslim country with traditions of its own—tolerance of Jews, for example—truly civilized. Meanwhile the FLN and the political left in France, especially the Communist party and the left-bank intellectuals, Sartre above all, thought that the destruction of colonial rule justified, sanctioned, proved the worth, of violence and cruelty of every sort. Frantz Fanon— you have heard of him? No? Never mind.—was one of the loud voices shouting for violent revolution, the ruin of all religion, Islam as well as Christianity, what he called 'new men' proving they owned the future by murdering the present. He wrote a terrifying book, *The Damned of the Earth*, which Sartre recommended to the world. Marx mixed with Nietzsche, the driving force, naturally, resentment. You see?"

"I see", Bernard said. "Or I begin to see."

"We hear them now, these loud voices, do we not? Murder and torture your way to the new Caliphate, to the perfection of Islam on earth. That is the plan of Daesh. These Salafists know that if you shout loudly enough your message will be heard by disaffected young men in the *banlieues*, and not only in the *banlieues*. In the respectable bourgeois bedrooms of children like your sister. They probably don't know that they have more in common with Nietzsche and Hitler, Stalin and Sartre, than with anything in real Islam. And on the other side, shouting in France equally loudly, what do we have? The *Front National*. Marine le Pen. Her father, Jean-Marie le Pen is a terrible man. Where does he come from? Where do you think?"

Bernard shook his head. He wasn't even sure that le Pen was still alive.

"*Action française*, Pétain the hero, Vichy to be admired. And torture in Algeria."

"Really?"

"Really. He was an interrogator during the war. In Algiers. Probably when I was in that prison. Then he founded the *Front National* with an officer from the OAS. And now who shouts on the right? His daughter. Against foreigners, against Muslims, against what is good and kind in Europe. Like the people who shout in England to leave the European Union.

370

Like this dreadful man on the right in America, who also shouts hatred.

"So, you see, Bernard. The quiet voice is not heard."

Silence. Bernard raised his head.

Thamar suddenly looked white and very tired. His right hand was on his chest, as it had been last night.

"Thamar!"

The old man put the index finger of his other hand to his lips, sat absolutely still for a few seconds, and then relaxed, put both hands flat on the table, and smiled.

"It's nothing, Bernard. I have been talking too much, far too much, again. Forgive me. It's because you are here to be talked to."

"It's my fault, Thamar. I asked for your help with the next part of your book. Perhaps I should have just carried on, leaving a long gap if that was what you wanted."

"Did I?"

He looked at Bernard, thinking.

"Yes. Perhaps I did."

Then, less doubtfully, he said, "I think you should start again."

"What? You mean go back to the beginning?"

"No, no. Look how much work you've already done." Thamar spread a hand, palm upwards, above the neat pile of typescript. "No. I didn't mean that you should start the whole book again. Only that you should make a new start, Part 2, perhaps you could call it, beginning when I have at last got back to Africa. Choosing what to leave out, after all, is the essence of design."

He smiled again.

"Perhaps it is also the essence of living. See how much, here, in this house, I have left out. Nothing I leave out do I ever regret."

Félix raised his head, stood up stiffly from where he had been lying asleep in front of the fire, and came to stand between them, gazing at each of them in turn.

Thamar put a hand on the shaggy head. "You're quite right, old boy. Time to go out. I'm not going up to the château today. Bernard needs some fresh air. You can take him for a walk, Félix."

Bernard laughed, went out of the dining room into the passage, followed by Félix wagging his tail, and took his donkey jacket from its peg.

"So, tomorrow you begin Part 2?", Thamar said, without getting up from the table.

"No, Thamar. I begin Part 2 on Monday morning. Tomorrow I hope the rain will have stopped and I'll go back to Tournus. To think."

"Very good."

The rain stopped in the afternoon and, by the time Thamar had left, early on Sunday morning, to walk to Mass in Saint-Christophe, the sun was shining. A bright, cold January day.

Bernard pumped up the tyres on the château's bicycle, put on his donkey jacket, a scarf, his Breton fisherman's cap from Nantes, and some antique gloves of Thamar's, and set off on the long ride to Tournus.

Small roads, almost no traffic on a winter Sunday morning, vines in their rows neatly pruned before Christmas, no flowers, no sound of birds, leafless woods on either side of the road: Burgundy waiting for the spring, still months away. When he got off his bike to push it uphill, he stood for a moment and breathed in the cold air and the silence. Four or five times in the autumn he had come this way, watching the autumn turn, the leaves brown and fall. The hills of the Mâconnais were no less beautiful now.

He stopped at the top of the last hill, and smiled as he saw the two bell-towers of the abbey church, with their elegant round-headed arches and tall tiled steeples, waiting, like friends, above the tiled roofs and pale stone of the abbey church and the old town buildings gathered about it. "Those towers, those walls like fortress walls, have been there for a thousand years", Thamar had told him after his first visit. "The monks had enemies then. As what they stood for has enemies now."

He free-wheeled down to the town, made his way through ordinary traffic on ordinary roads, and reached the square, not really a square but a small, irregular space in front of the church, and stood beside his bicycle watching people coming out of the great west door, shaking hands with the priest, who was dressed as the priest had been in the Mass he had attended with Marie in Nantes. Some of these people. who were mostly in their seventies or eighties and looked, Bernard thought, like extras in a film from the 1950s, shook hands with each other before buttoning their coats, rewinding their scarves and setting off in different directions, no doubt towards their lunch. Two of the old men even put on felt hats as they walked away with their wives on their arms. He looked at his watch. Twelve-thirty. These old couples must have other people, probably equally old cooks, preparing lunch at home to make it possible for them to come to what was clearly the last Mass of the morning. Or daughters or daughters-in-law anxious over hot stoves. Bernard smiled at the unseriousness of the thought.

He walked with his bicycle, as he had done once before, all the way round the outside of the church. Its walls were built of grey, white, and creamy pink stone, the masonry mostly quite rough but here and there the stones arranged in patterns. The walls were complicated by some lesser buildings, each with its rusty-brown tiled roof, attached to the church. The little streets were quiet, except for four small boys kicking a football across the ancient stone flags of a paved space at the far end of the church. Their ball shot into his bicycle. He kicked it back to them and one of them thanked him. The walls, of the church and the other buildings, stood in the sunshine in a settled calm: centuries passed; countless generations of children played; the walls stood.

When he arrived back in the square everyone had vanished, though there was the noise of plates and glasses being brought to the tables of the crowded café, its windows steamy from the warmth inside, and an expensive car drew up behind two others outside the hotel-restaurant opposite, which was clearly also full for Sunday lunch.

Bernard wasn't hungry. He was looking for something that wasn't lunch.

He propped his bicycle against the stone wall round the corner from the formidable west front of the church. Then he stood for a moment a little way back from where half of the big west door was still open, to darkness inside, and looked up. The tremendous wall was broken not by windows until the towers began, but by narrow vertical slits, perhaps made for men, themselves invisible from the ground, to shoot arrows at Norsemen, or at wild Hungarians on horseback waving flaming torches, a thousand years ago. Instead of windows there was blind arcading, as plain as could be. No statues. No representation of anything but solid strength.

High up where the towers began was one cross-shaped window. He wanted to register again how far it was from the ground so that he could feel the height of the whole wall when he saw the cross-shaped window from the inside. As he looked he remembered how impressed he had been before by the thinness of almost all the stones. A few larger whiter stones were arranged in horizontal lines at the level of the top of the door. Otherwise all the stones, so carefully and durably laid one upon another, were longer and thinner than ordinary bricks.

He knew he was concentrating on the building, using up time and memory, not only because he loved it but in order to put off, push away, what he had come to Tournus for.

He had set out intending to think on the road from the village. But the effort and enjoyment of the ride had made it easy not to.

Now—

He put it off a bit longer by going inside the church.

He was expecting the shock of the massive plain pillars in the near-darkness in the narthex—by now he had learned some proper terms for the parts of a church—but they were a shock all the same: huge and round and entirely without carving or decoration of any kind. Nothing here, he thought, also not for the first time, for the girl he had met in Cluny, sitting on the floor of the museum drawing the finely carved capitals made by one master craftsman or another.

Here was only the anonymous stone of the ages. But he thought of them, the builders, so long ago, dozens of them, small, tough men with calloused hands, wheeling barrows of stone, packing them in slings for more small, tough men on half-built columns to haul up with pulleys, ropes creaking on wheels. Perhaps it wasn't like that. But it must have been, more or less. Worlds away from the pernickety carvers and gilders and plumbers at Versailles. How much he would have preferred to be building Tournus. For a moment he thought of Marie. Tournus was too old, too heavy, for her.

He climbed the worn steps of the spiral staircase to the chapel above the narthex, an even more astonishing space, twice as high, and with more massive, heavy, unadorned pillars, carrying the weight of plain, plain walls and vaults. Here at last were windows, as simple as everything else, one, high on the west wall, was the cross-shaped window he had looked for from the ground, dark then, now a cross of light.

Nothing and no one. Not a chair, not a bench. Nothing made of anything but stone. He sat on the floor. How far away and pointlessly new seemed the pile of typescript on the dining room table in Thamar's house, how unimportant his problem.

He was stuck. He didn't know how to go on with what, in the sections he had already done, had become his book. After what Thamar had told him yesterday, he thought he understood why the old man hadn't tried, anywhere in the hundreds of pages he had written, to describe the year, the several years, after his first return from Algeria.

But now Thamar wanted him to restart his story in Africa, after what Bernard knew was the most important moment of change in his grandfather's whole life, much more important to him than the two, quite different, breakings in his life that came later.

Thamar was right. But for the telling of the next bit of Thamar's story Bernard felt that he, Bernard, who he was, what he knew, what he had ever felt or thought himself, was wholly inadequate. He hadn't learned enough. Probably he never would learn enough. He also knew that he hadn't lost the scepticism, although by now he suspected that it was more instinctive than reasoned, in which he had been educated, by his father, his school, his university.

Didn't scepticism even identify him, as an adequately intelligent young man of his generation?

Wasn't he sure, in the end, that Thamar had been deluding himself all this time? What, where, who was the God he persuaded himself, or people had persuaded him, was more real than reality? Nowhere? Somewhere? Only in Thamar's brain and the brains of those who thought as he did?

Yet Thamar had struck him on that first day, last May, and getting to know him over months hadn't altered his first impression, as the least deluded person he had ever met.

Bernard sat on the floor in the cold, in the near-dark, his arms round his knees, inconsiderable amid the great weight of the round stone columns, the round stone arches. After a while he saw himself sitting there, a warmish bundle of flesh and blood and scruffy clothes. Someone coming up the stairs from the narthex might see him, sitting in the shadows at the dusty base of a cliff of stone, and think him a pile of old rags the builders left behind. Even his bones, he thought, looking up and up to the stones of the curved roof, wouldn't last long once he was dead. He unclasped his arms from his knees and spread his hands, palms down, in front of him. Bones, some flesh on them, not much, sinews, veins, nails which grew and had to be cut. He bent his fingers, his thumbs. How astonishing was a thumb and the difference it made to what fingers could do.

He clenched his hands, so cold that he almost pulled his gloves out of his pockets and put them on. No.

This inconsiderable bundle was what? Bernard Charpentier aged twenty-two, from Paris and Rouen and a village in Burgundy and another in the violet mountains of Kabylia and a shtetl in Galicia. With, probably, far to go.

Whereas old Thamar, with his steady weeks and years, his modest life, Félix and his garden to look after, the number of his days unknown but fast diminishing, understood that he was something Bernard had no sense that he himself was, or perhaps had no sense yet that he himself was, a soul in the hands of God.

Then Bernard realized that it wasn't the fear of not understanding Thamar that was holding him back from getting on with the book. It wasn't even the fear, justified though he knew it to be, of not being a good enough writer to cope with what lay ahead in the story of Thamar's life. It was fear of what he would have to face in himself, for himself, if he were adequately to describe the rest of Thamar's life. But it had to be faced. Otherwise he, who hated leaving anything untidy, unfinished, would have to go back to Paris without completing the job he had taken on. And let down Thamar, which he couldn't bear.

He got up, looked once more around him, above him, at the high stone chapel, waved at the bright cross of the window that had looked small and black from the ground, and went down the stairs.

For a moment he peered inside the main body of the church, so light after the chapel and the narthex, so tall and elegant, with its three files of pale plain columns, creamy pink and lit from two rows of plain windows, the sunshine pouring in from those on the south wall. There were four or five people in the church, looking up, pointing. One woman in a headscarf was sitting motionless half way up the nave.

He didn't stay. He went out into the square, and, suddenly really hungry, squeezed past the crowded tables in the café and bought at the bar a ham sandwich and a bottle of Coke. He collected his bike, putting his lunch in the basket, and rode a couple of hundred yards down a narrow street to the river.

He stood and ate his sandwich looking at the wide, slow, green Saône, swollen by some days of rain, flowing without a sound from his left to his right. One old man in a thick coat and a woolly hat was fishing, sitting on a folding stool. He looked up as Bernard crumpled the paper that had wrapped his sandwich.

"Bonjour, monsieur", Bernard said.

The old man put a gloved finger to his lips, as if, in a river that size, a fish could have been frightened away from his bait by Bernard's two words.

"Pardon", Bernard said, more quietly.

Then, saving his Coke for the ride home, he turned his bike and set off for the town, the ordinary traffic, and the lanes and hills beyond.

Tomorrow he would begin again.

Chapter 7

Thamar

November 1992 to January 1995

Most mornings, very early, he went to the Sisters' Mass, cele-
brated for them by one of the White Fathers in their little
chapel. He knelt at the back on the cool clean tiles, standing only for the Gospel and the Our Father, and not receiving
Holy Communion. No one paid him any attention: the nuns
and whichever priest it happened to be were used to his silent
presence.

The only mornings on which he missed Mass were those
that followed his occasional nights in the desert.

Walking alone one day, an hour away from the town, in the
cooler sunlight of late autumn, he had seen a large black hole,
wider than it was tall, about twelve feet above him in a rock
face. He had climbed up the rock without difficulty—the red
stone was ledged, not crumbly, with plenty of footholds—and
discovered that the hole was the entrance to a large cave, just
high enough for him to be able to stand up inside it. The cave
floor was almost flat, dusty red. After about three yards into
the cave, the roof was lower, the floor higher. On his hands
and knees he found, in the increasing darkness, that the space
between uneven rock floor and uneven rock roof soon became
no more than a long crack. There was no way of telling how far
it reached: he could investigate no further. He turned, crawled
back towards the brilliant light, stood for a moment and then
sat, his arms round his knees, and looked out at the desert.

No one. Nothing. Not a sound. The sand and rock across
which he had walked. The mountains that hid the town,
Ghardaia, and the other four fortified villages of the Mzab

378

valley, except for the tall, ancient minaret at Ghardaia's centre, which he could see above the tops of the hills. The time-worn path down which he had come was now too distant to be visible.

After some time, a line of laden camels appeared, perhaps a mile away to his right; from where he was sitting, the camels looked very small, black, emblematic like a line of Egyptian hieroglyphs, except that they were moving. He couldn't see clearly the Bedouin traders walking with them, one or two perhaps riding on one of the camels or on an accompanying mule. He thought he could see two mules, or perhaps donkeys, but wasn't sure. He watched them travelling slowly across the desert, no doubt towards the town, the market, the shops, towards haggling merchants and fresh coffee, as trains of camels had come out of the desert from the south for a thousand years. Or two thousand years. Who knew?

After many years in Africa, he had never stopped enjoying the moments that reminded him of the biblical pictures in the children's missal his grandmother had let him look at during Mass when he was very young.

He watched the camels' passage towards the mountains, into which in due course they disappeared. People in Ghardaia had told him that there were fewer camel trains than there used to be. In theory the town was a staging post on what was grandly called the Trans-Sahara Highway. In practice that meant that trucks did arrive from the north, even all the way, three hundred miles, from Algiers. So did military convoys, jeeps with soldiers in camouflage uniforms, guns at the ready from the sides and the back. Behind the guns, no doubt, were boys as scared as he had once been. These were government soldiers, looking for trouble that they were supposed to deal with. There had been, lately, so much trouble that the Fathers and the Sisters had met, twice, to discuss whether they should stay in the desert, where there was little protection from Islamist guerrillas with guns, or leave Ghardaia where they had been for more than a hundred years. At each meeting, they had decided to stay.

The road to the south wasn't yet good enough for trucks nor, much of it, even for jeeps, although it was supposed to cross the whole of the Sahara and eventually to reach as far as Lagos, another seventeen hundred miles from Ghardaia. At present, camels were as reliable as they had always been, on what was mostly the ancient desert road in its ancient condition. They were also less likely than trucks, or soldiers in jeeps, to be attacked. So, from the south, they came.

He stayed in the cave for nearly two hours.

After he lost sight of the camel train he saw only two more living things from his ledge at the mouth of the cave, a desert falcon high in the sky, smaller than the eagles, the Roman eagles, he had seen all those years ago, and terrifying in its sudden dive to the ground to catch some creature in the sand, and a lizard he noticed, not because he could feel it, on his shoe. He watched it, motionless, unimpressed by his presence, for a few moments. Then it vanished, swift and soundless, into the cave behind him.

The camels. The falcon. The lizard.

Then only the desert, the sunlight, the mountains to the north, and the silence. He had never known such silence in Burgundy: even in winter, even when there was snow on the ground, when no work was being done and the birds had stopped singing, there were always sounds, a car in the distance, a plane somewhere out of sight, a rabbit or a deer rustling in the woods, a pigeon flying, or dear old Baron, nosing about in the undergrowth. His grandmother had written to tell him, when he was living in Paris for the second time, that Baron had died. She had found him in the garden and at first thought he was asleep. That must have been in 1964 or 1965.

In Africa, wherever he was, there had always been sounds: among soldiers noise by day and by night; in the violet mountains and later in a village in Tunisia there had been the comforting sounds of village life: children, dogs, hens, donkeys; in Tunis, or Carthage as the Fathers liked to call it, and then in Tizi Ouzou, there had been a silent house perhaps, once the Fathers and the students were in bed, but, outside, the sounds of a big city, and then a smaller city, traffic, random shouts, faint music. Even in Ghardaia, where he was lucky to be, where he was happy—wasn't he?—there were the sounds of a town at night, the sounds of other people, the quiet shattered at any moment by a jeep on patrol or one young man on a motor-scooter accelerating away into a wider street.

He felt he was listening to all the noise, all the sounds of his life, even the worst, the screams of the prisoners being tortured in Algiers, the crack of the spade on the baked earth as the man in the village tried to dig a grave for his daughter, fade, fade into a silence which absorbed them, took them in, made them as if they had never been.

Here, only here, the silence was absolute. So was his still-ness as he sat, his arms round his knees, and couldn't hear his heart beat or his breathing. He found after a while that he was listening to the silence as if it were a sound.

Was listening to silence as if silence were a sound like paying attention to the absence of God as if absence were presence?

He remembered that one of the priests who taught him during the second year of his formation, in Carthage, had told the class of novices that the Arabic word, *sukun*, for the silence between prayers was from the same root as the Hebrew word *shekinah*, which means the presence of God. The same priest had recommended to the class that they should read a book called *Waiting for God* or perhaps *The Wait for God*, he couldn't remember exactly. The priest had been warning the class that from time to time their sense of God being close to them, caring for them, being anywhere at all, might disappear. Any of them might find, from one day to the next, that he felt himself to be all alone, with the vocation, the call from God that had impelled him so far, having faded into silence. If this happened, the priest had said, and from time to time it almost certainly would happen, they mustn't feel to blame; they mustn't try too hard to bring their minds, their souls, back to where they thought they should be. They should be patient, stick to the routine of every day, and wait for God.

He hadn't read the book. It seemed, when he looked for it, to have vanished from the library, and when he asked the librar-ian, an austere and very strict young Father, whether someone had borrowed the book, he was told not to bother with it. "The author was a Jew, you know, and refused to be baptized a

Catholic." He reported this to his tutor, who shrugged. "Well, there you are. But I'm sorry to hear that, so late in the day. Albert Camus called her 'the only great spirit of our times.' Never mind. I'll find you something even better."

This turned out to be Pascal's *Pensées*. The priest had half a dozen copies on the shelf in his cell. Lending one to Jacques, he said: "This is one of the great books. If you find yourself alone and wondering what you are doing here with the White Fathers, or here in Africa, or here on the planet, read some of this book, almost anything you happen to find in it, and you will discover that you are not alone. It's all bits and pieces because poor Pascal died before he had time to organize what he had written, so it doesn't matter where you start or stop."

The priest was right. Jacques found in Pascal another companion: he had already, in the White Fathers' college in France where he had spent his first year of formation, decided that St Augustine was his friend.

Pascal, like Jacques, had been raised as a good Catholic. Much more intelligent than Jacques would ever be, he had become a mathematician, a brilliant scientist, famous in France. What he taught Jacques to understand was that there are two kinds of knowledge. Both come from learning but the kinds of learning are different. The mind's knowledge is delivered to the mind by the mind, by reason and experiment and adventurous thinking. It is certain, but only for the time being: it changes as progress is made by minds working together or in opposition to each other. The heart's knowledge is given by God, and is to be received and loved, indeed can be received and loved, only by the faithful heart. It is different. It is more certain. It comes and goes only as we pay more, or less, attention. What is attention? Waiting.

No one had ever suggested, before this, that he should read Pascal. He didn't think he had even heard his name mentioned. But he remembered that in Saint Étienne-du-Mont, the church near the Sorbonne where he had begun to go to Mass, after so many years, in 1968, the church outside which he had stopped running with Sylvie, both of them out of breath, on the night of the riot, the church in which he had heard a White Father preach the homily about Africa that had changed his life, there was a simple stone in the wall recording the fact that Pascal was buried in the church. So good, he thought, far away in Augustine's Carthage, reading the *Pensées*, that Pascal lay in a church, where he belonged, and not, a hundred yards away, in the Panthéon, the secular temple of glory.

What had happened to change Pascal, the great mathematician, the great inventor, into someone who could speak of the truth of God, was what he called his night of fire, the night in which he knew, knew for sure, that Christ is God, the God of Abraham, Isaac and Jacob, come to us, to our world, as a man.

Nothing remotely like Pascal's night of fire had ever happened to Jacques. But ever since he had read Pascal's prayer of praise, written on that night and afterwards carried with him until the day he died, he had taken Pascal's word for the reality, the truth, of what had been given to him on that night.

So, in whatever darkness, whatever storms of confusion and despair, such as, three years ago, had almost overwhelmed him, he had been able to remember Pascal's encouragement, Pascal's confidence that Christ would never desert anyone still longing to know him. Pascal, in a beautiful meditation on Jesus's suffering in the garden of Gethsemane, wrote something he imagined Jesus saying: "Be comforted; you would not seek me if you had not found me." Jacques thought of this sentence often.

Now, as he sat on the ledge of rock at the mouth of the cave, he listened to the silence of the desert and heard it as the silence of God. Into which, once and always, God has sent, sends, his Christ, speaks his word.

This is the word, he thought, not for the first time, that the Muslims don't, can't, hear. Their sense of God was so deep, so impressive, even when, like Monsieur Sadi, they didn't pray five times a day and had never done the Hajj, that it put to shame most of the Christians, or so-called Christians, Jacques had ever come across. The same was surely true, down the ages, of the Jews. The Jews thought of Christ as a teacher, a great rabbi. The Muslims thought of Christ as a teacher, a great prophet. Neither could think of him as the word of God made flesh, the image made real, living and breathing, laughing and crying, and dying, of the unseen God.

If only, he thought, as the White Fathers had trained him to think, if only the Christians had not for centuries and centuries treated the Jews and the Muslims with cruelty and contempt, it might have been more possible for them to see in Christians what Christ was, is. Instead—what have they seen in Christians?

He remembered reading somewhere that Abd el Kader, the noble hero of Algerian resistance to the French conquest, had said to a French general, "Make haste and build your church, for not until we see it shall we believe that you worship God and that we can put faith in your word." Building the church so that Muslim people could believe that Christians also could be faithful to God without bullying, without scorn for other believers, was exactly what Cardinal Lavigerie and his White Fathers had set themselves to do. Perhaps, after the horrors of the war in which he himself had had to take part, after the further horrors of civil war, in which so many had died and which wasn't yet over, the little groups of White Fathers and White Sisters that were left in Algeria could manage to show that what Lavigerie had intended was still, just, here and there, possible.

He remembered being told, no doubt by one of the Fathers in Tunis, that Lavigerie, years before he had even thought of founding a society of priests in Africa, had visited Abd el Kader in Damascus, where the ageing fighter against France was living in exile and had saved thousands of Christians from being murdered by Muslims in the bloody riots of 1860. Lavigerie was so much impressed by the wisdom and humanity of this representative of Islam that he recognized him as an example many Christians would do well to follow.

Thamar, as he had chosen to be called when he left Tizi Ouzou, was working in Ghardaia for the White Sisters, looking after their garden, mending for them things that broke, running errands for them in the town, helping in their little hospital when heavy patients, heavy equipment, needed lifting, above all maintaining in good repair the water system that filled the taps, irrigated the garden, flowed through the drains. It had been constructed centuries ago by the practical Berbers of the town, and, if it was kept an eye on, it still worked well.

He knew that living close to a community of nuns and doing useful chores for them was exactly what Charles de Foucauld had done when, before he chose to live in the Sahara, he had worked for the Poor Clares in Nazareth and then, for more Poor Clares, on the road, Jesus's road, between Bethany and Jerusalem. Thamar was pleased from time to time to remember this, and to know that, far though he was from anything like the holiness of de Foucauld, he was a more competent odd job man.

On most days, busy from dawn to nightfall, he had little time to think. Today was All Saints Day, and the Sister in charge of the house had told him, after Mass, to take a day off. "It's a great feast, Thamar, a holiday. It's not good to work every single day." So he had set off to walk. And here he was, listening to the silence of the desert from the edge of his cave, and, with the sadness that returned every time he took, as it were, a step back from his ordinary responsibilities, thinking of the life and death of Anir, one lost boy in whose life, and death, had been concentrated the long history of this most beautiful, most abused land.

Why had it so completely failed, the aspiration that he had often, in the army and afterwards, heard called "the civilizing mission" of France? He had recognized ever since Monsieur Sadi and the village in the violet mountains that there was something badly wrong with the very phrase: the assumption that other people, any other people but particularly Africans, had no civilization of their own, that the superiority of what France was bringing to other people was self-evident. One reason for his sense of belonging among the White Fathers was that "the civilizing mission" was a phrase they never used. From the college in Carthage they had taken the novices on the long bus ride to Kairouan to see the Great Mosque. People who were not Muslims were not allowed inside the mosque, but, from the huge, calm space of the court they enclosed, the ancient sand-coloured buildings that seemed to have risen from the desert itself, and were begun less than forty years after the death of the Prophet, were powerfully impressive. How was this not a work of civilization? And how was the even more ancient tradition of Berber self-government, self-respect, peaceful cooperation, that he had seen in Monsieur Sadi's village and that, astonishingly after all the political troubles and the wars, was still the pattern of life in Ghardaia, not also a work of civilization?

In the silence of the desert, he understood properly, perhaps for the first time, that the failure had been caused not only by the assumption that France was civilized while Africa was not, but also, and more destructively, by what it was that, in 1830 and ever since, had been taken, by the French themselves, to be French civilization: railways and paved roads and hospitals and better methods of farming, though the hospitals were mostly for the *colons* and the better methods of farming were those used by the *colons* on the better land, stolen from Arabs and Berbers whose families had farmed it for generations. Thousands of acres of vineyards, worked, as Mathieu had pointed out long ago, by people who didn't drink wine, to make fortunes for the *grands colons*: this was exploitation, not civilization.

And education? After many decades, the French authorities at last changed their minds about educating some Muslims in French civilization. Perhaps the result, which would be some Muslim *lycéens*, some Muslim graduates from the French university in Algiers, a few qualified doctors, lawyers, scientists, would be more useful than it would be threatening? And there were those, of course, who actually believed in educating Muslims as an essential part of "the civilizing mission".

What happened? Sometimes what happened was Monsieur Sadi, or Mouloud Feraoun. But more often the results were not hopeful but ominous for the future. Clever Muslim boys were taught about the Enlightenment and the splendid benefits of the Revolution: liberty, equality, fraternity. They were not taught that freedom of the soul under God, the equal value of every person in the eyes of God, the imperative to treat others as you would wish to be treated yourself, were not ideas, ideals, invented in the eighteenth century, but were ideas, ideals, that properly belonged to religion. Given the pride and selfishness inborn in every human being, they were unrealizable and, further, rationally unjustifiable, without the belief in God that Muslims actually shared with Christians, and both Muslims and Christians shared with Jews. Meanwhile, every day of their lives, the Muslims of *Algérie française* were being shown that liberty, equality and fraternity were not for them but only for the French, the Europeans, the "Christians" who had invaded their country, made as much money as possible from it, and regarded them as for ever inferior, not least because of their faith.

It was hardly surprising that some of those who collected from their French education the notions of liberty, equality and fraternity as valuable possibilities to be fought for, against privilege, injustice and contempt, should become the revolutionary leaders of the FLN whose prime objective was to rid their country of the French. They had collected from intellectual France, before and after the Second World War, the scorn for religion of Marx, Nietzsche, Sartre and the rest, and a baseless confidence in a utopian socialist future in which religion would wither away. So it was equally unsurprising that these same leaders, educated in French *laïcité*, should, after defeating the French, have neglected, even despised, the old faith of most of their fellow-countrymen. That was why, for years now, there had been this bitter war between the government, which really meant the army, still striving for a French secular republic, and the people, an actual majority of the people, who had been driven to support an embattled modern Islam of intolerance, vindictiveness and cruelty, the Islamists who won the first genuinely open election Algeria had ever known, and were then deprived of their victory by the government and the army. The FIS, they were called, the Islamic Salvation Front. What had driven so many people, most of them in the cities and on the coast, though fewer in Kabylia and fewer still in the desert, to support the FIS? Surely the answer was their sense that, in their faith and their old-fashioned practice, the praying, the fasting and all the rest, they were patronized and humiliated by the careless government in Algiers no less than they had been for a hundred years, and for the same reasons, by the French. These were people who had not been given by anyone anything better to believe in than the merciful Allah to whom they and their forefathers had always prayed.

But the militancy, the violence, recently the actual terrorism, of the FIS and more extreme Islamists, like the GIA, the Armed Islamic Group, were not part of this tradition, were new, foreign and horrible. And actually, Thamar, with the time to think, now saw that they owed more to Nietzsche and his will to power than to anything in ancient Islam.

He thought of a wise old Muslim he had met in one of the smaller towns of the Mzab valley, who had told him, "The government, ever since the end of the war with France, have shown that they do not respect Islam. They do not respect the past. There is no meaning in the life they offer to the young, only the possibility, which will always be denied to most of these boys who have no proper work, of too much money, fast cars, noisy music, girls on the beach who can be slept with once or twice and then abandoned. And as for these new murdering Islamists, as the French call them: they do not respect the real Islam of the past either. Who do they think they are? They know nothing. They persuade simple people, who are not scholars, who may not be able to read and write, that they, the Islamists, and they alone are the true followers of the Prophet, peace be upon him, and that other Muslims are heretics and traitors who deserve to be killed. They seem to recommend nothing but killing: killing foreigners, killing intellectuals who speak French, killing women in the wrong clothes, of course killing Christians above all. And what does France do? France supports the army, which is no less cruel, very often, than the Islamists, because the army is the government and the government is secular. So the army must be good, as the French think that all Muslims are the same, and that all Muslims are bad."

The old man said this with a smile. Thamar felt honoured to be trusted with this smile, which showed that the old man recognized in Thamar the traditional White Fathers' acknowledgement that Allah is God and that many Muslims are pious, virtuous and truthful.

"And the world", the old man added, "allows France to say what the world should think about Algeria because the world has been told that France knows and understands Algeria. It does not understand us, because it never wished to and so it never did.

"We in the Mzab towns are Ibadite Muslims as you know. We have down the ages from time to time been persecuted by other Muslims. That is why we are here, in our mountains in the desert, so far from the sea. But we are an ancient part of Islam, from soon after the death of the Prophet, peace be upon him, from before Islam divided into Sunni and Shia. Other Muslims we have never persecuted, although we have had many other Muslims, Berbers, naturally, but Arabs also, in our towns. We have always had Tuareg from the desert. Since who knows how many centuries ago, we have always had Jews in the Mzab, and we did not persecute the Jews. Who was it who welcomed the Jews when the Christians drove them out of Spain? The Muslims in North Africa.

"It was the French who destroyed this kindly life, you know. For years they didn't bother with us. They couldn't see ways of making money in the desert, so no *colons* came. Our Jews were never given French citizenship as the Jews in Algiers were. Not that it helped them in the time of Vichy. Our Jews were intended to resent this distinction between the Jews of the coast, the cities, and the Jews of the desert. It was a piece of effective and cruel manipulation: the French wanted our Jews to object to their treatment, to show that they were more deserving of privileges than us, the Muslims they had lived among since who knows when?. The manipulation succeeded. We, the Muslims who had so much reason to make common cause with the Jews, allowed the French to encourage hatred and suspicion between us. And then there was Israel, for them to go to. So they left. Almost all of them. You know Doctor Ephraim?"

"I do, yes", Thamar said.

Doctor Ephraim, who was over eighty years old, was the best-qualified, most experienced doctor in Ghardaia. The

Sisters occasionally asked for his help with difficult cases.

"Exactly. He stayed. He is a good man. So our Jews left. Some went to France, with the *colons* who had to leave at the end of the war. Some went to Israel. A few were so unhappy that they came back. In France they were too poor to be respected. In Israel they were too dark-skinned and too backward to be acceptable, or so the advanced, modern Israelis thought. Alas.

"We had lived together for hundreds of years without difficulty. Now that is all in the past. In any case, the French never counted us desert people, Muslims or Jews, as people: what were we to them? A mystery they did not care to explore because there was nothing we had that they wanted. What was the Sahara to *Algérie française*? Then, before, or perhaps during, the war with the French, I'm not sure exactly when, they found oil in the desert. Aha! Money for France. This oil I fear even more, now that the French have gone, because it means a great deal of money, which they haven't had to work for, for a small number of people. That isn't good, ever."

The old man paused, and smiled again at Thamar, who had brought him some medicine that he needed, which the Sisters had managed to get sent from Algiers.

"There were exceptions, of course. In the mercy of Allah there are always exceptions. There was the Christian *marabout* long ago in the desert. He came here once or twice. My grandfather told me when I was young that he had met this *marabout*, and that he himself and all the good Muslims of the desert were horrified and ashamed when he was murdered. He was a truly holy man and never did he say to a Muslim that Islam was a false religion. And the White Fathers, and the Sisters of course, were gentle and helpful to us as they were to everyone. One or two of the Fathers seemed to dislike the Jews, but they treated us Muslims well. As they still do."

Soon after this conversation the old man had died. Thamar, hearing of his death from the Sisters, had gone to stand outside the house on the day after the death, and then to join the small crowd of men who followed the body, wrapped in a white cloth and carried aloft by his sons and sons-in-law, to the Ibadite cemetery outside the village walls. Before they reached the gate in the walls, Jacques left the crowd for a narrow, deserted street, a street mostly of steps as so many in the Mzab villages were: he didn't want to embarrass anyone by his presence. He felt deeply grateful to this old man for the confidence in him that he had shown, telling Thamar so much that he didn't know, about the Mzab valley and its history, about the sadness remaining for so many, and about the complicated reasons for the recent murderous fighting. It had been as if he hadn't counted Thamar as a Frenchman, and that was something that moved and pleased him very much.

Who was he, in any case, by now? A Frenchman who wasn't, and didn't want to be, any longer a Frenchman. A White Father who wasn't, and couldn't imagine himself ever again being, a White Father. A gardener and porter and odd job man for a group of nuns, who knew almost nothing about him, and would no doubt have been shocked if they had known more. They were grateful to him for his work. They asked him no questions. They were devoted to each other and to their patients, but not to him. They didn't pay him but they gave him his meals, the simple meals that they made for the patients, in the hospital kitchen, and they made sure that he had enough clothes and a blanket or two in the winter to keep him warm on the floor of the pink limestone outhouse where he slept. a cool building with one unglazed window, as plain as every other house in the town. On its wall, beside the window so that it couldn't be seen from outside, was his crucifix, which had been made for him by a metalsmith in a Tunisian village who had become his friend because Thamar, then Père Jacques, had sat with him through a long night as the metalsmith's old father was dying.

The Fathers in Ghardaia knew, more or less, why he was no longer Père Jacques. But they seemed to have been able to forget what they knew of his story almost as soon as he had reached the town. A few doubtful looks during his first weeks, then nothing. They asked no more questions than the Sisters did, and very soon it was as if he had always been there, in the background, doing this and that, bothering no one. It was almost as lonely as being alone, but more ordinarily useful because of his day-to-day work, and that was fine. He was happy. How real was his happiness? It was, at least, the absence, usually and more or less, of pain. For this absence he was grateful to God.

The light began to change as the sun, out of sight to his left, threw a lengthening shadow, to his right, of the strangely shaped mass of rock that held him in its cave. The upper slopes of the hills, and among them the top of Ghardaia's minaret, were lit in the gold light from the west. He looked at his watch and realized that he should start on the walk back: darkness fell quickly in the desert and he didn't know the path up the mountain well enough to be sure of finding it once the daylight had gone.

He turned, stiff from sitting still for so long, to face the rock in order to climb down. As he lowered himself over the edge, his hand brushed against something that moved. Not a living creature. Not a stone. He pulled himself up a foot or so, and stretched out his hand, sweeping the dusty rock in the darkness of the cave. He touched whatever it was and it rolled a few inches further away. He had to climb right back into the cave to get hold of it and when he did it cut his hand.

It was a rusty can that looked as if it had been in the cave for years. The rust was inside, but he didn't like the look of the jagged top, which had cut him. Someone had opened the can, long ago, with a knife. Three fingers of his right hand were bleeding. Blood was good, cleaning the wounds. He thought of a boy who had trodden on a rusty nail in a village twenty miles from Tizi Ouzou. The boy's mother had pulled the nail out of his foot, but the wound had killed him. Infection, poison, fever, death. It had taken five days. The Berber doctor who helped the White Fathers in Tizi Ouzou said afterwards that if the gangrened foot had been cut off soon enough it might have been possible to save the boy's life. By the time someone with a truck had driven him from the village to the town it was too late.

Now, Thamar held his hand up until the blood became sticky and then awkwardly, with his left hand, wound round the cut fingers a moderately clean handkerchief from his pocket. He couldn't tie the handkerchief but tucked the end, as firmly as he could, into the bandage he had made.

He picked up the can, holding it with his left hand. The label, which looked as if it had been printed a hundred years ago, was still legible. Condensed milk. From a factory in Normandy. He almost laughed at how far this tin had travelled, and how long ago, and because he remembered reading that Charles de Foucauld, when he had been living at Tamanrasset deep in the Sahara, had been pleased when condensed milk reached him in occasional parcels from France. Condensed milk, which was a luxury for the *marabout*, with sometimes a tin of tea, unkown in the desert, arrived packed up with the needles and simple medicines he could give to the Tuareg tribesmen who venerated him for his holiness.

This can couldn't of course be his. Some French soldier or traveller, long ago, had found this cave, stayed there, as he had, for perhaps an hour or two, and drunk his can of milk.

Jacques threw the can down to the sand at the foot of the rock, turned back to face the ledge he had been sitting on, lowered his legs to find footholds and climbed carefully down, with more difficulty than he had climbed up because he could see only the rock in front of him and because of his injured hand.

He jumped down the last couple of feet into the sand, crouched a little way from the rock, and, with his left hand scooped a hole and buried the can a foot down. In a sandstorm, he knew, it might come to the surface again and bowl across the desert to who knew where. Good luck to it. He set off to walk back to the town.

When he was half way up the steep path darkness fell, but an almost full moon, too bright for him to see the stars, gave him enough light for him to find his way. His hand was more and more painful. He forgot his meditation in the cave and could think only of Anir, who had died, not slowly and in pain like the child with the poisoned foot, but suddenly and horribly.

Did he think of him every day? Perhaps, by now, he didn't, but it was as if he did. He tried to explain this to himself but it was difficult. When he remembered Anir the pain was the same as it had been for more than three years now, no less, no easier to bear. But for days, even for weeks, he forgot him, forgot the pain altogether. He forgot, as he had been certain he never would, both the pain and the joy, that in his memory as in the real time during which he found him and lost him, were not separable.

He got back to the Sisters' kitchen in time to be given, as usual, his supper, couscous and vegetables, and a glass of clear water from the supply he was in charge of keeping in good order. He ate with a fork in his left hand.

"You look tired, Thamar", the Sister who did the cooking said as she took his empty bowl.

He looked up and by mistake put his right hand on the table.

"What have you done to your hand?"

"It's nothing. I cut my fingers."

"Thamar! There's a lot of blood. And you shouldn't have it bandaged in that dirty old rag."

She turned to a younger nun who was washing dishes behind her.

"Leave that, Sister Marie-Jean. Go and find Sister Pauline and tell her that Thamar needs his hand dressing in the infirmary."

No doubt she was right, though he hadn't wanted to admit he had hurt himself.

"These are wicked cuts", Sister Pauline said, as she washed his fingers with stinging disinfectant. "What have you been doing, Thamar?"

He was probably twenty years older than Sister Pauline, who was a trained nurse, Dutch, brisk and efficient, but because she was talking to him as if to a small child, he found he was nearly in tears on account of a pang of homesickness, something he almost never felt.

His grandmother had died many years ago, while he was a novice in Carthage—Père Bonnard had written to tell him, a formal, pious letter—and he hadn't been back to Burgundy since the last time he visited her, more than a year before her death. He had no idea what had happened to her house.

At least his grandmother had been pleased with his decision to ask to join the White Fathers, though she couldn't understand why, if he had a vocation to the priesthood, he couldn't have stayed in the archdiocese of Lyon so that she could have been proud of him, "my grandson, the priest", in his clerical collar and his black suit, visiting the village to say Mass when he was allowed a holiday. "France needs young priests just as much as Africa does", she had said. "Probably more. It would have been considerate towards me, Jacques, not to go so far away when I'm not getting any younger."

"This is your right hand, Thamar", Sister Pauline said. "You are right-handed, aren't you? So you have not cut your fingers with a tool?"

"No, sister. I found a cave."

"A what?"

"A cave in a sort of cliff, but easy to climb up to. I was walking in the desert. I stayed for a while in the cave. I was beginning to climb down when I cut my hand on an old tin someone else, a long time ago, had left there. But I shall go to the cave again."

"There", she said, having neatly bandaged each of his three cut fingers separately. "Come back to me if your hand gets more painful or if you become feverish. Why would you return to this cave?" Her French was correct, a little stiff.

"Because it's a beautiful place."

"You must be more careful, Thamar. Beauty isn't everything, you know. Look at your hand. Caves are dangerous in any case. There might be snakes, or scorpions."

Beauty may not be everything but it is a great deal, he thought and didn't say.

So he did go back to the cave. Every two or three months, over the next two years, he asked the Sisters if he could have an afternoon and the morning of the next day off work—" But where will you go, Thamar? Have you a friend to stay with?" He shook his head and didn't answer—so that he could go to the cave and sleep there and wake up to the sun rising over the desert. The first time he did this he woke very cold, and hungry, so after that he took his blanket, rolled up with a bottle of water and a chunk of bread, and tied to his back with twine.

He went to the cave for the silence, and the desert, and the sky, and as a kind of memorial pilgrimage for Anir. It was a way of concentrating his memories and his grief, and what was left of his guilt, into a place and a time that concerned no one except himself, and therefore perhaps God, into whose hands he felt, on each of his visits to the cave, more and more able to put the complexities of the story he knew he was never going to be able to tell to any other human being.

When, in 1969, he had his first interview with the White Fathers, he was asked whether he had ever been in love. He hesitated.

"I don't know", he said.

"Come along, Monsieur Thomas. You are—" This priest, the youngest of the three sitting in a row at a long table, facing Jacques, looked down at the paper in front of him. "Twenty-eight years old. Almost twenty-nine. You must know whether or not you have been in love."

He thought of Tanifa. Love? Not exactly. He thought of that one evening with Sylvie in the riot. Certainly not. He thought of Mathieu and the sadness at his loss, which had lasted for years. Perhaps.

"No", he said. "Not really." This didn't seem to be enough. So he added, "I suppose I have been quite lonely."

There was a pause. Was what he had said, which was as truthful as he could make it, good or bad? What did they want to hear, from men of his age who thought they might have a missionary vocation? He had no idea.

"I see from what you have said on your form that you never knew your father". This was the priest who, sitting between the other two, seemed to be the most important.

"That's right, father. I was born during the war. My father was, almost certainly, killed by the Germans."

"Was he a soldier?"

"I don't think so. He—disappeared, in Paris, during the Occupation."

"Was he a Jew?"

"Yes."

He saw the third, the oldest, priest wince. This priest then said, "A foreign Jew?"

"Yes."

The priest in the centre of the table said, quite firmly, "None of us chooses his parents." Then, "And your mother? I see that your family address is in Burgundy. Is your mother still alive?"

Jacques hadn't been expecting these questions.

"My mother went to South America after the war. I don't know whether she is still alive."

"Ah", the priest said. He knows, Jacques thought, why people went to South America after the war. But, without any change in his expression, the priest went on, "So you don't remember her clearly?"

"No, father."

"And your grandmother, your mother's mother, brought you up in Burgundy. Is that correct?"

"Yes, father. She is alive. She is a good Catholic. In the past, all through my childhood, she went to Mass every day. She is too old, now, to walk that far—there is a convent a mile or so from her house—and she isn't very well."

"I understand. What does she think of your idea that you might have a missionary vocation?"

"I haven't told her. I thought—well, I thought the White Fathers, you, father, might not accept me, and I didn't want to raise her hopes and then disappoint her."

"Quite. That was kind of you."

The older priest was looking at the paper in front of him.

"Do you have a recommendation from your parish priest, your grandmother's parish priest, that is, in Burgundy?"

"No, father. He doesn't know me now, though he knew me when I was a child. I was an altar boy in the village church. But—"

"But?"

"A lot has happened since then."

"Of course. To you, as to us all." This was, again, the priest in the centre.

"There was—" Jacques said, and started again. "I might have been able to ask the nuns' chaplain for a letter to you. I knew him better, or, rather, he knew me better, but he died several years ago."

Old Père Louis hadn't known Jacques well, but Jacques had never forgotten his promise to remember him before the Blessed Sacrament.

A pause.

The priest in the middle of the table said, "As an adult, you didn't get on with your grandmother's parish priest?"

"That was my fault, no doubt, not his."

"Possibly", said the priest, who was looking again at the paper in front of him, which was Jacques's story of his life. He had sent it with his letter asking if he might be considered as a possible missionary priest.

"Tell us, Monsieur Thomas", he said, "about your time as a soldier. 1960 to 1963, I see. You were sent to Algeria, no doubt?"

"Yes, father. I was in Algeria for the last fifteen months of the war, though I was sent home for three of those months."

"You were wounded?"

How to reply?

"Yes, father." This was true, after all.

"You must have had a very difficult time in Algeria at the end of the war. I was there myself for some of the war. I'm sure that all the conscripts had a difficult time. Was your faith of help to you then?"

Jacques thought. He knew that the truth was necessary, and that it would be good to find the words for it.

"What I had learned, as a child, seemed to have nothing to do with—with what we had to—what we were ordered to do, as soldiers. Even before that, at the *lycée*, and when I was working in Paris, I had—well, I had lost connection with the faith of my grandmother. I didn't go to Mass, except when I was at home, when I went to Mass with my grandmother so as not to upset her. I felt free—freed, I suppose, from what I had been told was true but for which I could see no evidence."

There was a pause. Then the younger priest said, "That is normal."

"But—", Jacques began, and didn't know how to go on.

"But?" The presiding priest again.

Jacques cleared his throat, looked down at his hands, folded on his lap to keep him calm, and decided to try. Still looking down, he said, "When I was wounded, I was cared for, until the wound healed, in a Berber village in Kabylia. The father of— the family was a good and kind man, faithful to Allah though there was no mosque in the village and I don't know whether he prayed five times a day. But his faith impressed me more— more than—" He couldn't go on.

"I think I understand", the priest said. "What this man, this Muslim, had made you feel was that there was a space, an emptiness, something missing in yourself. Is that right?"

"Yes. But it wasn't clear to me, what this meant, let alone what might fill the emptiness, until much later, several years later, that is."

"In a young man of your age, several years is a long time."

"Yes, father."

There was an unasked question in the silence. During those years—what? Should he try to answer this question? It seemed important to try.

But then, across the silence, "Monsieur Thomas", the old priest said. "If your wound healed while you were in Algeria, why were you sent home for three months?"

"Because—because I wasn't well. I couldn't deal with what we were being ordered to do. The army doctor said I needed to go home to get better."

"You broke down?"

"Yes, father."

All three priests wrote something on the paper each had in front of him.

That's that, Jacques thought. They won't accept me.

"Would you say", the younger priest said, "that afterwards you completely recovered from this—period of illness?"

All three priests were looking at him, as if the answer to this question were of great importance. Jacques saw that, from their point of view, of course it was. He also saw that an attempt to answer it might also be an attempt to answer the question, about those blank years, that no one had actually asked.

"After—after the end of the war in Algeria, I was sent to Berlin, where there was little for us to do, until my time in the army was up. Then I went home for a short time, and soon I was back in Paris. I had worked in a bookshop before my military service, and they took me on again. I still work there now, in a more responsible job. All this time I was—I was not ill, exactly."

"Your wound troubled you, perhaps?" This was the priest in the middle of the table.

"No. I was physically quite all right. But I did my work, got through the days, ate meals, went back to my room in the Boulevard Raspail, slept, more or less, as if I were watching someone else do all these things. As if they scarcely concerned me. I'm sorry. I can't explain."

"I think I understand", the priest said. "The effect of being in Algeria, no doubt. You were not alone, you know. War, particularly that war, did no young man any good."

Jacques nodded.

"What changed?", the priest said. "What returned you to health? What, in fact, returned you to the faith, to God?"

Jacques thought, carefully, for some moments. This he must get right.

"I will try, father, to explain. It was *les événements*, the demonstrations, the riots, last summer in Paris, in the Latin Quarter. Such rage and fury among the students, marching in the streets, tearing up the cobble stones, building barricades, a great deal of noise, and on the other side the riot police, fierce to begin with, then just watching, almost laughing, until suddenly they were fierce again, clubbing students, swinging their capes. I saw it all. We had students hiding in the bookshop, being pulled out by the police. The students thought they were rioting in a grand tradition. They thought they were *Communards* as in 1870. They thought they were Communists fighting authority, any authority, the university, the police, their parents. The real Communists, the Trades Unions, didn't think the students anything but irresponsible idiots, and, from what I saw, it was obvious that the real Communists were right."

"So", the priest said. "You weren't tempted to join in?"

"Absolutely not. I was only a few years older than the students but I felt much, much older. What had they seen, what had they known? I was caught up in the riot in the Latin Quarter in 1960, just by chance, you understand. I knew, then, very little about what was driving the violence, *Algérie française* on one side, defending the *colons*, the students on the other side demonstrating for freedom for the Arabs, the Muslims, even the Berbers of whom, no doubt, they'd never heard. I saw the riot police and which side they were on, and their cruelty to the students made me certain that the students were on the side of right. When I got to Algeria as a soldier I began to understand more, and to see that there was no clear line between what was right and what was wrong. The Arabs deserved their freedom, no doubt, but the *colons*, the poor not the rich, were facing the end of the only life they had ever known: how much idea of that did the students in the Boul'Mich have? In Algeria life and death were truly at stake on both sides.

"Last summer was not the same, not at all the same. There was nothing serious at issue. The students were a bunch of spoiled kids rioting for more sex, more drugs, fewer rules, fewer exams too, for all I know. Were they interested in anything beyond their own freedom to do as they wanted? I don't think so. It certainly wasn't anything like a revolution, which they called it. They were claiming that Trotsky was their inspiration. He would have thought them no more than expendable children of the frivolous bourgeoisie."

He stopped. Why was he saying all this?

"So, Monsieur Thomas", the priest said. "The effect on you of the *événements* was?"

"I'm sorry father."

"Try to tell us. The effect was clearly important to you."

Jacques looked down at his clasped hands, looked up at the patient face of the priest, noticed that the older priest was writing something on the paper in front of him, and took a deep breath.

"Afterwards", he said, "Very soon afterwards, when they were still sweeping the debris from the streets and resetting the cobbles, I realised that—that I had given up thinking, given up trying to understand—to understand anything. For six years, ever since I came back from Algeria, I had been like a sleep-walker. My eyes were open but I was seeing nothing. I had no more reason for getting up in the morning, doing my work in the shop, getting my lunch and my supper, than to keep going until the next day, which would be the same. In other words, I had no more serious reason for staying alive than the students had for rioting. There was nothing in their heads beyond more fun. There was nothing in my head beyond looking as if I were alive when in truth I was barely present in my own life.

"So the next Sunday I went to Mass. Just to see, to try—I'm not sure what I expected, or what, really, I wanted. But I went."

"Where did you go? Which church did you go to?"

"I could have gone to Saint Sulpice. I pass it every day on my way to work. It's too grand, too big. I went to Saint Étienne-du-Mont. I remembered—that there were lights and singing there on the night of the riot in 1960.

"That Sunday last summer was Pentecost. I didn't know, of course. I wasn't paying any attention to the feasts of the Church. But there I was, standing at the back—there were lots of people—and the Mass was beautiful. It was also very strange to me because it was in French, and I could hear and understand every word. When I was an altar boy, I knew the Latin words more or less, the ones I could hear, but I don't think I ever knew properly what they said. And then, that morning in Saint-Étienne, the priest preached about what it meant, that the people at Pentecost could all hear the Holy Spirit speaking to them in the languages they already knew. He said something like, 'You think you can't understand, but you can, because the Spirit uses who you are and where you have been and what you have done, the language you already know, to speak to you, one by one.' I can't remember his exact words, but what he said—well, together with the French instead of Latin, it seemed to be the first time someone had recognized who I was, where I was, perhaps ever. Though of course the priest had no idea who I was or that I was there in his church."

402

"Ah", the older priest said, sourly Jacques thought, "A Vatican II convert."

Jacques didn't know what this meant.

A long silence. Then the younger priest said, "Very good. This showed you that what the priest was saying was true?"

Jacques nodded. He had been understood. Almost, he was in tears.

"And after that?", said the priest in the middle.

Jacques swallowed the tears.

"After that I took to going to Mass every Sunday, and sometimes on weekday mornings early, with a few old ladies dressed in black. One or two of them smiled at me, but I always left the church quickly after Mass so as not to have to talk to anyone. All the time I was learning, as if I had learned nothing earlier in my life, which, in a way, was true. I bought a Bible, a Bible in ordinary French, something I hadn't known existed, and I tried to follow the Mass readings by looking up the whole chapters they came from, to understand them better."

"You were not receiving Holy Communion?" This was the priest in the middle.

"No. Of course not. There was too much, too much in me, in what I had seen and done for me to—I thought I was too much implicated in sin, or perhaps only too confused. I thought I always would be."

"But later?" the younger priest said.

"Nine months ago, at the beginning of Advent, the priest at Saint Étienne stopped me as I was going out of the church one day when I had been too slow to leave. He asked me my name and said it had been good to see me so often at Mass. Then he said, 'Are you Catholic?' I didn't know what to answer. I said something like, 'Yes. No. Not yet.' I can't remember exactly. 'Are you baptised?' he said. I must have nodded because he said, 'Then you are Catholic.' He looked at me carefully and said, 'Come and see me sometime after Mass on a weekday. Perhaps before Christmas?' That was kind because I was scared and it gave me some time to decide."

"So you did?", the younger priest again.

"So, a few days before Christmas, I did. We talked, and after a while he took me into the church and I made my confession."

After all, it had been not difficult, brief, almost disappointing. The priest, having listened, without saying much, to what Jacques had told him across the presbytery fire, on the other side of the grille had said even less. When Jacques had done his best to describe the carelessness of years, the not caring about the truth, which, much more than what had happened with Tanifa, he knew to be his gravest sin, the priest said, "For your penance, say three Our Fathers." Jacques found he remembered the act of contrition from his childhood. Then the priest gave him absolution. Jacques was getting up from his knees when the priest added, "When you say your penance, pay attention to the words. They are Christ's. Where are we in the Church's year? Where are you in your life? *Adveniat regnum tuum*: this is your prayer. Now go."

Jacques left the church grateful, resolved. He also felt very tired, and knew that he had a long journey ahead of him at the end of which he might, or might not, realize properly what he had just done.

But he remembered, now, nine months later at his interview with the White Fathers, that when he received Holy Communion at the midnight Mass on Christmas Eve, he had felt, for a few moments, that he, like the untidy world, was, without understanding the gift, let alone deserving it, receiving God himself. He was afraid, as the shepherds watching over their sheep in the night had been afraid. After Mass, the priest invited him and four others, including two old tramps who were more or less sober, to the presbytery for the meal his housekeeper had cooked. When he left, he thanked the priest, who said, "Don't thank me, my son. Thank God."

"This is all very well. And thanks be to God for your return to the Church", the old White Father said. "But why are you here?"

"Because in the spring a White Father came to Saint Étienne one Sunday and in his homily told us the story of Cardinal Lavigerie and the White Fathers in Algeria and Tunisia and then in all of Africa, and how they had freed so many slaves and looked after orphans and educated so many children and helped people who were poor and sick. I knew very little about them, about you, fathers. I remembered, from a book my grandmother gave me to read before I joined the army, that the White Fathers were kind to—to Père de Foucauld in Algeria. But that was long in the past. And here was a priest, quite young, telling us of his own life, his own work. He had come, I realized, to raise some money from Catholics in Paris for whom North Africa meant only the war and the defeat of France and the poor Algerians in the *banlieues*. I talked to him at the end of Mass, just for a few minutes, you understand. I asked him whether there were White Fathers still in North Africa. He said there were a few, that it was dangerous for them in Algeria, but that there were many people who perhaps more than ever needed their presence, their help.

"After that, I couldn't escape the idea that maybe I should at least find out more about—about your work, fathers, your life. I did try—"

"To escape? Or to find out?" This was the younger priest.

"Both, of course. But I meant that I tried to escape."

"Why?"

"Because only a few months earlier, not much more than a year ago, I wasn't even a Catholic. I thought I had left the Church, left the Mass, left believing in God behind me for good. That I would never be able to go back—I suppose, in reality, to go forward—to something that seemed too simple, too hopeful, to have anything to do with truth. And now here I was, here I am, looking at the possibility—the possibility that you might consider training me to be a White Father, for—for—the rest of my life. The idea terrified me and I tried to forget about it, to work harder at the shop, to do other things, go to more films, talk to strangers in bars, anything to fill the time. But I couldn't escape the feeling, the belief even, that this, exactly this, was being asked of me, by God. So I am here."

"Do you know", the priest in the middle said, after a silence in which it seemed to Jacques that all three Fathers wanted to be sure he had nothing to add, "why you were terrified?"

"O, yes", Jacques said. "I was terrified, sometimes I am still terrified, that I might be wrong."

"Wrong about your vocation?" The priest leant forward over the table and said, "You must understand, young man, that it is far from unknown for a person to mistake another motive, another impulse, for a vocation. But, should we accept you as a postulant, your first year with us will make it clear to you as well as to us whether or not your vocation is truly a summons from God."

"Of course, father. I do understand that. But I meant—I really meant that my fear, sometimes, has been that I am wrong about everything. That I have deluded myself, because I have been lonely, because I so badly needed a reason for being alive, into believing that truth can be found in the teaching of the Church, in the Bible, when in reality there is no such thing as the truth. And definitely not a set of truths so strange as those declared in the Creed."

Silence.

"That's the end", Jacques thought. "Now they've lost any interest in me that they might have had."

But the priest in the middle sat back in his chair as if this were a less serious concern than Jacques's fear that he might not after all have a vocation.

"I doubt", the priest said, "if there are many thoughtful Christians in our times who have not looked into the darkness you describe. That you are familiar with this darkness shows me that you are aware of the scale of the difference it makes, to everything, whether there is such a thing as truth, or not. I assure you that this is a good beginning to a Christian life."

"Thank you, father", Jacques said, not knowing if this was an appropriate reply.

"Just one more question, if I may, father", said the young priest.

"By all means, Père Denis", the priest in the middle said.

"Monsieur Thomas", the young priest said. "Do you think that it might be because of your experiences in the war in Algeria that you are particularly drawn to the idea of the priesthood in Africa? As a way, perhaps, of making amends in some measure for—for the past history of France in Algeria, for example?"

Even as Jacques wondered what kind of answer to this question might be most favourably received by the Fathers, he was struck by the fact that he hadn't asked himself the same question. Stupid of him, he now saw. Tell them the truth, he thought again.

"I hadn't made the connection, Father", he said to the young priest. "But now that you have made it for me, yes. There is too much terrible history"—he remembered often the book about General Bugeaud that he had read before he joined the army—" over too many years for anyone, now, to be able to make amends. But I see that you are right, father. I myself would like to do anything I can, anything that is possible, for the people of Algeria. And the White Fathers—"

"Exactly", the priest in the middle said, as he gathered together the papers in front of him and stood up. The other two priests, and Jacques, also stood.

"Thank you, Monsieur Thomas. We shall be writing to you shortly. We may well decide to invite you to our house in France, first of all to visit us, to have a look at our life in community, and then, if you have liked what you see, perhaps to begin your first year of formation as a missionary of Africa. If that is our decision, you are, of course, entirely free to change your mind and let us know that you do not wish to embark upon this journey of discernment. For that, to begin with, is what it would be."

"I understand. Thank you, fathers."

Jacques looked at each priest in turn, met the eyes of each and bowed his head a little. The young priest gave him a friendly smile, then came forward and, with a nod, led him out of the room, which was in a university building close to where Jacques lived, and then to a side door into the street.

Jacques walked to the nearest café and sat over a coffee on the terrace, watching the tourists walking by—it was August, and there seemed to be more foreigners than French people in Paris—and wondering if he hadn't just demonstrated that he was entirely unsuited to the priesthood. For one thing, he had talked too much. He knew that this was because he hardly ever talked properly to anyone. Had he talked properly to anyone since the few conversations, so long ago, it seemed, that he had had with Monsieur Sadi? Or, really, since he had talked and talked to Mathieu, even longer ago, although in the cafés and on the park benches of the Left Bank, close to where he was sitting now.

He had been very much impressed by the three White Fathers who had interviewed him, even by the old man who was clearly suspicious of him, and now he was surprised by the strength of his hope that his own uncertainties, and what he realized must have seemed to the three of them the laziness of his mind for so long, hadn't already lost this possible future.

On a winter night in 1994 he sat in his cave, wrapped in his blanket, and smiled at the memory of the bare white room where the three Fathers had questioned him twenty-five years ago, a quarter of a century, almost half his lifetime, the last moment when he could have, might have, decided to do something quite different. But what else could he have chosen to do that was any real improvement on his harmless job in the bookshop, or that would have given him the sense of dedication to God in work that was useful and unselfish that his life with the White Fathers had brought him? And then, in any case, nothing, and, perhaps more to the point, no one, had seemed as attractive, as positive, as the project, the possibility of living as a priest, far away from France, far away from Paris, devoted to other people, to the poor, to the sick, to children, above all to those who for generations had been oppressed and despised by France.

A week later the letter had come, inviting him, if he still wished to try his vocation with the Missionaries of Africa, to come to the French house of studies on a date in October, at first only for a month, and telling him what he should bring with him. Very little.

He found his trial month natural and easy, and he was asked to return in the following spring, if he hadn't changed his mind, to start in earnest his years of formation.

And so it began, his life as a student of philosophy in France, becoming accustomed to living in an orderly community which was austere but not gloomy. He liked the other students, with one or two exceptions, and kept a careful distance from each of them, as the custom of the house required. After this first year, he spent a year as a novice in Tunis, delighted to be back in North Africa, and in a city, St Augustine's Carthage, kinder than he could imagine Algiers had ever been, studying theology and Arabic and Islam. Tunisia had been an independent country for only fifteen years but its freedom had been achieved, while the war in Algeria was already raging, without bloodshed, no doubt partly because it had been under French rule for a much shorter time, and there were many fewer *colons*.

For his two years of what they called apostolic experience Jacques was delighted to stay in Tunisia: he had thought it likely that he would be sent to another African country. With three Fathers, a novice, younger than he was, from Mozambique, and two Brothers, he lived far from a big city in a small town, really only a village, where all the people were Muslim. He learned to help in a school for local boys, and even a few girls, and was given some basic medical training. Sometimes he was sent to visit the sick, or to help a family in difficulty, often because a widowed mother was trying to keep at home a son who wanted to leave the countryside for Tunis or even Paris. He learned more Arabic, because he had to speak and understand it every day, and he also, for the first time in his life, began to learn, from one of the Brothers, about gardening, which he much enjoyed, and particularly to learn about irrigation and the cherishing of water in near-desert land. He remembered his delight when he was told that the clementine, the small tangerine which grew on pretty little trees in the Fathers' garden, had been invented, even if by accident, by Brother Clément in the garden of a White Fathers' orphanage in Algeria.

His studies continued in Rome, where he felt himself to be part of the Church of the whole world, the Church that was opening its heart and its imagination to the whole world after the Council. He and his class had to study the documents of the Second Vatican Council: their tutor, a middle-aged French Father, was enthusiastic about them, particularly about *Nostra*

409

aetate . "It would have been much easier for us in the past if Rome had spoken about Islam with such respect. And let us hope and pray that this will be the end of anti-Semitism in the Church." Jacques saw that the White Fathers in Rome were mostly delighted by the decisions of the Council, and much admired Pope Paul, though one or two elderly Fathers grumbled a good deal.

He enjoyed almost every day of these years as a student and a novice. At first to his surprise—he hadn't sat in a classroom since he was at the *lycée* and had never attended a lecture delivered to adults—he discovered that he enjoyed learning. He got better at taking notes, reading the right parts of difficult books in libraries, and writing essays that stuck to the point and weren't far too long. He also enjoyed, as he recognized with some shame, not being responsible for anything beyond being faithfully present at the Mass, the prayers and the scripture study of each day, and doing the work he was set to do as well as he could

He completed his studies, took, in due course, the Missionary Oath, in the chapel of a beautiful White Fathers' house north of Paris, in a village close to a river, after a thirty-day retreat which he remembered as an intense and glowing time of silence and deep attention to Jesus, the man and the Christ. He tried to read and think his way through the gospels as if he had never heard or read them before, and they moved him into a place where he so much wished he could stay that the next six months, as he was prepared in the house of studies for ordination, seemed to him only white, black and grey, as if he had left behind with the river, the Oise, that flowed in spring sunshine through the woods and fields, the irrecoverable colour and warmth of his retreat.

White Fathers were usually ordained in their home parishes. He had no home, and no one he could invite to his ordination, so he was ordained with an African and a Vietnamese, also without families in France, in the chapel of the house by the Oise.

As a priest, he regained, occasionally and unpredictably at the altar celebrating Mass, what he had discovered on that retreat, the presence of Christ, beside him as Christ, unrecognized, had been beside the travellers on the road to Emmaus. Most of the time, although he did everything asked of him and enjoyed, as his Arabic became fluent and easy, helping more experienced Fathers look after the sick, growing vegetables and fruit, teaching children simple mathematics and the French that their parents, despite the humiliations of the past, still wanted them to learn, he found that again he felt as if he were observing himself from the outside. He saw a harmless man, leading a moderately useful life, doing all right. Little more than this.

His formation had taken years. His life as a priest had lasted more years, eighteen years of hard work, the difficulties, sometimes, of living with two or three other priests. not always the same ones, who found him, he knew, too reserved, too self-contained, to be a friendly companion. He felt that people took his silence for aloofness or disapproval when it was only silence.

Then, while he was living with four other White Fathers and two Brothers in Tizi Ouzou, the Berber town where Tanifa's father had been a schoolboy at the *lycée*, so in Kabylia but not, alas, in the violet mountains, he had fallen in love.

When he recognized what had happened, which was not until for several weeks he had been teaching a class of which Anir was a member, he knew that it was a disaster. He also knew that he was alive again, alive day after day, and no longer observing himself as if from outside, as he hadn't been alive since the retreat before he took the Missionary Oath. And this was stronger, deeper, much more difficult to deal with than what he had felt during his retreat. It was more like his first recognition that actual truth might be there in the faith, the Church, after the stupidity and violence of the shallow rebellion on the Left Bank in 1968. That was when he allowed himself to suspend his cynicism and learn. Now, he found, he had suspended his caution, the caution of all his life, without even noticing that he had allowed himself to.

Anir was eighteen years old. He lived in a village a few miles from Tizi Ouzou and bicycled into the town every weekday

411

to learn French in the class the White Fathers ran for about fifteen boys, all Muslims, all ambitious to leave home one day for Algiers and to find a job in a government service or in the oil industry. Jacques had discovered over the years that he liked teaching and was reasonably good at it. So he was pleased when he was asked to take this class on three mornings a week.

Anir was noticeable, not at once, but after two or three weeks. He was a quiet, serious boy, quicker to learn and with a better memory than any of the others. He sat very still, listened carefully, and produced an answer, usually the right answer, to a question only after several others had failed. The rest of the class were respectful of him and at the same time irritated by him. They exchanged resigned, slightly mocking, looks when he got something right, again. He paid them little attention. Only his eyes, full of intelligence, were also full of vitality and an ironic smile that came and went, as if inside him were a life of thought and a detachment from classrooms and lessons that distanced him from his fellow-pupils and from what was going on around him. He was a little older than some, roughly the same age as most, and seemed considerably older than all the others.

The classes always ended at midday, so that the boys could pray and then go home to the work they would normally be doing in these hot summer months when the schools were on holiday. Anir, after three weeks, would wait in the classroom for a few moments as the others left, as if to collect himself in a brief silence. Jacques would stay sitting at the teacher's desk—the whitewashed classroom, with a blackboard, plain blinds for the windows, and bare walls, was a simple version of an ordinary French schoolroom—until Anir stood, picked up his textbook and notepad and gave Jacques a brief, formal nod, before leaving to go home.

One day, on an impulse so uncharacteristic that it surprised him every time he remembered it, Jacques followed Anir out into the bright stony sunlight of the street and said, "Your French, Anir, is improving very quickly. Perhaps you would like to borrow one or two books to read from the Fathers' library?"

Jacques had said this in Arabic, to be friendly.

Anir looked at him with his remote amusement and said, in French, "I prefer to speak in French, father. We speak in Tamazight, the language of the Berbers, you know, although in school everything had to be done in Arabic. The government's Arabic is not even North African Arabic but Arabic from the east, from Syria, Egypt, wherever. This is not our language."

Jacques had never heard Anir say so much. He knew that the government's policy for years had been to replace French with classical Arabic, and to ignore the Berber language, forbidding its use in schools, so that it would die. This was why the White Fathers' French classes were popular with the ambitious young, particularly among the Berbers, who preferred to an alien Arabic the French spoken and written by the educated of their parents' and grandparents' generations. The classes were very unpopular with the government, although they hadn't actually been forbidden, since French speakers were, after all, useful.

Ever since the village in the mountains, and Tanifa and her father, more than thirty years before, Jacques had wanted to learn the Berber language. When he was studying in Carthage and in Rome he had discovered in serious books of French scholarship, mostly written in the nineteenth century, that what he had assumed to be immemorial legend when he had heard it from Monsieur Sadi turned out to be historical fact. The Berbers had always been there in North Africa, and everyone else had come and stayed, or come and gone, or a mixture, while the Berbers had watched and suffered and usually resisted whatever power was asserted over them, as they quietly outlasted invaders and settlers and the languages and institutions of empires and ideologies.

In French Jacques now said, "What does your father do, Anir?"

"My father is dead. He belonged to the FLN from the very beginning, He was killed in Algiers as the war was ending. I was nine months old when he died and so I do not remember him."

"I am sorry."

"No. People who remember the end of the war are more to be pitied than those who were young enough not to have known what the war was."

Jacques was too stricken by the truth of this, and by Anir's unyouthful perception, to be able to reply.

"Yes", he said, after a pause.

Anir seemed to be expecting Jacques to say something more.

"And your mother?" eventually Jacques said.

"My mother after some years married another man. I have five half brothers and sisters. Their father, her husband, you understand, wishes me to go away and live for myself somewhere. He has enough children to work on his olives and his vines. So I try to improve my French."

"Where would you like to go?"

Anir half-smiled, and shrugged.

"Who knows?", he said. "Paris? The moon?"

That was all. It was enough.

After Jacques's next class, Anir waited a moment as usual. They left the room together, without exchanging even a look, and out in the sunshine Anir said, as if four days had not gone by, "Yes, father. I would be pleased to borrow a book, if you will choose one for me."

Jacques merely nodded.

"Thank you", Anir said, with his little bow of the head, and then took his bike from where it was propped against a wall and rode off at speed.

Jacques spent a long time in the Fathers' modest library looking for the perfect book for Anir. In the end, on another impulse that, looking back, he thought he should probably be ashamed of, he borrowed for him Saint-Exupéry's *Terre des hommes* and *Le petit prince*.

"But this is a book for children", Anir said, looking at the pictures in *Le petit prince*, and then at Jacques, his expression almost offended.

Jacques shook his head. "Not really, or not only, for children. Read it and you will see."

At the end of Jacques's next lesson, Anir, once the rest of the class had gone, brought the books to the teacher's desk and put them down in front of Jacques.

"My French is not strong enough for me to read easily *Terre des hommes*, but I have tried and I have understood, I think, quite a lot. He was a lonely man."

"Yes", Jacques said. "But he found friends."

Anir looked at him, without irony in his eyes, and said, "Is everyone lonely, father?"

Jacques looked down at the books, and after a moment said, "Perhaps. But then—the little prince. Even in the desert."

Anir's slight smile.

"Perhaps", he said. Then, "May I borrow them again, these books?"

"Of course."

He picked them up, bent his head as always, and left the classroom.

After this, to his delight and also to his horror, Jacques found that he could think of almost nothing but when he was going to see Anir again, how he could find ways to see him more, how he could discover more about him.

In crowded streets, in the market when Jacques was buying vegetables and fruit for the kitchen, he kept thinking he saw Anir, walking away from him, at stalls choosing oranges or onions. Always the boy he saw turned out to be someone else. All day he longed to see him, to talk to him. At night he thought of him when he was awake, dreamed about him when he was asleep, woke ashamed and exalted.

He knew he had discovered in himself something that must always have been there but that he had never before recognized. What he had discovered explained, he now understood, his desolation when he had lost Mathieu, and also explained how, when he had left the village in the mountains and lost Tanifa, he had worried about her, and about the consequences for her of what had taken place between them after the expedition to Djémila, but had never felt despair at the certainty that he would never see her again.

At present, his delight in the existence of Anir, in his beauty, his mysterious subtlety, his quick understanding, was already so mixed with despair that on the mornings when it was his turn to celebrate Mass for the community, he lay on his bed and groaned. He knew, or thought he knew, that he should not

415

celebrate Mass while he was suffering, or enjoying—which?—feelings that were surely sinful. But was it forbidden, should it be forbidden, to offer to God with the bread and the wine his own sinfulness, his own love, to be transformed into Christ, even if the love and the sinfulness were the same? Wasn't the Eucharist all about love, God's love for us, our thanks to him for his love, his grace, the beauty of his creation, his truth? Was love divisible into the good and the wicked? Yes, indeed, he knew that they are. On the other hand, surely he was bringing to God at the altar both himself and Anir, both imperfect, both far from grace, for God's healing and love? Could this be shameful? These moments at the altar were the best, and also the worst.

And was Anir's effect on him—of which he was almost certain that Anir was entirely unaware—no more and no less than the revelation that he was, and supposed that he always had been, tainted, stained, not just by the original sin of every human being, but by—what? A sinfulness, or a tendency to sin, that he had himself done nothing to provoke or encourage. Somewhere from the back of his mind there had returned to him the words "gravely disordered".

Was he understanding this rightly?

He remembered a pair of boys in the *lycée* at Mâcon. They were friends. They sat next to each other in class, exchanged notes when they thought no one was looking, stood together at the edge of the playground and never joined rough games, were teased and mocked by other boys. He felt sorry for them, and never joined the bullying. Now he remembered that they also made him feel afraid. He hadn't known why.

He remembered a fellow novice in his first year of formation, a sallow young man who laughed too easily and was often on his knees alone in the chapel, more evidently pious than anyone else. After three or four months he disappeared. Jacques asked another novice why the boy had gone. A shrug was the answer, and "Not suited to the missionary life. Pretty obviously, don't you think?" He had forgotten all about him, and this unstated implication, until now.

He also remembered how, living during the 1960s on the

416

Left Bank, he had looked with fascination and, again, some fear, at the extravagantly dressed, evidently homosexual, older men, to be seen in the streets of Saint-Germain-des-Prés. Sometimes he watched, he now thought with something like envy, one or another of them in animated conversation with a handsome student across a café table.

He thought of the Christian men, the writers, who had for years been his friends, his guides, Augustine and Pascal. What would either of them say, what had either of them said, about the temptation, the wild happiness, the anxiety, and the guilt crowding in on him now? Pascal? No help from him, only a calm, right down to the depths of his soul, that must have protected him from this kind of storm, these terrifying waves that swept the surface of everyday life so violently as to drown a person. A person who couldn't swim.

And Augustine, who was familiar, for sure, with such storms, such waves? In his youth Augustine had known misery over the death of a friend, another man, who had died in the midst of a misunderstanding which Augustine couldn't put right and of which he was deeply ashamed. When Augustine's mother sent his wife—what other word was there for the woman who had shared his life for seventeen years and borne his son?—back to Carthage because she was too poor, too embarrassingly African, for a public marriage, he was so desperately unhappy, and no doubt also so full of guilt, that he couldn't bring himself to use her name when he wrote about her. But of the kind of love that was torturing Jacques with its collision of exaltation and fear Augustine, so far as he could remember, had never written anything.

For Jacques this was, again, a matter of truth, different from the old question of whether God himself was there, some-where, or not, but no less insistent and more immediately painful. He was haunted by the words of Jesus which, when he had first heard them, or first listened to them, at Saint-Étienne all those years ago, had rung for him with encouragement: "You will know the truth and the truth will set you free". Now these words were bitter, and seemed only contrary to what he was actually experiencing. What he had discovered about himself, deep inside himself, was and must always have been true, and this truth had him bound, constricted, tied in a tangle of conflicting feelings that he had no idea how to escape. Not free. The opposite of free.

Was this only an unexpected intensification of the state of sinfulness with which all human beings have to deal, and from which they can be rescued only by the grace and mercy of God? He was accustomed to the daily examination of conscience enjoined upon every novice, even every properly informed Christian. Laziness, resentments, inattention to liturgy and scripture reading which was inattention to God, boredom: all these were the sins of every day, any day, that he had for years acknowledged to himself and to his confessors. But this storm of feeling, so exhilarating, so dangerous, was something altogether different. How could it be only sinful when it had woken him from what seemed like years of numbness, almost of sleep—to what? To a sense of wonder at the beauty of the world which he thought he had left long ago in Burgundy or on the day of the walk to Djémila, and had briefly regained on that retreat by the spring river. And lost, he had thought, for good.

One hot early morning when he had walked outside the town to deliver a message to a family whose sick child was recovering in the Fathers' hospital, he had stopped to look at an ancient, twisted olive tree by the road. A tree that seemed never to have been pruned. A tree that had grown and thickened and twisted in the sun and the wind but whose green and silver leaves were as delicate and fresh as the leaves on an olive tree four or five years old. He sat beside the dusty road to look up at the leaves, the branches, and saw, as if he had never noticed them before, the mountains surrounding Tizi Ouzou in a light more clear and still than he had ever before thought it. He longed for the presence of Anir beside him, and was moved almost to tears by the absolute impossibility of his presence beside him, ever.

What would he say to a penitent who came to him for advice on a difficulty of this kind? "You must banish these feelings. Do not allow into your mind pictures and scenes which you know would be sinful if they became reality. Fill your days with work so that when you go to bed you are too tired to think, too tired for anything but sleep. Put your suffering in the hands of God and allow him to take it from you." He said all this to himself, and the words made no impression on him, and Anir filled his mind and his heart.

The community's life in Tizi Ouzou was very busy. Jacques's days were full. He helped every afternoon with the line of people, old men, women with children, men with injuries from accidents and occasionally from fights, who came for first aid, for medicine, for encouragement, from the Father who was almost a doctor. He helped to look after the garden, where another Father was in charge of growing vegetables and fruit. He had learned to drive in Tunisia and was often asked to take the Fathers' jeep out of the town on errands to villages. All the time, now, he did everything required of him while allowing Anir, his black eyes, his equivocal expression, his disappearing smile, to occupy his mind and his imagination.

Among the few rules all White Fathers had to observe, although the Society had never had such a thing as a formal Monastic Rule, was that none of them should ever be alone in a room with a woman or a child. Another was that no Father should ever live by himself, but always with two or more companions. But to be alone with a young man, for a while, a short while, which was, at present, his goal, his ambition, his desire, every day, every hour—no one had ever warned him against such a thing. If they had, would he have known enough to avoid this pain, this joy?

"Would it be useful", he said one day to the other Fathers when they were drinking their coffee after lunch, "if I were to learn some Tamazight?"

"Of course it would", Père Charles said. He had lived in Kabylia for many years and spoke the local language well. "There are so many people needing our help who know neither French nor Arabic. We do have a Tamazight grammar somewhere. It's a difficult language but it wouldn't be hard for you to learn more than the basics you've already picked up. At least it's written in French script, not in Arabic letters."

"There's a boy in the class, exceptionally intelligent, whose French is improving rapidly and whose first language is Tamazight. I thought of asking him to give me some lessons, if he has the time."

"What is his name?" said Père Alain, the oldest of the other priests in the house, who had taught generations of boys in Tizi Ouzou.

"His name is Anir Izdarasen."

"Ah", Père Alain said. "We were warned about him, you know, when we submitted to the district office the list of boys who wanted to join the class."

Warned? Jacques was aware of blushing. He was nearly fifty years old and he was blushing. He wiped his face with the back of this hand.

But the old priest went straight on, "The police say he's mixed up with Berber extremists and could be dangerous—not to us, but possibly to the police or the army if he and his friends were to get hold of guns or landmines. I decided to let him join the class anyway: better to keep these idealistic boys close than to push them into isolation from everything positive."

"I'm sure—", Jacques began.

"Yes, father?"

"I'm sure he's not—not the kind of young man who would take to violence, or plan murders, or anything of that kind."

"With the Berbers", Père Charles said, "one can never tell. Resistance is what they do best, though violence isn't really in their nature. The early enthusiasts of the FLN were almost all from Kabylia, you know. Do you know what 'Mazigh' means, Père Jacques? The root word of 'Tamazight', the usual word for the language."

"No, father."

"It means 'a free man' 'the free man', 'the defender'. 'Berber' is the same word as 'barbarian', ancient, ancient Greek for everyone else, everyone who didn't speak Greek. The Berbers have always known this. They are the Imazighem, the free. Those young Berbers who joined the FLN at the beginning: all they wanted was a free Algeria. Alas. This new Islamism, Muslim fundamentalism, whatever you call it, was nowhere in their plans, and in those days in any case it didn't exist in Algeria. The Berbers now, those who are interested in politics, are most concerned to save their language, their traditions, their mild, ancient, Islam from both the government and the extremists. The young, like all the young here, have seen violence all around them, in the papers and on the television, though not in the streets of Tizi Ouzou recently, thank God. And the slaughter here nine years ago won't be forgotten in a hurry. Disappointment over generations does terrible things to people."

"Anir Izdarasen"—Jacques enjoyed even saying his name—" tells me he is learning French so as to be able to leave Algeria, and perhaps work in France."

"That's what they all say. And no doubt most of them are telling the truth. But French is still necessary to those ambitious for power and influence in this country, as you know, and a clever young Berber—well, he may see himself as some kind of leader in the future, some kind of hero."

"Look at his name", said Père Jean, the most acute of Jacques's four companions. "Anir Izdarasen. It means 'powerful angel', 'angel of power'. It can't be his real name: the government has outlawed Berber names."

Jacques looked up in surprise and met the keen glance of Père Jean, a little younger than Père Alain and Père Charles but the superior of their little community. For something to do, Jacques picked up his coffee cup and drained it as if it were not already empty.

"If you really want to learn Tamazight, Père Jacques", Père Alain said, "there's a retired schoolmaster in the town who knows how to teach and would no doubt give you lessons if you asked him. He's an old friend."

They know, Jacques was suddenly sure. He remembered the pale novice who disappeared, the pair of boys at school. He also remembered the old priest at his first interview: "Was your father a Jew?", and the presiding priest saying: "None of us chooses his parents." This he hadn't chosen either.

So he didn't ask Anir to teach him Tamazight. And he was careful not to let anyone see that he could think of almost nothing, now, but seeing Anir in his class on three mornings every week, and exchanging a word or two with him at the end of the lesson.

Anir brought back the two books by Saint-Exupéry. At the end of a class, when the other students had gone, he came up to Jacques's desk and put the books in front of him.

"Thank you, father", he said. And then, after a pause, and looking down at Jacques, he added, "I shall not forget him, the little prince, when I can't see him. As he says."

Jacques couldn't answer.

"Would you please borrow something else for me to read? In French that is not too difficult, if possible. There are no French books to buy here. I see for sale only books about Islam. Books in Arabic."

"Willingly", Jacques said. "I will look for something that you might find interesting."

"Thank you, father."

His formal nod. His footsteps through the classroom and out into the midday sunshine. Jacques pretended, to himself, to sort the papers, French sentences written out by the students, on his desk.

At the end of the next class, Anir came to the desk, and said nothing.

"I have a book for you to try", Jacques said, and took a book out of the desk drawer. He held on to it as he said, "Have you heard of a writer called Albert Camus?"

Anir shook his head. "No, father." His smile, for a moment. "I know very little."

"But you understand what you know. That is rare."

Anir's polite nod.

"Albert Camus", Jacques said, "was a very good writer. He died, too young, in an accident."

 * "Like Monsieur de Saint-Exupéry?"

"Yes. Only not in a war. In a traffic accident."

It was difficult to go on.

"And then?" Anir said, and, as if to help Jacques, "Tell me. About Monsieur Camus."

"He was a *colon*."

422

Anir winced, and drew back from the desk.

"No", Jacques said. "He was a good man. And a very intelligent man. He suffered with everyone whom he saw suffer, before the war against France, and during the war. He suffered with the poor *colons*—his own family was very poor; his father was killed in the Great War when he was a baby and his mother was illiterate—" "Like mine", Anir said.

Jacques looked at him, and nodded. After a moment, he went on, "And he suffered also with the Arabs, and with the Berbers. He wrote of the misery in Kabylia when few people in France knew or cared about what France had done to Algeria, and almost no one had ever heard of Kabylia."

In the Fathers' library Jacques had found for Anir not one of Camus's novels but the *Chroniques Algériennes*, with Camus's essays on Kabylia that he wrote in 1939. Jacques put a hand on the book, which he had reread in the last three days.

"You will find here writing of great beauty and great sympathy for your country and your people."

"But if he was a *colon*—?"

"Ah. The *colons* turned against him, although he was their most famous son, because he understood the suffering of everyone."

"Was he a Christian?", Anir said.

"Not exactly, although when he was young he wrote about St Augustine—have you heard of him?"

Anir shook his head again.

"A great man, also a great writer. Sixteen hundred years ago. He was a Berber."

"Really?"

"Really."

"Did he speak in Tamazigh?"

"Probably. His mother certainly did. Mostly he spoke Latin, and he wrote in Latin."

"He was a Roman?"

"That's right. He was a Berber who was also a Roman."

"And Monsieur Camus was a *colon* who was also a French writer?"

"Yes. These things are possible, Anir. Camus was a Christian

423

child. As an adult he was not any longer a Christian, and he was not, of course, a Muslim either. But he believed most profoundly in the existence of the truth, and of goodness. And of beauty. As Christians do. As Muslims do."

Anir looked down at the book and, after a moment, at Jacques, and said, "Was this Monsieur Camus also a lonely man?"

"In the end, yes, he was. Because he condemned all violence, all terrorism, all killing, particularly of innocent civilians who had no weapons, there were always people who felt passionately that he should have been on their side and was not. He lost his intellectual Marxist friends in Paris because he hated the cruelties of Soviet Russia. He lost the friends he had once had in the FLN because he condemned the FLN's brutality to wretched *colons*, his own people after all. And he lost the confidence of his own people because he condemned the cruelty of the French army fighting for *Algérie française*. So yes, in the end he was lonely. For the last few years of his life, and he died before the end of the war here, he wrote nothing about Algeria. The silence of a lonely man."

Anir pulled a classroom chair from behind a desk.

"May I sit?", he said.

"Of course."

He sat for a minute or two, quite still, with his head bent and his hands resting on his knees, his faded jeans.

"I don't understand", he said. "I think that I don't understand. If this Monsieur Camus was a good man, as you say, father, why did he not take the part of liberty? Why did he not support the cause of liberty, for example for the Berbers, who have never known liberty?"

"He did, I'm sure. Or he would have. He was torn in half by his loyalties. He wanted above all that the killing should stop. He says somewhere in this book—"

Jacques picked up the book and turned over a few pages at the beginning. He found the place. "Yes. Here. He says, 'The real question is not how to die separately but how to live together'. You see? He thought there was room for everyone to live in liberty in Algeria if only people would recognize each other as human beings. As children of Allah, a religious person, whether Jewish or Christian or Muslim, would say. If each child of Allah is of equal value in the sight of Allah, to kill in the name of Allah is always wrong. Just as it is wrong to kill in order to hold on to land or wealth that has been stolen in the first place. And it is wrong to kill in the name of liberty."

He saw that Anir was struggling with this.

The boy leant forward to object.

"But killing has to be answered with killing. What else can we do?"

"Anir, listen to me. There is much else that can be done. To talk, to argue, to put a good case for what we deserve—perhaps to find clever and honest and brave people who will talk and argue for us: this takes perseverance and patience and some trust in those we can persuade to listen. It will take time and will often seem to be useless, but in the end it is the only way that leads to peace. What does killing lead to? More killing."

"Too much time has been wasted already. Hundreds and hundreds of years for us, and we are still not free, to be ourselves."

Anir leant further forward and clasped his hands together on the teacher's desk..

"And those who more and more rely on Allah, father", he said, "will kill more, and die more, thinking they will go to Paradise. The Islamic Salvation Front: have you heard of it?"

"I have. Do you belong to this party, Anir?"

"No. Certainly I do not. I will not fight for a kind of Islam that is not our own. I will fight for us, for our liberty and our language. This is politics. It is not religion."

Jacques looked at Anir's now lively face, his shining eyes.

"Politics, certainly, but French politics, Anir", he said. "Liberty and equality: people have fought and died to achieve them, for two whole centuries since the Revolution. But to hold them together requires so much of the third grand French word, fraternity, that people have failed in all those years to make the ideal, the dream come true. Usually, the more liberty, the less equality, or the more equality, the less liberty: one or the other is the result, and, I'm afraid, more often than not, neither. As for fraternity: only forty years after the Revolution came the French conquest of Algeria which had nothing to do with any ideal whatsoever. No, Anir. I am a Frenchman, of course, and a Christian, evidently. But from what I have seen myself, the Berber tradition of orderly self-government and unselfish cooperation is stronger and better than the wild ambitions of French politics. You should be proud of the Berber tradition, and keep it safe."

Anir got up, angry now.

"Were you here in 1980?"

"Yes, I was."

"In that case, you saw what happened then, to peaceful Berber cooperation. I wasn't here. I was a child, in my village. But we all know what happened in Tizi Ouzou, and we will never forget."

This was what Père Charles had called "the slaughter". Jacques remembered it, of course.

A conference had been arranged in the university, the brand-new university, where everything was taught and learned in Arabic. The subject of the conference was to be the language and poetry of the Berbers and the most famous Berber writer, Mouloud Mammeri, was to speak. The government in Algiers cancelled the conference. The students and teachers protested, peacefully. The government sent police and soldiers to clear them out of the university and bully them off the streets. More than a hundred were killed, many more were injured, and more than a thousand were arrested. Jacques, helping to deal with shot and beaten students brought to the Fathers by their friends, had found himself almost blinded by tears of rage as he tried to stop the bleeding of wounds and comfort terrified boys. His anger was with the French example which had taught the Algiers government how to do this: the example of the Vichy-trained, therefore Nazi-trained, riot police on the Left Bank in the riot of 1960; the same example which the FLN followed when they tortured and killed French soldiers because French soldiers were torturing and killing them; the same example that the OAS thugs followed when they murdered the French conscripts in Algiers in 1961. That night in Tizi Ouzou was one more horror in the whole long bloody story which seemed to be the story of his life.

"No", he said to Anir. "You won't forget, and you shouldn't forget. But more killing will not set you free, from injustice and oppression. You must be braver than that. Read this book. Please."

"I will try."

Anir stood up, returned his chair to its place, and took the book from Jacques's hands. He stood solemnly in front of the desk for a moment, and said, before his usual little bow of the head, "But we must also be ready to fight." Then he left the classroom without looking back.

For the next few days, Jacques, doing his ordinary work with care but with no attention, went over and over this conversation in his mind. Dressed, as always, in his white gandoura with his black rosary round his neck, he felt that what they had said to each other had dismantled the barrier between him and the other person that the gandoura and the rosary had for much of his life represented. A useful barrier in all ordinary circumstances.

He wished he had asked Anir whether he himself had chosen his Tamazight name. Much more, he wished he had asked Anir whether he could find some time to give Jacques lessons in his language: the Fathers, after all, had not quite forbidden him to do this. He longed and longed to be alone with Anir, somewhere, anywhere not in the classroom. Under the magical, ancient olive tree for example.

Two more lessons Anir came to, behaved exactly as usual among the other students, didn't say anything to Jacques about Camus's book, and left with the others at the end of the class.

Jacques, now thinking about nothing but this clever, passionate boy with his brilliant black eyes, felt his hold on everything else slipping. Should he go to one of the other Fathers and confess—what? He had done nothing wrong. Was allowing himself to acknowledge that he was what he now knew he had always been itself a sin for which he need absolution? How could he find in himself the firm purpose of amendment without which he should not even ask to be confessed? How could be amend something in himself which he had not chosen and could not change?

Perhaps he should pretend to be ill and ask to be relieved of his teaching, or even ask to be moved to another place, another country? He didn't think he could pretend to be ill convincingly. And if not here in Tizi Ouzou, if not Anir, then, wherever else he might be, who else might appear in his life, and seduce him into this storm of feeling just by his presence in the same room?

Was he losing everything, his faith, his knowledge for twenty years that he was doing what God wanted him to do and that what he was doing was good?

To keep his balance, more or less, he allowed himself, most of the time, nothing more than to hope that Anir would bring back the book and want to talk about it.

The third lesson was a week after their conversation, the only real conversation they had had.

Anir wasn't there. Jacques waited for three or four minutes before beginning the class. Then he had to start teaching, from the page of the French grammar book for non-French speakers that they had reached.

At a couple of minutes before midday on the classroom clock, which he could see and the students couldn't, he closed the book.

"Does anyone know whether Anir is ill?", he said.

Silence. A kind of silence that frightened Jacques.

"Well?" he said.

"Anir is dead", a boy said.

"What?" Jacques was only glad that he was sitting down. It was important that he should show no reaction.

"How?", he said. "How did he die?"

"There was an explosion", another boy said. "Anir and his friend were both killed."

"An explosion? Where? Why?"

A shrug from the second boy. No one else responded.

"This is terrible news", Jacques managed to say. Then, "Now it's time for you to go and pray."

In silence they left the classroom. One of them shut the door.

Jacques sat for a long time with his arms on the desk in front of him, his head resting on his arms, his eyes shut, in a darkness of his own. He heard someone open the door and then, without coming into the room, shut it.

He thought he would like to die, here, now, his head heavy on his arms, in the chair where he had talked to Anir. He wanted to follow him into wherever he had gone.

He stood up, eventually, stiff and old and trembling, left the school and walked very slowly back through the blazing light of Africa to the White Fathers' house which was supposed to be his home.

He said nothing at the midday meal, and ate almost nothing. Before the end of the meal he had to leave the refectory to be sick. He was shivering, with the effort not to weep.

He was sitting on a bench in the passage leading to the chapel when Père Alain walked past, stopped, walked back to him, and said, "Are you ill, father?"

"No, father." Then, thinking it might help him, he said, "Perhaps."

"What is it?"

Jacques looked up and said, "Do you know what has happened to Anir Izdarasen?"

"Ah. The boy in your class. I hear he died in an accident a couple of days ago."

"An accident?"

"There were two of them. Izdarasen and a friend. Apparently they were making some kind of bomb. No doubt they were intending to blow up a military patrol on the road or something of that kind. Whatever they were trying to make exploded and killed both of them instantly." The old priest sighed. "What a waste of young lives. And Izdarasen an unusually gifted young man, I gather. When will violence in this country ever end?"

"Excuse me, father." Jacques got up quickly and almost ran to the sacristy next to the chapel where he was sick again, into the sink.

Over the next few days Jacques's health collapsed as it had when he was in the military prison all those years ago. He couldn't eat without being sick. He was trembling with cold except when he was hot and sweating under the blankets they gave him in the hospital's small room kept for Fathers who were sick. The nursing Sisters brought him orange juice and tried to get him to drink it: he could manage only water, a little water, later a little more. The water in his glass became too warm to drink. This made him cry, if no one was in the room. He cried a lot. He couldn't read because he couldn't concentrate. He couldn't sleep for the pictures that haunted him, of Anir's face and body shattered by flying fragments of the bomb he had been putting together.

He was angry all the time, with himself for not getting to know Anir properly in time to prevent him doing something so stupid and dangerous; with the Berber nationalists for encouraging boys to make bombs; with the young man who had died with Anir—whoever he was, Jacques hated him—and above all with Anir himself for the childish heroics that had killed him.

Several times each day, more times each night, he tried to pray. For what? He couldn't pray for peace in his mind, in his soul, when he was more angry with God than even with Anir.

Doctor Djeddi, a Berber of about his own age, trained in Algiers and an old friend of the White Fathers in Tizi Ouzou, came to see him every day, took his pulse, listened with his stethoscope to his chest, asked him simple questions which he answered, and went away again.

Beside his bed, on the small white table with his glass of water, was his big rosary, in a jumbled heap. Sometimes, when he woke from muddled sleep, it looked threatening, like a snake or a giant spider poised to strike.

He didn't need to touch his rosary for the prayers he had said hundreds, thousands, of times to the moving of beads through his fingers, to flow through his mind until, soon, they had him in tears. Even the Apostles' Creed, so deep inside him and yet also outside him as the story of everything that made sense of the world, stopped him at "He descended into hell". Had Jacques ever before understood these words? Christ,

God, descended into the darkness, the place where there is no hope, no love, only death and despair. The place where Jacques was. The idea of Christ being here with him made him cry, for Christ as for himself. Shouldn't it make all the difference for him to know that Christ had been where he was, and had on the third day risen, in his new but still scarred body, to the garden where Mary Magdalene failed to recognize him? It should, but it didn't. Christ was without sin. He, Jacques, now, in his desolation at Anir's death, knew that he was, and always had been, and always would be, a sinner. He wasn't scarred, like Christ, by wounds inflicted by others, but he was a sinner in every cell of his body which had yearned for the body of a beautiful boy forbidden to him by the Church, by his responsibility as a teacher, and now by death. But the sin remained.

He lay in his hospital bed, too cold or too hot, in the light of the African day or in the dark of night, and he found that the rosary was a presence that he both feared and needed. He had several times almost thrown it to the floor where he wouldn't be able to see it. He imagined the noise it would make, the splash of beads on the tiles, and he couldn't do it. But also he couldn't bear to pick it up and go back to the beginning with the angel coming to Mary. If he couldn't repent what he hadn't done and hadn't chosen, how could he even say the Our Father? How could he ask for forgiveness when he couldn't forgive God himself for what had happened to him?

He could pray only for Anir because he was dead and because Anir, at least, had escaped any harm that Jacques might have done to him had he lived.

When he had been in his hospital room for a week, and the Sister looking after him had shaken her head sadly when he ate a little couscous she brought him and, yet again, immediately vomited, Père Jean came to see him.

"Doctor Djeddi tells me he can't find anything physically wrong with you, Père Jacques. He is sure, after a week, that you have none of the infections or diseases we have to watch for here."

The priest picked up the small chair from close to the wall, brought it to beside Jacques's bed, and sat down. After a minute or two, he said, "I deduce that it's your soul that is sick, father. Am I right?"

Jacques swallowed the tears rising in his throat.

"Yes", Père Jean said. "I see that I'm right. Can you tell me what it is that is making you suffer so?"

Jacques shook his head.

After a pause, the priest tried again.

"Is it something that you have done?"

Jacques shook his head again.

"Is it perhaps the absence of God? Sometimes I think we all fall into a hollow place where his absence is hard to bear."

The tears at least were now under control.

"I wish it were that. The absence of God, that is. I have known his absence. I have learned to wait, only to wait. No. If he were absent, I would not feel his—his cruelty as I do."

Père Jean looked at Jacques long and kindly, and then said, "Père Jacques, if you think it would help you, please try to tell me what it is that is causing you so much distress?"

"I can't, father. I ask your forgiveness, but I can't."

"My forgiveness you will always have, of course. But I am unable to give you any help unless I have some idea of what is troubling you—troubling you so severely that you are here in the hospital, not eating, not sleeping properly, the Sisters tell me, when you are not ill."

"And not working, father. I know. Doing nothing for the house or the people. I have become a priest, a missionary, incapable of being of any use, any service, to anyone. Perhaps this will now always be so."

"Nonsense, Père Jacques. You will recover. We shall help you. But I do need—"

Suddenly Jacques knew that he had to speak, and realized that he could. He sat up in his bed, light-headed because of the effort, drank from his glass a little warm water which made his stomach turn, and, looking not at his superior but at the bright, blank square of the window with its blind, he said, "I fell in love, father. With Anir Izdarasen. A boy in the French class. I am a homosexual. I didn't know. Anir is dead. I don't know his real name. And all these years I have not known my real self. I am nothing now. I have nothing. Anir with his invented name is dead, and my life as a priest, as a White Father representing Christ—perhaps this life has always been no less invented. In any case, it is also dead. Anir and I, both of us unreal people on the face of the earth."

"Stop, Père Jacques. You are not yourself. You are not well. However—"

Père Jean's voice had changed. Jacques had to look at him.

"It is necessary for me to ask you: did you—was there any physical contact between you and this boy?"

"No, father. There was not."

"This is the truth?"

"This is the truth. Not that—"

He couldn't go on.

"Not that?", Père Jean said.

Jacques swallowed one mouthful of warm water. "Not that I did not crave it. But there was none."

"That's good. The White Fathers can do nothing in Africa unless they are respected, as they have always been."

A long silence.

"So, Père Jacques, my concern is you. The boy, alas, is dead, another victim of this country's terrible history. You will remember him before God, naturally, and you should be thankful that no harm came to him through you. But you, yourself—"

Jacques waited. He realized that he was neither shivering nor sweating, that he was feeling better than he had since he was told that Anir was dead. The storm had quietened. Perhaps, after all, there was someone who knew what he should think, what he should do.

"You are not alone, you know", at last Père Jean said. "In the first place, none of us is ever alone. In Christ, God is with us, in suffering, and also in love, which can present itself as suffering even while it may also bring us joy. In the second place, you are not the first priest to find himself in your exact situation, and you will not be the last. We do not discuss these matters, probably because we are too busy, though no doubt when you were in the seminary some tutor gave a talk which then you thought had nothing to do with you."

Père Jean leant forward, with his hands on his knees.

"I want you to remember one thing: celibacy is a decision, and a promise. Chastity is a virtue. It is a grace, a gift of God, which we have to be ready to receive. What—what you have recently discovered about yourself does not make the hope, the prayer, for this grace any more difficult for you than for anyone else. You don't believe me now, I can see by your face."

"But the Church—", Jacques said. "How can I be a priest, ever again, when the Church regards me as a—as someone who is not sound, not whole, not a real man—"

The tears were back.

"You have committed no grave sin in connection with this boy."

"Yes, I have. If a man looks with lust on a woman, Christ said, he has already committed adultery. How much more sinful if he looks with lust on a man."

"No, Jacques. You were tempted, and you resisted the temptation."

Jacques noticed that Père Jean had used only his name, hadn't called him "father". He felt encouraged in his effort to be truthful.

"I didn't. There wasn't time. There wasn't anywhere—He wanted to be a hero and he died in an explosion that was his own fault. I resisted nothing. I loved him. I was determined to find a way—a way to him. Those were not the worst but the best few weeks of my whole life, the very best. I am not the man I thought I was, the man you, all of you, thought I was, when I was ordained priest. I am someone else, not fit to be a priest, not fit to—"

Now there were tears streaming down Jacques's face.

Père Jean took a clean white handkerchief out of the pocket of his gandoura and gave it to Jacques.

After a long silence while Jacques blew his nose, mopped his face, and lay back on his pillow with his eyes closed, Père Jean said:

"First, you must recover your health. Sleep, eat, rest, until you are strong again. I think that now you will find you are able to. Then it may be better, for you and for the rest of us, if you leave Tizi Ouzou, at least for a while. I will talk to Tunis and see what can be found for you. Until you feel that you can clear from your soul this boy, may he rest in peace, and what you have felt for him, you should, on the question of your priestly duties, follow your conscience."

Père Jean stood up, put his chair back against the wall, and, beside Jacques's bed, said. "God bless you, Père Jacques. I shall pray for you. I shall tell the others in the house only that you have been ill and that I have no doubt that you will recover soon."

It was as Père Jean had predicted. After a day and a night of extreme weakness and much sleeping, Jacques awoke hungry, and soon, to the delight of the Sisters, regained his strength. Two weeks later, in ordinary clothes, having returned his gandouras and his burnous to the cupboard in Tizi Ouzou where the spare habits were kept, he travelled beside the driver of a trader's truck carrying barrels of olives to Ghardaia, where he had lived ever since. He took with him his rosary, his crucifix, and, having asked permission from Père Alain, who looked after the library, one of the house's two copies of *Le petit prince*.

He did not clear Anir from his soul. He never would. He did not, therefore, ask for his confession to be heard. He went to Mass, did not receive Holy Communion, was never questioned by anyone in Ghardaia, and lived, mostly, in a calm, occupied routine that he saw no reason to change for the rest of his life. He was fifty years old, he was useful, he did no harm. He thanked God, now, without difficulty. He said without difficulty, every night on his knees, a decade of the rosary.

Every so often he set out from the town, climbed the rock into his cave, watched the sun set in memory of Anir, and soon allowed himself to diminish to a speck of consciousnes on his shelf of rock as he looked at the brilliant desert stars in the black sky. "The stars are beautiful", the little prince had said, "because of a flower that you do not see." Afterwards, wrapped in his blanket, he slept in the cave, and woke to the miraculous light of the risen sun.

On 26 December 1994 Thamar took his blanket to the cave in the afternoon. On the day after Christmas, the feast having been hard work for everyone, the Sisters told him to take some time off: they knew he liked to walk to his cave from time to time, and always warned him to look out for snakes.

The night was colder than any he had spent in the desert, and in the morning the sun looked strange, too red, too large, with thin, high bands of cloud above and below. It didn't look as if it would rain, alas. Rainfall was always precious to everyone in Ghardaia.

He ate a piece of bread, drank the rest of his water, rolled the bottle in his blanket, tied the bundle to his back, and carefully, as always, climbed down from the cave. As he walked back to the town, the sun gradually recovered its ordinary winter gentleness.

As he turned the corner of the White Sisters' street, he saw a small crowd of people at the door of the house. Two or three women were crying, clutching their shawls to their mouths. An old man was sitting on the steps with his head in his hands.

Jacques walked past him and found the door locked, which it never was in the daytime. He pulled the string which rang a bell inside. After a minute or two, Sister Marie-Jean came to the door and let him in, shutting and locking the door behind him. She was white and shaking and had clearly been crying.

"Whatever is it, sister?"

"O, Thamar, it is so terrible. We heard an hour ago on the telephone. The Fathers in Tizi Ouzou are dead, all four of them, shot. We are in the chapel now, Père Philippe is saying Mass for them, but what can we do?"

"Who shot them?"

"We don't know. The Islamist terrorists, perhaps, who killed the nuns in Algiers two months ago? But we don't know. Come."

He followed her to the chapel and knelt at the back until the end of the Mass. He thought most of all of Père Jean, of his care for him, his goodness.

In the days that followed there were new discussions about whether the Fathers and Sisters in Ghardaia should leave Algeria. None of them wanted to. "Not in Ghardaia. It wouldn't happen here. We've been here so long. The people need us. They don't hate us. They've never hated us. We're far away in the desert."

The Fathers, however, had an anonymous letter, which came through the mail from Tizi Ouzou, saying that they would be next. "All Christians and Jews who have chosen to remain in Algeria will be killed." Then there were two telephone calls. "Not long now, cross-bearers." A voice, speaking Arabic.

On Sunday 8 January, twelve days after the murders in Tizi Ouzou, the GIA came to Ghardaia.

Thamar, who had been to Mass early in the Sisters' chapel, was in the small courtyard of the Fathers' house with a few local Muslims calling themselves a "group for self-defence". The Fathers were at Mass. Everyone knew there might be an attack. "These murderers are wicked. This is not Islam. The Fathers are not crusaders. We must protect them." But they had no guns.

A jeep drew up in the street. Three young men in dirty camouflage uniforms and black balaclavas ran shouting into the courtyard, waving old Kalashnikov rifles. One was brought down by two of the local defenders. His gun skidded over the stony ground. The others ran into the house. Thamar tried to run after them but was stopped by more defenders. "No. No. Too dangerous."

They heard shots.

The attackers appeared in the doorway, their guns to their shoulders. Everyone ran towards the street, Thamar, older than the rest, ran too slowly.

When he came to, in a hospital bed with Sister Pauline watching him, he had no idea what had happened. He had an intense headache. He couldn't open his mouth to speak. His face was completely bound in bandages. With the eye that wasn't covered he saw the Sister's face, her smile.

"Thamar, you are awake."

She sat on his bed and took his hand.

"If you can hear me, squeeze my hand."

He could. He did.

"That's very good. Listen, Thamar."

She bent forward and smiled again.

"Do you remember that attackers came to the Fathers' house?"

He squeezed her hand.

"That was two days ago. By the mercy of God, no one was killed. They shot Père Philippe and he was hurt, not badly. When he fell down, it seems that the boys with guns panicked. Everyone else got out of the chapel and the courtyard safely except you, poor Thamar. You were very unlucky. I'm afraid your face is badly injured. Your jaw is broken, and your cheekbone, and your eye-socket. We asked Doctor Ephraim to have a look at you. He has bandaged your face as best he could. He says you need a specialist surgeon to set the broken bones, but that means a proper hospital in Algiers, and we may not be able to get you there in time for the bones to be mended properly."

Two months later, Thamar, his face scarred and twisted, his courage, this time, he thought, destroyed beyond repair, was accompanied from Algiers to Paris by a French White Father he didn't know who was flying home for his mother's funeral. Thamar travelled on to Mâcon on a train, his face almost completely wrapped in a scarf.

Chapter 8

Bernard

May to June 2016

"Tonight", Thamar said, "we have a little celebration."

"Do we? Have you guessed?"

"Have I guessed what?"

"I think I've got to the end of what you wanted me to call Part 2."

"Have you indeed? You're a good boy, Bernard, and you work hard."

"There's more to do, I know. I need to go back and look carefully at everything I've written so far, change things, add things, leave things out. How is one ever sure that a piece of writing is as good as it's going to get? But there's a lot more to do. Before you read it. And I think that the book needs one more section, Part 3, perhaps, which should be quite short."

"Ah", Thamar said. "I'm glad. Not, you understand because you have more work to do, when you have done so much, but because you will stay a little longer. I know you have promised your parents to return to Paris in the summer, and get on with what your father thinks of as your real life. You must keep your promise. But I fear I am becoming a selfish old man and for me it is good, more than good, that you will be here—for what? Perhaps for another couple of months?"

"I will. Don't worry." Bernard looked at his grandfather across the table in the summerhouse. The old man had just come back, with Félix, from the château, and sat down, stretching his back as he sat, in the other chair.

"How did you know", Bernard said, "that I'd got to the end of Part 2?"

"I didn't know. Our celebration is for the anniversary."

"Really? Anniversary of what?"

"The sixth of May. The day you walked into this house and began the year which has become the happiest year, I think, that I have ever had."

Bernard couldn't answer this.

"It's true, Bernard. Every day, I thank God for this year, for you."

"It has been, for me too, the—" He couldn't go on.

Thamar got to his feet, gripping hard the arms of the wicker chair.

"Enough", he said. "I'm going to cook something good, I hope, for supper. It should be ready in an hour or so."

He paused for a moment, his hand on the table, before going down the two steps and walking through the grass and the fallen apple blossom to the house. Bernard, and Félix, who had stayed at the bottom of the steps, watched him as he walked. Bernard was anxious, now, about the old man's health, but had learned not to ask how he was. Once he had suggested a visit to the doctor. The suggestion had been received with scorn. "I'm getting old. That's all. I don't need a doctor to tell me." And it was true that Thamar still walked every day to the château and worked in the garden. He came back later, so more slowly, and increasingly tired.

Perhaps this evening he could ask his grandfather a question he had been putting off for weeks, not knowing how to get it into the right words, and afraid that it might be tactless, clumsy, upsetting for Thamar, to raise something that in all the hundreds of pages of writing that Bernard was now so familiar with, he had never once mentioned. He must have said nothing about it because silence, on this subject, was what he preferred. But why? When he had written so candidly about so much, why hadn't he explained what Bernard felt was the last piece of the jigsaw, the missing piece of the thousand, or the nine hundred and ninety-nine that he had worked over the months to fit together.

When Bernard, followed by Félix, went into the kitchen an

hour later, there was a wonderful smell.

"What have you made, Thamar?"

"Ah. Wait and see. Will you make a salad, Bernard, and lay the table? There are tomatoes in the bowl, good ones from Provence, and they're best if you slice them just before you eat them. Only some oil and salt. And open that bottle of wine."

Thamar had made an onion tart, sweet and creamy, with crisp pastry.

After they'd eaten, and had their cheese with some grapes that Thamar must have bought that morning, Bernard tidied up the table, sat down again, and said, "There's one thing I do need to ask you."

"What is it?" The old man looked a little wary.

"I'm sorry, Thamar, if this is difficult, perhaps something you would rather not tell me, or something you would like to be left out of the book. But I'm interested, myself, because of how much I have already learned from you. And because, you know, I'm at last beginning to learn a little about the Church. About how it is, really, for ordinary people."

Thamar smiled his crooked smile, not wary now.

"Ah. The Church is complicated. But it is also simple."

In the months since Bernard had returned to the village in January, he had, very tentatively at first, allowed his grandfather to bring him a little way towards the Church, towards, even, the possibility that what Christianity declared might have in it the kind of truth that Bernard, since he was a fifteen-year-old schoolboy in his father's *lycée*, had been certain did not and could not exist.

Of course it was his work on the book, his long effort to imagine, which was to understand, Thamar's becoming, as a damaged young man in Paris, a Catholic again, and his conviction that to allow his life to be reconstructed as the life of a White Father was what he was, somehow, intended by God, if God existed, to do—it was all this that had made Bernard think, as seriously as he could, about things that had never before reached the surface of his mind in any coherent way. He found himself thinking, for example, that the mysteriousness

441

of time and fallible memory, something that had struck him as a child, could be resolved only as Augustine resolved it in his *Confessions*: time—the past doesn't exist because it is over; the future doesn't exist because it hasn't yet arrived—is only the present, too swift for us to grasp it, but present always in eternity, as time was created out of eternity. So the question of whether all that each of us has forgotten is merely lost into the dark of nothingness, or is not, is answered: what is unremembered is not lost but is always present in God's eternity. Struggling with Thamar's muddled manuscript, struggling to get to know properly a man who had tried his best to write down what he knew of himself, his life, but whose memory was as partial, as imperfect, as everyone's memory is, Bernard saw that only in God, by God, is a man truly known. As Augustine said, over and over again, in different ways.

So, a few weeks earlier, in the middle of March, Bernard had said, one Saturday evening, "May I come with you to Mass tomorrow?"

A long, questioning look.

"Because you think it would please me? Because it would help you to understand some things in the book that are strange, outlandish, inexplicable to you?"

"Well—", Bernard said.

"Or perhaps because you would like to discover something of what it is that holds the loyalty of an old man like me, in spite of—in spite of so much?"

Bernard said, truthfully, "All three."

Thamar laughed.

"Good. Good. And honest. But that you always are, Bernard. Of course you can come with me. We have Mass in the village tomorrow, so it's not even a long walk. Nine o'clock."

Bernard got up to put two more logs on the fire. He was in charge, now, of the fuel supply. He brought back fallen branches when he walked in the woods, sawed and chopped them into logs and kindling, and stored the logs, neatly stacked, under a tarpaulin at the bottom of the garden to dry out.

He sat down in his comfortable chair and they went back to reading their books. Or Thamar did. Bernard, after looking into the fire for a few minutes, said, "Thamar."

The old man looked up, serious.

"You know that, since I was five or six, I've only been to Mass once before", Bernard said, "in the cathedral in Nantes a year ago. I understood absolutely nothing. What should I know before I come with you tomorrow?"

Thamar laughed.

"Very little. Or a very great deal. The Mass, as someone said of the Bible, is shallow enough for a child to paddle in, deep enough for an elephant to swim in."

"Who said that? It's wonderful."

"I can't remember. Augustine, I expect. It sounds like him and, being an African, he knew about elephants."

Was he avoiding Bernard's question?

He went on, "Though all Romans did, I suppose, because of Hannibal. Africa, again."

He was avoiding Bernard's question.

Then Thamar said, "I'm sorry, Bernard. This is important. For both of us. But you mustn't worry about what you know and what you don't know, or what you don't yet know. Without doubt, you will have picked up more than you realize from dealing with the chaos I gave you to sort out in the book."

He looked across the quietly burning fire at Bernard.

"But—"

He stopped, and wiped a hand across his mouth and his bearded chin.

"But?", Bernard said.

Thamar laughed, a little.

"Here I am", he said, "a trained missionary with many years of experience, teaching and preaching and all the rest of it. I want to give you something precious, and useful, and I don't know where to start."

He bent his head, and, after sitting for a few minutes in the stillness that was to Bernard now very familiar, looked up at last and began.

"To be present at Mass is to be, in a particular and God-given way, in the presence of Christ. It is a crossing of time and eternity, as the coming of Christ into ordinary human life

443

was his coming out of eternity into time, as, for us, in all time, Christ, the image, the visibility, of God, bears his character and brings his redemption into the sinfulness and confusion in which we live. There—you look thoroughly baffled, my poor Bernard."

Bernard shook his head. "Not exactly—though it's a lot—"

"Of course it is. It is so much that it makes all the difference to everything."

Silence for a few moments.

"Let me start again", Thamar said. "Among many other things, the Mass is a story. We arrive in the church. We clear our souls and our minds by admitting our sinfulness and confusion and asking for God's mercy. Then we listen to bits of the Bible being read, a bit of the Old Testament and a psalm, which is a song, also from the Jewish Bible, and then a bit of a letter, usually by St Paul from the very early days of the Church, and then a bit of one of the Gospels, about Christ himself, what he does, what he says. There's a short address to us by the priest, who tries, sometimes well, sometimes badly, to make something fresh of what we've just heard. We say the Creed, which is a list, a careful list which took centuries to form, of the statements about God's dealings with the world that Christians believe to be true. You'll have to just listen to this list, for the time being.

"Now we're a small crowd, very small here, as you'll see, waiting for Jesus to be present, now, in the moment that, in this life, is all we have. We sing what the crowd sang when Jesus was arriving in Jerusalem to be killed: Blessed is he who comes in the name of the Lord, with an ancient Jewish greeting, Hosanna.

"The story continues, mixing up times, as stories do. The priest asks for the blessing of the Holy Spirit, the Spirit of God, as the Spirit blessed Jesus when he was baptized, blesses all of us when we are baptized, blessed you, Bernard. Then we are at the Last Supper with Jesus and his disciples before he is crucified. He gives them the bread and wine which are on the table, and says he is giving to them, giving to us as we watch and listen, himself, his body and blood, yet to be given up, yet to be shed, in the bread and the wine. So, in this mystery we shall never wholly understand, he is with us.

"The prayer afterwards that every Christian knows—maybe these are the first words you should learn by heart—is the Our Father, which tells the whole story again in a few short sentences. God sends his Son to us so that the kingdom of heaven may begin on earth. His Son does his will, as we pray we may. We pray to be fed, with the truth as with bread, to be forgiven, not to be misled, to be protected from evil. And then we look up to the crucifix over the altar, Christ killed by the sinfulness of human beings, the lamb of God who takes away the sins of the world."

Both of them looked up at Christ on the cross, above the fire.

"Why", Bernard said, "is he called the lamb of God?"

"Because he is innocent. Because he has given himself as a sacrifice, for us."

"I don't understand."

"Of course you don't. But then, really, who does?" A half-smile. "After that, the people go up to the priest to receive Holy Communion, the body and blood of Christ."

"So they believe."

"That's right. So they believe. Just before they do that, they say one more prayer. 'Lord I am not worthy to receive you—' It's a good prayer because it's always true of all of us, whether we receive Holy Communion or not, and specially if we do not."

"Like me?"

"Like you. And, for many years, like me. I have been encouraged, often, when I've remembered that the man who first said those words was an outsider, not a Jew, a Roman centurion. Jesus offered to come to the centurion's house, to cure his servant who was very sick, and this was what the centurion said. You remember some Latin, Bernard? So, the centurion said to Jesus, 'Domine, non sum dignus ut intres sum tectum meum sed tantum dic verbo, et sanabitur puer meus'. You see, the faith of this man?"

"Say them again, Thamar, his words." Bernard's Latin wasn't quick enough.

"'Domine, non sum dignus ut intres sub tectum meum.' 'Lord'—this is a fairly senior Roman officer, speaking to a poor Jewish teacher—'Lord, I am not worthy that you should enter my house.' 'Sed tantum dic verbo, et sanabitur puer meus.' 'But only speak the word, and my boy will be cured.' it's a remarkable moment and there we have it, always, in the Mass."

"And was he?"

"Was who?"

"Was the boy cured?"

"He was cured."

Thamar sat back in his armchair and smiled at Bernard.

"I'm sorry, Bernard", he said. "I have probably said too much, more than you will be able to remember tomorrow, or perhaps ever. But if you remember that you will be there, in the presence of an unfolding story that took place long ago, and that takes place in every Mass, you won't go far wrong."

"Thank you, Thamar, again. I will do my best."

"I know."

Thamar got to his feet.

"Time to go to bed", he said.

Bernard tidied up the fire and put in front of it the old iron guard, which had probably been in the winter room since Thamar was a child.

Thamar turned out the lights. As Bernard went up the stairs, ahead, because he moved more quickly, he just heard the old man say, "And who knows? Perhaps my boy too—".

There were fifteen people in the church: Bernard counted them. Two thirds of the rows of chairs, with their rush seats, each with a kneeler that folded down from the chair in front, were empty. Most of the people were old or very old. Only two of the old people, not counting Thamar, were men. There was one young family. The youngest child, a little boy of perhaps two years old, ran up and down the aisle for a while, until his father picked him up. He cried, and his father took him outside and didn't come back. The middle-aged woman who read the first passages from the Bible had forgotten her reading spectacles and stumbled over the words.

446

Bernard found it difficult to concentrate, and more difficult to remember what Thamar had described to him, which seemed impossibly remote and grand compared to what he was seeing and hearing.

Two moments impressed him enough for him to have to think about them afterwards. In the Gospel story he heard that Jesus shamed, by asking them if they were themselves sinless, upholders of the law who wanted to stone to death a woman caught committing adultery. One by one they went away and, alone with the woman, Jesus didn't condemn her and told her to go away and not to sin again. It seemed to Bernard a story of light being shed into darkness. But why did Jesus, twice, write on the ground with his finger? The picture of him doing this stayed with Bernard for days.

He did remember, more or less, what Thamar had said about the collision, in the Mass, of the past, the present and the future, when, into the silence of the kneeling people in the church, a silence which seemed to have collected a new density, and not only because the two-year-old had been taken outside, the priest spoke Jesus's words over the bread and then the wine. "This is my body, which will be given up—This is my blood, which will be shed—" Now, and tomorrow and always, and the dead figure on Thamar's cross.

But then, kneeling still, and watching as the line of people, Thamar the last of them, shuffled up to the altar and received the little round piece of bread from the priest and, for a moment, the cup from the elderly man standing beside the priest, Bernard felt only sorry for them, poor deluded people, persuaded by long, long tradition that they were doing something so much more than what they were actually doing, eating a piece of bread, swallowing a sip of wine. And Thamar, as deluded as the rest? Yes. No. The extreme difference was dizzying, like the difference between seeing rabbits and seeing Greek vases in a trick picture: impossible, unnervingly impossible, to see both at the same time.

"You were disappointed, Bernard. I'm sorry", Thamar said as they walked back to the house. "I pitched it wrongly for you, last night. I should have warned you that a little parish Mass is also a humble, ordinary affair, which is one of the reasons for my faithfulness to it. I know these old people by sight. They know me by sight. We nod, and say 'Bonjour', and that's all. It has been so for many years. But the Church is not a solitary thing. 'Where two or three meet in my name', Jesus says, 'I am there'. There is—how to put it?—there is a warmth in a little congregation, even of strangers, even in a cold church, which is good."

Bernard stopped in the road, so Thamar also stopped.

"No", Bernard said. "I wasn't disappointed. Not exactly. Your description of what to notice was so—so large, so full of—. And here and there I caught it. But then I lost it again. I'm just confused, I suppose. More confused than ever. I can't—" But he couldn't explain, about the rabbits and the Greek jars.

"Never mind. What I think you should do is persist. For a little longer in any case. Come with me to Mass again, perhaps next Sunday when you will hear read aloud—not, alas, very well—what happens when Jesus arrives in Jerusalem and rides through the cheering crowds, and then the whole story of his arrest, his trial and his death. The week that follows is called Holy Week. On Thursday Jesus gives himself in the bread and wine to his friends at the Last Supper. On Friday he is crucified. On Sunday he rises from the dead."

Bernard looked at the ground.

"Come along", Thamar said. "Time for some coffee."

Neither of them said anything until, twenty minutes later, they were sitting at the kitchen table with, in front of them big breakfast cups of coffee with hot milk, and chunks of yesterday's bread.

"It's no good, Thamar", Bernard said. "I can't do it. It's too strange, too difficult to hold steady. I simply can't believe it's all true. And obviously, if it isn't all true, none of it is."

Thamar drank some coffee, put his cup down carefully and looked at Bernard.

"I think you should persevere, all the same, Bernard. If only for a few weeks. Wait. One moment."

He got up, left the kitchen and went into his winter room. At once he came back, with an old red book in his hands, a book with the thin gold horizontal lines of a Pléiade edition on its back.

"Pascal", he said. "You haven't read him."

"No. Only some sentences you quote in your book."

"Well. Listen to this."

Still standing, across the kitchen table, the old man searched, for two or three minutes, backwards and forwards through the pages of the book.

"It's in the nature of this book", he said as he searched, "that what you are looking for could be anywhere."

He smiled across the kitchen table at Bernard. "How often is that true of all sorts of things?"

He searched in the book some more. "Ah. Here it is. A famous passage called 'Pascal's Wager'. Never mind why—it's all to do with mathematics. But at the end of a very brilliant argument, he says this."

Another pause, while he read.

"Essentially, he says this: Since you have everything to gain and nothing to lose by taking a chance on Christianity being true, try it. Learn from people who have behaved as if they believed until they did." He looked over the top of his spectacles at Bernard. "Me, perhaps." He looked down again at the book.

"Then he says—" Here he read from the book. "'What harm will come to you from taking this course? You will be faithful, honest, humble, grateful, kind, a sincere, true friend.' Well, Bernard, I would say you are already half way there. And then he winds up the whole case like this: 'And you will realize in the end that you have bet on something certain, something infinite, for which you have lost nothing.'"

So Bernard tried it.

The next Sunday, they walked the three kilometres to Saint-Roch, a smaller village with a smaller church, and Bernard stood, holding the palm he had been given, and listened to the story of Jesus riding into Jerusalem as the people cheered, and then to the long account of Jesus's last supper with his friends, of his trial at the Jewish council and then his trial before Pilate, of his crucifixion and burial. To his surprise, the story, which he had never before read or heard, struck him as clearly a historical account. About the angel appearing in the garden to give Jesus courage no one could have known. Otherwise the story was as vivid and full of exact detail as a good newspaper report by a journalist who was there to see and hear what happened. Perhaps the centurion who watched Jesus die and declared that he was a just man was the same centurion who had earlier thought himself unworthy to ask him into his house?

Bernard said nothing about that Sunday Mass to Thamar.

On the Friday of that week, Holy Week, Thamar didn't go to the château but sat in the silence of his winter room, without lighting the fire, while Bernard took Félix for a long walk through the woods, where birds sang and green shoots were piercing the litter of dead leaves and ferns were beginning to uncurl. Félix chased rabbits in vain.

After a lunch consisting of bread and water and no coffee, Thamar and Bernard walked all the way to Saint-Christophe and, in a bigger church with more people in the congregation, and the same priest, Bernard heard Sunday's story again, this time with better readers. The same story, differently told. Like reading another journalist's account in a different newspaper; what had happened was clearly what had happened. When the priest carried a large crucifix through the church to the altar, Bernard looked at Thamar to see if it was all right for him to follow the line of people walking up to kiss the foot of the cross. Thamar nodded.

Back in the dining room, trying to find a way of putting into fewer and calmer words Thamar's several muddled accounts of his brief obsession with Anir, he gave up the effort, shut his laptop, and wondered why, at the back of the line of people who seemed grief-stricken by what had happened to Jesus, he had followed Thamar to the cross.

Beside his laptop on the plush tablecloth was the booklet of the Good Friday Liturgy which Thamar had said he could take home from the church.

Yes. It was partly because of the words being sung by the choir, four oldish men and two women singing only fairly well.

Extraordinary words. "My people, what have I done to you? How have I offended you?" It seemed to Bernard as if the figure on the cross were reproaching the people in the church, the people standing and watching as he died, all the people in the world. And there was also—he turned back a few pages in the booklet to check—the moment when Pilate said, "What is truth?" Bernard had no idea that so long ago a man who was obviously a powerful Roman official could be asking this question, a question Bernard had assumed was only modern, only asked by philosophers confronting the shifting certainties of science, the shifting uncertainties of a world that had left religion behind.

He looked at the booklet again. What had Jesus said to provoke Pilate's question? "I came into the world to bear witness to the truth. Whoever is of the truth hears my voice." So Pilate couldn't hear, couldn't recognize, the truth of God in this man standing in front of him, any more than the crowd could, the crowd shouting for him to be crucified. If, of course, it were true—again the question—that Jesus was bearing witness to the truth.

And Bernard, now? He didn't know. On the one hand, according to Thamar, God came into the world as Christ, a man whose death cancelled the sins, the sinfulness, of the whole human race, his death the witness to the truth that asks to be heard. On the other hand, couldn't all this be no more than the story, even if probably the true story, of an unusually good man who was unjustly killed? What he did now know was that this was the central question. He gave up. It was all too difficult.

Still he said nothing to Thamar.

The next day, Saturday, Thamar asked him to dig over the vegetable patch in the garden of the house and fork farmyard manure into each trench. Bernard had dug the whole patch properly in the autumn, so it was less hard work, now, to collect forkfuls of cow dung mixed with straw from the heap by the garden wall, chuck each forkful into the turned earth and cover it with a few inches of soil. A farmer, who, Thamar said, had kindly done this for years, had last month tipped the dung

451

over the wall from a trailer behind his tractor. Bernard enjoyed the work, convinced of the rich fertility of the stuff he was forking in. It smelt good, not disgusting as he had expected. The sun was shining and the grass, trees, flowers, birds, insects, he could see, feel and hear coming back to life with the spring as he trudged backwards and forwards the length of the garden with his barrow of manure, fork stuck in to the load, wearing Thamar's oldest, cracked, boots.

"Today is the strangest day of the year", Thamar had said at breakfast. "A day of absence. Christ is among the dead." That was all.

In the evening, when Bernard, dirty and tired, had had a bath and appeared in the kitchen for supper, Thamar said, "There is a beautiful liturgy tonight, the vigil, the watch before the dawn, when a great candle is lit in the darkness. But it's in Saint-Christophe, where there are more people, and I'm too old to walk there and back so late. We'll go to Mass in the village in the morning. Easter Day."

On Sunday, at the nine o'clock Mass, the priest was tired; the reader, today with the right spectacles, still read in a flat, joyless voice; the two-year-old yelled when his mother wouldn't give him the chocolate he was asking for. Bernard did his best, to concentrate, to listen, to believe that Jesus had returned from the dead and was alive among his friends, and that that made all the difference to everything, but most of all to the sinfulness of the world. It was no good. Jesus remained for him the lifeless figure on the cross, over the fire in Thamar's winter room, and in the church at Saint-Christophe where Bernard had knelt and kissed the cross in his own insignificant reparation for the injustice and cruelty of this death. How could this one good man, of all human beings in the whole of time, have left the grave—the Gospel reading at Mass had told of his followers finding his tomb empty—and been alive again for them to see and listen to and eat with?

"It's useless", he said to Thamar when they were back at the kitchen table eating their Sunday lunch with—a rare treat bought in the village shop by Thamar for Easter—peaches and ice cream after their soup and cheese.

"What's useless?"

"It's me that's useless, no doubt. I can't do it."

"What do you mean, Bernard?"

What exactly did he mean?

"They were delicious, the peaches and the ice cream. Thank you, Thamar", Bernard said, giving himself a moment to think.

A nod of acknowledgement.

"Well. Easter is the great feast, you know" Thamar said. "The feast that is the meaning of every Sunday all the year, of every Mass."

Bernard had to try to explain.

"That's what I can't do, I mean, that's what my brain, my mind, I myself I suppose, can't accept, can't believe. I could believe last Sunday, and on Good Friday, that the story is true, that these things did happen, described differently by different people, that Pilate did say 'What is truth?' because he couldn't see, couldn't accept, the authority of the man he was supposed to be deciding about, while the centurion could. Do you think it was the same centurion, Thamar?"

Thamar smiled. "I have often wondered, myself. Perhaps it was. I hope it was. We shall never know. God knows."

Ah. This Bernard could cope with. It was or it wasn't the same centurion. Only God knows, but God does know. It didn't help, with Easter.

"But today—the empty tomb", he said. "Peter saying that he and other chosen people had seen Jesus alive, eating and drinking, and that his resurrection makes him the judge and also the one who forgives—I can't, I don't, believe it."

Thamar folded his hands in front of him on the kitchen table, looked down at them, motionless and far away from Bernard in his stillness, and after a long silence, raised his head, and said, "That's not surprising, Bernard, not surprising at all. Today was the third time in your life that you have been there at Mass, the fourth if you count sitting beside your friend in the cathedral at Nantes, which I certainly do. You have come far, and taken in a lot, in a very short time. But the news of today, the news of Easter, which seems impossible, crazy, beyond all ordinary understanding, is at present too much for you. I know, I promise you, where you are. I have been there. I have been back there many times, even as a priest. All you can do is persevere. Try it, as Pascal said. Keep going—keep going to Mass. Wait patiently. And, perhaps, one day—you will discover that—"

Bernard waited. But Thamar didn't finish his sentence. Instead, he said, "Because this is the centre and heart and soul of it all. Saint Paul said, 'If Christ has not been raised from the dead, your faith is empty and you are still in your sins.'"

Bernard shook his head.

"There you are", he said. "The connection between Christ and our sins, even the connection between his death and our sins, never mind his coming back to life, doesn't make any sense to me. None at all. Saint Paul would say I have no faith, and he would be right."

Bernard was nearly in tears.

"I'm sorry, so sorry, Thamar."

"If you persist, I believe it will come. Belief, again, Bernard, different from deduction, different from proof. But belief, if it is given by God, is strong. And it comes first, *fides quaerens intellectum*, belief seeking understanding, not the other way round."

"But—"

"Enough. It is Easter Day. Make us some coffee."

Through what always afterwards seemed to him a blessed spring, he worked on what he planned to be the last section of Thamar's book. This was more difficult for him, by far, than the two long sections he had, he thought, more or less finished, although he found that he could improve almost every sentence when he read it again. He worked hard, and when he couldn't hear his sentences any more, he walked or bicycled through the woods and hills and vineyards as Burgundy became every day more beautiful. He went several times to Cluny and sat in the museum looking at the model of the abbey as it had been. Almost no one else visited the museum. He didn't go back to Tournus. He was afraid he wouldn't find again whatever it was that he had discovered there.

With the Mass he persevered. He walked with Thamar every Sunday morning, and knelt, towards the back of whichever church they had come to, watching Thamar, usually last in the line of people going up to receive Holy Communion, until he turned to come back, when Bernard bent his head and must have looked as if he were praying.

He also read, with real and growing interest, about Jesus's life, preaching, stories, cures, arguments. He had asked Thamar where to start. "Read Luke's Gospel, slowly. Then John's Gospel. Don't worry too much as you read. Just listen. Pay attention. It will all seem very long ago. But it's not."

So he read a chapter every night, sitting up in bed so as not to fall asleep before he had got to the end.

He had been surprised by how brief and how fresh Luke's account of Jesus's life was. And how believable. Bernard was sure that Mary and Joseph had lost the twelve-year-old Jesus in Jerusalem, and that worry and relief, as with any ordinary parents, made them angry with him when they found him. And that, even as a boy, Jesus was clever enough to be talking intelligently with scholars, rang true. How quick and how effective was Jesus's answer to enemies who wanted to trick him into some kind of opposition to the authority of the Romans: the coin with Caesar's portrait on it was clearly Caesar's, so paying it in tax to the Romans was returning it to its owners. Bernard, the morning after he read about this, looked at the coins in his hand when he bought himself a coffee at the Café de la Paix so that he could email his mother, and thought, "money belongs to the Republic, not to me, and that's good".

Later, after he had read carefully through Luke's account of Jesus's trial and death, the same account that he had heard on Palm Sunday at the second Mass he had been to with Thamar, he envied the two puzzled travellers who had been joined by Jesus on the road. Although he talked to them as they walked and explained who he was and what had been foretold about him, they didn't recognize him until, at supper, he broke the bread and gave it to them. So had they been there, these two, at the last supper? Or had they only heard about it? If they had only heard about it, they were lucky, blessed, whatever was the right word, to see that Jesus was alive, was there with them, just as he disappeared. Could that have happened? Either it did or it didn't. Either Jesus was there, now, when the priest broke the bread at the altar. Or he wasn't. Again.

The very end of Luke's Gospel he couldn't understand at all. The risen Jesus had returned to heaven was what it said. Why wasn't this a disaster for his friends? Why weren't they sad to lose him? Yesterday, Thursday, was the feast remembering this disappearance, the Ascension. Bernard had gone with Thamar to the nine o'clock Mass in the village for the feast, and couldn't see why it was a celebration. He said nothing.

Thamar hadn't asked him how he was getting on with his reading, and Bernard had kept quiet about this too: he wanted to seem, or to become, less childish before he asked Thamar to explain anything in the gospels. Tonight he would read the first chapter of John's Gospel.

And now, after their anniversary supper, Thamar said, "Well, Bernard. What did you want to ask me?"

Bernard took a sip of his wine.

"I think it's a question about the Church. As well as a question about you, Thamar, of course. How is it that, after everything you wrote in your book about—about Anir and what you discovered then, and how you had to stop being a White Father and work for the Sisters in Ghardaia, and then came here and lived, well, as you live now—how is it that when you go to Mass you go up to receive Holy Communion with the other people?"

A long silence, Thamar looking down at the table. Damn, damn, Bernard thought. He had made a mess of asking the question. And he shouldn't have asked it. He almost hadn't asked it

"I'm sorry", Bernard eventually said. "I shouldn't have mentioned something you never wrote about. Forgive me, Thamar."

Thamar looked up, brought his gaze back to Bernard's from somewhere far away.

"No, Bernard. You should, have asked me this. It's an important question. You see—"

He paused again, but this time not for long.

"For many years, in Ghardaia and then when I came home, so for nearly twenty years, I stayed, so to speak, on the edge of the Church, because that was where I was certain I had to be. The Church says that homosexual people are 'intrinsically' or 'objectively' 'disordered'. I could not, I cannot, change who I am."

"But, Thamar—" Bernard couldn't help interrupting, and immediately wished he hadn't.

"But?", the old man said, shaking his head and looking at Bernard as if he had thought he was alone. Damn again: he shouldn't have stopped him, startled him.

"I'm so sorry", he said. "I shouldn't have interrupted you. I was shocked. How can something no one can help be described as 'intrinsically disordered'? What a horrible phrase, by the way. If someone has short sight, or is deaf, or has Down's Syndrome are they to be described as intrinsically disordered? No one can help any of these things, any more than a person can help being gay. Are all these people intrinsically disordered? Fascists would think so, I suppose. Maybe the *Front National*, who probably think black people, North Africans, Muslims, Jews, intrinsically disordered. But Christians?"

"Ah, Bernard. You are young. The way people of your age think about these things is so much better, so much kinder, than the way people used to think."

"But this is real stuff, not just fashion, changing times. This is you, Thamar, in your life. If that's what the Church says about being gay, I can't understand why you didn't just leave the Church altogether."

"No. Of course you can't. But I couldn't leave the Church, not then, not ever, because, to me, that would mean deserting the truth. The Church is a human institution. It is fallible, even wrong, even cruel, about some things, some rules, some definitions, which may change in time. Some of its rules and definitions have changed, you know, down the centuries. But the Church is where the truth is, where Christ is to be met, to be loved. You know quite enough about me by now to see that I could not abandon it. Even if, when, it seemed that it had abandoned me. I don't have, I have never had, a Protestant soul." He stopped, shook his head as if to collect his thoughts, and started again.

"In any case, as I was trying to explain—"

"I'm sorry, Thamar."

Now he smiled at Bernard and waved a deprecating hand.

"Here I lived, as I had lived in Ghardaia, beyond the reach of the sacraments—you don't know what that means, Bernard. It means that I could not be absolved of my sins, reconciled to the Church, because my most serious sin seemed to be who I am. I couldn't turn my back on who I am and decide to be someone else, as one might turn one's back on a vice or a bad habit or a nursed resentment. So I could not receive Holy Communion at Mass, and if I had died— well, who knows? But then—"

He paused.

"But then?" Bernard said.

"This will sound very strange to you, I know, because you can't, or perhaps—" His crooked smile across the table. "Or perhaps you can't yet, have any idea of what it actually is to be a Catholic. In any case, in the summer of 2013, nearly three years ago, I read in *Le Monde* that the new Pope had said in an aeroplane to the journalists who were travelling back with him from Brazil something entirely new about homosexuality. I remember his words exactly. He said, 'The question is: if a person who has that condition, has good will, and looks for God, who are we to judge?' I sat at the table outside on the terrace, with *Le Monde* in front of me, and everything looked different because of the Pope's words.

"I think I understood in that moment that, while homo-sexual people—like, as you say, the blind or the deaf or the damaged—can be called intrinsically disordered, so can every single human being in the world. We are incomplete, liable to sin at any moment, responsible directly or indirectly for harm to others, lazy, selfish, proud. Of course we are intrin-sically, objectively, disordered, all of us. Augustine knew this very well. The sacraments help us to make new beginnings, to come closer to Christ. They are for the disordered, not for the

458

perfect, since the perfect human being does not exist. I had known this, I thought, for many, many years. Perhaps I had never really known it."

He stopped, remembering, Bernard saw, that one moment with *Le Monde* at the table under the summer flowers on the terrace.

"So I asked Monsieur le curé at Saint-Christophe to hear my Confession, as I have done regularly since then, and I began again to receive Holy Communion."

Bernard saw that this was the end of what Thamar had to say. He thought he more or less understood, but this last piece, or what he had seen as this last piece, of the puzzle that was Thamar's life was somehow an anti-climax, perhaps because he couldn't imagine exactly what resuming his life as an unbanished Catholic, or however it should be described, had meant to Thamar. A great deal? Probably.

"I think I understand", he said after a few moments. "Thank you, Thamar."

But he sat at the kitchen table and wondered whether the last section of the book he was trying to write perhaps didn't exist, shouldn't be written. Perhaps the book should just stop at Thamar's return to the village more than twenty years ago with his damaged face and his quiet, harmless life beginning as it had continued all this time.

"Does this help, Bernard?", Thamar said.

"It does, of course. But—"

"But?"

He wasn't going to say anything about the book.

"I wanted to ask you something quite different."

"Of course."

"How do you imagine that the Church in France is going to survive for people younger than you are? All the Catholics seem to be old. How many young people do we see at Mass in the three churches here? How many children? And the poor priest of Saint-Christophe, Monsieur le curé, who's quite old himself, and so tired, with too many churches to look after: he can't live for ever. Quite soon, won't all the little churches in the country be closed?"

Thamar spread his hands, palms upwards, above the kitchen table.

"What is to be done?" He said this with his crooked smile, and went on, "You are right, Bernard, of course. And yet—I have a kind of hope, I don't know whether or not it is a reasonable hope, that some young people will begin to see that they need, that's to say they may notice that there is something inside them that needs, more than whatever it is that modern life throws at them all day, every day. They need a sane and sensible faith in what is good and true, in what does not change, even in what the coming of Christ means to the world, to sustain them. I have read in *Le Monde*, which does report on what is happening even if it is a newspaper for secular intellectuals, that more young people are beginning to go to Mass in Paris, although their parents, their grandparents, may never have been to Mass except for the occasional funeral. *Le Monde* suggests that this is because these young people are frightened of Islam. It doesn't occur to the kind of people who write in *Le Monde* that these young people may be frightened of nothingness, truthlessness, the secular void. And of course there are many Muslims who are horrified by the terror attacks, and by what is happening in Syria and Iraq, and, alas, in poor Libya, who understand that the extremists are not real Muslims and that they themselves must be more, not less, faithful to what is good and true in Islam, which of course is a great deal.

"It is the young who need to think again about the false god of *laïcité* which they have been brought up to worship. This word, this sacred word—how much irony is there here?— should be used only of the state. The state, the Republic, is lay, in itself secular. Therefore *laïcité* should be used as a means to allow religious people to learn, to think, to worship God without being ordered to by anyone. Instead, now, the word *laïcité* is used as a means to bully Muslims, and even sometimes to bully Catholics, because they are religious. If this goes on, the atmosphere in France will get even worse, even more dangerous. Good Catholics and good Muslims must understand that what they share, a trust in God and a reliance on his mercy, is more important than anything that divides them. And the young must learn this too, if France is to become a gentler, a more civilized country than it is at present. There is hope, I think, I trust. After all—"

Thamar smiled as he heard himself say this. "That's what my grandmother used to say", he said. "Always, to calm herself. After all."

"I know", Bernard said.

"Well, after all, you have found my mixed and untidy life interesting enough to work on it for months, haven't you? And I hope not only because I happen to be your grandfather. And—you are young. So there is hope, represented by Bernard Charpentier. No?"

"Perhaps. But I hope so", Bernard said.

"There you are", Thamar said, as if he had proved something.

"But I'm still so confused about so much. Working on the book has taught me a great deal about things I knew nothing about, absolutely nothing, or so it now seems to me. But there's much more to learn. And by the summer, well, by early in July, I suppose, when the holidays start, the time when I came here to start on the book last year, I will have to go back to Paris and try to find some work of a kind my father will think serious."

Then he added what he felt most of all.

"And I wish the book were better."

The next morning, Saturday, Bernard went to email his mother and have some coffee at the Paix, as he did every Wednesday and Saturday. It suited both of them to stick to a simple routine for messages.

"Morning, Bernard", said Hortense from behind the bar as he opened the door from the terrace where the little tables were already set out in the sunshine.

"Café au lait?", she said, as always.

"Please. And a croissant. It's such a beautiful day." The croissant was a treat he allowed himself occasionally.

Hortense, and so the whole village, knew he was staying with Monsieur Thamar, and helping him to write a book. It had been easier to tell the truth when Hortense first asked him why he was there. She also knew that he was Madame

Charpentier's son—"the charming lady who visited us in the spring"—but that was all she knew.

"How's it going, Bernard?", she said as she brought him his coffee. "How is Monsieur Thamar?"

"He's fine, thank you, madame. And the work's going reasonably well. I should have finished the book quite soon."

"Then you'll be going back to Paris?"

"That's right."

"We shall miss you. The village could do with more nice, well-brought-up boys like you. The young ones who do well at school all leave the village. They go to Chalon, or Lyon, or even Paris, to work in offices and that, and we don't see them again. Girls as well as boys. It's a shame."

"Yes, it is a shame." He opened his laptop and she went through the door into the kitchen.

"Give me a shout, Bernard, if a customer comes in."

There was, as usual, an email from his mother. He opened it.

Bernard. There is terrible news. The police came this evening when Papa and I got back from school. Joséphine is in prison—in detention, they called it—because she is a suspected terrorist. She is in Paris. They say she has been in Paris for months—can you believe it?—living with some North African boys in Ivry. They have all been arrested. Guns and home-made bombs in their flat, the police say. Your father is in despair. One of us is allowed to see her on Monday. I think it should be me. Please come home if you can.

Maman

His mother had sent the message the evening before, Friday evening, when he and Thamar had been eating their anniversary dinner.

Bernard replied at once:

Maman—I am so very sorry. How dreadful for you and papa. How could she be so stupid? I will come home today of course. I will call you from Mâcon. B

462

He hadn't got his little mobile phone with him, and he hadn't charged the battery for weeks.

He picked up his coffee cup, and put it down untasted. His poor parents. They didn't deserve this. No parents did. He was furious with Joséphine. At the same time he realized that he wasn't all that surprised. The wretched girl had never been interested in anything except the most superficial rubbish, pop music, clothes, endless chatting to her friends on the internet. Perhaps this news proved that she had been drawn into sinister propaganda she found online. Or—and Bernard thought this more likely—she had met and fallen for some fanatical young man on her travels. He groaned. What to do next, now this minute? Poor Thamar.

He looked round the empty, familiar, friendly bar of the café. He might be seeing it for the last time.

He got up, crossed the room and knocked on the kitchen door.

"Hortense!"

"Coming!"

She appeared, wiping her hands on a tea towel. As always. "What is it, Bernard? Not a customer?"

"Hortense, I've had bad news from home. I have to go to Paris today. Can you let me use your telephone? And have you the number of a taxi in Mâcon?"

"Not your mother? Your father?"

"No. They are well. But I have to get home."

She looked hard at him. He saw her decide not to ask any more questions.

"Here", she said. The telephone was behind the bar. "There are the taxi numbers, just behind the phone."

"Thank you."

He asked the taxi to pick him up in half an hour.

He was leaving the café without his laptop when Hortense called him back.

"Don't forget this. And, Bernard, drink your coffee. You have a lot to do."

He drank a little of his coffee, found money in his pocket.

"I'm sorry", he said. "This is for everything, and the telephone call."

"No, Bernard. You're not paying for the telephone. Out of the question. And take the croissant. Eat it on the way back to Monsieur Thamar's. Here's your change."

As he left, she said, "I hope we'll see you back very soon."

Thamar was in the garden, tying straggling stems of climbing plants to hazel sticks which Bernard, under detailed instruction, had cut in the woods in March, and arranged in two rows in a richly manured patch of the vegetable plot. "For sweet peas. Wait and see." The seedlings had grown through the winter on the sill of the dining room window. Now they were three or four feet high, and flower buds were showing.

Félix bounded over to the gate when Bernard opened it, led him to Thamar and didn't lie down. The dog stood, tail wagging, gazing up at Bernard. Time for a walk.

"No, Félix, I'm sorry", Bernard said.

Thamar, bending over to cut lengths of twine from the ball at his feet, straightened up, almost losing his balance.

"Bernard, what is it?", he said. "You look terrible."

"Thamar, my sister has been arrested, in Paris. It seems she has been in Paris for months. I must go home."

"Arrested? For what?"

"Terrorism."

"No!"

The old man dropped the knife he was holding. Both hands went to his chest. For a moment he gasped for breath. Bernard stepped forward to stop him falling. Thamar shook his head before Bernard touched him.

"It's all right", he said. "I must sit."

Bernard picked up the knife. Slowly they walked up the garden to the terrace. Thamar sat. Bernard fetched a glass of water.

"Thank you."

After drinking some water and taking some slow breaths, Thamar said, "Your poor mother. You must go home, of course."

"Yes. I'm sorry, Thamar. I have a taxi coming to take me to the station."

"Naturally. Go and get your things ready. Félix will stay with me."

It was unlike him to show that he was perhaps afraid. But he looked a bit better.

Ten minutes later Bernard was ready.

"You will come back?"

"Of course. I haven't finished the book. I've left my winter clothes and other stuff in my room. And the printed sections of the book are still on the dining room table."

A smile.

"The book is of no importance. But—I'm glad you will be coming back."

"Yes, Thamar. I will come back. I don't know when, obviously, but as soon as I can. And the book is of much importance—to me in any case."

When the taxi driver banged on the door, Bernard hugged Félix, put a hand for a moment on Thamar's shoulder, and left them on the terrace.

"God bless you, my boy. God bless all of you."

In Paris, Bernard's parents were as he expected them to be: his mother was brave, tearful, reproaching herself for not having been close enough to Joséphine in the year before she disappeared; his father was angry with everything, with the government, with the "useless" President, with *Charlie Hebdo* for provoking Muslims, with the whole of France for supporting *Charlie Hebdo*, with America and Britain for invading Iraq when France had the sense not to join in, and with the city authorities in Paris who for generations had tidied away the North Africans in the slums of the *banlieues* in order not to upset the tourists. Underneath all this rage, of which Bernard could see his mother had already had more than enough, was his father's fury with Joséphine, and with himself for more or less telling her that, as far as he was concerned, the *baccalauréat* was the only important goal of an eighteen-year-old's life.

"Jean-Claude", his mother said, when, still on Saturday, they had finished eating dinner, without noticing what they

465

were eating, and his father had been ranting for ten minutes, "That's enough. We are where we are. We have to think of something, anything, we might be able to do to help Joséphine now. Bernard, you have said almost nothing—"

With both his parents looking at him as if he could somehow produce a constructive idea, Bernard said, "Tell me exactly what the policemen said last night. You said there were two of them?"

His father, as if he couldn't bring himself to go over it all again, waved at Bernard's mother.

"That's right", she said. "They were quite polite to us. The older one was obviously sorry for us. Apparently, they arrested Joséphine yesterday, early in the morning, because a neighbour, a Vietnamese woman, they said, had reported that she'd seen one of the boys in the flat buying in the local ironmonger's what the police called 'suspicious items'. They didn't say what they were. They searched the flat. They can search anywhere, just like that, at present, because of the state of emergency after the attacks. They found four guns and stuff, 'primitive materials', they said, for making bombs. Three boys and Joséphine, living in two rooms, the younger boys only nineteen. The oldest boy, who is twenty-seven, seemed to be Joséphine's boyfriend. Nearly ten years older than she is. Oh—"

She stopped, pulled out a handkerchief, blew her nose and sniffed.

"I'm sorry, Bernard. After all this time, nearly a year, it's so horrible to find—The worst thing is to find that she's been living in Paris all this time and never told us, never called us, even to say she was alive—"

She blew her nose again, wiped her eyes with the handkerchief.

Bernard's father scraped back his chair and got up.

"This is just upsetting your mother, Bernard. I'm going out for some fresh air."

He left the kitchen. The front door of the flat banged shut.

His mother gazed after him and then turned to Bernard and said, "Thank goodness. He may feel better if he goes for a brisk walk."

"I'm so sorry, maman, about all this. Papa being so angry isn't helpful, I can see. But it isn't surprising. I'm sure he's mostly angry because he's blaming himself, which neither of you should be doing. Whoever has led Joséphine into this nightmare is to blame, not you or papa. "

His mther looked sadly across the kitchen table at him.

"We didn't lead her, that's true, but did we push her? Did we turn her away from us, turn her towards whatever horrible ideas or people have got hold of her now, because we only wanted her to be the sort of daughter we expected her to be? Could I have tried harder to get her to talk to me? I don't know."

Bernard couldn't answer these questions, so he said, "What else did the policemen say?"

"They said she is being held—whatever that means, in a prison I suppose, or a police cell—by the anti-terrorist police until they, and the examining magistrate, have finished inter-rogating her. Then they will decide whether to charge her, and what to charge her with."

"How long?"

"How long is this likely to take? I asked them. They said 'it depends'. Weeks, certainly, perhaps months. 'The state of emergency, you understand, madame.' That's all they said."

"Has she got a lawyer?"

"Papa asked them that. Apparently they asked her if she wanted a particular lawyer. Of course she had no idea, so she was allotted one, from a list. We don't even know who he, or I suppose she, is. There seems to be nothing, absolutely nothing, we can do to help her. But one of us is allowed to see her on Monday. Papa wants me to go."

"Much better than him going. I wish I could come with you."

"O, Bernard. So do I. But I'm afraid it's not allowed. As it is, I have to take time off work, and I don't know what to tell Doctor Picard."

Doctor Picard was the director of the *lycée*, a remote figure whom Bernard, being a good boy at school, had never properly met, though his mother had been his secretary for years.

"Tell him the truth, maman."

She looked at him in amazement.

467

"I can't Bernard. I can't. Papa would be furious, even more furious than he is already."

"Never mind papa. You need support, help. Both of you do. Monsieur Picard has known papa for twenty years and you for—what?—at least ten. He must be aware that a number of children of respectable, bourgeois parents like you, with no religious background, no education in Islam, have decided to run away from home, to be jihadists or whatever Joséphine thinks she is."

His mother looked at him for a long moment, and slowly nodded.

"You're right, of course. Why isn't papa here? He would have to agree. I will tell Doctor Picard the truth. He will be horrified. But he may know—he may even know how we can find her a good lawyer, experienced in these dreadful things, and not just someone from a list."

She stretched a hand across the table and put it on Bernard's.

"You know, maman", he said, "we must be grateful that at least she's safe in Paris, even if she's in detention, and not in Syria or Iraq, in terrible danger, or even dead."

"What a comfort you are, Bernard. Thank God you weren't in North Africa and could easily come home."

He saw her realize that, in the hours since he arrived, she hadn't said anything about Burgundy, about the book, about her father.

"I'm so sorry, darling. I haven't even asked you how he is, Monsieur Thomas. Was he very shocked about Joséphine?"

"Of course. But perhaps not very surprised. He was mostly anxious about you."

"Not surprised, you say?"

"He has seen a lot, lived through a lot, and he thinks every day about the world, about France, about Islam too. I have learned a great deal from him."

"He must have been sad that you had to leave him, for such an unpleasant reason, too."

"Yes. But I promised to go back. I haven't quite finished the book."

"Are you pleased with it, with what you've done so far?"

"I don't know. It's difficult to tell whether it's any good when you're so close to it, and to the person who really wrote it, though what he wrote was a terrible muddle."

"What does he think of it?"

"He hasn't read it."

"What? You've been doing all this work and he hasn't read it?"

"No. I don't know if he ever will. I think in some way he wants it to be entirely separate from him, from how he lives now. He's a complicated man."

"Are you fond of him, Bernard?"

His mother's phrase didn't come close to what, after almost a year, he felt about Thamar.

"Of course", he said. "I couldn't have lived with him, alone with him, all these months if I didn't love him. And after all",— he smiled as he said this—"he is my grandfather."

She smiled.

"I know", she said. "It's still difficult for me to grasp—exactly that. So, in any case, you haven't been bored, out in the country with only one old man to talk to?"

"I haven't been bored. I've been interested, every day."

On Monday afternoon, Bernard was waiting for his mother to come back from the headquarters of the anti-terrorist police where Joséphine was being held. After a silent breakfast with his parents, who had left for work before eight in the morning, he had spent most of the day walking.

Yesterday, Sunday, he had wanted to go to Mass because he wanted to see what the Church would tell everyone now that Christ had gone back to heaven and the Holy Spirit hadn't yet arrived: Thamar had told him that at Pentecost, the feast that Thamar had blundered into long ago in Saint Étienne-du-Mont, the Holy Spirit would come. And Bernard was now in the habit—he remembered what Thamar had told him about habits—of going to Mass on Sunday mornings.

But he couldn't further upset his parents by doing something so strange. His father would certainly blame Thamar for leading Bernard into, at best, romantic nostalgia, at worst, dangerous right-wing superstition. And Bernard, who had spent all his childhood in the same flat, played and gone to school in the same neighbourhood, didn't know where the nearest church was.

But today he was alone. So he walked, across the bottom of the Champ de Mars, up to the Invalides where he had some coffee at a little table in the park, under the trees, their new leaves pale, fresh green, and thought the golden dome had never shone so brightly. He walked along the Rue de Varenne, past the grandest houses in Paris, hidden behind their carriage doors and courtyards, turned towards the Seine, and reached the Latin Quarter. At the crossroads of the Boulevard Saint-Germain and the Boulevard Saint-Michel, he stood on the corner with his back to the Musée de Cluny—why was it called the Musée de Cluny? He had no idea—and watched the buses, taxis, cars stop at the red lights, move forward all together when the lights changed. If someone were a couple of seconds slow to move, the driver behind hit his horn. Otherwise order prevailed. Students, half of them looking at phones, old ladies shopping, a few tourists, some pointing their phones to take photographs, some old enough to have maps in their hands, walked at different speeds on the wide pavements. Bernard shut his eyes to listen to the shouting, the sirens, the loudspeakers, the thud of batons and swung lead-lined capes on bodies, the chant of *Algérie française* and the cries of the injured, from long ago at this crossroads. Thamar had been so young, younger than Bernard was now.

He opened his eyes. Calm, tidy, early May on the Left Bank. He started walking. As he turned left off the Boulevard Saint-Michel towards the Panthéon, where he had been once, on a school trip when he was about ten, he saw four policemen, or, more likely, soldiers, watchful with machine-guns, at the doors.

Wretched Joséphine and his frightened mother: what would they say to each other?

He found the church of Saint-Étienne-du-Mont. It was much grander than he expected, and larger too, only small in comparison to the huge bulk of the Panthéon. The stone pediment over the central door was like the pediment on a Greek temple, thick with sculpture and supported by four ribbed and banded stone pillars. The wall on the right must have been the wall against which Thamar and Syrie caught their breath when they had escaped the riot. Then, there were lights in the church. They hadn't gone inside. Now, the main door and the smaller doors to each side were all shut and locked. He stood and gazed at the elaborately carved front. He felt homesick for the village churches of Burgundy.

He thought of Chapaize. Two weeks ago, on his Saturday bike ride, he had arrived at Chapaize, on Thamar's recommendation, at about this time of day. Late morning. A little village of stone houses with weathered red-tiled roofs. Trees in new leaf. A minibus and one car parked near the church. And the church—pale grey, almost white, simple stone, grey stone roof-tiles, a beautiful bell tower, tall over the village, with two rows of double, round-headed window arches at the top, He went inside. Plain, heavy rough stone pillars, round arches, thick, heavy masonry, no decoration, no elaboration. Best of all, a small congregation of monks in black habits—for a moment Bernard wondered if they were real—and Mass being said at the altar. They had reached what he had learned to call the Sanctus, which they said gently, all together. He knelt at the back for the rest of Mass. As the monks left the church, one of them smiled and said "good morning". Then, although Bernard had said only "good morning, Father" in reply, the monk said. "We are on a little tour of monastic churches in Burgundy. Chapaize was a Benedictine priory, you know. They built this church a thousand years ago." The monks got into their minibus and drove away.

When he got home, Bernard said to Thamar, "Chapaize is a perfect church." "Ah", Thamar said, "that's why I didn't want you to see it too soon."

A group of Japanese tourists arrived at Saint-Étienne-du-Mont. They gathered obediently round their guide, some of them listening, some of them taking photographs, while she talked, in Japanese, presumably about the history of the church.

Bernard waited. Perhaps a priest, or a caretaker, would arrive and open the church. No one came.

After some time he looked at his watch. Nearly midday. He walked through narrow streets to the river, emerged opposite Notre Dame, bought a ham sandwich and a Coca-Cola in a bar on the *quai*, crossed the Pont de l'Archevêché and sat on a bench to eat his lunch in the cathedral garden as Thamar had sat with Mathieu more than half a century ago.

Was the book any good? It was certainly a tidier story than Thamar was ever going to manage to tell, but would anyone want to read it? The old? There was so much they didn't want to remember, didn't, if they hadn't known it, want to know. The young? Bernard thought of the students in Nantes. Were they, even those of them who were supposed to be studying history or philosophy, interested in what had happened in the lives of their grandparents? Very little. Were they interested in the questions which Thamar had thought about all his life? Even less. And yet what was happening now in France, among the Muslims in particular, was serious—how many of them wanted to fight France, here or anywhere, how many of them were in prison encouraging each other in hatred and resentment, how many of them felt only neglected and condemned for nothing they had done? How much did Bernard's contemporaries care?

Why should a publisher take a chance on a book written by someone nobody had ever heard of, a true story about someone else nobody had ever heard of? How much did Thamar mind if the book were never published? Bernard realized he had no idea. And how much did he mind himself? It would matter to his father: this whole year out of Paris, out of what his father regarded as real life, could only be justified in his father's eyes if the book were published, if it sold some copies, if it helped Bernard to find what his father would see as a proper job.

What did he want to do with his life? It struck him for the first time, sitting on his bench among the neat tulips and mown grass of the park, with its low fences to keep children and dogs from untidying the grass, that he had less idea now that he had had a year ago. It also struck him for the first time that what he wanted most was to find someone else, someone who was not Thamar whom he loved, to teach him how to be a Catholic.

He crumpled the paper that had wrapped his sandwich and threw it into the litter bin because Mathieu had, and started walking home along the *quais*. There was plenty of time. His mother had been told to arrive at the police headquarters at three o'clock. He didn't know for how long she would be allowed to see Joséphine.

Joséphine. He walked beside the Seine, opposite the Louvre, opposite the Tuileries gardens, all the way to the Pont des Invalides, then turned left and was nearly back at the Champ de Mars, a few minutes from home. He had stopped noticing Paris, noticing the passers-by, noticing the spring. He was worrying about his mother, wondering if anything could be done to save Joséphine from the consequences of her own folly, more and more furious with her for putting both their parents through an ordeal that wasn't going to be over for months, years, perhaps ever.

Now he was waiting. He had read, without concentrating, some of his parents' *Le Figaro*. He went to the shop on the corner to buy *Le Monde* because he was used to it, and it was good to get it on the right day. Thamar's was always yesterday's paper. He couldn't concentrate on *Le Monde* either.

He made some coffee, not as good as Thamar's, and tried to read the American news in *Le Monde*.

At last he heard his mother's key in the door. He jumped up.

She came in, threw her bag on a chair and almost collapsed into another.

"O, Bernard."

"Maman, you look done in. I'll get you some coffee."

"Make me a tisane, there's a good boy. Verveine—there should be some in the top cupboard."

He made her tea, put the cup and saucer beside her on the little table, and sat down opposite her.

She sipped the tea, wincing because it was too hot.

"It was terrible, Bernard. She looks quite different, much more than a year older, and so thin. Dreadful prison clothes, of course, and long dirty hair—you know how she used to fuss about her hair."

"What did she say?"

"Very little. There was a guard, a woman, there all the time. Very grim. Not a smile for either of us in half an hour."

"Poor maman."

She sipped her tea.

"Was she pleased to see you, at least?"

"She cried when she saw me. I thought that was a good sign. But quickly she stopped. We were separated by a kind of wide bench. I couldn't hug her or even touch her. This woman was watching, to see that I didn't give her anything, I suppose.

"When she pulled her hands down her face to get rid of the tears, I saw what looked like a wedding ring. It reminded me of—"

"Reminded you of what?"

"Of something Monsieur Thomas told me. Never mind. So, Joséphine. I asked her if she is married. She said, 'Not really. But it helps with the others.' What can that mean?"

After a moment, Bernard said, "Did you ask her where she's been all this time?"

"Of course I did. She only said, 'We've been in Paris since November.' She looked at the guard and then said, 'They know that anyway, because of the neighbours.' I asked her, 'Who is "we"?' She shook her head, and said, 'You wouldn't understand.' She said that several more times. She would hardly look at me. O, Bernard, it was horrible. She's not herself, not Joséphine, silly and irresponsible. Not even cross and sulky. Just someone different. Imagine her being in Paris for six months and not getting in touch, not a call, not a message, nothing."

"Did you ask her where she was before she came back to Paris?"

"She wouldn't say."

"Anything about the boyfriend?"

"Just 'You wouldn't understand.'"

"Did they tell you anything about what will happen next? Or how long all this is likely to take?"

His mother miserably shook her head.

"I asked, of course, at the desk where they searched my bag. I was searched on the way in, and searched on the way out. The answer was nothing but a shrug. 'It depends', the officer said, exactly like the policeman on Friday, but didn't tell me what it depends on. She's allowed one visit a week. I said to her that perhaps Papa could come to see her next week. She said, 'No. Not papa. Please.' I thought perhaps next week, Bernard, you might go."

"Did you suggest that to her?"

"No. Because—"

"Because probably she would have said no?"

"Well, yes. I didn't want to give her the opportunity to say no. It's possible she'll talk a little more to you. You're young. She might not feel so—so angry with you as she seems to feel with us."

Bernard looked at his watch, stupidly he knew at once, because he wanted to get back to Thamar as soon as he could. His mother noticed.

"What is it? You're not going out?"

"No. Not at all."

"You want to go back, to Monsieur Thomas? Sooner than next week, I can tell."

"Maman, I'm sorry. I do want to go back, yes, because I want to finish the book in the next few weeks so that I can come back to Paris properly in July, as I promised papa I would. But I'll stay, now, as long as you think I can help. And of course I'll go to see Joséphine next Monday, if you think perhaps she might talk to me. Even if she won't, it would save you from repeating this awful afternoon, so soon. By the way, how did Doctor Picard take all this? You did tell him?"

"Yes. You were quite right. He was very kind. And he's going to see whether he can help us. He knows a lawyer, quite a famous lawyer apparently, whose children were at the *lycée* some time ago, who might know an expert lawyer who could be persuaded to take Joséphine's case. That would be wonderful, particularly for Papa."

Lawyers.

"You haven't told them in Rouen?", he said.

She almost laughed. "Absolutely not. Can you imagine their reaction? What would their friends say?"

"Joséphine's name hasn't been in the papers?"

"No, thank God. The boyfriend's name was in the *Figaro* on Saturday. Habib something. And the names of the two other young men. Arab names, of course. They were all arrested together. But Joséphine was just 'Joséphine C,' I think because she's so young. Long may it last. In Rouen they only read *Ouest France* in any case."

So Bernard spent the rest of the week in Paris. He had spent the whole of his childhood in the city. But on the fine days of this peculiar week, when he was staying at home only in order to see Joséphine, he walked the city as if he had never explored it before, because he hadn't.

His parents from Tuesday to Friday were out at work. Every day he did some shopping in the local street market for his mother, and some cooking for their dinner: he had learned from Thamar some useful ways of cooking vegetables, cheese, eggs. He left the meat for his mother to cook. Otherwise, his mother, at least, was expecting nothing from him except that he would be there in the flat when she got back from the *lycée*.

So he walked. Once he had done the breakfast dishes, he set out, always in the same direction, the Champ de Mars and then the Seine, the *quais* of the Left Bank as far as the Île de la Cité, and then into the Latin Quarter. After almost a year in the deep country, he felt like a tourist, a visitor, himself, as he passed, was passed by, so many people, heard so many languages, avoided those so wrapped up in whatever they were saying into their telephones that they weren't looking where they were going. There were beggars on the *quais*, in the Luxembourg Gardens, on the steps of important buildings: men in suits, women in suits, pressed buttons beside polished doors and went inside paying the beggars no attention. There were old drunks asleep, as in his childhood, but also Romanian gypsy mothers with babies and toddlers, Arab boys playing guitars, a young man with bandaged eyes, a notice hanging on his chest saying "blinded in Syria", with a scruffy dog asleep beside him. Bernard put some coins in the dirty baseball cap in front of him and the dog growled.

On Tuesday morning, he set out with no particular intention, and soon found that he was looking at, looking for, churches.

Notre-Dame, he thought. He had never been inside it. He sat on a bench among the tourists, the school parties and the pigeons for a while, looking at the great west front of the cathedral, the massive towers, the three huge doors, one with a slow line of visitors approaching it. There were pairs of watchful soldiers, with guns, at each door. He didn't go in. He thought perhaps he would look at the Sainte-Chapelle: he had sent that postcard of it to Thamar, because it was a church, but had never seen it, and it was a couple of minutes away. When he got there, he saw another line of tourists queuing at the entrance, and more soldiers. He remembered the blue and gold of the picture on the postcard. Again, he didn't go in.

He walked to the western end of the île de la Cité along the Quai des Orfèvres, looking up at the windows, one of which must have been the window of Maigret's office. His father had recommended Simenon's stories to Bernard as holiday reading when he was about fourteen; ever since, Maigret had been to him almost a real person. The barges on the Seine that Maigret was always watching from his window had gone. Leaning on the balustrade of the Pont Neuf, Bernard looked towards the Pont des Arts, the Louvre, the Pont du Carrousel: the river glittered in the spring sunshine as it flowed away from him, but there were no boats except for one half-empty *bateau mouche* chugging its way upstream towards Notre-Dame.

He walked a short distance back along the *quai* to cross the Pont Saint-Michel to the Left Bank. He stopped to read a new-looking memorial stone set into a wall near the bridge. "To the memory", it said, "of many Algerians killed in the bloody repression of the peaceful demonstration of 17 October 1961."

He stood still and read the words again.

There it was, an acknowledgement, so many years later, of the killings here, in Police Headquarters or on the *quai*, the killings Mademoiselle Gaillard had told Thamar about when he came back to Paris and couldn't find Mathieu. "Many Algerians": no number, no names. "The dead deserve names", a sentence of Thamar's. He stood a little longer.

He walked into the Latin Quarter, avoiding the Panthéon, to Saint-Étienne-du-Mont. Today the church was open. He went inside. No tourists, or at least no groups of tourists being lectured to by guides. One old woman, and far away from her, one old man were sitting, perhaps in prayer. A middle-aged foreign couple, English or German, were standing in front of a tomb, the man reading to his wife from a guidebook. Bernard didn't like the inside of the church any better than he had liked the outside. The elaborate extravagance of the carving everywhere, the carved stone screen like a bridge, the two carved spiral staircases: there was too much decoration, and it seemed to him to have little to do with the building being a church. But he'd better find Pascal's tomb, for Thamar's sake.

He waited for the serious German couple to leave, but the tomb they'd been looking at turned out to be Racine's. How much did he remember about Racine? They had read *Andromaque* and *Phèdre* at the *lycée*. He vaguely remembered stretches of formal, distant verse in formal, distant language, and also an impression of hysterical women in one emotional crisis after another: some of the girls in the class had loved all this, most of the boys, including Bernard, had been bored.

He turned his back on Racine's tomb and looked round the now quiet but over-cluttered, somehow expensive, church. Then he saw it, a simple plaque on the wall. Pascal. So young when he died, thirty-nine. 1662, the time of Louis XIV, Cardinal Richelieu, Versailles, everything he most disliked about French history, including Racine. What a world for Pascal to live and write in. He stood for a few minutes, in homage, for Thamar nearly fifty years ago.

"You have everything to gain and nothing to lose by taking a chance on Christianity being true": something like that, Thamar had read to him. "So try it."

But not here. Bernard looked at his watch. He had seen near the door a notice of Mass times in Saint Étienne. Twelve-fifteen today. In half an hour. He didn't want to stay for it.

Where next? He was in a part of Paris he had never been to. Knowing that most people of his age would have consulted a phone for directions, he was pleased to pull out of his pocket a folding street map that had always been beside the telephone in his parents' flat. He found the Rue Mouffetard, where Thamar had lived in a little room over a charcuterie. It was close by.

He walked all the way down what was now clearly a smart, expensive shopping street, with some real market stalls only at the far end. There were several charcuteries: it was impossible to tell where Thamar had lived, and no doubt the shop and his room had been 'developed', horrible word, out of recognition. In a very grand cheese shop with hundreds of different cheeses, he bought a small piece of Thamar's favourite Burgundian cheese as a treat for his parents, remembering that when Thamar was first living alone, just here, he used to eat camembert too ripe to be sold to proper customers.

Bernard was hungry. He walked between the surprisingly unforbidding exteriors of the *Grandes Écoles* whose doors no one he knew, except perhaps Doctor Picard, had ever entered, and, again avoiding the Panthéon, reached the Boulevard Saint-Michel, and crossed it into the Luxembourg Gardens. At a café table under trees, in now almost hot sunshine, he ate another ham sandwich, drank another Coca-Cola, watched small children playing on the grass while their mothers or nannies—impossible, as in Nantes, to tell the difference—talked at other tables, one or two spoon-feeding babies in pushchairs. Students were eating sandwiches at some tables, mostly alone, mostly reading or tapping at laptops and smartphones. More students wandered by, a boy and a girl holding hands, two boys talking, one of them shaking his head in firm disagreement, three girls laughing. A boy and a girl lay entwined under a tree not far away. An elderly man was reading *Le Figaro* at another table; he put the paper down, took off his spectacles and sighed. Bernard met his glance. The old man frowned.

After almost a year alone in the country with Thamar, Bernard watched these strangers in the middle of their unknown lives as if he had never before sat in a park at lunchtime surrounded by people old and young. He had done exactly this, often, in Nantes, though perhaps not in Paris. Briefly, he wished that he were still a student, with imminent examinations requiring organized work, looking forward to dancing with Marie, holding her hand as he walked her back through quiet streets to her hostel, treating her carefully so as not to upset her. He glanced at the couple kissing under their tree, and found that he was not envious, not at all, but pleased to be alone. And yet. What had happened to him during all those months in the village with Thamar, thinking and learning and talking about things that, when he was a student, he knew nothing about? He looked round at the café tables. Was there a girl he might join, talk to politely, perhaps like, perhaps take to a film? There were several girls by themselves at different tables. One, working on her laptop, was prettier than the others. She had long hair and glasses, like the girl he had met drawing in the museum at Cluny. He looked at his watch. There was time to go to an afternoon showing of a film and be back at the flat before his parents got home from work. Then he shook his head, finished his coca cola and stood up, leaving the money for his lunch and a tip on the table. He didn't want to pick up a girl. Not in the least. But, as he hadn't for months, he was missing Marie, her laugh, her happiness, her hand in his.

He set off towards the Seine, past the little lake in the middle of the park, past the Palais du Luxembourg, joining the people going back to offices after their lunch.

He knew what he wanted. He wanted to find a church that wasn't like Saint-Étienne-du-Mont, that was like the churches in Burgundy which he had got used to, kneeling beside Thamar and following what was happening in the Mass with more and more—what? Familiarity, yes. Interest, yes. Engagement of some kind with what was going on? Sometimes. But also moments of his old certainty, the conviction which he had collected from his father, his schools, his university, and which until now had never been tested, that this quiet ceremony to console a few old people who had known it all their lives, was just that, harmless, attractive in its way, but without substance, without reality, retelling an old story that was nothing more than an old story.

He wasn't going to find a plain, uncomplicated church in Paris. He looked at his watch again. Nor was he going to find a Mass at two o'clock on a Tuesday afternoon. He passed a big, ornate church, Saint-Sulpice, and didn't go inside, and then emerged from ordinary streets into the Boulevard Saint-Germain, a little way west of the crossroads with the Boulevard Saint-Michel where Thamar and Sylvie had been caught in the riot. There were crowds of tourists on the pavements on both sides of the wide street. This was guidebook three-star Paris, where he had almost never been. Here were the cafés he had read about, the Deux Magots and the Café de Flore—he was surprised to see them both still there—where years ago Sartre and de Beauvoir and Camus and Picasso had held forth and shown off: it had been exhilarating to find in Thamar's book that he, and even sceptical Mathieu, had, exactly when existentialism was the height of fashion among the young, taken it much less than seriously. On the pavement terraces of both the famous cafés, early in the afternoon, the tables were full, with people standing and waiting for a free chair or two. He stood in front of the Café de Flore terrace and saw, across the Boulevard, opposite the Deux Magots but set back from the street behind other buildings, a strong, plain church tower that was like the towers of Tournus.

He stood still, no longer noticing the tourists passing by, the cars, buses, lorries, motorbikes starting and stopping at the traffic lights in the Boulevard. The heavy, square tower was built, as at Tournus, like a castle keep: high up were arrow slits, or perhaps thin lights for a stone spiral staircase; at the top of the tower was the bell-chamber, a smaller square, with only one layer, instead of the two at Tournus, of colonnaded round arches; the pointed roof, naturally, was made of the grey-blue slate of Paris instead of the rust-coloured tiles of Burgundy.

He crossed the road and walked over a paved space with a couple of stalls selling popcorn, fizzy drinks, bicycle pennants and black and white postcards of 1950s film stars. The church had one large, open door. No armed police. He went inside, and through the next door into the church.

He took a deep breath, and breathed out slowly. This was exactly what, without knowing it, he had been looking for, and not expecting to find anywhere in Paris. The round arches and plain masonry of the nave and the transepts held in the stone the ancient simplicity he had learned to love in Tournus, had come upon in Chapaize, and had seen in some of the smaller churches, connected to Cluny, that he had visited on his bike rides in Burgundy. The church was darker than Tournus and some of the surfaces were coloured and patterned; he could see, too, that the choir had been built quite a bit later.

But he felt at home. There were only a few tourists, scattered, quiet. He walked slowly round the church and then sat for some time on one of the straw-bottomed chairs towards the back of the nave, wondering why he had been looking all day, without really intending to, for this particular kind of stillness.

Eventually, he had to look at his watch. He was going to have to walk fast to get home before his mother might reach the flat: she usually left the *lycée* before his father.

On his way out of the church he saw a framed notice giving a brief history of the building. An abbey church—of course, like Tournus, like poor destroyed Cluny, and the peaceful ruins of the abbey of his childhood in the green bend of the Seine—and more ancient than all of them. "Founded in 543." He looked back down the nave to the high altar. Not this building, obviously. But a church, nevertheless, so very long ago, and, here, now, in this most secular, most dismissive, most intellectual and un-Christian part of Paris, still a real and alive church. Mass—another, smaller notice, in the porch—Monday to Saturday at twelve-fifteen. Tomorrow. And at lunchtime so that his parents wouldn't know.

He walked briskly home.

As he put his key in the lock, he realized that he hadn't given Joséphine one minute's thought since he left the flat in the morning.

On Wednesday it rained all day, the Paris streets as grey as the sky, so, once he had done his mother's shopping, Bernard stayed indoors and worked at his laptop on the kitchen table.

He went back to the beginning of what he had written, and, reading slowly, made a number of very small changes, trying to leave out more words than he was adding, in accordance with the instructions of his French literature teacher at the *lycée* who, on the subject of essay-writing, had said to Bernard's class: "There's no merit in length for length's sake. Avoid adjectives. And, whatever else you do, avoid colourful adverbs."

The sun was shining again on Thursday. Today, Bernard had a plan.

He bought a postage stamp while he was shopping, returned to the flat and wrote a note to Thamar saying that he had to stay in Paris for a few more days because he had promised to visit his sister on Monday. But he would be back in the village on Tuesday, or Wednesday at the latest. "My mother sends her love", he added, although she knew nothing of this note. And he ended his message with a simple "B."

He put the letter in a postbox on his way to the river and walked, again, towards Notre-Dame along the *quais* of the Left Bank, enjoying the rinsed freshness of the city after the rain. He was going to be too early for Mass at Saint-Germain-des-Prés, so he crossed the Pont Neuf, nodded to Maigret's window on the Quai des Orfèvres, walked past the cathedral with its queue and its armed guards, and crossed the Pont Saint-Louis. And there, still there, on the point of the Île Saint-Louis, was the Alsatian brasserie where Thamar had failed to meet Mathieu, failed to say goodbye, on the night of the riot. Bernard stood for a moment, in memory of that disappointment, and then continued his walk to the other end of the island, back to the Left Bank across the Pont de Sully and along the whole first half of the Boulevard Saint-German, through the Place Maubert where the violence of the *Algérie française* riot had begun, across the Boulevard Saint-Michel and on to Saint-Germain-des-Prés. He reached the church at midday, as he had intended, and sat still, at the back of rows of chairs, for fifteen minutes, while a small, as usual mostly elderly, congregation assembled, waiting for the Mass he now thought he had been looking for since he arrived in Paris five days ago.

The Mass was quiet, calm, satisfying because he found that he didn't once doubt that he was present at a mystery that had in it meaning and a real connection to the truth of God, although as yet he wasn't able to understand how or why. This sense of security, new to him, was given to him partly by the

Gospel, a passage from St John in which Jesus was talking to God, his Father, about his hopes for the love and unity of his people stretching far into the future as the love between God and Jesus stretched back to the foundation of the world. "The world has not known you, but I have known you", Jesus said. Bernard thought of Thamar, and, with sudden longing for her company, among these words of promise, of his mother. Would he ever be able even to talk to her about all this?

The old priest celebrating Mass added, in one sentence, to Bernard's sense of security. When he had finished the Gospel reading, the priest took off his spectacles, looked up from the lectern at the dozen or so people in front of him, and said only, "You see, brothers and sisters, in these days of waiting for the coming of the Holy Spirit, it is fitting that we should give thanks for the prayer, which was and is for us, of Jesus himself."

After the Mass, Bernard went back to the children, the mothers and nannies, the students with their laptops, in the Luxembourg gardens, ate his sandwich, drank his coca cola, and thought about nothing. Then he walked home and went to sleep for two hours.

His mother woke him when she came back to the flat.

"Are you all right, Bernard?"

"I'm very well, maman. I walked quite far today. I had a—" But it was quite impossible for him even to begin to tell her about his day.

"You met someone?"

"Not exactly. But it was a good day."

"I'm glad. At least you are enjoying being in Paris for a few days, aren't you?"

"I am, yes. Thank you, maman."

"When papa gets home he may have some news for us. Doctor Picard asked to see him at the end of classes today."

"Is that good?"

She laughed.

"Not usually. But today it might be."

It was. When his father came home, he told Bernard and his mother that Doctor Picard had arranged for him to see a lawyer, not the one who had had children in the *lycée* but a colleague of his, who specialized in defending the interests of Arabs accused of terrorist activities.

"But Joséphine isn't an Arab. Or—"

"No. Joséphine is not an Arab. And even though—well, she doesn't look even the quarter Arab that she is."

"Berber", Bernard said.

"What?" his father said.

"It doesn't matter."

"In any case", his father went on, irritated now, "She needs a good lawyer even more than an Arab would. French children getting mixed up in terror plots are not popular with the authorities."

"When", Bernard's mother said, "is your appointment with the lawyer, Jean-Claude?"

"After school tomorrow. At five o'clock."

Bernard could see that his father was not looking forward to this meeting, so he wasn't surprised when his father said, "And you, Bernard. What have you been doing with yourself these last three days?"

"Not much, papa. Mostly walking. Yesterday it was wet so I did some work on the book."

"You do realize that being in Paris on account of Joséphine is an excellent opportunity for you to think about your future, don't you? If you still think you want to be a journalist, you should be making enquiries at newspaper offices, radio stations, wherever you think you might get a trainee job after the summer holidays."

"Yes, papa."

"Poor Bernard", his mother said. "He's been working very hard, you know, for—for my father. He deserves a few days off."

"We mustn't be too indulgent with him as well, Jamila. So you haven't taken any steps to find out about possible work, Bernard?"

"Not yet. No. I'm sorry, papa."

"You do realize that whatever you've been doing for your grandfather, helping him to write this book and so on, won't be of any use to you unless or until the book is published? Do you think that's likely?"

485

"It's difficult for me to tell."

"Exactly. And while we're on the subject of your future, how long are you intending to stay in Paris?"

"I'm going to see Joséphine on Monday. Then, unless there seems to be anything useful I can do to help you and maman deal with this mess, I thought I would go back to Burgundy on Tuesday so that I can finish the book and come home properly when I promised to, at the beginning of the holidays, or just before, so that perhaps I can find a job that I could start when everyone comes back at the end of August."

"That sounds sensible enough", his father said, without much enthusiasm. "And I do understand that, having done all this work, you must finish the book." He smiled, for the first time since he had come into the flat. "And who knows, perhaps it will turn out to be a masterpiece and you will make all our fortunes."

The next day, Friday, his last day alone, Bernard didn't go back to the Mass at Saint-Germain-des-Prés. He didn't want to risk a difference, a difference in him, a different priest, that would make it, after Thursday's Mass, a disappointment.

Instead he went to the museum, at the crossroads of Thamar's riot and not two hundred yards further than the Abbey of Saint-Germain-des-Prés, that he had never heard of until finding it in Thamar's account of that evening. The Musée de Cluny: he had done some simple research on his laptop and discovered that for hundreds of years it had been the Paris house of the abbots of Cluny, that the Roman baths underneath and beside it could still be seen, and that the museum had in it the national collection of medieval art and objects. He couldn't believe it: why had his schools taken him in various classes to the Louvre several times, to the Musée d'Orsay twice, to a number of other museums, but never to the Musée de Cluny? The usual laïcité priorities? Probably.

He spent a morning of enchantment in the museum. Everything was beautiful, interesting, from the irregular cobbled courtyard to the smallest jewels, reliquaries, illuminated manuscripts—"illuminated", what a perfect word for the bright colours, the red and blue and gold, of the tiny pictures—and pieces of stained glass windows, to the sculpture and, most amazing of all, the flowery pink and green tapestries of the Lady and the Unicorn, in a room by themselves where Bernard sat for an hour, some of the time alone. In the solid Roman bath-house he found capitals from a big church, like the capitals the girl had been drawing that day in Cluny. These were from Saint-Germain-des-Prés. Well!

Eating his sandwich for lunch, in a different café in the Luxembourg Gardens, he made a decision. When he came back from Burgundy to start what his father regarded as his real life, he would try to get a job in the Musée de Cluny. He had seen the museum attendants, one in each of the rooms, some old, some young, almost none middle-aged. Each one sat on a chair keeping an eye on the visitors. Obviously they were there to spring forward, set off an alarm, shout, or whatever, if a visitor looked like trying to steal or damage an exhibit or do anything dangerous to other visitors or the building. Dull work. Badly paid, no doubt. But, he imagined, almost always uneventful. Was it possible to do the job and read a book at the same time? He wasn't sure whether he had noticed anyone reading a book, though one or two certainly had open newspapers.

He would like to be surrounded all day not just by beautiful things but by these beautiful things, and by an atmosphere that Thamar would be able to explain better than he could himself. And such an undemanding job would give him time and space to do what he really wanted: to learn, to discover, to build on everything he had learned from Thamar. It would be difficult to persuade his father to accept that a year, say, doing something so unambitious while he set himself to study for what he might later become, wasn't a bad or a lazy idea. But he could try. His father wouldn't object to him living at home, and would approve of him earning enough to contribute a bit to the family finances. And his mother would be pleased.

He went back to the museum after his lunch. They let him in on the ticket that he had bought in the morning, and he walked slowly, again, through all the rooms, and the Roman baths, almost convincing himself that he was already working there.

His father got home after six o'clock that evening. He had been to see the lawyer recommended by Doctor Picard, in his chambers.

"That is another world", he said as he sat down heavily in his armchair. "His room, for a start. Panelling, leather-bound books, the nineteenth century."

"Jean-Claude", Bernard's mother said as she came in from the kitchen. "What happened? Did he say he would take Joséphine's case?"

"Yes, he says he will take the case, though how we're going to pay his bills, I have no idea."

"But it's good that he will help, isn't it?"

"I hope so. But it's all going to take months, I'm afraid. Perhaps more. Maître Lebrun told me that terror suspects can be detained, under the emergency powers, for a year before they're tried."

"A year? A whole year? But that's appalling, Jean-Claude. Can it be true? In France?"

"Specially in France. Since the attacks in Paris in November. Maître Lebrun will interview Joséphine as soon as the formalities to do with her changing her lawyer are complete—I've signed forms and she has to sign them too—but he's not at all hopeful that she'll be allowed to come home. Could we control her if she did? A good question. He asked it. I couldn't answer. The police will ask it. So I'm afraid things are likely to stay as they are for some considerable time."

His father was, not for the first time, sounding like a lawyer himself, Bernard thought.

"But", Bernard's mother said, "this Maître Lebrun, he can't think that Joséphine, at her age and with her kind of family, can possibly have been plotting to kill people. Can he?"

"Don't you see, Jamila? At this stage, he has no more idea than we have as to what she was or wasn't plotting. Perhaps she will talk to him truthfully when he interviews her."

"She'd better", Bernard said. His father didn't appear to notice.

"Perhaps there'll be what he called 'extenuating circumstances', a degree of coercion'. Something like this seemed to be the best hope of her avoiding a conviction and a prison sentence. For the time being, all we can do is wait and see."

"Jean-Claude, you look exhausted. Let me get you a cognac?"

"Thank you, Jamila. That would be very good."

On Monday afternoon, Bernard went to the terrorist police headquarters to see Joséphine.

The weekend had been difficult. Bernard hadn't been brave enough to say anything about his museum plan. On Sunday morning, Pentecost, the coming of the Holy Spirit, the day that had changed Thamar's life so long ago, he wished it had been possible to be back in the village with Thamar. He wished he could go to Mass in Saint-Germain-des-Prés, but couldn't either say that that was what he was doing or invent a reason for going out for an hour and a half. He didn't want to lie, about this in particular. And, so as not to upset his mother, he didn't want to provoke his father into an attack on Thamar as a bad influence as well as a waste of time: he could easily imagine his father's response to the museum idea, and his even worse response to Bernard saying he was going to Mass.

So when his father said, on Sunday morning, "Let's go out to lunch at Gaston's"—a Provençal restaurant close by, where family treats had taken place for years—"and try and forget about Joséphine for an hour or two", Bernard had tried to look pleased. His mother had looked actually pleased. They had managed a reasonably cheerful lunch, had talked about politics, the unimpressiveness of the candidates for the presidency of the republic next year, and the dire possibility that, particularly if more terrorist attacks happened, Marine le Pen and the Front National might win the presidential election. The subjects of Joséphine and Bernard's future were both carefully avoided.

The processing of prisoners' visitors at the anti-terrorist police headquarters was, as his mother had described, cheerless. Bernard was searched. The two books his mother had produced for him to take to Joséphine—trashy girls' novels he had hardly looked at—were shaken, leafed through, almost broken in half, presumably to see that they didn't contain drugs or messages; the officer said they would be given to Joséphine when he had gone.

His half-hour with his sister was supervised. Probably the set-faced woman guard was the one his mother had found so grim.

Joséphine, as his mother had said, looked older and thinner. But her hair was clean.

"O", she said when she was brought in to sit opposite him, "I thought maman would come."

"She was very sad after she saw you last week."

"Really? She never cared about me much before—before I went away."

"How can you say that, Joséphine? You know it's not true."

"It's true for me. So it's true. She always preferred you."

Bernard couldn't answer this, so he said, "She sent you some books. They'll give them to you after I've gone."

"Books? What sort of books? I don't need books."

Silence.

"Joséphine. How could you be so cruel to them—to be in Paris for so many months without a word when they didn't know whether you were alive or dead? Why didn't you just let them know you had come back?"

"Why do you think?"

More silence. He didn't want to get her to say something that would make her situation worse. Even worse.

"It's all very well for you, Bernard", she suddenly said. "You've always done what they wanted. I couldn't get anything right, according to them. They only wanted me to be the same as them. To disappear. That's what people like them always want, so-called normal French people. They want all Muslims to disappear. Like maman has. To be the same as them. Or else."

He had never heard Joséphine say anything like this.

"But you're not a Muslim."

"I am now."

"I—I think I see what you mean, about French people wanting, or hoping, that Muslims would become just like them", he said, carefully. "But surely the answer can't be to—"

She wasn't listening.

490

"Well, I'm not going to disappear. We refuse to disappear. They think they have everything and we have nothing. It's them who have nothing. We have Allah."

"God the merciful", Bernard said.

Joséphine looked at him properly for the first time.

"Where did you learn that?", she said.

"It doesn't matter." He had decided before he came not to tell her about Thamar, whatever happened between them.

"Allah will avenge his people", she said. "His people have been victims everywhere. Islam is conquest. The infidels will—" Then she stopped and looked sideways at the guard, whose eyes were fixed on the wall straight ahead of her.

"You wouldn't understand", Joséphine said.

"I might", Bernard said, and then, regretting what he had said, looked at the guard as Joséphine had. No sign of a reaction.

"No. You wouldn't."

A long silence.

"Papa will come to see you next week. He may have some news that will be helpful to you."

"I don't need help. Not from papa. Not from anyone. In any case he can't come on Monday afternoon when he's teaching his precious *bac* classes. And I don't want to see him. I don't want to see maman either. Or you. Just go away, Bernard, and get on with your boring life."

She wouldn't say another word. He asked her if there was anything she would like their mother to bring. No reply. He asked her if she would like him to give a message to any of her old friends. No reply. He asked her if she were afraid of what might happen to her next. At this she looked at him again, and said, "We don't do fear."

He had expected, if she said anything to him, confusion. There was no confusion.

So, before he was told that the time allowed was over, he stood up and said, "Goodbye, Joséphine. Think carefully." She said nothing and didn't raise her head.

On Tuesday afternoon, Bernard got home—the house in the village was, now, home—before it was time for Thamar to come back from the château.

He made some coffee and sat on the terrace, where more flowers had bloomed since he went to Paris, and breathed in the silence of the garden. His laptop was on the table in front of him. He didn't open it.

His mother, saying goodbye before he took the métro to the Gare de Lyon, hugged him, crying a little. "See you soon, darling. In a few weeks, I hope." His father, on Monday evening, had said, "You must have a plan for your future, Bernard, before we see you again."

It was so good to be back that he almost fell asleep in the old basket chair on the terrace.

He heard the front door open. He got to his feet. Félix bounded along the passage and through the kitchen, jumping up and putting his big white paws on Bernard's shoulders. A growl, almost like Félix's own, from Thamar had the dog back on all fours wagging his tail.

"We are delighted to see you, Bernard", the old man said. "But there are limits."

Over supper, which they cooked together, Thamar at last said, "How is your mother?"

"Brave. She can't understand what's happened to Joséphine. Nor, for different reasons, can my father."

"Can you?"

"Partly, perhaps. I saw her, yesterday. In the prison, the detention cells of the terrorist police. That's why I stayed so long. She's allowed one visit a week. My mother went last week and was only upset at the change in Joséphine."

"And you?"

"She is certainly different. Someone has fed her the simplest propaganda and she has absorbed it thoroughly, I suppose because there was nothing much in her head before. 'Islam is conquest', she said."

"Did she, indeed? Do you know, Bernard, what the word 'Islam' truly means?"

Bernard shook his head.

"It means 'submission to the will of Allah', the will of God, as in 'Thy will be done'. Almost the exact contrary of 'Islam is conquest'. These wretched children, your sister and so many others, we hear, seduced into murder and suicide. They want to destroy, bu they have no idea, because, really, they know nothing about Islam, that what they destroy first is Islam itself."

"She also said, 'The French have nothing; we have Allah.'"

Thamar laughed, ruefully. "There, of course, she has a point. An important point, if only the Allah they think they have discovered weren't such a distortion of the Allah of genuine Islam. It is at least more accurate to say this than to say, as apparently the so-called Caliphate said last year after the terrible murders in Paris, that Paris is the leading carrier of the banner of the cross in Europe. Very far from the truth. Alas."

"Did they really say that? But how could anyone think—?"

"President Bush's Crusade. And he wasn't the first. Did I ever tell you what happened many years ago, in 1930—the centenary, you understand, of the French invasion of Algeria—when the Church held a Eucharistic Congress in Carthage? The Muslim leaders in Tunis were invited. I've told you how much Augustine is respected in North Africa. So they came. And senseless *colons* dressed as Crusaders marched in the streets. The White Fathers were horrified. This nonsense of the clash of civilizations. So stupid. Civilizations don't clash. They are more, or less, civilized. The Ottomans ruled over Muslims and Jews and Christians. Mostly quite peacefully.

"And now French civilization has to be defined by its *laïcité*. And the word has been turned into a weapon. In *Le Monde* I have seen the phrase *laïcité de combat*: the politicians use it to show how religion is to blame for everything; the Front National use it to disguise their hatred of Muslims, black Africans, Jews."

Bernard waited. Thamar was talking too much, because he was pleased to see him.

"And your mother is well?"

And also because he wanted to ask this question again.

"She is very upset about Joséphine, of course. But I think she's beginning to understand that what's happened isn't her fault. My mother's fault, that is. Although—"

"Although?"

"Joséphine is full of resentment. I saw that yesterday."

"Resentment is a terrible thing. Do you know what Augustine said about resentment?"

"No."

"He said 'resentment is like taking poison and hoping someone else will die.'"

Bernard had to think about this for a moment.

"What an extraordinary man he was", he said.

"He was. And another extraordinary man, mostly a force for evil and not for good, saw that resentment is at the root of the will to power. Humiliation leads to resentment. Resentment leads to the will to power. It is surely this that drives the fanatics of the Caliphate."

"Nietzsche?"

"That's right. But Bernard, why should your sister be full of resentment? She has had the same good family life as you."

"That's not what she feels. In fact, she feels almost the opposite. She thinks our parents always preferred me to her."

"Did they?"

"My father certainly didn't. I worried him less than Joséphine did, because I was better at doing what he expected of his children. But there was always—always a sense that Joséphine belonged to his family, to Rouen and my other grandparents, whereas I didn't. I suppose because I am darker and I reminded them that their son had married a poor Arab girl."

"Do you resent that?"

"No. Hardly at all." Bernard laughed. "I don't have enough in common with them to mind. Which proves that they're right, doesn't it?"

"And your mother?"

"My mother?"

"Did she, does she, prefer you to Joséphine?"

"No. Not in the way she brought us up. Not at all. But yes, in another way, perhaps she does. Only because I am more like her than Joséphine is. Not just to look at, but really more like her."

A pause, while Thamar studied Bernard's face.

"What else did you do in Paris?" He never missed an

implication.

"It was strange. I found I was looking for a church. Not just any church, but somewhere—"

"Somewhere that reminded you of Burgundy?"

"Exactly."

"And did you find it?"

"I did, in the end. Because of its tower."

"Ah. Saint-Germain-des-Prés."

"Exactly. How did you know?"

"Because of its tower."

Both of them laughed.

"And did you go to Mass there?"

"I did, yes. On Thursday. Quiet and beautiful, it was. I wanted very much to go to Mass on Sunday, for Pentecost, but of course I couldn't."

"Of course?"

"My parents were at home because it was Sunday. I couldn't tell them I was going to Mass. And I couldn't tell them a direct lie."

"Could you have told your mother?"

"I don't think so. Not while she's so desperately worried about Joséphine. My mother is afraid of the Church. My father only thinks it's of no interest, an irrelevance."

In one of his moments of stillness, Thamar, looking down at the kitchen table, said nothing for some time.

Then he said: "You have difficulties ahead, Bernard."

For a minute or two, Bernard was furious with the old man, as he had never been before. How dare he assume—and what was it that he was assuming?

He shook his head, and said, "I haven't—you know—I haven't made up my mind—about anything."

Thamar smiled, reached a hand towards Bernard and put it flat on the table.

"I know. I know. And it is your mind to make up. But you will need more—more experience and more knowledge before you do make up your mind. And finding that will not be easy when you go back to Paris. That's all I meant to say. I'm sorry. I upset you. I understand why."

"No, Thamar. Forgive me. You always understand."

"In any case, it's time to go to bed. You look tired, Bernard."

Together they washed the few dishes, dried them and put them away.

"You go up first. It's going to be another fine day tomorrow. Goodnight, Bernard."

He went upstairs and from his room heard his grandfather open the kitchen door to the terrace, send Félix out into the garden, walk slowly along the passage to lock the front door, and then return to let Félix in and lock the kitchen door. As every night. But the sound of him coming upstairs had changed: he was taking the stairs one by one, first one foot, then the other on the same step, and pausing several times.

How could he have been angry with him, even for a moment?

Nine days later, on 26 May, Bernard spent the morning in the summer house, listening to the gentle rain on the roof, looking up now and then to see and smell the garden responding to the rain, but mostly hard at work on a first draft of the last section of the book. He was finding it very difficult. There was no writing of Thamar's to help, yet Bernard was sure that the book needed a final chapter describing Thamar's eccentric, solitary life in the village, calm, orderly, and, as far as Bernard could tell, happy. He knew he needed some events to make the story interesting, and there weren't any, or there weren't any that he knew about.

Towards the end of the morning the rain stopped and the sun came out, lighting the drops on the leaves, grass, flowers, so that the whole garden that he could see between the summer house and the terrace glittered. He was watching a butterfly, red, gold, black, zig-zagging above the bed where Thamar's kitchen herbs grew, the chives already with purple flowers, when he hit the summer house table with his clenched fist.

"That's it. That's what I have to do", he almost said aloud.

Without having properly formulated the question, he had suddenly seen the answer. The event, the events, of Thamar's life, here in the village after all he had known and suffered in

496

Africa, were the appearance, here in the summer house, of his daughter, whose very existence he had never suspected, and then the presence, for a whole year, of his grandson. Thamar hadn't written, was never going to write, anything about these events. But Bernard himself? Would this be a possible way of framing Thamar's story, not from Thamar's point of view, unrecoverable by Bernard, but with Thamar's story enclosed so that his life would remain, as it must, at the book's centre?

Bernard was now walking, fast, along the road out of the village in the opposite direction from the château, the road he loved, between the meadows and the vineyards on the slopes beyond the meadows, with here and there groups of white cattle in the flowery grass under a few trees in new leaf. He wasn't looking. He was thinking as he walked.

He knew his plan was the right one: why had it taken him so long to think of it? Before he turned round at the bottom of the wood he had seen one problem. What would Thamar think, if the book were to change its very nature? Hadn't it always been intended to be his book, told from what he had written on all those pieces of paper?

But did he need to know? He hadn't read the sections Bernard had printed for him: while Bernard had been in Paris for those ten days on account of Joséphine, Thamar hadn't touched the neat pile of sheets on the dining room table. Bernard was sure now that Thamar wasn't going to read the book, probably not even when, if, it were published. Would it be in any way deceiving him to write a frame he had no idea of? No, Bernard decided: if Thamar ever discovered what he had done, wouldn't he be pleased rather than upset? But he couldn't consult the old man, or discuss the idea with him. So he was alone with his plan.

The other problem—he was nearly back in the village when this struck him—was that he wouldn't have enough time, any-thing like enough time, to finish the book as he saw it should be, before he had to go back to Paris and whatever he could persuade his father to accept as the beginning of a career. He was going to have to start the book differently, to set up the frame. That would take weeks, probably months, of work. He

497

stopped in the middle of the road. How could he get a job, learn what he wanted to learn without his parents noticing, and do the work that he now understood needed to be done on the book—all at the same time? He started to imagine the kind of day he would have to plan for himself in Paris: how early could he get up to work on the book? If it turned out to be possible to get the sort of job he hoped for at the Musée de Cluny, how many hours of the day would it take? Would it be possible to go to the twelve-fifteen Mass at Saint-Germain-des-Prés? They must give the museum staff a lunch break? And what about the reading, the finding someone to teach him?

Lost in these calculations, he had to jump out of the way when a car approaching the village hooted and sped past him. A new Mercedes. A Lyon number plate. No doubt one of the rich outsiders with a modernized cottage only used at week-ends, so disliked by Hortense.

She had been pleased to see him the day before, Wednesday, when he went to the café as usual to read his mother's email.

I saw Joséphine on Monday. Papa couldn't cope with a visit. She was angry with papa for finding Maître Lebrun to help her. She said, "I don't need a horrible know-all lawyer who thinks he understands everything about me when he hasn't any idea. I signed the beastly paper they brought, but I wish I hadn't. Tell papa to get rid of Maître Lebrun." The worst thing she said was, "We should be dead by now anyway. That was what it was all for." What does this mean, Bernard? I haven't told papa what she said. All we can do is to hope that Maître Lebrun will be able to show that she doesn't know what she has done. He told Papa that the boyfriend has been in prison before and that Joséphine met him in Turkey when he was on his way back to France from Syria.

Keep well, darling, and work hard so that you can come back for good in July.

He was walking briskly through the village, to get back to the summer house and his laptop so that he could start to plan—he did like plans—the new frame for the book, when he saw Félix galloping towards him across the top of the square.

Félix by himself?

The dog stopped in front of him, barking and barking. In cold premonition Bernard followed Félix back to the house. He went in and called Thamar, then into the garden, calling again. Silence. Félix didn't follow him but stood in the passage, whining now, beside Bernard's bike.

He took his bike into the road, and set off, as fast as he could pedal, Félix galloping alongside him, towards the château. The road. The drive. In the kitchen garden, a hundred yards from the back of the house, Félix ran to where Thamar was lying face down, a hoe dropped beside him. Bernard, on his knees, turned the old man over, with difficulty although he wasn't heavy. His eyes were open. Bernard put his ear to Thamar's chest, to his mouth. No heartbeat. No breath. Nothing. Félix stood panting, whining, beside the body.

"Stay, Félix", Bernard said, and walked, his legs heavy, to the château. The porter helped him carry Thamar upstairs to an empty room where they laid him down on the bed. Bernard closed his grandfather's eyes, and made the sign of the cross on his forehead with his thumb. The porter crossed himself.

Bernard went down the wide, carpeted stairs of the château, meeting no one—he could hear that it was lunchtime in the nursing home—and knocked on the door of the office. The secretary was eating a sandwich. He told her what had happened and asked if he could use her telephone. He left a message on his mother's mobile, not telling her of Thamar's death, but saying he would call her at six when she was home from work. Seeing the printer on its table, Bernard suddenly began to cry because Thamar would now never read the book.

"Sit down, Bernard", the secretary said. "I am so sorry. Poor Monsieur Thamar. He has worked here for so many years. The patients will miss him. All of us will miss him. Now, you are not to worry about anything. We are accustomed to deaths here. I will speak to the director and I'm sure he will agree that we will help you to make the necessary arrangements."

Bernard pulled himself together, blew his nose hard, thanked the secretary and went to find Félix.

The dog was lying where he had left him, beside the hoe.

"Come, Félix. We must go home."

At six o'clock, from the empty terrace of the café, he told his mother.

Thamar's funeral took place the following Wednesday.

Once the nursing home had dealt with the practical things that had to be done, Bernard bicycled to Saint-Christophe to talk to the priest, whom he had never met beyond a friendly nod at the end of Mass. He turned out to know more about Thamar than Bernard expected. "He was a good man, who had suffered much. I think it was a blessing that his death came as it did. And I am glad that you have been company for him, young man, in the last year of his life. You are his grandson, are you not?"

"That's right. Yes, father."

"Very good. Will your mother be able to come to the Requiem?"

"She will come."

Bernard felt he should say more.

"She didn't know—that's to say, she hardly knew her father. Also she is not a Catholic."

"I know that. She is a Muslim, perhaps?"

"No. She was brought up with no religion. But—"

"But?"

"She is a good person, and—" How could he put into words what he had always sensed in his mother, but knew more clearly after living with Thamar all this time? "She understands that people have souls, not just brains."

"Then she will perhaps be comforted by the Mass even if she knows little about its meaning?"

"I hope so, yes. I think she will."

She arrived the evening before the funeral. She had asked Bernard to arrange for her to stay in the Café de la Paix. "They were so kind to me last year. And I want to remember my father's house as I saw it then." Bernard understood that she felt shy about staying in the house that Bernard knew so well, and perhaps having to sleep in Thamar's own bed.

He was waiting for his mother on the café terrace, Félix

500

asleep beside him, when her taxi crossed the square and drew up beside the terrace. His mother got out, carrying a small overnight bag and a bunch of white roses.

He hugged her. Félix wagged his tail.

"O! His dog—what will happen to him now?"

Bernard looked down at the dog, and realized that he hadn't thought that his mother—of course—would expect him to go back to Paris very soon, to leave the village, the house. Perhaps for ever. And Félix?

Hortense appeared.

"Welcome, madame." Hortense and his mother shook hands. "We are delighted to see you again, although on so sad a day. What beautiful roses—for tomorrow, no doubt. I will put them in water for you. What can I get you?

"Thank you, madame. A coffee would be very nice. Bernard?"

"A beer, please, Hortense."

She took the flowers and they waited at the little table in the evening sunshine for her to come back with coffee and beer, and leave them. Inside, the café was noisy. The terrace, except for them, was empty.

"So, darling, have you been all right, through these days?"

"Yes, sad, of course, but—I think he understood, you know, that he might die at any time. He wasn't afraid. He left everything in perfect order, his clothes, his books, the cupboards in the kitchen, his rosary on the table by his bed—"

Bernard, who hadn't cried since he caught sight of the printer in the office at the château, was now almost crying.

"Poor Bernard", his mother said. "You're bound to be upset after all these months. I'm so sorry."

Bernard shook his head, blew his nose. "No. I'm glad I was here when he died. I'm glad—"

"You're glad that you knew him. Of course you are. We both have my mother to thank for that. And so did he."

Hortense came back to the terrace.

"Would you like to have dinner here, madame? With Bernard?"

His mother looked at Bernard. He nodded, smiled.

"We should like that very much. Thank you, madame."

When she had gone again, Bernard said, "He left a will, a proper will, witnessed by the parish priest a couple of months ago. I had no idea."

"I never thought of that, although papa said—"

"What did papa say?"

"O, you know your father. He only said, 'I don't suppose he made a will. I don't suppose he had any money, in any case. But what will happen to the house?' He wasn't being unkind, of course. Just practical, as he always is."

"Well. Thamar said in this will, that the house was for you, and for me. If we want to sell it, he wished us to make sure to sell it to someone local, not to an outsider. If you, or I, might one day want to live in the house, he says we should rent it out, again to someone local, until it might be possible to come back to it."

They said nothing while Hortense returned, laid their table for dinner, and again disappeared.

His mother said, "That is so kind, and so careful."

"He was, both of those things."

"We'll have to see what papa thinks."

"Of course. But one day—"

"One day you can imagine yourself living in Monsieur Thamar's house?"

"It would be what I would like, more than anything, one day—But maman, there would be quite a lot of money if we sold the house. And Joséphine, and the lawyer—it's all going to cost a lot, isn't it?"

"Bernard. We're not going even to think about it until we get back to Paris."

"Meanwhile, shall I talk to the Mairie about some tenants, just for the time being? I may have to go to Chalon or Mâcon and see a notary and probably a house agent too. Anyway, I'll find out what has to be done."

"Of course. I'm sure you can manage all that. Thank goodness you are a sensible boy."

At the Requiem Mass next morning in the village church, Bernard and his mother sat alone in the front row of chairs.

Half a dozen of the old people who always came to Mass sat behind them, with the director, the secretary, the porter and two patients from the nursing home. Thamar's coffin was in front of the altar, with Jamila's roses and a bunch of sweet peas Bernard had brought from the garden, white and pink and pale blue, laid on its top. The Easter candle, tall and lit, stood beside the coffin.

Bernard felt his mother's nervousness: she glanced at him often to make sure that she wasn't doing anything wrong. She listened intently to the words of the Mass. The priest paid a brief tribute to Thamar, at the point in the Mass where the homily would normally be. Bernard was surprised. He had never before been to a Catholic funeral: at his grandmother's funeral, in a crematorium chapel in Paris, there had been a few words spoken, some kind of prayer, he now supposed, and nothing said about his grandmother. He couldn't remember anyone even mentioning her name.

The priest said that Monsieur Thamar had been a faithful Catholic, a good and brave man, and a skilled and devoted gardener for many years at the nursing home. He also said that the last year of his life had been made happy by the presence of his grandson, Bernard Charpentier, who had come to help him with some work he was doing.

At this there was a stir in the congregation, and Bernard's mother, beside him, put both her hands to her face.

At the exchange of peace, Bernard kissed her cheek, and two old women Bernard had often seen in the village came forward to shake his hand, his mother's hand. When the parishioners, the porter, and one of the patients filed up to receive Holy Communion, his mother looked at Bernard and he shook his head.

Afterwards the director, who had agreed to allow Thamar to be buried beside his grandmother in the old nuns' cemetery among trees at the far end of the château's garden, followed the hearse in his car, with Bernard's mother beside him and the secretary and Bernard in the back seat. The priest took his own car and the porter drove the patients back to the château. Four men from the village, whose names Bernard didn't know, carried the coffin from the church to the hearse, and from the end of the château's back drive to the neatly dug grave. At the graveside, Bernard stood with his arm round his mother's shoulders—she was quietly weeping now—while the priest read the prayers of committal. Bernard listened but heard only a few of the words. "—that we may serve you in union with the whole Church, sure in faith, strong in hope, perfected in love."

When the priest gave the blessing, as at the end of every Mass, Bernard crossed himself, for the first time in his life.

The four men lowered the coffin into the grave.

"You may throw a little earth on the coffin, madame", the priest said. "Or perhaps a flower?"

She took a rose from her bunch, which a bearer had given her to hold, kissed it and threw it into the grave: it fell on the coffin with a little tap. Bernard knelt in the grass and reached down to put all the sweet peas, without a sound, on the coffin.

At the Café de la Paix—the priest had driven them back from the château but declined Bernard's invitation to have lunch with them—Hortense had laid their table for them on the terrace. She came out to greet them—" All went well? Very good."—followed by Félix, wagging his tail. Bernard had asked Monsieur Chaumont to look after him while they were at the funeral.

When Hortense had brought them their first course, Jamila picked up her knife and fork and put them down again.

"Bernard, have you become a Catholic?"

"No, maman. Not yet. Perhaps not ever. But I have been to Mass with Thamar a few times and—well, I have got used to it. I like the quiet, and I like to listen and learn, about Christ and about God. I have learned a great deal from Thamar, you know."

His mother started to eat.

"I understand. I think I understand. I was surprised, myself, just now, at how—how gentle and calm it was in the church. I was expecting music and singing and—I don't know—people to be disapproving."

She looked at Bernard across her plate.

"Did you go to church in Paris?", she said.

"Once, yes."

She ate a little more.

"But you were at home only for two Sundays, so how—?"

"Mass happens every day somewhere."

"Does it? I didn't know. Eat your *jambon persillé*, Bernard. It's delicious."

When Hortense had taken their plates and replaced them with plates of chicken casserole—" No wine, madame? Bernard? Anyhow, enjoy my stew."—Jamila said, "What are you going to tell papa?"

"Do I need to tell him anything? You know how he dislikes possibilities, things that haven't happened yet. And, in this case, may never happen."

She ate a little chicken.

"Would you have told me", she said, "if—if Monsieur Thomas hadn't died and I hadn't come to his funeral?"

"I don't know, maman. Yes, I would, when, if, I become more certain. One of these days."

"Don't let's say anything to papa now. You know how he would see it: 'We should never have let Bernard get involved with your father. Didn't I tell you he must have been a priest?' That's what he would say. And, with Joséphine in such trouble, he would think that he's lost his other child to religion too."

"Maman, seriously, there's no religion, nothing that deserves to be called religion, in what Joséphine has got mixed up with. I've learned enough from Thamar to know this for sure. The poor kids in the *banlieues*, with no work, nothing to do but hang about on street corners and sell drugs—I've seen them— may sometimes feel that all they have, all they are, is being Muslim. Islam gives them a little pride, and why not? What else do they have to be proud of? That's why some of the girls start wearing headscarves, even the burka, which their mothers don't. But being obviously Muslim only makes them less French, more despised. Which is France's fault. But the ones who become terrorists have no connection with what Islam really is. Most of them haven't had a religious upbringing. They don't know the Koran. They don't pray. They begin as ordinary street criminals. And they become fanatical Muslims only because they're furious, furious with a society, French society, and law-abiding Muslim society too, that they think doesn't want them or need them, furious with the colonial powers that despised them, furious with their parents who are disappointed in them—that bit is Joséphine, isn't it? Joséphine and papa and the wretched *bac*—and so what they want is revenge, and meaning, and glory. And wicked people persuade them that God has chosen them to win all three in a violent death that takes with it as many bystanders as possible. This is not religion."

"O, Bernard", his mother said. "Poor papa. But why Joséphine? Hundreds of girls and boys like her mess up the *bac* every year and they don't—"

"Chance, accident, bad luck. She runs away with the other girl, just so as not to face the music at home. Who knows what happens next? At some point she meets this man—maybe he rescues her from another man or when she's run out of money—and he fills her head with justification for her own rebellion, and gives her a glamorous part to play in the history of the world. And there you are."

A pause, while his mother looked at him. Then she said, "You have changed, Bernard, grown up, I suppose, being here all this time. I expect you're right. You seem to know so much more than I—more than we—have been able to understand. It will be a comfort to have you at home."

Hortense reappeared and took their plates. "Some cheese, madame? Dessert?"

"Just some coffee, please, madame. For both of us." Then she said, "How long will you have to stay here, Bernard, before you come back to Paris?"

"Not long. A few days, perhaps. Enough time to sort out what will happen immediately to the house." And to collect the few things he knew Thamar would like him to have: the crucifix over the fireplace, the old copy of Pascal, Thamar's pages of writing, the coffee grinder. The rosary from beside his bed. Someone else would have to tell him, one day, how to use the rosary to pray. If he got that far.

His mother looked at her watch.

"My taxi is coming in a quarter of an hour. I must go upstairs to collect my things. And I must pay Monsieur Chaumont."

Bernard watched the taxi cross the square and turn right on the road to Saint-Christophe and Mâcon. As it disappeared, he realized that the whole story was Jamila's story. It should start and end with her.

He poured himself the last of the coffee Hortense had brought them. Three young men came out of the café, climbed into a farm truck parked in the square and set off, no doubt back to work.

Work. That was a problem he would face when he got back to Paris.

Monsieur Chaumont appeared in the café doorway. Félix, lying at Bernard's feet, pricked up his ears and wagged his tail.

"May I?", Monsieur Chaumont said, and sat down at Bernard's table.

"Will you be going back to Paris, Bernard?"

"Yes. I'm afraid I must. I shall be sad to leave the village."

"Of course. Who wouldn't be? Hortense will miss you."

"That's kind."

"What are you going to do with Félix? Take him with you to Paris?"

"No. I would like to take him but—our flat, my parents' flat, is not a good place for a big dog. And Félix is used to the country. Do you, Monsieur Chaumont—" Bernard put his hand on Félix's familiar head. He was suddenly too anxious about what would happen to him to go on. He made himself go on.

"Do you know anyone in the village who might like to take him, to give him a home?"

"That's what I came out to say. He's a beautiful dog and very obedient. He's quite old, isn't he? He won't change his ways now. We'll give him a home, here in the Paix. He would be a fine guard dog at night. And Hortense thinks it would be good for me"—Monsieur Chaumont patted his paunch—"to take him for a walk in the morning and a walk in the evening before the bar gets busy. What do you think?"

Bernard found himself thinking that this was a blessing from God. He also thought of what would have been Thamar's mixed response to the idea that Pierre Chaumont, son of a villain of the Occupation, should be Félix's new master.

"I think that's a marvellous idea", he said. "I shall be very happy to think of him here when I've gone. Thank you, Monsieur Chaumont, and Hortense too, of course."

They stood and shook hands across the little table. Félix thumped his tail on the ground.

"I'll be here for a few more days. I have things to sort out. I'll let you know which day I'm leaving and bring Félix then."

"That's perfect."

Chapter 9

Jamila

August 2016

On 2 August, a Tuesday morning, Jamila was having breakfast, in what she always thought of as the unnaturally tidy kitchen of her mother-in-law's house in Rouen.

She was alone.

Jean-Claude and his father had already had their breakfast and had gone for the short walk, today in intermittent rain, that her father-in-law took every day of his life, with his elegant walking stick and his two dachshunds on leads. Jean-Claude's mother always had her coffee in her bedroom and didn't appear until 10 o'clock.

To Jamila's amazement, Bernard, busy in Paris with his holiday job in the Louvre, had telephoned at six o'clock the evening before, and asked his grandmother if he could stay the night in the house in Rouen. Jamila's mother-in-law—like Jean-Claude, and also like Bernard—was always irritated by surprises, alterations to what she was expecting: she had made an effort to look pleased after Bernard's call, but was fussing, at once, about there not being enough dinner for five people. Jamila was relieved that Bernard at least wasn't late for dinner. There was plenty of food.

The evening had passed reasonably well: Bernard was able to explain how much he was looking forward to his diploma course at the Louvre, in museum management, on which he had succeeded in securing a late place, and which was starting in September. His grandparents were moderately impressed, probably because of the word "management". "We had no idea that you were interested in art, Bernard", his grandmother said.

"This must be a new enthusiasm. It's to be hoped that it will last."

Jamila saw that her father-in-law was wondering how the course was going to be paid for. She and Jean-Claude had told his parents only what they had agreed, a year ago, to tell them: that Bernard had been in the country, helping an elderly writer finish a book. They had also agreed that Jean-Claude, at an appropriate moment, would tell his parents that the writer had recently died and left Bernard some money. Actually she and Bernard, with Jean-Claude's approval, had managed, with the help of an agency in Mâcon, to let the house in the village to a local couple with a small child who had been living in Saint-Christophe with the woman's parents. The rent would more or less pay for Bernard's course. Jean-Claude would have liked them to sell the house, but, although Bernard had said, "Of course it should be sold if we really need the money", Jamila had seen Jean-Claude understand Bernard's attachment to the house. And Jean-Claude had settled the issue by saying, "We needn't make any decisions yet, Bernard. We'll manage Joséphine's difficulties somehow, and see how you and your mother feel about the house in a year or two." As so often, Jamila was deeply grateful to him, but didn't say so.

She had had no chance to ask Bernard why he had suddenly decided to come to Rouen.

"Very unlike Bernard, to turn up at no notice", Jean-Claude had said to her the night before when they were getting ready for bed. "I know he's never much enjoyed coming here. And on a Monday night, too."

"There'll be a reason. Bernard always has a reason."

She hoped he would come downstairs before Jean-Claude and her father-in-law returned from their walk. She looked towards the kitchen door and Bernard came in, cautiously, making sure there was no one there but her.

"Good morning, maman". He kissed her, and poured himself some coffee and sat down at the table.

"Bernard, tell me quickly why you're here."

"I came for the funeral. It's in half an hour."

"Whose funeral?"

"Père Hamel. Père Jacques, as Thamar might have been, all those years."

"What are you talking about? O, is that the priest who was murdered last week?"

"That's right. There is a great Requiem for him this morning, in the cathedral here."

"That huge cathedral? So famous. I never wanted to go inside it. But why, Bernard? Why do you want to go to this funeral? I don't understand."

"For Thamar, maman. Père Hamel was ten years older than Thamar, almost to the day as it happens, and of course they never met. But his life, his good and generous life, was so like Thamar's, so like what Thamar's should have been. As a young man Père Hamel was a conscript in the war in Algeria, like Thamar. And also I want to go to the cathedral for those boys, Algerian boys, who cut his throat at the altar, and were shot by the police. As of course they had to be. And Père Jacques was a friend of the Muslims in his town, and worked with them for peace. A terrible, terrible thing. The sins of the fathers."

"What do you mean?"

"The long past. Never mind, now."

Jamila drank a little more coffee, and then said, "What went wrong with Monsieur Thomas's life, Bernard? Was it the injury to his face?"

"Ah. One day, you must read the book, his book, my book. The injury was only part of the story—I think it was more a symbol to him, of the course of his life, a kind of metaphor. But you will see."

Something about Bernard this morning made her say, "Bernard, are you a Catholic now?"

He looked at her, as he used to look at her when he was a small boy and she had said something only he understood.

"Yes, maman. I think I am. Don't say anything to papa. Not yet, while Joséphine is still in detention."

"But what persuaded you? How did you—?"

"Thamar, and his book. And since I came back to Paris I've been talking to a priest from time to time, at Saint-Germain-des-Prés. A nice man. Very cautious and calm. You would like him. Even papa would quite like him, I think. You must meet him one day."

Bernard drank his coffee and stood up.

"I must go", he said. "The radio said that hundreds of people are coming to the funeral."

"What shall I tell papa? About this morning? This visit?"

"Tell him, tell them, I've come to Rouen to see a friend. I must go back to Paris afterwards. I only got the morning off work. Thank grandmother for me."

"Bernard—"

She followed him into the hall.

"You must take an umbrella. It's raining again."

"Never mind. I've got my Breton cap."

"We'll see you next weekend when we get back to Paris?"

"On Sunday, yes. On Saturday I'm going to Nantes for the day. To see a friend." He smiled as he kissed her. "Really to see a friend."

"A girl?"

"A girl. She's called Marie."

He waved as he went out into the rain and shut the front door behind him.

349 : ∅

350f: crying a
t elsewher substitute

93: too much 2!

362: history

131: misprints

408: alteriore

133: Muriel/ Anne Jeanne

413: Tawnright

167: Pols ✓

415: unconvincing
on gay sexuality

169: anti-postmodern

173: X pols

443-4: Mass θεοι

452: not right on gays

179: X p.r

462: you only wanted her to be
the sort of doctor you expected
her to be

181: Aug

493: θεοι

192: Itm The prob with the moralism
of R. Short & Essays ;-)

349: Pols

351: X

353: too self-lacerating

391: ?

402: gap in his life I don't
believe in.

Lightning Source UK Ltd.
Milton Keynes UK
UKHW01f0215040718
325198UK00002B/42/P